The Selected Writings of
Jean Genet

The Selected Writings of

JEAN GENET

◄O►

EDITED AND WITH AN
INTRODUCTION
BY EDMUND WHITE

THE ECCO PRESS

THE ECCO PRESS
100 West Broad Street
Hopewell, NJ 08525

Published simultaneously in Canada by
Penguin Books Canada Ltd., Ontario
Printed in the United States of America

Designed by Janis Owens

ISBN: 978-0-88001-420-5

Library of Congress Cataloging-in-Publication Data

Genet, Jean, 1910–1986
[Selections. English. 1993]
The selected writings of Jean Genet /
edited by Edmund White.
p.   cm. — (Ecco companions)

1. Genet, Jean, 1910–1986—Translations into English.   I. White,
Edmund, 1940–   . II. Title. III. Series.
PQ2613.E53A28   1993
842'.912—dc20   93-2408
CIP

The text of this book is set in 10 point Janson

Page 461 constitutes a continuation of this copyright page.
05 06 07 RRD 10 9 8 . 7 6 5 4 3 2

Contents

◄o►

IV

ESSAY

V

FILM

VI

MEMOIR

VII

LETTERS

VIII

INTERVIEW

Introduction

◄O►

JEAN GENET (1910–1986) was a writer of unusual versatility. He wrote five novels, a hefty volume of memoirs *(Prisoner of Love)*, several long dramatic poems, several one-act plays, including *The Maids*, which can be seen as a taut condensation of a five-act drama, three full-length plays, numerous film scripts, hundreds of letters, and a few essays (including one about sculptor Alberto Giacometti that Picasso called the best art essay ever written). In addition, after 1968 Genet wrote dozens of political essays, articles, and speeches. In 1950 he made an erotic silent film, twenty minutes long in black and white *(A Song of Love)*. He prepared a speech for radio about delinquent boys called "The Criminal Child" (which was never broadcast because it was banned by the state). He even devised the story line for a ballet, *'Adame Miroir*, in which two sailors dance together (one is meant to be the other's reflection) until Death (or at least a menacing figure) arrives to put an end to the fun.

Few people in the English-speaking world (or even in France) ascribe to Genet this sort of versatility; until now he has been known primarily as a novelist and playwright. In France, due to contractual disputes between two of his publishers, his writings were generally available only in an expensive and austere edition of his complete works. Not until the mid-1970s was the legal conflict resolved; then for the first time his novels and plays began to appear in widely distributed paperbacks, but by then he had been lost to a whole generation of general readers.

In the United Kingdom and the United States, Genet's most popular works were already in paperback in the 1960s, but the extent and diversity of the rest of his work remained hidden longer than in France. His essays and poems were either not translated at all or were published in obscure or fugitive journals or in editions not widely available.

Even in France, approximately a quarter of Genet's extant writing is still awaiting publication. Nevertheless, his French publisher, Gallimard, is slowly bringing out volume after volume of his *Complete Works* which, despite the name, is in reality a judicious selection of Genet's total output, some of which is of uneven quality or (in the case of Genet's political statements) repetitious.

Which is not to suggest that Genet was an unconscious demiurge, a primitive who churned out both inspired and flat pages that wiser editors must now winnow. I mention this notion (in order to dismiss it) only because some critics, despite all evidence to the contrary, continue to see Genet as a self-educated diamond in the rough.

Quite the contrary. Genet may have received a formal education only until the age of twelve, but he was first in his class. He was a constant reader. In Alligny-en-Morvan, the village near Dijon in which he lived with foster parents until the age of twelve, he refused to perform manual labor of any sort. The most he would condescend to do was to watch a cow as it grazed. Genet spent his time reading books from the school library, including many nineteenth-century boys' adventure stories, action-packed tales that would have a complex influence on Genet's own novels.

By age sixteen, Genet was condemned because of a few petty thefts to an unusually harsh reform school, where the authorities specifically forbade the adolescent inmates to engage in any studies beyond the bare rudiments. The institution was supposed to prepare future laborers, field hands, and soldiers, who would presumably be given ideas above their lowly station if they read novels or learned geometry. Despite these strictures, Genet discovered the Renaissance poet Ronsard, whose elevated diction and sentiments gave him a thrillingly exalted vision of the power of literature. Buried in Genet's prose are many small echoes of Ronsard's verse as well as of his poetic erotic writing.

At nineteen, Genet, in order to cut short his reform-school sentence, joined the army, and for the next six years he was a soldier with long hours to kill. Those hours he devoted to reading, especially the works of Dostoevsky, who became one of his favorite authors. Like Genet, Dostoevsky had been a prisoner and, in *The House of the Dead*, had written about incarceration. Like Genet, Dostoevsky was fascinated by religion and royalty—and by pure evil. But what Genet (who late in life wrote an essay about Dostoevsky) most admired was what he called Dostoevsky's "buffoonish" way of undermining his own moral points, his practice of creating distinct characters only to blur and distort them later or to let them drift out of focus. Genet declared that he liked only works of art that destroyed themselves, that were both player and target in an artistic shooting gallery.

Throughout the 1930s, while Genet was in his twenties, he wandered the world. As a soldier he was sent to Damascus and Morocco. Subsequently, as a vagabond, he wandered through Spain, Italy, Eastern Europe, Holland, and Belgium. Those who knew him in Czechoslovakia recall that among his few belongings were manuscripts he was constantly working on. He had met the French novelist and essayist André Gide and had written him a long, confused, self-conscious letter (which, typically, ended with a request for money.)

Genet may have been the thief, homosexual prostitute, and beggar that he pictures himself as being in his last novel, *The Thief's Journal*, but such a self-portrait is only a partial view. At the same time he was also a voluminous reader with serious literary ambitions, a part-time tutor of French and French literature, and someone hungry for information about the Paris literary scene.

The only traces we have of Genet the writer before 1940 are fragmentary—and suggest he was a stilted and affected stylist. He sent six long letters to Anne Bloch, a German–Jewish refugee living in Czechoslovakia whom he had tutored in French. These letters reveal a writer given to ready-made sentiments and stock phrases. Although Genet was a homosexual who never had sexual relations with women, in these letters he was trying to convince himself he was in love with Madame Bloch, a virtuous, married woman who would never have dreamed of granting her favors to her strange little French teacher with his dirty clothes and elegant manners. In his letters to her from Paris, he speaks of Gide, the Decadent novelist Rachilde—and especially of Rimbaud.

There are many examples of Genet's fascination with Rimbaud. He tore out of a book the pages containing Rimbaud's long poem *The Drunken Boat* and sent them to Anne Bloch. Genet pretended he had joined the army, like Rimbaud, in order to receive an initial bonus before deserting after three days. Although Rimbaud in fact did serve just three days, Genet spent nearly six years in the army during several different engagements. Like Rimbaud, Genet had grown up nursing fantasies of artistic success in faraway Paris. Like Rimbaud, when Genet at last arrived in Paris, he terrorized the older, middle-class poets he encountered. Rimbaud bullied Verlaine, just as Genet intimidated Jean Cocteau, the versatile man-about-Paris who discovered Genet and paid for the publication of Genet's first novel. Somewhat in the manner of Rimbaud, who abandoned poetry at age nineteen, Genet wrote with great intensity during short periods and more than once renounced his craft. Already in the nineteenth century Rimbaud embodied the model of the homosexual hoodlum and self-created genius, given to extravagant behavior and revolutionary literary feats, whom Genet emulated some seventy years later.

Ronsard, Dostoevsky, Rimbaud—these are only three of the several gods in Genet's pantheon. The one Genet revered the most was Mallarmé, the hermetic, nearly abstract nineteenth-century poet.

Genet was discovered by Jean Cocteau at the beginning of 1943, and Cocteau arranged for his first novel, *Our Lady of the Flowers*, to be published a year later—sold under the counter in an expensive edition limited to some three hundred copies. When Genet encountered Cocteau he had already written several plays and scenarios as well as a long poem, *The Man Condemned to Death*, which Genet himself had paid to have printed up by a man he had met in prison. The printer, apparently, had been sentenced for having forged food-ration coupons, a grave offense during World War II. When he was released, he printed a hundred copies of the poem for Genet, who was still behind bars. It is interesting that Genet (contrary to what Sartre asserts in his massive study, *Saint Genet*) was already working in several different forms at the very beginning of his career—drama, film, poetry, and fiction.

Very quickly, Genet (who was in prison off and on for petty thefts during the wartime years, when he wrote his first two novels, *Our Lady of the Flowers* and *Miracle of the Rose*) became a celebrity whom few Parisians had met and even fewer had read. His celebrity was sparked during a trial in July 1943, at which Genet, as a multiple offender, faced a heavy sentence. Cocteau got him off lightly—with just a three-month sentence—by intimidating the judge and proclaiming Genet the greatest writer of the modern period. Cocteau compared Genet to Rimbaud and sternly reminded the judge that one did not imprison a Rimbaud. Only in France, of course, would such a legal defense work (which is all to the glory of the country).

The period 1942–1947 was an extremely productive one for Genet and can be considered one of the most condensed bursts of creativity in literary history. During these years Genet wrote all his major poems, including *The Fisherman of Suquet* presented here; all five of his novels *(Our Lady of the Flowers, Miracle of the Rose, Funeral Rites, Querelle,* and *The Thief's Journal)* and several plays, including *Deathwatch* and *The Maids.*

This was a time when Genet either was actually behind bars or felt he was living in the shadow of prison. Even after 1944, when he served out his last term, Genet still had a sentence outstanding that had never caught up with him due to the confusion of the war years. He had written his first two novels in noisy cells filled with other prisoners. He had crouched in a corner and written on his knees, usually in student notebooks—once on paper intended to be made into bags by prisoners. When fifty pages were confiscated by an angry prison guard, Genet reconstructed the entire missing text from memory—this time on the proper paper. Not only did Genet work with the constant threat of prison hanging over his head, he also wrote his first two books on an empty stomach. Wartime shortages (and a deliberate Nazi policy to starve prisoners into extinction) meant that Genet was consumed by hunger during the composition of *Our Lady of the Flowers* and especially *Miracle of the Rose.* In letters to one of his early editors he repeatedly called for packages of food. Fully aware of his talent, Genet declared in these letters that he was giving France some of its most glorious pages of literature, pages that were genuinely "marvelous," in the original, overwhelming sense of the word; in return he angrily demanded a minimum of food for survival.

Genet was not overestimating the dimensions of his achievement as a writer. His style, rich with unexpected metaphors and animated by a strong poetic sensibility, is unmistakably original. No one had ever written like this before, and most of the genuine artists who read Genet were quick to recognize his genius. Cocteau passed along *Our Lady of the Flowers* in manuscript to many writers. Simone de Beauvoir and Jean-Paul Sartre announced that Genet gave them new confidence in the future of the novel; Sartre published excerpts from Genet's work in his review *Les Temps modernes,* arranged for Genet to win a prestigious literary award, and agreed to write a book-length essay to introduce Genet's *Complete Works.* Sartre's *Saint Genet,* published in 1952, was a long "existential psychoanalysis" of Genet, a tracing out of the various stages the orphan Genet must have gone through in order to move from criminal to esthete, writer, and saint. Some twenty years later Genet was once again the subject of another book-length investigation by a major philosopher—*Glas* by Jacques Derrida.

Genet's fiction appeals to philosophers because of the originality and density of the prose, equalled in line-by-line intelligence only by that of Marcel Proust, whose *Remembrance of Things Past* was Genet's main inspiration. One day, probably in 1941, Genet was participating in a covert exchange of books with other prisoners during an exercise period. Being the last to arrive, Genet was forced to take a dull-looking volume no one else wanted—*The Guermantes Way*, a volume in Proust's saga. As soon as Genet read the first page he closed the book because he wanted to savor its treasures slowly over the days to come. He later admitted in an interview that his reading of Proust at age thirty-one or thirty-two was the decisive stimulus that made him begin writing. Indeed, Genet can be seen as the Proust of the criminal class.

Unlike Proust—or most novelists for that matter—Genet felt no obligation to do justice to his subjects, to explain or apologize, to produce the illusion of reality, to document a milieu, or to demonstrate his own moral fineness. To be sure, his writing can be sociologically accurate, as in his portrait of gay culture in Montmartre, just as it can be extremely moralistic, as it is toward the end of *The Thief's Journal*. But neither the sociological nor the moral impulse in Genet resembles that of any other author. Like Proust, Genet has a thoroughly philosophical turn of mind and gives pride of place to reflection on the meaning of events rather than a mere recounting of an anecdote.

Genet never stops reminding his reader, especially in *Our Lady of the Flowers*, that all the characters (Divine, Darling, Our Lady, Seck Gorgui) whom he is so stunningly inventing, are mere fabrications of his imagination, figments he fleshes out only in order to excite himself while masturbating. Genet would like to suggest that he's the irresponsible god of his universe, animating and abandoning characters at will in a purely improvisational way.

But in fact the structures underlying Genet's fiction are ambiguous and complex. After he tells us repeatedly that his characters are masturbation fantasies, he's quite capable of saying, "When I met Divine at Fresnes Prison," or "Darling's real name is Paul Garcia." The level of reality in Genet's fiction is constantly in question.

The organization of Genet's fiction, equally original, bears a resemblance to film montage. Often Genet would be at work on two or three different novellas, which he initially conceived of as independent entities, but which eventually he would intercut in order to form one book. In *Our Lady of the Flowers* there are three different narrative strands. The "frame tale," as students of narrative put it, is about Genet in prison awaiting a trial that will determine his future as convict or free man. We are repeatedly reminded that the date of the trial is rapidly approaching. The second narrative is about Genet's puppets: the drag queen–prostitute Divine; her pimp Darling; the handsome young thief, nicknamed Our Lady, who comes to live with them in Montmartre; and a black man named Seck Gorgui, who eventually drops Divine and takes up with Our Lady. These narratives begin (out of sequence) with Divine's funeral, when her coffin is accompanied to the cemetery by an honor guard of transvestites. It ends with Our Lady's trial, when he is condemned to death for killing an old man (Our Lady, horrified by his own impulsive words, blurts out his confession). The third narrative strand is the story of Divine's childhood as the boy Louis Culafroy. It comprises scenes loosely based on Genet's own childhood in the Morvan, a densely wooded region east of Paris. (Genet took Divine's boyhood name from Louis Cullaffroy, a boy Genet actually knew in the village in which he grew up.)

These are not only three different, almost unrelated stories, they are also quite different *sorts* of stories: a romantic confessional in which Genet speaks of his own approaching trial; a constantly interrupted and undermined picture of tacky Montmartre gay life just before the war; and a much more carefully constructed and consistent picture of a boy growing up as a sissy in a backwoods village.

Genet's relationship to the reader is problematical—and dramatic. He makes very clear, in all his novels except *Querelle*, that he is addressing a middle-class, respectable, heterosexual male reader, whom he alternately cajoles and menaces, seduces and shocks, wins over and repels. This pierce-and-parry *is* the action of Genet's novels—an uneasy and ever-changing relationship.

Although Genet presents his novels as autobiographical, they all take great liberties with the facts. Nevertheless, they do cover some of the major periods in his life. In *Our Lady of the Flowers*, he writes of his childhood in the village. In *Miracle of the Rose*, he documents with great care the reform school, Mettray, where he was detained from September 1926 to March 1929. In *Funeral Rites*, he covers his romantic, wartime friendship with a Résistant, Jean Decarnin, who died during the Liberation of Paris in August 1944. And in *The Thief's Journal*, he writes about his time in Spain (late in 1933 in real life) and his great, year-long hegira on foot from Italy to Albania, Yugoslavia, Czechoslovakia, Germany, Holland, and Belgium (which actually occurred in 1936 and 1937). He is careful not to mention his years as a soldier (too normal, not glamorous enough), to make his short stay in Spain sound like a long one, and to leave out all mention of his voluminous reading, literary correspondence, and friendships with cultivated people.

By the time Genet finished *The Thief's Journal*, his last novel, he had exhausted all his colorful autobiographical material as a beggar, thief, and prostitute and worked his way up dangerously close in time to his current celebrity as a Parisian artistic figure—a figure not at all in keeping with the "Golden Legend" he had forged for himself.

The only novel that does not fit into this series is *Querelle*, although Lieutenant Seblon's journal, contained within the novel, seems to echo many of Genet's thoughts. Genet does not figure as a first-person narrator or character under his own name, however. *Querelle* is apparently a wholly invented, made-up novel. Genet had been briefly imprisoned in the French seaport of Brest, where the action takes place, and the city's past as a place from which galley ships manned by prisoners had sailed certainly intrigued him. The decisive moment in Genet's erotic history had surely been Mettray; all the rest of his life he sought out in life and in art an all-male, hierarchical, military-style community in which male heterosexuals, being deprived of female company, are forced to have sex with one another. Their sex also serves as a game of domination and submission. The army, the navy, North Africa, the French penal colony on Devil's Island, the world of penniless male prostitutes—these were just some of the populations or situations that fired Genet's erotic fantasies about virile, occasionally sadomasochistic homosexuality. *Querelle* is an elaborate staging of these fantasies.

The Maids—which was first staged in Paris on April 19, 1947, but which had been conceived a few years earlier and had gone through several major rewrites—was Genet's decisive move away from homosexuality as a theme. As he said much later in an interview, he had decided to recast his personal concerns as a homosexual into other themes of oppression in his theater. In his plays, Genet treated the humiliation of family servants *(The Maids)*, the splendors and miseries of whores *(The Balcony)*, as well as the smoldering rage of colonized black Africans *(The Blacks)* and Arabs *(The Screens)*. In a screenplay written in this period *(The Penal Colony)*, which was never produced or published, he dealt with prison life on Devil's Island.

A seven-year period, from 1948 to 1955, elapsed between the time Genet composed his novels and the time he began to write his three full-length plays *(The Balcony, The Blacks, The Screens)*. During this period, he was plunged into a nearly suicidal depression. He later blamed this depression on Sartre's *Saint Genet*, but it had been published in 1952, a good four years after the depression and creative sterility had begun. What actually triggered Genet's despair was, paradoxically, a presidential pardon that he had received. In July 1948, some of the most distinguished artistic names in Paris, everyone from Picasso to Paul Claudel, had signed a petition drafted by Jean-Paul Sartre and Jean Cocteau to the president of France, asking him to pardon Genet from the sentence that was hanging over his head with the threat of life imprisonment. A year later, on August 12, 1949, the president issued a pardon. Now Genet could no longer picture himself as an outcast and criminal; he had to recognize that, magically, through the power of his pen, he had beaten the system. Nothing is so depressing as success.

His fiction had been founded on his feeling of being singular, marginal, and in an adversarial relationship with his intimidated middle-class reader. Now this particular formulation could no longer work, and Genet was plunged into a nearly vegetable-like state during which he found it difficult to shave, eat, or even get out of bed.

The end of this gloomy period came when Genet made two discoveries. He met the sculptor Alberto Giacometti, and by 1955 the two men had become inseparable. Genet wrote a brilliant essay about Giacometti, a man above or beyond all vanity, who lived for his work and accepted his common humanity. Giacometti provided Genet with an image of how to grow old if not gracefully at least fiercely and with integrity. This encounter was seconded by a nearly mystical experience Genet had in a train, when he was seated opposite a repellent little man. Genet felt in a literal sense an exchange of souls back and forth between himself and this miserable specimen—and this exchange revealed to him that he, Genet, was not a singular, extraordinary being but in fact someone much like everyone else. This realization in turn directed Genet toward the theater. Whereas fiction can induct a reader into the strange mental world of an eccentric writer, the theater reports dialogue and displays actions, devoid of all commentary, before an audience acutely aware of itself as a group. Theater is a social form of art and depends on a social conception of the individual.

In 1955, the year Genet became very friendly with Giacometti, he wrote a first draft of *The Balcony*, began *The Blacks*, tossed off a one-act play called *Elle*, and worked on *The Penal Colony*. It was also the year in which he met Abdallah, a young circus performer whom Genet trained as a high-wire artist and who became his lover. Genet's essay "The High-Wire Artist" indirectly compares the aerial acrobat to the writer. Both are engaged in a performance art that involves great risk.

Genet pushed his lovers to dangerous limits and beyond. Abdallah fell twice from the high wire, drifted into depression and inactivity, and finally committed suicide in the spring of 1964. This date marks the beginning of Genet's second long silence. Overcome with remorse, Genet swore he would never write again and literally refused to hold a pen in his hand. Curiously enough, during this period of personal grief, his plays were enjoying a growing international fame. A national scandal was created by the French premiere in 1966 of *The Screens*. Presented in a state-subsidized theater not long after the Algerian War, *The Screens* infuriated French soldiers who had fought to retain the colony and had lost. They disrupted performances by leaping on stage, setting off smoke bombs, and interrupting the action, although not a single performance was cancelled during the run.

Genet's theatrical writing was not only scandalous, it was also genuinely revolutionary in an artistic sense. The Theater of Ritual, which became an artistic rallying cry in avant-garde performance-art circles in the United States during the 1960s, was virtually invented by Genet. *The Maids*, the opening scenes of *The Balcony*, and the entire action of *The Blacks* are elaborate rituals designed to accomplish an act—a murder, the identification of a private individual with a public role, the exorcism of race hatred. Genet's plays are not didactic or even politically committed; they do not suggest a revolutionary program or a progressive course of action, and Sartre disliked them precisely because they were not sufficiently *engagé*. They do, however, manage to isolate inflammatory topics, and they have been used by oppressed people for political purposes. For instance, when *The Blacks* was performed in the United States in the early 1960s, its cold fury served to remind audiences that the Civil Rights era had only tapped, not expressed, the rage of black Americans.

Genet was as drawn to the cinema as he was to the theater but with fewer visible results. In 1950 he directed a twenty-minute black-and-white silent film, *A Song of Love*, using amateur actors and professional technicians. The result was a homosexual erotic film of great poetic beauty about prison life. One of the most memorable images is of two men in adjoining cells who exchange cigarette smoke through a straw inserted into a hole in the wall that separates them.

During the next thirty-five years Genet was to write several long film scripts, including *Forbidden Dreams* (on which Tony Richardson's *Mademoiselle* was based), *The Penal Colony, The Language of the Wall* (about Mettray), and *Nightfall*, a fiction film about the single day an Arab immigrant spends in Paris. None of these scripts, except the one for *Mademoiselle*, was produced, usually because Genet himself got cold feet shortly before they were to be shot and pulled out of the deal. Nevertheless, thoughts about film shaped all of Genet's writing. A selection in this anthology, drawn from *The Penal Colony*, contains Genet's striking thoughts on cinema.

In the last sixteen years of his life, from 1970 to 1986, Genet, the eternal phoenix, emerged from silence and depression to take up the causes of the Black Panthers and the Palestinians. He traveled extensively throughout the United States during the first half of 1970 to speak on behalf of the Panthers, and he subsequently spent long months living among the Palestinians in Jordanian camps. But except for occasional manifestos and interviews on behalf of his twin causes, Genet wrote nothing—certainly nothing long and ambitious. He traveled all over the world— Japan, North and South America, Morocco, Greece, England, Germany, Jordan, Syria, and Lebanon—but he was afraid he would never be able to write the book he had promised to write for the Panthers and the Palestinians. Then in 1979 he learned he had throat cancer, and he became more than ever aware his time was running out. (Time is something, he had declared, that is in a television interview, "sacred" and must not be wasted.)

What finally triggered his last great creative flowering was a visit he made in September 1982 to Beirut. There he witnessed the appalling results of a massacre of Palestinian civilians in the camps of Shatila and Sabra; Genet was the first European to observe the hundreds of brutally slaughtered bodies. He broke his literary silence and wrote an essay, "Four Hours at Shatila," which was so powerful that he knew he could write a book. In 1983 he began work on *Prisoner of Love;* when he died during the night of April 14, 1986, he had just finished correcting the proofs. The book came out in May, a month after his death.

Like four of his five novels, it is written in the first person, it is based on his personal experiences and observations, and it is cinematically composed through the use of montage. But in most other ways *Prisoner of Love* marks a real break with Genet's earlier prose. Whereas the novels throw golden dust in the bewitched eyes of the reader, in *Prisoner of Love* Genet addresses the reader simply, sincerely. No longer is Genet systematically reversing all normal human values; now he is writing about the normal virtues of courage, tenacity, loyalty—although he continues to insist on his own status as an outsider. He tells the reader that even if he, Genet, wants to support the Palestinian cause, he has never been wholly engaged all at once, body and mind.

Prisoner of Love is an old man's book: ruminative, not very sensuous, composed in an idiosyncratic shorthand, and reduced to the main points. Now Genet is more concerned with communicating than dazzling, with convincing than intimidating. The highly metaphorical style of the novels, with its constant (and shockingly ambiguous) references to the church and the aristocracy, is abandoned in favor of a conversational, repetitive style reminiscent of Céline's and built up out of little touches. The references are to anything and everything, including Mozart's *Requiem*, sex-change operations, and Japanese Shinto ceremonies for the dead.

The book testifies to Genet's genuine devotion to the Palestinians and the Black Panthers, two causes that long seemed dangerous or at least quixotic to many Europeans. Genet was frank about his erotic fascination with the young black and Arab militants, but he didn't actually have relations with members of either group; in any event his sexual interest accompanied, rather than preceded, his political commitment. No, what attracted Genet was that both groups were *lost* causes, nations without a land, Davids fighting Goliaths. The Goliath in both cases was the United States, according to Genet; he ranked the enemies of the Palestinians as, first, the United States, second, the other Arab states, and only finally Israel. Genet averred that the day the Palestinians regained their lost land he would lose interest in them.

Genet was buried in Larache, a town in northern Morocco, within sight of the house of his last lover, Mohammed El Katrani. Since he was not Muslim he had to be interred in a long-since abandoned Spanish cemetery. The grave, appropriately enough, is on a hill above the sea and close to the local prison and whorehouse. The grave diggers, Muslims themselves, unthinkingly oriented the tomb toward Mecca. When a sightseer stole the original, chiseled plaque, someone very close to Genet rewrote the inscription in black paint on the headstone. Since that person, Jacky Maglia, had been brought up by Genet, his handwriting was almost identical to Genet's. The result is that Genet seems to have signed his own grave.

This final statement—Muslim and Christian, Arab and European, sacred and profane, public and solipsistic—is consistent with Genet's contradictory and idiosyncratic enterprise. No other writer has been at once so moralistic and so immoral, so estranged from popular, middle-class wisdom yet so uncompromising in enforcing his personal code, so harsh in rejecting the good son who has stayed at home and so loving of the broken body of the prodigal.

This book contains generous selections from all five of Genet's novels; a new translation of a long poem; key scenes from *The Maids* and *The Balcony*; a new translation of one of Genet's best essays; never before published—in any language—notes on the cinema; a long section of Genet's memoirs; two previously unpublished letters; and an interview, given here in its entirety in English for the first time. The selections from the plays and four of the novels were translated by Bernard Frechtman between 1948 and the time of his death in 1967.

I

FICTION

Our Lady of the Flowers

◄○►

Genet's first novel was written in 1941 and 1942. By the end of 1942, the book had been completed. Parts of it were written in prison. On December 10, 1941, Genet had been arrested for stealing fabric samples from a tailor (one of the witnesses of the arrest was a bookstore owner from whom Genet had stolen an edition of Proust's works). Genet was sentenced to three months and one day in prison.

When he was freed on March 10, 1942, he helped out a friend who was tending a bookstall along the Seine on the Left Bank across from Notre Dame. It was there that Genet met two young intellectuals, Jean Turlais and Roland Laudenbach, who were fascinated by the exconvict's culture. They introduced him to intellectual figures in Paris. On April 14, 1942, Genet was arrested again, for stealing books, and this time was sentenced to eight months in prison. He was freed early, on October 15. Soon afterward, he finished his novel. While working on Our Lady of the Flowers, *he was also writing numerous film scenarios and a now-lost play,* Heliogabalus, *the story of the decadent Roman emperor. At this time he also wrote his first long poem,* The Man Condemned to Death.

On February 14, 1943, Genet was introduced to Jean Cocteau. Genet read The Man Condemned to Death *out loud to Cocteau and, two days later, read him extracts from* Our Lady of the Flowers. *At first, Cocteau was shocked by the subject matter of the novel but, after passing a sleepless night rereading the text, the ever-generous Cocteau recognized that he had simply been jealous of Genet's achievement. Cocteau arranged for the novel to be published by his own secretary, Paul Moribien. The following December, Moribien, in collaboration with the publisher Robert Denoël, printed* Our Lady of the Flowers (Notre Dame des Fleurs)—*anonymously and in secret. The puritanical Nazis, still occupying Paris, would never have approved publication of this scandalous, homosexual text. The book was not distributed openly, however, until after the Liberation of Paris in August 1944. Even then, it was sold under the counter for a high price, mainly to rich, homosexual collectors. This was not the general audience Genet longed for. For a normally priced version Genet had to wait until 1948, when Ar-balète Editions brought out a second, more generally available edition of the novel.*

Genet based the childhood scenes of Louis Culafroy on his own boyhood memories. Even the adult transvestite, Divine, is loosely based on Genet's own experiences as a male prostitute in Montmartre. At least, Genet once showed a photograph of himself with long hair to a friend and said, "This is a picture of me when I was Divine."

WEIDMANN APPEARED BEFORE YOU in a five o'clock edition, his head swathed in white bands, a nun and yet a wounded pilot fallen into the rye one September day like the day when the world came to know the name of Our Lady of the Flowers. His handsome face, multiplied by the presses, swept down upon Paris and all of France, to the depths of the most out-of-the-way villages, in castles and cabins, revealing to the mirthless bourgeois that their daily lives are grazed by enchanting murderers, cunningly elevated to their sleep, which they will cross by some back stairway that has abetted them by not creaking. Beneath his picture burst the dawn of his crimes: murder one, murder two, murder three, up to six, bespeaking his secret glory and preparing his future glory.

A little earlier, the Negro Angel Sun had killed his mistress.

A little later, the soldier Maurice Pilorge killed his lover, Escudero, to rob him of something under a thousand francs, then, for his twentieth birthday, they cut off his head while, you will recall, he thumbed his nose at the enraged executioner.

Finally, a young ensign, still a child, committed treason for treason's sake: he was shot. And it is in honor of their crimes that I am writing my book.

I learned only in bits and pieces of that wonderful blossoming of dark and lovely flowers: one was revealed to me by a scrap of newspaper; another was casually alluded to by my lawyer; another was mentioned, almost sung, by the prisoners—their song became fantastic and funereal (a *De Profundis*), as much so as the plaints which they sing in the evening, as the voice which crosses the cells and reaches me blurred, hopeless, inflected. At the end of the phrases it breaks, and that break makes it so sweet that it seems borne by the music of angels, which horrifies me, for angels fill me with horror, being, I imagine, neither mind nor matter, white, filmy, and frightening, like the transluscent bodies of ghosts.

These murderers, now dead, have nevertheless reached me, and whenever one of these luminaries of affliction falls into my cell, my heart beats fast, my heart beats a loud tattoo, if the tattoo is the drum-call announcing the capitulation of a city. And there follows a fervor comparable to that which wrung me and left me for some minutes grotesquely contorted, when I heard the German plane passing over the prison and the burst of the bomb which it dropped nearby. In the twinkling of an eye, I saw a lone child, borne by his iron bird, laughingly, strewing death. For him alone were unleashed the sirens, the bells, the hundred-and-one cannon shots reserved for the Dauphin, the cries of hatred and fear. All the cells were atremble, shivering, made with terror; the prisoners pounded the doors, rolled on the floor, shrieked, screamed blasphemies, and prayed to God. I saw, as I say, or thought I saw, an eighteen-year-old child in the plane, and from the depths of my 426 I smiled at him lovingly.

I do not know whether it is their faces, the real ones, which spatter the wall of my cell with a sparkling mud, but it cannot be by chance that I cut those handsome, vacant-eyed heads out of the magazines. I say vacant, for all the eyes are clear and must be sky blue, like the razor's edge to which clings a star of transparent light, blue and vacant like the windows of buildings under construction, through which you can see the sky from the windows of the opposite wall. Like those barracks which in the morning are open to all the winds, which you think are empty and pure when they are swarming with dangerous males, sprawled promiscuously on their beds. I say empty, but if they close their eyes, they become more disturbing to me than are huge prisons to the nubile maiden who passes by the high-barred windows, prisons behind which sleeps, dreams, swears, and spits a race of murderers, which makes of each cell the hissing nest of a tangle of snakes, but also a kind of confessional with a curtain of dusty serge. These eyes, seemingly without mystery, are like certain closed cities—Lyons, Zurich—and they hypnotize me as much as do empty theaters, deserted prisons, machinery at rest, deserts, for deserts are closed and do not communicate with the infinite. Men with such faces terrify me, whenever I have to cross their paths warily, but what a dazzling surprise when, in their landscape, at the turning of a deserted lane, I approach, my heart racing wildly, and discover nothing, nothing but looming emptiness, sensitive and proud like a tall foxglove!

I do not know, as I have said, whether the heads there are really those of my guillotined friends, but I have recognized by certain signs that they—those on the wall—are thoroughly supple, like the lashes of whips, and rigid as glass knives, precocious as child pundits and fresh as forget-me-nots, bodies chosen because they are possessed by terrible souls.

The newspapers are tattered by the time they reach my cell, and the finest pages have been looted of their finest flowers, those pimps, like gardens in May. The big, inflexible, strict pimps, their members in full bloom—I no longer know whether they are lilies or whether lilies and members are not totally they, so much so that in the evening, on my knees, in thought, I encircle their legs with my arms—all that rigidity floors me and makes me confuse them, and the memory which I gladly give as food for my nights is of yours, which, as I caressed it, remained inert, stretched out; only your rod, unsheathed and brandished, went through my mouth with the suddenly cruel sharpness of a steeple puncturing a cloud of ink, a hat pin a breast. You did not move, you were not asleep, you were not dreaming, you were in flight, motionless and pale, frozen, straight, stretched out stiff on the flat bed, like a coffin on the sea, and I know that we were chaste, while I, all attention, felt you flow into me, warm and white, in continuous little jerks. Perhaps you were playing at coming. At the climax, you were lit up with a quiet ecstasy, which enveloped your blessed body in a supernatural nimbus, like a cloak that you pierced with your head and feet.

Still, I managed to get about twenty photographs, and with bits of chewed bread I pasted them on the back of the cardboard sheet of regulations that hangs on the wall. Some are pinned up with bits of brass wire which the foreman brings me and on which I have to string colored glass beads.

Using the same beads with which the prisoners next door make funeral wreaths, I have made star-shaped frames for the most purely criminal. In the evening, as you open your window to the street, I turn the back of the regulations sheet toward me. Smiles and sneers, alike inexorable, enter me by all the holes I offer, their vigour penetrates me and erects me. I live among these pits. They watch over my little routines, which, along with them, are all the family I have and my only friends.

Perhaps some lad who did nothing to deserve prison—a champion, an athlete—slipped in among the twenty by mistake. But if I have nailed him to my wall, it was because, as I see it, he had the sacred sign of the monster at the corner of his mouth or the angle of the eyelids. The flaw on the face or in the set gesture indicates to me that they may very possibly love me, for they love me only if they are monsters—and it may therefore be said that it is this stray himself who has chosen to be here. To provide them with a court and retinue, I have culled here and there, from the illustrated covers of a few adventure novels, a young Mexican half-breed, a gaucho, a Caucasian horseman, and, from the pages of these novels that are passed from hand to hand when we take our walk, clumsy drawings: profiles of pimps and Apaches with a smoking butt, or the outline of a tough with a hard-on.

At night I love them, and my love endows them with life. During the day I go about my petty concerns. I am the housekeeper, watchful lest a bread crumb or a speck of ash fall on the floor. But at night! Fear of the guard who may suddenly flick on the light and stick his head through the grating compels me to take sordid precautions lest the rustling of the sheets draw attention to my pleasure; but though my gesture may be less noble, by becoming secret it heightens my pleasure. I dawdle. Beneath the sheet, my right hand stops to caress the absent face, and then the whole body, of the outlaw I have chosen for that evening's delight. The left hand closes, then arranges its fingers in the form of a hollow organ which tries to resist, then offers itself, opens up, and a vigorous body, a wardrobe, emerges from the wall, advances, and falls upon me. Crushes me against my straw mattress, which has already been stained by more than a hundred prisoners, while I think of the happiness into which I sink at a time when God and His angels exist.

No one can tell whether I shall get out of here, or, if I do, when it will be.

So, with the help of my unknown lovers, I am going to write a story. My heroes are they, pasted on the wall, they and I who am here, locked up. As you read on, the characters, and Divine too, and Culafroy, will fall from the wall onto my page like dead leaves, to fertilize my tale. As for their death, need I tell you about it? For all of them it will be the death of him who, when he learned of his from the jury, merely mumbled in a Rhenish accent: "I'm already beyond that" (Weidmann).

This story may not always seem artificial, and in spite of me you may recognize in it the call of the blood: the reason is that within my night I shall have happened to strike my forehead at some door, freeing an anguished memory that had been haunting me since the world began. Forgive me for it. This book aims to be only a small fragment of my inner life.

Sometimes the cat-footed guard tosses me a hello through the grate. He talks to me and, without meaning to, tells me a good deal about my forger neighbors, about arsonists, counterfeiters, murderers, swaggering adolescents who roll on the floor screaming: "Mama, help!" He slams the grate shut and delivers me to a tête-à-tête with all those fine gentlemen whom he has just let slip in and who twist and squirm in the warmth of the sheets and the drowsiness of the morning to seek the end of the thread which will unravel the motives, the system of complicity, a whole fierce and subtle mechanism which, among other neat tricks, changed a few pink girls into white corpses. I want to mingle them too, with their heads and legs, among my friends on the wall, and to compose with them this children's tale. And to refashion in my own way, and for the enchantment of my cell (I mean that thanks to her my cell will be enchanted), the story of Divine, whom I knew only slightly, the story of Our Lady of the Flowers, and, never fear, my own story.

Description of Our Lady of the Flowers: height, 5 ft. 7 ins., weight 156 lbs., oval face, blond hair, blue eyes, matt complexion, perfect teeth, straight nose.

Divine died yesterday in a pool of her vomited blood which was so red that, as she expired, she had the supreme illusion that this blood was the visible equivalent of that black hole which a gutted violin, seen in a judge's office in the midst of a hodge-podge of pieces of evidence, revealed with dramatic insistence, as does a Jesus the gilded chancre where gleams His flaming Sacred Heart. So much for the divine aspect of her death. The other aspect, ours, because of those streams of blood that had been shed on her nightshirt and sheets (for the sun, poignant on the bloody sheets, had set, not nastily, in her bed), makes her death tantamount to a murder.

Divine died holy and murdered—by consumption.

It is January, and in the prison too, where this morning, during the walk, slyly, among prisoners, we wished each other a happy New Year, as humbly as servants must do among themselves in the pantry. The chief guard gave us each a little half-ounce packet of coarse salt as a New Year's gift. Three hours after noon. It has been raining behind the bars since yesterday, and it's windy. I let myself drift, as to the depth of an ocean, to the depths of a dismal neighborhood of hard and opaque but rather light houses, to the inner gaze of memory, for the matter of memory is porous. The garret in which Divine lived for such a long time is at the top of one of these houses. Its large window propels the eyes (and delights them) toward the little Montmartre Cemetery. The stairway leading up to it plays an important role today. It is the antechamber, sinuous as the hallways of the Pyramids, of Divine's temporary tomb. This cavernous hypogeum looms up, pure as the bare marble arm in the darkness which is devouring the queen to whom it belongs. Coming from the street, the stairway mounts to death. It ushers one to the final resting place. It smells of decaying flowers and already of the odor of candles and incense. It rises into the shadow. From floor to floor it dwindles and darkens until, at the top, it is no more than an illusion blending with the azure. This is Divine's landing. While in the street, beneath the black haloes of the tiny flat umbrellas which they are holding in one hand like bouquets, Mimosa I, Mimosa II, Mimosa the half-IV, First Communion, Angela, Milord, Castagnette, Régine— in short, a host, a still long litany of creatures who are glittering names—are waiting, and in the other hand are carrying, like umbrellas, little bouquets of violets which make one of them lose herself, for example, in a reverie from which she will emerge bewildered and quite dumbfounded with nobility, for she (let us say First Communion) remembers the article, thrilling as a song from the other world, from our world too, in which an evening paper, thereby embalmed, stated:

"The black velvet rug of the Hotel Crillon, where lay the silver and ebony coffin containing the embalmed body of the Princess of Monaco, was strewn with Parma violets."

First Communion was chilly. She thrust her chin forward as great ladies do. Then she drew it in and wrapped herself in the folds of a story (born of her desires and taking into account, so as to magnify them, all the mishaps of her drab existence) in which she was dead and a princess.

The rain favored her flight.

Girl-queens were carrying wreaths of glass beads, the very kind I make in my cell, to which they bring the odor of wet moss and the memory of the trail of slime left on the white stones of my village cemetery by snails and slugs.

And all of them, the girl-queens and boy-queens, the aunties, fags, and nellies of whom I am speaking, are assembled at the foot of the stairway. The girl-queens are huddled together, chattering and chirping around the boy-queens, who are straight, motionless, and vertiginous, as motionless and silent as branches. All are dressed in black: trousers, jacket, and overcoat, but their faces, young or old, smooth or crinkly, are divided into quarters of color like a coat of arms. It is raining. With the patter of the rain is mingled:

"Poor Divine!"

"Would you believe it, my dear! But at her age it was fatal."

"It was falling apart. She was losing her bottom."

"Hasn't Darling come?"

"Hi there!"

"Dig *her!*"

Divine, who disliked anyone's walking over her head, lived on the top floor of a middle-class apartment house in a sober neighborhood. It was at the foot of this house that the crowd belonging to this backstage conversation shuffled about.

Any minute now the hearse, drawn perhaps by a black horse, will come to take away Divine's remains and carry them to the church, then here, close by, to the little Montmartre Cemetery, which the procession will enter by the Avenue Rachel.

The Eternal passed by in the form of a pimp. The prattle ceased. Bareheaded and very elegant, simple and smiling, simple and supple, Darling Daintyfoot arrived. There was in his supple bearing the weighty magnificence of the barbarian who tramples choice furs beneath his muddy boots. The torso on his hips was a king on a throne. Merely to have mentioned him is enough for my left hand in my torn pocket to . . . And the memory of Darling will not leave me until I have completed my gesture. One day the door of my cell opened and framed him. I thought I saw him, in the twinkling of an eye, as solemn as a walking corpse, set in the thickness—which you can only imagine—of the prison walls. He appeared standing before me with the same graciousness that might have been his lying naked in a field of pinks. I was his at once, as if (who said that?) he had discharged through my mouth straight to my heart. Entering me until there was no room left for myself, so that now I am one with gangsters, burglars, and pimps, and the police arrest me by mistake. For three months he regaled himself with my body, beating me for all he was worth. I dragged at his feet, more trampled on than a dust mop. Ever since he has gone off free to his robberies, I keep remembering his gestures, so vivid they revealed him cut out of a faceted crystal, gestures so vivid that you suspected they were all involuntary, for it seems utterly impossible that they were born of ponderous reflection and decision. Of the tangible him there remains, sad to say, only the plaster cast that Divine herself made of his cock which was gigantic when erect. The most impressive thing about it is the vigor, hence the beauty, of that part which goes from the anus to the tip of the penis.

I shall say that he had lace fingers, that, each time he awoke, his outstretched arms, open to receive the World, made him look like the Christ Child in his manger—with the heel of one foot on the instep of the other—that his eager face offered itself, as it bent backward facing heaven, that, when standing, he would tend to make the basket movement we see Nijinsky making in the old photos where he is dressed in shredded roses. His wrist, fluid as a violinist's, hangs down, graceful and loose-jointed. And at times, in broad daylight, he strangles himself with his lithe arm, the arm of a *tragedienne*.

This is almost an exact portrait of Darling, for—we shall see him again—he had a talent for the gesture that thrills me, and, if I think about him, I can't stop praising him until my hand is smeared with my liberated pleasure.

A Greek, he entered the house of death walking on air. A Greek, that is, a crook as well. As he passed—the motion was revealed by an imperceptible movement of the torso—within themselves, secretly, Milord, the Mimosas, Castagnette, in short, all the queens, imparted a tendril-like movement to their bodies and fancied they were enlacing this handsome man, were twining about him. Indifferent and bright as a slaughterhouse knife, he passed by, cleaving them all into two slices which came noiselessly together again, though emitting a slight scent of hopelessness which no one divulged. Darling went up the stairs two at a time, an ample and forthright ascension, which may lead, after the roof, on steps of blue air, up to heaven. In the garret, less mysterious since death had converted it into a vault (it was losing its equivocal meaning, was again assuming, in all its purity, that air of incoherent gratuity that these funereal and mysterious objects, these mortuary objects lent it: white gloves, a lampion, an artilleryman's jacket, in short, an inventory that we shall list later on), the only one to sigh in her mourning veils was Divine's mother, Ernestine. She is old. But now at last the wonderful, long-awaited opportunity does not escape her. Divine's death enables her to free herself, by an external despair, by a visible mourning consisting of tears, flowers and crape, from the hundred great roles which possessed her. The opportunity slipped between her fingers at the time of an illness which I shall tell about, when Divine the Gaytime Girl was still just a village youngster named Louis Culafroy. From his sickbed, he looked at the room where an angel (once again this word disturbs me, attracts me, and sickens me. If they have wings, do they have teeth? Do they fly with such heavy wings, feathered wings, "those mysterious wings"? And scented with that wonder: their angels' name which they change if they fall?), an angel, a soldier dressed in light blue, and a Negro (for will my books ever be anything but a pretext for showing a soldier dressed in sky blue, and a brotherly Negro and angel playing dice or knuckle bones in a dark or light prison?) were engaged in a confabulation from which he himself was excluded. The angel, the Negro, and the soldier kept assuming the faces of various schoolmates and peasants, but never that of Alberto the snake fisher. He was the one Culafroy was waiting for in his desert, to calm his torrid thirst with that mouth of starry flesh. To console himself, he tried, despite his age, to conceive a kind of happiness in which nothing would be winsome, a pure, deserted, desolate field, a field of azure or sand, a dumb, dry, magnetic field, where nothing sweet, no color or sound, would remain. Quite some time before, the appearance on the village road of a bride wearing a black dress, though wrapped in a veil of white tulle, lovely and sparkling, like a young shepherd beneath the hoar frost, like a powdered blond miller, or like Our Lady of the Flowers whom he will meet later on and whom I saw with my own eyes here in my cell one morning, near the latrines—his sleepy face pink and bristly beneath the soapsuds, which blurred his vision—revealed to Culafroy that poetry is something other than a melody of curves on sweetness, for the tulle snapped apart into abrupt, clear, rigorous, icy facets. It was a warning.

He was waiting for Alberto, who did not come. Yet all the peasant boys and girls who came in had something of the snake fisher about them. They were like his harbingers, his ambassadors, his precursors, bearing some of his gifts before him, preparing his coming by smoothing the way for him. They shouted hallelujah. One had his walk, another his gestures, or the color of his trousers, or his corduroy, or Alberto's voice; and Culafroy, like someone waiting, never doubted that all these scattered elements would eventually fuse and enable a reconstructed Alberto to make the solemn, appointed, and surprising entrance into his room that a dead and alive Darling Daintyfoot made into my cell.

When the village *abbé*, hearing the news, said to Ernestine: "Madame, it's a blessing to die young," she replied: "Yes, your Lordship," and made a curtsy.

The priest looked at her.

She was smiling in the shiny floor at her antipodal reflection which made her the Queen of Spades, the ill-omened widow.

"Don't shrug your shoulders, my friend, I'm not crazy."

And she wasn't crazy.

"Lou Culafroy is going to die shortly. I feel it. He's going to die, I can tell."

"He's going to die, I can tell," was the expression torn alive—and helping her to fly—from a book, and bleeding, like a wing from a sparrow (or from an angel, if it can bleed crimson), and murmured with horror by the heroine of that cheap novel printed in tiny type in newsprint—which, so they say, is as spongy as the consciences of those nasty gentlemen who debauch children.

"So, I'm dancing the dirge."

He therefore had to die. And in order for the pathos of the act to be more virulent, she herself would have to be the cause of his death. Here, to be sure, morality is not involved, nor the fear of prison, or of hell. With remarkable precision, the whole mechanism of the drama presented itself to Ernestine's mind, and thereby to mine. She would simulate a suicide. "I'll say he killed himself," Ernestine's logic, which is a stage logic, has no relationship with what is called verisimilitude, verisimilitude being the disavowal of unavowable reasons. Let us not be surprised, we shall be all the more astonished.

The presence of a huge army revolver at the back of a drawer was enough to dictate her attitude. This is not the first time that things have been the instigators of an act and must alone bear the fearful, though light, responsibility for a crime. This revolver became—or so it seemed—the indispensable accessory of her gesture. It was a continuation of her heroine's outstretched arm, in fact it haunted her, since there's no denying it, with a brutality that burned her cheeks, just as the girls of the village were haunted by the brutal swelling of Alberto's thick hands in his pockets. But—just as I myself would be willing to kill only a lithe adolescent in order to bring forth a corpse from his death, though a corpse still warm and a shade sweet to hug, so Ernestine agreed to kill only on condition that she avoid the horror that the here below would not fail to inspire in her (convulsions, squirting blood and brain, reproaches in the child's dismayed eyes), and the horror of an angelic beyond, or perhaps to make the moment more stately—she put on her jewels. So in the past I would inject my cocaine with a cut-glass syringe shaped like the stopper of a decanter and put a huge diamond on my index finger. She was not aware that by going about it in this way she was aggravating her gesture, changing it into an exceptional gesture, the singularity of which threatened to upset everything. Which is what happened. With a kind of smooth sliding, the room descended till it blended with a luxurious apartment, adorned with gold, the walls hung with garnet red velvet, the furniture heavy but toned down with red faille curtains; here and there were large beveled mirrors, adorned with candelabra and their crystal pendants. From the ceiling—an important detail—hung a huge chandelier. The floor was covered with thick blue and violet carpets.

One evening, during her honeymoon in Paris, Ernestine had glimpsed from the street, through the curtains, one of those elegant, well-heated apartments, and as she walked demurely with her arm in her husband's—demurely still—she longed to die there of love (phenobarbital and flowers) for a Teutonic knight. Then, as she had already died four or five times, the apartment had remained available for a drama more serious than her own death.

I'm complicating things, getting involved, and you're talking of childishness. It *is* childishness. All prisoners are children, and only children are underhanded, wily, open, and confused. "What would top it all," thought Ernestine, "would be for him to die in a fashionable city, in Cannes or Venice, so that I could make pilgrimages to it."

To stop at a Ritz, bathed by the Adriatic, wife or mistress of a Doge; then, her arms full of flowers, to climb a path to the cemetery, to sit down on a simple flagstone, a white, slightly curved stone, and, all curled up in fragrant grief, to brood!

Without bringing her back to reality, for she never left reality, the arrangement of the setting obliged her to shake off the dream. She went to get the revolver, which had long since been loaded by a most considerate Providence, and when she held it in her hand, weighty as a phallus in action, she realized she was big with murder, pregnant with a corpse.

You, you have no idea of the superhuman or extralucid state of mind of the blind murderer who holds the knife, the gun, or the phial, or who has already released the movement that propels to the precipice.

Ernestine's gesture might have been performed quickly, but, like Culafroy in fact, she is serving a text she knows nothing about, a text I am composing whose *dénouement* will occur when the time is ripe. Ernestine is perfectly aware of how ridiculously literary her act is, but that she has to submit to cheap literature makes her even more touching in her own eyes and ours. In drama, as in all of life, she escapes vainglorious beauty.

Every premeditated murder is always governed by a preparatory ceremonial and is always followed by a propitiatory ceremonial. The meaning of both eludes the murderer's mind. Everything is in order. Ernestine has just time to appear before a Star Chamber. She fired. The bullet shattered the glass of a frame containing an honorary diploma of her late husband. The noise was frightful. Drugged by sleeping pills, the child heard nothing. Nor did Ernestine. She had fired in the apartment with the garnet red velvet, and the bullet, shattering the beveled mirrors, the pendants, the crystals, the stucco, the stars, tearing the hangings—in short, destroying the structure which collapsed—brought down not sparkling powder and blood, but the crystal of the chandelier and the pendants, a gray ash on the head of Ernestine, who swooned.

She came back to her senses amidst the debris of her drama. Her hands, freed from the revolver, which disappeared beneath the bed like an axe at the bottom of a pond, like a prowler into a wall, her hands, lighter than her thoughts, fluttered about her. Since then, she has been waiting.

That was how Darling saw her, intoxicated with the tragic. He was intimidated by her, for she was beautiful and seemed mad, but especially because she was beautiful. Did he, who himself was handsome, have to fear her? I'm sorry to say I know too little (nothing) about the secret relations between people who are handsome and know it, and nothing about the seemingly friendly but perhaps hostile contacts between handsome boys. If they smile at each other over a trifle, is there, unknown to them, some tenderness in their smile, and do they feel its influence in some obscure way? Darling made a clumsy sign of the cross over the coffin. His constraint gave the impression that he was deep in thought; and his constraint was all his grace.

Death had laced its mark, which weighs like a lead seal at the bottom of a parchment, on the curtains, the walls, the rugs. Particularly on the curtains. They are sensitive. They sense death and echo it like dogs. They bark at death through the folds that open, dark as the mouth and eyes of the masks of Sophocles, or which bulge like the eyelids of Christian ascetics. The blinds were drawn and the candles lighted. Darling, no longer recognizing the attic where he had lived with Divine, behaved like a young man on a visit.

His emotion beside the coffin? None. He no longer remembered Divine.

The undertaker's assistants arrived almost immediately and saved him from further embarrassment.

In the rain, this black cortege, bespangled with multicolored faces and blended with the scent of flowers and rouge, followed the hearse. The flat, round umbrellas, undulating above the ambulating procession, held it suspended between heaven and earth. The passersby did not even see it, for it was so light that it was already floating ten yards from the ground; only the maids and butlers might have noticed it, but at ten o'clock the former were bringing the morning chocolate to their mistresses and the latter were opening the door to early visitors. Besides, the cortege was almost invisible because of its speed. The hearse had wings on its axle. The *abbé* emerged first into the rain singing the *dies irae*. He tucked up his cassock and cope, as he had been taught to do at the seminary when the weather was bad. His gesture, though automatic, released within him, with a placenta of nobility, a series of sad and secret creatures. With one of the flaps of the black velvet cope, the velvet from which are made Fantômas' masks and those of the Doges' wives, he tried to slip away, but it was the ground that gave way under him, and we shall see the trap into which he fell. Just in time, he prevented the cloth from hiding the lower part of his face. Bear in mind that the *abbé* was young. You could tell that under his funereal vestments he had the lithe body of a passionate athlete. Which means, in short, that he was in travesty. In the church—the whole funeral service having been merely the "do this in memory of me"—approaching the altar on tiptoe, in silence, he had picked the lock of the tabernacle, parted the veil like someone who at midnight parts the double curtains of an alcove, held his breath, seized the ciborium with the caution of an ungloved burglar, and finally, having broken it, swallowed a questionable host.

From the church to the cemetery, the road was long and the text of the breviary too familiar. Only the dirge and the black, silver-embroidered cope exuded charms. The *abbé* plodded through the mud as he would have done in the heart of the woods. "Of what woods?" he asked himself. In a foreign country, a forest of Bohemia. Or rather of Hungary. In choosing this country, he was no doubt guided by the precious suspicion that Hungarians are the only Asiates in Europe. Huns. The Hunis. Attila burning the grass, and his soldiers warming between their brutal and colossal thighs (like those, and perhaps even larger than those, of Alberto, Darling, and Gorgui) and their horses' flanks the raw meat that they will eat. It is autumn. It is raining in the Hungarian forest.

Every branch that he has to push aside wets the priest's forehead. The only sound is the patter of the drops on the wet leaves. Since it is evening, the woods become more and more alarming. The priest draws the gray coat more tightly about his splendid loins, the great cape, like his cope of today, which envelopes him over there.

In the forest is a sawmill; two young men work it and hunt. They are unknown in the region. They have (the *abbé* knows this as one knows things in dreams without having learned them) been around the world. And so here the *abbé* was chanting the dirge as he would have sung it there when he met one of the strangers, the younger, who had the face of the butcher of my village. He was on his way back from hunting. In the corner of his mouth, an unlit butt. The word "butt" and the taste of the sucked tobacco made the *abbé's* spine stiffen and draw back with three short jerks, the vibrations of which reverberated through all his muscles and on to infinity, which shuddered and ejaculated a seed of constellations.

The woodcutter's lips came down on the *abbé's* mouth, where, with a thrust of the tongue more imperious than a royal order, they drove in the butt. The priest was knocked down, bitten, and he expired with love on the soggy moss. After having almost disrobed him, the stranger caressed him, gratefully, almost fondly, thought the *abbé*. With a heave, he shouldered his game bag, which was weighted down with a wildcat, picked up his gun, and went off whistling a raffish tune.

The *abbé* was winding his way among mausoleums; the queens were stumbling over the stones, getting their feet wet in the grass, and among the graves were being angelicized. The choirboy, a puny lad with ringworm, who hadn't the slightest suspicion of the adventure the *abbé* had just had, asked him whether he might keep his skullcap on. The *abbé* said yes. As he walked, his leg made the movement peculiar to dancers (with one hand in their pockets) as they finish a tango. He bent forward on his leg, which was slightly advanced on the tip of the toe; he slapped his knee against the cloth of the cassock, which flapped back and forth like the bell-bottomed trousers of a swaying sailor or gaucho. Then he began a psalm.

When the procession arrived at the hole which had already been dug, perhaps by the grave digger Divine used to see from her window, they lowered the coffin in which Divine lay wrapped in a white lace sheet. The *abbé* blessed the grave and handed his sprinkler to Darling, who blushed to feel it so heavy (for he had to some degree returned, after and beyond Divine, to his race, which was akin to that of young Gypsies, who are willing to jerk you off, but only with their feet), then to the queens, who turned the whole area into a squealing of pretty cries and high giggles. Divine departed as she would have desired, in a mixture of fantasy and sordidness.

Divine is dead, is dead and buried . . .
. . . is dead and buried.

Since Divine is dead, the poet may sing her, may tell her legend, the Saga, the annals of Divine. The Divine Saga should be danced, mimed, with subtle directions. Since it is impossible to make a ballet of it, I am forced to use words that are weighed down with precise ideas, but I shall try to lighten them with expressions that are trivial, empty, hollow, and invisible.

What is involved for me who is making up this story? In reviewing my life, in tracing its course, I fill my cell with the pleasure of being what for want of a trifle I failed to be, recapturing, so that I may hurl myself into them as into dark pits, those moments when I strayed through the trap-ridden compartments of a subterranean sky. Slowly displacing volumes of fetid air, cutting threads from which hang bouquets of feelings, seeing the Gypsy for whom I am looking emerge perhaps from some starry river, wet, with mossy hair, playing the fiddle, diabolically whisked away by the scarlet velvet portiere of a cabaret.

I shall speak to you about Divine, mixing masculine and feminine as my mood dictates, and if, in the course of the tale, I shall have to refer to a woman, I shall manage, I shall find an expedient, a good device, to avoid any confusion.

Divine appeared in Paris to lead her public life about twenty years before her death. She was then thin and vivacious and will remain so until the end of her life, though growing angular. At about two A.M. she entered Graff's Café in Montmartre. The customers were a muddy, still shapeless clay. Divine was limpid water. In the big café with the closed windows and the curtains drawn on their hollow rods, overcrowded and foundering in smoke, she wafted the coolness of scandal, which is the coolness of a morning breeze, the astonishing sweetness of a breath of scandal on the stone of the temple, and just as the wind turns leaves, so she turned heads, heads which all at once became light (giddy heads), heads of bankers, shopkeepers, gigolos for ladies, waiters, manager, colonels, scarecrows.

She sat down alone at a table and asked for tea.

"Specially fine China tea, my good man," she said to the waiter.

With a smile. For the customers she had an irritatingly jaunty smile. Hence, the "you-know-what" in the wagging of the heads. For the poet and the reader, her smile will be enigmatic.

That evening she was wearing a champagne silk short-sleeved blouse, a pair of blue trousers stolen from a sailor, and leather sandals. On one of her fingers, though preferably on the pinkie, an ulcer-like stone gangrened her. When the tea was brought, she drank it as if she were at home, in tiny little sips (a pigeon), putting down and lifting the cup with her pinkie in the air. Here is a portrait of her: her hair is brown and curly; with the curls spilling over her eyes and down her cheeks, she looks as if she were wearing a cat-o'-nine-tails on her head. Her forehead is somewhat round and smooth. Her eyes sing, despite their despair, and their melody moves from her eyes to her teeth, to which she gives life, and from her teeth to all her movements, to her slightest acts, and this charm, which emerges from her eyes, unfurls in wave upon wave, down to her bare feet. Her body is fine as amber. Her limbs can be agile when she flees from ghosts. At her heels, the wings of terror bear her along. She is quick, for in order to elude the ghosts, to throw them off her track, she must speed ahead faster than her thought thinks. She drank her tea before thirty pairs of eyes which belied what the contemptuous, spiteful, sorrowful, wilting mouths were saying.

Divine was full of grace, and yet was like all those prowlers at country fairs on the lookout for rare sights and artistic visions, good sports who trail behind them all the inevitable hodge-podge of side shows. At the slightest movement—if they knot their tie, if they flick the ash of their cigarette—they set slot machines in motion. Divine knotted, garrotted arteries. Her seductiveness will be implacable. If it were only up to me, I would make her the kind of fatal hero I like. Fatal, that is, determining the fate of those who gaze at them, spellbound. I would make her with hips of stone, flat and polished cheeks, heavy eyelids, pagan knees so lovely that they reflected the desperate intelligence of the faces of the mystics. I would strip her of all sentimental trappings. Let her consent to be the frozen statue. But I know that the poor Demiurge is forced to make his creature in his own image and that he did not invent Lucifer. In my cell, little by little, I shall have to give my thrills to the granite. I shall remain alone with it for a long time, and I shall make it live with my breath and the smell of my farts, both the solemn and the mild ones. It will take me an entire book to draw her from her petrifaction and gradually impart my suffering to her, gradually deliver her from evil, and, holding her by the hand, lead her to saintliness.

The waiter who served her felt very much like snickering, but out of decency he did not dare in front of her. As for the manager, he approached her table and decided that as soon as she finished her tea, he would ask her to leave, to make sure she would not turn up again some other evening.

Finally, she patted her snowy forehead with a flowered handkerchief. Then she crossed her legs; on her ankle could be seen a chain fastened by a locket which *we* know contained a few hairs. She smiled all around, and each one answered only by turning away, but that was a way of answering. The whole café thought that the smile of (for the colonel: the invert; for the shopkeepers: the fairy; for the banker and the waiters: the fag; for the gigolos: *"that"* one; etc.) was despicable. Divine did not press the point. From a tiny black satin purse she took a few coins which she laid noiselessly on the marble table. The café disappeared, and Divine was metamorphosed into one of those monsters that are painted on walls—chimeras or griffins—for a customer, in spite of himself, murmured a magic word as he thought of her:

"Homoseckshual."

That evening, her first in Montmartre, she was cruising. But she got nowhere. She came upon us without warning. The habitués of the café had neither the time nor, above all, the composure to handle properly their reputations or their females. Having drunk her tea, Divine, with indifference (so it appeared, seeing her), wriggling in a spray of flowers and strewing swishes and spangles with an invisible furbelow, made off. So here she is, having decided to return, lifted by a column of smoke, to her garret, on the door of which is nailed a huge, discolored muslin rose.

Her perfume is violent and vulgar. From it we can already tell that she is fond of vulgarity. Divine has sure taste, good taste, and it is most upsetting that life always puts someone so delicate into vulgar positions, into contact with all kinds of filth. She cherishes vulgarity because her greatest love was for a dark-skinned Gypsy. On him, under him, when, with his mouth pressed to hers, he sang to her Gypsy songs that pierced her body, she learned to submit to the charm of such vulgar cloths as silk and gold braid, which are becoming to immodest persons. Montmartre was aflame. Divine passed through its multicolored fires, then, intact, entered the darkness of the promenade of the Boulevard de Clichy, a darkness that preserves old and ugly faces. It was three A.M. She walked for a while toward Pigalle. She smiled and stared at every man who strolled by alone. They didn't dare, or else it was that she still knew nothing about the customary routine: the client's qualms, his hesitations, his lack of assurance as soon as he approaches the coveted youngster. She was weary; she sat down on a bench and, despite her fatigue, was conquered, transported by the warmth of the night; she let herself go for the length of a heartbeat and expressed her excitement as follows: "The nights are mad about me! Oh the sultanas! My God, they're making eyes at me! Ah, they're curling my hair around their fingers (the fingers of the nights, men's cocks!). They're patting my cheek, stroking my butt." That was what she thought, though without rising to, or sinking into, a poetry cut off from the terrestrial world. Poetic expression will never change her state of mind. She will always be the tart concerned with gain.

There are mornings when all men experience with fatigue a flush of tenderness that makes them horny. One day at dawn I found myself placing my lips lovingly, though for no reason at all, on the icy banister of the Rue Berthe; another time, kissing my hand; still another time, bursting with emotion, I wanted to swallow myself by opening my mouth very wide and turning it over my head so that it would take in my whole body, and then the Universe, until all that would remain of me would be a ball of eaten thing which little by little would be annihilated: that is how I see the end of the world. Divine offered herself to the night in order to be devoured by it tenderly and never again spewed forth. She is hungry. And there is nothing around. The pissoirs are empty; the promenade is just about deserted. Merely some bands of young workmen—whose whole disorderly adolescence is manifest in their carelessly tied shoelaces which hop about on their insteps—returning home in forced marches from an evening of pleasure. Their tight-fitting jackets are like fragile breastplates or shells protecting the naïveté of their bodies. But by the grace of their virility, which is still as light as a hope, they are inviolable by Divine.

She will do nothing tonight. The possible customers were so taken by surprise that they were unable to collect their wits. She will have to go back to her attic with hunger in her belly and her heart. She stood up to go. A man came staggering toward her. He bumped her with his elbow.

"Oh! sorry," he said, "terribly sorry!"

His breath reeked of wine.

"Quite all right," said the queen.

It was Darling Daintyfoot going by.

Description of Darling: height, 5 ft. 9 in., weight 165 lbs., oval face, blond hair, blue-green eyes, matt complexion, perfect teeth, straight nose.

He was young too, almost as young as Divine, and I would like him to remain so to the end of the book. Every day the guards open my door so I can leave my cell and go out into the yard for some fresh air. For a few seconds, in the corridors and on the stairs, I pass thieves and hoodlums whose faces enter my face and whose bodies, from afar, hurl mine to the ground. I long to have them within reach. Yet not one of them makes me evoke Darling Daintyfoot.

When I met Divine in Fresnes Prison, she spoke to me about him a great deal, seeking his memory and the traces of his steps throughout the prison, but I never quite knew his face, and this is a tempting opportunity for me to blend him in my mind with the face and physique of Roger.

Very little of this Corsican remains in my memory: a hand with too massive a thumb that plays with a tiny hollow key, and the faint image of a blond boy walking up La Canabière in Marseilles, with a small chain, probably gold, stretched across his fly, which it seems to be buckling. He belongs to a group of males who are advancing upon me with the pitiless gravity of forests on the march. That was the starting point of the daydream in which I imagined myself calling him Roger, a "little boy's" name, though firm and upright. Roger was upright. I had just got out of the Chave prison, and I was amazed not to have met him there. What could I commit to be worthy of his beauty? I needed boldness in order to admire him. For lack of money, I slept at night in the shadowy corners of coal piles, on the docks, and every evening I carried him off with me. The memory of his memory made way for other men. For the past two days, in my daydreams, I have again been mingling his (made-up) life with mine. I wanted him to love me, and of course he did, with the candor that required only perversity for him to be able to love me. For two successive days I have fed with his image a dream which is usually sated after four or five hours when I have given it a boy to feed upon, however handsome he may be. Now I am exhausted with inventing circumstances in which he loves me more and more. I am worn out with the invented trips, thefts, rapes, burglaries, imprisonments, and treachery in which we were involved, each acting by and for the other and never by or for himself, in which the adventure was ourselves and only ourselves. I am exhausted; I have a cramp in my wrist. The pleasure of the last drops is dry. For a period of two days, between my four bare walls, I experienced with him and through him every possibility of an existence that had to be repeated twenty times and got so mixed up it became more real than a real one. I have given up the daydream. I was loved. I have quit, the way a contestant in a six-day bicycle race quits; yet the memory of his eyes and their fatigue, which I have to cull from the face of another youngster whom I saw coming out of a brothel, a boy with firm legs and ruthless cock, so solid that I might almost say it was knotted, and his face (it alone, seen without its veil), which asks for shelter like a knight-errant—this memory refuses to disappear as the memory of my dream-friends usually does. It floats about. It is less sharp than when the adventures were taking place, but it lives in me nevertheless. Certain details persist more obstinately in remaining: the little hollow key with which, if he wants to, he can whistle; his thumb; his sweater; his blue eyes . . . If I continue, he will rise up, become erect, and penetrate me so deeply that I shall be marked with stigmata. I can't bear it any longer. I am turning him into a character whom I shall be able to torment in my own way, namely, Darling Daintyfoot. He will still be twenty, although his destiny is to become the father and lover of Our Lady of the Flowers.

To Divine he said:
  "Terribly sorry!"
  In his cups, Darling did not notice the strangeness of this passerby with his aggressive niceness:
  "What about it, pal?"
  Divine stopped. A bantering and dangerous conversation ensued, and then everything happened as was to be desired. Divine took him home with her to the Rue Caulaincourt. It was in this garret that she died, the garret from which one sees below, like the sea beneath the watchman in the crow's nest, a cemetery and graves. Cypresses singing. Ghosts dozing. Every morning, Divine will shake her dustrag from the window and bid the ghosts farewell. One day, with the help of field glasses, she will discover a young grave digger. "God forgive me!" she will exclaim, "there's a bottle of wine on the vault!" This grave digger will grow old along with her and will bury her without knowing anything about her.
  So she went upstairs with Darling. Then, in the attic after closing the door, she undressed him. With his jacket, trousers, and shirt off, he looked as white and sunken as an avalanche. By evening they found themselves tangled in the damp and rumpled sheets.
  "What a mess! Man! I was pretty groggy yesterday, wasn't I, doll?"
  He laughed feebly, and looked around the garret. It is a room with a sloping ceiling. On the floor, Divine has put some threadbare rugs and nailed to the wall

the murderers on the walls of my cell and the extraordinary photographs of good-looking kids, which she has stolen from photographers' display windows, all of whom bear the signs of the power of darkness.

"Display window!"

On the mantelpiece, a tube of phenobarbital lying on a small, painted, wooden frigate is enough to detach the room from the stone block of the building, to suspend it like a cage between heaven and earth.

From the way he talks, the way he lights and smokes his cigarette, Divine has gathered that Darling is a pimp. At first she had certain fears: of being beaten up, robbed, insulted. Then she felt the proud satisfaction of having made a pimp come. Without quite seeing where the adventure would lead, but rather as a bird is said to go into a serpent's mouth, she said, not quite voluntarily and in a kind of trance: "Stay," and added hesitantly, "if you want to."

"No kidding, you feel that way about me?"

Darling stayed.

In that big Montmartre attic, where through the skylight, between the pink muslin puffs which she has made herself, Divine sees white cradles sailing by on a calm, blue sea, so close that she can make out their flowers from which emerges the arched foot of a dancer. Darling will soon bring the midnight blue overalls that he wears on the job, his ring of skeleton keys and his tools, and on the little pile which they make on the floor he will place his white rubber gloves, which are like gloves for formal occasions. Thus began their life together in that room through which ran the electric wires of the stolen radiator, the stolen radio, and the stolen lamps.

They eat breakfast in the afternoon. During the day they sleep and listen to the radio. Toward evening, they primp and go out. At night, as is the practice, Divine hustles on the Place Blanche and Darling goes to the movies. For a long time, things will go well with Divine. With Darling to advise and protect her, she will know whom to rob, which judge to blackmail. The vaporish cocaine loosens the contours of their lives and sets their bodies adrift, and so they are untouchable.

Though a hoodlum, Darling had a face of light. He was the handsome male, gentle and violent, born to be a pimp, and of so noble a bearing that he seemed always to be naked, save for one ridiculous and, to me, touching movement: the way he arched his back, standing first on one foot, then on the other, in order to take off his trousers and shorts. Before his birth, Darling was baptized privately, that is, beatified too, practically canonized, in the warm belly of his mother. He was given the kind of emblematic baptism which, upon his death, was to send him to limbo; in short, one of those brief ceremonies, mysterious and highly dramatic in their compactness, sumptuous too, to which the Angels were convoked and in which the votaries of the Divinity were mobilized, as was the Divinity Itself. Darling is aware of this, though only slightly; that is, throughout his life, rather than anyone's telling him such secrets aloud and intelligibly, it seems that someone whispers them to him. And this private baptism, with which his life began, gilds his life as it unfolds, envelops it in a warm, weak, slightly luminous aureole, raises for this pimp's life a pedestal garlanded with flowers, as a maiden's coffin is bedecked with woven ivy, a pedestal massive though light, from the top of which, since the age of fifteen, Darling has been pissing in the following position: his legs spread, knees slightly bent, and in more rigid jets since the age of eighteen. For we should like to stress the point that a very gentle nimbus always isolates him from too rough a contact with his own sharp angles. If he says, "I'm dropping a pearl," or "a pearl slipped," he means that he has farted in a certain way, very softly, that the fart has flowed out very quietly. Let us wonder at the fact that it does suggest a pearl of dull sheen: the flowing, the muted leak, seems to us as milky as the paleness of a pearl that is slightly cloudy. It makes Darling seem to us a kind of precious gigolo, a Hindu, a princess, a drinker of pearls. The odor he has silently spread in the prison has the dullness of the pearl, coils about him, haloes him from head to foot, isolates him, but isolates him much less than does the remark that his beauty does not fear to utter. "I'm dropping a pearl," means that the fart is noiseless. If it rumbles, then it is coarse, and if it's some jerk who drops it, Darling says, "My cock's house is falling down!"

Wondrously, through the magic of his high blond beauty, Darling calls forth a savanna and plunges us more deeply and imperiously into the heart of the black continents than the Negro murderer will plunge me. Darling adds further:

"Sure stinks. I can't even stay near me . . ."

In short, he bore his infamy like a red-hot brand on raw flesh, but this precious brand is as ennobling as was the fleur-de-lis on the shoulders of hoodlums of old. Eyes blackened by fists are the pimp's shame, but Darling says:

"My two bouquets of violets." He also says, regarding a desire to shit:

"I've got a cigar at the tip of my lips."

He has very few friends. As Divine loses hers, he sells them to the cops. Divine does not yet know about this; he keeps his traitor's face for himself alone, for he loves to betray. When Divine met him, he had just got out of jail, that same morning, having served a minimum sentence for robbery and receiving stolen goods, after having coldly ratted on his accomplices, and on some other friends who were not accomplices.

One evening, as they were about to release him from the police station to which he had been taken after a raid, when the inspector said to him, in that gruff tone that makes one think they won't go any further: "You wouldn't happen to know who's going to pull a job? All you have to do is stooge for us, we can come to some arrangement," he felt, as *you* would say, a base caress, but it was all the sweeter because he himself regarded it as base. He tried to seem nonchalant and said:

"It's a risky business."

However, he noticed that he had lowered his voice.

"You don't have to worry about that with me," continued the inspector. "You'll get a hundred francs each time."

Darling accepted. He liked selling out on people, for this dehumanized him. Dehumanizing myself is my own most fundamental tendency. On the first page of an evening paper he again saw the photograph of the ensign I mentioned earlier, the one who was shot for treason. And Darling said to himself:

"Old pal! Buddy!"

He was thrilled by a prankishness that was born from within: "I'm a double crosser." As he walked down the Rue Dancourt, drunk with the hidden splendor (as of a treasure) of his abjection (for it really must intoxicate us if we are not to be killed by its intensity), he glanced at the mirror in a shop window where he saw a Darling luminous with extinguished pride, bursting with this pride. He saw this Darling wearing a glen plaid suit, a felt hat over one eye, his shoulders stiff, and when he walks he holds them like that so as to resemble Sebastopol Pete, and Pete holds them like that so as to resemble Pauley the Rat, and Pauley to resemble Teewee, and so on; a procession of pure, irreproachable pimps leads to Darling Daintyfoot, the double crosser, and it seems that as a result of having rubbed against them and stolen their bearing, he has, you might say, soiled them with his own abjection; that's how I want him to be, for my delight, with a chain on his wrist, a tie as fluid as a tongue of flame, and those extraordinary shoes which are meant only for pimps—very light tan, narrow and pointed. For, thanks to Divine, Darling has gradually exchanged his clothes, which were shabby from months in a cell, for some elegant, worsted suits and scented linen. The transformation has delighted him. For he is still the child-pimp. The soul of the ill-tempered hoodlum has remained in the castoffs. Now he feels in his pocket, and strokes with his hand, better than he used to feel his knife near his penis, a .38 calibre gun. But we do not dress for ourselves alone, and Darling dressed for prison. With each new purchase, he imagines the effect on his possible prison mates at Fresnes or the Santé. Who, in your opinion, might they be? Two or three hoods who, never having seen him, could recognize him as their peer, a few wooden-faced men who might offer him their hand or, from a distance, during the medical examination or while returning from the daily walk, would rap out of the corner of their mouth, with a wink: " 'lo, Darling." But most of his friends would be jerks who were easily dazzled. Prison is a kind of God, as barbaric as a god, to whom he offers gold watches, fountain pens, rings, handkerchiefs, scarves, and shoes. He dreams less of showing himself in the splendor of his new outfits to a woman or to the people he meets casually in daily life than of walking into a cell with his hat tilted over one eye, his white silk shirt open at the collar (for his tie was stolen during the search), and his English raglan unbuttoned. And the poor prisoners already gaze at him with respect. On the basis of his appearance, he dominates them. "I'd like to see the look on their mugs!" he would think, if he could think his desires.

Two stays in prison have so molded him that he will live the rest of his life for it. It has shaped his destiny, and he is very dimly aware that he is ineluctably consecrated to it, perhaps ever since the time he read the following words that someone had scribbled on the page of a library book:

Beware:
First: Jean Clément, known as the Queen,
Second: Robert Martin, known as the Faggot,

Third: Roger Falgue, known as Nelly.
The Queen has a crush on Li'l Meadow (society sis),
The Faggot on Ferrière and Grandot,
Nelly on Malvoisin.

The only way to avoid the horror of horror is to give in to it. He therefore wished, with a kind of voluptuous desire, that one of the names were his. Besides, I know that you finally tire of that tense, heroic attitude of the outlaw and that you decide to play along with the police in order to reassume your sloughed-off humanity. Divine knew nothing about this aspect of Darling. Had she known it, she would have loved him all the more, for to her love was equivalent to despair. So they are drinking tea, and Divine is quite aware she is swallowing it the way a pigeon swallows clear water. As it would be drunk, if he drank it, by the Holy Ghost in the form of a dove. Darling dances the java with his hands in his pockets. If he lies down, Divine sucks him.

When she talks to herself about Darling, Divine says, clasping her hands in thought:

"I worship him. When I see him lying naked, I feel like saying mass on his chest."

It took Darling some time to get used to talking about her and to her in the feminine. He finally succeeded, but he still did not tolerate her talking to him as to a girlfriend. Then little by little he let her do it. Divine dared say to him:

"You're pretty," adding: "like a prick."

Darling takes what comes his way in the course of his nocturnal and diurnal expeditions, and bottles of liquor, silk scarves, perfumes, and fake jewels accumulate in the garret. Each object brings into the room the fascination of a petty theft that is as brief as an appeal to the eyes. Darling steals from the display counters of department stores, from parked cars; he robs his few friends; he steals wherever he can.

On Sunday, Divine and he go to mass. Divine carries a gold-clasped missal in her right hand. With her left, she keeps the collar of her overcoat closed. They walk without seeing. They arrive at the Madeleine and take their seats among the fashionable worshipers. They believe in the bishops with gold ornaments. The mass fills Divine with wonder. Everything that goes on there is perfectly natural. Each of the priest's gestures is clear, has its precise meaning, and might be performed by anyone. When the officiating priest joins the two pieces of the divided host for the consecration, the edges do not fit together, and when he raises it with his two hands, he does not try to make you believe in the miracle. It makes Divine shudder.

Darling prays, saying:

"Our Mother, Which art in heaven . . ."

They sometimes take communion from a mean-looking priest who maliciously crams the host into their mouths.

Darling still goes to mass because of its luxuriousness.

When they get back to the garret, they fondle each other. Divine loves her man. She bakes pies for him and butters his roasts. She even dreams of him if he is in the toilet. She worships him in any and all positions.

A silent key is opening the door, and the wall bursts open just as a sky tears apart to reveal The Man, like the one Michelangelo painted nude in *The Last Judgment*. When the door has been closed, as gently as if it were made of glass, Darling tosses his hat on the couch and his cigarette butt any old place, though preferably to the ceiling. Divine leaps to the assault, clings to her man, licks him, and envelopes him; he stands there solid and motionless, as if he were Andromeda's monster changed to a rock in the sea.

Since his friends keep away from him, Darling sometimes takes Divine to the Roxy Bar. They play poker-dice. Darling likes the elegant movement of shaking the dice. He also likes the graceful way in which fingers roll a cigarette or remove the cap of a fountain pen. He gives no thought to either his seconds or his minutes or his hours. His life is an underground heaven thronged with barmen, pimps, queers, ladies of the night, and Queens of Spades, but his life is a Heaven. He is a voluptuary. He knows all the cafés in Paris where the toilets have seats.

"To do a good job," he says, "I've got to be sitting down."

He walks for miles, preciously carrying in his bowels the desire to shit, which he will gravely deposit in the mauve tiled toilets of the Café Terminus at the Saint-Lazare station.

I don't know much about his background. Divine once told me his name; it was supposed to be Paul Garcia. He was probably born in one of those neighborhoods that smell of the excrement which people wrap in newspapers and drop from their windows, at each of which hangs a heart of lilacs.

Darling!

If he shakes his curly head, you can see the earrings swinging at the cheeks of his predecessors, the prowlers of the boulevards, who used to wear them in the old days. His way of kicking forward to swing the bottoms of his trousers is the counterpart of the way women used to kick aside the flounces of their gowns with their heels when they waltzed.

So the couple lived undisturbed. From the bottom of the stairs, the concierge watches over their happiness. And toward evening the angels sweep the room and tidy up. To Divine, angels are gestures that are made without her.

Oh, I so love to talk about them! Legions of soldiers wearing coarse sky blue or river-colored denim are hammering the azure of the heavens with their hobnailed boots. The planes are weeping. The whole world is dying of panicky fright. Five million young men of all tongues will die by the cannon that erects and discharges. Their flesh is already embalming the humans who drop like flies. As the flesh perishes, solemnity issues forth from it. But where I am I can muse in comfort on the lovely dead of yesterday, today, and tomorrow. I dream of the lovers' garret. The first serious quarrel has taken place, which ends in a gesture of love. Divine has told me the following about Darling: when he awoke one evening, too weary to open his eyes, he heard her fussing about in the garret.

"What are you doing?" he asked.

Divine's mother (Ernestine), who called the wash the wash basin, used to do the wash basin every Saturday. So Divine answers:

"I'm doing the wash basin."

Now, as there was no bathtub in Darling's home, he used to be dipped into a wash basin. Today, or some other day, though it seems to me today, while he was sleeping, he dreamed that he was entering a wash basin. He isn't, of course, able to analyze himself, nor would he dream of trying to, but he is sensitive to the tricks of fate, and to the tricks of the theater of fear. When Divine answers, "I'm doing the wash basin," he thinks she is saying to mean "I'm playing at being the wash basin," as if she were "doing" a role. (She might have said: "I'm doing a locomotive.") He suddenly gets an erection from the feeling that he has penetrated Divine in a dream. In his dream he penetrates the Divine of the dream of Divine, and he possesses her, as it were, in a spiritual debauch. And the following phrases come into his mind; "To the heart, to the hilt, right to the balls, right in the throat."

Darling has "fallen" in love.

I should like to play at inventing the ways love has of surprising people. It enters like Jesus into the heart of the impetuous; it also comes slyly, like a thief.

A gangster, here in prison, related to me a kind of counterpart of the famous comparison in which the two rivals come to know Eros:

"How I started getting a crush on him? We were in the jug. At night we had to undress, even take off our shirts in front of the guard to show him we weren't hiding anything (ropes, files, or blades). So the little guy and me were both naked. So I took a squint at him to see if he had muscles like he said. I didn't have time to get a good look because it was freezing. He got dressed again quick. I just had time to see he was pretty great. Man, did I get an eyeful (a shower of roses!). I was hooked. I swear! I got mine (here one expects inescapably: I knocked myself out). It lasted a while, four or five days . . ."

The rest is of no further interest to us. Love makes use of the worst traps. The least noble. The rarest. It exploits coincidence. Was it not enough for a kid to stick his two fingers in his mouth and loose a strident whistle just when my soul was stretched to the limit, needing only this stridency to be torn from top to bottom? Was that the right moment, the moment that made two creatures love each to the very blood? "Thou art a sun unto my night. My night is a sun unto thine!" We beat our brows. Standing, and from afar, my body passes through thine, and thine, from afar, through mine. We create the world. Everything changes . . . and to know that it does!

Loving each other like two young boxers who, before separating, tear off each other's shirt, and, when they are naked, astounded by their beauty, think they are seeing themselves in a mirror, stand there for a second open-mouthed, shake— with rage at being caught—their tangled hair, smile a damp smile, and embrace each other like two wrestlers (in Greco-Roman wrestling), interlock their muscles in the precise connections offered by the muscles of the other, and drop to the mat until their warm sperm, spurting high, maps out on the sky a milky way where other constellations which I can read take shape: the constellations of the Sailor, the Boxer, the Cyclist, the Fiddle, the Spahi, the Dagger. Thus a new map of the heavens is outlined on the wall of Divine's garret.

Divine returns home from a walk to Monceau Park. A cherry branch, supported by the full flight of the pink flowers, surges stiff and black from a vase. Divine is hurt. In the country, the peasants taught her to respect fruit trees and not to regard them as ornaments; she will never again be able to admire them. The broken branch shocks her as you would be shocked by the murder of a nubile maiden. She tells Darling how sad it makes her, and he gives a horselaugh. He, the big-city child, makes fun of her peasant scruples. Divine, in order to complete, to consummate the sacrilege, and, in a way to surmount it by willing it, perhaps also out of exasperation, tears the flowers to shreds. Slaps. Shrieks. In short, a love riot, for let her touch a male and all her gestures of defense modulate into caresses. A fist, that began as a blow, opens, alights, and slides into gentleness. The big male is much too strong for these weak queens. All Seck Gorgui had to do was to rub lightly, without seeming to touch it, the lump his enormous tool made beneath his trousers, and none of them were henceforth able to tear themselves away from him who, in spite of himself, drew them straight home as a magnet attracts iron filings. Divine would be fairly strong physically, but she fears the movements of the riposte, because they are virile, and her modesty makes her shy away from the facial and bodily grimaces that effort requires. She did have this sense of modesty, and also a modesty about masculine epithets as they applied to her. As for slang, Divine did not use it, any more than did her cronies, the other Nellys. It would have upset her as much as whistling with her tongue and teeth like some cheap hood or putting her hands in her trousers pockets and keeping them there (especially by pushing back the flaps of her unbuttoned jacket), or taking hold of her belt and hitching up her trousers with a jerk of the hips.

The queens on high had their own special language. Slang was for men. It was the male tongue. Like the language of men among the Caribees, it became a secondary sexual attribute. It was like the colored plumage of male birds, like the multicolored silk garments which are the prerogative of the warriors of the tribe. It was the crest and spurs. Everyone could understand it, but the only ones who could speak it were the men who at birth received as a gift the gestures, the carriage of the hips, legs and arms, the eyes, the chest, with which one can speak it. One day, at one of our bars, when Mimosa ventured the following words in the course of a sentence: ". . . his screwy stories . . .," the men frowned. Someone said, with a threat in his voice:

"Broad acting tough."

Slang in the mouths of their men disturbed the queens, although they were less disturbed by the made-up words peculiar to that language than by expressions from the ordinary world that were violated by the pimps, adapted by them to their mysterious needs, expressions perverted, deformed, and tossed into the gutter and their beds. For example, they would say: "Easy does it," or "Go, thou art healed." This last phrase, plucked from the Gospel, would emerge from lips at the corner of which was always stuck a crumb of tobacco. It was said with a drawl. It would conclude the account of a venture which had turned out well for them. "Go . . .," the pimps would say.

They would also say curtly:

"Cut it."

And also: "To lie low." But for Darling the expression did not have the same meaning as for Gabriel (the soldier who is to come, who is already being announced by an expression which delights me and seems suitable only to him: "I'm running the show."). Darling took it to mean: you've got to keep your eyes open. Gabriel thought: better clear out. A while ago, in my cell, the two pimps said: "We're making the pages." They meant they were going to make the beds, but a kind of luminous idea transformed me there, with my legs spread apart, into a husky guard or a palace groom who "makes" a palace page just as a young man makes a chick.

To hear this boasting made Divine swoon with pleasure, as when she disentangled—it seemed to her that she was unbuttoning a fly, that her hand, already inside, was pulling up the shirt—certain pig-latin words from their extra syllables: edbay, allbay.

This slang had insidiously dispatched its emissaries to the villages of France, and Ernestine had already yielded to its charm.

She would say to herself: "A Gauloise, a butt, a drag." She would sprawl in her chair and murmur these words as she inhaled the thick smoke of her cigarette. The better to conceal her fantasy, she would lock herself up in her room and smoke. One evening, as she opened the door, she saw the glow of a cigarette at the far end of the darkness. She was terrified by it, as if she were being threatened by a gun, but the fright was short-lived and blended into hope. Vanquished by the hidden presence of the male, she took a few steps and collapsed in an easy chair, but at the same time the glow disappeared. No sooner had she entered than she realized that she was seeing in the mirror of the wardrobe opposite the door, isolated by the darkness from the rest of the image, the glow of the cigarette she had lit, and she was glad that she had struck the match in the dark hallway. Her true honeymoon might be said to have taken place that evening. Her husband was a synthesis of all men: "A butt."

A cigarette was later to play her a shabby trick. As she walked down the main street of the village, she passed a young tough, one of those twenty faces I have cut out of magazines. He was whistling; a cigarette was stuck in the corner of his little mug. When he came abreast of Ernestine, he lowered his head, and the nodding gesture made him look as if he were ogling her tenderly. Ernestine thought that he was looking at her with "impertinent interest," but the fact is he was going against the wind, which blew the smoke into his eyes and made them smart, thus causing him to make this gesture. He screwed up his eyes and twisted his mouth, and the expression passed for a smile. Ernestine drew herself up with a sudden movement, which she quickly repressed and sheathed, and that was the end of the adventure, for at that very moment the village hood, who had not even seen Ernestine, felt the corner of his mouth smiling and his eye winking. With a tough-guy gesture, he hitched up his pants, thereby showing what the position of his true head made of him.

Still other expressions excited her, just as you would be moved or disturbed by the odd coupling of certain words, such as "bell and candle," or better still "a Tartar ball-hold," which she would have liked to whistle and dance to the air of a java. Thinking of her pocket, she would say to herself: "My pouch."

While visiting a friend: "Get a load of that." "She got the works." About a good-looking passerby: "I gave him a hard-on."

Don't think that Divine took after her in being thrilled by slang, for Ernestine was never caught using it. "To get damned sore," coming from the cute mouth of an urchin, was enough to make both mother and son regard the one who said it as a sulking little mug, slightly husky, with the crushed face of a bulldog (that of the young English boxer Crane, who is one of my twenty on the wall).

Darling was growing pale. He knocked out a pink-cheeked Dutchman to rob him. At the moment, his pocket is full of florins. The garret knows the sober joy that comes from security. Divine and Darling sleep at night. During the day, they sit around naked and eat snacks, they squabble, forget to make love, turn on the radio, which drools on and on, and smoke. Darling says shit, and Divine, in order to be neighborly, even more neighborly than Saint Catherine of Siena, who passed the night in the cell of a man condemned to death, on whose prick her head rested, reads *Detective Magazine.* Outside, the wind is blowing. The garret is cosily heated by a system of electric radiators, and I should like to give a short respite, even a bit of happiness, to the ideal couple.

The window is open on the cemetery.

Five A.M.

Divine hears church bells ringing (for she is awake). Instead of notes, which fly away, the chimes are strokes, five strokes, which drop to the pavement, and, on that wet pavement, bear Divine with them, Divine who three years before, or perhaps four, at the same hour, in the streets of a small town, was rummaging through a garbage can for bread. She had spent the night wandering through the streets in the drizzling rain, hugging the walls so as to get less wet, waiting for the angelus (the bells are now ringing low mass, and Divine relives the anguish of the days without shelter, the days of the bells) which announces that the churches are open to old maids, real sinners, and tramps. In the scented attic, the morning angelus violently changes her back into the poor wretch in damp tatters who has just heard mass and taken communion in order to rest her feet and be less cold. Darling's sleeping body is warm and next to hers. Divine closes her eyes; when the lids join and separate her from the world which is emerging from the dawn, the rain begins to fall, releasing within her a sudden happiness so perfect that she says aloud, with a deep sigh: "I'm happy." She was about to go back to sleep, but the better to attest her marital happiness she recalled without bitterness the memories of the time when she was Culafroy, when, having run away from the slate house, she landed in a small town, where, on golden pink, or dreary mornings, tramps with souls—which, to look at them, one would call naïve—of dolls, accost each other with gestures one would also call fraternal. They have just got up from park benches on which they have been sleeping, from benches on the main square, or have just been born from a lawn in the public park. They exchange secrets dealing with Asylums, Prisons, Pilfering, and State Troopers. The milkman hardly disturbs them. He is one of them. For a few days Culafroy was also one of them. He fed on crusts, covered with hair, that he found in garbage cans. One night, the night he was most hungry, he even wanted to kill himself. Suicide was his great preoccupation: the song of phenobarbital! Certain attacks brought him so close to death that I wonder how he escaped it, what imperceptible shock—coming from whom?—pushed him back from the brink. But one day there would be, within arm's reach, a phial of poison, and I would have only to put it in my mouth; and then to wait. To wait, with unbearable anguish, for the effect of the incredible act, and marvel at the wondrousness of an act so madly irremediable, that brings in its wake the end of the world which follows from so casual a gesture. I had never been struck by the fact that the slightest carelessness—sometimes even less than a gesture, an unfinished gesture, one you would like to take back, to undo by reversing time, a gesture so mild and close, still in the present moment, that you think you can efface it—Impossible!—can lead, for example, to the guillotine, until the day when I myself—through one of those little gestures that escape you involuntarily, that it is impossible to abolish—saw my soul in anguish and immediately felt the anguish of the unfortunate creatures who have no other way out than to confess. And to wait. To wait and grow calm, because anguish and despair are possible only if there is a visible or secret way out, and to trust to death, as Culafroy once trusted the inaccessible snakes.

Up to that time, the presence of a phial of poison or a high-tension wire had never coincided with periods of dizziness, but Culafroy, and later Divine, will dread that moment, and they expect to encounter it very soon, a moment chosen by Fate, so that death may issue irremediably from their decision or their lassitude.

There were random walks through the town, along dark streets on sleepless nights. He would stop to look through windows at gilded interiors, through lacework illustrated with elaborate designs: flowers, acanthus leaves, cupids with bows and arrows, lace deer; and the interiors, hollowed out in massive and shadowy altars, seemed to him veiled tabernacles. In front of and beside the windows, taperlike candelabra mounted in a guard of honor in still leafy trees which spread out in bouquets of enamel, metal, or cloth lilies on the steps of a basilica altar. In short, they were the surprise packages of vagrant children for whom the world is imprisoned in a magic lattice, which they themselves weave about the globe with toes as hard and agile as Pavlova's. Children of this kind are invisible. Conductors do not notice them on trains, nor do policemen on docks; even in prison they seem to have been smuggled in, like tobacco, tattooing ink, moonbeams, sunbeams, and the music of a phonograph. Their slightest gesture proves to them that a crystal mirror, which their fist sometimes bespangles with a silvery spider, encages the universe of houses, lamps, cradles, and baptisms, the universe of humans. The child we are concerned with was so far removed from this that later on all he remembered of his escapade was: "In town, women in mourning are very smartly dressed." But his solitude made it possible for him to be moved by petty miseries: a squatting old woman who, when the child suddenly appeared, pissed on her black cotton stockings; in front of restaurant windows bursting with lights and crystals and silverware, but still empty of diners, he witnessed, spellbound, the tragedies being performed by waiters in full dress who were dialoguing with a great flourish and debating questions of precedence until the arrival of the first elegant couple which dashed the drama to the floor and shattered it; homosexuals who would give him only fifty centimes and run off, full of happiness for a week; in stations at major junctions he would observe at night, from the waiting rooms, male shadows carrying mournful lanterns along multitudes of tracks. His feet and shoulders ached; he was cold.

Divine muses on the moments which are most painful for the vagabond: at night, when a car on the road suddenly spotlights his poor rags.

Darling's body is burning. Divine is lying in its hollow. I do not know whether she is already dreaming or merely reminiscing: "One morning (it was at the crack of dawn), I knocked at your door. I was weary of wandering through the streets, bumping into ragpickers, stumbling over garbage. I was seeking your bed, which was hidden in the lace, the lace, the ocean of lace, the universe of lace. From the far end of the world, a boxer's fist sent me tumbling into a tiny sewer." Just then, the angelus tolled. Now she is asleep in the lace, and their married bodies are afloat.

Here I am this morning, after a long night of caressing my beloved couple, torn from my sleep by the noise of the bolt being drawn by the guard who comes to collect the garbage. I get up and stagger to the latrine, still entangled in my strange dream, in which I succeeded in *getting my victim to pardon me*. Thus, I was plunged to the mouth in horror. The horror entered me. I chewed it. I was full of it. My young victim was sitting near me, and his bare leg, instead of crossing his right, went through the thigh. He said nothing, but I knew without the slightest doubt what he was thinking: "I've told the judge everything, you're pardoned. Besides, it's me sitting on the bench. You can confess. And you don't have to worry. You're pardoned." Then, with the immediacy of dreams, he was a little corpse no bigger than a figurine in an Epiphany pie, than a pulled tooth, lying in a glass of champagne in the middle of a Greek landscape with truncated, ringed columns, around which long, white tapeworms were twisting and streaming like coils, all this in a light seen only in dreams. I no longer quite remember my attitude, but I do know that I believed what he told me. Upon waking, I still had the feeling of baptism. But there is no question of resuming contact with the precise and tangible world of the cell. I lie down again until it's time for bread. The atmosphere of the night, the smell rising from the blocked latrines, overflowing with shit and yellow water, stir childhood memories which rise up like a black soil mined by moles. One leads to another and makes it surge up; a whole life which I thought subterranean and forever buried rises to the surface, to the air, to the sad sun, which give it a smell of decay, in which I delight. The reminiscence that really tugs at my heart is that of the toilet of the slate house. It was my refuge. Life, which I saw far off and blurred through its darkness and smell—an odor that filled me with compassion, in which the scent of the elders and the loamy earth was dominant, for the outhouse was at the far end of the garden, near the hedge—life, as it reached me, was singularly sweet, caressing, light, or rather lightened, delivered from heaviness. I am speaking of the life which was things outside the toilet, whatever in the world was not in my little retreat with its worm-eaten boards. It seemed to me as if it were somewhat in the manner of floating, painted dreams, whereas I in my hole, like a larva, went on with a restful, nocturnal existence, and at times I had the feeling I was sinking slowly, as into sleep or a lake or a maternal breast or even a state of incest, to the spiritual center of the earth. My periods of happiness were never luminously happy, my peace never what men of letters and theologians call a "celestial peace." That's as it should be, for I would be horrified if I were pointed at by God, singled out by Him; I know very well that if I were sick, and were cured by a miracle, I would not survive it. Miracles are unclean; the peace I used to seek in the outhouse, the one I am going to seek in the memory of it, is a reassuring and soothing peace.

At times it would rain. I would hear the patter of the drops on the zinc roofing. Then my sad well-being, my morose delectation, would be aggravated by a further sorrow. I would open the door a crack, and the sight of the wet garden and the pelted vegetables would grieve me. I would remain for hours squatting in my cell, roosting on my wooden seat, my body and soul prey to the odor and darkness; I would feel mysteriously moved, because it was there that the most secret part of human beings came to reveal itself, as in a confessional. Empty confessionals had the same sweetness for me. Back issues of fashion magazines lay about there, illustrated with engravings in which the women of 1910 always had a muff, a parasol, and a dress with a bustle.

It took me a long time to learn to exploit the spell of these nether powers, who drew me to them by the feet, who flapped their black wings about me, fluttering them like the eyelashes of a vamp, and dug their branchlike fingers into my eyes.

Someone has flushed the toilet in the next cell. Since our two latrines are adjoining, the water stirs in mine, and a whiff of odor heightens my intoxication. My stiff penis is caught in my underpants; it is freed by the touch of my hand, strikes against the sheet, and forms a little mound. Darling! Divine! And I am alone here.

It is Darling whom I cherish most, for you realize that, in the final analysis, it is my own destiny, be it true or false, that I am draping (at times a rag, at times a court robe) on Divine's shoulders.

Slowly but surely I want to strip her of every vestige of happiness so as to make a saint of her. The fire that is searing her has already burned away heavy bonds; new ones are shackling her: Love. A morality is being born, which is certainly not the usual morality (it is consonant with Divine), though it is a morality all the same, with its Good and Evil. Divine is not beyond good and evil, there where the saint must live. And I, more gentle than a wicked angel, lead her by the hand.

Here are some "Divinariana" gathered expressly for you. Since I wish to show the reader a few candid shots of her, it is up to him to provide the sense of duration, of passing time, and to assume that during this first chapter she will be between twenty and thirty years of age.

DIVINARIANA

Divine to Darling: "You're my Maddening Baby!"

—Divine is humble. She is aware of luxury only through a certain mystery which it secretes and which she fears. Luxury hotels, like the dens of witches, hold in thrall aggressive charms which a gesture of ours can free from marble, carpets, velvet, ebony, and crystal. As soon as she accumulated a little money, thanks to an Argentine, Divine trained herself in luxury. She bought leather and steel luggage saturated with musk. Seven or eight times a day, she would take the train, enter the Pullman car, have her bags stacked in the baggage racks, settle down on the cushions until it was time for the train to leave, and, a few seconds before the whistle blew, would call two or three porters, have her things removed, take a cab and have herself driven to a fine hotel, where she would remain long enough to install herself discreetly and luxuriously. She played this game of being a star for a whole week, and now she knows how to walk on carpets and talk to flunkeys, who are luxury furnishings. She has domesticated the charms and brought luxury down to earth. The sober contours and scrolls of Louis XV furniture and frames and woodwork sustain her life—which seems to unroll more nobly, a double stairway—in an infinitely elegant air. But it is particularly where her hired car passes a wrought-iron gate or makes a delicious swerve that she is an Infanta.

—Death is no trivial matter. Divine already fears being caught short for the solemnity. She wants to die with dignity. Just as that air-force lieutenant went into combat in his dress uniform so that, if the death that flies overtook him in the plane, it would find and transfix him as an officer and not a mechanic, so Divine always carries in her pocket her oily, gray diploma for advanced study.

—He's as dumb as a button, as a button on . . . (Mimosa is about to say: your boot).
Divine, blandly: on your fly.

—She always had with her, up her sleeve, a small fan made of muslin and pale ivory. Whenever she said something that disconcerted her, she would pull the fan from her sleeve with the speed of a magician, unfurl it, and suddenly one would see the fluttering wing in which the lower part of her face was hidden. Divine's fan will beat lightly about her face all her life. She inaugurated it in a poultry shop on the Rue Lepic. Divine had gone down with a sister to buy a chicken. They were in the shop when the butcher's son entered. She looked at him and clucked, called the sister and, putting her index finger into the rump of the trussed chicken that lay on the stall, she cried out: "Oh, look! Beauty of Beauties!" and her fan quickly fluttered to her blushing cheeks. She looked again with moist eyes at the butcher's son.

—On the boulevard, policemen have stopped Divine, who is tipsy. She is singing the *Veni Creator* in a shrill voice. In all the passersby are born little married couples veiled in white tulle who kneel on tapestried prayer stools; each of the two policemen remembers the time he was best man at a cousin's wedding. In spite of this, they take Divine to the station. Along the way she rubs against them, and they each get a hard-on, squeeze her more tightly, and stumble on purpose in order to tangle their thighs with hers. Their huge cocks are alive and rap sharply or push with desperate, sobbing thrusts against the door of their blue woollen pants. They bid them open, like the clergy at the closed church door on Palm Sunday. The little queens, both young and old, scattered along the boulevard, who see Divine going off, borne away to the music of the grave nuptial hymn, the *Veni Creator*, cry out:
"They're going to put her in irons!"
"Like a sailor!"
"Like a convict!"
"Like a woman in childbirth!"
The solid citizens going by form a crowd and see nothing, know nothing. They are scarcely, imperceptibly, dislodged from their calm state of confidence by the trivial event: Divine being led away by the arm, and her sisters bewailing her.
Having been released, the next evening she is again at her post on the boulevard. Her blue eyelid is swollen:
"My God, Beauties, I almost passed out. The policemen held me up. They were all standing around me fanning me with their checked handkerchiefs. They were the Holy Women wiping my face. My Divine Face. 'Snap out of it, Divine! Snap out of it,' they shouted, 'snap out of it, snap out of it!' They were singing to me.
"They took me to a dark cell. Someone (Oh! that SOMEONE who must have drawn them! I shall seek him throughout the fine print on the heavy pages of adventure novels which throng with miraculously handsome and raffish page boys. I untie and unlace the doublet and hip boots of one of them, who follows Black-Stripe John; I leave him, a cruel knife in one hand and his stiff prick clutched in the other, standing with his face to the white wall, and here he is, a young, fiercely virgin convict. He puts his cheek to the wall. With a kiss, he licks the vertical surface, and the greedy plaster sucks in his saliva. Then a shower of kisses. All his movements outline an invisible horseman who embraces him and whom the inhuman wall confines. At length, bored to tears, overtaxed with love, the page draws . . .) had drawn dear ladies, a whirligig of ah! yes yes, my Beauties, dream

and play the Boozer so you can fly there—I refuse to tell you what—but they were winged and puffy and big, sober as cherubs, splendid cocks, made of barley sugar. Ladies, around some of them that were more upright and solid than the others, were twined clematis and convolvulus and nasturtium, and winding little pimps too. Oh! those columns! The cell was flying at top speed! It drove me simply mad, mad, mad!"

The sweet prison cells! After the foul monstrousness of my arrest, of my various arrests, each of which is always the first, which appeared to me in all its irremediable aspects in an inner vision of blazing and fatal speed and brilliance the moment my hands were imprisoned in the steel handcuffs, gleaming as a jewel or a theorem, the prison cell, which now I love as one loves a vice, consoles me, by its being, for my own being.

The odor of prison is an odor of urine, formaldehyde, and paint. I have recognized it in all the prisons of Europe, and I recognized that this odor would finally be the odor of my destiny. Every time I backslide, I examine the walls for the traces of my earlier captivities, that is, of my earlier despairs, regrets, and desires that some other convict has carved out for me. I explore the surface of the walls, in quest of the fraternal trace of a friend. For though I have never known what friendship could actually be, what vibrations the friendship of two men sets up in their hearts and perhaps on their skin, in prison I sometimes long for a brotherly friendship, but always with a man—of my own age—who is handsome, who would have complete confidence in me and be the accomplice of my loves, my thefts, my criminal desires, though this does not enlighten me about such friendship, about the odor, in both friends, of its secret intimacy, because for the occasion I make myself a male who knows that he really isn't one. I await the revelation on the wall of some terrible secret: especially murder, murder of men, or betrayal of friendship, or profanation of the dead, a secret of which I shall be the resplendent tomb. But all I have ever found has been an occasional phrase scratched on the plaster with a pin, formulas of love or revolt, more often of resignation: "Jojo of the Bastille loves his girl for life." "My heart to my mother, my cock to the whores, my head to the hangman." These rupestral inscriptions are almost always a gallant homage to womanhood, or a smattering of those bad stanzas that are known to bad boys all over France:

When coal turns white,
And soot's not black,
I'll forget the prison
That's at my back.

And those pipes of Pan that mark the days gone by!
And then the following surprising inscription carved in the marble under the main entrance: "Inauguration of the prison, March 17, 1900," which makes me see

a procession of official gentlemen solemnly bringing in the first prisoner to be incarcerated.

—Divine: "My heart's in my hand, and my hand is pierced, and my hand's in the bag, and the bag is shut, and my heart is caught."

—Divine's kindness. She had complete and invincible confidence in men with tough, regular faces, with thick hair, a lock of which falls over the forehead, and this confidence seemed to be inspired by the glamour these faces had for Divine. She had often been taken in, she whose critical spirit is so keen. She realized this suddenly, or gradually, tried to counteract this attitude, and finally intellectual scepticism, struggling with emotional consent, won out and took root in her. But in that way she is still in error, because she now takes it out on the very young men to whom she feels attracted. She receives their declarations with a smile or ironic remark that ill conceals her weakness (weakness of the faggots in the presence of the lump in Gorgui's pants), and her efforts not to yield to their carnal beauty (to make them dance to her tune), while they, on the other hand, immediately return the smile, which is now more cruel, as if, shot forth from Divine's teeth, it rebounded from theirs, which were sharper, colder, more glacial, because in her presence their teeth were more coldly beautiful.

But, to punish herself for being mean to the mean, Divine goes back on her decisions and humiliates herself in the presence of the pimps, who fail to understand what's going on. Nevertheless, she is scrupulously kind. One day, in the police wagon, on the way back from court, for she often slipped, particularly for peddling dope, she asks an old man:
"How many?"
He answers:
"They slapped me with three years. What about you?"
She's down for only two, but answers:
"Three years."

—July Fourteenth: red, white, and blue everywhere. Divine dresses up in all the other colors, out of consideration for them, because they are disdained.

Divine and Darling. To my mind, they are the ideal pair of lovers. From my evil-smelling hole, beneath the coarse wool of the covers, with my nose in the sweat and my eyes wide open, alone with them, I see them.

Darling is a giant whose curved feet cover half the globe as he stands with his legs apart in baggy, sky blue silk underpants. He rams it in. So hard and calmly that anuses and vaginas slip onto his member like rings on a finger. He rams it in. So hard and calmly that his virility, observed by the heavens, has the penetrating force of the battalions of blond warriors who on June 14, 1940, buggered us soberly and seriously, though their eyes were elsewhere as they marched in the dust and sun. But they are the image of only the tensed, buttressed Darling. Their granite prevents them from being slithering pimps.

I close my eyes. Divine: a thousand shapes, charming in their grace, emerge from my eyes, mouth, elbows, knees, from all parts of me. They say to me: "Jean, how glad I am to be living as Divine and to be living with Darling."

I close my eyes. Divine and Darling. To Darling, Divine is barely a pretext, an occasion. If he thought of her, he would shrug his shoulders to shake off the thought, as if the thought were a dragon's claws clinging to his back. But to Divine, Darling is everything. She takes care of his penis. She caresses it with the most profuse tenderness and calls it by the kind of pet names used by ordinary folk when they feel horny. Such expressions as Little Dicky, the Babe in the Cradle, Jesus in His Manger, the Hot Little Chap, your Baby Brother, without her formulating them, take on full meaning. Her feeling accepts them literally. Darling's penis is in itself all of Darling: the object of her pure luxury, an object of pure luxury. If Divine is willing to see in her man anything other than a hot, purplish member, it is because she can follow its stiffness, which extends to the anus, and can sense that it goes farther into his body, that it is this very body of Darling erect and terminating in a pale, tired face, a face of eyes, nose, mouth, flat cheeks, curly hair, beads of sweat.

I close my eyes beneath the lice-infested blankets. Divine has opened the fly and arranged this mysterious area of her man. Has beribboned the bush and penis, stuck flowers into the buttonholes of the fly. (Darling goes out with her that way in the evening.) The result is that to Divine, Darling is only the magnificent delegation on earth, the physical expression, in short, the symbol of a being (perhaps God), of an idea that remains in heaven. They do not commune. Divine may be compared to Marie Antoinette, who, according to my history of France, had to learn to express herself in prison, willy-nilly, in the slang current in the eighteenth century. Poor dear Queen!

If Divine says in a shrill voice: "They dragged me into court," the words conjure up for me an old Countess Solange, in a very ancient gown with a train of lace, whom soldiers are dragging on her knees, by her bound wrists, over the cobblestones of a law court.

"I'm swooning with love," she said.

Her life stopped, but around her life continued to flow. She felt as if she were going backward in time, and wild with fright at the idea of—the rapidity of it—reaching the beginning, the Cause, she finally released a gesture that very quickly set her heart beating again.

Once again the kindness of this giddy creature. She asks a young murderer whom we shall eventually meet (Our Lady of the Flowers) a question. This casual question so wounds the murderer that Divine sees his face decomposing visibly. Then, immediately, running after the pain she has caused in order to overtake it and stop it, stumbling over the syllables, getting all tangled up in her saliva, which is like tears of emotion, she cries out:

"No, no, it's me."

The friend of the family is the giddiest thing I know in the neighborhood. Mimosa II. Mimosa the Great, the One, is now being kept by an old man. She has her villa in Saint-Cloud. As she was in love with Mimosa II who was then a milkman, she left her her name. The II isn't pretty, but what can be done about it? Divine has invited her to high tea. She came to the garret at about five o'clock. They kissed each other on the cheek, being very careful to make sure their bodies did not touch. She greeted Darling with a male handshake, and there she is sitting on the couch where Divine sleeps. Darling was preparing the ladies' tea; he had his little coquetries.

"It's nice of you to have come, Mimo. We see you so seldom."

"That's the least I could do, my dear. Besides, I simply adore your little nook. It has quite a vicarage effect with the park in the distance. It must be awfully nice having the dead for neighbors!"

Indeed, the window was very lovely.

When the cemetery was beneath the moon, at night, from her bed, Divine would see it bright and deep in the moonlight. The light was such that one could clearly discern, beneath the grass of the graves and beneath the marble, the spectral unrest of the dead. Thus, the cemetery, through the fringed window, was like a limpid eye between two wide-open lids, or, better still, it was like a blue glass eye—those eyes of the fair-haired blind—in the hollow of a Negro's palm. It would dance, that is, the wind stirred the grass and the cypresses. It would dance, that is, it was melodic and its body moved like a jellyfish. Divine's relations with the cemetery: it had worked its way into her soul, somewhat as certain sentences work their way into a text, that is, a letter here, a letter there. The cemetery within her was present at cafés, on the boulevard, in jail, under the blankets, in the pissoirs. Or, if you prefer, the cemetery was present within her somewhat as that gentle, faithful, submissive dog was present in Darling, occasionally giving the pimp's face the sad, stupid look that dogs have.

Mimosa is leaning out the window, the bay window of the Departed, and is looking for a grave with her finger pointing. When she has found it, she yelps:

"Ah! You hussy, you harlot, so you finally kicked off! So now you're good and stiff beneath the icy marble. And I'm walking on your rugs, you bitch!"

"You're wackeroo," muttered Darling, who almost bawled her out in whore (a secret language).

"Darling, I may be wacky with love for you, you great big terrible Darling, but Charlotte's down there in the grave! Charlotte's right down there!"

We laughed, for we knew that Charlotte was her grandfather who was down in the cemetery, with a grant in perpetuity.

"And how's Louise (that was Mimosa's father)? And Lucie (her mother)?" asked Divine.

"Ah! Divine, don't talk to me about them. They're much too well. The dumb bitches'll never kick off. They're just a couple of filthy sluts."

Darling liked what the faggots talked about. He especially liked, provided it was done in private, the way they talked. While preparing the tea, he listened, with a gliding caravel on his lips. Darling's smile was never stagnant. It seemed forever twitching with a touch of anxiety. Today he is more anxious than usual, for tonight he is to leave Divine; in view of what is going to happen, Mimosa seems to him terrible, wolflike. Divine has no idea of what is in store. She will learn all at once her desertion and of Mimosa's shabby behavior. For they have managed the affair without losing any time. Roger, Mimosa's man, has taken a powder.

"My Roger's off to the wars. She's gone to play Amazon."

Mimosa said that one day in front of Darling, who offered, in jest, to replace Roger. Well, she accepted.

Our domestic life and the law of our Homes do not resemble your Homes. We love each other without love. Our homes do not have the sacramental character. Fags are the great immoralists. In the twinkling of an eye, after six years of union, without considering himself attached, without thinking that he was causing pain or doing wrong, Darling decided to leave Divine. Without remorse, only a slight concern that perhaps Divine might refuse ever to see him again.

As for Mimosa, the fact of hurting a rival is enough to make her happy about the pain she is causing.

The two queens were chirping away. Their talk was dull compared to the play of their eyes. The eyelids did not flutter, nor did the temples crinkle. Their eyeballs flowed from right to left, left to right, rotated, and their glances were manipulated by a system of ball bearings. Let us listen now as they whisper so that Darling may draw near and, standing beside them, pachyderm that he is, make titanic efforts to understand. Mimosa whispers:

"My dear, it's when the Cuties still have their pants on that I like them. You just look at them and they get all stiff. It drives you mad, simply mad! It starts a crease that goes on and on and on, all the way down to their feet. When you touch it, you keep following the crease, without pressing on it, right to the toes. My love, you'd think that the Beaut was going straight down. For that, I recommend sailors especially."

Darling was smiling faintly. He knows. The Big Beaut of a man does not excite him, but he is no longer surprised that it excites Divine and Mimosa.

Mimosa says to Darling:

"You're playing hostess. To get away from us."

He answers:

"I'm making the tea."

As if realizing that his answer was too noncommittal, he added:

"No news from Rogerboy?"

"No," said Mimosa, "I'm the Quite-Alone."

She also meant: "I'm the Quite-Persecuted." When they had to express a feeling that risked involving an exuberance of gesture or voice, the queens contented themselves with saying: "I'm the Quite-Quite," in a confidential tone, almost a murmur, heightened by a slight movement of their ringed hand which calms an invisible storm. Old-timers who, in the days of the great Mimosa, had known the wild cries of freedom and the mad gestures of boldness brought on by feelings swollen with desires that contorted the mouth, made the eyes glow, and bared the teeth, wondered what mysterious mildness had now replaced the disheveled passions. Once Divine began her litany, she kept on until she was exhausted. The first time Darling heard it, he merely looked at her in bewilderment. It was in the room; he was amused; but when Divine began again in the street, he said:

"Shut up, chick. You're not gonna make me look like an ass in front of the boys."

His voice was so cold, so ready to give her the works, that Divine recognized her Master's Voice. She restrained herself. But you know that nothing is so dangerous as repression. One evening, at a pimp's bar on the Place Clichy (where, out of prudence, Darling usually went without her), Divine paid for the drinks, and in picking up the change, forgot to leave a tip on the counter for the waiter. When she realized it, she let out a shriek that rent the mirrors and the lights, a shriek that stripped the pimps:

"My God, I'm the Quite-Giddy!"

Right and left, with the merciless speed of misfortune, two slaps shut her up, shrank her like a greyhound, her head no longer even as high as the bar. Darling was in a rage. He was green beneath the neon. "Beat it," he said. He, however, went on sipping his cognac to the last drop.

These cries (Darling will say: "She's losing her yipes," as if he were thinking: "You're losing money," or, "You're putting on weight.") were one of the idiosyncracies of Mimosa I that Divine had appropriated. When they and a few others were together in the street or a queer café, from their conversations (from their mouths and hands) would escape ripples of flowers, in the midst of which they simply stood or sat about as casually as could be, discussing ordinary household matters:

"I really am, sure sure sure, the Quite-Profligate."

"Oh, Ladies, I'm acting like such a harlot."

"You know (the *ou* was so drawn out that that was all one noticed), *yoouknow*, I'm the Consumed-with-Affliction."

"Here here, behold the Quite-Fluff-Fluff."

One of them, when questioned by a detective on the boulevard:

"Who are you?"

"I'm a Thrilling Thing."

Then, little by little, they understood each other by saying: "I'm the Quite-Quite," and finally: "I'm the Q-Q."

It was the same for the gestures. Divine had a very great one: when she took her handkerchief from her pocket, it described an enormous arc before she put it to her lips. Anyone trying to read something into Divine's gesture would have been infallibly mistaken, for two gestures were here contained in one. There was the elaborated gesture, which was diverted from its initial goal, and the one that contained and completed it by grafting itself on just at the point where the first ceased. Thus, in taking her hand out of her pocket, Divine had meant to extend her arm and shake her unfurled lace handkerchief. To shake it for a farewell to nothing, or to let fall a powder which it did not contain, a perfume—no, it was a pretext. This tremendous gesture was needed to relate the following oppressive drama: "I am alone. Save me who can." But Darling, though unable to destroy it completely, had reduced the gesture, which without, however, becoming trivial, had turned into something hybrid and thereby strange. He had, in overwhelming it, made it overwhelming. Speaking of these constraints, Mimosa had said:

"Our males have turned us into a garden of rheumatics."

When Mimosa left the garret, Darling tried to pick a quarrel with Divine so he could leave her. He found nothing to quarrel about. That made him furious with her. He called her a bitch and left.

So Divine is alone in the world. Whom shall I give her for a lover. The Gypsy I am seeking? The one whose figure, because of the high heels of his Marseilles pumps, resembles a guitar? About his legs there coil and climb, the better to hug him coldly at the buttocks, the trousers of a sailor.

Divine is alone. With me. The whole world that stands guard around the Santé Prison knows nothing, has no desire to know anything, of the distress of a little cell, lost amidst others, which are all so much alike that I, who know it well, often mistake it. Time leaves me no respite; I feel it passing. What shall I do with Divine? If Darling comes back, it will not be long before he leaves again. He has tasted divorce. But Divine needs a few jolts which squeeze her, pull her apart, paste her back together, shatter her, till all I have left of her is a bit of essence which I am trying to track down. That is why M. Roquelaure (127, Rue de Douai, an employee of the Municipal Transport Company), when he went down at seven A.M. to get the milk and morning papers for himself and Mme Roquelaure, who was combing out her hair in the kitchen, found in the narrow hallway of the house, on the floor, a trampled fan. The plastic handle was encrusted with fake emeralds. He kicked at the rubbish boyishly and kept shoving it out on to the sidewalk and then into the gutter. It was Divine's fan. That very evening Divine had met Darling quite by chance and had gone with him, without reproaching him for his flight. He listened to her, whistling as he did, perhaps a bit contrite. They happened to run into Mimosa. Divine bent to the ground in a deep bow, but Mimosa, in a voice that sounded male to Divine for the first time, screamed:

"Get the hell out of here, you dirty whore, you dirty cocksucker!"

It was the milkman . . . This is not an unfamiliar phenomenon, the case of the second nature that can no longer resist and allows the first to break out in blind hatred. We wouldn't mention it were it not a matter of showing the duplicity of the sex of fags. We shall see the same thing happen again in the case of Divine.

So it was quite serious. Here again, Darling, with magnificent cowardice (I maintain that cowardice is an active quality, which, once it assumes this intensity, spreads like a white dawn, a phantasm, about handsome young cowards who move within it in the depths of a sea), did not deign to take sides. His hands were in his pockets.

"Go on, kill each other," he said with a sneer.

The sneer, which still rings in my ears, was uttered one evening in my presence by a sixteen-year-old child. This should give you an idea of what satanism is. Divine and Mimosa fought it out. Leaning against the wall of a house, Divine gave little kicks and beat down on the air with her fists. Mimosa was the stronger and hit hard. Divine managed to break away and run, but Mimosa caught her just as she reached the half-open door of a house. The struggle continued in the hallway with hushed voices and pulled punches. The tenants were asleep; the concierge heard nothing. Divine thought: "The concierge can't hear anything because her name is Mme Muller." The street was empty. Darling, standing on the sidewalk with his hands still in his pockets, was gazing thoughtfully at the garbage in the can that had been put outside. Finally, he made up his mind and left.

"They're both frigging idiots."

On the way, he thought: "If Divine's got a shiner, I'll spit in her dirty mug. Boy, fags are rough." But he came back to live with Divine.

So Divine found her pimp again, and her friend Mimosa. And resumed her life in the garret, which was to last another five years. The garret overlooking the dead. Montmartre by night. The Shame-on-Me-Crazy. We're approaching thirty . . . With my head still under the covers, my fingers digging into my eyes and my mind off somewhere, there remains only the lower part of my body, detached, by my digging fingers, from my rotting head.

A guard who goes by; the chaplain who comes in and doesn't talk of God. I no more see them than I know that I'm in the Santé Prison. Poor Santé which goes to the trouble of keeping me.

Darling loves Divine more and more deeply, that is, more and more without realizing it. Word by word he grows attached. But more and more neglects her. She stays in the garret alone; she offers up to God her love and sorrow. For God—as the Jesuits have said—chooses a myriad of ways to enter into souls: the golden powder, a swan, a bull, a dove, and countless others. For a gigolo who cruises the tearooms, perhaps He has a way that theology has not catalogued, perhaps He chooses to be a tearoom. We might also wonder, had Churches not existed, what form the sanctity (I am not saying her path to salvation) of Divine and of all the other Saints would have taken. We must realize that Divine does not live with gladness of heart. She accepts, unable to elude it, the life that God makes for her and that leads her to Him. But God is not gilt-edged. Before His mystic throne, useless to adopt artful poses, pleasing to the Greek eye. Divine is consumed with fire. I might, just as she admitted to me, confide that if I take contempt with a smile or a burst of laughter, it is not yet—and will it some day be?—out of contempt for contempt, but rather in order not to be ridiculous, not to be reviled, by anything or anyone, that I have placed myself lower than dirt. I could not do otherwise. If I declare that I am an old whore, no one can better that, I discourage insult. People can't even spit in my face anymore. And Darling Daintyfoot is like the rest of you; all he can do is despise me. I have spent whole nights at the following game: working up sobs, bringing them to my eyes, and leaving them there without their bursting, so that in the morning my eyelids ache, they feel hard and stony, as painful as a sunburn. The sob at my eyes might have flowed into tears, but it remains there, weighing against my eyelids like a condemned man against the door of a cell. It is especially then that I realize how deeply I suffer. Then it's the turn for another sob to be born, then another. I swallow them all and spit them out in wisecracks. So my smile, which others may call my whistling in the dark, is merely the inordinate need to activate a muscle in order to release an emotion. We are, after all, familiar enough with the tragedy of a certain feeling which is obliged to borrow its expression from the opposite feeling so as to escape from the myrmidons of the law. It disguises itself in the trappings of its rival.

To be sure, a great earthly love would destroy this wretchedness, but Darling is not yet the Chosen One. Later on, there will come a soldier, so that Divine may have some respite in the course of that calamity which is her life. Darling is merely a fraud ("an adorable fraud," Divine calls him), and he must remain one in order to preserve my tale. It is only on this condition that I can like him. I say of him, as of all my lovers, against whom I butt and crumble: "Let him be steeped in indifference, let him be petrified with blind indifference."

Divine will take up this phrase and apply it to Our Lady of the Flowers.

This movement makes Divine laugh with grief. Gabriel himself will tell us how an officer who loved him, unable to do better, used to punish him.

Our Lady of the Flowers here makes his solemn entrance through the door of crime, a secret door, that opens on to a dark but elegant stairway. Our Lady mounts the stairway, as many a murderer, any murderer, has mounted it. He is sixteen when he reaches the landing. He knocks at the door; then he waits. His heart is beating, for he is determined. He knows that his destiny is being fulfilled, and although he knows (Our Lady knows or seems to know it better than anyone) that his destiny is being fulfilled at every moment, he has the pure mystic feeling that this murder is going to turn him, by virtue of the baptism of blood, into Our Lady of the Flowers. He is excited as he stands in front of, or behind, the door, as if, like a fiancé in white gloves . . . Behind the wood, a voice asks:

"What is it?"

"It's me," mutters the youngster.

Confidently, the door opens and closes behind him.

Killing is easy, since the heart is on the left side, just opposite the armed hand of the killer, and the neck fits so neatly into the two joined hands. The corpse of the old man, one of those thousands of old men whose lot it is to die that way, is lying on the blue rug. Our Lady has killed him. A murderer. He doesn't say the word to himself, but rather I listen with him in his head to the ringing of chimes that must be made up of all the bells of lily-of-the-valley, the bells of spring flowers, bells made of porcelain, glass, water, air. His head is a singing copse. He himself is a beribboned wedding feast skipping, with the violin in front and orange blossoms on the black of the jackets, down a sunken April road. He feels himself, youngster that he is, leaping from flowery vale to flowery vale, straight to the mattress where the old man has tucked away his little pile. He turns it over, turns it back, rips it open, pulls out the wool, but he finds nothing, for nothing is so hard to find as money after a premeditated murder.

"Where does the bastard keep his dough?" he says aloud.

These words are not articulated, but, since they are only felt, are rather spat out of his throat in a tangled mass. It is a croak.

He goes from one piece of furniture to the next. He loses his temper. His nails catch in the grooves. He rips fabrics. He tries to regain his composure, stops to catch his breath, and (in the silence), surrounded by objects that have lost all meaning now that their customary user has ceased to exist, he suddenly feels himself in a monstrous world made up of the soul of the furniture, of the objects; he is seized with panic. He swells up like a bladder, grows enormous, able to swallow the world and himself with it, and then subsides. He wants to get away. As slowly as he can. He is no longer thinking about the body of the murdered man, nor the lost money, nor the lost time, nor the lost act. The police are probably lurking somewhere. Got to beat it fast. His elbow strikes a vase standing on a commode. The vase falls down and twenty thousand francs scatter graciously at his feet.

He opened the door without anxiety, went out on the landing, leaned over, and looked down the silent stairwell, between the apartments, at the glittering ball of cut crystal. Then he walked down the nocturnal carpet and into the nocturnal air, through the silence which is that of eternal space, step by step, into Eternity.

The street. Life is no longer unclean. With a feeling of lightness, he runs off to a small hotel which turns out to be a dive, and rents a room. There, to assuage him, the true night, the night of the stars, comes little by little, and a touch of horror turns his stomach: it is that physical disgust of the first hour, of the murderer for the murdered, about which a number of men have spoken to me. It haunts you, doesn't it? The dead man is rigorous. Your dead man is inside you: mingled with your blood, he flows in your veins, oozes out through your pores, and your heart lives on him, as cemetery flowers sprout from corpses . . . He emerges from you through your eyes, your ears, your mouth.

Our Lady of the Flowers would like to vomit out the carcass. The night, which has come on, does not bring terror. The room smells of whore. Stinks and smells fragrant.

"To escape from horror, as we have said, bury yourself in it."

All by itself the murderer's hand seeks his penis, which is erect. He strokes it through the sheet, gently at first, with the lightness of a fluttering bird, then grips it, squeezes it hard; finally he discharges into the toothless mouth of the strangled old man. He falls asleep.

To love a murderer. To love to commit a crime in cahoots with the young half-breed pictured on the cover of the torn book. I want to sing murder, for I love murderers. To sing it plainly. Without pretending, for example, that I want to be redeemed through it, though I do yearn for redemption. I would like to kill. As I have said above, rather than an old man, I would like to kill a handsome blond boy, so that, already united by the verbal link that joins the murderer and the murdered (each existing thanks to the other), I may be visited, during days and nights of hopeless melancholy, by a handsome ghost of which I would be the haunted castle. But may I be spared the horror of giving birth to a sixty-year-old corpse, or that of a woman, young or old. I am tired of satisfying my desire for murder stealthily by admiring the imperial pomp of sunsets. My eyes have bathed in them enough. Let's get to my hands. But to kill, to kill you, Jean. Wouldn't it be a question of knowing how I would behave as I watched you die by my hand?

More than of anyone else, I am thinking of Pilorge. His face, cut out of *Detective Magazine*, darkens the wall with its icy radiance, which is made up of his Mexican corpse, his will to death, his dead youth, and his death. He spatters the wall with a brilliance that can be expressed only by the confrontation of the two terms that cancel each other. Night emerges from his eyes and spreads over his face, which begins to look like pines on stormy nights, that face of his which is like the gardens where I used to spend the night: light trees, the opening in a wall, and iron railings, astounding railings, festooned railings. And light trees. O Pilorge! Your face, like a lone, nocturnal garden in Worlds where Suns spin round! And on it that impalpable sadness, like the light trees in the garden. Your face is dark, as if in broad daylight a shadow had passed over your soul. It must have made you feel slightly cool, for your body shuddered with a shudder more subtle than the fall of a veil of tulle known as "gossamer-fine tulle," for your face is veiled with thousands of fine, light, microscopic wrinkles, painted, rather than engraved, in crisscross lines.

Already the murderer compels my respect. Not only because he has known a rare experience, but because he has suddenly set himself up as a god, on an altar, whether of shaky boards or azure air. I am speaking, to be sure, of the conscious, even the cynical murderer, who dares take it upon himself to deal death without trying to refer his acts to some power of a given order, for the soldier who kills does not assume responsibility, nor does the lunatic, nor the jealous man, nor the one who knows he will be forgiven; but rather the man who is called an outcast, who, confronted only with himself, still hesitates to behold himself at the bottom of a pit into which, with his feet together, he has—curious prospector—hurled himself with a ludicrously bold leap. A lost man.

Pilorge, my little one, my friend, my liqueur, your lovely hypocritical head has got the axe. Twenty years old. You were twenty or twenty-two. And I am . . . I envy you your glory. You would have done me in, as they say in jail, just as you did in the Mexican. During your months in the cell, you would have tenderly spat heavy oysters from your throat and nose on my memory. I would go to the guillotine very easily, others have gone to it, particularly Pilorge, Weidmann, Angel Sun, and Soclay. Besides, I am not sure that I shall be spared it, for I have dreamed myself in many agreeable lives; my mind, which is eager to please me, has concocted glorious and charming adventures for me, made especially to order. The sad thing about it is, I sometimes think, that the greater part of these creations are utterly forgotten, though they constitute the whole of my past spiritual concert. I no longer even know that they existed, and if I happen now to dream one of these lives, I assume it is a new one, I embark upon my theme, I drift along, without remembering that I embarked upon it ten years earlier and that it sank down, exhausted, into the sea of oblivion. What monsters continue their lives in my depths? Perhaps their exhalations or their excrements or their decomposition hatch at my surface some horror or beauty that I feel is elicited by them. I recognize their influence, the charm of their melodrama. My mind continues to produce lovely chimeras, but so far none of them has taken on flesh. Never. Not once. If I now try to indulge in a daydream, my throat goes dry, despair burns my eyes, shame makes me bow my head, my reverie breaks up. I know that once again a possible happiness is escaping me and escapes me because I dreamed it.

The despondence that follows makes me feel somewhat like a shipwrecked man who spies a sail, sees himself saved, and suddenly remembers that the lens of his spy-glass has a flaw, a blurred spot—the sail he has seen.

But since what I have never dreamed remains accessible, and as I have never dreamed misfortunes, there remains little for me to live but misfortunes. And misfortunes to die, for I have dreamed magnificent deaths for myself in war, as a hero, covered elsewhere with honors, and never by the gallows. So I still have something left.

And what must I do to. get it? Almost nothing more.

Our Lady of the Flowers had nothing in common with the murderers of whom I have spoken. He was—one might say—an innocent murderer. To come back to Pilorge, whose face and death haunt me: at the age of twenty he killed Escudero, his lover, in order to rob him of a pittance. During the trial, he jeered at the court; awakened by the executioner, he jeered at him too; awakened by the spirit of the Mexican, sticky with hot, sweet-smelling blood, he would have laughed in its face; awakened by the shade of his mother, he would have flouted it tenderly. And so Our Lady was born of my love for Pilorge, with a smile in his heart and on his bluish white teeth, a smile that fear, which made his eyes start out of his head, will not tear away.

One day, while idling in the street, Darling met a woman of about forty who suddenly fell madly in love with him. I sufficiently hate the women who are in love with my lovers to admit that this one powders her fat red face with white face powder. And this light cloud makes her look like a family lamp shade with a transparent, pink muslin lining. She has the slick, familiar, well-heeled charm of a lamp shade.

When he walked by, Darling was smoking, and a slit of abandon in the woman's hardness of soul chanced just then to be open, a slit that catches the hook cast by innocent looking objects. If one of your openings happens to be loosely fastened or a flap of your softness to be floating, you're done for. Instead of holding his cigarette between the first joint of the forefinger and middle finger, Darling was pinching it with his thumb and forefinger and covering it with the other fingers, the way men and even small boys usually hold their pricks when they piss at the foot of a tree or into the night. The woman (when he spoke to Divine about her, Darling referred to her as "the floozy" and Divine called her "that woman") was unaware of the virtue of the position itself. But its spell therefore acted upon her all the more promptly. She knew, though without quite knowing why, that Darling was a hard guy, because to her a hard guy was, above all, a male with a hard-on. She became mad about him. But she came too late. Her round curves and soft femininity no longer acted upon Darling, who was now used to the hard contact of a stiff penis. At the woman's side, he remained inert. The gulf frightened him. Still, he made an effort to overcome his distaste and keep the woman attached to him in order to get money from her. He acted gallantly eager. But a day came when, unable to bear it any longer, he admitted that he loved a—earlier he might have said a boy, but now he has to say a man for Divine is a man—a man then. The lady was outraged and uttered the word fairy. Darling slapped her and left.

But he did not want his dessert to escape him (Divine was his steak), and he went back to wait for her one day at the Saint-Lazare station, where she got off, for she came in every day from Versailles.

The Saint-Lazare station is the movie-stars' station.

Our Lady of the Flowers, still and already wearing the light, baggy, youthful, preposterously thin and, in a word, ghostlike gray flannel suit that he was wearing the day of the crime and that he will be wearing the day of his death, came there to buy a ticket for Le Havre. Just as he got to the platform, he dropped his wallet which was stuffed with the twenty thousand franc notes. He felt it slip from his pocket and turned around just in time to see it being picked up by Darling. Calmly and fatally, Darling examined it, for though he was a genuine crook, nevertheless he did not know how to be at ease in original postures and imitated the gangsters of Chicago and Marseilles. This simple observation also enables us to indicate the importance of dreaming in the life of the hoodlum, but what I want particularly to show you by means of it is that I shall surround myself only with roughnecks of undistinguished personality, with none of the nobility that comes from heroism. My loved ones will be those whom you would call "hoodlums of the worst sort."

Darling counted the bills. He took ten for himself, put them into his pocket and handed the rest to Our Lady, who stood there dumbfounded. They became friends.

I leave you free to imagine any dialogue you please. Choose whatever may charm you. Have it, if you like, that they hear the voice of the blood or that they fall in love at first sight, or that Darling, by indisputable signs invisible to the vulgar eye, betrays the fact that he is a thief . . . Conceive the wildest improbabilities. Have it that the depths of their being are thrilled at accosting each other in slang. Tangle them suddenly in a swift embrace or a brotherly kiss. Do whatever you like.

Darling was happy to find the money. However, with an extreme lack of appropriateness, all he could say, without unclenching his teeth, was: "Guy's no dope." Our Lady was boiling. But what could he do? He was too familiar with Pigalle-Blanche to know that you must not put on too bold a front with a real pimp. Darling bore, quite visibly, the external marks of the pimp. "Have to watch my step," Our Lady felt within him. So he lost his wallet, which Darling had noticed. Here is the sequel: Darling took Our Lady of the Flowers to a tailor, a shoe shop, and a hat shop. He ordered for both of them the bagatelles that make the strong and terribly charming man: a suede belt, a felt hat, a plaid tie, etc. Then they stopped at a hotel on the Avenue de Wagram. Wagram, battle won by boxers!

They spent their time doing nothing. As they walked up and down the Champs-Elysées, they let intimacy fuse them. They made comments about the women's legs, but, as they were not witty, their remarks had no finesse. Since their emotion was not torn by any point, they quite naturally skidded along on a stagnant ground of poetry. They were child-roughnecks to whom chance had given gold, and I enjoy giving it to them, just as I enjoy hearing an American hood—it's amazing—say the word dollar and speak English. When they were tired, they went back to the hotel and sat for a long time in the big leather chairs in the lobby. Even there, intimacy evolved its alchemy. A solemn marble stairway led to corridors covered with red carpets, upon which one moved noiselessly. During a high mass at the Madeleine, when Darling saw the priests walking on carpets, after the organ had stopped playing, he began to feel uneasy at the mystery of the deaf and the blind, the tread upon the carpets that he recognizes in the grand hotel, and as he walks slowly over the moss, he thinks, in his guttersnipe language: "Maybe there's something." For low masses are said at the end of the halls of big hotels, where the mahogany and marble light and blow out candles. A mingled burial service and marriage takes place there in secret from one end of the year to the other. People move about like shadows. Does this mean that my ecstatic crook's soul lets slip no opportunity for falling into a trance? Oh to feel yourself flying on tiptoe while the soles of humans move flat on the ground! Even here, and at the Fresnes Prison, the long fragrant corridors that bite their tails restore to me, despite the precise, mathematical hardness of the wall, the soul of the hotel thief I long to be.

The stylish clients moved about the lobby in front of them. They took off their furs, gloves, and hats, drank port, and smoked Craven cigarettes and Havana cigars. A bellboy scurried about. They knew they were characters in a movie. And so, mingling their gestures in this dream, Darling and Our Lady of the Flowers quietly wove a brotherly friendship. How hard it is for me not to mate the two of them better, not to arrange it so that Darling, with a thrust of the hips—rock of unconsciousness and innocence, desperate with love—deeply sinks his smooth, heavy prick, as polished and warm as a column in the sun, into the waiting mouth of the adolescent murderer who is pulverized with gratitude.

That too might be, but will not. Darling and Our Lady, however rigorous the destiny I plot for you, it will never cease to be—oh, in the very faintest way—tormented by what it might also have been but will not be because of me.

One day, Our Lady, quite naturally, confessed to the murder. Darling confessed to his life with Divine. Our Lady, that he was called Our Lady of the Flowers. Both of them needed a rare flexibility to extricate themselves without damage from the snares that threatened their mutual esteem. On this occasion, Darling was all charm and delicacy.

Our Lady of the Flowers was lying on a couch. Darling, seated at his feet, watched him confess. It was over, as far as the murder was concerned. Darling was the theater of a muted drama. Confronting each other were the fear of complicity, friendship for the child, and the taste, the desire for squealing. He still had to admit to the nickname. Finally he got to it, little by little. As the mysterious name emerged, it was so agonizing to watch the murderer's great beauty writhing, the motionless and unclean coils of the marble serpents of his drowsy face moving and stirring, that Darling realized the gravity of such a confession, felt it so deeply that he wondered whether Our Lady was going to puke pricks. He took one of the child's hands, which was hanging down, and held it between his own.

". . . You understand, there were guys that called me . . ."

Darling held on to his hand. With his eyes, he was drawing the confession toward him:

"It's coming, it's coming."

During the entire operation, he did not take his eyes off the eyes of his friend. From beginning to end, he smiled with a motionless smile that was fixed on his mouth, for he felt that the slightest emotion on his part, the slightest sign or breath, would destroy . . . It would have broken Our Lady of the Flowers.

When the name was in the room, it came to pass that the murderer, abashed, opened up, and there sprang forth, like a Glory, from his pitiable fragments, an altar on which there lay, in the roses, a woman of light and flesh.

The altar undulated on a foul mud into which it sank: the murderer. Darling drew Our Lady toward him, and, the better to embrace him, struggled with him briefly. I would like to dream them both in many other positions if, when I closed my eyes, my dream still obeyed my will. But during the day it is disturbed by anxiety about my trial, and in the evening the preliminaries of sleep denude the environs of myself, destroy objects and episodes, leaving me at the edge of sleep as solitary as I was one night in the middle of a stormy and barren heath. Darling, Divine, and Our Lady flee from me at top speed, taking with them the consolation of their existence, which has its being only in me, for they are not content with fleeing; they do away with themselves, dilute themselves in the appalling insubstantiality of my dreams, or rather of my sleep, and become my sleep; they melt into the very stuff of my sleep and compose it. I call for help in silence; I make signals with the two arms of my soul, which are softer than algae, not, of course, to some friend firmly planted on the ground, but to a kind of crystallization of the tenderness whose seeming hardness makes me believe in its eternity.

I call out: "Hold me back! Fasten me!" I break away for a frightful dream which will go through the darkness of the cells, the darkness of the spirits of the damned, of the gulfs, through the mouths of the guards, the breasts of the judges, and will end by my being swallowed very very slowly by a giant crocodile formed by the whiffs of the foul prison air.

It is the fear of the trial.

Weighing upon my poor shoulders are the dreadful weight of legal justice and the weight of my fate.

How many policemen and detectives, with their teeth on edge, as is so aptly said, for days and nights, were making relentless efforts to unravel the puzzle I had set? And I thought the affair had been shelved, whereas they kept plunging away, busy themselves about me without my being aware of it, working on the Genet material, on the luminous traces of the Genet gestures, working away on me in the darkness.

It was a good thing that I raised egoistic masturbation to the dignity of a cult! I have only to begin the gesture and a kind of unclean and supernatural transposition displaces the truth. Everything within me turns worshiper. The external vision of the props of my desire isolates me, far from the world.

Pleasure of the solitary, gesture of solitude that makes you sufficient unto yourself, possessing intimately others who serve your pleasure without their suspecting it, a pleasure that gives to your most casual gestures, even when you are up and about, that air of supreme indifference toward everyone and also a certain awkward manner that, if you have gone to bed with a boy, makes you feel as if you have bumped your head against a granite slab.

I've got lots of time for making my fingers fly! Ten years to go! My good, my gentle friend, my cell! My sweet retreat, mine alone, I love you so! If I had to live in all freedom in another city, I would first go to prison to acknowledge my own, those of my race, and also to find you there.

Miracle of the Rose

◄○►

When Genet signed his first literary contract with Paul Morihien, on March 1,
1943, he alluded to two other novels he was planning: The Children of Un-
happiness *(the first title for* Miracle of the Rose*) and* The Thief's Journal.
He also named the titles of five plays he was writing, among them an early ver-
sion of Deathwatch. *Genet was in prison from July 19 to August 30, 1943, and*
at that time he was already working on Miracle of the Rose.

The book was finished in another prison, the Camp des Tourelles, in the first
month of 1944. Genet had been transferred to this transitional prison, which was
for detainees about to be sent to concentration camps in Germany. Genet had been
condemned to this camp because he was considered a person without a fixed resi-
dence or profession. His life was saved by Cocteau and his friends, who
intervened on his behalf. Thanks to their manipulations, although Genet re-
mained a prisoner, he received permission to have pencils and paper.

The book weaves together two separate narrative strands—an extremely accu-
rate account of Genet's adolescence at the Mettray reform school, and a highly
romanticized version of Genet's adult prison life. Although Genet was never actu-
ally incarcerated in the prison of Fontevrault, scene of this strand of the novel, he
was attracted to the site because it had been, before the French Revolution, a royal
abbey. Richard the Lion-Hearted, Eleanor of Aquitaine, and other Plantagenets
were buried there, and Genet fancied he was linked to them through his name.

Genet was inspired in writing this book by a late nineteenth-century manual
on the symbolism of the rose, which he was reading at the time.

Miracle of the Rose *was not published until 1946, when it was brought out*
in a luxurious edition by Arbalète.

O F ALL THE STATE PRISONS of France, Fontevrault is the most disqui-
eting. It was Fontevrault that gave me the strongest impression of anguish and
affliction, and I know that convicts who have been in other prisons have, at the

mere mention of its name, felt an emotion, a pang, comparable to mine. I shall not try to define the essence of its power over us: whether this power be due to its past, its abbesses of royal blood, its aspect, its walls, its ivy, to the transient presence of convicts bound for the penal colony at Cayenne, to its prisoners, who are more vicious than those elsewhere, to its name—none of this matters. But to all these reasons was added, for me, another: that it was, during my stay at the Mettray Reformatory Colony, the sanctuary to which our childhood dreams aspired. I felt that its walls preserved—the custodial preserving the bread—the very shape of the future. While the boy I was at fifteen twined in his hammock around a friend (if the rigors of life make us seek out a friendly presence, I think it is the rigors of prison that drive us toward each other in bursts of love without which we could not live; unhappiness is the enchanted potion), he knew that his final form dwelt behind them and that the convict with his thirty-year sentence was the fulfilment of himself, the last transformation, which death would make permanent. And Fontevrault still gleams (though with a very soft, a faded brilliance) with the lights emitted in its darkest heart, the dungeon, by Harcamone, who was sentenced to death.

When I left Santé Prison for Fontevrault, I already knew that Harcamone was there, awaiting execution. Upon my arrival I was therefore gripped by the mystery of one of my fellow inmates at Mettray who had been able to pursue the adventure of all of us to its most tenuous peak: the death on the scaffold which is our glory. Harcamone had "succeeded." And as this success was not of an earthly order, like fortune or honors, his achievement filled me with amazement and admiration (even the simplest achievement is miraculous), but also inspired the fear that overwhelms the witness of a magical operation. Harcamone's crimes might have meant nothing to me had I not known him at close range, but my love of beauty (which desired so ardently that my life be crowned with a violent, in fact bloody death) and my aspiration to a saintliness of muted brilliance (which kept it from being heroic by men's standards) made me secretly choose decapitation, which has the virtue of being reproved, of reproving the death that it gives and of illuminating its beneficiary with a glory more somber and gentle than the shimmering, silvery velvet of great funerals; and Harcamone's crimes and death revealed to me—as if taking it apart—the mechanism of that glory which had at last been attained. Such glory is not human. We have never heard of any executed criminal whose execution alone haloed him as the saints of the Church and the glories of the age are haloed, but yet we know that the purest of those who were given that death felt, within themselves and on their severed head, the placing of the amazing private crown which was studded with jewels wrested from the darkness of the heart. Each of them knew that the moment his head fell into the basket of sawdust and was taken out (by the ears) by an assistant whose role seems to me strange indeed, his heart would be garnered by fingers gloved with modesty and be carried off in a youngster's bosom that was adorned like a spring festival. I thus aspired to heavenly glory, and Harcamone had attained it before me, quietly, as the result of murdering a little girl and, fifteen years later, a Fontevrault guard.

I arrived at the prison with my hands and feet chained. I had been prepared by a very long and rough trip in the armored police train. There was a hole in the seat, and when my gripes got too violent because of the jolting, I had only to unbutton. It was cold. I rode through a countryside numbed with winter. I imagined the hard fields, the hoarfrost, the impure daylight. My arrest had taken place in midsummer, and my most haunting memory of Paris is of a city completely empty, abandoned by the population which was fleeing from the invasion, a kind of Pompeii, without policemen at the crossings, a city such as the burglar dares dream of when he is tired of inventing ruses.

Four traveling-guards were playing cards in the corridor of the train. Orléans ... Blois ... Tours ... Saumur. The car was detached and switched to another track, and we were at Fontevrault. There were thirty of us, because the police car had only thirty cells. Half of the convoy was composed of men of about thirty. The rest ranged from eighteen to sixty.

While the passengers looked on, we were attached in pairs, and with our hands and feet chained we got into the Black Marias that were waiting for us at the station. I had time to note the sadness of the crop-headed young men who watched the girls go by. My chainmate and I entered one of the narrow cells, a vertical coffin. I noticed that the Black Maria was divested of its charm, that air of haughty misfortune which, the first few times I had taken it, had made it a vehicle of exile, a conveyance fraught with grandeur, slowly fleeing, as it carried me off, between the ranks of a people bowed with respect. It is no longer a vehicle of royal misfortune. I have had a clear vision of it, of a thing which, beyond happiness or unhappiness, is splendid.

It was there, upon entering the prison wagon, that I felt I had become a true, disenchanted visionary.

The wagons drove to the prison. I cannot tell how it looked from the outside—I can tell this about few prisons, since those which I know, I know only from the inside. The cells of the wagon were closed, but from a jolt of the vehicle as it mounted a paved slope I gathered that we had gone through a gate and that I was in the domain of Harcamone. I know that the prison is at the bottom of a valley, of an infernal gorge from which a miraculous fountain gushes, but nothing stops us from thinking that it is at the top of a high mountain; here, in this place, everything leads me to think that it is at the top of a rock, of which the ramparts are a continuation. Although this altitude may be ideal, it is all the more real, for the isolation it grants is indestructible. Neither the walls nor the silence has anything to do with it. We shall see this in the case of Mettray Reformatory, which is as far-flung as the prison is high.

Night had fallen. We arrived amidst a mass of darkness. We got out. Eight guards, lined up like footmen, were waiting for us on the lighted steps. At the top of a flight of two stairs the wall of darkness was breached by a huge, brightly illuminated arched door. It was a holiday, Christmas perhaps. I had barely time to catch a glimpse of the yard, the black walls of which were covered with mournful ivy. We passed an iron gate. Behind it was a small inner yard lit up by four electric lamps: the bulb and shade, in the form of an Anamite hat, are the official lamp of all French prisons. At the end of this yard, where, even in the darkness, we sensed an unwonted architecture, we passed another iron gate, then went down a few steps lit by lamps of the same kind and suddenly we were in a delightful square garden adorned with shrubbery and a fountain around which ran a cloister with delicate little columns. After mounting a stairway sculpted in the wall, we found ourselves in a white corridor and then proceeded to the record office, where we remained a long time in a state of disorder before our chains were taken off.

"You there, you going to put out your wrists?"

I extended my wrist, and the chain pulled up the hand, sad as a captured animal, of the fellow to whom it was attached. The guard fumbled at the lock of the handcuffs; when he found it and inserted the key, I heard the slight click of the delicate trap that was freeing me. And that deliverance to enter captivity was to us a first affliction. The heat was stifling, but no one thought it would be so hot in the dormitories. The door of the office opened into a corridor that was lit up with cruel precision. The door was unlocked. A convict on the maintenance staff, probably a sweeper, pushed it slightly, put his smiling face in, and whispered:

"Say, boys, if any of you have butts, better let me have 'em, because . . ."

He broke off and disappeared. Probably a guard was coming. Someone shut the door from the outside.

I listened to hear whether the voice would cry out, but I heard nothing. Nobody was being tortured. I looked at one of the fellows who were with me. We smiled. We had both recognized the whisper which would be for a long time the only tone in which we could speak. We sensed all around us, behind the walls, a stealthy, silent but zealous activity. Why in the dead of night? In winter, darkness came on quickly, and it was only five in the afternoon.

Some moments later, likewise muffled but remote, a voice, which sounded to me like that of the inmate, cried out:

"Regards to your fanny from my dick!"

The guards in the office heard it too but didn't bat an eyelash. Thus, as soon as I arrived I realized that no convict's voice would be clear. It is either a murmur low enough for the guards not to hear, or else a cry muffled by a thickness of walls and anguish.

As soon as each of us gave his name, age, occupation, and distinguishing marks and signed with the print of his forefinger, he was taken by a guard to the wardrobe. It was my turn:

"Name?"

"Genet."

"Plantagenet?"

"I said Genet."

"What if I feel like saying Plantagenet? Do you mind?"

" . . . "

"Christian name?"

"Jean."

"Age?"

"Thirty."

"Occupation?"

"No occupation."

The guard gave me a dirty look. Perhaps he despised me for not knowing that the Plantagenets were buried in Fontevrault, that their coat of arms—leopards and the Maltese Cross—is still on the stained-glass windows of the chapel.

I had barely time to wave a stealthy good-bye to a youngster who had been in the convoy and whom I had singled out. It is less than fifty days since I left him, but though I would like to adorn my grief with the memory of him, to linger over his face, he flees me. In the Black Maria that took us from the station to the prison, he managed to get into the same narrow cell (the guards made us enter in pairs) as a tough-looking pimp. In order to be chained to the pimp, he had resorted to a trick that made me jealous of both of them and that still bothers and, owing to a deep mystery, attracts me, tearing a veil so that I have a luminous insight. And ever since, when time hangs heavy, I mull over this memory in my prison, but I cannot get to the heart of it. I can imagine what they did and said, what plans they made for the future, I can fabricate a very long life for their love. But I weary quickly. Developing this brief incident—the child's maneuvre and his entering the little cell—adds nothing to my knowledge of it, in fact destroys the charm of the lightning maneuvre. In like manner, when Harcamone hurried past me, the beauty of his face lit me up, but when I observed it at great length, in detail, the face faded. Certain acts dazzle us and light up blurred surfaces if our eyes are keen enough to see them in a flash, for the beauty of a living thing can be grasped only fleetingly. To pursue it during its changes leads us inevitably to the moment when it ceases, for it cannot last a lifetime. And to analyze it, that is, to pursue it in time with the sight and the imagination, is to view it in its decline, for after the thrilling moment in which it reveals itself it diminishes in intensity. I have lost that child's face.

I picked up my bundle: two shirts, two handkerchiefs, a half-loaf of bread, a songbook. And, with an already plodding gait, not saying a word to them, I left my traveling companions, crashers, pimps, hoodlums, thieves sentenced to three years, five years, ten years, and lifers, and went to join other crashers, other lifers. I walked in front of the guard through very clean, white hallways which were brightly lit and smelled of fresh paint. I passed two trusties who were carrying on a stretcher the eight monumental registers containing the names of the eleven hundred and fifty prisoners. They were followed by a young guard and a clerk. The two prisoners walked in silence, their arms straining beneath the weight of the giant volumes which could have been reduced to a small notebook. In shuffling along on their selvaged slippers, they bore the full weight imparted by so much sadness and thus seemed to be thudding the floor, lumberingly, with rubber boots. The two guards observed the same silence and walked with equally solemn steps. I almost saluted, not the jailers, but the books which contained the so illustrious name of Harcamone.

"Hey, you going to salute?"

This was said by the turnkey who was escorting me, and he added:
"Unless you already feel like getting the works."

Prisoners are required to salute the guards. As I neared them I ventured, with difficulty, the ridiculous salute which is so incompatible with our flabby, gliding gait on heelless slippers. We passed other guards, who didn't even look at us. The prison lived like a cathedral at midnight of Christmas eve. We were carrying on the tradition of the monks who went about their business at night, in silence. We belonged to the Middle Ages. A door was open at the left. I entered the wardrobe. When I took off my clothes, I felt that the brown homespun prison outfit was a robe of innocence which I was putting on in order to live near, in fact under the very roof of the murderer. Trembling like a thief, I lived for days on end in a state of wonder which none of the lowliest daily preoccupations was able to destroy: neither the crappers nor the stew nor the work nor the confusion of the senses.

After assigning me to a dormitory, Number 5, they assigned me to the workshop where camouflage nets were being made for the German army which was then occupying France. I had made up my mind to keep out of the intrigues of the big shots, of the guys who pay for larceny, who pay for murder, but in the wardrobe I was given a pair of trousers that had belonged to a bruiser—or an inmate who must have acted like one. He had made two slits in it for false pockets, which were forbidden. They were waist-high and cut on the bias, like those of sailors. When I walked, or was inactive, that was where, in spite of myself, I put my hands. My gait became what I hadn't wanted it to be, that of a big shot. The outfit included a brown homespun jacket without collar or pockets (though a convict had pierced the lining and thus made a kind of inner pocket). It had buttonholes, but all the buttons were missing. The jacket was very threadbare, but less than the trousers, which had been mended with nine patches, all more or less worn with age. There were thus nine different shades of brown. The two false pockets had been cut diagonally at stomach-level with, I imagine, a paring knife from the shoemaking shop. The trousers were supposed to be held up by the buttons alone, without belt or braces, but the buttons were all missing, which made the outfit look as sad as a wrecked house. In the shop, two hours after my arrival, I made myself a raffia belt in the form of a rope, and, as it was confiscated every evening by a guard, I would make another the following day. There are inmates who make a new one every single morning, that is, say, for ten years, three thousand times. The trousers were too short for me. They reached only to my calves, so that my long underpants and pale white legs were visible. The underpants were white and the letters A.P., which stand for *administration pénitentiaire*, were stamped on them in thick ink. The undershirt was made of homespun, also brown, and had a small pocket on the right side. The coarse linen shirt was collarless. The sleeves had no cuffs. Nor buttons either. There were rust spots on the shirt which I feared were shit stains. It was stamped A.P. We changed shirts every two weeks. The slippers were made of brown homespun. They would get stiff with sweat. The flat forage cap was made of brown homespun. The handkerchief had blue and white stripes.

I add the fact that Rasseneur, whom I had met in another prison, recognized me and, without consulting me, got me into a mob. Apart from him, I recognized no one from Santé or the other prisons. Harcamone was the only one who had been with me at Mettray, but he remained invisible in the death cell.

I shall try to tell what Harcamone meant to me, and thereby what Divers meant to me, and above all Bulkaen, whom I still love and who finally indicates my fate to me. Bulkaen is the finger of God; Harcamone is God, since he is in heaven (I am speaking of the heaven I create for myself and to which I am devoted body and soul). Their love, my love for them persists within me, where it acts and stirs my depths, and though what I felt for Harcamone may be mystic, it is nonetheless violent. I shall try to tell as well as I can what it is about these handsome thugs that charms me, the element which is both light and darkness. I shall do what I can, but all I can say is that "they are a dark brightness or a dazzling darkness." This is nothing compared to how I feel about it, a feeling which the most worthy novelists express when they write: "The black light . . . the blazing shade . . .," trying to achieve in a short poem the living, apparent synthesis of Evil and the Beautiful. Through Harcamone, Divers, and Bulkaen I shall again relive Mettray, which was my childhood. I shall revive the abolished reformatory, the children's hell that has been destroyed.

Can it be that the world was unaware of, did not even suspect, the existence of three hundred children who were organized in a rhythm of love and hate in the fairest spot of fairest Touraine? There, among the flowers (those garden flowers and those which I offer to dead soldiers, anxiously, lest they not suffice, have been, ever since, my infernal props) among the flowers and rare varieties of trees, the Colony led its secret life, worrying the peasants for fifteen miles around, for they feared that a sixteen-year-old colonist might escape and set fire to their farms. Furthermore, as every peasant was given a fifty-franc reward for each runaway child he brought back, the Mettray countryside was the scene, night and day, of an actual child-hunt, complete with pitchforks, shotguns, and dogs. If a colonist went out at night, he strewed terror through the fields. Rio, whom I cannot think of without being moved by his maidenly sweetness, was about eighteen when he tried to run away. He dared set fire to a barn so that the panic-stricken peasants would get up and run to the fire in their nightshirts without taking time to lock the door. He entered unseen and stole a jacket and pair of trousers in order to get rid of the white canvas breeches and blue-twill smock that were the uniform of the Colony and that would have singled him out. The house blazed away magnificently. Children, so it was reported, were burned to a crisp, cows perished, but the bold, remorseless child got as far as Orléans. It is a known fact that young countrywomen always leave a jacket and pair of trousers on the clothesline in the hope and fear that a runaway will steal them, move the line, which rings a bell, and so be caught. Traps laid by women's hands surrounded the Colony with an invisible, undetectable danger which threw pairs of frightened kids into a wild panic. The mere memory of this causes me, within my affliction, a greater affliction, fills me with frightful gloom at the thought that this childhood world is dead. Only one phrase can express my sadness, the one that is always written at the end

of a prince's visit to the scenes of his former loves or the scenes of his glory:
". . . and he wept . . ."

Fontevrault, like Mettray, could be rendered by a long list of the couples which
were formed by names:

> Botchako and Bulkaen
> Sillar and Venture
> Rocky and Bulkaen
> Deloffre and Toscano
> Mouline and Monot
> Lou Daybreak and Jo
> Bulkaen and I
> Divers and I
> Rocky and I.

I lived for a week in the bewilderment of arrival, familiarizing myself with the
prison discipline and regimen. A simple regimen, a life that would be easy if it
were not lived by us. We got up at six. A guard opened the door. We went to the
stone-flagged corridor to get our clothes which we had left there before going to
bed. We then got dressed. Five minutes in the washroom. We drank a bowl of soup
in the refectory and then left for the shop. Work until noon. Then back to the
refectory until one-thirty. Again to the shop. At six o'clock, mess. At seven, to the
dormitory. I have just set down, exactly, the daily schedule at Mettray. On Sunday
we would stay in the shops, inactive, sometimes reading the list of names of the
abbesses, appointed by royal decree, who had reigned over Fontevrault. To go to
the refectory at noon, we had to cross yards that were infinitely sad, sad because
of the abandonment that already dooms to death the admirable Renaissance
façades. Black faggots are heaped in a corner, near the abbey chapel. Dirty water
flows into gutters. The grace of some architectural jewel is sometimes wounded.
I got involved in the complications of love affairs, but the daily preoccupations
with work, meals, exchanges, the occasional devices whereby a convict craftily
carries on a private life behind his official, visible life, and, in addition, a rapid
acquaintanceship with the inmates, did not prevent me from bearing, almost
painfully, the weight of Harcamone's presence. One day, at meal time, I couldn't
refrain from whispering to Rasseneur:

"Where is he?"

And he, in a breath:

"In Number 7. Special cell."

"You think he'll get it?"

"Sure thing."

A kid at my left who guessed we were talking about that death put his hand to
his mouth and muttered:

"It's great to die gloriously!"

I knew he was there, and I was full of hope and fear, when I had the privilege of witnessing one of his appearances. It happened during a recreation period. We were lined up near the death cell, waiting our turn to be shaved by a convict (we were shaved once a week). One of the superintendents had opened Harcamone's door. He was accompanied by a guard who was casually entwining his gestures with a thick chain, as thick as those by which the chairs are attached to the walls. The superintendent entered. Though we were facing the wall, we could not help looking, despite the fact that we weren't allowed to. We were like children whose heads are bowed during evening service and who look up when the priest opens the tabernacle. It was the first time I had seen Harcamone since leaving Mettray. He was standing, with the full beauty of his body, in the middle of the cell. He was wearing his beret, not drooping over his ear as at Mettray but set almost on his eyes and bent, forming a peak, like the vizor of the caps of old-time hooligans. I received such a shock that I can't tell whether it was caused by the change in his beauty or by the fact that I was suddenly confronted with the exceptional creature whose story was familiar only to the well-guarded chamber of my eyeballs, and I found myself in the situation of the witch who has long been summoning the prodigy, lives in expectation of it, recognizes the signs that announce it and suddenly sees it standing before her and—what is even more disturbing—sees it as she had announced it. It is the proof of her power, of her grace, for the flesh is also the most obvious means of certainty. Harcamone "appeared unto me." He knew it was recreation time, for he put out his wrists, which the guard attached with the short chain. Harcamone dropped his arms, and the chain hung in front of him, below his belt. He walked out of the cell. As sunflowers turn to the sun, our faces turned and our bodies pivoted without our even realizing that our immobility had been disturbed, and when he moved toward us, with short steps, like the women of 1910 in hobble skirts, or the way he himself danced the java, we felt a temptation to kneel or at least to put our hands over our eyes, out of decency. He had no belt. He had no socks. From his head—or from mine—came the roar of an airplane engine. I felt in all my veins that the miracle was under way. But the fervor of our admiration and the burden of saintliness which weighed on the chain that gripped his wrists—his hair had had time to grow, and the curls had matted over his forehead with the cunning cruelty of the twists of the crown of thorns—caused the chain to be transformed before our unastonished eyes into a garland of white flowers. The transformation began at the left wrist, which it encircled with a bracelet of flowers, and continued along the chain, from link to link, to the right wrist. Harcamone kept walking, heedless of the prodigy. The guards saw nothing abnormal. I was holding the pair of scissors with which, once a month, we were allowed, each in turn, to cut our fingernails and toenails. I was therefore barefooted. I made the same movement that religious fanatics make to seize the hem of a cloak and kiss it. I took two steps, with my body bent forward and the scissors in my hand, and cut off the loveliest rose, which was hanging by a supple stem near his left wrist. The head of the rose fell on my bare foot and rolled on the pavestones among the dirty curls of cut hair. I picked it up and raised my enraptured face, just in time to see the horror stamped on that of Harcamone, whose nervousness had been unable to resist that sure prefiguration of his death. He almost fainted. For a very brief instant, I found myself on one knee before my idol, who was trembling with horror, or shame, or love, staring at me as if he had recognized me, or merely as if Harcamone had recognized Genet, and as if I were the cause of his frightful emotion, for we had each made exactly the gestures that might be so interpreted. He was deathly pale, and those who witnessed the scene from a distance might have thought that this murderer was as delicate as a Duke of Guise or a Knight of Lorraine, of whom history tells us that they fainted, overwhelmed by the smell and sight of a rose. But he pulled himself together. His face—over which a slight smile passed—grew calm again. He continued walking, with the limping gait of which I shall speak later, though it was attenuated by the fetters on his ankles, but the chain that bound his hands no longer suggested a garland and was now only a steel chain. He disappeared from my sight, whisked away by the shadow and the bend of the corridor. I put the rose into the false pocket that was cut in my jacket.

This, then, is the tone I shall adopt in speaking of Mettray, Harcamone and the prison. Nothing will prevent me, neither close attention nor the desire to be exact, from writing words that sing. And though the evocation of Bulkaen may bring me back to a more naked view of events, I know that, as soon as it ceases, my song, in reaction against this nakedness, will be more exalted. But let there be no talk of improbability or of my having derived this phrase from an arrangement of words. The scene was within me, I was present, and only by writing about it am I able to express my worship of the murderer less awkwardly. The very day following this prodigy, I forgot all about it in my infatuation with Bulkaen.

Blond, close-cropped hair, eyes that were perhaps green but certainly grim-looking, a thin, lithe body—the expression that best renders it is: "grace in leaf and love at rest"—an air of being twenty years old: that's Bulkaen. I had been at Fontevrault a week. I was going down for the medical examination when, at a turn of the stairway, I saw him. He was dressing or undressing. He must have been swapping his homespun jacket for a newer one. I had time enough to see, spread across his golden chest and wide as a coat of arms, the huge wings of a blue eagle. The tattoo wasn't dry, and the scabs made it stand out in such relief that I thought it had been carved with a chisel. I was seized with a kind of holy terror. When the youngster stood up straight, his face was smiling. It was gleaming with stars. He was saying to the crony with whom he was making the swap, ". . . and besides, I've been given a ten-year injunction."[1] He threw his jacket over his shoulders and kept it there. I was holding a few cigarette butts in my hand, which was on a level with his eyes because of our positions on the stairs—I was on the way down. He looked at them and said, "Someone's got cigarettes." I said, "I have," and kept going, feeling a little ashamed of smoking Gauloises. The cigarette is the prisoner's gentle companion. He thinks of it more than of his absent wife. His charming friendship

---

[1] In the original, *interdiction de séjour:* a punishment, which does not exist in English and American law, whereby a criminal is banished from an area for a given time.—Translator's note.

with it is largely due to the elegance of its shape and the gestures it requires of his fingers and body. It was boorish of me not to offer Bulkaen one of my white maidens. That was our first meeting. I was too struck by the brilliance of his beauty to dare say another word. I spoke of him to no one, but I carried off in my eyes the memory of a dazzling face and body. I prayed for him to love me. I prayed for him to be the kind of person who could love me. I already knew he would lead me to death. I know now that this death will be beautiful. I mean that he was worthy of my dying for him and because of him. But may he lead me to it quickly. In any case, sooner or later it will be because of him. I shall die worn out or shattered. Even if, at the end of this book, Bulkaen proves to be contemptible because of his stupidity or vanity or some other ugly quality, the reader must not be surprised if, though aware of these qualities (since I reveal them), I persist in changing my life by following the star to which he points (I am using his terms, despite myself. When he sent me notes later on, he would write: "I've got my star . . .") for his role of demon requires that he show me this new direction. He brings a message which he himself does not quite understand but which he implements in part. Fatality will first utilize my love of him. But when my love—and Bulkaen—disappear, what will be left?

I have the nerve to think that Bulkaen lived only so that I could write my book. He therefore had to die, after a life I can imagine only as bold and arrogant, slapping every paleface he came across. His death will be violent and mine will follow close on his. I feel that I'm wound up and heading for an end which will blow us to bits.

The very next day, in the yard, during recreation, Rasseneur introduced us to each other, at a moment when several fellows were plaguing a homely, unlikeable old queer. They were pushing him around, bullying him, making fun of him. The most spiteful of all, possessed of a cruelty that seemed completely unwarranted, was Botchako, who had the reputation of being the most formidable crasher in Fontevrault, a brutal individual who usually said nothing to the jerks and even less to the queers, whom he seemed unaware of, and I wondered why he had suddenly let loose on this one. It was as if he were all at once giving vent to insults that had been accumulating a long time. His irregular but firm teeth seemed to be curling his lips. His face was freckled. One imagined he was red-headed. He hadn't the shade of a beard. He wasn't jeering with a smile, as were the others; he was nasty and insulting. He wasn't playing but seemed to be taking revenge. Rage set him ablaze. He was regarded as the biggest fucker in the jug. Ugliness is beauty at rest. When he spoke, his voice was hoarse and hollow. It also had some acid scratches which were like cracks, like fissures, and, considering the beauty of his voice when he sang, I examined his speaking voice more attentively. I made the following discovery: the irritating hoarseness, forced by the singing, was transformed into a very sweet, velvety strain, and the fissures became the clearest notes. It was somewhat as if, in unwinding a ball of wool at rest, these notes had been refined. A physicist can easily explain this phenomenon. As for me, I remain disturbed in the presence of the person who revealed to me that beauty is the projection of ugliness and that by "developing" certain monstrosities we obtain the purest ornaments. Under the spell of his words, I expected to see him strike the jerk, who dared not make a movement, not even of fear. He instinctively assumed the sudden, shifty, prudent immobility of a frightened animal. Had Botchako made a single move to strike, he might have killed him, for he would not have been able to check his fury. It was known in the prison that he never stopped fighting until he was completely exhausted. The features of his pug-nosed face manifested the power of a solid, stocky, unflinching body. His face was like a boxer's, tough and firm, hardened by repeated blows, beaten like wrought iron. There was nothing soft or drooping about its flesh. The skin clung to dry muscle and bone. His forehead was too narrow to contain enough reason to stop his anger once it got going. His eyes were deep set and the epidermis of his chest, which was visible through the opening of the shirt and homespun jacket, was white and healthy-looking and absolutely hairless.

Above the yard, on a kind of raised catwalk, Randon made his rounds without stopping. From time to time he would look down into the yard where we were standing about. He was the meanest of the guards. In order that he not notice the cruelty of the scene—he would have had the guilty ones punished for the sake of virtue—the big shots and the jerk himself made their attitudes and gestures look inoffensive, even friendly, while their mouths were spewing insults, though in a muffled voice that veiled their malevolence. The queer was smiling with the utmost humility, as much to put off the guard as to try to mollify Botchako and his cronies.

"You bitch, you swallow it by the mouthful!"

With a single twist, unique in the world, Botchako hitched up his pants.

"I'd shoot it up your hole, you punk!"

Bulkaen was leaning against the wall with his elbow, in such a way that his head was under his arm, which looked as if it were a crown. This crown-arm was bare, for his jacket was, as always, simply thrown over his shoulders, and that enormous coil of muscle, his baron's coronet on the light head of a child of the North, was the visible sign of the ten years of banishment that weighed on his delicate pate. He wore his beret the way Harcamone did. At the same time, I saw his neck, the skin of which was shadowy with grime; from his round shirt collar emerged a wing tip of the blue eagle. His right ankle was crossed over the left, the way Mercury is always depicted, and the heavy homespun trousers, as worn by him, had infinite grace. His smiling lips were parted. From his mouth came a breath which could only be perfumed. His left hand was poised on his hipbone as on the handle of a dagger. I haven't invented this posture. That's how he stood. I add that he had a slender figure, broad shoulders and a voice strong with the assurance that came from the awareness of his invincible beauty. He was watching the scene. Botchako was still spitting insults and getting more and more nasty.

Lou Daybreak, the most isolated of us because of his name, made a vague gesture. Lou's name was a vapor that enveloped his entire person, and when you pierced the softness and approached him, when you passed through his name, you scraped against the thorns, against the sharp, cunning branches with which he bristled. He was blond, and his eyebrows looked like spikes of rye stuck to his stylized brow. He was a pimp, and we didn't like him. He hung out with other pimps, whom we called "Julots" or "Those Gentlemen" . . . and they often get into brawls with our mobs.

We thought that this gesture—his hand dropping on Botchako's shoulder—was an attempt to make peace, but he said, with a smile:

"Go on, marry him! You're in love with him. Anyone can see it!"

Botchako's face expressed exaggerated disgust. There was no reason for Lou to talk as he did, for though the pimps and the crashers, who formed distinct groups, did speak to each other about trivial matters having to do with work and life in common, they never took the liberty of going too far. I was waiting for Botchako to go for Lou, but he turned away and spat. Lou smiled. There was a movement of hostility in the group of crashers. I looked at Bulkaen. He was smiling and shifting his gaze back and forth from Botchako to the jerk. Amused perhaps. But I dared not think I was in the presence of two guys (Bulkaen and the queer) who were basically identical. I was watching Bulkaen to see his reaction to the queer's gestures. I tried to detect a correspondence between their gesticulations. There was nothing mannered about Bulkaen. His excessive vivacity made him seem somewhat brutal. Was he carrying within him an abashed and quivering fag who resembled the pathetic jerk that everyone despised?

Would he love me? My spirit was already flying off in quest of my happiness. Would some unexpected happening, some blunder, alike and equally miraculous, link us by love as he was linked with Rocky? He related the great event to me later on. I translate his language: Rocky and he had met at Clairvaux Prison. They were released the same day and decided to work together. Three days later, their first burglary made them rich: a wad of banknotes. "Sixty thousand francs," said Bulkaen. They left the rifled apartment and went out into the street and the night, floating with elation. They dared not count and split the booty in the lighted street. They entered the garden of the Square d'Anvers, which was deserted. Rocky took out the bills. He counted them and gave thirty to Bulkaen. The joy of being free and rich gave them wings. Their souls tried to leave their cumbrous bodies, to drag them heavenward. It was real joy. They smiled with glee at their success. They rose to the occasion, as if to congratulate each other, not upon their skill but their luck, as one congratulates a friend who has come into money, and this happy impulse made them embrace. Their joy was so great that there is no knowing its essence. Its origin was the successful job, but a small fact (the embrace, the accolade) intervened amidst the joyous tumult, and despite themselves it was this new fact that they considered the source of the happiness which they named love. Bulkaen and Rocky kissed. They could not break away from each other, for happiness never produces a movement of withdrawal. The happier they were, the more deeply they entered each other. They were rich and free—they were happy. They were in each other's arms at the moment of deepest happiness: they loved each other. And as this merging was energized by the mute fear of being caught, and also because their mutual solitude made them seek a friend as a shelter in which to hide, they married.

Bulkaen's gaze turned away from the scene that pained me and it settled on Rasseneur, the friend who had introduced us—but his head had to make a quarter turn and his gaze met mine on its way to Rasseneur. I thought for a moment that he had recognized me as the fellow of the day before. My face remained impassive, indifferent, and his, now that I recall it, was, I think, somewhat arch. He started a conversation. When the ten-minute recreation period was over, I shook hands with him without wanting to seem as if I were bothering to look at him, and I made a point of this calculated indifference by pretending to be overjoyed to see a friend who was going by, but I carried Bulkaen off in the depths of my heart. I went back to my cell, and the abandoned habit of my abandoned childhood took hold of me: the rest of the day and all night long I built an imaginary life of which Bulkaen was the center, and I always gave that life, which was begun over and over and was transformed a dozen times, a violent end: murder, hanging or beheading.

We saw each other again. At each of our meetings he appeared before me in a bloody glory of which he was unaware. I was drawn to him by the force of love, which was opposed by the force of supernatural but brawny creatures who kept me from going to him by fettering my wrists, waist, and ankles with chains that would have kept a cruiser anchored on a stormy night. He was always smiling. Thus, it was through him that the habits of my childhood took hold of me again.

My childhood was dead and with it died the poetic powers that had dwelt in me. I no longer hoped that prison would remain the fabulous world it had long been. One day I suddenly realized from certain signs that it was losing its charms, which meant perhaps that I was being transformed, that my eyes were opening to the usual view of the world. I saw prison as any ordinary roughneck sees it. It is a dungeon where I rage at being locked up, but today, in the hole, instead of reading "Tattooed Jean" on the wall of the cell, I read, because of a malformation of the letters carved in the plaster, "Tortured Jean." (It's because of Harcamone that I've been in the hole for a month, and not because of Bulkaen.) I walked by the murderer's cell too often, and one day I was caught. Here are a few details: The carpentry shop and the shops where camouflage nets and iron beds are made are in a court in the north part of the former abbey. They are one-story buildings. The dormitories are on the first and second floors of the left wing, which is supported by the wall of the former chapter house. The infirmary is on the ground floor. In order to get there, I had to go by way of the sixth or seventh division, where the death cells are located, and I always went by way of the seventh. Harcamone's cell was at the right. A guard, who sat on a stool, would look inside and talk to him or read a newspaper or eat a cold meal. I would look straight ahead and keep going.

It must seem odd that I walked through the prison all by myself. The reason is that I had arranged things, first with Rocky, who was an attendant in the infirmary, and then, when he left prison, with his successor. While at work, I would pretend that something was wrong with me, and the attendant would send for me to be treated. The guard in the shop would merely ring up his colleague and let him know I was coming.

The exact vision that made a man of me, that is, a creature living solely on earth, corresponded with the fact that my femininity, or the ambiguity and haziness of my male desires, seemed to have ended. If my sense of wonder, the joy that suspended me from branches of pure air, sprang chiefly from my identifying myself with the handsome thugs who haunted the prison, as soon as I achieved total virility—or, to be more exact, as soon as I became a male—the thugs lost their glamour. And though my meeting Bulkaen revives dormant charms, I shall preserve the benefit of that march toward maleness, for Bulkaen's beauty is, above all, delicate. I no longer yearned to resemble the hoodlums. I felt I had achieved self-fulfillment. Perhaps I feel it less today, after the adventures I am describing, but I felt strong, not dependent, free, unbound. Glamorous models ceased to present themselves. I strode jauntily in my strength, with a weightiness, a sureness, a forthright look which are themselves proofs of force. The hoodlums no longer appealed to me. They were my equals. Does this mean that attraction is possible only when one is not entirely oneself? During those years of softness when my personality took all sorts of forms, any male could squeeze my sides with his walls, could contain me. My moral substance (and physical substance, which is its visible form, what with my white skin, weak bones, slack muscles, my slow gestures and their uncertainty) was without sharpness, without contour. I longed at the time— and often went so far as to imagine my body twisting about the firm, vigorous body of a male—to be embraced by the calm, splendid stature of a man of stone with sharp angles. And I was not completely at ease unless I could completely take his place, take on his qualities, his virtues. When I imagined I was he, making his gestures, uttering his words: when I *was* he. People thought I was seeing double, whereas I was seeing the double of things. I wanted to be myself, and I was myself when I became a crasher. All burglars will understand the dignity that arrayed me when I held my jimmy, my "pen." From its weight, material, and shape, and from its function too, emanated an authority that made me a man. I had always needed that steel penis in order to free myself completely from my faggotry, from my humble attitudes, and to attain the clear simplicity of manliness. I am no longer surprised at the arrogant ways of youngsters who have used the pen, even if only once. You may shrug your shoulders and mutter that they're scum. Nothing will prevent them from retaining the jimmy's virtue, which gives, in every circumstance, a sometimes astounding hardness to their youthful softness. Those who have used it are marked men. Bulkaen had known the jimmy, I could tell at once. These kids are crashers, therefore men, as much by virtue of the kind of nobility conferred upon them by the jimmy as of the risks, sometimes very great, which they have taken. Not that any particular courage is needed—I would say, rather, an unconcern, which is more exact. They are noble. A crasher cannot have low sentiments (I intend, starting here, to generalize. You will read later on about the baseness of hoodlums), since he leads a dangerous life with his body, for only the crasher's body is in danger, he does not worry about his soul. You are concerned for your honor, your reputation, you devise ways and means of saving them. But the crasher takes risks in the practice of his trade. His ruses are the ruses of a warrior and not of a sharper. It is noteworthy that during the war of 1940 real burglars did not try to live by what became common among bourgeois and workers, by what was then called the "black market." They knew nothing about business. When the prisons were filled with honest people who had been driven from the woods by hunger, they lost their fine, lordly bearing, but the crashers remained a haughty aristocracy. The great evil of this war has been its dissolving the hardness of our prisons. The war has locked up so many innocent people that the prisons are merely places of lamentation. Nothing is more repugnant than an innocent man in prison. He has done nothing to deserve jail (these are his own words). Destiny has made an error.

I did not get my first jimmy from a yegg, I bought it in a hardware store. It was short and solid, and, from the time of my first robbery, I held it as dear as a warrior his weapons, with a mysterious veneration, as when the warrior is a savage and his weapon a rifle. The two wedges, which lay next to the jimmy in a corner of my room—the corner quickly became magnetic, hypnotic—lightened it and gave it that air of a winged prick by which I was haunted. I slept beside it, for the warrior sleeps armed.

For my first burglary I chose a few houses in Auteil and looked up the names of the tenants in the phone book.[2] I had decided to operate as luck would have it. I would break in if nobody was home. I casually passed the concierge's window in the first apartment house. In my trousers against my thigh, were my jimmy and wedges. I started on the fifth floor so as to run less risk of being disturbed. I rang once. No one answered. I rang twice. Finally I set up a peal that lasted two minutes so as to be sure the apartment was empty.

If I were writing a novel, there might be a point in describing the gestures I made, but the aim of this book is only to relate the experience of freeing myself from a state of painful torpor, from a low, shameful life taken up with prostitution and begging and under the sway of the glamour and charm of the criminal world. I freed myself by and for a prouder attitude.

I had trained myself by breaking open doors in safe places, my own door and those of my friends. I therefore carried out the present operation in quick time, perhaps three minutes. Time enough to force the bottom of the door with my foot, insert a wedge, force the top with the jimmy and insert the second wedge between the door and the jamb, move up the first wedge, move down the second, wedge the jimmy near the lock, and push . . . When the lock cracked, the noise it made seemed to me to resound through the building. I pushed the door and went in. The noise of the lock as it gives way, the silence that follows, and the solitude that always besets me will govern my criminal entrances. These are rites, the more important as they are inevitable and are not mere adornments of an action whose

[2]There is a Paris directory arranged by street and house number.—Translator's note.

essence is still mysterious to me. I entered. I was the young sovereign who takes possession of a new realm where all is new to him but where there surely lurks the danger of attacks and conspiracies, a danger hidden along the road he takes, behind every rock, every tree, under the rugs, in the flowers that are tossed and the gifts offered by a people invisible by virtue of their number. The entrance was large. It heralded the most sumptuous home I had ever seen. I was surprised that there were no servants. I opened a door and found myself in the big drawing room. The objects were waiting for me. They were laid out for the robbery, and my passion for plunder and booty was inflamed. To speak properly of my emotion I would have to employ the same words I used in describing my wonderment in the presence of that new treasure, my love for Bulkaen, and in describing my fear in the presence of the possible treasure, his love for me. I would have to allude to the trembling hopes of the virgin, of the village fiancée who waits to be chosen, and then to add that this light moment is threatened by the black, pitiless, single eye of a revolver. For two days I remained in the presence of Bulkaen's image, with the fearful shyness of one who carries his first bouquet in its lace-paper collar. Would he say yes? Would he say no? I implored the spiders that had woven such precious circumstances. Let their thread not snap!

I opened a glass cabinet and carried off all the ivories and jades. Perhaps I was the first crasher ever to leave without bothering about cash, and it was not until my third job that I felt the sense of power and freedom that comes from discovering a sheaf of bills that you stuff into your pocket. I closed the door behind me and went downstairs. I was saved from bondage and low inclinations, for I had just performed an act of physical boldness. I already held my head high as I walked down the stairs. I felt in my trousers, against my thigh, the icy jimmy. I amiably wished that a tenant would appear so that I could use the strength that was hardening me. My right hand closed on the jimmy:

"If a woman comes along, I'll lay her out with my pendulum."

When I got to the street, I walked boldly. But I was always accompanied by an agonizing thought: the fear that honest people may be thieves who have chosen a cleverer and safer way of stealing. This fear disturbed my peace of mind in my solitude. I dismissed the idea by means of shrewd devices, which I shall describe.

I was now a man, a he-man. The broad-shouldered kids and pimps, the children of sorrow with bitter mouths and frightening eyes, were of no further use to me. I was alone. Everything was absent from the prisons, even solitude. Thus, my interest in adventure novels wanes insofar as I can no longer seriously imagine myself being the hero or being in his situation. I stopped plunging into those complications in which the slightest feat, criminal or otherwise, could be copied, be carried over into life, be utilized personally and lead me to wealth and glory. Thus, it was now extremely difficult for me to re-immerse myself in my dream-stories, stories fabricated by the disheartening play of solitude, but I found—and still find, despite my new plunge—more well-being in the true memories of my former life. Since my childhood is dead, in speaking of it I shall be speaking of something dead, but I shall do so in order to speak of the world of death, of the

Kingdom of Darkness or Transparency. Someone has carved on the wall: "Just as I'm guarded by a prison door, so my heart guards your memory . . ." I shall not let my childhood escape.

Thus, my heaven had emptied. The time to become who I am had perhaps arrived. And I shall be what I do not foresee, since I do not desire it, but I will not be a sailor or explorer or gangster or dancer or boxer, for their most glorious representatives no longer have a hold on me. I stopped wanting, and I shall never again want, to go through the canyons of Chile, for I have stopped admiring the clever and sturdy Rifle King who scaled their rocks in the illustrated pages of my childhood. The excitement was over. As for things, I began to know them by their practical qualities. The objects here in jail have been worn out by my eyes and are now sickly pale. They no longer mean prison to me, since the prison is inside me, composed of the cells of my tissues. It was not until long after my return here that my hands and eyes, which were only too familiar with the practical qualities of objects, finally stopped recognizing these qualities and discovered others which have another meaning. Everything was without mystery for me, but that bareness was not without beauty because I establish the difference between my former and present view of things, and this displacement intrigues me. Here is a very simple image: I felt I was emerging from a cave peopled with marvelous creatures, which one only senses (angels, for example, with speckled faces), and entering a luminous space where everything is only what it is, without overtones, without aura. What it is: useful. This world, which is new to me, is dreary, without hope, without excitement. Now that the prison is stripped of its sacred ornaments, I see it naked, and its nakedness is cruel. The inmates are merely sorry creatures with teeth rotted by scurvy; they are bent with illness and are always spitting and sputtering and coughing. They go from dormitory to shop in big, heavy, resounding sabots. They shuffle along on canvas slippers which are eaten away and stiff with filth that the dust has compounded with sweat. They stink. They are cowardly in the presence of the guards, who are as cowardly as they. They are now only scurrilous caricatures of the handsome criminals I saw in them when I was twenty. I only wish I could expose sufficiently the blemishes and ugliness of what they have become so as to take revenge for the harm they did me and the boredom I felt when confronted with their unparalleled stupidity.

And it grieved me to discover this new aspect of the world and of prison at a time when I was beginning to realize that prison was indeed the closed area, the confined, measured universe in which I ought to live permanently. It is the universe for which I am meant. It is meant for me. It is the one in which I must live (for I have the organs one needs to live in it), to which I am always being brought back by the fatality that showed me the curve of my destiny in the letters carved on the wall: "M.A.V."[3] And I have this feeling (so disheartening that after my mentioning it to Rasseneur he exclaimed: "Oh! Jean!" in a tone of such poignant sadness that I felt an instant expression of his friendship), I have this feeling during

---

[3] M.A.V., *mort aux vaches*, death to the cops.—Translator's note.

the medical checkup or during recreation when I meet friends, new and old, those to whom I am "Jeannot with the Pretty Ties," those I knew at the Mousetrap, in the corridors of Santé and Fresnes prisons, even outside. It is so natural for them to make up the population of prison and I discover I have such close ties with them (professional relations, relations of friendship or hatred) that since I feel so much a part of this world, it horrifies me to know that I am excluded from the other, yours, just when I was attaining the qualities by means of which one can live in it. I am therefore dead. I am a dead man who sees his skeleton in a mirror, or a dream character who knows that he lives only in the darkest region of a being whose face he will not know when the dreamer is awake. I now act and think only in terms of prison. My activity is limited by its framework. I am only a punished man. To the usual hardships of prison has been added hunger, and not a child's hunger—for our hunger at Mettray was the gluttony natural to children who are never sated, even by abundance. Hunger here is a man's hunger. It bites the bodies (and gnaws the minds) of the least sensitive brutes. Behind the walls, the war, which is mysterious to us, has shrunk our loaf of bread, our food allowance, and the big shots have been hit in the rightful object of their pride, their muscles. Hunger has transformed the prison into a Great North where wolves howl at night. We live at the confines of the Arctic polar circle. Our skinny bodies fight among themselves, and each, within itself, against hunger. This hunger, which at first helped to disenchant the jail, has now become so great that it is a tragic element which finally crowns the prison with a savage, baroque motif, with a ringing song that is wilder than the others and may dizzy me and make me fall into the hands of the powers summoned by Bulkaen. Despite this affliction—for though I take a man's stand, I realize that I am leaving a larval world of prodigious richness and violence—I want to try to relive my moments at Mettray. The atmosphere of the prison quickly impelled me to go back—in going back to Mettray—to my habits of the past, and I do not live a single moment on earth without at the same time living it in my secret domain, which is probably similar to the one inhabited by the men who are being punished, who walk round and round with their heads bent and their eyes looking straight ahead. And the fury with which I once turned on Charlot has not yet emptied me of the hatred I vowed him, despite my air of indifference, when, in the shop, because I reacted vaguely, or perhaps not at all, to one of his jokes, he shook me by the shoulder and said, "You in a fog or something?" I instantly felt the hatred we can bear a person who violates our dearest secrets, those of our vices.

At times, each of us is the theater of a drama which is occasioned by several elements: his real loves, a fight, his jealousy, a projected escape, which merge with dream adventures more brutal than real ones, and the men who are then wracked by the drama suddenly thrash about, but in silence. They make stiff gestures. They are brusque, taut, set. They hit out as if fighting an invisible soldier. Suddenly they relapse into their torpor; their very physiognomy sinks to the bottom of a swamp of dreams. Though the warden may say we are sluggish, the more subtle guards know that we are deep in these gardens and they no more disturb the submerged convict gratuitously than a Chinese disturbs an opium-smoker. Charlot was not an absolute tough. He therefore could not permit himself to screw me. And though he could later knock hell out of anyone who needled him, there hung over him the infamy of having made with his own hands, when he was broke, a black satin dress so that his girl could cruise for trade. I hated him for that blemish and for his shrewdness. In fact, my nerves couldn't stand the provocations, however slight, of a jerk or weakling. I would let my fists fly at the merest trifle. But there would have been no need to let fly at a tough, and it was not only because of fear, but because the toughs never even annoyed me. There issues from those I call "toughs" a potency that still dominates, and that soothes me. At Mettray I beat the daylights out of a little jerk who ran his hands over the windowpanes with a squeaking sound. A few days later, Divers did the very same thing and thus tugged at all my nerves, which wound about him and climbed lovingly over his body. If my memories of the Colony are awakened by Bulkaen in particular, by his presence, by his effect on me, the danger will be doubled, for my love of him already threatened to deliver me to the former powers of the Prison. And because in addition to this danger is that of the language I shall use in talking of Mettray and Fontevrault. For I tear my words from the depths of my being, from a region to which irony has no access, and these words, which are charged with all the buried desires I carry within me and which express them on paper as I write, will re-create the loathsome and cherished world from which I tried to free myself. Furthermore, as the insight I acquired into commonplace things enables me to indulge in the play and subtleties of the heart, my heart is caught in a veil again, incapable of fighting back when the lover practices his wiles. Charms master and throttle me. But I am glad to have given the loveliest names, the most beautiful titles (archangel, child-sun, my Spanish evening) to so many youngsters that I have nothing left with which to magnify Bulkaen. Perhaps, if words do not meddle too much, I shall be able to see him as he is, a pale, lively hoodlum, unless the fact of remaining solitary, alone with himself, unnamable and unnamed, charges him with an even more dangerous power.

The green faces of the plague-stricken, the world of lepers, the nocturnal sound of rattles, a voice against the wind, a tomblike atmosphere, a knocking on the ceiling, do not repel, do not horrify so much as do the few details which make an outcast of the prisoner, the deported convict or the inmate of a reformatory. But within the prison, at its very heart, are solitary confinement and the disciplinary cell from which one emerges purified.

The origin—the roots—of the great social movements cannot possibly lie in goodness, nor can they be accounted for by reasons which are openly avowable. Religions, the Frankish and French royalty, the freemasonries, the Holy Empire, the Church, national socialism, under which people still die by the axe and whose executioner must be a muscular fellow, have branched out across the globe, and the branches could have been nourished only in the depths. A man must dream a long time in order to act with grandeur, and dreaming is nursed in darkness. Some men take pleasure in fantasies whose basic contents are not celestial delights.

These are less radiant joys, the essence of which is Evil. For these reveries are drownings and concealments, and we can conceal ourselves only in evil or, to be more exact, in sin. And what we see of just and honorable institutions at the surface of the earth is only the projection, necessarily transfigured, of these solitary, secret gratifications. Prisons are places where such reveries take shape. Prisons and their inmates have too real an existence not to have a profound effect on people who remain free. For them, prisons are a pole, and, in prison, the dungeon. I shall therefore tell why I tried to have Bulkaen—for whom my love was so recent—sent to the hole.

But first, here is why I was sent to the punishment cell, where I began to write this account.

Just as when you walk at someone's side, his elbow and shoulder, despite your trying to walk straight, shift you to the right or left, and may make you bump against walls, so a force shifted me, despite myself, in the direction of Harcamone's cell. The result was that I often found myself in his vicinity and thus rather far from my dormitory and workshop. I would leave with a definite goal, though on the sly, either to bring some bread to a crony, or to get a cigarette in another shop, or for some other practical reason, and most of the time the goal was quite far from the seventh division, where the death cells are located, but the same force always made me go out of my way, or go too far, and I also noticed that as I approached the secret goal, which was hidden behind the mask of a reasonable decision, my pace grew slower, my gait more supple and lighter. More and more I would hesitate to go farther. I was both pushed forward and held back. Finally I would so lose control of my nerves that if a guard came along I would be unable to dash out of sight, and if he questioned me, I had no explanation to account for my presence in the seventh division. So that the guards imagined God knows what whenever they found me there alone, and one of them, Brulard, once nabbed me.

"What are you doing here?"

"You can see for yourself. I'm going by."

"You're going by? Where are you going? . . . And besides, I don't like your tone. Take your hands out of your belt."

I was on a horse.

Even when I am very calm, I feel as if I were being swept by a storm. This may be due to my mind's stumbling over every unevenness of surface because of its rapid pace, or to my desires, which are violent because they are almost always repressed, and when I live my inner scenes, I have the exhilaration that comes from always living them on horseback, on a rearing and galloping steed. I am a horseman. It is since I have known Bulkaen that I live on horseback, and I enter the lives of others on horseback as a Spanish grandee enters the Cathedral of Seville. My thighs grip the flanks. I spur my mount, my hands tighten on the reins.

Not that it happens quite that way, I mean not that I really know I'm on horseback, but rather I make the gestures and have the spirit of a man on horseback: my hand tightens, I toss back my head, my voice is arrogant. The sensation of riding a noble, whinnying animal overflowed into my daily life and gave me what is called a cavalier look and what I considered a victorious tone and bearing.

The guard reported me, and I was brought up before the warden, in the prison court. He hardly looked at me. He read the charge, put a pair of dark glasses over his pince-nez and pronounced sentence:

"Twenty days in the hole."

A guard took me there, without letting go of my wrist, which he had held all through the hearing.

When a man in prison does all he can to make trouble for his friends who have remained free and is responsible for their being caught, he is called malicious, whereas the fact is that in such a case the malice is composed of love, for he lures his friends to prison in order to sanctify it by their presence. I tried to have Bulkaen punished, to have him sent to the disciplinary cell, not in order to be near him, but because it was essential that we both be doubly outcast at the same time, for people can love each other only on the same moral level. It was thus one of the usual mechanisms of love that made me a rat.

Bulkaen was never sent to the disciplinary cell. He died—shot—without getting there.

I am going to talk once again about this twenty-year-old crasher with whom the whole prison was in love. Mettray, where he had spent his youth, elated both of us, united and merged us in the vapors of our memory of monstrously exquisite hours. In our relations with each other we had fallen back, though not deliberately, into the ways and habits of the reformatory; we used the colonists' gestures, and even their language; and around us, at Fontevrault, there was already a group of big shots who had been at Mettray, whether friends of ours or not, but fellows we had known well, who were united by the same likes and dislikes. Everything was a game to him, even the most serious matters. He once whispered to me on the stairs:

"We used to plan escapes. For the slightest reason, with another little guy, Régis . . . We'd feel like eating apples, and off we'd go! Or it was the grape season, so we'd go for grapes. Sometimes it was to screw, sometimes for no reason at all. And sometimes we'd plan real ones, escapes, escapes for good. We'd manage so they didn't work out. All in all, we had a great time."

The prison regulations state that any convict who commits an offense or a crime must serve his penalty in the institution where he committed it. When I arrived at Fontevrault, Harcamone had been in irons for ten days. He was dying, and that death was more beautiful than his life. The death throes of certain monuments are even more meaningful than their period of glory. They blaze before going out. He was in irons. I remind you that repressive measures are practiced within the prisons: the simplest is loss of canteen privileges, then dry bread, solitary confinement, and, in the state prisons, the disciplinary cell. The Cell is a kind of big shed, the floor of which has a high polish—I don't know whether it's polished by brushes and floor wax or by the canvas slippers of generations of punished men who walk in a circle and are so spread as to occupy the entire perimeter of the hall without anyone's being first or last, and who walk circles the way punished colonists at Mettray walked round and round the yard (with one difference, though a disturbing one: the drill had got complicated. Here, we walk at a more rapid pace than at Mettray, and we have to keep within boundary lines that go around the hall, making our circuitous march resemble a childish and difficult game), to such a degree that at Fontevrault it seemed to me I had grown up without stopping in my round. The walls of the Mettray yard have fallen about me; those of the prison have sprung up, walls on which I read, here and there, words of love carved by convicts and phrases written by Bulkaen, the most singular of appeals, which I recognize by the abrupt pencil strokes, as if each word were a matter of solemn decision. Ten years have gone by and a ceiling has covered the sky of Touraine. In short, without my realizing it, the setting was transformed as I aged and circled. It also seems to me that every step taken by a convict is only the step, complicated and continued for as long as ten or fifteen years, which was taken by a Mettray colonist. What I mean is that Mettray, though now destroyed, carries on, continues in time, and it seems to me too that the roots of Fontevrault are to be found in the vegetable world of our children's hell.

At regular intervals, two yards from and parallel to the walls, is a series of masoned blocks with rounded tops, like the bitts of boats and wharves, on which the punished men sit for five minutes every hour. A husky assistant, one of the punished prisoners, supervises the drill. In a corner, behind a little wire cage, a guard reads his newspaper. At the center of the circle is the can into which the men shit, a recipient three feet high in the form of a truncated cone. It has two ears, one on each side, on which you place your feet after sitting down, and a very low backrest, like that of an Arab saddle, so that when you drop a load you have the majesty of a barbaric king on a metal throne. When you have to go, you raise your hand, without saying anything; the assistant makes a sign, and you leave the line, unbuttoning your trousers, which stay up without a belt. You sit on the top of the cone with your feet on the ears and your balls hanging. The others continue their silent round, perhaps without noticing you. They hear your shit drop into the urine, which splashes your bare behind. You piss and get off. The odor rises up. When I entered the room, what struck me most was the silence of the thirty inmates and, immediately, the solitary, imperial can, center of the moving circle.

If the assistant had been at rest while supervising the drill, I would not have recognized his face, but sitting on the throne, with his brow wrinkled by the effort, he looked as if he were worried, as if he were straining with a difficult thought, and he recaptured the mean look of his youth—gathering his features—when his eyebrows, contracted by anger or bad temper, almost came together and I recognized Divers. Perhaps if I had been less in love with Bulkaen it would have pained me, even after fifteen years, to meet, in such a posture, the person I had loved so ardently at Mettray. Though perhaps not, for nobility was so apparent in his slightest movements that it was difficult, if not impossible, for him to seem humiliated. He got up without wiping himself. The odor—his odor—rose up, vast and serene, in the middle of the room, and, after buttoning himself, he resumed the rigid immobility of command.

"One . . . two! One . . . !"

It is still the same guttural voice, a big shot's voice, that issues from a throat encumbered with oysters which he can still spit violently in the face of a jerk. It is the same cry and voice he had at Mettray. From my cell, I still hear him yelling. The pace of the marching will remain a hundred and twenty steps a minute.

I arrived in the morning from a punishment cell in order to enjoy by means of words the memory of Bulkaen, who had remained above, in order to caress him by caressing the words which are meant to recall him to himself by recalling him to me, I had begun the writing of this book on the white sheets with which I was supposed to make paper bags. My eyes were startled by the light of day and smarting from the night's dream, a dream in which someone opened a door for Harcamone. I was in the dream, behind the door, and I motioned to Harcamone to cross the threshold, but he hesitated, and his hesitation surprised me. Awakened by the guard during this episode in order to go from the hole to the big cell, I was still under the influence—which was painful, I don't know why—of the dream when, at about eight o'clock, I went to take my place in the circle.

After punishment in the disciplinary cell there is the severe one of being put in irons. This can be imposed only by the Minister of the Interior, at the warden's request. It consists of the following: The ankles are held by a ring which is attached to a very heavy chain; the ring is snapped shut by a guard. The wrists are bound by a lighter, slightly longer chain. This is the stiffest punishment of all. It precedes the death penalty and is, in fact, its forerunner, since, from the day sentence is pronounced until the day of execution, the feet of men condemned to death are in irons day and night, and their wrists and feet are chained at night and whenever they leave the cell.

Before speaking more fully about Bulkaen and Divers, who were the pretext for my book, I want to introduce Harcamone, who, when all is said and done, remains its sublime and final cause. I felt, as he did, the shock and dismal sound of the formula "preliminary hearing to confirm the mandatory sentence of life imprisonment."[4] When a man is convicted of theft for the fourth time, with mandatory penalties, that is, more than three months in prison, he is sentenced to "transportation." Now that the penal colony has been abolished, he will have to spend the rest of his life in prison. Harcamone was sentenced to "transportation." And I am going to speak of his death sentence. I shall explain later the miracle whereby I witnessed, at certain times, his entire inner, secret, and spectacular life, but here and now I offer my thanks for this to the God we serve, who rewards us by the attentions that God reserves for his saints. It is saintliness too that I am returning to seek in the unfolding of this adventure. I really must go in quest of a God who is mine, for as I looked at pictures of the penal colony my heart suddenly clouded with nostalgia for a land which I knew elsewhere than in Guiana, elsewhere than on maps and in books, and which I discovered within myself. And the picture

---

[4]Life imprisonment, *rélégation perpétuelle. Rélégation,* confinement in a place of detention, formerly included transportation of habitual offenders to a penal colony.—Translator's note.

showing the execution of a convict in Cayenne made me say: "He stole my death."
I still remember my tone of voice: it was tragic, that is, the exclamation was
directed to the friends I was with—I wanted them to believe me—but the tone was
also slightly muted because I was voicing a deep sigh, a sigh which came from afar,
which showed that my regret came from afar.

To speak of saintliness again in connection with transportation will set your
teeth on edge, for they are not used to an acid diet. Yet the life I lead requires the
giving up of earthly things that the Church, and all churches, require of their
saints. Then saintliness opens, in fact forces a door which looks out on the
marvelous. And it is also recognized by the following: that it leads to Heaven by
way of sin.

Those who are sentenced to death for life—the "transportees"—know that the
only means of escaping horror is friendship. By abandoning themselves to it, they
forget the world, *your* world. They raise friendship to so high a plane that it is
purified and remains alone, isolated from the creatures who fathered it, and
friendship—on this ideal level, in the pure state, as it must be if the lifer is not to
be carried away by despair, as one is said to be carried off (with all the consequent
horror) by galloping consumption—friendship becomes the individual and very
subtle sentiment of love which every predestined man discovers (in his own hiding
places) for his inner glory. Living in so restricted a universe, they thus had the
boldness to live in it as passionately as they lived in your world of freedom, and
as a result of being contained in a narrower frame their lives became so intense,
so hard, that anyone—journalists, wardens, inspectors—who so much as glanced
at them was blinded by their brilliance. There the most potent pimps hew out—
that's exactly the word—a dazzling celebrity, and when one feels, behind the wall
that is more fragile than the past and equally impassable, the proximity of your
world (paradise lost) after witnessing the scene which is as frighteningly fabulous
as God's wrathful threatening of the punished couple, the audacity to live (and to
live with all one's might) within that world whose only outlet is death has the
beauty of the great maledictions, for it is worthy of what was done in the course
of all the ages by the Mankind that had been expelled from Heaven. And this, in
effect, is saintliness, which is to live according to Heaven, in spite of God.

It is by Harcamone that I am taken there, that I am transported beyond the
appearances I had attained at the molting time of which I have spoken. My faith
in Harcamone, my devotion to him and my profound respect for his achievement
strengthened my bold will to penetrate the mysteries by performing the rites of
the crime myself, and it must have been my abhorrence of the infinite that
accorded me this faith and trust. If we are free—available—and without faith, our
aspirations escape from us, as light does from the sun, and, like light, can flee to
infinity, for the physical or metaphysical sky is not a ceiling. The sky of religions
is a ceiling. It ends the world. It is a ceiling and screen, since, in escaping from my
heart, the aspirations are not lost; they are revealed against the sky, and I, thinking
myself lost, find myself in them or in the images of them projected on the ceiling.
Abhorring the infinite, religions imprison us in a universe as limited as the universe

of prison—but as unlimited, for our hope in it lights up perspectives just as sudden, reveals gardens just as fresh, characters just as monstrous, desert, fountains; and our more ardent love, drawing greater richness from the heart, projects them on the thick walls; and this heart is sometimes explored so minutely that a secret chamber is breached and allows a ray to slip through, to alight on the door of a cell and to show God. Harcamone's crimes—the earlier murder of the girl and, closer to us, the murder of the jailer—will appear to be foolish acts. Certain slips of the tongue in the course of a phrase give us sudden insight into ourselves by substituting one word for another, and the unwelcome word is a means whereby poetry escapes and perfumes the phrase. These words are a danger to the practical understanding of discourse. In like manner, certain acts. Faults sometimes—they are deeds—produce poetry. Though beautiful, these deeds are nonetheless a danger. It would be difficult for me—and impolite—to present a report here on Harcamone's mental faculties. I am a poet confronted with his crimes, and there is only one thing I can say: that those crimes gave off such a fragrance of roses that he will be scented with them, as will his memory and the memory of his stay here, until our waning days.

And so, when he killed the guard, Harcamone was taken to a special cell, where he remained until the hearing in the Criminal Court, and it was not until late afternoon, after the death sentence, that he was placed, for the forty-five days of the appeal period, in the death cell. It was from that cell, where I see him as a kind of Dalai Lama, invisible, potent, and present, that he emitted throughout the prison those waves of mingled joy and sadness. He was an actor whose shoulders bore the burden of such a masterpiece that one could hear the creaking. Fibers tore. My ecstasy was shot through with a slight trembling, with a kind of wave frequency that was my alternate and simultaneous fear and admiration.

Every day he had a one-hour recreation period in a special yard. He was in chains. The yard was not very far from the punishment cell where I am writing. And what I often took for the sound of my pen against the inkwell was the very faint, indeed one might say, as of any mournful sound, the very delicate sound of the condemned man's chains. An attentive or predisposed or pious ear was required to perceive it. The sound was intermittent, for I sensed that Harcamone dared not walk too much lest he make known his presence in the yard. He would take a step in the wintry sun and then stop. He hid his hands in the sleeves of his homespun jacket.

There is no need to invent stories of which he is the hero. His own suffices, and, what is quite exceptional in prison, his truth is more becoming than any lie. For convicts lie. Prisons are full of lying mouths. Everyone relates fake adventures in which he plays the role of hero, but these stories never continue in splendor to the very end. The hero sometimes gives himself away, for he needs sincerity when he talks to himself, and we know that when the imagination is vivid it may cause the inmate to lose sight of the dangers of his real life. It masks the reality of his situation, and I don't know whether he is afraid of falling into the depths of the imagination until he himself becomes an imaginary being or whether he fears a collision with the real. But when he feels imagination overcoming him, invading him, he reviews the real risks he runs, and, to reassure himself, he states them aloud. Bulkaen used to lie, that is, of the thousand adventures he invented, which composed a light and fantastic lacework skeleton and organism for him, loose ends stuck out of his mouth and eyes. Bulkaen did not lie to advantage. He was not calculating, and, when he tried to be, he made errors in calculation.

Though my love for Divers and my adoration of Harcamone still excite me, Bulkaen, despite the levity I discovered in him, was the thing of the moment. He was he who is, I did not imagine him, I saw him. I touched him, and, thanks to him, I could live on earth, with my body, with my muscles. Shortly after seeing him with the queer, I met him on the stairs. The stairway, which goes from the floors on which the workshops and refectories are installed, to the ground floor, where the offices, prison court, medical room, and visitors' room are located, is the main meeting place. It is cut into the stone of the wall and unwinds in shadow. That was where I almost always saw Bulkaen. It was the lovers' trysting place, particularly ours, and it still vibrates with the sound of the kisses exchanged there. Bulkaen ran down the stairs two at a time. His shirt was dirty, bloodstained, open in the back as the result of a stab. At the bend, he stopped short. He turned around. Had he seen me or sensed my presence? He was shirtless; his torso was naked beneath the jacket. It was another inmate—a new one—who had passed me, had, in silent flight on his slippers, passed Bulkaen, had, in the twinkling of an eye, come between the kid and me and, in so brief a time, had once again sparked the thrill of seeing Bulkaen in the theatrical conclusion that I wished for him. He turned around and smiled.

I pretended, for two reasons, not to recognize him. Firstly, so that he did not regard my eagerness as a sign of my love—which would have put me in an awkward position in relation to him. Though the fact is, I was wasting my time, for he admitted to me later that he had read everything in my eyes the first time we met. "I could tell right away. I could see you got a kick out of being next to me." Secondly, because I had seen him until then in the company of big shots, particularly pimps who couldn't admit me to their clan since I was a newcomer, and I didn't want to look as if I were playing up to them by associating too openly with one of them whom I had no right to treat otherwise than I did them. Furthermore, I had a feeling that the crashers were at odds with the pimps. . . . It was he who came up to me and put out his hand.

"Hello, Jean!"

I still don't know how he knew my name.

"Hello," I answered casually, in a tone of indifference and in a very low voice—but I stopped:

"Well?"

His lips remained slightly parted after whispering that word. There was no telling what his question was about, and his body was hardly at rest for his whole body was questioning. "Well?" meant "How goes?" or "What else is new?" or "What's up, kid?" or all of them together. I didn't answer.

"Say, you look healthy! I don't know how the hell you manage, but you always seem rarin' to go!"

I shrugged slightly. A prisoner who did not know us stopped on our stair on his way down. Bulkaen looked him in the eyes in such a way that he dared not say a word to us; he dashed off. Bulkaen's gaze delighted me with its hardness. I could tell what my fate would be if ever such a gaze transfixed me, and what followed frightened me more, for in order to alight on me his eyes grew milder until they were only a moonbeam quivering with leaves, and his mouth smiled. The walls crumbled, time turned to dust. Bulkaen and I remained standing on a column which kept raising us higher. I don't think I even had a hard-on. The prisoners continued on their way down in silence, one by one, invisible to our solitary encounter. There was a great rustling of leaves, and Bulkaen screamed at me:

"How the hell do you manage? You probably eat your head off!"

I still didn't answer. He continued his whispering, very low, without ceasing to smile, for we realized that behind the bend of the stairway the guards were counting the prisoners on their way down to recreation. Behind the walls, the commissary, the offices. We had to speak very low. Also behind, the Warden, the countryside, the free people, the towns, the world, the seas, the stars, everything was close to us though we were far away. They were on the watch, they could take us by surprise. His smile tried to put them off the track; Bulkaen muttered quickly:

"You've always got cigarettes. . . ."

At last he was telling me what obsessed him. He showed what was on his mind. . . .

"It gets me down not having cigarettes. I'm not fit for the ash can. No butts, not a thing, not a thing. . . ."

As his smile reached these last words, it gradually faded. He had to talk quickly and quietly, we were in a hurry, almost the whole division had gone down. A guard might have come up and found us there. Under that double pressure, Bulkaen's voice and what it was saying seemed to be reeling off a drama, a crime story.

"I'll croak if it goes on. . . ."

My attitude didn't encourage him. I still kept my mouth shut. At times I couldn't understand his whispers. I cocked my ear, I listened carefully. Behind the walls I could sense the presence of our past life, of our days in prison, our sorrowful childhood. He said:

"You don't have a butt on you, do you, Jean?"

Without letting my face show any feeling, though I was annoyed, I simply put my hand into my jacket pocket and took out a fistful of butts, which I handed him. He seemed not to believe they were all for him, but his face was beaming. And I went down, still not saying a word, with a casual shrug. I was already downstairs, outside, when he finally arrived. We were locked up in the same little yard. He came straight to me and thanked me, then immediately, to justify his chiseling, informed me that he had been in prison from the age of twelve. And he specified:

"From twelve to eighteen I was in a reformatory. . . ."

I asked: "Where?"

"At Mettray."

I remained calm enough to ask:

"What family? Joan of Arc?"

He answered "that's right," and we reminisced about Mettray. He accompanied each of his important but rare remarks with a broad, open, flat movement of his left hand, which seemed to come down suddenly on the five strings of a guitar. A male gesture whereby the guitarist mutes the vibrations of the strings, but it is a calm gesture of possession, and one that produces silence. I gave way to my passionate nature. The love I had been damming up for several days broke through its reserve and flowed out in the form of great pleasure in finding a Mettray colonist in my division. The word pleasure isn't quite right. Neither is joy, nor the other synonyms, nor satisfaction, nor even felicity or delight. It was an extraordinary state since it was the fulfilment of what I had been desiring (though with a vague desire that remained obscure to me until the day of my encounter) for twenty years: to find in someone other than myself the memory of Mettray, as much perhaps in order to relive Mettray as to continue it in my adult life by loving in accordance with the ways of the past. But added to that state of happiness was the fear that a slight wind, a slight shock, might undo the result of that encounter. So often had I seen the fondest dreams turn to dust that I never dared dream of Bulkaen, of a young, hale, handsome boy with a faithful heart and stern gaze, and who would love me. A youngster who would love robbery enough to cherish thieves, contemptuous enough of women to love a hoodlum, and also honest enough to remember that Mettray was a paradise. And suddenly, at the same time as the Colony showed me that despite my talent and training as a dreamer I had never ventured the fairest of dreams (I did approach it at times!), prison life was confronting me with the living fulfilment of that dream.

Bulkaen came from the depths of Mettray, sent forth by her, born God knows how, bred in the faraway, dangerous world of tall ferns, learned in evil. He brought me the most secret perfumes of the Colony, where we found our own odors.

But when I work on the fabric of our love, I shall know that an invisible hand is at the same time undoing the stitches. In my cell, I wove; the hand of destiny destroyed. Rocky destroyed. Although at the time of those first two meetings I did not know that he had loved, I did know that he had been loved. I sensed it. It did not take me long to learn of Rocky's existence in his life. When, for the first time, I wanted to ask a guy in his shop whether Bulkaen had gone downstairs, I tried to describe him, since I didn't know his name. The guy replied:

"Oh, you mean the little crasher who pukes on dough! Rocky's girl. Or, if you prefer, Bulkaen. . . ."

Rocky's "girl." . . . The crasher who pukes on dough! The convict thus informed me of one of Bulkaen's most amazing peculiarities: whenever he discovered cash while doing a job, a kind of nausea made him vomit on the bills. The whole prison knew it, and no one ever dreamed of joking about it. It was as strange as Harcamone's limp or Botchako's epileptic fits, as Caesar's baldness, as the Viscount of Turenne's fear, and this strangeness aggravated his beauty. Hersir destroyed. As did Divers's presence. I invented the most curious designs for our love, but I sensed beneath the loom the fatal hand that unknotted the kinks. Bulkaen would never belong to me, and I could not weave firmly on the mere basis of a single meeting, even of a whole night of love. The following is the usage of the expression "It was too good to be true." I had the feeing that no sooner had life brought us together than it would separate us, to my shame and sorrow. And life was so cruel as to make Bulkaen disappear just as I was putting out my arms to his apparition. But for the time being I enjoyed tremblingly the precarious happiness that was granted me.

So I could see him whenever I liked, could go up to him, shake his hand, give him what I had. I had the most avowable of pretexts for approaching him: my fellowship with a former colonist and my fidelity to Mettray. That same evening he called out to me from his row:

"Hey, Jean!"

I imagined him smiling in the darkness. When he smiled, we all felt our knees give way.

I was lying down. I hadn't the force to spring up and rush to the door, and I yelled back:

"Yes, what do you want?"

"Nothing. How goes?"

"All right. And you?"

"All right."

A tough voice broke sharply through the silence:

"Don't worry, he's imagining your little mug and beating his meat."

Bulkaen seemed not to have heard this comment.

He said to me: "Good night, Jean." When he finished, his voice was prolonged by a kind of chant. It was a cry from another window:

"Boys, this is Roland talking! They let me have it! Hard labor for life. So long, boys! I'm pushing off tomorrow for Melun! So long!"

The silence closed again over the last word. All the beauty of the evening and of Bulkaen's cry will be contained in that child's noble farewell to his life. Though the windows are shut, the waves he whips up will transmit his peaceful sadness to the depths of our sleep. It is the commentary on Bulkaen's cry of greeting.... "So long, boys, I'm pushing off tomorrow...." The simplest—the reader knows what I mean by simple—the simplest of us is praying. It is an orison, the state that makes you forgive, since it leaves you powerless when confronted with the greatest crimes, that is, men's judgments, for that is why it was granted us that evening to hear the very voice of afflicted love. I then had to take a piss. Suddenly I was flooded with the complete memory of so full a day, and I had to hold my prick with both hands for it was too heavy. Bulkaen! Bulkaen! The name enchanted me, though I still don't know his given name. Will he love me? I remembered his mean look and his ever so gentle look, and his shifting from one to the other when he looked at me was so frightening that, in order to escape the fear, my body found nothing better to do than sink into sleep.

Harcamone was given a life sentence after his fourth theft.

I cannot tell exactly how the idea of death occurred to him. I can only invent it. But I know him so well that I am likely to be right. I myself knew the tremendous despair of a life sentence, and it was even worse that morning, for I had the feeling that I was being damned forever.

I have just read the amorous scribbles on the wall of the punishment cell. Almost all of them are addressed to women, and, for the first time, I now understand them, I understand those who carved them, for I would like to proclaim my love for Bulkaen on all the walls, and if I read them, or if someone reads them aloud, I hear the wall telling me of my love for him. The stones speak to me. And it was amidst hearts and flowers that the inscription M.A.V. suddenly brought me back to my cell at Petite Roquette, where, at the age of fifteen, I saw those mysterious initials. I had long since—from the time I learned their exact meaning—ceased to be affected by the sinister glamour of the carved letters: M.A.V., B.A.A.D.M., V.L.F. When I read them, I merely read *mort aux vaches* (death to the cops), *bonjour aux amis du malheur* (greetings to friends in need), and now, all at once, a shock, a sudden loss of memory, makes me feel uneasy at the sight of M.A.V. I now see these letters only as a strange object, an inscription on an ancient temple. I feel the same sense of mystery as in the past, and, when I become conscious of it, I have the added feeling of being replunged into unhappiness, into the grief that was the substance of my childhood, and this feeling is even more painful than what I felt in the disciplinary cell when I took my place in a marching circle that seemed eternal, for I realize that it is within myself that nothing has changed, that my misfortune does not obey external laws but that it is within me, a permanent fixture, immobile, and faithful to its function. So I feel that a new era of misfortunes is opening in the very heart of the happiness caused by my love for Bulkaen, a love which is enhanced by his death. But this feeling of sorrow, along with the discovery of the signs that accompany it, was aroused perhaps by my amorous passion, which had the external form of my passions at Mettray. This ardor was involved in the same childish and tragic complications. I was thus going to live in the unhappy mode of my childhood. I am caught in the mechanism of a cycle. It is a period of misfortune— and not misfortunes—which is opening when another is about to end, and there is nothing to prove that it will not be succeeded by a third—and so on throughout eternity.

When a man has been condemned to spend the rest of his days in jail, death is at the heart of prison life, and prison is the worst misfortune that can befall natures which are still enraptured with the taste of freedom—I have said prison and not solitude. At first, Harcamone wanted to escape. Like the rest of us, he wanted, as soon as he arrived, to make a calendar which would be valid for his entire confinement, but not knowing the date of his death, he thus did not know the date of his release. I too made a calendar, at first a ten-page notebook, with two pages for each year, in which every day would be marked. To go through it, I had to turn the pages, and that takes time. In order to get an overall view of their twenty years of detention, the hardened criminals detach all the pages and paste them on the wall. I did the same. With a single glance I can scan my penalty, can possess it. Over those twenty years they indulge in the most frightfully complicated mathematics. They multiply, divide, juggle the number of months, days, weeks, hours, minutes. They want to arrange those twenty years in every possible way, and it seems as if the twenty years were going to be extended from the numbers in purer form. Their calculations will end on the eve of their release, with the result that the twenty years will appear to have been necessary in order to know the combinations contained in twenty years, and the aim and justification of the imprisonment will be these calculations which, placed flat against the wall, look as if they were being slowly swallowed up in the darkness of the future and the past and, at the same time, seem to be shining with so unbearable a present brightness that this brightness is its own negation.

Harcamone was unable to have a calendar. His dead life followed its course to infinity. He wanted to flee. He quickly considered all possible means, including escape. In order to escape, what was required, in addition to help from the outside, which Harcamone had never been able to arrange for, because he was as dull in free life as he was dazzling in prison (allow me to say a word about this brilliance. I would like to compare hardened convicts to actors—and even to the characters they impersonate—who, in order to reach the highest pitch, require the freedom provided by the stage and by its fabulous lighting, or the situation, which is outside the physical world, of Racine's princes. This brilliance comes from the expression of their pure feelings. They have time to be tragic and the necessary "income of a thousand francs"), what was required was a show of boldness, a constant will to take cunning precautions, which the sparkle that I have mentioned made difficult, impossible. A man with a powerful personality is incapable of cunning or guile or of putting on an act.

Harcamone therefore came round to death as the only way of shortening his captivity. He first thought of it in perhaps a literary way, that is, by talking about it, by hearing other inmates say to him, "It's better to croak," and his lofty nature, which was hostile to sordidness, took over the idea and ennobled it in the only effective way, by making it familiar, by making it an absolute necessity, whereby it escaped moral control. He conversed with this idea of death in a tone of intimacy, a tone that was practical and never romantic. But as facing his death was a grave act, he did it with gravity, and when he spoke of it, he did so without grandiloquence, though one could nevertheless detect ceremonious attitudes in his voice.

As for ways of taking his own life, the revolver and poison had to be discarded. He could have thrown himself from the top of one of the upper galleries. . . . One day he went to the railing and climbed over. Squatting for a moment at the edge of the void, he moved back a little, dazzled by the horror of it. With his arms slightly behind him, he beat the air a while and, for a brief moment, he was like an eagle flying from its rock. Finally, mastering his dizziness, he turned away, sickened no doubt by the sight of his shattered limbs on the ground. He did not see Rasseneur, who reported the scene to me. Rasseneur was alone with him on the gallery, but he had stepped back, hugging the wall so as to leave Harcamone with the impression of his solitude.

Harcamone chose to commit what was for him a rather trivial act, one which, through the working of a fatal mechanism stronger than his will, would cause his death. He murdered, in an almost calm moment, the guard, a man insolent with mildness and beauty, who had bullied him least during his two years at Fontevrault. We know that Harcamone died nobly during the four months following this murder. He had to erect his destiny, as one erects a tower, had to give this destiny tremendous importance, towering importance, unique and solitary, and had to build it of all his minutes. It seems to you impossible that I dare ascribe to a petty thief the act of building his life minute by minute, witnessing its construction, which is also a progressive destruction. Only a rigorously trained mind seems to you capable of that. But Harcamone was a former colonist of Mettray who had built his life there minute by minute, one might say stone by stone, as had all the others, in order to bring to completion the fortress most insensitive to men's blows. He approached Rose-wood (I learned all about the murder immediately), who suspected nothing, least of all that anyone might kill him, and least of all cut his throat, even if the cutthroat were Harcamone. Perhaps he could not admit the possibility of a jailor's becoming a victim, that is, a hero who was already idealized since he was dead and reduced to the state of a pretext for one of those brief poems which are the crime items in newspapers. I have no way of knowing how Harcamone happened to be present when the guard passed by, but he was said to have rushed up behind and grabbed him by the shoulder, as if he had wanted to kiss him from behind. I've done the same thing to my friends more than once in order to plant a kiss on their childish necks. (In his right hand he held a paring knife which he had stolen from the shoemaking shop.) He struck a blow. Rose-wood fled. Harcamone ran after him, caught up with him, grabbed him again by the shoulder and this time cut his carotid. The blood spurted on his right hand, which he had not withdrawn in time. He was in a sweat. Though he tried hard to be calm, he must have suffered extremely at being borne all at once to the climax of his destiny and carried back to the time when he murdered the little girl, though he had the luck to perform his later murder with gestures other than those with which he had committed the earlier one, thus safeguarding himself from too great a misfortune. Since he avoided repetition, he was less aware of sinking into misfortune, for all too often people overlook the suffering of the murderer who always kills in the same way (Weidmann and his bullet in the back of the neck, etc.), since it is most painful to invent a new and difficult gesture.

He wanted to wipe his wet face, but his hand smeared it with blood. The scene was witnessed by some inmates whom I didn't know. They allowed the murder to be carried out and they overpowered Harcamone only when they were quite certain that Rose-wood was dead. Finally, Harcamone thought of doing something very difficult, more difficult than the murder: he fainted.

Hewn out of the rock, embellished by a thousand cruelties, constructed with boys who erect their lives stone by stone, the Mettray Colony nevertheless sparkles in the mists of an almost continuous autumn which bathe that existence, and autumn likewise bathes ours, in which everything has the tints of dead leaves. We ourselves, in our prison homespun, are dead leaves, and it is with a certain sadness that one moves about in our presence. We fall silent. A slight melancholy—slight not because it is infrequent but because it weighs little—hovers about us. Our weather is gray, even when the sun is shining, but the autumn within us is artificial, and terrible, because it is constant, because it is not a transition, the end of a beautiful day, but a finished state, monstrously immobilized in the mist of the walls, the homespun, the odors, the stealthy voices, the indirect looks. Mettray sparkled through the same sadness. I cannot find the words that would present it to you lifted from the ground, borne by clouds, like the fortified cities in old paintings, suspended between heaven and earth and beginning an eternal assumption. Mettray swarmed with children, children with charming faces and bodies and souls. I lived in that cruel little world: at the top of a slope, a pair of colonists, outlined against the sky; a thigh swelling out a pair of canvas trousers; the toughs and their open flies from which there escaped, in whiffs that turned your stomach, the scent of tea roses and wisteria fading into evening; a simple child kneeling on the ground as if he were about to take aim, in order to watch a girl go by between the trees; another youngster who means to talk about his beret but thinks of his cap and says "my fez, my hood, my toupee"; Harcamone as a child, swathed in princely poverty; the bugle opening in his sleep the gates of dawn; the playless yards (even in winter, the snow isn't used for fights); but also the dark machinations, the walls of the mess hall painted with tar up to the level of a child's head (what infernal mind, what gentle-mannered director, conceived the idea of painting them, and of delicately painting in black the inner walls of the cells in the quarter? And who was it who thought of painting half-white and half-black the walls of the cells of Petite Roquette, where almost all of us had been before coming to Mettray?); in the quarter, a mournful Corsican song reverberating from cell to cell; a pair of torn trousers revealing a knee of piercing beauty ... and lastly, among the flowers in the Big Square, the vestiges of the schooner where the sadness of being here, locked up, makes me seek refuge at night. In the past, it was rigged and masted, with sails and wind, amidst the roses, and colonists (all of whom joined the navy when they left Mettray) used to learn there, under the orders of an ex-sailor, how to handle a boat. For a few hours a day, they were transformed into cabin boys. And throughout the Colony one still hears the words topman, watch, first mate, frigate (this word designates a chicken, a queer); for a long time, the language and habits retained the imprint of this practice, and anyone on a quick visit to the Colony might have thought it had been born, like Amphitrite, of the sea. This language in itself, and what remained of the customs, created a fantastic origin for us, since it was a very old language and not the one which had been invented by generations of colonists. The children had an extraordinary power of creating words as well. Not extravagant words, but in order to designate things, words which children repeat to each other, thus inventing an entire language. The colonists' words, invented for a practical purpose, had an exact meaning; "a gear" was an excuse. They would say, "Not a bad gear." "To fox" meant to grumble. The others escape me. I shall mention them later, but I wish to state that these words were not argot. It was Mettray that invented and used them, for they are not to be found in the vocabularies of any of the other reformatories or of the state prisons or of the penal colony. By mingling with other words whose authentic nobility goes back to time immemorial, these relatively new ones isolated us from the world even more. We were a land that had been spared by a very ancient cataclysm, a kind of Atlantis which preserved a language that had been taught by the gods themselves, for I use the word "gods" to mean the glamorous, formless powers, such as the world of sailors, the world of prisons, the world of Adventure, by which our entire life was ordered, from which our life drew even its sustenance, its life. Even the word "guy," which is a naval term, upsets me. Thinking about the idea would relieve me, but merely touching upon it makes me feel uneasy at the thought that Guy comes from so far away. My chest. . . .

Indeed it seems that when tragedians, while performing, reach the heights of tragedy, their chests swell because of the rapidity of their breathing. The rhythm of their life is quickened. Their speech seems to be rushing headlong even when it slows up, even when they wail softly, and the spectator, who is a victim of this art, feels similar movements within himself, and, when he does not feel them spontaneously, he thinks he will enjoy the tragedy more if he provokes them. He parts his lips, he breathes rapidly, he gets excited . . . and so, when I think, by way of Guy, of Bulkaen's gentler moments, of his actual death, of his deaths as imagined in the secrecy of my nights, of his states of despair, of his falls, hence of his culminant beauty—since I have said it was elicited by the wretched disorder of his face—though I lie motionless in bed, my chest swells, I breathe more quickly, my lips are parted, my bust feels as if it were straining toward the tragedy which the boy experienced, the rhythm of my circulation quickens, I live faster. I mean that all this seems to me to *be*, but I actually think that I haven't moved and that it is rather the representation of myself, one of my images which *I see*, confronted with the image of Bulkaen in his loftiest attitude.

Thus, Bulkaen had taken increasing possession of me. He had surged into me, for I had let slip the avowal of a love which he had long been aware of, perhaps as much from the song in my eyes as from my gifts to him. He seemed so independent of the world around us that he appeared to me unaware not only of the strangeness of Harcamone's situation but of his presence here, his existence in our midst. He seemed to be unaffected by this influence, and perhaps no one but me—and, for other reasons, Divers—was affected by it. Botchako, whom I sometimes saw when I passed the overheated tailor shop, where he worked stripped to the waist like a Chinese executioner, was much more glamorous. The reason is that blood purifies, that it raises the one who sheds it to unwonted heights. By virtue of his murders Harcamone had attained a kind of purity. The authority of the big shots is lewd. They are men who can still get a hard-on, whose muscles are of flesh. The member and the flesh of murderers are of light. I mentioned him to Bulkaen:

"You've never seen Harcamone?"

"No."—He looked indifferent, and he added, without seeming to attach any importance to the question:

"Have you?"

The light flared. He suddenly seemed its purest essence.

At four in the afternoon, when darkness set in, the lights went on and the prison seemed engaged in an activity whose purposes were extraterrestrial. The flick of a switch sufficed: before, the semidarkness in which human beings were things, in which things were dumb and blind; after, the light in which things and people were their own intelligence anticipating the question and resolving it before it was raised.

The look of the stairway changed. It was a well rather than a stairway. There were exactly fourteen steps from floor to floor (there were three stories). The white stone stairs were worn away in the middle, and so the guards, whose hobnailed shoes tended to slip, had to go down very slowly, grazing the wall, which, to be more exact, was a partition. It was painted ocher and adorned with scribbles, hearts, phalli, arrows, etc., which were quickly engraved by a feckless rather than ardent fingernail and quickly effaced by a trusty at the order of a turnkey. At elbow and shoulder level, the ocher was rubbed off. At the bottom, it flaked off. In the middle of each landing was an electric bulb.

In the light, I replied:

"Me? Yes. We were pals at Mettray."

That was false, and the light made my voice ring false. We had never been friends at Mettray. Harcamone, who already possessed the kind of glory he was to develop to its apotheosis, maintained a silence that seemed disdainful. The truth, I believe, is that he could neither think nor talk, but who cares about the reasons for an attitude that composes a poem? Bulkaen hitched up his pants with one hand and put the other on his hip:

"No kidding? Is he from Mettray too?"

"That's right."

Then he left without showing further curiosity. And I suffered the shame of feeling for the first time that I was turning away from my chosen divinity. It was the following day that Bulkaen sent me his first note. Almost all his letters began as follows: "Young tramp." If he had surmised that I was sensitive to the charm of the expression, he had surmised rightly, but in order to have realized it, he would have had to detect on my face or in my gestures certain signs or mannerisms that showed my contentment. But he hadn't, since he was never present when I read his letters and I would never have been foolish enough to tell him. The first time I had occasion to talk to him, I remembered that he was in for a jewel robbery and, not knowing his name yet, I called out: "Hey. . . . Hey . . . Jewel! Hey, Jewel!" He turned around, his face lit up. "Excuse me," I said, "I don't know your name. . . ." But he said very fast and in a low voice: "You're right, call me Jewel, that's all right." And then, almost immediately, so that I wouldn't suspect the pleasure it gave him to be called Jewel, he added: "Like that we'll be able to talk and the guards won't know who it is."

I learned that his name was Bulkaen a little later when I heard a guard rebuke him for walking too slowly, and it was on the back of a photo that I saw his given name "Robert." Anyone but me would have been surprised that at first he told people to call him "Pierrot" and later "Jewel." I was neither surprised nor annoyed. Hoodlums like to change names or distort their real ones until they are unrecognizable. Louis has now become Loulou, but ten years ago it was transformed to P'tit Louis (Li'l Louis), which in turn became "Tioui."

I have already spoken of the virtue of the name. A Maori custom requires that two tribal chiefs who esteem and honor each other exchange names. It was perhaps a similar phenomenon that made Bulkaen swop Robert for Pierrot[5]—but who was Pierre? Was it Hersir, about whom he spoke to me in spite of himself? Or, since it is customary for hoodlums to be called only by a familiar form of their name, had he chosen Pierrot because there was no suitable nickname for Robert? But again, why precisely Pierrot?

His naïve joy was hale and hearty, because of his youth, but even though I felt it when he called me "young tramp," I had to refrain from displaying the same joy. Therefore, he himself must have felt the slight thrill produced by these words when they are uttered affectionately: "young tramp," comparable, for me, to the caress of a broad hand on the back of a boy's neck.

We were still at the bend of the stairway, in the shadow.

I shall never sing sufficiently the pleated stairway, and its shadow. The fellows used to meet there. The toughs—those whom the judges call hardened offenders—the "black-ties" (because all or almost all of them have appeared in Criminal Court and wore, for the hearing, the little black bow tie sold at the canteen, for the assizes are a more formal ceremony than the hearings in police court) find shelter there for a few seconds from the guards who hound them (and from the jerks who might squeal on them—though informing is more to be feared from a tough than from a jerk), and they concoct escapes. As for their past life and the setbacks that have marked it, they choose to talk about such things in bed, from cell to cell, from chicken coop to chicken coop (the dormitory is a huge room with two facing rows of narrow cells—each of which has only one bed—separated by a brick partition but covered with a wire netting and closed by a grating. They are called the chicken coops). The first evening, after the rounds had been made, I heard a strange invocation; it was phrased by an amazingly elegant voice: "Oh my solid, oh my fierce, oh my burning one! Oh my Bees, watch over us!"

---

[5]Pierrot is the familiar form of Pierre.—Translator's note.

A chorus of grave and fervent voices, which were moved to the depths of the soul that dwells in the voice, responded:

"Amen."

The lone voice that had sung out was that of Botchako the bandit. His invocation had been addressed to his jimmy, to the pry and wedges, and all the crashers in the dormitory had responded. No doubt the invocation was a parody, which it aimed to be, for amidst the cluster of voices a few other yeggs heightened the buffoonery (one of them even said: "bring your dough," and another added: "bring your fanny"), but in spite of itself the buffoonery remained *profoundly* grave. And my whole being, both body and soul, turned to my jimmy, which lay motionless though vibrant in my room in Paris. It still seems to me that those vibrations made that corner of my room a bit hazy, blurred, as if they had spread a kind of golden mist which was the halo of the jimmy—officers' scepters and batons are pictured that way in conventional imagery. It vibrates like my indignant and wrathful prick.

Bulkaen asked me whether I had received his note.

"No, I didn't get anything."

He seemed annoyed, for he had given it to a trusty who was to have passed it on to me. I asked him what it said.

"Do you need something?"

"No no," he said.

"No? Then what was it about?"

"Oh, nothing."—He looked embarrassed. I understood his embarrassment, which was perhaps feigned so that I would insist or question him further, or so that I would guess without asking questions. But I insisted. We both felt a deep shyness in the other's presence, a shyness hidden behind rough gestures, but it was the very essence of the moment since it was what remains in my memory when my gestures have been scraped away. I insisted:

"Then why'd you write if you don't need anything? I don't get it."

"I sort of wrote about my friendship for you . . ."—I had a feeling that my love had been discovered. I saw I was in danger. Bulkaen was kidding me. I was being made a fool of. This attitude, which, along with meanness, is the core of my nature, permits me to say a word about that meanness. When I was poor, I was mean because I was envious of the wealth of others, and that unkindly feeling destroyed me, consumed me. I wanted to become rich in order to be kind, so as to feel the gentleness, the restfulness that kindness accords (rich and kind, not in order to give, but so that my nature, being kind, would be pacified). I stole in order to be kind.

I made a final effort to lock myself in behind a door that might have revealed my heart's secret and enabled Bulkaen to enter me as he would a conquered country, mounted, in boots and spurs, holding a whip, with an insult on his lips, for a youngster is never gentle with a man who worships him. I therefore replied roughly:

"Your friendship? Who the hell wants your friendship!"

He was suddenly abashed, and his gaze lost its hard fixity, its razorlike sharpness. He said, painfully, word by word, he wavered: "Thank you, Jean, you're nice. . . ." I was immediately ashamed of what I took for my toughness but what was simply meanness, revenge on a kid who had just "got the better of me." As a result of entering the prison at night, when the lights were on, I shall retain, throughout the present narrative, a kind of inwardness and the surprise of living a monstrous Christmas eve—during the day too. Bulkaen would be the Redeemer, the gracious and living, even familiar Redeemer. I was anxious lest everything stop and collapse. I wanted to atone for my dull-witted remark, and I said, laying a hand on his shoulder (that was my first friendly gesture, I touched Bulkaen for the first time):

"Pierrot my boy, you're imagining things. If I'm nice to you, it's because we were both at Mettray. I've got to be nice because of Mettray. You can have all the pals you like, you can be friends with them . . ."—but what I was about to utter was too painful to me—since it would also be painful to write it—it touched too much on my love, endangered it by allowing Bulkaen to be unaware of it and to love whomever he liked—and suddenly I felt within me one of the far too many lacerations that lay my soul bare. I said:

"If I've got a crush on you, forget about it."

He took both my hands and said:

"No, Jean, I won't forget about it. It's important to me."

"It's not."—I was trembling. The mass might end, the organs might stop playing. But a choir of young voices went on with its canticles. He said:

"It is, Jean. You'll get to know me."

These words filled me with hope. We were pals, and I even asked him to send me another note. I was capitulating. It was then that we began to exchange the love letters in which we spoke of ourselves, of plans for robberies, of prodigious jobs and, above all, of Mettray. He signed his first letter "Illegible," as a matter of caution, and I began my reply with "Dear Illegible." Pierre Bulkaen will remain for me the indecipherable. It was always on the stairs, where he waited for me, that we handed each other the slips of paper. Though we were not the only couple who carried on that way, we were probably the most painfully agitated. Fontevrault was thus full of those furtive exchanges which swelled the prison as if with repressed sighs. At Fontevrault, the amorous nuns and sisters of God came to life again in the form of pimps and crashers. There are things one could say about destinies, but note the strangeness of that of monastries and abbeys (which prisoners call the bee[6]): jails and preferably state prisons! Fontevrault, Clairvaux, Poissy! . . . It was God's will that these places shelter communities of only one sex. After the monks (they too in homespun) had chiseled the stone, the convicts modeled the air with their contortions, gestures, calls, their cries and modulations, their sea-cow vociferation, the silent movements of their mouths; they torture the air and sculpt the pain. The monasteries all belonged to a Lord—or Sire—who possessed true

---

[6] *Abbaye* (abbey) and *abeille* (bee) are pronounced almost alike.—Translator's note.

wealth, namely men and their souls, and the men gave him the best of themselves. They carved wood, painted leaded glass windows and cut stone. Never would a lord have dared collect rood lofts or stalls or any polychrome wooden statue in a room of his castle. Today, Fontevrault is ravaged of its jewels of stone and wood. People without nobility, incapable of winning souls, have bought them for their apartments. But another and more splendid debauch fills the prison. It is the dance in the darkness of two thousand convicts who shout, sing, sizzle, suffer, die, froth, spit, dream, and love each other. And amongst them Divers. I had read his name on the list of men who were in the disciplinary cell. And so here he was again, he who for so long (his absence itself was indiscreet) obsessed the little Mettray colonist. I recognized him on the can, as I have said, and I spontaneously associated his presence with Harcamone's death sentence. However, I never said a word to Divers about the murderer. Not a single one, for by the time I could speak to him freely I had already been informed that there was a painful relationship between them. No one knew the details, but the whole prison felt uneasy about it. And this silence was observed everywhere. It was so absolute that it was disturbing, for a particularly important event was taking place in the prison, an event of which everyone spoke and thought about but of which Divers and I said nothing, though it was perhaps the thing that drew us closer together. This silence was comparable to that of well-bred people when they suddenly smell the odor of a silent fart in a drawing room.

When Divers returned to Mettray, he was introduced to me with great pomp, in the presence of the crowd, with all the display befitting the occasion, with the ceremonial that fate cannot resist when it wants to deal one of its great blows. When I was taken to the Mettray Reformatory, I was fifteen years and seventeen days old and I had come from Petite Roquette. At present, the kids who are at Fontevrault come from Lily Street (which is what we call the corridors of the ninth and twelfth divisions of Santé Prison, where the cells of the minors are located). In the mess hall, a few moments after my arrival—I was in a state of nervous tension that evening (or perhaps I did it to prove I was very daring)—I threw a plate of soup in the face of the head of the family (I shall say a few words about the division of the Colony into "families"). I was no doubt admired for this gesture by the big shots who were stronger than I, but I was already distinguishing myself by a merely moral courage, knowing full well that I would not be beaten for such a gesture but would be punished according to law, whereas I was so afraid of being hit that I would not have dared to fight with another colonist. Besides, the bewilderment of being a newcomer in a world of boys who you feel are hostile is paralyzing. Bulkaen himself admitted this to me. He was given a thrashing the day of his arrival, and it was not until a month later that he dared fight back. He said to me:

"I suddenly realized I could fight. You can imagine what a lift it gave me. I was gay as a lark. I was alive again! All I had to do was get started in order to know I had the stuff."

It was the impossibility of killing my opponent, or at least of mutilating him hatefully enough, that kept me from fighting in the beginning; to fight in order to hurt him seemed to me ridiculous. I would not have minded humiliating him, but if I had lorded it over him, he would have felt no shame, for the victor was haloed with little glory. Only the act of fighting was noble. It was not a matter of knowing how to die but rather how to fight, which is finer. Nowadays, the soldier knows only how to die, and the bumptious individual retains the manly bearing of the fighter, all the hodgepodge of his trappings. I had to impress Bulkaen by something other than this moral courage, which he would not have understood. I sensed as much from the tone of his letters. The first of them was surprisingly amiable. He wrote about Mettray, about Old Guépin, and I learned that he had almost always worked in the fields. Here is the second, which I managed to preserve:

> Dear Jean,
> "Thanks for your note. I enjoyed it. But excuse me for not being able to write letters like yours. I'm not educated enough for that, because that wasn't the kind of thing I could learn at Mettray with Old Guépin. You know what I mean since you were there too, so excuse me, but believe me when I say I really like you, and if it's possible I'd like to go off with a fellow like you, someone who likes to go bumming and who's got big ideas real big ones. . . .
> "I want you to believe me when I say I probably see things the same way you do. Age has nothing to do with it, but I don't like kids. I'm twenty-two, but I've seen enough since the age of twelve to know what life's about. . . . I've sold all I had in order to eat and smoke because at my age it's hard to live on what they feed you here. . . .
> "Don't ever think I'll laugh at you, I'm not like that, I'm frank and when I've got something to say I don't care who hears it, and besides I've suffered too much myself to joke about your friendship which I'm sure is sincere.

A few words which he wanted to emphasize were put into brackets or set off by quotation marks. My first impulse was to point out to him that it was ridiculous to put slang words and expressions between quotation marks, for that prevents them from entering the language. But I decided not to. When I received his letters, his parentheses made me shudder. At first, it was a shudder of slight shame, disagreeable. Later (and now, when I reread them) the shudder was the same, but I know, by some indefinable, imperceptible change, that it is a shudder of love—it is both poignant and delightful, perhaps because of the memory of the word shame that accompanied it in the beginning. Those parentheses and quotation marks are the flaw on the hip, the beauty mark on the thigh whereby my friend showed that he was himself, irreplaceable, and that he was wounded.

Another flaw was the word "kiss" with which the note ended. It was scrawled rather than written. The letters were muddled and made it almost indecipherable. I could see the horse that rears when a shadow falls.

He also said a few words about his robberies, his work outside, and how he loved it, and he displayed great artfulness in letting me know he was hungry. We are all hungry because of the war, about which we receive news which is so remote that

it seems like ancient history; the rations have been cut in half, and everyone
engages in an amazingly ruthless traffic. The war? The open countryside—the
open countryside beneath a pink September evening. People are whispering, bats
are flitting by. Far away, *at the borders,* soldiers grouse and see the dream flit by. But
I was gleaming, and gleaming visibly. Being used to prisons, I knew how to get a
double food ration; I bought bread and cigarettes from a few turnkeys, whom I paid
in stamps. Bulkaen, without knowing how I did it, saw on my body the reflection
of my wealth. Without asking me, he hoped for some bread. When he begged me
for cigarette butts on the stairs, he had already opened his homespun jacket,
revealing his naked torso, and, running his hands over his sides, had shown me how
thin he was, but I was so struck at the time by the fact that the tattoo, which I had
taken for an eagle tooled in the round, was the head of a whore whose hair spread
right and left like two wings, that I wasn't aware of my annoyance. I was therefore
disappointed again when I realized the ill-concealed meaning of his letter. I made
a great effort to overcome my annoyance, of which I was conscious this time, by
telling myself that hunger was general, that the toughest, sternest pimps were
tortured by it, and that I had the privilege of witnessing one of the prison's most
painful experiences, since the usual tone was raised to a pitch of tragic paroxysm
by a physical suffering which added a grotesque element. I told myself too that
friendship need not be absent from a relationship in which self-interest also had
its place, and, instead of being brutal with him, I realized that Pierrot was young
and that his very youth, and it alone in him, demanded bread. The next morning
I gave him a roll, along with a friendly note. I wanted to hand it to him with a smile.
I felt it would have been delicate not to speak, to make my offering lightly. I tried
hard to be gracefully casual, but I was weighed down by all that love and I
remained solemn. Love made me ascribe infinite importance to every gesture,
even those to which I would rather not have done so. I pulled a long face in spite
of myself and made a solemn gesture.

A little later he wanted my beret.

"I'm hot for that beret of yours," he said. And I exchanged it for his. The next
day, it was my trousers.

"I'm itchy for your pants," he said, with a leer which I couldn't resist. And on
the stairs we quickly took off our trousers and exchanged them. The men going
by showed no surprise at seeing us bare-legged in the shadow. In seeming thus to
scorn adornments, in casting off my own, I was moving toward the state of
tramphood which lies almost wholly in appearances. I had just committed a new
blunder. The exchange of notes became a habit. I slipped him one every day as
he passed me his. He wrote admiringly about brawls and brawlers. And that was
after the eagle's metamorphosis into a woman made me fear he was more virile
than was apparent from his face. I had to avoid acts of moral courage that might
have made me lose sight of physical courage. I return to Divers.

At Mettray, after the soup incident, I was given two weeks on dry bread (four
days on a starvation diet and one day with a bowl of soup and a piece of bread),
but the gravest comment was that of the heads of families and other colonists who

told me, after my throwing the bowl, that I resembled Divers. Physically, it seems. The Colony was still full of that gala event, his stay among us. And when I wanted to know who Divers was, everyone agreed that he was a tough customer, a thug, an eighteen-year-old big shot, and immediately, without knowing any more about him, I cherished him. The fact that his name was Divers endowed him with an earthly and nocturnal dream quality sufficient to enchant me. For one isn't called Georges Divers, or Jules or Joseph Divers, and that nominal singleness set him on a throne as if glory had recognized him when he was still in the children's hell. The name was almost a nickname, royal, brief, haughty, a convention. And so he galloped in and took possession of the world, that is, of me. And he dwelt within me. Henceforth, I enjoyed him as if I were pregnant with him. Carletti told me, one day when we were alone in a cell, that he had once had an experience that was like a counterpart of mine. One morning, in prison (upon awakening, his conscious personality was still entangled with night), he slipped into the blue trousers, which were too big for him, of a hefty sailor who was in his cell and whose clothes (which are left outside the door for the night) had been mixed up with his by a turnkey whose blunder had been planned by the gods.

"I was his kid," he said.

And I, having only the name Divers as a visible, prehensible asperity for grasping the invisible, shall contort it so as to make it enter mine, mingling the letters of both. Prison, particularly a state prison, is a place which makes things both heavier and lighter. Everything that pertains to it, people and things alike, has the weight of lead and the sickening lightness of cork. Everything is ponderous because everything seems to sink, with very slow movements, into an opaque element. One has "fallen," because too heavy. The horror of being cut off from the living precipitates us—the word calls for precipice (note the number of words relating to prison that evoke falling, "fall" itself, etc.). A single word that a convict utters transforms and deforms him before our very eyes. When I saw Divers again in the big cell, he was going up to a big strapping fellow to whom he said:

"Cut the strong-arm stuff." To which the yegg replied, nonchalantly:

"My arms are 6/35's." That was enough to transform the bruiser then and there into a dispenser of justice and to make Divers a promised victim. When he was mentioned to me, upon my arrival at Mettray, he was in prison at Orléans. He had once escaped, but the police caught him in Beaugency. It was rare for a colonist to be able to go farther in the direction of Paris. Then suddenly one day he returned to the Colony, and after a rather brief stay in the quarter, he was let out and was assigned to Family B, mine. That evening I could smell on his breath the pungent odor of the butts he had picked up among the laurels, an odor as heartbreaking as it was the first time I ever smelled it. I was ten years old. Walking on the sidewalk, with my head upturned, I bumped into a passerby, a young man. He was coming toward me, holding between his fingers, chest-high, hence on a level with my mouth, a lighted cigarette, and my mouth stuck to it when I stumbled against his legs. That man was the heart of a star. The creases formed by the trousers when one is seated converged at his fly and remained sharp, like the rays of a shadowy sun. When I raised my eyes, I saw the young hoodlum's brutal, irritated look. I had extinguished his cigarette between my teeth. I cannot tell which pain supplanted the other, the burn on my lips or in my heart. It was not until five or ten minutes later that I began to notice the smell of the cigarette and that, on licking my lips, my tongue encountered a few grains of ash and tobacco. I recognized that smell on the warm breath that Divers blew at me. I knew how hard it was even for members of "families" to get tobacco, let alone the colonists who were being punished in the quarter. Rare were the big shots to whom this luxury was accorded. Of what sovereign race was Divers? I belonged to him from the very first day, but in order to celebrate our marriage I had to wait until Villeroy, my boss at the time, left for Toulon to join the navy. The ceremony took place on a clear, freezing, sparkling night. The door of the chapel was slightly opened from within. A youngster put out his shaved head, looked into the yard and inspected the moonlight, and less than a minute later the procession emerged. Description of the procession: twelve pairs of doves or colonists between the ages of fifteen and eighteen. All handsome, even the homeliest. Their skulls were shaven. They were twenty-four beardless Caesars. At the head of it ran the groom, Divers, and I, the bride. I wore on my head neither a veil nor flowers, nor a crown, but around me, in the cold air, floated all the ideal attributes of weddings. We had just been married secretly in the presence of the assembled Family B, except, of course, the jerks, or bums. The colonist who usually acted as chaplain had stolen the key of the chapel, and we had entered it around midnight to perform the mock marriage. The rites were parodied, but true prayers were murmured from the depths of the heart. And that night was the loveliest of my life. Silently, because they were barefooted in plain cloth slippers and because they were too cold and too afraid to talk, the members of the procession made their way to the stairway of Family B, an outer wooden stairway which led to the dormitory. The faster we went and the lighter grew the moment, the faster our hearts beat and the more our veins swelled with hydrogen. Overexcitement generates magic. At night, we were light-footed. During the day, we moved in a torpor due to the fact that our acts were performed reluctantly. The days were the Colony's. They belonged to that indefiniteness of dreams which produces suns, dawns, dew, breezes, a flower, things which are indifferent because they are ornaments of the other world, and through them we felt the existence of your world and its remoteness. Time was multiplied there by time.

A few creakings of the wood barely indicated to the indifferent night that something unusual was going on. In the dormitory, the couples coiled round themselves in their hammocks, warmed themselves, made and unmade love. I thus knew the great happiness of being solemnly though secretly, bound until death, until what we called death, to the handsomest colonist of Mettray Reformatory. That happiness was a kind of light vapor which raised me slightly above the floor, which softened what was hard: angles, nails, stones, the looks and fists of the colonists. It was, if a color can be ascribed to it, pale gray, and like the exhalation, scented with envy, of all the colonists who recognized I had the right to be who

I was. It was composed of the knowledge I had of my power over Divers, of his power over me. It was composed of our love. Though there was never any question of "love" at Mettray. The sentiment one felt was not named, and all that was known there was the brutal expression of physical desire.

Mention of the word love between Bulkaen and me aged us. It made me realize that we were no longer at Mettray and that we were no longer playing. But at Mettray we obviously had more gusto, for the fact of not naming our feelings, out of shyness and ignorance, made it possible for us to be dominated by them. We submitted to them entirely. But when we knew their names, it was easy for us to speak of feelings that we could think we were experiencing when we had named them. It was Bulkaen who first uttered the word love. I had never talked to him about anything but friendship (it should be noted that when I let slip my confession on the stairs I did so in a form that hardly committed me):

"If I've got a crush . . . ," for I was not yet sure of the attitude he would adopt. I remained on guard because of the tattoo. Moreover, if he accepted me as his friend, whom was he dropping? Or who had dropped him? What was Rocky's place in the hierarchy of the toughs, Rocky, whom he had known at Clairvaux and for whom he fought? And, above all, who was Hersir and how had he loved him? It was not until later that he informed me that Hersir had been, some time before himself, Rocky's boy.

"Did you love him?"

"No. It was he who loved me."

"Rocky who loved the other one?"

"That's right."

"Then what the hell does it matter? Why are you always talking to me about that Hersir of yours?"

He gestured with his elbow, then with his shoulder. He said, with his usual scowl:

"Oh, it's nothing, it's nothing."

The first time I tried to kiss him, the expression on his face, which was very close to mine, became so hostile that I realized there was a wall between us which would never be broken down. My forehead knocked against his withdrawal and he himself collided, as I could see, with his aversion for me, which was perhaps his physical aversion for men. It's true that I imagine him, in all likelihood, with a girl at his arm, and I'm sure that, at first, he was a chicken only because of his good looks (and later, in addition, because of his enthusiasm for strength, his loyalty to friendship, his goodheartedness). So he drew back a bit. He still looked hostile. I said:

"Let me kiss you."

"No Jean, not here. . . . I assure you, outside, you'll see."—He was explaining his refusal by the fear of being seen by a guard (we were still on the stairs), but he knew very well that there was little chance of that. He started to leave and, perhaps to console me for staying so short a time, he said:

"Jean, you'll see, I'll have a surprise for you in a week." He said this with his usual graciousness, the graciousness that emanated from each of his gestures, from his scowls, from his words, even when he wasn't thinking of you. Another remarkable thing was that his graciousness seemed to spring from his toughness, or rather to have the same origin. It was sparkling.

I acted as if I weren't too disappointed and I didn't want to be so cruel as to tell him what he was at Fontevrault, what role he played among the big shots, or what he had been at Clairvaux, as I happened to learn from another convict (from Rasseneur himself):

"He was taken for what he was, but you can't say he wasn't respected."

I forced a smile, as if Bulkaen's refusal were unimportant, and shrugged slightly at the surprise he promised me, but though my smile meant to be simple and casual, it could not remain so for long. I was too upset and hurt. I could feel tragedy welling up within me, for I felt I was rushing to my doom, and when I said:

"You little rat, you're stringing me along . . . ," I was already half-way up the altitude to which resentment was carrying me. Perhaps my words were sharp, my tone of voice—which I wanted to be bantering—shaken with emotion, quivering. He mistook the meaning of my words—unless, because of that shaken voice, he really discerned the true meaning which I wanted to conceal from myself—he said:

"You can stop giving me bread and cigarettes if you think I'm your pal just in order to get something out of you. I won't take anything more."

"Come off it, Pierrot. You can always pull the friendship line on me. You'll have your bread."

"No no, I don't want it, keep it."

I snickered:

"You know very well that won't stop me. You can play me for a sucker as much as you like, I'll always give you what you need. And it's not because I've got a crush, it's because I've got to. It's out of loyalty to Mettray."

I was about to resume the slightly literary tone that would alienate me from him, that would cut the too immediate contact, for he would be unable to follow me. But, on the contrary, what I actually did was to quarrel with him in a sordid way, to reproach him for what I gave him. I didn't want to be strung along. My haughtiness, my magnanimity—which were feigned—were exasperating him. I added:

"Your good looks, which I can't help seeing, are payment enough."

I have since realized that this remark clearly expressed the passion I was trying to conceal. At the expression "good looks" he made a gesture of annoyance, a rough gesture, which showed how he felt about me, a gesture which told me to go to hell. He said:

"So what . . . so what . . . my good looks, my good looks, what about it? That's all you talk about!"—His voice was hostile, lewd, and hollow, as always, and muted out of cautiousness. I was about to reply; a guard was coming up the stairs. We parted hastily, without a word, without looking at each other. The situation seemed to me more ominous because it had been cut short. I felt my abandonment, my loneliness, when the dialogue between us no longer maintained me ten feet above the ground. If he had been simply a queer, I would have immediately known what act to put on: I would have "played it tough," but Pierrot was a smart crasher, a kid who was perhaps sore at heart—and cowardly, as males are. Had I been brutal, he would have perhaps responded likewise, whereas he could still be caught in the trap of unexpected gentleness. His meanness, his trickiness, his violent reversals, his straightforwardness, those were his sharp angles. They were his brilliance. They fascinated. They hooked my love. As Bulkaen could not be without his meanness, could not be that demon without it, I had to bless it.

I remained upset for a long time, less because of his apparent indifference to what I gave him and still less because of the rejected kiss, which was proof of his lukewarm attitude toward me, than because of my discovering a hard, granitelike element which was often visible to me and which made his face a landscape of white rocks beneath a sky devoured by an African sun. Sharp edges can kill. Bulkaen, without realizing it (or realizing it), was heading for death and was leading me to it too. And in abandoning myself to his order, I moved a little further away from Harcamone's. The feeling—in the course of a conversation with Pierrot—of having begun to undergo rather than to decide—continued in what might be called a normal way. I belonged, it seems, to Pierrot.

Tonight, as I sit and write, the air is sparkling. The most sorrowful female head, with the softest blonde hair I have ever seen, the saddest woman in the world, is nodding slightly. The Prison is in her brain, under the brainpan, like an abscess. It causes what she calls her "vapors." Let the Prison emerge from her forehead, or ear, or mouth, and the woman will be cured, and the prison itself will breathe a purer air. We see the frost on the windows, and that splendor is a mockery since it is all we are allowed to admire, without being able to indulge in the cosy joys that usually accompany it. We have no Christmas, no chandeliers in our living rooms, no tea, no bearskins. Thinking so much about Bulkaen has worn me to a frazzle. When I lie down, I feel tired all over, especially in the arms, near the shoulders, and the following expression flits across my mind: "my arms are weary of hugging you and of not being able to hug you." In short, I am so obsessed by desire that all words and each of their syllables evoke love. "To push back the aggressor" suggests "to push back shit," aggravated by an idea of grease'.... I suffer at never having possessed Bulkaen. And death now prevents all hope. He refused on the stairs, but I invent him more docile. His eyes, his eyelids are trembling. His whole face is giving way. Does he consent? But what prohibition weighs upon him? While a stern will thrusts aside the images which are not of him, my mind strains eagerly toward a vision of the most enticing details of his body. I am obliged to invent the amorous postures he would assume. This requires great courage, for I know that he is dead and that this evening I am violating a corpse (it is probably a "rape followed by violation without deflowering," as the Judge sometimes says

---

[7] The sound of the word *graisse* (grease) is contained in the word *agresseur* (aggressor).—Translator's note.

of a little girl who has been tumbled, but the fact remains that death terrifies and imposes its morality, and that the image of Bulkaen which I conjure up has its real double in the realm of the infernal gods). I would need all my virility—which is mainly a mental attitude rather than physical courage and appearance. But just as I am about to enter him in thought, my member softens, my body grows limp, my mind drifts. . . . I live in so closed a universe, the atmosphere of which is thick, a universe seen through my memories of prisons, through my dreams of galleys and through the presence of convicts: murderers, burglars, gangsters, that I do not communicate with the usual world or, when I do perceive it, what I see of it is distorted by the thickness of the wadding in which I move with difficulty. Each object in your world has a meaning different for me from the one it has for you. I refer everything to my system, in which things have an infernal signification, and even when I read a novel, the facts, without being distorted, lose the meaning which has been given them by the author and which they have for you, and take on another so as to enter smoothly the otherworldly universe in which I live.

The air is sparkling. My pane is frosted over, and it is indeed a joy to see the frost. From the dormitory we never see a nocturnal sky. The windows are forbidden us, since at night we occupy small cells in a big room which are laid out in two facing rows. And sometimes we commit an offense so as to be sent to the hole where at night we can see through the skylight, which is often unmasked, a patch of starry sky and, even more rarely, a piece of moon. The air is sparkling. Mettray suddenly takes the place—not of the prison in which I live—but of myself, and I embark, as formerly deep in my hammock, on the remains of the half-destroyed, unmasted ship among the flowers of the Big Square at Mettray. My longing for flight and love disguises her as a mutinous galley that has escaped from a penal colony. She is the *Offensive*. I have roamed the South Seas on her through the branches, leaves, flowers, and birds of Touraine. At my order, the galley cleared out double-quick. She sailed beneath a sky of lilacs, each cluster of which was heavier and more charged with anguish than the word "blood" at the top of a page. The crew, now composed of all the moguls from here, who were formerly big shots at Mettray, bestirred itself slowly, with pain and difficulty. Perhaps it wanted to be roused, for it was oppressed by the princely authority of the captain who kept watch at the post which is called, on galleys, the Tabernacle. The captain's past will remain mysterious to you, as it is to me. What crimes brought him to the naval colony and what faith enabled him to stir up the galley? I ascribe everything to his good looks, to his blond curls, his cruel eyes, his teeth, his bare throat, his exposed chest, to the most precious part of him. But all I have just said exists through words, whether flat or luminous. Will it be said that I'm singing? I am. I sing Mettray, our prisons and my hoodlums, to whom I secretly give the pretty name "petty tyrants." Your song has no object. You sing the void. Words may conjure up for you the pirate I want to speak of. To me he remains invisible. The face of him who commanded the galley of my childhood is forever lost to me, and in order to speak accurately to you about him I have a right to use as a model a handsome German soldier—I even desire him—who shot a bullet into the charming neck of a fifteen-year-old kid and who returned to his barracks no less clean, no less pure, heroized even more by that useless murder. He remains pale in his funereal uniform, and is so proud when he sees his bust emerge from his tank that I thought I was seeing the captain at his post. He will serve as model for my description of that figurehead whose face and body have worn away, but if I start using this subterfuge to revive my galley, am I quite sure that all of Mettray will not be described according to models quite different from the reality and chosen, as chance would have it, from among my lovers? But what does it matter! If I restore such a limbo bit by bit, it is because I carried it scattered within me. It is because the Colony is contained in my loves or else my only loves are those that can revive it.

The sailors, the pirates of the galley, had the same bearing as the captain, though without that crown of darkness. We were sailing on a fair sea and would not have been surprised to see the waters open with the thrill of carrying such a burden and swallow it up. The ship swarmed with muscular torsoes, brutal thighs, heads of hair, necks from which polished oak tendons projected as they turned; also, one could tell that behind the daring trousers were the loveliest tools in the Royal Navy, and I was reminded of them in prison by the equally heavy member of Divers, which was darker and yet more radiant than ever, so that I wonder whether its brilliance was not due to the proximity of Harcamone, who daily moved toward death. I never knew anything definite about Divers's relations with Harcamone. Though the whole prison was darkened with a kind of sadness when it associated those two names, nobody could tell the reason why. We felt there was a link between them, and we suspected it was criminal since it remained secret. The old-timers were at one in remembering that Harcamone, continuing to live in his world (of higher lineage than ours), used to humiliate the trusties. Not that he refused to obey, but by his subdued gestures—for his gesticulation was very sober—he assumed in their presence, without meaning to, insolently authoritative poses which made him dominate the turnkeys and inmates. Divers was aware of his authority (at Mettray, the head of the family once ordered a newcomer, a sickly boy, to read the family's greetings to the director on New Year's Day, and it was on this occasion that Divers uttered the famous saying: "It's not fair!"). No doubt he was thinking of the power that should have been his because of his beauty, because of its superiority to all other virtues. Being jealous, he may have wanted to appropriate Harcamone's artful gestures of command and, in order to make them more effective with his flock, to eliminate the true lord, to provoke the fight that ended in the death of the guard. You, the reader, now know that we were wrong.

I had become particularly friendly with the pilot. (Note how I speak of that galley on which, though I could have been the master, I accorded myself only the lowliest post, that of cabin boy, and sought the friendship of my mates. You'll say that I wanted to be a cabin boy so as to enjoy the love of the whole crew, but you ask why I didn't choose, by inventing some other story, of kidnapping or of boarding a boat, to be a fair captive.) Perhaps I had vowed the pilot this friendship because of the melancholy, of the loneliness too, which never left him and so made me think he was gentler, more tender, more affectionate than the other sailors. For all the buccaneers were brutes, which I wanted them to be. I continued on ship the life I had led at Mettray, but with even more cruelty, with such cruelty that I could thereby project my real life and perceive its "double," which too often was invisible. I was the only cabin boy on board. In the evening, with my calves abraded and my hands sore from coiling the stiff ropes (precisely those which we use in our shops at Fontevrault to make the camouflage nets that will be the enormous tulle which veils the phalli of the Nazi cannons when they spit), I would go and squat beside the pilot (if the captain did not allow me to stretch out on my bed). I stayed on until it was rather late. The *Subtle* plunged ahead into a fog of stars. I pointed with my toe to the Big Dipper, then, bumping my forehead into sails, stumbling over capstans and anchors, I went back to my hammock. In the Mettray dormitory my hammock was near the window. Beneath the moon and stars I could see the chapel, the Big Square, and the little cottages of the ten families. Five of them form one side of the square, the other five form the side opposite, the chapel stands on a third, and, facing it, the lane of chestnut trees runs down to the road that leads to Tours.

My head is spinning, I'm pitching with dizziness. I have just written the words "chestnut trees." The yard of the Colony was planted with them. They bloomed in the spring. The flowers covered the ground and we walked on them, we fell on them, they fell on us, on our caps, on our shoulders. Those April flowers were bridal, and chestnut blossoms have just bloomed in my eyes. And all the memories that crowd on me are obscurely chosen, in such a way that my stay at Mettray seems to have been only a long mating broken by bloody turmoils in which I saw colonists whack each other and become a mass of bleeding flesh, red or pale, and hot, with a savage fury, ancient and Greek, to which Bulkaen, more than any other, owed his beauty. Indeed, his fury was constant. And though his youth seemed to me too young, too weak and fresh, I bear in mind that the old crashers, who are strong and clever, were once young and that in order to have become what they are they had to be as tough as he when they were his age. He lived in a state of unrest. He was the arrow that keeps vibrating and will not come to a stop before the end of its course, which will be the death of someone, and his own. Though I never knew anything definite about his skill as a crasher, I can sense it from his suppleness and trickiness—though the kind of cleverness necessary on the outside is different from what works here. He was no doubt the furtive crasher who casts a rapid look about and whose gesture was of the same nature. He had a casual gait, but if he came upon a corridor or bare wall, a quick and sudden leap thrust him to the right or left and concealed him. Those brusque movements which flared up in his supple casualness destroyed it; they were streaks of lightning that clung to his elbows, to his broken bust, his knees, his heels. As for me, I'm a crasher of a different kind. None of my movements is more rapid than another. I do all things without sudden haste. My gait is slower and calmer, more reposed and staid, more certain. But, like me, Pierrot loved robbery. The crasher's joy is a physical joy. The whole body is involved. Pierrot must have hated racketeering, though he naïvely admired the great racketeers, just as he admired books and their authors, without loving them. When he was burgling, he thrilled from top to toe. "He lubricated."

He burst into a silent laugh.

"Cut it out, Jean. You slay me."

"What. . . ."

"But even all alone . . ." (his voice is a murmur, he barely speaks, I have to listen carefully, to draw closer. Night is coming on. The stairway is dark.)

". . . Jean, I did most of my jobs *solo,* because with someone else, you understand. . . ."

I understand and I note his gesture of disappointment!

"I did them *solo!*"

The child was teaching me that the true stuff of Parisian slang is gentle sorrow. I said to him, as I did every time I left him:

"Got anything to smoke?"

He did not answer my question but smiled faintly and whispered, holding out his hand:

"Come on, give with the butt! Cough up! Clear the horizon!"—Then he made an ironic military salute and ran off.

The very day after the mysterious nuptials which I have described, I left the Colony forever without having been able to spend a single night with Divers, my first encounter with whom I have not yet related. One May evening, amidst the fatigue of a holiday in honor of Saint Joan of Arc, with the oriflammes drooping beneath the weight of a ceremony that was at last over and the sky already changing color like a lady's makeup at the end of a ball, when nothing more was expected, he appeared.

The first directors of the Colony must have realized what a magnificent garden the yard became when it was decked with the national colors, because for a long time any holiday was seized as a pretext for pinning flags on the trees and walls, in the rosebushes and wisteria. Red cotton and cheesecloth inflamed the chestnut trees; the bright greens of the early branches were shot through with red, blue, and especially white, for the Colony did not forget that its founders were nobles and that its benefactors, whose names are still inscribed on the walls of the chapel, were: His Majesty the King, Her Majesty the Queen, Their Royal Highnesses the Princes of France, The Royal Court of Rouen, The Royal Court of Nancy, The Royal Court of Agen, all the royal courts of France, the Countess de La Rochejaquelein, the Count de La Fayette, the Prince de Polignac, in fact a list of five or six hundred lilied names, written out in full and accompanied by titles, as can still be seen on the most beautiful tombstone in the little cemetery, between the poor mound of Taillé (eleven years old) and that of Roche (twenty years old): "Marie Mathilde Julie Herminie de Saint Crico, Viscountess Droyen de Lhuys, Lady of the Orders of Maria Luisa of Spain, Theresa of Bavaria and Isabella of Portugal." Interspersed among the tricolored flags were white and pale blue oriflammes with gold *fleurs de lis.* They were generally arranged in clusters of three, the one in the middle being blue and white. On Joan of Arc Day, this fabric instilled a light joy into the newness of spring and the fresh greenery, it purified the air. On the trees in the Big Yard, the souls of a race of handsome young cocksmen, seemingly indifferent to an apotheosis among the branches, fierce-eyed lads with violent bodies and hostile loves, spurting abominable insults between their white teeth, were moistened with a gentle dew. But on Assumption Day, however, those same cloths became, in the sun and dust and amidst dead flowers, a kind of demented bunting. They presided with haughty weariness over some royal ceremony of which we witnessed only the preparations or, if you like, the settings, for the personages were too sublime—and their dramas too grave—to be seen by us.

It was in the middle of this kind of huge, unused altar that new colonists sometimes made their first appearance. Around five in the afternoon (for that was also when boys who had been punished and who were to be reprieved were let out), I immediately noticed a colonist nobler than the others. He had both hands in his pockets, thus raising the front of his blue smock, itself rather short, and revealing to the dumbfounded afternoon a fly lacking a button, which must have popped off under the heavy shock of a fag's stare, the kind of kid about whom one says:

"You've got eyes that make fly buttons pop!"

I noticed this and also the dirt around the opening of the fly. Then I was struck by the toughness of his expression. I remember too his . . . and I cannot, even mentally, without a frightful pain in my chest, conclude the word . . . smile. I shall burst into tears if I utter in their entirety the words which betoken a single one of his charms, for I realize that in mentioning them I would be depicting Pierrot. But he had what Pierrot doesn't have: his cheekbones, his chin, all the prominent parts of his face, were, perhaps because of the compact blood vessels, darker than the rest. He seemed to be wearing a black tulle veil, or only the shadow of that veil. This is the first article of mourning that will adorn Divers. And the face was human, but, to be accurate, I am obliged to say that it was continued in movements that made it cease to be so and that changed it into a griffon, and even into a plant. It remained in my mind like the faces of angels engraved on glass and painted on stained-glass windows, faces that end, with the hair or neck, in the form of an acanthus leaf. Anyhow, Divers had that crack, which was intended by the architect, as was the pathetic breach in the Coliseum which causes eternal lightning to flash over its mass. I later discovered the meaning of the crack, which was a second sign of mourning, and of the even more theatrical one that furrows Bulkaen, that furrows all the big shots, from Botchako to Charlot—Charlot to whom my hatred clung and still clings, whom I felt within me, certain that some day a pretext would be found for that hatred to discharge violently.

We entered the mess hall. A little yegg said to me:

"Did you see her? One of them is back!"

"Who? Who's back?"

"A doe."

You now understand the meaning of the expression "to doe."[a] A person who runs away, a person who escapes, is a doe. Quite naturally, and without anyone's daring to make a gesture or say a word, Divers sat down at the first table, that of the big shots. As the tables were set out like those of pupils in a classroom, with four colonists, on one side only, facing the desk of the head of the family, I beheld the back of that prodigy who deigned to eat and even to show delicate dislikes after coming out of the hole. Indeed, he pushed a few bits of undercooked vegetables to the edge of his iron plate, whereas all the others ate everything. When we went out into the yard for afternoon recreation, which lasts only a few minutes, he joined the group of Toughs who—an extremely rare thing—shook hands with him. It was not customary at Mettray for colonists to shake hands openly. I think that this is to be regarded as a secret agreement on their part to reject whatever recalls civilian life and might make them miss it. It should also be regarded as a certain reluctance felt by a "tough" who wants to become a "man" and is therefore averse to any show of friendship. And perhaps the colonists were somewhat ashamed to perform among themselves a gesture which was habitual among the guards but from which the guards excluded them. As soon as he drew near the group, the released colonist saw all hands reach out to him. He was breaking customs by his mere presence, though he himself was still attached to them, for he was somewhat abashed at the sight of the open hands, hardly realizing that they were held out for him. We shall have occasion to note that the colonists who come out of the "punishment quarter" at Mettray, or out of the "disciplinary cell" here, spontaneously assume the self-satisfied, arrogant attitude of a tough, just as, during the war, any French soldier assumed the pretentious air of a man who had died on the field of honor. I was watching the new colonist from the top of the stairs at the entrance of the mess hall; I was standing with my back against the door frame, but that slightly leaning posture, and that support, and that pedestal, made me look too important. I walked a few steps away, with my head bowed. I dared not ask who he was, lest I seem silly—for though I was not a big shot, nevertheless the fact of my being the elder brother's chicken gave me a kind of status as a well-protected *grande dame*, and in order to maintain my prestige in the eyes of the jerks it was important that I not seem ignorant of what all the big shots knew (toughs and big shots are the two terms that designated, as they do here, the masters, the chiefs). The bugle blew taps. To get to the dormitory, which was on the first floor, we lined up in double file at the bottom of the outside stairway, of which I have spoken, and marched up the stairs. The newcomer stepped into line beside me. As he approached, he wet his lips; I thought he was going to speak, but he said nothing. The gesture was only a tic. I was not yet aware that he resembled me, for I did not know my face. We went up the wooden stairs. I did not have the audacity, in his presence, to put my hands into my pockets (fear of seeming too much like a big shot and too much his equal). I let them hang. That was humbler. He stumbled against the iron edge of a stair and I said to him, trembling slightly,

---

[a] *Se bicher* (to clear out); *biche* (a doe).—Translator's note.

"Watch out. The elder brother'll get after you, especially since you've just got out of the hole." He turned his head to me and answered with a smile: "To do that he'd have to have a little more hair on his chest." Then he added: "Is he your big shot? Tell him to go pad his knees." I didn't answer, but I lowered my head, and I would like the cause to have been an obscure sense of shame at having a big shot other than this insolent tough. He also uttered between his teeth the words *"Maldonne"* and *"la Caille,"** expressions not used in the families, and he seemed to me to have returned from far away, from a dangerous adventure, for those words, coming from him, were like the black velvet seaweed that a diver brings up around his ankles. One feels he was involved in games or struggles that partake of amorous play and the fancy-dress ball. He was, in effect, a residue of the underworld. The quarter thus had a life even more secret than ours, a life to which the rest of the Colony seemed impervious. It appeared to me less vicious because more turbid. The hardness and limpidity of Bulkaen's expression were due perhaps to sheer stupidity, to shallowness! Intelligence has vacillations that stir the depths of the eyes, that veil them. This veil passes for mildness, which perhaps it is. Mildness, a hesitation?

A hammock next to mine was free and was assigned to the newcomer by the head of the family himself. That same evening, I gave him a stunning present. During drill in the dormitory (the rite of going to bed), all noise except the rhythmic clicking of our heels on the floor was forbidden. The elder brother in charge of the drill was at the other end of the dormitory, near the head of the family. In taking from its slot the spar from which the hammocks hung, Divers knocked it against the wall. The head of the family growled:

"You there, can't you watch what you're doing?"

"Who did that?" yelled the elder brother.

For some seconds the silence in the dormitory grew more intense. I did not look at Divers.

"He won't own up, no danger of that!"

Then I turned slightly and raised my hand.

"Well, which of the two?"

I looked at Divers in amazement. He too had raised his arm, though reluctantly, and was already lowering it.

"It's me," I said.

"You should have said so. K.P. for you tomorrow."

Divers had a quizzical smile at the corner of his mouth and the gleam of a conqueror in his eyes.

For a brief moment the same gesture had made us accomplices in a slight imposture, and now I stood there alone, stupidly, with my hands emptied of their offering. After drill, when we were in bed, we chatted for a moment. He courted me slightly while Villeroy, the elder brother of the family and my personal big

Maldonne, literally misdeal, conveys the idea of "barking up the wrong tree"; *la Caille* might be rendered as: "that creep."—Translator's note.

shot, was reporting to the head of the family, in the latter's room, on the day's events (perhaps he was playing stool pigeon). I hardly answered, for I was afraid of revealing my preoccupation: "Tell me about the quarter where Divers still is." I was waiting for the captive male to talk about himself, and first about the quarter, which was still mysterious to me. I dared not look at him, but I could imagine his little head raised above the hammock. I said in a whisper:

"Were you there long?"

"There where?" he said sternly. I got flustered.

"Where? In the quarter . . . where you were . . ."

I awaited his answer anxiously, amidst a silence that was beginning to rustle softly.

"In the quarter? For a month."

A month. I dared not tell him that I had been at the Colony more than a month and had never seen him there before. I was afraid of annoying him and of his remaining silent. There was whispering around us. Life was starting. Taps had blown. Despite myself, I said simply:

"But . . ."

"Well, I'm back. With the nippers, you know, handcuffs. They put 'em on me, the rats! But it didn't get me down. You can be sure of that. I purposely let the chain hang in front of me, like a fancy bracelet. People were squinting at me, you can imagine, since Beaugency."

If, twenty years from now, while walking along the beach I met a stroller wearing a big coat and if I spoke to him about Germany and Hitler, he would look at me without answering, and suddenly, seized with panic, I would pull up the flaps of the coat and see a swastika on his lapel. I would stammer: "So you're Hitler?" Thus did Divers appear to me, as great, as evident, as pure as divine injustice. In short, I was confronted at the same time with the disturbing mystery of Divers and of the quarter. It was little guys like him that I heard marching in the yard the day of my arrival, when I was taken to the council room to see the director. He was sitting at the table with the green cover, beneath the crucifix. I could hear the clacking of the little but heavy sabots that were moved by the little feet of colonists. The director made a sign and the guard pushed the window. The director scowled with annoyance. His jowls quivered, and the guard shut the window completely. We could still hear the sound of the little sabots. I could see the director's face growing angrier and angrier and his gray jowls moving more and more and faster and faster. I felt no desire to smile because I wasn't really sure that he hadn't sent for me to punish me already.

"You are here . . ."

His voice tried to cover the sound of the sabots.

". . . You will not be unhappy. The other boys . . . The Mettray Colony is not a penitentiary, it's a big family."

He spoke more and more loudly, and I suddenly felt myself blushing for him. I took upon myself his shame and suffering, I felt the same uneasiness as when I heard attempts to jam a radio broadcast (German at the beginning of the war,

English at the end), those desperate efforts to destroy a dangerous message, to prevent its being received, though it gets through anyway and succeeded in sending out its call.

During our stay at Mettray, Divers did not use all his ways and means of surprising me. The very afternoon when I saw him again, fifteen years later, on top of the can in the disciplinary cell, one of the guys whispered to me as I was about to return to my coop:

"Riton-la-Noïe is asking for you."—"La Noïe" means night.—I answered likewise in a whisper:

"Riton-la-Noïe? Never heard of him."

"He's the trusty. There he is, behind you."—I turned around. It was Divers. He was leaning against the wall and looking at me. His right hand was hanging at his thigh, back side out, the very position in which he used to take hold of his prick.

Hiding from the guards, we made a few invisible movements of approach. I went straight over to him, unhesitatingly, as a friend, as a pal. Despite that gesture and posture which were all too reminiscent of the big shot of the old days, my love for Bulkaen did not allow anything but friendship. No doubt, when I saw him again (Bulkaen was still alive, above my head, working in the shop, sleeping in the dormitory), there was no element of tenderness in my friendship, though a slight tenderness did seem to well up or to disappear far off in the depths of me.

Thus, Mettray blossomed curiously in the heavy shadow of Fontevrault. The Colony was ten or fifteen miles from the prison and its race of vicious bruisers. It had a dangerous glamour for us, a glamour of cabinets in which poison is stored, of powder magazines, of embassy antechambers. Bulkaen disregarded my allusions to the Colony and talked about the future. In reply to a letter in which I told him about my passion for distant journeys, for going places, he spoke of plans for fleeing, for escaping, for a free life, in which I was involved. Then he went on to talk about women and confided to me that after making love he felt like bashing their heads in with the bidet, but all these passages in the letter were silenced by the one that revealed his misery: ". . . When the job was over, my pals would go see the girls and I'd go off by myself, all alone." How could he who was so charming write such a thing? Could it really and truly be, and was it possible that no one realized how miserable the child was? In another letter he added: "You know, Jean, I wasn't a jerk. Lots of big-timers were proud to be seen with me." He was not unaware of the glamour he possessed. He had had the experience of Mettray.

We lived beneath the stern gaze of the Prison, like a village at the foot of a feudal castle inhabited by steel-clad knights, and we wanted to be worthy of them. In order to resemble them, we observed the orders that reached us secretly from the castle. Through whom? I cannot help saying that everything was in league with the children that we were: the flowers spoke, the swallows and even the guards were, willingly or not, our accomplices. Like Mettray, the Prison was guarded by a race of old jailers to whom beastliness was natural. To them we were dregs. They openly hated the inmates, but cherished them in secret. In addition, they were—

they are—the jealous guardians of loathsome ways and customs. Their comings and goings wove the limits of an inhuman domain, or rather the meshes of a trap in which abjection was caught. Some of them live for a quarter of a century, and often more, amidst hoodlums whom at the same time they contain. Every new convict was immediately not merely pushed around by brutal gestures, but, even worse, was drowned in the mockery and snarling words that ordered all the vile measures, from the shearing of the hair to the wearing of the hood, and one feels that the guards are on intimate terms with the hoodlums, not because there is intimacy between them in the usual sense of the word but because there wells up from the hoodlums the horror in which the guards are caught, in which they melt. A family air merges them, as it merges masters and old servants, who are the seamy side of the masters, their opposite and, in a way, their unwholesome exhalations. The disease with which they were inoculated was kept alive not only by the regulations, but even more by the habits of the inmates and their personalities, by the finical punctuality of the guards, who were sick with the sickness of the big shots, and also by the stagnating immobility, or, if you like, the running around in circles in that tightly closed domain.

We obeyed the men of the castle, and we were even bolder than they. Even if, by virtue of some strong predisposition, a boy had not loved the Prison, he would have been carried away, would have been carried toward it, by the wave of love that rose up to it from the Colony. At every moment a colonist would have shown him what made it lovable. Before long he would have realized that it was the perfect expression of his truth. Legend, which embellishes everything, embellished the Prison and its big shots and all that pertained to them, even, and above all, their crimes. A word was sufficient, if uttered by a Tough of the Family, in such a tone . . .

Though we were moved by tragic spirits, the tragedy was stricken with an extraordinary malady of love. Our heroism was stained with acts of baseness, acts of fascinating cowardice. It was not uncommon for the fiercest toughs to play up to the guards with the repulsive purpose of getting special consideration. Informers are often found among the toughs. They are so sure of their power that they know a betrayal will not affect them, but the other little guys cannot for a single moment slacken in their will to be "regular." The slightest lapse would be fatal to them. They cling to loyalty as do others to virility. At noon, on a heavy, broad-rumped, hairy-legged nag that was still wearing its brass and leather harness, Harcamone, riding sidesaddle with his legs dangling at the left, crossed the Big Square on his way back from cartage or work in the fields. He had had the audacity to hook at the edge of his tilted cap, near his ear and almost covering his left eye with a trembling, mauve leucoma, two huge bunches of lilac. He must have been quite sure of his integrity. In the Colony, he alone could coyly adorn himself with flowers. He was a true male. The apparent rectitude of Bulkaen was due perhaps to his profound weakness. I know that he never compromised with the adversary. He often told me how he hated squealers, but I never saw his hatred so clearly as the time he spoke to me about "fairies," about the "little queers" of Pigalle and

Blanche. We were on the stairs. Resuming in a low voice the conversation we had begun during the medical examination, he said:

"Don't go to those joints, Jean. The guys who go there aren't for you. They're the kind who sell, and they're all squealers."

He was wrong about queers being informers, but he wanted to show me how he hated stool pigeons and also that he didn't want to be confused with fags. If those words are still so clear in my memory, it is because they were followed by others that were even more disturbing. He said to me:

"We'll beat it, Jean! As soon as we get the hell out of here, we'll head for Spain."

He freely let his dreams escape. He sat down on the stairs and remained there with his head in his hand and his eyes closed.

"Jean, listen, imagine us in Cannes, on a pedal boat, in the water . . . it's sunny there . . . We'll be happy."

In the sentences that followed, he uttered the word happiness a number of times. He also said: "Down there we'll be as quiet as mice." I resisted the desire to take his shaven head in my warm hands and, as I was on a lower step, to rest it on my knees, which were on the step above. I felt the same grief I had often felt at Mettray when confronted with my helplessness. There was nothing I could do for him but caress him, and I had the impression that my caresses even aggravated his sadness, as in the past my caress had saddened Villeroy when he had the blues. He said, in wonderment, with only the barest hint of anxiety: "Do you think the guys in our cell know that we . . . ?"

Villeroy was at Mettray because he had killed his father, a pork butcher. Villeroy was my man. As elder brother of Family B (each family, all of whose members occupied one of the ten cottages on the Big Square, which was covered with lawn and planted with chestnut trees, was called Family A, B, C, D, E, F, G, H, J, or L. Each of the cottages housed about thirty children who were ordered about by a colonist huskier and more vicious than the others. He was picked by the head of the family and was called the "elder brother." The elder brother was supervised by the head of the family, who was usually some retired civil servant, a noncommissioned officer, an ex-trooper), he had in his service a kid who was something like his squire, or page, or female attendant, or lady, and who worked in the tailor shop.

Mettray, now as I write, has been emptied of its fierce and charming demons. And for whom does Fontevrault have a bone? Our heaven has been depopulated. If we climb to our transoms, our eager eyes no longer have the luck to think they see the belfry around which the colonists must be playing in the Touraine countryside. And as our life is without external hope, it turns its desires inward. I cannot believe that the Prison is not a mystic community, for the death cell, in which a light burns night and day, is the chapel to which we direct our silent prayers. It is true that the more hard-boiled of the hoodlums pretend to deny Harcamone's grandeur, for the purity attained by blood—one speaks of the baptism of blood—offends them, but I have noticed more than once in the course of conversation a sign which showed that those least prone to respect felt a certain reluctance to use harsh words when talking about the murderer. In fact, one day, during the medical checkup, Lou Daybreak, Botchako, Bulkaen, and others were standing in front of the infirmary and talking about the death of Rose-wood and the act of killing. Each of them expressed his opinion of Harcamone's worth. I had, so I thought, completely freed myself from his hold. But I didn't talk about him. However, the discussion was cut short by a single word from Bulkaen:

"He's what I call a man!"

He said it quietly, though with a slightly comic intonation. Immediately the former power swooped down on me. Flowing from my love of Bulkaen, waves of submission to Harcamone broke over my head. I made a slight movement, as if I were going to bend, or stoop. No one challenged the boy's remark. We felt that only the youngest and handsomest of us could decide whether Harcamone was a man. It was for him to offer the palm branch—the palm of Stephen the deacon— for that palm, which was within us, was awarded by what was most youthful in us. Bulkaen was the visible form of the quality that made us pay deference to Harcamone's act.

"He's what I call a man," he said. And, after a silence, he added:

"And him, at least, he shovels it up. He gets all the grub and wine he wants."

Then he stood there, a little foolishly, with his legs too far apart, like a young colt or a little calf. Indeed, Harcamone received a double and even triple ration of bread and soup. He was being fattened in his cell, like the ancient kings of the Isle of Nemi who were elected for a year and then immolated. And Pierrot, whose belly was devoured by hunger when he thought of Harcamone, must have been struck mainly by the latter's air of prosperity. Harcamone was stout. He was being bred. To the heartbreaking sweetness of being out of the world before death, was added, in Pierrot's mind, the pleasantness of the mild torpor that lulls a sated body to sleep.

Funeral Rites

◄o►

Perhaps the most shocking of all Genet's novels is Funeral Rites, *which Genet wrote in honor of his friend Jean Decarnin, who had died on the barricades during the Liberation of Paris in August 1944.*

Before Decarnin's death, Genet had already been working on a text about the young maid who loses her baby, buries it in her village, and is raped by the grave diggers. This grotesque and melancholy tale was inspired by Genet's childhood friend Solange Comte, who had lost a baby when she was still an adolescent.

After Decarnin died, Genet decided to make the little maid into Decarnin's fiancée and the lost baby their child. Although Genet claims that he and Decarnin were lovers, mutual friends of the period doubt that they ever were sexual partners. Nevertheless, Genet's feelings for Decarnin ran so deep that even as an old man he was incapable of talking about him. Indeed, Decarnin and Abdallah, the high-wire artist, were the most revered figures in Genet's personal pantheon.

The book is outrageous because it embraces Decarnin's enemies, Nazis of all sorts, including Hitler himself, in order to propitiate Decarnin's ghost. In fact, the book can be read as an elaborate ritual designed to resuscitate Decarnin. Yet, even viewed as a piece of magic, the book retains its shocking aspects. The original publisher waited till 1947 to bring it out, and then published it without a publisher's name on the title page.

THE NEWSPAPERS THAT appeared at the time of the liberation of Paris, in August 1944, give a fair idea of what those days of childish heroism, when the body was steaming with bravura and boldness, were really like.

"PARIS ALIVE!" "PARISIANS ALL IN THE STREETS!" "THE AMERICAN ARMY IS ON THE MARCH IN PARIS." "STREET FIGHTING CONTINUES." "THE BOCHES HAVE SURRENDERED." "TO THE BARRICADES!" "DEATH TO THE TRAITORS!"

Bernard Frechtman had completed the first draft and first revisions of this translation at the time of his death. The final editing and verification of the text was completed by Helen R. Lane.

As we turn the pages of the old sheets, we see once again the stern and smiling faces, gray with the dust of the streets, with fatigue, with four or five days' growth of beard. Shortly thereafter, these papers bring before us the Hitlerian massacres and the games, which others call sadistic, of a police that recruited its torturers from among the French. Photographs still show dismembered, mutilated corpses and villages in ruins, Oradour and Montsauche, burned by German soldiers. It is within the framework of this tragedy that the event is set: the death of Jean D., which is the ostensible reason for this book.

When I returned from the morgue where his fiancée had taken me (she was an eighteen-year-old housemaid, an orphan from the age of twelve. She used to stand next to her mother and beg in the Bois de Boulogne, offering to the passerby, with a dull face of which only the eyes were beautiful, a few songs in a beggar-girl's voice. Her humbleness was already such that at times she would accept only the small coins of the money that the ladies offered her as they strolled by. She was woebegone, and so dejected that in all seasons one saw around her the stiff rushes and pure puddles of a swamp. I don't know where Jean picked her up, but he loved her), when I returned alone from the morgue, darkness had set in. As I walked up the Rue de la Chaussée-d'Antin, swimming on waves of sadness and grief and thinking about death, I raised my head and saw a huge stone angel, dark as night, looming up at the end of the street. Three seconds later, I realized it was the bulk of the Church of the Trinity, but for three seconds I had felt the horror of my condition, of my poor helplessness in the presence of what seemed in the darkness (and less in the August darkness of Paris than in the thicker darkness of my dismal thoughts) to be the angel of death and death itself, both of them as unyielding as rock. And a moment ago, when writing the word "Hitlerian," in which Hitler is contained, it was the Church of the Trinity, dark and formless enough to look like the eagle of the Reich, that I saw moving toward me. For a very brief instant, I relived the three seconds in which it was as if I were petrified, appallingly attracted by those stones, the horror of which I felt but from which my trapped gaze could not flee. I felt it was evil to gaze in that way, with that insistence and that abandon, yet I kept gazing. It is not yet the moment for me to know whether the Führer of the Germans is, in general, to personify death, but I shall speak of him, inspired by my love for Jean, for his soldiers, and perhaps shall learn what secret role they play in my heart.

I shall never keep close enough to the conditions under which I am writing this book. Though its avowed aim is to tell of the glory of Jean D., it perhaps has more unforeseeable secondary aims. To write is to choose among the materials that are offered you. I wonder why I was willing to set down in words one fact rather than another of equal importance. Why is my choice limited and why do I see myself depicting before long the third funeral in each of my three books? Even before I knew Jean, I had chosen the funeral of the bastard child of the unwed mother which, disguised by the words, prettified, decorated by them, disfigured, you will read about later. It is disturbing that a gruesome theme was offered me long ago so that I would deal with it today and incorporate it, despite myself, into a work meant to decompose the gleam of light (composed mainly of love and pain) that is projected by my grieving heart. I am writing this book near a monastery that stands deep in the woods, among rocks and thorns. As I walk by the torrent, I enjoy relieving the anguish of Erik, the handsome Boche tank driver, of Paulo, of Riton. I shall write freely. But I wish to emphasize the strangeness of the fate that made me describe at the beginning of *Our Lady of the Flowers* a funeral I was to conduct two years later in accordance with the secret rites of the heart and mind. The first was not exactly the prefiguration of the second. Life brings its modifications, and yet the same disturbance (though one that, paradoxically, would spring from the end of a conflict—for example, when the concentric waves in a pond move away from the point at which the stone fell, when they move farther and farther away and diminish into calm, the water must feel, when this calm is attained, a kind of shudder which is no longer propagated in its matter but in its soul. It knows the plenitude of being water). The funeral of Jean D. brings back to my mouth the cry that left it, and its return causes me an uneasiness that is due to having found peace once again. That burial, that death, the ceremonies lock me up in a monument of murmurs, of whisperings in my ear, and of funeral exhalations. They were to make me aware of my love and friendship for Jean when the object of all that love and friendship disappeared. Yet now that the great eddying is over, I am calm. One of my destinies seems to have just been fulfilled. Jean's mother appeared to understand this when she said to me:

"That set you off."

"Set me off?"

She was arranging books on the sideboard. She hesitated a bit, nervously pushed a volume that struck the photograph of her husband, and, without looking at me, she uttered a sentence of which I understood only the last words:

". . . the candles."

I made no reply, perhaps out of laziness, and, it seems to me, so as to be less alive. Indeed, every act that was too precise, too explicit, put me back into the life from which my grief tried to uproot me. I felt ashamed, at the time, of still living when Jean was dead, and it caused me great suffering to rise to my own surface. Nevertheless, in my pitiful, illogical mind, which was drifting more and more into vagueness, those two words, which probably referred to the candles on the sideboard, arranged themselves in the following sentence:

"You're setting yourself off amidst the candles."

No longer remembering what preceded these few words, I am surprised to recall the following statement by Jean's mother, who was staring at me:

"People can say what they like but breeding will tell."

I looked at her and said nothing. Her chin was cupped in the hollow of her right hand.

"Jean took after his grandmother a bit in that respect."

"Yes, he might have been distinguished. He was quite refined."

Her gaze turned away from me and rested on the polished surface of a service plate, lying on the sideboard, in which, with her head bent forward, she was admiring herself as she tucked her hair back into place:

"My mother was very distinguished. She was a society woman. It was I who inherited the aristocracy in the family."

A gesture with which she arranged the candles had released that confidence. The mother wanted to prove to me that she was worthy of such a son and her son worthy of me.

She raised her head and, without looking at me, left silently. She was going to inform Erik of my arrival. She had never loved Jean, but his sudden death nevertheless glorified her maternal conscience. Four days after the funeral I received a letter from her thanking me—did she mean to thank me for my grief?—and asking me to come to see her. It was the little housemaid who opened the door to me. Jean's mother had taken her in despite her disgust at the fact that the girl was a maid and the daughter of a beggar. Juliette ushered me into the living room and left. I waited. Jean's mother was no longer in mourning. She was wearing a white, very low necked, sleeveless dress. She wore mourning, that is, in the manner of queens. I knew that she had been hiding a German soldier in her small three-room apartment since the insurrection of Paris, but an emotion very much akin to fear gripped my throat and heart when Erik appeared at her side.

"Monsieur Genet," she said, simpering and putting out her white, flabby, plump hand, "this is my friend."

Erik was smiling. He was pale despite the memory of a sun tan. When he tried to be attentive, his nostrils grew tense and white. Without consciously formulating the thought that he must have been quick tempered, I felt the kind of discomfort one feels in the presence of a man who is ready to bite. Undoubtedly he had been the lover of the Berlin executioner. His face, however, was veiled with a kind of shame in my presence, and that shame later led me to imagine him in a posture which I shall speak of. He was wearing civilian clothes. I first saw his frightening neck, which emerged from a blue shirt, and his muscular arms in his rolled-up sleeves. His hand was heavy and steady though the fingernails were bitten. He said:

"I know about your friendship with Jean . . ."

I was very surprised to hear a very soft, almost humble, voice speak to me. Its timbre had the roughness of Russian voices, but it was softened by a kind of gentleness when I discerned in it what might be called shrill notes, the vibrations of which he tried—deliberately or not—to muffle. The smiles of both the woman and the soldier were so hard, perhaps because of the stiffness and immobility of the curl of the lips, that I suddenly felt as if I were caught in a trap and being watched by the smiles, which were as alarming as the inevitable jaw of a wolf trap. We sat down.

"Jean was so gentle . . ."

"That's true, Monsieur. I don't know anyone . . ."

"But you're not going to call each other Monsieur," said the mother laughingly. "After all, you're a friend. And besides, it's too long. It makes for endless formality."

Erik and I looked at each other hesitantly. For a moment, we were ill at ease. Then, moved by some force or other, I immediately put out my hand first and smiled. Confronted with mine, the two other smiles lost their cruelty. I crossed my legs and a really friendly atmosphere was created.

Erik coughed. Two dry little gasps that were in perfect harmony with his pallor.

"He's very shy, you know."

"He'll get used to me. I'm not a monster."

The word "monster" must have been awakened by the echo of the words "get used to." Was it possible that in my personal life I was accepting without anguish one of those against whom Jean had fought to the death? For the quiet death of that twenty-year-old Communist who, on August 19, 1944, was picked off at the barricades by the bullet of a charming young collaborator, a boy whose grace and age were his adornment, puts my life to shame.

I ruminated for perhaps six seconds on the words "get used to" and felt a kind of very slight melancholy that can be expressed only by the image of a pile of sand or rubbish. Jean's delicacy was somewhat akin (since it suggests it) to the grave sadness that issues—along with a very particular odor—from mortar and broken bricks which, whether hollow or solid, are made of apparently very soft clay. The youngster's face was always ready to crumble, and the words "get used to" have just crumbled it. Amidst the debris of buildings being demolished, I sometimes step on ruins whose redness is toned down by the dust, and they are so delicate, discreet, and fragrant with humility that I have the impression I am placing the sole of my shoe on Jean's face. I had met him four years before, in August 1940. He was sixteen at the time.

At present, I am horrified with myself for containing—having devoured him—the dearest and only lover who ever loved me. I am his tomb. The earth is nothing. Dead. Staves and orchards[1] issue from my mouth. His. Perfume my chest, which is wide, wide open. A greengage plum swells his silence. The bees escape from his eyes, from his sockets where the liquid pupils have flowed from under the flaccid eyelids. To eat a youngster shot on the barricades, to devour a young hero, is no easy thing. We all love the sun. My mouth is bloody. So are my fingers. I tore the flesh to shreds with my teeth. Corpses do not usually bleed. His did.

He died on the barricades of August 19, 1944, but his staff had already stained my mouth with blood in May, in the orchards. When he was alive, his beauty frightened me, as did the chastity and beauty of his language. At the time, I wanted him to live in a grave, in a dark, deep tomb, the only dwelling worthy of his monstrous presence. It would be lit by candle, and he would live in it on his knees or crouching. He would be questioned through a slit in the slab. Is that the way he lives inside me, exhaling through my mouth, anus, and nose the odors that the chemistry of his decaying accumulates within me?

I still love him. Love for a woman or girl is not to be compared to a man's love

---

[1] "Staves and orchards" renders an untranslatable play on words: *les verges et les vergers*. *Verge* is the zoological word for penis.—Translator's note.

for an adolescent boy. The delicacy of his face and the elegance of his body have crept over me like leprosy. Here is a description of him: his hair was blond and curly, and he wore it very long. His eyes were gray, blue, or green, but extraordinarily clear. The concave curve of his nose was gentle, childish. He held his head high on a rather long, supple neck. His small mouth, the lower lip of which had a distinct curl, was almost always closed. His body was thin and flexible, his gait rapid and lazy.

My heart is heavy and succumbs to nausea. I puke on my white feet, at the foot of the tomb which is my unclothed body.

Erik had sat down in a chair with his back to the window draped with long, white-lace curtains. The air was dense, painful. It was obvious that the windows were always kept closed. The soldier's legs were spread, so that the wooden front of the chair on which he put his hand was visible. The blue workman's trousers he was wearing were too tight for his thighs and behind. Perhaps they had been Jean's. Erik was handsome. I don't know what suddenly made me conceive the notion that his sitting on a straw-bottomed chair cramped his *"oeil de Gabès."*[2] I remembered an evening on the Rue des Martyrs, and in a few seconds I relived it. Between the dizzying cliffs of the houses the street climbed uphill toward a stormy sky that paid heed to the melody of the gait and gestures of the group of three kids and a *bataillonnaire*, who were all delighted with a story the soldier was telling. As they went by, the shopping bags of the bareheaded women hit against their calves.

". . . that was all I wanted, so I stuck my finger in his eye."

The *Joyeux* pronounced *oeil* (eye) like *ail* (garlic). The three youngsters, who were walking at the same pace, with their heads down and shoulders slightly bent and their hands in their pockets pressing against the muscles of their taut thighs, were a bit winded by the climb. The *Joyeux's* story had a fleshy presence. They said nothing. Within them hatched an egg from which emerged an excitement charged with cautious lovemaking under a mosquito net. Their muteness allowed the excitement to make its way quiveringly to their very marrow. It would have taken very little for the kind of love that was developing within them for the first time to escape from their mouths in the guise of a song, poem, or oath. Embarrassment made them curt. The youngest walked with his head high, eye pure, lips slightly parted. He was nibbling his nails. Because of his weakness he was not always able to be calm or self-controlled, but he felt deeply grateful to those who brought him peace by dominating him.

He turned his head a little. His open mouth was already a fissure through which all his tenderness passed and through which the world entered to possess him. He gazed docilely at the *Joyeux*. The sensitive *Joyeux* understood and was pained by

[2]A few French terms have been retained in this and the following paragraphs. *L'oeil de Gabès* (the eye of Gabès) was African Battalion slang for the anus. A member of the Battalion, which was referred to familiarly as the Bat-d'Af (Bataillon d'Afrique), was a *bataillonnaire* or, familiarly, a *Joyeux* (a Merry Boy).—Translator's note.

the excitement he had aroused. He drew his head back proudly. His little foot, which was surer, mastered a conqueror. He snickered a bit:

". . . In the oye, I'm tellin' ya, in the oyye!"

He came down hard on the *o* so as to let the *yye* stream out. Then, a slight silence. And he ended the sentence so bombastically that the story became the relation of a deed witnessed in the land of the gods, at Gabès,[3] or at Gabes in the broiling, sumptuous country of a lofty disease, of a sacred fever. Pierrot stumbled over a stone. He said nothing. Without moving the fists in his pockets, the soldier again threw back his round little burned head, which was as brown as a pebble of the wadis, and added with his hoarse laugh, in which the blue tattooed dot at the outer angle of his left eyelid seemed to be painted:

". . . of Gabès! In the eye of Gabès! And bango!"

It is not a matter of indifference that my book, which is peopled with the truest of soldiers, should start with the rarest expression that brands the punished soldier, that most prudent being confusing the warrior with the thief, war with theft. The *Joyeux* likewise gave the name "bronze eye" to what is also called the "jujube," the "plug," the "onion," the "meanie," the "tokas," the "moon," the "crap basket." Later, when they return to their hometowns, they secretly preserve the sacrament of the Bat-d'Af, just as the princes of the Pope, Emperor, or King glorified in having been, a thousand years ago, simple brigands in a heroic band. The *bataillon-naire* thinks fondly of his youth, of the sun, of the blows of the guards, of the prison queers, of the prickly-pear trees, the leaves of which are also called the *Joyeux*'s wife; he thinks of the sand, of the marches in the desert, of the flexible palm tree whose elegance and vigor are exactly those of his prick and his boyfriend; he thinks of the grave, of the gallows, of the eye.

The veneration I feel for that part of the body and the great tenderness that I have bestowed on the children who have allowed me to enter it, the grace and sweetness of their gift, oblige me to speak of all this with respect. It is not profaning the most beloved of the dead to speak, in the guise of a poem whose tone is still unknowable, of the happiness he offered me when my face was buried in a fleece that was damp with my sweat and saliva and that stuck together in little locks of hair which dried after lovemaking and remained stiff. My teeth went at it desperately at times, and my pupils were full of images that are organizing themselves today where, at the back of a funeral parlor, the angel of the resurrection of the death of Jean, proud, aloft in the clouds, dominated in his fierceness the handsomest soldier of the Reich. For at times it is the opposite of what he was that is evoked by the wonderful child who was mowed down by the August bullets, the purity and iciness of which frighten me, for they make him greater than I. Yet I place my story, if that is what I must call the prismatic decomposition of my love and grief, under the aegis of that dead boy. The words "low" and "sordid" will be meaningless if anyone dares apply them to the tone of this book which I am writing in

[3]*Gabès is in southern Tunisia.—Translator's note.*

homage. I loved the violence of his prick, its quivering, its size, the curls of his hairs, the child's eyes, and the back of his neck, and the dark, ultimate treasure, the "bronze eye," which he did not grant me until very late, about a month before his death.

On the day of the funeral, the church door opened at four in the afternoon on a black hole into which I made my way solemnly or, rather, was borne by the power of the grand funeral to the nocturnal sanctuary and prepared for a service which is the sublime image of the one performed at each grieving of the fallen prick. A funereal flavor has often filled my mouth after love.

Upon entering the church:

"It's as dark here as up a nigger's asshole."

It was that dark there, and I entered the place with the same slow solemnity. At the far end twinkled the tobacco-colored iris of the *"oeil de Gabès,"* and, in the middle of it, haloed, savage, silent, awfully pale, was that buggered tank driver, god of my night, Erik Seiler.

Despite the trembling of the tapers, from the black-draped church door there could be discerned on Erik's chest, as he stood on top of an altar supporting all the flowers of a stripped garden, the location of the mortal hole that will be made by a Frenchman's bullet.

My staring eyes followed Jean's coffin. My hand played for a few seconds with a small matchbox in the pocket of my jacket, the same box that my fingers were kneading when Jean's mother said to me:

"Erik's from Berlin. Yes, I know. Can I hold it against him? One's not responsible. One doesn't choose one's birthplace."

Not knowing how to answer, I raised my eyebrows as if to say, "Obviously."

Erik's hand, which was between his thighs, was pressed against the wood of the chair. He shrugged and looked at me with somewhat anxious eyes. Actually I was seeing him for the second time, and had long known that he was Jean's mother's lover. Since his force and vigor compensated for what (despite great austerity) was too frail in Jean's grace, I have ever since made great efforts to live his life as a Berlin youngster, but particularly when he stood up and went to the window to look into the street. With a gesture of needless caution he held one of the double, red-velvet curtains in front of his body. He stood that way for a few seconds, then turned around without letting go of the curtain, so that he was almost completely wrapped in its folds, and I saw an image of one of the young Nazis who paraded in Berlin with unfurled flags on their shoulders, wrapped in folds of red cloth buffeted by the wind. For a second, Erik was one of those kids. He looked at me, again turned his head with a brief movement toward the closed window from which the street could be seen through the lace, then let go of the curtain so that he could raise his wrist and see the time. He realized that he no longer had a watch. Jean's mother was standing quietly by the sideboard and smiling. She saw his gaze—I did too—and the three of us immediately looked in the direction of a small table near a couch where two wristwatches were lying side by side.

I blushed:

"Look, your watch is over there."

The mother went to get the smaller one and brought it to the soldier. He took it without a word and put it into his pocket.

The woman did not see the look he gave her, and I myself did not understand the meaning of it. He said:

"It's all over."

I thought that everything was over for him, me, and Jean's mother. Nevertheless, I said:

"Not at all, nothing's over."

This was an obvious answer, but I hardly thought about what I was saying, since, inspired by the image of Erik in the folds of the curtain, I was in the process of going back to his childhood, of living it in his stead. He sat down on the chair again, fidgeted, stood up, and sat down a third time. I knew that he had hated Jean, whose severity did not allow for indulging his mother. Not that he condemned her, but the child who went all over Paris with valises full of guns and anti-German pamphlets had no time to smile. He also realized that the slightest truckling, the slightest witticism, might relax his attitude, which he wanted to keep rigid. I even wonder whether he felt any tenderness toward me.

On the sideboard in a frame adorned with flowers and shellwork foliage was a portrait photograph of him. When I went to see him at the morgue, I was hoping that his perfectly scrubbed, clean, naked, white skeleton, which was composed of very dry scraped bones, of a skull admirable in shape and matter, and particularly of thin finger joints that were rigid and severe, had been laid out on a bed of roses and gladiolas. I had bought armfuls of flowers, but they were at the foot of the trestle that supported the coffin. They were stuck in a roll of straw and formed, with the oak or ivy leaves that had been added, ridiculous wreaths. I had got my money's worth, but the fervor with which I myself would have strewn the roses was lacking. It was indeed roses that I had wanted, for their petals are sensitive enough to register every sorrow and then convey them to the corpse, which is aware of everything. A huge straw cushion, lastly, decorated with laurel leaves, was leaning against the coffin. Jean had been taken from the refrigerator. The reception room of the morgue, which had been transformed into a mortuary chapel, was thronged with people walking through it. Jean's mother, who was sitting next to me veiled in crape, murmured to me:

"Before, it was Juliette. Now it's my turn."

Four months earlier, Juliette had lost a newborn baby, and the fact that Jean was its father had infuriated his mother. She had cursed them, foolishly, and now she herself was a child weeping over her son's death.

"It's hardly . . . ," she added.

The phrase was completed by a tremendous sigh, and though my thoughts were far away I gathered that she meant: "Hardly worth my being in charge of the funeral."

My grief did not prevent me from seeing beside me the young man I had met beside the tree near which Jean had died. He was wearing the same fur-lined leather coat. I was sure he was Paulo, Jean's very slightly older brother. He said nothing. He was not crying. His arms hung at his side. Even if Jean had never spoken about it, I would have recognized his nastiness. It gave great sobriety to all his gestures. He had a tendency to put his hands into his pockets. He stood there without moving. He was shutting himself up in his indifference to evil and unhappiness.

Despite the crowd, I bent forward to contemplate the child who, by the miracle of machine-gun fire, had become that very delicate thing, a dead youth. The precious corpse of an adolescent shrouded in cloth. And when the crowd bent over him at the edge of the coffin, it saw a thin, pale, slightly green face, doubtless the very face of death, but so commonplace in its fixity that I wonder why Death, movie stars, touring virtuosi, queens in exile, and banished kings have a body, face, and hands. Their fascination is owing to something other than a human charm, and, without betraying the enthusiasm of the peasant women trying to catch a glimpse of her at the door of her train, Sarah Bernhardt could have appeared in the form of a small box of safety matches. We had not come to see a face but the dead Jean D., and our expectation was so fervent that he had a right to manifest himself, without surprising us, in any way whatever.

"They don't go in for style these days," she said.

Heavy and gleaming, like the most gorgeous of dahlias, Jean's mother, who was still very beautiful, had raised her mourning veil. Her eyes were dry, but the tears had left a subtle and luminous snail track on her pink, plump face from the eyes to the chin. She looked at the pine wood of the coffin.

"Oh, you can't expect quality nowadays," replied another woman in deep mourning who was next to her.

I was looking at the narrow coffin and at Jean's leaden face, which was overlaid with flesh that was sunken and cold, not with the coldness of death, but the iciness of the refrigerator. At twilight, accompanied by the muted fanfares of fear, almost naked and knowing I was naked in my corduroy trousers and under my coarse, blue, V-necked shirt, the sleeves of which were rolled up above my bare arms, I walked down silent hills in sandals, in the simple posture of the stroller, that is, with one hand closed in my pocket and the other leaning on a flexible stick. In the middle of a glade, I had just offered funereal worship to the moon that was rising in my sky.

An assistant brought in the lid of the coffin and I was torn apart. It was screwed on. After the rigidity of the body, the ice of which was invisible, breakable, even deniable, this was the first brutal separation. It was hateful because of the imbecility of a pine board, which was fragile and yet absolutely reliable, a hypocritical, light, porous board that a more depraved soul than Jean's could dissolve, a board cut from one of the trees that cover my slopes, trees that are black and haughty but frightened by my cold eyes, by the sureness of my footing beneath the branches, for they are the witnesses to my visits on the heights where love receives me without display. Jean was taken away from me.

"It has no style."

It was an agony for me to see the boy go off in the dissolution of a ceremony whose funereal pompousness was as much a mocking as familiarity would have been. The people walked around the coffin and left. The undertaker's assistants took the coffin, and I followed the black-clad family. Someone loaded the hearse with wreaths the way one garners bundles of hay. Each action wounded me. Jean needed a compensation. My heart was preparing to offer him the pomp that men refused him. No doubt the source of this feeling was deeper than defiance of the shallow sensitivity indicated by men's acts, but it was while I was following the coffin that friendship rose within me as the star of the dead rises at night in the sky. I stepped into the hearse. I gave the chauffeur twenty francs. Nothing was preventing the inner revelation of my friendship for Jean. The moon was more solemn that evening and rose slowly. It spread peace, but grief too, over my depopulated earth. At a crossing, the hearse had to stop so that an American convoy could pass, and it took another street, when suddenly the silence, contained amidst the houses, welcomed me with such nobility that I thought for a moment death would be at the end of the street to receive me and its valets would lower the running board. I put my right hand to my chest, under my jacket. The beating of my heart revealed the presence within me of a tribe that dances to the sound of the tom-tom. I was hungry for Jean. The car turned. Undoubtedly I was made aware of my friendship by the grief that Jean's death was causing me, and little by little I became terribly afraid that since the friendship would have no external object on which to expand itself it might consume me by its fervor and cause my death. Its fire (the rims of my eyelids were already burning) would, I thought, turn against me, who contain and detain Jean's image and allow it to merge with myself within me.

"Monsieur! Monsieur! Hey! Monsieur, please stay with the men!"

Of course, I must stay with the men. The director of the funeral was wearing knee breeches, black stockings, a black dress coat, and black pumps and was carrying an ivory-headed cane entwined with a black silk cord at the end of which was a silver tassel. Someone was playing the harmonium.

Paulo was walking stiffly in front of me. He was a monolithic block, the angles of which must have scraped space, the air, and the azure. His nastiness made one think he was noble. I was sure that he felt no grief at his brother's death, and I myself felt no hatred for that indifference against which my tenderness was about to crash.

The procession stopped for a second, and I saw the profile of Paulo's mouth. I mused upon his soul, which cannot be defined better than by the following comparison: one speaks of the bore of a gun,[4] which is the inner wall—less than the wall itself—of the gun. It is the thing that no longer exists, it is the gleaming, steely, icy vacuum that limits the air column and the steel tube, the vacuum and the metal; worse: the vacuum and the coldness of the metal. Paulo's soul was perceptible in his parted lips and vacuous eyes.

[4]The French word *âme* means both "soul" and "bore" of a gun.—Translator's note

The procession stirred, then got under way again. Paulo's body hesitated. He was his brother's chief mourner, as a king is a king's, and led the cortege like a caparisoned horse charged with a nobility of fire, silver, and velvet. His pace was slow and heavy. He was a lady of Versailles, dignified and unfeeling.

When Jean had diarrhea, he said to me, "I've got the trots." Why did that word have to come back to me just as I was watching Paulo's solemn and almost motionless backside, why did I have to call the barely indicated dance the trots?

Roses have the irritability, curtness, and magnetic edginess of certain mediums. It was they who were performing the actual service.

The coffin was slid onto the catafalque through an opening at one end. This sudden theatrical stunt, the conjuring away of the coffin, greatly amused me. Acts without overtones, without extension, empty acts, were reflecting the same desolation as the death being reflected on the black-draped chairs, on the little trick of a catafalque, on the *Dies Irae*. Jean's death was duplicating itself in another death, was making itself visible, was projecting itself upon trappings as dark and ugly as the details with which interments are surrounded. It seemed to me an inane, doubly useless act, like the condemnation of an innocent man. I deeply regretted that processions of handsome boys, naked or in underpants, sober or laughing—for it was important that his death be an occasion for play and laughter—had not accompanied Jean from a bed of state to his grave. I would have loved to gaze at their thighs and arms and the backs of their necks, to have imagined their woolly sex under their blue woolen underpants.

I had sat down. I saw people kneeling. Out of respect for Jean, I suppose, and in order not to attract attention, I wanted to kneel too. I mechanically put my hand into my jacket pocket and encountered my little matchbox. It was empty. Instead of throwing it away, I had inadvertently put it back into my pocket.

"There's a little matchbox in my pocket."

It was quite natural for me to recall at that moment the comparison a fellow prisoner once made while telling me about the packages which the inmates were allowed to receive:

"You're allowed one package a week. Whether it's a coffin or a box of matches, it's the same thing, it's a package."

No doubt. A matchbox or a coffin, it's the same thing, I said to myself. I have a little coffin in my pocket.

As I stood up in order to kneel, a cloud must have passed in front of the sun, and the church was darkened by it. Was the priest censing the catafalque? The harmonium played more softly, or so it seemed, as soon as I was on my knees, with my head between my hands. This posture immediately brought me into contact with God.

"Dear God, dear God, dear God, I melt beneath your gaze. I'm a poor child. Protect me from the devil and God. Let me sleep in the shade of your trees, your monasteries, your gardens, behind your walls. Dear God, I have my grief, I'm praying badly, but you know that the position is painful, the straw has left its mark on my knees . . ."

The priest opened the tabernacle. All the heralds in blazoned velvet jerkins, the standard-bearers and pikemen, the horsemen, the knights, the S.S., the Hitler Youth in short pants paraded through the Führer's bedroom and on into his quarters. Standing near his bed, with his face and body in the shadow and his pale hand leaning on the flounced pillow, he watched them from the depths of his solitude. His castration had cut him off from human beings. His joys are not ours. Out of respect, the parade performed in the deep silence reserved for the sick. Even the footsteps of the stone heroes and the rumbling of the cannons and tanks were deadened by the woolen rugs. At times, a slight rustling of cloth could still be heard, the same sound that is made in the darkness by the stiff, dry cloth of the uniform of American soldiers when they move fast on their rubber soles.

". . . Dear God, forgive me. You see me as I am, simple, naked, tiny."

I was praying spontaneously, from my heart and lips. This attitude estranged me from Jean, whom I was betraying for too lofty a personage. I seized upon this pretext of a delicate sentiment to avoid creasing my trousers. I sat down and thought about Jean with far greater ease. The star of my friendship rose up larger and rounder into my sky. I was pregnant with a feeling that could, without my being surprised, make me give birth to a strange but viable and certainly beautiful being, Jean's being its father vouched for that. This new feeling of friendship was coming into being in an odd way.

The priest said:

". . . He died on the field of honor. He died fighting the invader . . ."

A shudder ran through me and made me realize that my body was feeling friendship for the priest who was making it possible for Jean to leave me with the regrets of the whole world. Since it was impossible for me to bury him alone, in a private ceremony (I could have carried his body, and why don't the public authorities allow it? I could have cut it up in a kitchen and eaten it. Of course, there would be a good deal of refuse: the intestines, the liver, the lungs, the eyes with their hair-rimmed lids in particular, all of which I would dry and burn—I might even mix their ashes with my food—but the flesh could be assimilated into mine), let him depart then with official honors, the glory of which would devolve upon me and thus somewhat stifle my despair.

The flowers on the catafalque grew exhausted from shedding their brightness. The dahlias were drooping with sleep. Their stomachs were glutted when they left the funeral parlor. They were still belching.

I followed the priest's oration:

". . . this sacrifice is not wasted. Young Jean died for France . . ."

If I were told that I was risking death in refusing to cry "Vive la France," I would cry it in order to save my hide, but I would cry it softly. If I had to cry it very loudly, I would do so, but laughingly, without believing in it. And if I had to believe in it, I would; then I would immediately die of shame. It doesn't matter whether this is due to the fact that I'm an abandoned child who knows nothing about his family or country; the attitude exists and is intransigent. And yet, it was nice to know that France was delegating its name so as to be represented at Jean's funeral. I was so overwhelmed with the sumptuousness of it all that my friendship went to my head (as one says: reseda goes to my head). Friendship, which I recognize by my grief at Jean's death, also has the sudden impetuousness of love. I said friendship. I would sometimes like it to go away and yet I tremble for fear it will. The only difference between it and love is that it does not know jealousy. Yet I feel a vague anxiety, a weak remorse. I am tormented. It is the birth of memory.

The procession—where could that obscure child have made so many friends?—the procession left the church.

The matchbox in my pocket, the tiny coffin, imposed its presence more and more, obsessed me:

"Jean's coffin could be just as small."

I was carrying his coffin in my pocket. There was no need for the small-scale bier to be a true one. The coffin of the formal funeral had imposed its potency on that little object. I was performing in my pocket, on the box that my hand was stroking, a diminutive funeral ceremony as efficacious and reasonable as the Masses that are said for the souls of the departed, behind the altar, in a remote chapel, over a fake coffin draped in black. My box was sacred. It did not contain a particle merely of Jean's body but Jean in his entirety. His bones were the size of matches, of tiny pebbles imprisoned in penny whistles. His body was somewhat like the cloth-wrapped wax dolls with which sorcerers cast their spells. The whole gravity of the ceremony was gathered in my pocket, to which the transfer had just taken place. However, it should be noted that the pocket never had any religious character; as for the sacredness of the box, it never prevented me from treating the object familiarly, from kneading it with my fingers, except that once, as I was talking to Erik, my gaze fastened on his fly, which was resting on the chair with the weightiness of the pouch of Florentine costumes that contained the balls, and my hand let go of the matchbox and left my pocket.

Jean's mother had just gone out of the room, I uncrossed my legs and recrossed them in the other direction. I was looking at Erik's torso, which was leaning slightly forward.

"You must miss Berlin," I said.

Very slowly, ponderously, searching for words, he replied:

"Why? I'll go back after the war."

He offered me one of his American cigarettes, which the maid or his mistress must have gone down to buy for him, since he himself never left the small apartment. I gave him a light. He stood up, not straight but leaning slightly forward, so that in drawing himself up he had to throw his torso backward. The movement arched his entire body and made his basket bulge under the cloth of his trousers. He had at that moment, despite his being cloistered, despite that sad, soft captivity among women, the nobility of a whole animal which carries its load between its legs.

"You must get bored."

We exchanged a few more trivialities. I could have hated him, but his sadness made me suddenly believe in his gentleness. His face was slightly lined with very fine wrinkles, like those of twenty-five-year-old blonds. He looked very handsome, very strong, and his sadness itself expressed the lasciviousness of the whole body of this wild animal that was reaching maturity.

He spoke to me very quietly. Perhaps he was afraid I might denounce him to the police. I wondered whether he was carrying a gun. My eyes furtively questioned his blue-denim trousers, pausing over every suspect bulk. Though I intended my gaze to be light, it must have weighed on the fly, for Erik smiled, if I may say so, with his usual smile. I blushed a little and looked away, trying to veil my blush by exhaling a cloud of smoke. He took advantage of this to cross his legs and say in a casual tone:

"Jean was very young. . . ."

He said "Dijan," pronouncing the "an" very curtly.

I did not reply. He said:

"*Aber,* you too, you Jean."

"Yes."

I was thinking of the warm, wide, heavy Louis XV bed covered with Venetian point lace in which Jean's mother pressed against Erik at night and no doubt during the day, either in a nightgown or naked. The bed was alive in the darkness of the bedroom, was emitting its rays, which reached me despite the walls. It was certain that one day or another Erik's and Paulo's thighs would constrict me there, they themselves getting their bellies all raddled with the maid and the mother, in a room watched over by the memory of Jean.

At the end of my fourth visit, Erik accompanied me alone to the entryway. It was late, it was getting dark. The entryway was very narrow. He pressed against my back. I felt his breath on my neck, and, close to my ear, he murmured:

"See you tomorrow, nine o'clock, Jean."

He took my hand and insisted:

"Nine o'clock, yes!"

"Yes."

The gesture of surprise he had just made on realizing that the two names were the same tightened the trousers against his buttocks and enhanced them. The outline of the muscles excited me. I tried to imagine what his relationship had been with Jean, whom he hated and who hated him. Erik's strength probably enabled him to seem very mild as he bullied the child. I looked at his eyes and composed in my mind the following sentence:

"So many suns have capsized beneath his hands, in his eyes . . ."

When I left the apartment after our first meeting, I attempted to retrace the course of his life and, for greater efficiency, I got into his uniform, boots, and skin. Drunk with the somewhat blurry vision of a tall, young Negro behind the windows of the café on the Boulevard de la Villette where he was leaning against a jukebox listening to javas and popular waltzes, I wormed my way into his past, gently and hesitantly at first, feeling my way, when the iron toe-plates of one of my shoes accidentally struck the curb. My calf vibrated, then my whole body. I raised my head and took my hands out of my pockets. I put on the German boots.

The fog was thick and so white that it almost lit up the garden. The trees were caught. Motionless, attentive, pale, nude, captured by a net of hair or a singing of harps. A smell of earth and dead leaves gave reason to think that all was not lost. The day would see the reign of God. A swan flapped its wings on a lake. I was eighteen, a young Nazi on duty in the park, where I was sitting at the foot of a tree. Since the seat of my riding breeches (I was preparing for the artillery) was leather-lined, I did not mind the dampness of the grass. Far off, behind me, an automobile drove by in the Siegesallee with its lights off, its noises muffled. Five o'clock was about to strike. I started to get up. A man was coming toward me. He was walking on the grass, ignoring the footpaths. His hands were in his pockets. He was heavy and yet light, for each of his angles was imprecise. He looked like a walking willow, each stump of which is lightened and thinned by an aigrette of young branches. He had a revolver. A force prevented me from getting up. The man was very close. His forehead was narrow, his nose and entire face were flattened, but their muscles were firm, as if wrought by a hammer. He was about thirty-five. He had the face of a brute. As he neared the tree under which I was sitting, he raised his head.

"Why is that man walking on the grass of the lawns?" I thought to myself.

"Say, he oughtn't to be there," thought the man, referring to me. "He's crossed the boundary."

He was smoking. Upon seeing me, he straightened up and threw back his chest with a strong, calm movement of his shoulders. He saw that I was a member of the Hitler Youth.

"You're going to get cold."

"I'm on guard."

"What are you guarding?"

"Nothing."

The man was satisfied with this reply. He was not sad, but indifferent or interested in other things than what he seemed to be. I was watching him. Though he was very close, I still could not see him clearly.

"Here."

He took a cigarette from his trouser pocket and handed it to me. I removed my gloves, took it, and stood up in order to light it from his. I was no stronger standing than sitting. The mere bulk of the man crushed me. I could tell that under his clothes, under his open shirt, was a terrific set of muscles. Despite his bulk and shape, he was lightened by the fog, his outline was blurred. It was also as if the morning mist were a steady emanation from his extraordinarily powerful body, a body strong with such glowing life that the combustion caused that motionless, thick, and yet luminous white smoke to seep out through all its pores. I was caught. I dared not look at him. Germany, stunned and staggering, was just managing to recover from the deep, rich drowsiness, the dizziness, the suffocation fertile in the new prodigies into which it had been plunged by the perfumes and charms emitted slowly and heavily by that strange curly poppy, Dr. Magnus Hirschfeld.

In the triangle of the V-necked shirt, in the middle of a tuft of hair that implied a fleece all over him, I saw, snug and warm, a little gold medallion cuddling in that wool, which was fragrant with the odor of armpits, like a plaster Jesus in the straw and hay dazed by the smell of the droppings of the ox and the ass. I shivered.

"Are you cold?"

"Yes."

The executioner said with a laugh that he had more heat than he needed, and, as if wanting to play, he drew me to him and put his arms around me. I dared not move. My long pale lashes fluttered a bit when the killer grabbed me and looked at me at closer range. A slight quiver ruffled the part of the face which is so sensitive in adolescents: the puffy surface around the mouth, the spot that will be covered by the mustache. The executioner saw the trembling. He was moved by the youngster's timorous flutter. He hugged him more gently, he softened his smile and said:

"What's the matter? Are you scared?"

I was wearing the wristwatch I had stolen the day before from one of the other boys. Was I scared? Why had he asked me that question point-blank?

More out of delicacy than pride, I almost answered no, but immediately, sure of my power over the brute, I wanted to be mean and I said yes.

"Did you recognize me?"

"Why?"

Erik was surprised at hearing slightly hesitant inflections in his voice which he had not been aware of and, at times, under the stress of greater anxiety, a slight trembling over a few notes that were too high for his usual timbre.

"Don't you recognize me?"

I kept my lips parted. I was still in the embrace of that unyielding fellow whose smiling face was armed with the glowing cigarette and bent over mine.

I had recognized him. I dared not say so. I replied:

"It's time for me to be getting back to the barracks."

"Are you scared because I'm the executioner?"

He had spoken until then in a hollow voice, in keeping with the blurriness of things or perhaps because he feared a danger might be hidden behind the fog, but when he uttered those words, he laughed with such violence and clarity that all the watchful trees suddenly came to attention in the wadding and recorded the laugh. I dared not move. I looked at him. I inhaled smoke, took the cigarette from my mouth and said:

"No."

But my "no" betrayed fear.

"No, you mean it, you're not scared?"

Instead of repeating the word no, I shook my head and, lightly tapping the cigarette twice with my forefinger, dropped a bit of ash on his foot. The casualness of these two gestures gave the boy such an air of detachment, of indifference, that the executioner felt humiliated, as if I had not deigned even to see him. He hugged me harder, laughingly, pretending that he wanted to frighten me.

"No?"

He peered into my eyes and dived right in. He blew the smoke in my face.

"No? Are you sure?"

"Of course I am, why?" And, to mollify the executioner, I added: "I haven't done any harm." The stolen watch on my wrist was punctuating my uneasiness.

It was cold. The dampness was penetrating our clothes. The fog was rather thick. We seemed to be alone, characters without a past or future, composed simply of our respective roles of Hitler Youth and executioner, and united to each other not by a succession of events but by the play of a grave gratuitousness, the gratuitousness of the poetic fact: *We were there,* in the fog of the world.

Still holding me by the waist, the executioner walked a few steps with me. We went down a path and then walked up onto another lawn to reach a clump of trees that made a dark spot in the pale dawn. I could have repeated that my duty obliged me to stay on the footpath. All I wanted was to have a smoke. I said nothing. But my chest was tight with fear and swollen with hope. I was one long, silent moan.

"What will be born of our lovemaking? What can be born of it?"

Until then I had known only unexciting play with a friend who was too young. Today it is I whom a fellow over thirty, a headsman, is leading imperiously to love, at an hour when one gets the axe, in the seclusion of a clump of trees, near a lake.

The Berlin executioner was about six feet one. His muscular build was that of an executioner who chops on a block with an axe. His brown hair was cropped very close, so that his completely round head was that of a beheaded man. He was sad despite his smile, which was meant to brave me and tame me. His sadness was profound, its source was deeper than his profession, being, rather, in his strength itself. He lived alone in a comfortable apartment which was tastefully furnished and resembled any other bourgeois apartment in Berlin. Every morning an old woman came to do the cleaning and left in a hurry. He ate in a restaurant. On days when capital punishment was scheduled, he did not go home in the evening. He would stay in a cabaret until daybreak, then wander in the dawn and dew through the lanes and lawns of the Tiergarten. The day before he met Erik and led him beneath the branches of a diamond-studded fir tree, he had detached a murderer's head from its trunk. Our faces were breaking the gossamer.

Now that I was sitting opposite Erik and seeing the beauty of his buttocks and the elegant impatience of his movements, not only was it obvious to me that his adventure had been lived, but, in addition, it fitted him so perfectly that I felt a kind of peace, the deep satisfaction of being present at the revelation of a truth. But my forsaking Jean, or rather granting his enemies such favor, delicately tortured my mind, into which remorse had worked its way and which it then ground, though very gently, with a few gentle writhing movements. I knew that I ought not abandon the boy whose soul had not yet found rest. I ought to have helped him. A few of the crabs he had probably picked up from a whore still clung to me. I was sure that the insects had lived on his body, if not all of them at least one whose brood invaded my bush with a colony that was digging in, multiplying, and dying in the folds of the skin of my balls. I saw to it that they stayed there and in the vicinity. It pleased me to think that they retained a dim memory of that same place on Jean's body, whose blood they had sucked. They were tiny, secret hermits whose duty it was to keep alive in those forests the memory of a young victim. They were truly the living remains of my friend. I took care of them as much as possible by not washing, not even scratching. At times, I would pluck one of them out and hold it between my nail and skin: I would examine it closely for a moment, with curiosity and tenderness, and then replace it in my curly bush. Perhaps their brothers were still living in Jean's hairs. The morgue keeps bodies for a long time. It has apparatus, refrigerators. Although Jean had been killed on the nineteenth, we did not know of his death until August 29. He was buried on September 3. I had been informed of some of the circumstances of his death by his comrades in the Communist Party, who had also told me where he had been killed. I was forced there by anxiety. On the afternoon of the first of September, I walked to Belleville and then to Ménilmontant, both of which I had forgotten about. The heat of the struggle was still visible on people's faces, but in the few days that had gone by they had lost their vigor. Their faith was slackening. The weather was hot. Although I kept my eyes lowered, I could see the open shops. Wicker baskets, chairs, and mats were being woven in the sky, people were eating fruit in the street, workers were smoking cigarettes made with Virginia tobacco. Nobody was aware of my pilgrimage. A huge sigh congested my chest and throat and might have caused my death. I was on the sunny side of the street. I asked a girl:

"Is this the way to the Boulevard Ménilmontant?"

She seemed not to know about my anguish, and the constipated look on my mug could not tell her the cause of it. Yet she did not seem shocked at my not addressing her more politely. As for me, I felt I was entitled to everything. People, even those who did not know me, owed me the greatest respect, for inside I was in mourning for Jean. Although I had always accepted the costume of widows in deep mourning, nevertheless its reduction to the status of a symbol, the black arm band, the strip of crepe on a lapel, the black cockade on the brim of workmen's caps, had previously seemed ridiculous to me. Suddenly I understood their necessity: they advise people to approach you with consideration, to be tactful with you, for you are the repository of a divinized memory.

". . . It's almost at the corner of the Rue de Belleville, opposite number sixty-four, sixty-six, or sixty-eight. I know about it from the fellow in the Party. You'll see a delicatessen."

I did not know the flavor of human flesh, but I was sure that all sausages and meat spreads would have a corpselike taste. I live frightfully alone and desperate, in a voracious society that protects a family of criminal sausage-makers (the father, mother, and probably three kids), mincers of corpses who feed all of France with dead young men and hide at the back of a shop on the Avenue Parmentier. I stepped onto the left-hand sidewalk, where the odd numbers are. I was at 23. It was time to cross. I turned toward the empty gutter, that river of dangerous light which separated me from Hell, and prepared to leave the shore. I was laden, encumbered with a more agonizing pain, with the fear of being alone amidst the passersby at an invisible theater where death had kidnapped Jean, where the drama—or mystery—had been performed, and the result of which I knew only through its negation. My pain was so great that it sought escape in the form of fiery gestures: kissing a lock of hair, weeping on a breast, pressing an image, hugging a neck, tearing out grass, lying down on the spot and falling asleep in the shade, sun, or rain with my head on my bent arm. What gesture would I make? What sign would be left me? I looked over to the other side of the street. First I saw, directly opposite me, a little girl of about ten who was walking quickly and clenching a stiff bouquet of white carnations in her little hand. I stepped down from the sidewalk, and a car that was going by on the other side, a little way up the street, suddenly exposed a French sailor whom I recognized by his white collar. He bent over toward the foot of a tree where a few people were standing and looking. The sailor's odd movement, which was accompanied by the passing of the girl, made my heart pound. When I reached the middle of the gutter, I could see better: at the foot of the tree were flowers in tin cans. The sailor had straightened up and was no longer a sailor. I had to make an effort to look at the number of the house opposite: 52. I still had a hope: someone else might have been killed there, at the same time as he. I put my hands into my pockets. Let it not be thought that I can be a party to this ridiculous plebeian tribute. Though they looked fresh from a distance and formed a kind of altar, from up close almost all the flowers were seen to be wilted. I was in the heart of China, in Japan, where the dead are honored in the streets, on the raods, on the sides of volcanoes, on the shores of rivers and the sea. I saw a big, damp spot and realized immediately it was the water from the flowers that was flowing. Nevertheless, I could not help thinking of all the blood Jean had lost. It was a lot of blood. Hadn't it dried since his death? An idiotic thought. Another: it was his piss. Or maybe the sailor had just relieved himself against the tree. Jean's piss! There's nothing to laugh about. Could he have died of fright? Not at all, one sometimes loses one's urine. No, it's not that. There were holes in the cans. The white shopfront . . . "Delica . . . Oh, God!"

I looked first at the sturdy sailor beaming in the middle of the spreading urine, and my eye took in the whole group: tree, flowers, and people. The sailor was a young fellow who had apparently been in the underground. His face was radiant: brown hair, though discolored by the sun, a straight nose, hard eyes. In order to put his hands into his pockets, he pushed back the flaps of a leather coat, a mackinaw, whose white furry collar—probably sheepskin—had misled me, for I had mistaken it for the light collar of a sailor. The little girl was still squatting in front of the tree, putting her white carnations into a can with a red and green label on which the word "Peas" was printed in black. I tried to recognize her face, but I had certainly never seen her before. She was alone. She was probably pretending that she was placing flowers on a grave. She had found a pretext for performing in everyone's presence the hidden rites of a nature cult and of a cult of the gods which childhood always discovers, but which it serves in secret. I was there. What gestures should I make? I would have liked to lean on the arm of the husky underground fighter. Does the tree perform marriages, or what if it records acts of adultery: its trunk is girdled with an official tricolored ribbon. The tree contains Jean's soul, which took refuge there when the shots from a machine gun riddled his elegant body. If I approach the fellow in the mackinaw, anger will make the plane tree shake its plume of leaves angrily. I dared not think of anyone other than Jean. I was in a cruel light, beneath the pitiless gaze of things. Since they know how to read every sign, every secret thought, they would condemn me if I had the slightest intention of acting. Yet I needed love. What to do? What gesture? Too much grief was pent up within me. If I opened a single, thin gate, the flood would sweep into my gestures and there's no telling what would happen. Crosses of Lorraine, tricolor cockades, and a few tiny pin-and-paper flags were stuck into the tree trunk around a sheet of lined note paper pinned to the bark. And on the sheet, in an awkward hand, was written the following: "A young patriot fell here. Noble Parisians, leave a flower and observe a moment of silence." Perhaps it wasn't he? I don't know yet. But what idiot wrote the word "young"? Young. I withdrew from the drama as far as possible. In order to weep, I had descended to the realm of the dead themselves, to their secret chambers, led by the invisible but soft hands of birds down stairways which were folded up again as I advanced. I displayed my grief in the friendly fields of death, far from men: within myself. No one was likely to catch me making ridiculous gestures; I was elsewhere. "Young" had been written in black ink, but it seemed to me that the certainty of Jean's death should not depend on a word that can be erased.

"And what if I erased it?" I realized at once that they wouldn't let me. Even the least hard-hearted would prevent me from checking fate. I would be depriving them of a dead person, and above all a dead person who was dear to them *by virtue* of his being dead. I thought of an eraser. The one I had in my pocket was a pencil eraser. What I needed was a harder, more granular one, an ink eraser. No. People would slap me. One doesn't try to resurrect bodies with an eraser.

"He's a Boche!" they would say. "A swine! A rat! A traitor! He's the one who killed him!" The mob would lynch me. Its cries welled up within me, rose all the way from my depths to my ears, which heard them backwards. The little girl who had been squatting stood up and went off, probably to her home twenty yards away. Could I be asleep? Are Belleville and Ménilmontant places in Paris where people venerate the dead by putting flowers into rusty, old tin cans and placing them at the foot of a dusty tree? Young! No doubt about it, I said to myself, it's here . . . I stopped there. The uttering of "here" and, even if only mentally, of the words meant to follow, "that he was killed," gave to my pain a physical precision that aggravated it. The words were too cruel. Then I said to myself that the words were words and did not in any way change the facts.

I forced myself to say over and over, inwardly, with the irritating repetitiveness of a saw, He-re, He-re, He-re, He-re.[5] My mind was being sharpened at the spot

[5]There is a play on the words *scie* (saw) and *ici* (here).—Translator's note.

designated by "Here." I was no longer even witnessing a drama. No drama could have taken place in an area too narrow for any presence. "He-re, He-re, He-re, He-re. That he was killed, that he was killed, that he was killed, that heels killed, that heels killed . . ." and I mentally composed the following epitaph: "Here that heels killed." People were watching. They no longer saw me, they were unaware of my adventures. An unkempt working-class woman was carrying a shopping bag. With a sigh, she drew from it a very tight little bunch of those ridiculous yellow flowers that are called marigolds. I looked at her. She was somewhat plump, and bold-looking. She bent over and put the bunch of marigolds into a rusty can in which there were wilted red roses. Everyone (five other persons, including the underground fighter, who was at my left) watched her performance. She straightened up and said, as if to herself, but it was meant for all of us:

"Poor things. Mustn't ask who it's for."

An old woman wearing a hat nodded. No one else made a gesture or uttered a word. The tree was acquiring an amazing bearing and dignity which heightened with each passing second. If that plane tree had grown on my estate or on the heights where I go to give thanks to love, I could have leaned against it, could have casually carved a heart in its bark, have wept, have sat down on the moss and fallen asleep in an air still blended with Jean's spirit, which had been reduced to powder by a burst of machine-gun fire. I turned around. In the glass of the shop front were two round, star-shaped holes. As everything was, at the time, a painful sign to me, the glass at once became sacred, forbidden. It seemed to be Jean's congealed soul, which, though pierced, retained its eternal transparency and protected the repulsive landscape of his flesh, which had been pounded, chopped, and cut up in the form of sausages and liver paté. I was about to turn around and thought the tree had perhaps lost its ridiculous adornment, the tin cans, the spreading urine, in short what one never sees at the foot of a tree and what could only be the doing of children or dreams. Everything, indeed, might have disappeared. Was it true that philosophers doubted the existence of things that were in back of them? How could one detect the secret of the disappearance of things? By turning around very fast? No. But faster? Faster than anything? I glanced behind me. I was on the watch. I turned my eyes and head, ready to . . . No, it was pointless. Things can never be caught napping. You would have to spin about with the speed of a propeller. You would then see that things had disappeared, and you with them. I stopped playing. With a feeling of gravity, I turned around. The tree was there. A lady who was going by made the sign of the cross. That little fête, at the foot of a tree that was pissing, was in bad taste. I refused everyone the right to invent such indelicate tributes. Let them stick to the polite, customary rites. The only thing lacking in that indecent spectacle was a wooden bowl draped with a crepe ribbon for collecting pennies for the widow and the kids. On a sunny day, with a delicate gesture, they could show that their hearts were in the right place, if they wanted to, though they kept their precious vases at home, and had the nerve to offer a naked hero graceless flowers in empty tins which they had stolen from garbage cans—and they hadn't even bothered to hammer down the sharp edges. While his soul was floating in the air, around the tree, Jean was heartbroken at still having that filthy wound, that damp, flowery canker whose rot stank in my nostrils. The canker was to blame for Jean's being kept on earth. He was unable to dissolve absolutely into the azure.

I looked at the fake sailor. He had put a cigarette into his mouth, no doubt mechanically, but very quickly removed it. Out of respect, I think. Thus, the patriot standing there in the August sun in a fur-lined leather coat open on a flexible waist and a broad chest pure as a banner was not, though I had hoped for a moment that he was, what death had achieved with Jean. He was not Jean transformed, disfigured, and transfigured, sloughing his hide and emerging with a new skin; for Jean, that soldier of the Year II, would not have dared make that inept gesture of respect.

I had never yet seen Jean's half brother. I was sure that it was he, as a matter of fact, whom I saw the following day at the funeral, with his mother.

He went off. For a moment I followed him with my eyes—not that I suspected what linked him to Jean—but because of his splendid bearing, which I shall speak about later. When he entered the room in which I was chatting with Erik for the first time, darkness was setting in. He said:

"Hello."

And he sat down in a corner, near the table. He did not look at either Erik or me. The first thing he did was to take the wristwatch that was lying on the table and put it on. His face expressed nothing in particular.

I was perhaps mistaken in supposing that the two watches lying back to back on a night table betrayed a shameful intimate relationship, but I had so often dreamed fruitlessly of intimate loves that the most desirable of these loves were signified, written, by things that are inanimate when alone and they sing—and sing only of love—as soon as they encounter the beloved, the song, ornaments of secret states of adornment. Paulo took a gun from his pocket and began to take it apart. The fact that he showed so little surprise meant that his mother must have informed him of my presence. She must have seen him when he came in. Erik had stopped talking. He did not look at Paulo. The mother came in by the same door as her son. She said to me, pointing at him:

"This is Paul, Jean's brother."

"Oh! I see."

The boy did not deign to make a movement. He did not say a word to me or even look at me.

"Can't you say hello? It's Monsieur Genet, you know, Jean's friend."

He did deign to stand up and come over to shake hands. I could tell he had recognized me, but he didn't smile at me.

"How goes it?"

He looked deep into my eyes. His face was grim, not because he was tired or out of indifference to my question or to me, but, I think, out of a violent will to exclude me, to drive me out. At that moment, Erik, who had left for twenty seconds, reappeared in the mirror and as he entered while Paulo was staring at me and gripping the weapon with one hand, I was seized with fear, a physical fear, as when one feels the imminence of a brawl. The grimness of that swarthy little face made me feel immediately that I was entering tragedy. Its hardness and sternness meant above all that there could be no hope and that I had to expect the worst. I hardly looked at him, yet I felt him living under very high tension, and on my account. He parted his lips but said nothing. Erik was behind him, ready, I felt, to back him up if, as once happened with a sailor, Paulo said to me, "Come outside," and joined me with a knife in his fist for a fight that would be fatal to me, not because of the blade but because it seemed to me impossible to soften all that hardness. I would have liked the inflexible frame that made Paulo mortally seductive to bend for me. But all I could do was be conscious of his elegant severity, the result of a disheartening failure (for if I can note here this kind of short poem, the reason is that it was not granted me to live a moment of happiness, because a sailor's face in front of me went blank when I asked him for a light). Paulo went to the table and started toying with his gun again. I watched his hands: not a single superfluous gesture. Not one of them, that did not do what it was meant to do. That precision created a disturbing impression of indifference to everything that was not the projected act. The machine could not make an error. I think that Paulo's meanness thus called attention to itself by a kind of inhuman severity. I turned to the mother:

"I'll be going."

"But you'll stay and have dinner with us. You're not going off just like that."

"I've got to go home."

"Is it urgent?"

"Yes, I've got to go home."

"But you'll come again. Come and see us again. Erik will be delighted to see you. All this war and killing is so unfortunate."

The maid was in the entryway. She opened the door for me to leave and looked at me without saying anything. In order to open it, she had to lift up a worn hanging that concealed it, and her hand grazed that of Jean's mother who drew back and said, apropos of so trivial a thing:

"Do watch what you're doing."

She too knew that the father of Juliette's child was not Jean but a former sergeant in the regular army who was now a captain in the Militia.

The maid opened the door. She neither smiled nor said good-bye, and I dared not speak to her about Jean.

I left. Jean had hardly spoken to me about his brother, who had gone off to Germany, then Denmark, and then Germany again. Yet, within me, I followed Paulo's adventures very attentively, waiting, so as to record them, in order for them to take on a particular meaning that would make them interesting, that is, capable of expressing me. My despair over Jean's death is a cruel child. It's Paulo. Let the reader not be surprised if in speaking of him the poet goes so far as to say that his flesh was black, or green with the greenness of night. Paulo's presence had the color of a dangerous liquid. The muscles of his arms and legs were long and smooth. One imagined his joints to be perfectly supple. That suppleness and the length and smoothness of his muscles were the sign of his meanness. I mean by "sign" that there was a connection between his meanness and his visible features. His muscles were elegant and distinguished. So was his meanness. His head was small and was set on a massive neck. The fixity of his gaze, which was worse than that of Erik, was that of an implacable judge, of a soldier, of an officer stupid to the point of sublimity. His face never smiled. His hair was smooth, but the locks overlapped. Or to put it another way, he seemed never to comb his hair but only to slick it down with his wet hands. Of all the little guys I like to stick into my books, he's the meanest. Abandoned on my bed, naked, polished, he will be an instrument of torture, a pair of pincers, a serpentine dagger ready to function, functioning by its evil presence alone and springing up, pale and with clenched teeth, from my despair. He is my despair embodied. He made it possible for me to write this book, just as he granted me the strength to be present at all the ceremonies of memory.

That visit to the home of Jean's mother left me in a state of exhaustion. To restore my peace of mind I had to organize and carry on the lives which I had fractured for a moment and integrate them into mine, but I was too weary to do it then. I had dinner in a restaurant, then went to a movie.

Suddenly the audience burst out laughing when the narrator said: "No, indeed, fighting on the rooftops doesn't fill a man's belly," for a militiaman had just appeared on the screen, a kid of sixteen or seventeen, frailer than Paulo. I said to myself: "He's frailer than Paulo," and this reflection proves that the adventure had got off on the right track. The kid was skinny but good-looking. His face had suffered. It was sad. It was trembling. One would have thought it expressionless. His shirt was open at the neck. There were cartridge loops on his belt. He was walking in socks too big for him. His head was down. I felt he was ashamed of his black eye. In order to look more natural, to deceive the paving stones in the street, he ran his tongue over his lips and made a brief gesture with his hand which was so closely related to that of his mouth that it traced his whole body, puckered it with very subtle waves, and immediately made me think the following:

"The gardener is the loveliest rose in his garden."

The screen was then filled by a single arm, which was fitted with a broad, heavy, very beautiful hand, then by a young French soldier who was shouldering the little traitor's rifle. The audience applauded. Then the militiaman reappeared. His face was trembling (particularly the eyelids and lips) from the cuffs he had received a few feet away from the camera. The audience was laughing, whistling, stamping. Neither the world's laughter nor the inelegance of caricaturists will keep me from recognizing the sorry grandeur of a French militiaman who, during the insurrection of Paris against the German army in August 1944, took to the rooftops with the Germans and for several days fired to the last bullet—or next-to-last—on the French populace that had mounted the barricades.

In the fierce eyes of the crowd, the disarmed, dirty, bewildered, stumbling, dazed, emptied, cowardly (it's amazing how fast certain words flow from the pen to define certain natures and how happy the author feels at being able to talk that way about his heroes), weary kid was ridiculous. A woman in light-colored rayon was thrashing about at my side. She was foaming at the mouth and bouncing her behind on her seat. She yelled:

"The bastards, rip their guts out!"

Confronted with the face of the little traitor (which was luminous just because the film had been shot against the sun), whose youth, caught in a deadly trap, was dazzling the screen, the woman was odious. I thought to myself that little fellows like him were being killed so that Erik might live. The audience was like the woman. It hated evil. My hatred of the militiaman was so intense, so beautiful, that it was equivalent to the strongest love. No doubt it was he who had killed Jean. I desired him. I was suffering so because of Jean's death that I was willing to do anything to forget about him. The best trick I could play on that fierce gang known as destiny, which delegates a kid to do its work, and the best I could play on the kid, would be to invest him with the love I felt for his victim. I implored the little fellow's image:

"I'd like you to have killed him!"

If one of my hands holds the lighted cigarette and the other clutches the armrest, they clasp each other even though they do not move. This gesture gives greater vigor to my wish, which is charged with a will and a forceful summons to transform itself into an invocation.

"Kill him, Riton, I'm giving you Jean."

My only gesture was to put my lighted cigarette to my lips, and my clasped fingers clenched each other to the breaking point. Scented with peril, my prayer rises to my head from the pit of my stomach, spreads beneath the vaulted ceiling of my skull, comes down again, emerges from my mouth, and turns my cry into a wail whose value I recognize—I mean something like musical value—and an "I love you, oh" issues from me. I don't hate Jean. I want to love Riton. (I can't tell why I *spontaneously* call the unknown young militiaman Riton.) I plead again as one crawls on one's knees over flagstones.

"Kill him!"

A frightful rending tore out my fibers. I would have liked my suffering to be greater, to rise to the supreme song, to death itself. It was ghastly. I did not love Riton, all my love was still for Jean. On the screen, the militiaman was waiting. He had just been picked up. What can one do to beauty that's so glaringly obvious? One cuts off its head. That's how the fool takes revenge on a rose he has plucked. The cop dares to say of a young thief he brings back in his clutches:

"I just plucked him on the pavement!"

So don't be surprised that I see Riton as a flower of the mountaintops, a gentle edelweiss. A movement of his arm showed that he was wearing a wristwatch, but the movement was rather feeble, unlike those of Jean. However, it might have been one of Paulo's though more effective. I was going to take off from that idea, and I realized more and more that Riton completed Paulo, but for my work of sorcery I needed perfect attention and had to make use of everything to achieve my end. The audience was whistling and yelling.

"He ought to be torn to bits!"

"Ought to give him another shiner!"

A soldier must have hit the militiaman, for he trembled and seemed to be trying to protect himself. His face clouded over. The beauty of the lily lies similarly in the amazing fragility of the little hood of pollen that trembles at the top of the pistil. A gust of wind, a clumsy finger, a leaf, can break and destroy the delicate equilibrium that holds beauty in balance. That of the child's face wavered a moment. Ruffled as it was, I feared it might not gain its composure. He was haggard. I looked at him closely and more quickly (one can, without taking one's eyes off an object, look very quickly. At that moment, my "gaze" swooped down on the image). In a few seconds he would disappear from the screen. His beauty and his gestures were the opposite of Jean's. I was at once lit up, with an inner light. A bit of love passed over to Riton. I really had the impression that love was flowing from me, from my veins to his. I called out inwardly:

"Riton, Riton, you can kill him, my child! My darling! Kill him!"

He turned his head a little. A colonel in front of me dared to say: "If I get my mitts on him . . ." Riton's gestures were killing Jean's, were killing Jean. Suddenly the people who were yelling and jeering ceased to be ridiculous. They were ugly with grief. The furious colonel and the women in tallow who was mad with rage and crimson under her bleached, yellow locks were being tracked down by the vengeance that compelled them to honor savagely, though with grandeur, by laughter, the death of a brother or son or lover. Nobody was ridiculous. Their invectives were an additional ovation to Riton's glory. The vise in which I was caught tightened. Another image (a marching army) was on the screen. I closed my eyes. A third silent invocation rose up from me and drew me out of myself:

"Bump him off, I'm letting you have him."

Another wave of love surged from my bent, still body slouching in the seat, and poured first on the face and then on the neck, chest, and entire body of Riton, confined in my closed eyes. I squeezed my eyelids tighter. I attached myself to the captive militiaman's body, which was violent despite its weariness. Beneath his debility, he was hard, fierce, and ever new, like a skillfully made machine. My inner gaze remained fixed on the image of him which I reconstructed in its natural violence, hardness, and ferocity. An unbroken flow of love passed from my body to his, which started living again and regained its suppleness.

I added:

"Go ahead. You can pick him off."

This time the very cast of the formula indicated that my will was going into action all by itself, was refusing the help of invocation. I kept my eyes shut. The same rivers of love poured over Riton, yet not a drop was withdrawn from Jean. I was preserving both youngsters under the double ray of my tenderness. The game of murder in which they will engage is rather a war dance in which the death of one of them will be accidental, almost involuntary. It is an orgy carried to bloodshed. I closed my eyes tighter. My gaze was glued to the militiaman's fly, the image of which was within me, and made it live, gave it weight, filled it with a vigorous monster that was swollen with hatred, and my gaze was the beam on which Riton rose up and returned to the rooftops. I loved him. I was going to marry him. It would perhaps be enough for me to be dressed in white, for the wedding, though with a decoration of large black crepe cabbage rosettes at each joint, at the elbows, the knees, the fingers, the ankles, the neck, the waist, the throat, the prick, and the anus. Would Riton accept me dressed that way and in a bedroom decked with irises? For the wedding celebration would then merge with my mourning and all would be saved. Was it necessary that I feel the victor's hardness in my hands? Though he was at the brink of the grave, I knew he was alive. Despite the walls, the streets, the calls, the breathing, the waves, and the automobile headlights, despite his flight to the back of the screen, my mind found him once again. He looked at me. He smiled.

"I killed him, you see. You're not sore at me?"

Had I uttered the words, "You did the right thing," I would have felt so ashamed of myself, of the excessively searing injustice of it all, that I would have rejected the adventure and lost what I'd won in the game. I replied to his image, which was now sharp and almost as firm to my eyes as a muscular body is to one's fingers.

"I gave him to you, Riton. Love him dearly."

I opened my eyes again. The orchestra was playing the national anthem of an ally. A heavier, richer odor was enveloping me. The glands between my thighs and those of my armpits and perhaps my feet had been working intensely. If I so much as stirred, that slightly acrid smell which I had been imprisoning for ten minutes would have escaped and poisoned the audience. I slipped a finger into the opening of my fly; the edges of my thighs were damp with sweat. I had just discovered how and in whose company Erik had spent the first five days of the Paris revolt before being able to shack up with his mistress. Riton will meet Erik, will fight at his side on the rooftops, but he first has to know Paulo. I'm trying to present these characters to you in such a way that you see them lit up by my love, not for their sake but for Jean's, and particularly in such a way that they reflect that love.

*   *   *

PUNY, RIDICULOUS LITTLE fellow that I was, I emitted upon the world a power extracted from the pure, sheer beauty of athletes and hoodlums. For only beauty could have occasioned such an impulse of love as that which, every day for seven years, caused the death of strong and fierce young creatures. Beauty alone warrants such improper things as hearing the music of the spheres, raising the dead, understanding the unhappiness of stones. In the secrecy of my night I took upon myself—the right way of putting it if one bears in mind the homage paid to my body—the beauty of Gérard in particular and then that of all the lads in the Reich: the sailors with a girl's ribbon, the tank crews, the artillerymen, the acres of the Luftwaffe, and the beauty that my love had appropriated was retransmitted by my hands, by my poor puffy, ridiculous face, by my hoarse, spunk-filled mouth to the loveliest armies in the world. Carrying such a charge, which had come from them and returned to them, drunk with themselves and with me, what else could those youngsters do but go out and die? I put my arm around Paulo and turned my body so that we faced each other, and I smiled. I was a man. The text of my stern gaze was inscribed on Paulo. That sternness of gaze corresponded to an inner vision, an amorous preoccupation; it signified attention to a kind of constant desire, in short to covetousness, in accordance with our arrangements straight out of a novel, it indicated that this little fellow never left to itself the living, gesticulating image of its double that stood at the tribune in Nuremberg. Paulo's teeth were clean. My mustache was now near him, and he could see it hair by hair. It was not only a sign—harmless or dangerous—of the pale, nocturnal blazon of a race of pirates, it was a mustache. Paulo was frightened by it. Could it be that a simple mustache composed of black hair—and dyed perhaps—meant: cruelty, despotism, violence, rage, foam, asps, strangulation, death, forced marches, ostentation, prison, daggers?

"Are you scared?"

With his whole inner being trembling, that being which vainly sought by fleeing, to drag along the flesh-and-blood being whose prisoner it was, Paulo replied, with a lump in his throat, "No."

The sonority of the word and the strange sound of his own voice made him more aware of the danger that lies in daring to enter dreams with one's actual flesh and blood, to have a private conversation with the creatures of night—a night of the heart that was poured out over Europe—with the monsters of nightmares. He felt a very slight throbbing at his temples—which I saw—a throbbing as clear as the vibration of crystal, and he yearned for an awakening, that is, for France. Then, the remoteness of France immediately gave him the same feeling of being abandoned that he would have felt had his mother died. Ramparts or rifles, cannons, trenches, electric currents, separated him from the world in which he was loved. Cunning and treacherous radios were lulling his friends to sleep, were denying the rumor of his death, were turning off his appeal, were consoling France for her loss. He felt he was a prisoner, that is, alone with destiny. He was sorry for France, and his sorrow included the following more particular regret: "I won't be able to tell the boys that I saw Hitler," and the inner fluttering that accompanied this regret was the finest tribute, the most touching poem addressed to the Fatherland.

Nevertheless, I smiled. I was awaiting death. I knew it was bound to come, in violent form, at the end of my adventure. For what could I desire in the end? There is no rest from conquest; one enters immortality standing up. I have already considered every possible kind of death, from the death by poison that an intimate friend pours into my coffee to being hanged by my people, crucifixion by my best friends, to say nothing of natural death amidst honors, brass bands, flowers, speeches, and statues, death in combat, by stabbing, bullets, but above all I dream of a disappearance that will astound the world. I shall go off to live quietly on another continent, observing the progress of, and the harm done by, the legend of my reappearance among my people. I have chosen every sort of death. None of them will surprise me. I have already died often, and always in splendor.

I sensed the child's distress, and, despite my delicacy, I could think of nothing to say that would reassure him.

"You're very good-looking," I said.

Paulo smiled wanly, with that extremely weary smile in which the teeth are not even bared. He did not take his eyes off mine, which had grown gentle. The gentleness that he could see in my gaze thrust me deeper into the region of foulness. I was a figure emerging from a silent cave. I seemed unhappy in the open, and it was evident from my attitude that I wanted to go back to my darkness. I think of that lair, the eye of Gabès.

"You're very good-looking," I repeated.

But I felt that the sentence did not have the amorous ring that would shatter the youngster's fear. And my graciousness found the following: I placed my two hands on his eyes, obliging his eyelids to close. I waited ten seconds, then I said, "Are you less afraid?"

I was laughing wildly, and at the same time my left hand was pressing Paulo's shoulder, forcing him to sit down on the bed. I paused to contemplate the folds of his ear, the head part of which was shiny, polished. My laughter widened his smile and made him show his teeth. That wider smile in which the teeth got a breath of air and the light infused a bit of intelligence into Paulo, banished his fear and some of the mortal beauty with which that fear covered up his fate. He was less close to death, less dominated by the rites that the heart devises for the killing, but his body thereby gained a little well-being, a slight relief. Anyway, the first gesture of a man and not of a shadow that he made—laying his cap on the rug—led him a little farther into the light. The deep silence in the room, which was no doubt insulated by cork, reassured him, for the slightest noise, even that of an alarm clock or of water dripping from a tap, would have been suspect to him and have meant invisible, hence supernatural, dangers. I took him by the neck, and our faces were against each other. I kissed him on the corner of his mouth. An anxiety of another order—though brief—came over him: although respect naturally froze him, advised him not to venture any intimate gesture, any caress, or even a too tender abandon, a quivering of the muscles or a contraction that would have brought his thighs close to mine, he wondered whether too tense an attitude might not wound the Master of the World. This thought made his smile, which saddened slightly, close slowly over his teeth and thereby take on the gentleness contained in all sadness. A touch of trust melted him, and he responded to my stroking his hair with an equally gentle caress on my shoulder, which, squeezed by the gabardine tunic, suddenly seemed to him as strong as a counterfort of the Bavarian Alps. Meanwhile he was thinking, word for word:

"But this bimbo's just a little old guy of fifty, after all."

However, he dared not continue the caress or the thought. He withdrew his hand, and this single shy token of kindness magnified my gratitude. I eagerly kissed his throat, temples, and the back of his neck—having made him turn around, with, for the first time, sovereign authority and self-assurance on my part. As we had been sitting on the edge of the bed, this movement left Paulo with his belly on the same edge, his face against the velvet, and his back supporting the German pasha. He found himself in that posture for the first time in his life. No longer supported or directed by my gaze, he was panting with unsatisfied pleasure. Like that of a drowning man, his whole life passed before his eyes. The sacred thought of his mother flashed upon him. But he realized the impropriety of such a posture for meditating upon a mother, father, or love affair. He thought of Paris, of the cafés, of the automobiles. The presence above him was total and tumultuous: his thighs, his legs had their exact burden of thighs and legs. His limbs accepted the domination, they rested in it. His body was compressed by the soft ridge of the bed. In an attempt to disengage himself he made a slight movement that raised his rump, and I responded to the summons with greater pressure. A new pain forced Paulo to repeat his movement, to relieve his stomach, and I shoved harder. He did the same thing again, and I squeezed him tighter. Then sharper and cleaner thrusts unleashed the surge that had been aroused by a misunderstanding. I went at him again ten times, and, though his stomach was being crushed, Paulo stopped. He had a hard-on, and when, a second later, I grabbed his hand and squeezed it tenderly, that big, broad, thick hand became tiny, docile, and quiet and murmured, "Thank you." My hand and I understood that language, for no sooner did I hear the words than I detached myself from the child's back. He had a feeling of relief because his guts had calmed down and were at ease again, but he suffered at being confronted with his regained wholeness, his free and lonely personality, the solitude of which was revealed to him by the detachment of God himself. Then and there he felt a pang that could be translated by the following question, which I ask in his stead: "What can you do now, without Him?"

His anguish was quickly destroyed by amazement. I gave him a push and roughly laid him down on his back. Paulo smiled at my smile. The mustache, the wrinkles, and the lock of hair suddenly took on human proportions, and, by the grace of unequalled generosity, the fabulous emblem of Satan's chosen people descended to inhabit that simple dwelling, the puny body of an old queen, a "faggot."

I was about to—I mean that there was no visible sign of my intention, though the latter had already made me more masterful by describing the movement from beginning to end within me and thus making me feel a lightness that would have enabled me to go backward in time—as I was saying, I was about to jump on the bed, but I immediately checked myself and, very deliberately, I lay down beside Paulo. I had made that brisk movement, which had remained an inner one and which I had and had not controlled, because my soul had meant to put itself on the level of Paulo's and my gestures to be those of someone his age. It was then that, in order to free my buttonholes, I had to turn my body slightly toward Paulo and push up his belly and then that my forelock, which was mysteriously composed of hair, grazed the nose of Paulo, who dared to raise the lock delicately with his fingertip, which had a black, bitten nail. Hitler was resplendent.

It was a rough-and-tumble—or rather a systematic labor—in which I tried in every possible way to return to the larval form by virtue of which one goes back to limbo. Paulo's behind was just a bit hairy. The hairs were blond and curly. I stuck my tongue in and burrowed as far as I could. I was enraptured with the foul smell. My mustache brought back, to my tongue's delight, a little of the muck that sweat and shit formed among Paulo's blond curls. I poked about with my snout, I got stuck in the muck, I even bit—I wanted to tear the muscles of the orifice to shreds and get all the way in, like the rat in the famous torture, like the rats in the Paris sewers which devoured my finest soldiers. And suddenly my breath withdrew, my head rolled and, for a moment, lay still on one buttock as on a white pillow.

I was sure of my strength. Yet I felt that that naked part of me in the room was vulnerable. I was being spied upon from all sides, and the enemy spies might worm their way in through that orifice. The Parisian youngster was doing his job valiantly. At first, he was afraid of hurting the Führer. The essential part of Paulo the torture machine was the penis. It had the perfection of clockwork, of a precision-tooled connecting rod. Its metal was solid, flawless, imperishable, polished by the work and the hard use it was put to: it was a hammer and a miner's bar. It was also without tenderness, without gentleness, without the trembling that often makes even the most violent ones quiver delicately. Paulo was overjoyed to feel the thrill of happiness and to hear the happy moan of Madame. The recognition of the beauty of his work made him proud and more ardent. The Führer was now lingering over it with veneration rather than simple respect. Being the object of such a cult, Paulo's rod was never more beautiful. It quivered with insolence, was set apart for deification, while, at the end of it, Paulo, now shy and simple, watched the ceremony without curiosity and was bored. Finally, Hitler gave it a more devout kiss. Then he put his right arm around it and cuddled it in the hollow, in the fold formed by the inner side of the elbow. Such a gesture would have made anyone other than Paulo let his prick be transformed into a babe in arms to be cuddled. He didn't bat an eyelash. Boredom made him flee the place, but the wheedling movement of my head brought him back. He did not put down his arms. He did not allow his naughty tool to lose any of its hardness, and I remained a poor fellow, a poor abandoned kid whom life sweeps up in a nausea of happiness and sadness.

"He's going to kill me," Paulo thought. "Since he won't be able to accuse me openly, I'll be poisoned. Or shot. They'll give me the works in a hurry, in a garden."

For a moment, hope welled up in Paulo, he had a feeling of confidence, of peace. Then suddenly, because upon turning around to button himself he saw on the wall a photograph of the Führer, who was so like the man whose death rattle he had just heard, with a hop, skip, and jump, fear came from the end of the world and sat on his shoulders. He took a step on the rug. Hitler was behind him, ready to intervene. Paulo was slowly buttoning himself up and waiting. His lips were parted and his eyes staring. He looked at the white porcelain bidet, the wallpaper, the cheap furniture. In the silence he could hear the earth rotating on its axis and revolving about the sun. He was filled with fear. He oozed fear. He was not trembling. From all his pores, traversing the cloth of his mechanic's overalls, seeped a very light but luminous vapor which enveloped his whole body and which he seemed to be emitting (as ships do their artificial fogs at sea) in order to camouflage himself, to disappear. Fear assured him invisibility. In the thickness of light in which he was shrinking to the size of a twig, he felt quite safe. His entire skin was pleating, like an accordion, and if, with a kind of superhuman courage (no doubt impossible amidst those milky and too blindingly bright jitters), he had dared to make the gesture of putting his hand to his fly, he would have seen his prick, which usually stuck such a long way out of his foreskin, withdraw into itself, as on cold days, completely covered by the skin. The piteous thing barely dangled. He walked to the window slowly and lifted the lace curtain where I watched the Seine flow slowly by.

Riton, who was constipated and whose whole digestive system had been upset by fatigue, felt a fart coming. He squeezed his buttocks, he tried to make it flow upward so that it would explode inside him, but his armor was too tight, and for several moments the gases which he was holding in for the sake of decency could no longer be controlled. He farted. This made a muffled and rather brief sound in the darkness, a sound which was quickly checked. The soldiers were behind him, in the room.

"They're Germans," he thought to himself. "Maybe they don't realize."

He hoped so. The soldiers weren't shy in his presence. For three days he had been at war, and close contact revealed that the sternest-looking warriors probably were rotten inside. In spite of their example, he dared not forget himself in their presence, dared not relieve himself openly, but his discomfort was too great that evening. Erik whispered "Sh!" as he rolled his eyes and pointed with his finger to indicate that the darkness could hear the slightest noise. Then he smiled a little. Riton felt his humanity more keenly. He was still in a world where one dared not fart. Death was not with us. The ears of the two friends were full of the crickets of silence. A shot rang out in the distance. Riton trembled. That fatal contraption was surmounted by a very beautiful head of curly hair. Erik recognized and did not recognize the little fellow in the subway. The picture he had of him and the sight of him that evening in battle dress made him compare Riton to an unhappy, newborn snail that he might have first met without its shell. A hermit without the cave in the rocks who is living out his fate. The kid of the subway and of all the encounters had not yet donned his tough-mindedness or parade dress to confront death, glory, and shame. The charming little creature of the past was perhaps a gentler sister of his. We know nothing about the prodigies that transform a passing child who sings and whistles into a delicate instrument of death whose slightest movement, even a frown, the too elegant play of an invisible fan, reveals a will to destruction. Erik had before him what, to a German, is the most amazing creation that there can be: a youngster betraying his country, but a madly courageous and bold little traitor. At that moment, he was on the alert so as to kill like a murderer.

"No, there's nothing," mumbled Riton.

"*Wie?* Nothing? *Nichts?*"

"*Nichts.*"

In order to utter this last word, which he pronounced "Nix," distorting it the way Paris street boys did, Riton turned his head all the way around and smiled. His smile reached Erik, who returned it. The sky above them was studded with stars. The shagginess of Riton's curls gave him an even crueler look, which the smile did not dispel. The darkness was working away on Erik's tired face. It was furrowing the eyebrows and hardening the fleshy parts, which seemed made of stone. It cast the shadow of the nose very low, and from the four-day growth of beard a very soft, blond light flowed. Separated by Riton's machine gun, they looked at each other in silence. The sergeant, who was behind them, approached in his stocking feet. His silence added, for a moment, to that of the other two. He asked Erik softly whether he had noticed anything suspect. There was nothing. He told him to go in, and, taking Riton by the hand, he succeeded in saying, talking to him very slowly: "You . . . should . . . take off . . . the bullets."

Riton tried to explain silently that he wanted to keep his coat of mail on, but the sergeant insisted. Riton turned around so as to go in behind the sergeant, and it was at that moment that his eyes spotted a strange thing which he had not yet noticed, a kind of rag hanging from a window of the house at the left. Leaning forward, he recognized the broad-striped American flag. He hardly thought it was on display, but rather that it was a secret signal. He went in. With infinite care Erik and the sergeant undid his metal bands. As they had just been operating in silence with cautious movements, the three of them had kept their mouths open. They needed a bit of water to moisten their dry palates.

"*Wasser* . . ."

Riton whispered, inverting his thumb above his mouth as if it were a faucet run dry, "*Wasser*, sergeant . . . I'm thirsty . . ."

"No."

"A drink . . ."

"No water . . ."

"In the kitchen?"

The sergeant made a broader grimace as his lips silently formed the word *nicht*, and he moved his forefinger back and forth in front of Riton's face. Riton was about to insist, not understanding why he was being refused water, but the sergeant went to the bedroom. He silently opened the wardrobe, took two armfuls of linen, carried it to the bathroom, where he made a kind of mattress of it in the bathtub, then went back to get Riton, whom he wanted to sleep there. Riton refused. A touch of pride bade him do so, as did the respect for German hierarchy which he had already acquired after two days of life in common with the Fritzes. The sergeant insisted.

"You are very little . . . very young."

In the darkness, clinging to the sergeant's arm so as to put his mouth against the other's ear, the kid tried to sound firm.

"No, sergeant," he whispered, "me a private, you a noncom."

And he added, beating his chest with broad silent slaps, "Me strong, me hefty."

But though the sergeant was worried for a few seconds about allowing him to be at liberty among the weapons (his plan was to lock him in the bathroom), he remembered how devoted Riton had been on the Rue de Belleville, and that reassured him. Finally, his own fatigue made him want the little bed he had just prepared in the bathtub. He went back to the dining room, again very quietly, to shut the windows. Riton looked for a glass in the darkness, found one on the shelf above the washbowl, and turned on the faucet. There was no water. He finally realized why the sergeant had refused. In desperation, fuming like a kid who feels his thirst more acutely, he went back to the dining room. The sergeant had already had time to mumble in German to Erik, who was sitting in a chair with his elbows on his knees and his head in his hand, "I'm leaving you with the Frenchman. So keep your eyes open."

He shook hands with Riton and went quietly back to the bathroom. For a few seconds the kid remained standing silently beside the table. Erik, who was at the back of the room, saw him outlined against the light background of the window. Disencumbered of his metal garment and his weapon, Riton realized how tired he was. Everything drained out of him at the same time—his pride, his shame, his hatred, his despair. All that remained was a poor, exhausted child's body overcome with weariness, and a mind disintegrating with fatigue. With minute attention to his movements, he moved forward to Erik's chair. He groped for a few seconds, grazed the hair, the collar, the shoulder. When he recognized the feel of the German insignia, he felt a discharge in his arm, in his shoulder, in his entire body. The monstrousness of his situation was more keenly apparent to him in the deep darkness. He was the prey of the insignia which, when he was a kid of twelve just before the war, had been the mark of the devil. No movement of withdrawal betrayed his anguish. At the first touch of a hand on his hair, Erik started as he recognized the little militiaman. He waited without moving so as to know the boy's intention. The hand seeking in the darkness found one of Erik's and squeezed it. As Riton bent forward until his breath lightly stroked the Fritz's neck, he murmured with a gentleness that more and more became his tone of voice, "*Gute Nacht*, Erik."

"*Gute Nacht*, good night, Riton."

'Good night.'

With the same caution Riton moved back to the window and lay down on the rug very quietly with his hands clasped behind his head. A very slight excitement had swollen his prick when he was next to Erik, but no sooner did he stretch out than he felt only the bliss of being in that position. Peace had entered him, and in order to prolong the enjoyment of it he kept his eyes open in the darkness and refused to fall asleep. His limbs and outstretched body grew heavier with fatigue; his bulk lay heavy on the rug, which was becoming the very stuff of his life, for the entire day had been one long fall. The feeling of certainty of his presence assembled his body from all parts of the horizon, sent out a call to arms toward an ideal point in the middle of himself by carrying to it, on a blissful surge, from the outermost tips of his fingers and toes to that imprecise point of the body (it is not the heart) where the lines of force converged, a message of peace and orderliness of the limbs, of the extremities, of the head itself. In exchange, that certainty of presence relieved the limbs of their function; it discharged them of all responsibility. Only his presence was awake, his muscles no longer existed. The goal of that day, to stretch out on the rug, had just been attained. That makeshift berth was more restful to the boy than a soft bed would have been. He felt secure in it. Every point of his body found a reassuring support in it. And also, the silence, the darkness, and the presence of the sleeping Erik, who was mightier by virtue of his sleep, protected his rest by thick walls, behind which, unfortunately, was enclosed, without anyone's being able to drive it away, a frightful anxiety: who was the tenant of that empty dwelling at the top of a house that was mined with the presence, on every floor, of hate-ridden Frenchmen bent on the greatest evil, who would blow up or set fire to the building in order to kill the pack of Boches, the swarm of wasps clinging to its summit? They wouldn't get out of the scrap unscathed. The only refuge was his trust in Erik. The breadth and strength of the dark chest, the hair of which Riton had seen through the opening of the shirt, was apparent to his mind's eye. Riton also hoped, for the space of one brief reverie, that all the tenants would be Germanophiles and that the flag at the window was there only to put people off. He even hoped that they would be decent and would not denounce him to the insurgents. He dared imagine that they had a greatness of soul larger than life. But no sooner did these hopes light up than they went out.

"No crap about it, we're done for. If we don't get the works tomorrow, we'll get it the next day."

Twenty seconds later, Erik, who was too uncomfortable in his chair, silently lay down beside Riton. Erik was dropping with sleep. As he bent down to lie at the right of the kid, over whose body he had just stepped, the leather of his new belt creaked slightly.

"Pretty supple," thought Riton, not knowing whether he was thinking the word about the leather or the athlete's torso. The creaking, which evoked muscular strength, the power of lithe and sturdy haunches, the perfect play of the joints, both reassured and disturbed him. Erik stretched out and turned slightly on to his right side because his pistol was in the holster on the left and would have been in the way, but he kept his legs straight and parallel. He was in his stocking feet. His right arm was pinned down, was being crushed on the floor by his body, and his left hand became aware, in his half-sleep, of its strength as it stroked his terrifying neck, which it circled, as if to polish it, though it was careful to be aware of what it was doing and remained conscious of that muscular neck beneath its palm and took pleasure in the back of it. It stroked his hardened face, which was softened by his blond beard. Then it returned and laid itself on his chest, where it remained, spread flat, with a few fingertips in the opening of the jacket and shirt touching his skin and golden hairs. Two fingers inspected the quality of the granite of that cellar flagstone. Erik, soothed by the slight contact with his body, fell into a deep sleep.

He could die the next day since he had acknowledged his beauty that evening. He hardly realized that he had turned to Riton, and it was in the position which I have just described that he fell asleep almost immediately. In the darkness, some blond hairs on the top of his raised toes caused the black waves of sleep and silence to break over the dead soldier. The bodies of the two boys were touching. Riton, lying on his back, was on Erik's shore. If he had a dizzy spell, he would fall into him and drown in the deep eddies that he sensed were rolling from the chest to the thighs, which were the more mysterious for being alive beneath that funereal cloth which also concealed a paraphernalia (such as is no doubt hidden behind a black curtain in special houses) of straps, belts, steel buckles, teamster's whips, boots, which the sound of the leather had conjured up, thighs, whose strength derived from a fascination with death. He lay still on his back, looking straight ahead at the far end of the room whose darkness his eyes were getting used to. He was seized with fright, for he was unable to see anything of Erik, though his whole body registered the other's presence. He stiffened with anxiety. Had he been lying on his right side, that is, with his back to the soldier and not grazed by him, it would not have been the same (his curled-up position would have made it possible for him to keep his usual Erik within himself). Had he lain on his back, he would have seen him in detail and been able at the same time to remain deep within himself, but apart from the fact that the power of that presence was too great for him not to be excited by it, his position left him exposed, defenseless, before the driving waves that rolled up to him from Erik's body and thrilled him to the point of dizziness. He got a hard-on. Not with a sudden swiftness, but slowly. It started the moment when he was most deeply conscious of his anxiety, that is, when Erik, whose clothes touched his, lay quite still. Then when the first thrill, the first thrust of extreme violence shook him, he became aware of his desire. A half-hour went by before Riton came to a decision or began the first movement, though his face had turned to Erik's. Suddenly the true meaning of his treason became apparent to him. If French rifles had been aiming at him for days, it was in order to prevent him from isolating himself at the top of the rock which all eyes had seen him climb to with that extraordinary mountaineer.

"So what?"

He was in love with a man. He quivered with pleasure at the thought of being so near the goal.

"I love him mad . . ."

Even in thought he did not complete the word "madly." The passion, born in the words "I love him," continued, increasing with wild speed and leaving him breathless halfway through that dizzying word which ended with the very shudder that quickened the beginning of it, shaking Riton's whole body as he mused, for the first time, but then greedily, with a kind of despair, on Erik's organ. He was too excited to imagine it precisely. The swollen crotch of the dark trousers was all he saw. Then he suddenly feared that Erik might know what he was thinking and be revolted at such a thought, but almost immediately his pride in his beauty restored his confidence.

"Since there're no girls around, maybe I'll be doing him a favor. He could find worse-looking guys than me."

By that thought alone he was bestowing his body on the soldier. He realized it, and, sweetly, naïvely too, he was willing to assume any posture to please him. Suddenly, he thought of the danger of such an adventure: he was afraid that all the soldiers might want to go down on him. They were German, squareheads, rough-hewn, and he, the youngest and weakest, alone and French.

He tried to conjure up Erik's prick more precisely. He imagined it huge and heavy in his closed hand. He made a slight movement to extend his arm, but he left his hand lying on his thigh. This venturing of a first gesture took his breath away. Behind the simple door that one opens perhaps there awakes a dragon whose body coils round itself several times. If you look a dog in the eye too intently, it may recite an astounding poem to you. You might have been mad for a long time and have realized it only at that moment. Is there perhaps a snake in the bag hanging from the coatrack? Beware. From the slightest patch of shadow, from a spot of darkness, there rise up prowlers armed to the teeth who tie you up and carry you off. Riton waited a bit in order to catch his breath. Erik's whole body from head to foot was lying against his. The fact that his love had been revealed to him at the moment of its greatest danger imparted such great strength that Riton felt he was brawny enough to crush dragons. The peril lay not in death but in love. He had the wit to feign sleep. He breathed noisily. The thought of Erik's prick became obsessive, and, with tears at the rims of his eyes, he wanted to extend his left hand, but, before making the movement, he realized, while executing it mentally, that it would be difficult for him to open the fly. He turned a bit on his left side.

"The fly, that's all I needed!"

So what! What did reproval of that love matter to Riton since he would be dead the following day, and what did life matter since he loved Erik! Very skillfully he pretended to be shifting in his sleep and put his right foot, on which was a soft, gray sock, across Erik's foot. He made the gesture very naturally, without any fear, but he felt it was the first phase of an embrace that could tighten to closest intimacy, when, with bated breath, he stretched out his right hand and laid it, hardly touching, on Eric's thigh.

"If he realizes, there'll be hell to pay!"

So what? We'll be killed tomorrow! A day of torture would be nothing. He pressed down with his hand gently, then a little harder. Unable to see the spot, he tried to figure out where it was. On the basis of the folds of the cloth and his own position he thought it was the middle of the thigh. If Erik woke up at that moment, he might think that sleep alone was responsible. Mad with fear and boldness, he moved lightly over the cloth, or rather he flew over the area. Erik slept on.

"You don't get a hard-on when you're asleep."

The hand moved upward with the same delicacy. It reached the fly and recognized it. Riton had difficulty breathing. The treasure was found. His light, fearful hand remained as if suspended for a moment. Not a sound in the room. He heard another shot, far away.

"It's fighting on the Rue de Buenos Aires," he thought. 'It's a hell of a way off." His hand assumed greater authority and it was blessing or was on the lookout for the next below. The hearts of the seven German soldiers must have been beating. Riton would surely be killed the next day, but before that he would bump off quite a lot of Frenchmen. He was in love.

"Those damn jerks. What the hell are they to me, they're just a bunch of idiots. I'm going to bump a few of them off . . ."

With, as it happens, that same right hand. He made the movement, despite himself, of pulling a trigger with his forefinger. His pinky struck the cloth—to have done so was to knock at the door of darkness and see that darkness open onto death, and it was with a closed fist that he remained there, first making its pressure light and then gradually letting it sink by its own weight into the moss.

The building was doomed. A face, a destiny, a boy, are said to be doomed. A sign of misfortune must have been inscribed somewhere, an invisible sign, for perhaps it was at the bottom of a door in the left corner, or on a window pane, or in the twitching of a tenant. Perhaps it was an object that at first sight was harmless—that a second look does not enable you to detect—it was a spider's web on the chandelier (there was a chandelier in the living room) or the chandelier itself. The house smelled of death. It was drifting toward an abyss. If that's what death is, it's sweet. Riton no longer belonged to anyone, not even to Erik. The fingers of his hand spread like the folioles of a sensitive plant in the sun. His hand was resting. He had placed his head under his left arm, and the graciousness of that posture was entering his soul. He had not killed enough Frenchmen, that is, not paid dearly enough for that moment. If the house blows up, that means it is thoroughly mined. If it burns, love is what fires it. With infinite delicacy Riton took his handkerchief from his pocket, wet it silently with saliva, and slipped it through his fly and between his legs, which were slightly drawn up so that he could clean his "bronze eye" properly.

"You think he'll stick it up me? Oh well, you never know." He wanted less to be ready for the act than to be ready for love. He rubbed a little, then took out the handkerchief so as to wet it again, happy to smell beneath his nostrils and on his lips the odor of sweat and shit. This discreet and careful grooming enchanted him.

Around the building and in the building itself, which was being undermined by mysterious insects, the nation was busying itself, as he would have desired. Multicolored paper garlands were being nailed to windows, flowers were being hooked onto electric wires, streamers and lanterns were being strung from window to window, cloth was being dyed in the darkness, women were sewing flags, children were preparing powder and bullets for the salvos. People were building up around the apartment a catafalque that was caught in the childish combinations of tricolored ribbons with more complicated intertwining than the arabesques of bindings which are called "fanfares." In the darkness, half of Paris was silently constructing the new funeral pyre of the seven males and the kid. The other half was on the lookout.

His hand opened. A harder fold made Riton think he was touching the prick. His chest collapsed. "If he's got a hard-on, it means he's not sleeping. In that case, I'm in the shit."

He decided to let his hand play dead. Its being there was no small joy, but the fingers had a life of their own and kept seeking, despite the rough cloth and the stiff edge of the fly where the buttons were. Finally they felt a warm, soft mass. Riton parted his lips. He stayed that way for a few seconds, straining his mind so as to be fully aware of his joy.

"He's got an octopus there between his legs."

"I'll just stay this way."

But the fingers wanted full particulars. They very delicately tried to distinguish the various parts of that mass whose abandon in his hands gratified him. All of Erik's power was contained in that little heap, which, though quiet and trusting, radiated despite its death. And all the might of Germany was contained in those sacred and peaceful though heavy and sleeping repositories which were capable of the most dangerous awakenings. They were watchful repositories which millions of soldiers carried preciously in freezing and scorching regions in order to impose themselves by rape. With the skill of a lacemaker, the hand above the dark cloth was able to sort out the confusion of the treasure which lay there all jumbled up. I prejudged its splendor in action and imprisoned it, sleeping little girl that it was, in my big ogre's paw. I was protecting her. I weighed her in my hand and thought, "There's hidden treasure in there." My cock stiffened out of pure friendliness. I was worthy of her. My fingers squeezed her a little more, with greater tenderness. They stroked her again. A slight movement of Erik's leg disturbed his immobility. I was filled with terrible fear, then immediately with hope, but first with fear. A mass of cries of fear rising from my belly tried to force open my throat and mouth, where my strong, clenched teeth were on the alert. Finding no outlets, those cries punctured my neck, which suddenly let flow the twenty white streams of my fear through twenty purple ulcers in the shape of roses and carnations. I kept the prick in my hand. If Erik awoke, I would take my chance. I even hoped he would. I squeezed a bit harder, and as soon as I did, I was astounded to feel the Fritz's cock swell between my fingers, harden, and quickly fill my hand. I stopped moving, but I left my hand there dead and dancing. Since my stroking had just given Erik such a violent hard-on, he was awake, and he did not rebel. I waited wonderful seconds, and it's amazing that there was not born of that waiting, from the moment that begins with the prick's awakening to happiness, the most fabulous of heroes, as Chrysaor sprang from the blood of Medusa, or new rivers, valleys, chimeras, in a leap on a bed of violets, hope itself in a white silk doublet with a feathered cap, a royal breast, a necklace of golden thorns, or tongues of flame, a new gospel, an aurora borealis over London or Frisco, a perfect sonata, or amazing that death itself did not make a fulgurant appearance between the two lovers. My hand squeezed the cock a second time; it seemed monstrously big.

"If he sticks the whole caboodle up my cornhole he'll wreck the works."

I squeezed a little harder. Erik did not stir, but I was sure he wasn't sleeping, because the regular sound of his breathing had stopped. Then I ventured a stroke over the cloth, and then another, and each time my gesture was more precise. Erik didn't make a move, he didn't say a word. Hope filled me with a boldness that amazed even me. I slipped the tip of my forefinger into one of the little interstices between the buttons. Erik was wearing neither jockey shorts nor boxer shorts. My finger first felt the hairs. It moved over them, then over the cock, which was as hard as wood, but alive. The contact thrilled me. In the state of ecstasy there is also an element of fear with respect to the divinity or his angels. The prick I was touching with my finger was not only my lover's but also that of a warrior, of the most brutal, most formidable of warriors, of the lord of war, of the demon, of the exterminating angel. I was committing a sacrilege and was conscious of it. That prick was also the angel's weapon, his dart, a part of those terrible devices with which he is armed. It was his secret weapon, the V-I on which the Führer relies. It was the ultimate and major treasure of the Germans. The prick was fiery. I wanted to stroke it, but my finger was not free enough. I feared lest my nail hurt it if I pressed. Erik had not moved. In order to make me think he was sleeping, he resumed his regular breathing. Motionless at the center of a state of perfect lucidity—so extraordinary that he feared for a moment lest the purity of his vision radiate outside him and illuminate Riton—he let the kid alone and was amused by his playing. I withdrew my finger and very skillfully succeeded in undoing two buttons. This time I put my whole hand in. I squeezed, and Erik recognized, I don't know how, that I was squeezing tenderly. He didn't stir.

The moon was veiled. Barefoot, I first walked on tiptoe, then I ran, I went up steps, I scaled houses so as to reach the most dangerous crossroad of the Albaïcin. Everybody in Granada was asleep. The few Gypsies who were prowling about in the darkness could not catch a glimpse of me. I was still swept up in my course, but as there was no way out of the square my movement continued in a silent whirl, on tiptoe. I felt, however, that a Gypsy had just awakened: ten houses away perhaps, beneath a porch. His big sleeping body had stirred in the brown woolen blanket. He was crawling. He grazed walls, went through alleys, stood up, walked over to meet me, finally leaped into the darkness. We were alone on the square. The moon was still veiled, but very thinly so. The Gypsy seized me by the waist, broke me, tossed me up, and then caught me smoothly and silently in his arms. The embroidery and white lace of my petticoats whirled in the darkness. With a flip of his cock the Gypsy tossed me up into the sky. From the whole land of Andalusia, from every ornament, from every lock there welled up a music that caressed me. It all took place in the morning. A few streaks of dawn kept watch on the hills. Their blue songs were still sleeping rolled up in the throats of the herdsmen. I fell astride the Gypsy's prick. The flounces of my skirts spread over the countryside like moss. It was April, and the moon lit up a vast stretch of flowering almond trees around Granada.

Anyway, completely reassured by Erik's immobility, I jerked him off quickly.

He was no doubt thinking of that girl's head which surmounted the strong and delicate body that held a tunic of bullets suspended over the frightened city. He beguiled the time by reconstructing her face in his imagination. The greatest happiness was granted him, since it was the kid himself who answered his secret call and came running up to impale himself. The old hallucination of my childhood obtruded itself, and I can render it only by the following image: *still rivers that do not mingle*, though they have a single source, rush into his mouth, which they spread and fill. One of the soldiers made a slight noise. Fearing that Riton might remove his hand, Erik took hold of it, pressed it down, and made it stay. There was another noise. They waited a moment.

I have killed, pillaged, stolen, betrayed. What glory I've attained! But let no run-of-the-mill murderer, thief, or traitor take advantage of my reasons. I have gone to too great pains to win them. They are valid only for me. That justification cannot be used by every Tom, Dick, and Harry. I don't like people who have no conscience.

The Führer sent his finest-looking men to death. It was his only way to possess them all. How often I have wanted to kill those handsome boys who annoyed me because I didn't have enough cocks to ream them all at one time, not enough sperm to cram them with! A pistol shot would, I feel, have calmed my desire-ridden, jealousy-ridden heart and body. Germany was a fiery stake that had been set up for Riton, a stake more beautiful than one of flames, cloth and paper. In fits and snatches, without regularity, the flames, embers, and brands were earning their living and their death, were biting, here and there, were menacing Hitler. A very slight displacement—ridding it of irony by means of words—is sufficient for humor to reveal the tragedy and beauty of a fact or of a soul. The poet is tempted by the game. Before the war, cartoonists caricatured Hitler as a Maid with clownish features and a movie comedian's mustache. "He hears voices," said the captions... Did the cartoonists feel that Hitler was Joan of Arc? They had been aware of the resemblance, and they noted it. Thus, the starting point of the features they gave him was that great similarity, since they had thought of it, whether clearly or confusedly, in making their drawings and comments. I regard that recognition as more of a tribute than a mockery. Their irony was the laughter you force for its arrow in order to puncture the agitation that would make you weep in certain moments of overpowering emotion. Hitler will perish by fire if he has identified himself with Germany, as his enemies recognize. He has a bleeding wound at the same level as Joan's on her prisoner's robe.

Like all the other boys of the Reich, Erik's face had retained something of the spatters of a royal sperm—a kind of shame, of deflowering, and at the same time a luster both bright and cloudy (like that of the pearl), precious and triumphant, opaline, the memory of which I thought I discerned in the beads of sweat on his forehead, which I took for tears of transparent sperm. No doubt it was owing to Nazism that Erik wore that thin veil of shame and light, but the executioner once actually did discharge in his face, and Erik was already overcome with dizziness and was sinking into the idea whose pressure was drowning him:

"He's darkening my sky!"

We were in bed. At the sight of the jet a very brief admiration coursed through him, perhaps with a bit of fear in regard to me whose oak, instead of being struck by lightning, issued the lightning, but when the drops which were still warm, touched his cheek and torso, I saw a gleam of hatred in his eyes.

The usual image appeared in the Führer's eyes: a fancy, white cradle. But at the very moment that he saw the lace and the muslin puffs, he noticed, around the pillow and covering it, the garland of white roses and ivy with which it had been adorned, since it contained a dead child. Hitler stood up. He wiped his fingers on his handkerchief. As always when he finished playing, he thought of his executioner, who must not be confused with the criminal executioner, the headsman, for we are referring to his private executioner, a killer with a revolver. It was by this male, who was, in short, the natural excrescence of a cruel animal, the poison gland and the dart, that he had had most of his victims executed—whether political victims or others—but every time that he had dealings with him, and even more often, he thought with anguish that there perhaps existed a list or a notebook with baffling information which this killer, in order to kill time, kept up-to-date.

After buttoning his fly, the Führer went to the conference room, where the generals, the admiral, and the cabinet ministers were waiting for him. Hitler's gracious and simple life was going to unleash terrible acts on the world, acts that would give rise to the most prodigious flowering of nightmares that a man has ever generated all by himself. High dignitaries, very noble ones, whose heads and shoulders were covered with gold, surrounded him, preserved him as priests preserve the gold of a relic. Hitler had secrets. Master magician that he was, he could float on carpets through several rooms whose walls were pierced by holes for the barrels of rifles.

"I'm just an old fossil," he thought, on his way back from the conference. He felt himself being a dusty fossil. Lovemaking had drained him. He dared not wipe his nose or even put a finger into it. Am I quite sure I *command* the world?

Riton will not kill himself . . . unless . . . We shall see. I am keen on his continuing until the last fraction of a second, by destruction, murder—in short, evil according to you—to exhaust, and for an ever greater exaltation—which means elevation—the social being or gangue from which the most glittering diamond will emerge; solitude, or saintliness, which is also to say the unverifiable, sparkling, unbearable play of his freedom. To anyone who may point out that Riton is not alone since he is in love, I wish to say that were it not for that love he would not have gone freely to the very top. It was necessity itself that made the militiamen—and especially our militiaman—fire on Frenchmen, but the only thing that counts is this: solitude being given and accepted. Rejection of it when it is inevitable is despair, a sin which is in conflict, I believe, with the second theological virtue. In any case, I am writing this book and proposing these things, and I climb limpingly and often tumble on my way up to my rock of solitude when, along with my eroticism, my friendship for the purest and most upright of adolescents, a saint according to men, conjures up the image of a haloed traitor. It is under the sway of the still-young death of Jean, red with that death and with the emblem of his party, that I am writing this book. The flowers that I wanted to be in profusion on his little grave which was lost in the fog are perhaps not faded, and I already recognize that the most important character glorified by the account of my grief and of my love for him will be that luminous monster who is exposed to the most splendid solitude, the one in whose presence I experience a kind of ecstacy *because* he discharged a burst of machine-gun fire into his body.

Riton continued his unhappy destiny which will never bring him out of a frightful misery contained in a very beautiful vase. When he joined up, he was still good-looking, and yet his life was ugly. Bear in mind that, weary, sweating, and livid, he took down the cat and put it into a canvas bag, which he closed; then, with all his might, he hammered away at that grotesque, mysterious, and plaintive mass. The cat was still alive. When Riton assumed that the head was smashed, he removed the still quivering animal. Finally, he attached it to the nail in the wall that I mentioned earlier and cut it up. The work took a long time. Hunger, which had disappeared for a moment, returned to Riton's stomach. The cat was still warm and steaming when he cut off the two legs and boiled them in a pot. With the mutilated remains before him, the skin of which was turned inside out like a glove and covered with blood, he ate a few pieces which were almost raw, and which were insipid, for he had no salt, and ever since that day Riton has been aware of the presence within him of a feline that marks his body and, to be more precise, his stomach, like the gold-embroidered animals on the gowns of ladies of former times. Either because the tom was sick, or had become sick—and had gone almost mad—as it was being tortured, or because its meat had not yet cooled, or also because the battle had unsettled the kid, Riton had pains during the night in his stomach and head. He thought he had been poisoned, and he offered up ardent prayers to the cat. The next day he joined the Militia. It pleases me to know that he is marked thus, in his in most flesh, with the royal seal of hunger. His movements were so nimble and sometimes so nonchalant that he himself thought occasionally that he was actuated by the cat he carried within him, and was already carrying when Erik met him. Later, Erik will confess to me that in Berlin the dogs growled at him when he was in a state of restrained or manifest anger.

"Dogs come sniffing at me. They jump all around me and try to bite me."

If, because of his anger, Erik became as disturbing an animal to dogs as the hedgehog or toad, the cat's presence in Riton could make him think he had been transformed, deformed, that he exuded a feline smell.

"The guy," he thought, when he felt Erik's chest against his back, "the guy must realize . . . His eyes were so bright that they looked black."

The funeral procession continued on its way. When it reached the open grave, the priest said a few more prayers, and the choirboys made the responses. Then the grave diggers lowered the little coffin. The hole was filled quickly. The hearse left with the priest. The choirboys withdrew a bit and sat down in the grass behind a granite vault to eat a ham sandwich. The only ones who stayed on were the two grave diggers and the little maid. She stood for a moment facing the grave in the same posture as the warbler when it remains suspended in midair, supported by the rapid flutter of its wings, with its body motionless in the strange flight that immobilizes it on a level with the branch and facing the nest where its young are chirping away as it watches them. A great tenderness startles it. "It could be caught by a bird of prey." Thus thought the little maid. She was flying. She was teaching to fly. A quivering prayer shook her soul and transported her "on the wings of prayer," as they say. She was sweetly advising her daughter to be bold, was calling her to the edge of the nest. She broke up the movements of her wings, thus giving the dead child the first lesson. Then she took off her hat, laid it on the ground, and sat down on the tombstone next to the grave. As she was not crying, the grave diggers did not think that she was the mother. One of them said:

"It's pretty hot even for July, eh? You'd think we were in Algeria."

He had turned naïvely to his fellow worker, but his tone of voice indicated that he was addressing the maid. With both hands in his pockets and his chest thrown back, he stamped with his heel, which clacked on the dry earth.

"It sure is warm," said the other. And he winked at his colleague in such a way that one would have thought he had just uttered a remark charged with weighty implications.

"What we need now is rain. It's hot enough for vegetables."

"And us, we need wine, don't you think?"

They both roared with laughter, and the one who had spoken first, a tall, brown-haired chap of about thirty with rolled shirt sleeves, laughing eyes, and flashing teeth, pushed away the star-shaped wreath that was lying on the tombstone and sat down beside the maid.

"You look tired, girly."

She seemed to be smiling, since fatigue made her grimace. Unlike Paulo, who was always grim, Riton was smiling. His was a joyous nature. When he made gestures such as getting on a bicycle and driving off fast with his body bent over the handlebars, or leaning against a railing, or watching girls in a casual way, or hitching up his trousers, men in the street would look at him with astonishment. And when he knew he was being observed, he would smile good-humoredly. With a smile on his face, he would accentuate the pose and thus succeed in being all coquetry. But let us go back to the maid. This book is true and it's bunk. I shall publish it so that it may serve Jean's glory, but which Jean? Like a silk flag armed with a golden eagle crowning darkness, I brandish above my head the death of a hero. Tears have stopped flowing from my eyes. In fact, I see my former grief behind a mirror in which my heart cannot be deeply wounded, even though it is moved. But it's a good thing that my sorrow, after having been so pitiful, triumphs in great state. May it enable me to write a cruel and beautiful story in which I keep torturing the mother of Jean's daughter.

Every grimace, if observed minutely, proves to be composed of a host of smiles, just as the color of certain painted faces contains a host of shades, and it was one of those puckers that the grave diggers saw. The maid did not answer. A kind of murmur continued inside her, though thought was foreign to her: that her foot hurt, and that Madame was, at that very moment, clearing the table.

"You can see she's sad," said the other man.

"Not at all, death's never serious, young lady. We see it every day."

He put his grimy, though broad and shapely, hand on the maid's knees, which were covered by the black dress. She was paralyzed with such indifference that she would have let her throat be slit without thinking of any reproach but the following:

"Well, well, so my time has come."

The man grew bolder. He put his arm around her waist. She made no movement to shake him off. In view of what seemed to be willingness on her part, the second grave digger regretted not being in on the fun, and he sat down on the stone on the other side of the maid.

"Ah, she's a very nice little girl," he said laughingly. And he put his arm around the maid's neck and pulled her to him, against his chest. No doubt an entreaty arose within her, but she found no word to formulate it. The sudden boldness of his mate excited the first fellow, who leaned over and kissed her on the cheek. Both men laughed, grew still bolder, and kept pawing her. Beside her little daughter's fresh grave, she allowed them to mistreat her, to open her dress, to stroke and fondle her poor indifferent pussy. Grief made her insensitive to everything, to her grief itself. She saw herself at the end of her rope, that is, on the point of flying away from the earth once and for all. And that grief which transcended itself was due not only to her daughter's death, it was the sum of all her miseries as a woman and her miseries as a housemaid, of all the human miseries that overwhelmed her that day because a ceremony, which, moreover, was meant to do so, had extracted all those miseries from her person in which they were scattered. The magical ceremony, which lies in polarizing around its paraphernalia all the reasons one has for being in mourning, was now delivering her up to death. She thought a little about her daughter and a little about her wretched lot. The men's hands met under her dress. They were laughing very loudly, and often their laughter was carved by a kind of death rattle, when desire was too great. But they did not particularly want to screw her. Rather, they were playing with her as with a docile animal, and in their play, in order to complete it, they placed on her head the wreath of glass beads which the tall one pushed down with a tap of his fist, while his friend, with another tap, knocked it down over her ear, where it remained until that evening, at the cocky angle at which militiamen and sailors sometimes wear their berets, pimps their caps, and Fritzes their black forage caps.

Flowers amaze me because of the glamour with which I invest them in grave matters and, particularly, in grief over death. I do not think they symbolize anything. If I wanted to cover Jean's coffin with flowers, it was perhaps simply as a gesture of adoration, for flowers are what one can offer the dead without danger, and if the practice did not already exist, a poet could invent this offering. The lavishing of flowers gives me a little rest from my grief. Though the youngster has now been dead for some time, the notes on which I base this book—which is meant to be a tribute to his glory—bring back the sadness of the early days, but the memory of flowers is sweet to me. As soon as I left the icy amphitheater, when I no longer saw his pale, narrow, terrifying face with the bands around it and his body with other linen, but in their stead the embellished, stylized, perfumed, and moving image of that spectacle, no sooner did I feel amazed and indignant at the wretched dryness and poverty of those remains, and suffer thereby, when I saw them and then wanted them to be covered with flowers. With my eyes still full of tears, I rushed to the nearest florist and ordered huge bouquets.

"They'll be delivered tomorrow," I thought, feeling calmer, "and they'll be laid all around his body and face."

The memory of those funeral flowers, furnishing a helmet for the soldiers who flee amidst the laughter of girls, cluttering the amphitheater, gives shape to the most beautiful expression of my love. If they adorn Jean, they will always adorn him in my mind. They bear witness to my tenderness, which made them spring from Erik's splendid whang. Dawn was breaking, what a dawn that haloed whang breaking out of the hoodlum's pants was, what a gloomy dawn!

I have no right to be joyful. Laughter desecrates my suffering. Beauty takes my mind off Jean, to whom the sight of vileness brings me back. Is it true that evil has intimate relations with death and that it is with the intention of fathoming the secrets of death that I ponder so intently the secrets of evil? But all these evils do not help me reason. Let us try in another key: is it possible, to begin with, if my grief diminishes when I contemplate evil (which I am willing, for the moment, to call evil according to conventional morality) that it does so because the distance is less great between this world which is decomposed by evil and Jean who is decomposed by death? Beauty, which is organization that has attained the height of perfection, turns me away from Jean. Better a fine living creature than a fine object, and my suffering increases. And I weep if I do not bind Jean to this world in which beauty lives.

Yet, though I take pleasure in the sight of so many ugly things which I make even uglier by writing about them, in that which Jean's death inspires me to write, there is an order to do no evil. Is it because life orders me to set off a death with a life, that is, with good (a word also employed in its usual sense), to balance death with life? But if I delight in examining evil and dead or dying things, how could I be implementing life? And as for the homage which I think I am rendering Jean when I grieve, when I weep, isn't it because I bring my state a little nearer his, because everything within me grows desolate and his solitude less great, a solitude that death accords with a suddenness that may chill the dead person's heart? That world without gaiety or beauty which I draw from myself slowly with the intention of organizing it as a poem that I offer to Jean's memory, that world lived within me, in a sunless, skyless, starless landscape. It does not date from today. My deep disgust and sadness have been wanting to express themselves for a long time, and Jean's death has finally given my bitterness a chance to flow out. Jean's death has made it possible for me, by virtue of the words that enable me to talk about it, to become more sharply aware of my shame about the following error: my thinking that the realms of evil were fewer than those of good and that I would be alone there. A few pages hence, Jean's death will continue to confront me with relations that seem to exist between, on the one hand, evil and death and, on the other, life and good. We know the command contained in my grief: do what is good. My taste for solitude impelled me to seek the most virgin lands. After my disappointing setback in sight of the fabulous shores of evil this taste obliges me to turn back and devote myself to good. I am disturbed by the encounter with these two pretexts that are offered me for departing from a path I had taken out of pride, out of a preference for singularity, but this book is not finished.

Ever since I began writing this book, which is completely devoted to the cult of a dead person with whom I am living on intimate terms, I have been feeling a kind of excitement which, cloaked by the alibi of Jean's glory, has been plunging me into a more and more intense and more and more desperate life, that has been impelling me to greater boldness. And I feel I have the strength not only to commit bolder burglaries but also to affront fearlessly the noblest human institutions in order to destroy them. I'm drunk with life, with violence, with despair.

Querelle

◄○►

Genet was no longer in prison, nor would he ever serve another sentence, when he began to write Querelle *in March 1945. While working on* Querelle, *he was simultaneously writing the early chapters of* The Thief's Journal.

Querelle *is the only novel Genet wrote that is not autobiographical and is not told by a first-person narrator named "Jean Genet."*

Genet had been a prisoner in Brest, where the action of the novel takes place, at the end of 1938. He had been arrested on October 15 for having stolen four bottles of liquor with an accomplice. Undoubtedly, Genet also transferred to the seaport of Brest many of his memories of the honky-tonk whores' section of Toulon, a Mediterranean port he had explored when he was younger.

Brest appealed to Genet as a poetic locale because it is blanketed in mists and had been the site of a famous prison, whence pairs of galley slaves, chained to each other for life, were sent out in royal barges. The legend of Brest as a prison town is only vaguely alluded to in this novel, but it formed part of Genet's imaginative excitement about the site. The fact that Brest had been destroyed by Allied bombers just before Genet began writing his novel also contributed to the poetic charm of the place. Genet often wrote about places and people that had only recently disappeared or died.

Because of his adolescent experiences at the reform school of Mettray, Genet first encountered homosexuality as a sadomasochistic struggle for dominance among young men who were usually heterosexual. These early experiences determined the shape of his erotic tastes, and the characters in Querelle *are predominantly heterosexual, sadistic, and homosexually involved with one another. Since* Querelle *is not autobiographical, nor linked to the facts of real-life experiences, in it Genet is free to release his erotic fantasies. The most persistent of these fantasies concerned gay sex between straight men, and* Querelle *dramatizes this preoccupation. Lieutenant Seblon can be seen as a stand-in for Genet himself, although the central character, Querelle, embodies Genet's anarchic and hostile impulses as well.*

Of all Genet's novels, Querelle *is the one that has invited the most commentary from critics, perhaps because it is the most fantastic. The book was virtually abandoned by Genet, who seems to have lost interest in the narrative as he approached the end of it. Perhaps he was frightened off by the monster of Frankenstein he had created in* Querelle. *His earlier heroes had been cowards and losers, but* Querelle *is a murderer who appears to be successful in the vengeance he wreaks on society.*

T HE NOTION OF murder often brings to mind the notion of sea and sailors. Sea and sailors do not, at first, appear as a definite image—it is rather that "murder" starts up a feeling of *waves.* If one considers that seaports are the scene of frequent crimes, the association seems self-explanatory; but there are numerous stories from which we learn that the murderer was a man of the sea—either a real one, or a fake one—and if the latter is the case, the crime will be even more closely connected to the sea. The man who dons a sailor's outfit does not do so out of prudence only. His disguise relieves him from the necessity of going through all the rigamarole required in the execution of any preconceived murder. Thus we could say that the outfit does the following things for the criminal: it envelops him in clouds; it gives him the appearance of having come from that far-off line of the horizon where sea touches sky; with long, undulating, and muscular strides he can walk across the waters, personifying the Great Bear, the Pole Star, or the Southern Cross; it (we are still discussing this particular disguise, as used by a criminal) it allows him to assume dark continents where the sun sets and rises, where the moon sanctions murder under roofs of bamboo beside motionless rivers teeming with alligators; it gives him the opportunity to act within the illusion of a mirage, to strike while one of his feet is still resting upon a beach in Oceania and the other propelling him across the waters toward Europe; it grants him oblivion in advance, as sailors always "return from far away"; it allows him to consider landlubbers as mere vegetation. It cradles the criminal, it enfolds him—in the tight fit of his sweater, in the amplitude of his bell-bottoms. It casts a sleep-spell on the already fascinated victim. We shall talk about the sailor's mortal flesh. We ourselves have witnessed scenes of seduction. In that very long sentence beginning "it envelopes him in clouds . . . ," we did indulge in facile poeticisms, each one of the propositions being merely an argument in favor of the author's personal proclivities. It is, admittedly, under the sign of a very singular inner feeling that we would set down the ensuing drama. We would also like to say that it addresses itself to inverts. The notion of love or lust appears as a *natural* corollary to the notion of Sea and Murder—and it is, moreover, the notion of *love against nature.* No doubt the sailors who are transported by ("animated by" would appear more exact, we'll see that later on) the desire and need to murder, apprenticed themselves first to the Merchant Navy, thus are veterans of long voyages, nourished on ships' biscuit and the cat-o'-nine-tails, used to leg irons for any little mistake, paid off in some obscure port, signed on again to handle some questionable cargo; and yet, it is difficult, in a city of fogs and granite, to brush past the huskies of the Fighting Navy, trained and trimmed by and for deeds we like to think of as daring, those shoulders, profiles, earrings, those tough and turbulent rumps, those strong and supple boys, without imagining them capable of murders that seem entirely justified by their deigning to commit them with their noble bodies. Whether they descend from heaven or return from a realm where they have consorted with sirens and even more fabulous monsters, on land these sailors inhabit buildings of stone, arsenals, palaces whose solidity is opposed to the nervousness, the feminine irritability of the waters (does not the sailor, in one of his songs, speak of how "... the sea's my best girl"?), by jetties loaded with chains, bollards, buoys, maritime paraphernalia to which, even when farthest from the sea, they know themselves anchored. To match their stature they are provided with barracks, forts, disused penitentiaries, magnificent pieces of architecture, all of them. Brest is a hard, solid city, built out of gray, Breton granite. Its rocklike quality anchors the port, giving the sailors a sense of security, a launching point when outward bound, a haven of rest after the continuous wave-motion of the sea. If Brest ever seems more lighthearted, it is when a feeble sun gilds the façades which are as noble as those of Venice, or when its narrow streets teem with carefree sailors—or, *then*, even when there is fog and rain. The action of this story starts three days after a dispatch boat, *Le Vengeur*, had anchored in the Roads. Other warships lie round her: *La Panthère*, *Le Vainqueur*, *Le Sanglant*, and around these, *Le Richelieu*, *Le Béarn*, *Le Dunkerque*, and more. Those names have their counterparts in the past. On the walls of a side chapel in the church of Saint-Yves, in La Rochelle, hang a number of small votive paintings representing ships that have been either lost or saved: *La Mutine*, *Le Saphir*, *Le Cyclone*, *La Fée*, *La Jeune Aimée*. These ships had had no influence whatsoever on Querelle who had seen them sometimes as a child, yet we must mention their existence. For the ships' crews, Brest will always be the city of La Féria. Far from France, sailors never talk about this brothel without cracking a joke and hooting like owls, the way they talk about ducks in China or weird Annamites, and they evoke the proprietor and his wife in terms like:

"Shoot a game of craps with you—like at Nono's, I mean!"

"That guy, for a piece of ass he'd do anything—he'd even play with Nono."

"Him there, he went to La Féria to *lose.*"

While the Madam's name is never mentioned, the names of "La Féria" and "Nono" must have traveled all around the world, in sarcastic asides on the lips of sailors everywhere. On board there never is anybody who would know exactly what La Féria really is, nor do they precisely know the rules of the game which has given it such a reputation, but no one, not even the greenest recruit, dare ask for an explanation; each and every seafarin' man will have it understood that he knows what it is all about. Thus the establishment in Brest appears ever in a fabulous light, and the sailors, as they approach that port, secretly dream of that house of ill repute which they'll mention only as a laughing matter. Georges Querelle, the hero of this book, speaks of it less than anyone. He knows that his own brother is the Madam's lover. Here is the letter, received in Càdiz, informing him of this:

> Good Bro.,
> I'm writing you these few lines to let you know that I'm back in Brest. I had planned on that dockyard job again, but, nothing doing. So there I was, stuck. And as you know, I'm none too good at finding the jobs, and besides, who wants to work his ass off anyhow. So, to get off the ground again, I went round to Milo's place and right after that the boss lady of La Féria was giving me the old eye. Did my best, we're getting along like a house on fire. The boss doesn't give a shit who goes with his woman, they're just business partners like they say. So, I'm in pretty good shape. Hope you're in good shape too, and when you get some furlough, etc.
>
> (Signed) Robert.

Sometimes it rains in September. The rain makes the light cotton clothes—open shirts and denims—stick to the skin of the muscular men working in port and Arsenal. Again, some evenings the weather is fine when the groups of masons, carpenters, mechanics come out from the shipyards. They are weary. They look heavily burdened, and even when their expressions lighten, their work shoes, their heavy steps seem to shatter the pools of air around them. Slowly, ponderously they traverse the lighter, quicker, more rapid hither-and-thither of sailors on shore leave who have become the pride of this city which will scintillate till dawn with their nautical swagger, the gusts of their laughter, their songs, their merriment, the insults they yell at the girls; with their kisses, their wide collars, the pompons on their hats. The laborers return to their lodgings. All through the day they have toiled (servicemen, soldiers or sailors, never have that feeling of having *toiled*), blending their actions in a network of common endeavor, for the purposes of an achieved work like a visible, tightly drawn knot, and now they are returning. A shadowy friendship—shadowy to them—unites them, and also a quiet hatred. Few of them are married, and the wives of those live some distance away. Toward six o'clock in the evening it is when the workmen pass through the iron gates of the Arsenal and leave the dockyard. They walk up in the direction of the railroad station where the canteens are, or down the road to Recouvrance where they have their furnished rooms in cheap hotels. Most of them are Italians and Spaniards, though there are some North Africans and Frenchmen as well. It is in the midst of such a surfeit of fatigue, heavy muscles, virile lassitude, that Sublieutenant Seblon of the *Vengeur* loves to take his evening walk.

They used to have this cannon permanently trained upon the penitentiary. Today the same cannon (its barrel only) stands mounted upright in the middle of the same courtyard where once the convicts were mustered for the galleys. It is astonishing that turning criminals into sailors used to be regarded as a form of punishment.

•   •   •

Went past La Féria. Saw nothing. Never any luck. Over in Recouvrance I caught a glimpse of an accordion—a sight I frequently see on board, yet never tire of watching—folding, unfolding on a sailor's thigh.

Se brester, *to brace oneself. Derives, no doubt, from* bretteur, *fighter: and so, relates to* se quereller, *to pick a fight.*

When I learn—if only from the newspaper—that some scandal is breaking, or when I'm just afraid that it may break upon the world, I make preparations to get away: I always believe that I shall be suspected of being the prime mover. I regard myself as a demon-ridden creature, merely because I have imagined certain subjects for scandal.

As for the hoodlums I hold in my arms, tenderly kissing and caressing their faces before gently covering them up again in my sheets, they are no more than a kind of passing thrill and experiment combined. After having been so overwhelmed by the loneliness to which my inversion condemns me, is it really possible that I may some day hold naked in my arms, and continue to hold, pressed close to my body, those young men whose courage and hardness place them so high in my esteem that I long to throw myself at their feet and grovel before them? I dare hardly believe this, and tears well up in my eyes, to thank God for granting me such happiness. My tears make me feel soft. I melt. My own cheeks still wet with tears, I revel in, and overflow with tenderness for, the flat, hard cheekbones of those boys.

That severe, at times almost suspicious look, a look that seems to pass judgment, with which the pederast appraises every young man he encounters, is really a brief, but intense meditation on his own loneliness. That instant (the duration of the glance) is filled with a concentrated and constant despair, with its own jagged frequency, sheathed in the fear of rebuff. "It would be so great . . . ," he thinks. Or, if he isn't thinking, it expresses itself in his frown, in that black, condemning look.

Whenever some part of his body happens to be naked, He (that is Querelle, whose name the officer never writes down—this not merely for the sake of prudence as regards his fellow officers and superiors, since in their eyes the contents of his diary would be quite sufficient to damn him) starts examining it. He looks for blackheads, split nails, red pimples. Irritated when he can't find any, he invents some. As soon as he has nothing better to do, he becomes engrossed in this game. Tonight he is examining his legs: their black, strong hairs are quite soft in spite of their vigorous growth, and thus they create a kind of mist from foot to groin, which softens the roughness and abruptness, one might almost say, the stoniness of his muscles. It amazes me how such a virile trait can envelop his legs with such great sweetness. He amuses himself by applying a burning cigarette to his hairs and then bends over them to savor the scorched smell. He is not smiling any more than usual. His own body in repose is his great passion—a morose, not an exultant passion. Bent over his body, he sees himself there. He examines it with an imaginary magnifying glass. He observes its minuscule irregularities with the scrupulous attention of an entomologist studying the habits of insects. But as soon as He moves, what dazzling revenge his entire body takes, in the glory of its motion!

• • •

He (Querelle) is never absentminded, always attentive to what he is doing. Every moment of his life he rejects the dream. He is forever present. He never answers: "I was thinking of something else." And yet the childishness of his obvious preoccupations astonishes me.

Hands in pockets, lazily, I would say to him, "Give me a little shove, just to knock the ash off my cigarette," and he would let fly and punch me on the shoulder. I shrug it off.

I should have been able to keep my sea legs or hang on to the gunwale, the ship wasn't rolling that hard, but quickly, and with pleasure, I took advantage of the ship's motion to sway and to allow myself to be shifted along, always in his direction. I even managed to brush against his elbow.

It is as if a fierce and devoted watchdog, ready to chew up your carotid artery, were following him around, trotting, at times, between the calves of his legs, so that the beast's flanks seem to blend with his thigh muscles, ready to bite, always growling and snarling, so ferocious one expects to see it bite off his balls.

After these few excerpts picked (but not entirely at random) from a private journal which suggested his character to us, we would like you to look upon the sailor Querelle, born from that solitude in which the officer himself remained isolated, as a singular figure comparable to the Angel of the Apocalypse, whose feet rest on the waters of the sea. By meditating on Querelle, by using, in his imagination, his most beautiful traits, his muscles, his rounded parts, his teeth, his guessed-at genitals, Lieutenant Seblon has turned the sailor into an angel (as we shall see, he describes him as "the Angel of Loneliness"), that is to say, into a being less and less human, crystalline, around whom swirl strands of a music based on the opposite of harmony—or rather, a music that is what remains after harmony has been used up, worn out, and in the midst of which this immense angel moves, slowly, unwitnessed, his feet on the water, but his head—or what should be his head—in a dazzle of rays from a supernatural sun.

They themselves tending to deny it, the strangely close resemblance between the two brothers Querelle appeared attractive only to others. They met only in the evenings, as late as possible, in the one bed of a furnished room not far from where their mother had eked out her meager existence. They met again, perhaps, but somewhere so deep down that they could not see anything clearly, in their love for their mother, and certainly in their almost daily arguments. In the morning they parted without a word. They wanted to ignore each other. Already, at the age of fifteen, Querelle had smiled the smile that was to be peculiarly his for the rest of his life. He had chosen a life among thieves and spoke their argot. We'll try to bear this in mind in order to understand Querelle whose mental makeup and very feelings depend upon, and assume the form of, a certain syntax, a particular murky orthography. In his conversation we find turns like "peel him raw!" "boy, am I flying," "oh, beat off!" "he better not show his ass in here again," "he got burnt all right," "get that punk," "see the guy making tracks," "hey, baby, dig my hard-on," "suck me off," etc., expressions which are never pronounced clearly, but muttered in a kind of monotone and as if from within, without the speaker really "seeing" them. They are not projected, and thus Querelle's words never reveal him; they do not really define him at all. On the contrary, they seem to enter through his mouth, to pile up inside him, to settle and to form a thick mud deposit, out of which, at times, a transparent bubble rises, exploding delicately on his lips. What one hears, then, is one of those bits of the argot.

As for the police in port and city, Brest lay under the authority of its Commissariat: in the time of our novel there were two Inspectors, joined together by a singular friendship, by the names of Mario Daugas and Marcellin. The latter was little more than an excrescence to Mario (it is well known that policemen always come in pairs), dull and painstaking enough, yet sometimes a source of great comfort to his colleague. However, there was yet another collaborator whom Mario had chosen, more subtle and more dear—more easily sacrificed, too, should that become necessary: Dédé.

Like every French town, Brest had its Monoprix store, a favorite stamping ground for Dédé and numerous sailors who circulated among the counters, coveting—and sometimes purchasing—pairs of gloves, of all things. To complete the picture, the old-time control by the Admiralty had been replaced by the services of the Préfecture Maritime.

Bought or stolen from a sailor, the blue denim pants belled over his entrancing feet, now motionless and arched after the final table-shaking stamp. He was wearing highly polished black shoes, cracked and crinkled at the point reached by the ripples of blue denim that ran down from the source of his belt. His torso was encased very tightly in a turtleneck jersey of white, slightly soiled wool. Querelle's parted lips slowly began to close. He started to raise the half-smoked cigarette to his mouth, but his hand came to rest halway up his chest, and the mouth remained half-open: he was gazing at Gil and Roger, who were united by the almost visible thread of their glances, by the freshness of their smiles; and Gil seemed to be singing for the boy, and Roger, like the sovereign at some intimate rite of debauch, to be favoring this young eighteen-year-old mason, so that with his voice he could be the hero of a roadside tavern for a night. The way the sailor was watching the two of them had the effect of isolating them. Once again, Querelle became aware of his mouth hanging half open. His smile became more pronounced at the corner of his mouth, almost imperceptibly. A tinge of irony began to spread over his features, then over his entire body, giving him and his relaxed posture leaning back against the wall an air of amused sarcasm. Altered by the raising of an eyebrow, to match the crooked smile, his expression became somewhat malicious as he continued his scrutiny of the two young men. The smile vanished from Gil's lips, as if the entire ball of string had been unrolled, and at the same moment expired on Roger's face; but four seconds later, regaining his breath and taking up the song again, Gil, once more on top of the table, resumed his smile, which brought back and sustained, until the very last couplet of the song, the smile on Roger's lips. Not for a second did their eyes stray from the eyes of the other. Gil was singing. Querelle shifted his shoulders against the wall of the bistro. He became aware of himself, felt himself pitting his own living mass, the powerful muscles of his back, against the black and indestructible matter of that wall. Those two shadowy substances struggled in silence. Querelle knew the beauty of his back. We shall see how, a few days later, he was to secretly dedicate it to Lieutenant Seblon. Almost without moving, he let his shoulders ripple against the wall, its stones. He was a strong man. One hand—the other remaining in the pocket of his peacoat—raised a half-smoked cigarette to his lips, still holding the half smile. Robert and the two other sailors were oblivious to everything but the song. Querelle retained his smile. To use an expression much favored by soldiers, Querelle shone by his absence. After letting a little smoke drift in the direction of his thoughts (as though he wanted to veil them, or show them a touch of insolence), his lips remained slightly drawn apart from his teeth, whose beauty he knew, their whiteness dimmed, now, by the night and the shadow cast by his upper lip. Watching Gil and Roger, now reunited by glance and smile, he could not make up his mind to withdraw, to enclose within himself those teeth and their gentle splendor, which had the same restful effect on his vague thoughts as the blue of the sea has on our eyes. Meanwhile, he was lightly running his tongue over his palate. It was alive. One of the sailors started to go through the motions of buttoning his peacoat, turning up the collar. Querelle was not used to the idea, one that had never really been formulated, that he was a monster. He considered, he observed his past with an ironic smile, frightened and tender at the same time, to the extent that his past became confused with what he himself was. Thus might a young boy whose soul is evident in his eyes, but who has been metamorphosed into an alligator, even if he were not fully conscious of his horrendous head and jaws, consider his scaly body, his solemn, gigantic tail, with which he strikes the water or the beach or brushes against that of other monsters, and which extends him with the same touching, heart-rending and indestructible majesty as the train of a robe, adorned with lace, with crests, with battles, with a thousand crimes, worn by a Child Empress, extends her. He knew the horror of being alone, seized by an immortal enchantment in the midst of the world of the living. Only to him had been accorded the horrendous privilege to perceive his monstrous participation in the realms of the great muddy rivers and the rain forests. And he was apprehensive that some light, emanating from within his body, or from his true consciousness, might not be illuminating him, might not, in some way from inside the scaly carapace, give off a reflection of that true form and make him visible to men, who would then have to hunt him down.

In some places along the ramparts of Brest, trees have been planted, and these grow in alleys bearing the perhaps derisive name of the "Bois de Boulogne." Here, in the summer, there are a few bistros where one can sit and drink at wooden tables swollen by rain and fog, under the trees or in arbors. The sailors had vanished into the shade of those trees, with a girl; Querelle let them, his buddies, take their turns with her, and then he came up to her as she lay stretched out on the grass. He proceeded to unbutton his fly, but after a brief, charming hesitation expressed in his fingers, he readjusted it again. Querelle felt calm. He had only to give the slightest turn of the head, to left or right, to feel his cheek rub against the stiff, upturned collar of his peacoat. This contact reassured him. By it, he knew himself to be clothed, marvelously clothed.

Later, when he was taking off his shoes, the bistro scene came back to Querelle's mind, who lacked the ability to assign it any precise significance. He could hardly put it into words. He knew only that it had aroused a faint sense of amusement in him. He could not have said why. Knowing the severity, the austerity almost, of his face and its pallor, this irony gave him what is commonly called a sarcastic air. For a moment or two he had remained amazed by the rapport that was established and understood and became almost an object between the eyes of those two: the one up on the table, singing there, his head bent down toward the other, who was sitting and gazing up at him. Querelle pulled off one of his socks. Apart from the material benefits derived from his murders, Querelle was enriched by them in other ways. They deposited in him a kind of slimy sediment, and the stench it gave off served to deepen his despair. From each one of his victims he had preserved something a little dirty: a slip, a bra, shoelaces, a handkerchief—objects sufficient to disprove his alibis and to condemn him. These relics were firsthand evidence of his splendor, of his triumphs. They were the shameful details, upon which all luminous but uncertain appearances rest. In the world of sailors with their striking good looks, virility, and pride, they were the secret counterparts of a greasy, broken-toothed comb at the bottom of a pocket; full-dress gaiters, from a distance impeccable as sails, but, like those, far from true white; a pair of elegant but poorly tailored pants; badly drawn tattoos; a filthy handkerchief; socks with holes in them. What for us is the strongest memory of Querelle's expression can best be described by an image that comes to mind: delicate metal strands, sparsely barbed, easily overcome, grasped by a prisoner's heavy hand, or grazing against sturdy fabric. Almost in spite of himself, quietly, to one of his mates, already stretched out in his hammock, Querelle said:

"Pair of fuckin' faggots, those two."

"Which two?"

"What?"

Querelle raised his head. His buddy, it seemed, didn't get it. And that was the end of the conversation. Querelle pulled off his other sock and turned in. Not that he wanted to sleep, or think over the scene in the bistro. Once he was stretched out, he had at last the leisure to consider his own affairs, and he had to think quick, in spite of his fatigue. The owner of La Féria would take the two kilos of opium, if Querelle only could get them out of the dispatch boat. The customs officials opened all sailors' bags, even the smallest ones. Coming ashore, all but the officers were subjected to a thorough search. Without cracking a smile, Querelle thought of the Lieutenant. The enormity of this idea struck him even while he was thinking what only he himself could have translated into:

"He's been giving me the old eye for some time now. Nervous like a cat on a hot tin roof. I got him hooked, I guess."

Querelle was glad to know that Robert was now living a life of Oriental ease and luxury; to know that he was a brothel Madam's lover as well as a friend to her obliging husband. He closed his eyes. He regained that region in himself where his brother was there with him. He let himself sink into a state where neither could be distinguished from the other. From this state he was able to extract, first, some words, and then, by a fairly elementary process, little by little, a thought—which, as it rose from those depths, again differentiated him from Robert and proposed singular acts, an entire system of solitary operations: quite gently these became his own, completely his, and Vic was there, with him, taking part. And Querelle, whose thoughts had overcome his personal autonomy in order to reach Vic, turned away again, re-entered himself, in the blind search for that inexpressible limbo which is like some inconsistent *pâté* of love. He was hardly touching his curled-up prick. He felt no urge. While still at sea, he had announced to the other sailors that once in Brest, he was sure going to shoot his wad; but tonight he wasn't even thinking about whether he should have kissed that girl.

Querelle was an exact replica of his brother. Robert, perhaps a little more taciturn, the other, a little hotter in temper (nuances by which one could tell them from each other, except if one was a furious girl). It so happens that we ourselves acquired our sense of Querelle's existence on a particular day, we could give the exact date and hour of—when we decided to write this story (and that is a word not to be used to describe some adventure or series of adventures that has already been lived through). Little by little, we saw how Querelle—already contained in our flesh—was beginning to grow in our soul, to feed on what is best in us, above all on our despair at not being in any way inside him, while having him inside of ourselves. After this discovery of Querelle we want him to become the Hero, even to those who may despise him. Following, within ourselves, his destiny, his development, we shall see how he lends himself to this in order to realize himself in a conclusion that appears to be (from then on) in complete accordance with his very own will, his very own fate.

The scene we are about to describe is a transposition of the event which revealed Querelle to us. (We are still referring to that ideal and heroic personage, the fruit of our secret loves.) We must say, of that event, that it was of equal import to the Visitation. No doubt it was only long after it had taken place that we recognized it as being "big" with consequences, yet there and then we may be said to have felt a true Annunciatory thrill. Finally: to become visible to you, to become a character in a novel, Querelle must be shown apart from ourselves. Only then will you get to know the apparent, and real, beauty of his body, his attitudes, his exploits, and their slow disintegration.

The farther you descend toward the port of Brest, the denser the fog seems to grow. It is so thick at Recouvrance, after you cross the Penfeld bridge, that the houses, their walls and roofs appear to be afloat. In the alleys leading down to the quayside you find yourself alone. Here and there you encounter the dim, fringed sun, like a light from a half-open dairy doorway. On you go through that vaporous twilight, until confronted once more by the opaque matter, the dangerous fog that shelters: a drunken sailor reeling home on heavy legs—a docker hunched over a girl—a hoodlum, perhaps armed with a knife—us—you—hearts pounding. The fog brought Gil and Roger closer together. It gave them mutual confidence and friendship. Though they were hardly aware of it as yet, this privacy instilled in them a hesitation, a little fearful, a little tremulous, a charming emotion akin to that in children when they walk along, hands in pockets, touching, stumbling over each other's feet.

"Shit—watch your step! Keep going."

"That must be the quay. Never mind 'em."

"And why not? You got the jitters?"

"No, but sometimes . . ."

Now and again they sensed a woman walking by, saw the steady glow of a cigarette, guessed at the outline of a couple locked in an embrace.

"Howzat . . . ? Sometimes what?"

"Oh come on, Gil, no need to take it out on me. It ain't my fault my sister wasn't able to make it."

And, a little quieter, after two more steps in silence:

"You can't have been thinking too much about Paulette, last night, dancing with that brunette?"

"What the fuck's that to you? Yeah, I danced with her. So what?"

"Well! You weren't just dancing, you took her home, too."

"So what, I'm not hitched to your sister, jack. Look who's talking. All I'm saying is, you could have made sure that she came along." Gil was speaking quite loudly, but none too distinctly, so as to be understood only by Roger. Then he lowered his voice, and a note of anxiety crept into it.

"So, what about it?"

"Gil, you know it, I just couldn't swing it for you. I swear."

They turned to the left, in the direction of the Navy warehouses. A second time they bumped into one another. Automatically, Gil put his hand on the boy's shoulder. It remained there. Roger slackened his pace, hoping that his buddy would stop. Would it happen? He was almost melting, feeling infinitely tender; but at that moment someone passed by—he and Gilbert were not in a place of perfect solitude. Gil let go of his shoulder and put his hand back into his pocket, and Roger thought that he had been rejected. Yet, when he took his hand away, Gil couldn't help bearing down a little harder, just as he let go, as if some kind of regret at taking it away had added to its weight. And now Gil had a hard-on.

"Shit."

He tried to visualize a sharp image of Paulette's face, and was immediately tempted by his erratic mind to concentrate on another point, on what Roger's sister had under her skirt, between her thighs. Needing an easily, immediately accessible physical prop, he said to himself, thinking in the inflections of cynicism:

"Well, here's her brother, right beside me, in the fog!"

It was then that it seemed to him it would be a delight to enter that warmth, that black, fur-fringed, slightly pursed hole that emits such vague, yet ponderous and fiery odors, even in corpses already cold.

"She gives me the hots, your sister, you know."

Roger smiled, from ear to ear. He turned his radiant face toward Gil.

"Aaahh . . ."

The sound was both gentle and hoarse, seeming to originate in the pit of Gil's stomach, nothing so much as an anguished sigh born at the base of his throbbing rod. He realized that there was a rapid, immediate line connecting the base of his prick to the back of his throat and to that muffled groan. We would like these reflections, these observations, which cannot fully round out nor delineate the characters of the book, to give you permission to act not so much as onlookers as creators of these very characters, who will then slowly disengage themselves from your own preoccupations. Little by little, Gil's prick was getting lively. In his pants pocket his hand had hold of it, flattening it against his belly. Indeed, it had the stature of a tree, a mossy-boled oak with lamenting mandrakes being born among its roots. (Sometimes, when he woke up with a hard-on, Gil would address his prick as "my hanged man.") They walked on, but at a slower pace.

"She gives you the hots, eh?"

The light of Roger's smile came close to illuminating the fog, making the stars sparkle through. It made him happy to hear, right there beside him, how Gil's amorous desire made his mouth water.

"You think that's funny, don'cha."

Teeth clenched, hands still in pockets, Gil turned to face the boy and forced him to retreat into a recess in the stone wall. He kept pushing him with his belly, his chest. Roger kept on smiling, a little less radiantly perhaps, hardly shrinking back from the thrust of the other young man's face. Gil was now leaning against him with his entire vigorous body.

"You think that's a scream, hey?"

Gil took one of his hands out of his pocket. He put it on Roger's shoulder, so close to the collar that the thumb brushed against the cool skin of the kid's neck. His shoulders against the wall, Roger let himself slide down a little, as if wanting to appear smaller. He was still smiling.

"So say something? You think it's funny? Eh?"

Gil advanced like a conqueror, almost like a lover. His mouth was both cruel and soft, like those movie seducers' mouths under their thin, black mustaches, and his expression turned suddenly so serious that Roger's smile, by a faint drooping of the corners of his mouth, now seemed a little sad. With his back to the wall, Roger kept on sliding, holding that wistful smile with which he looked to be sinking, submerging in the monstrous wave that Gil was riding, one hand still in pocket, clutching that great spar.

"Aaahh . . ."

Again, Gil voiced that groan, hoarse and remote, that we have had occasion to describe.

"Oh, yeah, I'd like to have her here, all right. And you bet your ass I'd screw her, and good, if I had her here, the way I've got you!"

Roger said nothing. His smile disappeared. His eyes kept on meeting Gil's stare, and the only gentleness he could see there was in Gil's eyebrows, powdered with chalk and cement dust.

"Gil!"

He thought: "This is Gil. It's Gilbert Turko. He's from Poland. He's been working at the Arsenal, on the gantry, with the other masons. He's in a rage."

Close to Gil's ear, under his breath which entered the fog, he murmured: "Gil!"

"Oh . . .! Oh . . .! I sure could use a piece of her, right now. You, you look alike, you know. You've got that same little mouth of hers."

He moved his hand closer to Roger's neck. Finding himself so the master, in the heart of the light mass of watery air, increased Gil Turko's desire to be tough, sharp, and heavy. To rip the fog, to destroy it with a sudden brutal gesture, would perhaps be enough to affirm his virility, which otherwise, on his return to quarters tonight, would suffer mean and powerful humiliation.

"Got her eyes, too. What a shame you ain't her. Hey, what's this? You passing out?"

As if to prevent Roger from "passing out," he pressed his belly closer still to his, pushing him against the wall, while his free hand kept hold of the charming head, holding it above the waves of a powerful and arrogant sea, the sea that was Gil. They remained motionless, one shoring up the other.

"What are you going to tell her?"

"I'll try to get her to come along tomorrow."

Despite his inexperience, Roger understood the extent, if not quite the meaning of his confusion, when he heard the sound of his own voice: it was toneless.

"And the other thing I told you about?"

"I'll try my best about that too. We going back now?"

They pulled apart, quickly. Suddenly they heard the sea. From the very beginning of this scene they had been close to the water's edge. For a moment both of them felt frightened at the thought of having been so close to danger. Gil took out a cigarette and lit it. Roger saw the beauty of his face that looked as if it had been picked, like a flower, by those large hands, thick and covered with powdery dust, their palms illuminated now by a delicate and trembling flame.

They say that the murderer Ménesclou used a spray of lilacs to entice the little girl closer to him so that he could then slit her throat; it is with hair, with his eyes—with his full smile—that He (Querelle) draws me on. Does this mean that I am going to my death? That those locks, those teeth are lethal? Does it mean that love is a murderer's lair? And could it mean that "He" is leading me on? And "for that"?

At the point of my going under, "in Querelle," will I still be able to reach the alarm siren?

(While the other characters are incapable of lyricism which we are using in order to recreate them more vividly within you, Lieutenant Seblon himself is solely responsible for what flows from his pen.)

I would love it—oh, I deeply wish for it!—if, under his regal garb, "He" were simply a hoodlum! To throw myself at his feet! To kiss his toes!

In order to find "Him" again, and counting on absence and the emotions aroused by returning to give me courage to address "Him" by his first name, I pretended to be leaving on a long furlough. But I wasn't able to resist. I come back. I see "Him" again, and I give "Him" my orders, almost vindictively.

He could get away with anything. Spit me in the face, call me by my first name.
    "You're getting overly familiar!" I'd say to "Him."
    The blow he would strike me with his fist, right in the mouth, would make my ears ring with this oboe murmur: "My vulgarity is regal, and it accords me every right."

By giving the ship's barber a curt order to clip his hair very short, Lieutenant Seblon hoped to achieve a he-mannish appearance—not so much to save face as to be able to move more freely among the handsome lads. He did not know, then, that he caused them to shrink back from him. He was a well-built man, wide shouldered, but he felt within himself the presence of his own femininity, sometimes contained in a chickadee's egg, the size of a pale blue or pink sugared almond, but sometimes brimming over to flood his entire body with its milk. He knew this so well that he himself believed in this quality of weakness, this frailty of an enormous, unripe nut, whose pale, white interior consisted of the stuff children call milk. The Lieutenant knew to his great chagrin that this core of femininity could erupt in an instant and manifest itself in his face, his eyes, his fingertips, and mark every gesture of his by rendering it too gentle. He took care never to be caught counting the stitches of any imaginary needlework, scratching his head with an imaginary knitting needle. Nevertheless he betrayed himself in the eyes of all men whenever he gave the order to pick up arms, for he pronounced the word "arms" with such grace that his whole person seemed to be kneeling at the grave of some beautiful lover. He never smiled. His fellow officers considered him stern and somewhat puritanical, but they also believed they were able to discern a quality of stupendous refinement underneath that hard shell, and the belief rested on the way in which, despite himself, he pronounced certain words.

The happiness of clasping in my *arms a body so beautiful, even though it is huge and strong!*
Huger and stronger than mine.

Reverie. Is this him? "He" goes ashore every night. When he comes back, "His" bell-bottom
pants—which are wide, and cover his shoes, contrary to regulations—look bespattered,
perhaps with jism mixed with the dust of the streets he has been sweeping with their frayed
bottoms. His pants, they're the dirtiest sailor's pants I've ever seen. Were I to demand an
explanation from "Him," "He" would smile as he chucked his beret behind him:
    "That, that's just from all the suckers going down on me. While they're giving me a blow
job, they come all over my jeans. That's just their spunk. That's all."
    "He" would appear to be very proud of it. "He" wears those stains with a glorious
impudence: they are his medals.

While it is the least elegant of the brothels in Brest, where no men of the Battle
Fleet ever go to give it a little of their grace and freshness, La Féria certainly is
the most renowned. It is a solemn gold-and-purple cave providing for the coloni-
als, the boys of the Merchant Navy and the tramp steamers, and the longshoremen.
Whereas the sailors visit to have a "piece" or a "short time," the dock workers and
others say: "Let's go shoot our wads." At night, La Féria also provides the imagina-
tion with the thrills of scintillating criminality. One may always suspect three or
four hoodlums lurking in the fog-shrouded *pissoir* erected on the sidewalk across
the street. Sometimes the front door stands ajar, and from it issue the air of a player
piano, blue strains, serpentines of music unrolling in the dark shadows, curling
round the wrists and necks of the workmen who just happen to be walking past.
But daylight allows a more detailed view of the dirty, blind, gray and shame-
ravaged shack it is. Seen only by the light of its lantern and its lowered Venetian
blinds, it could well be overflowing with the hot luxury of a bounty of boobs and
milky thighs under clinging black satin, bursting with bosoms, crystals, mirrors,
scents, and champagne, the sailor's dreams as soon as he enters the red-light
quarter. It had a most impressive door. This consisted of a thick slab of wood,
plated over with iron and armed with long, sharp spikes of shining metal—perhaps
steel—pointing outward, into the street. In its mysterious arrogance it was per-
fectly suited to heighten the turmoil of any amorous heart. For the docker or
stevedore the door symbolized the cruelty that attends the rites of love. If the door
was designed for protection, it had to be guarding a treasure such as only insensate
dragons or invisible genies could hope to gain without being impaled to bleed on
those spikes—unless, of course, it did open all by itself, to a word, a gesture from
you, docker or soldier, for this night the most fortunate and blameless prince who
may inherit the forbidden domains by power of magic. To be so heavily protected,
the treasure had to be dangerous to the rest of the world, or, again, of such a fragile
nature that it needed to be protected by the means employed in the sheltering of
virgins. The longshoreman might smile and joke about the sharp spear tips point-
ing at him, but this did not prevent his becoming, for a moment, the man who

penetrates—by the charm of his words, his face, or his gestures—a palpitating virginity. And from the very threshold, even though he was far from a true hard-on, the presence of his prick would make itself felt in his pants, still soft perhaps, but reminding him, the conqueror of the door, of his prowess by a slight contraction near the tip that spread slowly to the base and on to the muscles of his buttocks. Within that still flabby prick the docker would be aware of the presence of another, minuscule, rigid prick, something like the "idea" of horniness. And it would be a solemn moment, from the contemplation of the spikes to the sound of bolts slamming shut behind him. For Madame Lysiane the door had other virtues. When closed, it transformed her, the lady of the house, into an oceanic pearl contained in the nacre of an oyster that was able to open its valve, and to close it, at will. Madame Lysiane was blessed with the gentleness of a pearl, a muffled gleam emanating less from her milky complexion than from her innate sense of tranquil happiness illuminated by inner peace. Her contours were rounded, shiny, and rich. Millennia of slow attrition, of numerous gains and numerous losses, a patient economy, had gone into the making of this plentitude. Madame Lysiane was certain that she was sumptuousness personified. The door guaranteed that. The spikes were ferocious guardians, even against the very air. The lady of La Féria passed her life in a leisurely time, in a medieval castle, and she saw it often in her mind's eye. She was happy. Only the most subtle elements of the life outside found their way to her, to anoint her with an exquisite ointment. She was noble, haughty, and superb. Kept away from the sun and the stars, from games and dreams, but nourished by her very own sun, her own stars, her own games and dreams, shod in mules with high Louis Quinze heels, she moved slowly among her girls without so much as touching them, she climbed the stairs, walked along corridors hung with gilt leather, through astounding halls and salons we shall attempt to describe, sparkling with lights and mirrors, upholstered, decorated with artificial flowers in cut-glass vases and with erotic etchings on the walls. Molded by time, she was beautiful. Robert had now been her lover for six months.

"You pay cash?"

"I told you so already."

Querelle was petrified by Mario's stare. That stare and his general demeanor expressed more than indifference: they were icy. In order to appear to ignore Mario, Querelle deliberately looked only at the brothelkeeper, looked him straight in the eye. His own immobility was making him feel awkward too. He regained a little assurance when he had shifted his weight from one foot to the other; a modicum of suppleness returned to his body, just as he was thinking: "Me, I'm only a sailor. My pay's all I've got. So I've got to hustle. Nothing wrong with that. It's good shit I'm talking about. He's got nothing on me. And even if that one *is* a cop, I don't give a shit." But he felt that he wasn't able to make a dent in the proprietor's imperturbability: he showed hardly any interest in the merchandise offered, and none at all in the person offering it. The lack of movement and the almost total silence among these three characters was beginning to weigh on each one of them.

Querelle went on, in his mind: "I haven't told him that I'm Bob's brother. All the same, he wouldn't dare put the finger on me." At the same time he was appreciating the proprietor's tremendous build and the good looks of the cop. Until now, he had never experienced any real rivalry in the male world, and if he was not all that impressed by what he was confronted with in these two men—or unaware of his feelings in terms of such phraseology—he was at least suffering, for the first time, from the indifference of men toward him. So he said:

"And there's no heat on, is there?"

It had been his intention to demonstrate his contempt for the fellow who kept on staring at him, but he did not care to define that contempt too pointedly. He did not even dare so much as indicate Mario to the boss with his eyes.

"Dealing with me you don't have to worry. You'll get your dough. All you've got to do is bring those five kilos here, and you'll receive your pennies. OK? So get cracking."

With a very slow, almost imperceptible movement of the head the boss nodded toward the counter against which Mario was leaning.

"That's Mario, over there. Don't worry about him, he belongs to the family."

Without one twitch of his face muscles, Mario held out his hand. It was hard, solid, armored rather than ornamented with three gold rings. Querelle's waist was trimmer than Mario's, by an inch or so. He knew that the very moment he set eyes on the splendid rings: they seemed to be signs of great masculine strength. He had no doubt that the realm over which this character lorded it was a terrestrial one. Suddenly, and with a twinge of melancholy, Querelle was reminded that he possessed, hidden forr'ard in the soaking dispatch boat out in the Roads, all it needed to be this man's equal. The thought calmed him down a little. But was it really possible for a policeman to be so handsome, so wealthy? And was it possible that he would join forces with, no, join his beauty to the power of an outlaw (because that is what Querelle liked to think the brothelkeeper was)? But that thought, slowly unfolding in Querelle's mind, did not set it at rest, and his disdain yielded to his admiration.

"Hello."

Mario's voice was large and thick like his hands—except that it carried no sparkle. It struck Querelle slap in the face. It was a brutal, callous voice, like a big shovel. Speaking of it, a few days later, Querelle said to the detective: "Your pound of flesh, every time you hit me in the face with it . . ." Querelle gave him a broad smile and held out his hand, but without saying anything. To the proprietor he said:

"My brother isn't coming, is he?"

"Haven't seen him. Dunno where he is."

Afraid that he might seem tactless and rile the boss, Querelle did not pursue the question. The main parlor of the brothel was silent and empty. It seemed to be recording their meeting, quietly, attentively. It was three o'clock in the afternoon, the ladies would be having their meal in the "refectory." There was no one about. On the second floor, in her room, Madame Lysiane was doing her hair by the light of a single bulb. The mirrors were vacant, pure, amazingly close to the unreal, having nobody and nothing to reflect. The boss tilted and drained his glass. He was a formidably husky man. If he had never been really handsome, in his youth he had no doubt been a fine specimen, despite the blackheads, the hair-thin black wrinkles on his neck, and the pockmarks. His pencil-line mustache, trimmed "American style," was undoubtedly a souvenir of 1918. Thanks to those doughboys, to the Black Market, and to the traffic in women he had been able to get rich quick and to purchase La Féria. His long boat trips and fishing parties had tanned his skin. His features were hard, the bridge of his nose firm, the eyes small and lively, the pate bald.

"What time d'you think you'll get here?"

"I'll have to get organized. Have to get the bag out of there. No problem, though. I've got it figured out."

With a flicker of suspicion, glass in hand, the boss looked at Querelle. "Yeah? But, make no mistake, you're on your own. It's none of my business."

Mario remained motionless, almost absent: he was leaning against the counter with his back reflected in the mirror behind him. Without a word he removed his elbows from the counter, thus changing his interesting posture, and went to the big mirror next to the proprietor: now it looked as if he were leaning against himself. And now, faced with both men, Querelle experienced a sudden malaise, a sinking of the heart, such as killers know. Mario's calmness and good looks disconcerted him. They were on too grand a scale. The brothelkeeper, Norbert, was far too powerful-looking. So was Mario. The outlines of their two bodies met to form one continuous pattern, and this seemed to blur and blend their muscular bodies as well as their faces. It was impossible, the boss couldn't be an informer; but then it seemed equally out of the question for Mario to be anything but a cop. Within himself, Querelle felt a trembling, a vacillation, almost to the point of losing himself, by vomiting it all out, all that he really was. Seized by vertigo in the presence of these powerful muscles and nerves that he perceived as towering above him—as one might when throwing one's head back to appraise the height of a giant pine tree—that kept on doubling and merging again, crowned by Mario's beauty, but dominated by Norbert's bald head and bullish neck, Querelle stood there with his mouth half open, his palate a little dry.

"No, sure, that's all right. I'll take care of all that."

Mario was wearing a very plainly cut, double-breasted maroon suit, with a red tie. Like Querelle and Nono (Norbert), he was drinking white wine, but like a true cop he seemed completely disinterested in their conversation. Querelle recognized the authority in the man's thighs and chest, the sobriety of movement that endows a man with total power: this, again, stemming from an undisputed moral authority, a perfect social organization, a gun, and the right to use it. Mario was one of the masters. Once more Querelle held out his hand, and then, turning up the collar of his peacoat, he headed for the backdoor: it was indeed better to leave through the small yard at the back of the house.

"So long."

Mario's voice, as we have observed, was loud and impassive. On hearing it, Querelle felt reassured in some strange way. As soon as he left the house he compelled himself to be aware of his attire, his sailor's attributes: above all, of the stiff collar of the peacoat, which he felt protected his neck like armor. Within its seemingly massive enclosure he could feel how delicate his neck was, yet strong and proud, and at the base of that neck, the tender bones of the nape, the perfect point of vulnerability. Flexing his knees lightly he could feel them touching the fabric of his pants. Querelle was stepping out like a true sailor who sees himself as one hundred percent just that, a sailor. Rolling the shoulders, from left to right, but not excessively. He thought of hitching the coat up a bit and putting his hands in the vertical front pockets, but changed his mind and instead raised a finger to his beret and pushed it to the back of his head, almost to the nape of his neck, so that its edge brushed against the upturned collar. Such tangible certainty of being every inch a sailor reassured him and calmed him down. Nevertheless, he felt sad, and mean. He was not wearing that habitual smile. The fog dampened his nostrils, refreshed his eyelids and his chin. He was walking straight ahead, punching his weighty body through the softness of the fog. The greater the distance he put between himself and La Féria, the more he fortified himself with all the might of the police force, believing himself to be under their friendly protection now, and endowing the idea of "police" with the muscular strength of Nono, and with Mario's good looks. This had been his first encounter with a police officer. So he had met a cop, at last. He had walked up to him. He had shaken hands with him. He had just signed an agreement that would protect both of them against treachery. He had not found his brother there, but instead of him those two monsters of certainty, those two big shots. Nevertheless, while gaining strength from the might of the Police as he drew away from La Féria, he did not for one moment cease to be a sailor. Querelle, in some obscure way, knew that he was coming close to his own point of perfection: clad in his blue garb, cloaked in its prestige, he was no longer a simple murderer, but a seducer as well. He proceeded down the Rue de Siam with giant strides. The fog was chilling. Increasingly the forms of Mario and Nono merged and instilled in him a feeling of submission, and of pride—for deep down the sailor in him strongly opposed the policeman: and so he fortified himself with the full might of the Fighting Navy, as well. Appearing to be running after his own form, ever about to overtake it, yet in pursuit, he walked on fast, sure of himself, with a firm stride. His body armed itself with cannon, with a hull of steel, with torpedoes, with a crew who were agile and strong, bellicose and precise. Querelle became "Le Querelle," a giant destroyer, warlord of the seas, an intelligent and invincible mass of metal.

"Watch your step, you asshole!"

His voice cut through the fog like a siren in the Baltic.

"But it was you who . . ."

Suddenly the young man, polite, buffeted, thrown aside by the wake of Querelle's impassive shoulder, realized that he was being insulted. He said:

"At least you could be civil about it! Or open your eyes!"

If he meant "Keep your eyes open," for Mario the message was "Light up the course, use your running light." He spun around:

"What about my lights?"

His voice was harsh, decisive, ready for combat. He was carrying a cargo of explosives. He didn't recognize himself any more. He hoped to appeal to Mario and Norbert—no longer to that fantastic compound creature that consisted of the sum of their virtues—but in reality he had placed himself under the protection of that very idol. However, he did not yet admit this to himself, and for the first time in his life he invoked the Navy.

"Lookahere, buddy, I hope you ain't trying to get my goat, or are you? Because, let me tell you, us sailors won't let anybody get away with that kind of shit. Understand?"

"But I'm not trying to do anything, I was just passing . . ."

Querelle looked at him. He felt safe in his uniform. He clenched his fists and immediately knew that every muscle, every nerve was taking up its battle station. He was strong, ready to pounce. His calves and arms were vibrating. His body was flexed for a fight in which he would measure up to an adversary—not this young man intimidated by his nerve—but to the power that had subjugated him in the brothel parlor. Querelle did not know that he wanted to do battle *for* Mario, and *for* Norbert, the way one would do battle for a king's daughter and against the dragons. This fight was a trial.

"Don't you know you can't push us around, not us Navy guys?"

Never before had Querelle applied such a label to himself. Those sailors proud of being sailors, animated by the *esprit de corps*, had always seemed comical to him. In his eyes they were as ridiculous as the bigheads who played to the gallery and then got shown up for the braggarts they were. Never had Querelle said, "Me, I'm one of the guys from the *Vengeur.*" Or even, "Me, I'm a *French* salt . . ." But now, having done so, he felt no shame; he felt completely at ease.

"OK, scram."

He pronounced these words with a twisted sneer directed right at the landlubber, and with his face fixed in that expression he waited, hands in pockets, until the young man had turned and gone. Then, feeling good and even a little tougher than before, he continued on down the Rue de Siam. Arriving on board, Querelle instantly perceived an opportunity for the dispensation of rough justice. He was seized by sudden and violent fury on noticing that one of the sailors on the larboard deck was wearing his beret the very same way he thought Querelle alone should wear it. He felt positively robbed, when he recognized that particular angle, that lock of hair sticking up like a flame, licking the front of the beret, the whole effect of it as legendary, now, as the white fur bonnet worn by Vacher, the killer of shepherds. Querelle walked up, his cruel eyes fixed on those of the hapless sailor, and told him, in a matter-of-fact tone:

"Put it on straight."

The other one did not understand. A little taken aback, vaguely frightened, he stared at Querelle without budging. With a sweep of his hand Querelle sent the beret flying down on to the deck, but before the sailor could bend down to pick it up, Querelle pounded his face with his fists, rapidly, and with a vengeance.

Querelle loved luxury. It seems obvious that he had a feeling for the common beliefs, that he did glory in his Frenchness, to some extent, and in being a Navy man, susceptible like any male to national and military pride. Yet we have to remember some facts of his early youth, not because these extend across the entire psyche of our hero, but in order to make plausible an attitude that does not boil down to a simple matter of choice. Let us consider his characteristic manner of walking. Querelle grew up among hoodlums, and that is a world of most studied attitudes, round about the age of fifteen—when you roll your shoulders quite ostentatiously, keep your hands thrust deep into your pockets, wear your pants too tight and turned up at the bottoms. Later on he walked with shorter steps, legs tight and the insides of his thighs rubbing against each other, but holding his arms well away from his body, making it appear that this was due to overdeveloped biceps and dorsals. It was only shortly after he committed his first murder that he arrived at a gait and posture peculiar to himself: he stalked slowly, both arms stiffly extended, fists clenched in front of his fly, not touching it; legs well apart.

This search for a posture that would set him, Querelle, apart, and thus prevent him from being mistaken for any other member of the crew, originated in a kind of terrifying dandyism. As a child he had used to amuse himself with solitary competitions with himself, trying to piss ever higher and farther. Querelle smiled, contracting his cheeks. A sad smile. One might have called it ambiguous, intended for the giver rather than the receiver. Sometimes, in thinking about it, the image, the sadness Lieutenant Seblon must have seen in that smile, could be compared to that of watching, in a group of country choirboys, the most virile one, standing firm on sturdy feet, with sturdy thighs and neck, and chanting in a masculine voice the canticles to the Blessed Virgin. He puzzles his shipmates, made them uneasy. First, because of his physical strength, and secondly by the strangeness of his overly vulgar behavior. They watched him approaching, on his face the slight anguish of a sleeper under a mosquito net who hears the complaint of a mosquito held back by the netting and incensed by the impenetrable and invisible resistance. When we read "... his whole physiognomy had its changeable aspects: from the ferocious it could turn gentle, often ironic: his walk was a sailor's, and standing up, he always kept his legs well apart. This murderer had traveled a great deal ... ," we know that this description of Campi, beheaded April 30, 1884, fits like a glove. Being an interpretation, it is exact. Yet his mates were able to say of Querelle: "What a funny guy," for he presented them, almost daily, with another disconcerting and scandalous vision of himself. He shone among them with the brightness of a true freak. Sailors of our Fighting Navy exhibit a certain honesty which they owe to the sense of glory that attracts them to the service. If they wanted to go in for smuggling or any other form of trafficking they would not really know how to go about it. Heavily and lazily, because of the boredom inherent in their task, they perform it in a manner that seems to us like an act of faith. But Querelle kept his eye on the main chance. He felt no nostalgia for his time as a petty hoodlum—

he had never really outgrown it—but he continued, under the protection of the French flag, his dangerous exploits. All his early teens he had spent in the company of dockers and merchant seamen. He knew their game.

Querelle strode along, his face damp and burning, without thinking about anything in particular. He felt a little uneasy, haunted by the unformulated glimmer of a suspicion that his exploits would gain him no glory in the eyes of Mario and Nono, who themselves were (and were for each other) glory personified. On reaching the Recouvrance bridge he went down the steps to the landing stage. It was then that it occurred to him, while passing the Customs House, that he was letting his six kilos of opium go too cheap. But then again it was important to get business off to a good start. He walked to the quayside to wait for the patrol boat that would come to return seamen and officers to the *Vengeur* which was lying at anchor out in the Roads. He checked his watch: ten of four. The boat would be there in ten minutes. He took a turn up and down to keep warm, but chiefly because the shame he felt forced him to keep on the move. Suddenly he found himself at the foot of the wall supporting the coastal road that circles the port, and from which springs the main arch of the bridge. The fog prevented Querelle from seeing the top of the wall, but judging by its slope and the angle at which it rose from the ground, from the size and quality of its stones—details he was quick to observe—he guessed that it was of considerable height. The same sinking of the heart he had felt in the presence of the two men in the brothel upset his stomach a little and tightened his throat. But even though his obvious, even brutal physical strength appeared subject to one of those weaknesses that cause one to be called "delicate," Querelle would never dare to acknowledge such frailty—by leaning against the wall, for example: but the distressing feeling that he was about to be engulfed did make him slump a little. He walked away from the wall, turned his back on it. The sea lay in front of him, shrouded in fog.

"What a strange guy," he thought, raising his eyebrows.

Stock-still, legs wide apart, he stood and pondered. His lowered gaze traveled over the gray miasma of the fog and came to rest on the black, wet stones of the jetty. Little by little, but at random, he considered Mario's various peculiarities. His hands. The curve—he had been staring at it—from the tip of his thumb to the tip of the index finger. The thickness of his arms. The width of his shoulders. His indifference. His blond hair. His blue eyes. Norbert's mustache. His round and shiny pate. Mario again, one of whose fingernails was completely black, a very beautiful black, as if lacquered. There are no black flowers; yet, at the end of his crushed finger, that black fingernail looked like nothing so much as a flower.

"What are you doing here?"

Querelle jumped to salute the vague figure that had appeared in front of him. First and foremost, he saluted the severe voice that pierced the fog, with all the assurance emanating from a place that was light and warm and real, framed in gold.

"Under orders to report to the Naval Police, Lieutenant."

The officer came closer.

"You're ashore?"

Querelle held himself to attention but contrived to hide, under his sleeve, the wrist on which he was wearing the gold watch.

"You'll take the next boat back. I want you to take an order to the Paymaster's Office."

Lieutenant Seblon scrawled a few words on an envelope and gave it to the seaman. He also gave him, in too dry a tone of voice, a few commonplace instructions. Querelle heard the tension in his voice. His smile flickered over a still trembling upper lip. He felt both uneasy at the officer's unexpectedly early return and pleased about it; pleased, above all, at meeting him there, after emerging from a state of panic—the ship's Lieutenant, whose steward he was.

"Go."

Only this word the Lieutenant pronounced with regret, without that customary harshness, even without the serene authority that a firm mouth ought to have given it. Querelle cracked a cautious smile. He saluted and headed toward the Customs House, then once again ascended the steps to the main road. That the Lieutenant should have caught him unawares, before there was time for recognition, was deeply wounding: it ripped open the opaque envelope which, he liked to believe, hid him from men's view. It then worked its way into the cocoon of daydreams he had been spinning the past few minutes, and out of which he now drew this thread, this visible adventure, conducted in the world of men and objects, already turning into the drama he half suspected, much as a tubercular person tastes the blood in his saliva, rising in his throat. Querelle pulled himself together: he had to, to safeguard the integrity of that domain into which even the highest-ranking officers were not permitted any insight. Querelle rarely responded even to the most distant familiarity. Lieutenant Seblon never did anything—whether he thought he did, or not—to establish any familiarity with his steward; such were the excessive defenses the officer armored himself with. While making Querelle smile, he left it to him to take any step toward intimacy. As bad luck would have it, such awkward attempts only served to put Querelle out. A few moments ago he had smiled because his Lieutenant's voice had been a reassuring sound. Now a sense of danger made the old Querelle bare his teeth. He had gone off with a gold watch from the Lieutenant's cabin drawer, but it was only because he had believed that the Lieutenant had really departed on a long furlough.

"When he gets back, he'll have forgotten all about it," had been his reasoning. "He'll think he lost it some place."

As he climbed the steps Querelle let his hand drag along the iron guard rail. The image of the two guys at the brothel, Mario and Norbert, suddenly flashed back to his mind. An informer and a cop. The fact that they had not denounced him immediately made it even more terrifying. Perhaps the police forced them to act as double agents. The image of the two grew larger. Grown monstrous, it threatened to devour Querelle. And the Customs? It was impossible to get round the Customs. Again the same nausea that had previously deranged his innards: now it culminated in a hiccough that did not quite reach his mouth. Slowly he regained his calm, and as soon as it spread throughout his body he realized that he was home free. A few more steps, and he would be sitting down up there on the top step, by the side of the road. He might even take a little nap, after such a wonderful brainstorm. From this moment on he forced himself to think in precise terms:

"Boy, that's it! I've got it. What I need is some guy (Vic was the man, he'd already decided), a guy to let down a piece of string from the top of that wall. I get off the boat and hang around on the jetty for a while. Fog's thick enough. Instead of going on, past the Customs, I'll stay at the foot of the wall. And up there, on the road, there's that guy holding the string. Need about ten, twelve meters of it. Then I tie the package to it. The fog'll hide me. My buddy pulls it up, and I walk through Customs, clean as a whistle."

He felt deeply relieved. The emotion was identical with the one he felt as a child at the foot of one of the two massive towers that rise in the port of La Rochelle. It was a feeling of both power and the lack of it: of pride, in the first place, to know that such a tall tower could be the symbol of his own virility, to the extent that when he stood at the base of it, legs apart, taking a piss, he could think of it as his own prick. Coming out from the movies in the evening he would sometimes crack jokes with his buddies, standing there, taking a leak in the company of two or three of them:

"Now that's what Georgette needs!"

or:

"With one like that in my pants I could have all the pussy in La Rochelle,"

or:

"You're talking like some old guy! Some old Rochellois!"

But when he was by himself, at night or during the day, opening or buttoning his fly, his fingers felt they were capturing, with the greatest care, the treasure—the very soul—of this giant prick; he imagined that his own virility emanated from the stone phallus, while feeling quietly humble in the presence of the unruffled and incomparable power of that unimaginably huge male. And now Querelle knew he would be able to deliver his burden of opium to that strange ogre with the two magnificent bodies.

"Just need to get another guy to help. Can't do it without him."

Querelle understood, though hazily, that the entire success of the venture depended on this one sailor, and (even more vaguely, in the peace of mind afforded by this very remote and sweet idea, yet as insubstantial as the dawn), in fact, on Vic—whom he would enroll for the job, and it would be through him that he would be able to reach Mario and Norbert.

Now the boss seemed straight; the other one was too handsome to be a mere cop. Those rings were too nice for that.

"And what about me? And my jewels? If only that sonofabitch could see them!"

Querelle was referring to the treasure hidden away in the dispatch boat, but also to his balls, full and heavy, which he stroked every night, and kept safely tucked away between his hands while he slept. He thought of the stolen watch. He smiled:

that was the old Querelle, blooming, lighting up, showing the delicate underside of his petals.

The workmen went and sat down at a bare wooden table in the middle of the dormitory, between the two rows of beds. On it stood two large, steaming bowls of soup. Slowly Gild took his hand off the fur of the cat lying stretched on his knee; then put it back there. Some small part of his shame was flowing out into the animal and being absorbed by her. Thus, she was a comfort to Gil, like a dressing staunching a wound. Gil had not wanted to get into a fight when, on coming back, Theo had started poking fun at him. And that had been obvious from his tone of voice, so surprisingly humble when answering: "There's some words better left unsaid." As his retorts were usually dry and laconic, almost to the point of cruelty, Gil had been all the more conscious of his humiliation when he heard his own voice ingratiate itself, stretch out like a shadow round Theo's feet. To himself, to console his self-regard, Gil had remarked that one does not fight with such assholes, but the spontaneous sweetness of his voice reminded him too strongly that he had, in fact, given in. And his buddies? What the hell did they matter, fuck 'em. Theo, that was well known, Theo was a queer. He was tough and nervy all right, but he was a queer. No sooner had Gil started to work in the shipyard than the mason had showered him with his attentions, favors which sometimes were real masterpieces of subtlety. He also bought Gil glasses of the syrupy white wine in the bistros of Recouvrance. But within that steely hand slapping him on the back in the bar Gil sensed—and trembled at sensing—the presence of another, softer hand. The one wanted to subjugate him, so that the other could then caress him. The last couple of days Theo had been trying to make him angry. It riled him that he had not yet had his way with the younger man. In the shipyard Gil would sometimes look across at him: it was rare not to find Theo's gaze fixed on him. Theo was a scrupulous workman, regarded as exemplary by all his mates. Before placing it in its bed of cement, his hands caressed each stone, turned it over, chose the best-looking surface, and always fitted it so that the best side faced outward. Gil raised his hand, stopped stroking the cat. He put it down gently, next to the stove, on a soft spot covered with shavings. Thus he perhaps made his companions believe that he was a very sweet-tempered man. He even wanted his gentleness to be provoking. Finally, for his own benefit, he had to give the appearance of wishing to distance himself from any excessive reaction induced by Theo's insult. He went to the table, sat down at his place. Theo did not look at him. Gil saw his thick mop of hair and thick neck bent over the white china bowl. He was talking and laughing heartily with one of his friends. The overall sound was one of mouths lapping up spoonfuls of thick soup. Once the meal was finished, Gil was the first one to get up; he took off his sweater and went to work on the dirty dishes. For a few minutes, his shirt open at the neck, sleeves rolled up above elbows, his face reddened and damp from the steam, his bare arms plunging into the greasy dishwater, he looked like a young female kitchen worker in some restaurant. He knew, all of a sudden, that he was no longer just an ordinary workman. For several minutes he felt he had turned into a strange and ambiguous being: a young man who acted as a serving maid to the masons. To prevent any of them coming up to tease her, to smack her on the buttocks with great gusts of laughter, he made sure all his motions were brisk and busy. When he took his hands out of the now revoltingly tepid water, they no longer appeared soft like that at all—you could see the ravages wrought by plaster and cement. He felt some regret at the sight of these workman's hands, their cracked skin, their permanent white frosting, their fingernails crusted with cement. Gil had been storing up too much shame over the last couple of days to even dare think about Paulette at this point. Nor about Roger, either. He was unable to think of them warmly; his feelings had been soiled by shame, by a kind of nauseating vapor that threatened to mingle with all his thoughts in order to corrupt and decompose them. Yet he did think of Roger: with hatred. In that atmosphere, the hatred grew more noxious, grew so forcefully that it chased away the feeling of shame, squeezed it, rammed it into the remotest corner of his consciousness; there, however, it squatted brooding and reminding him of its presence with the heavy insistence of a throbbing abscess. Gil hated Roger for being the cause of his humiliation. He hated Roger's good looks, even, for providing Theo with ammunition for his evil sense of irony. He hated Roger for coming down to the shipyard, the previous day. True, he had smiled at him all through an evening, while singing, on a tabletop—but that was simply because Roger alone knew that the last song was the one Paulette liked to hum, and thus he was addressing her, through an accomplice

> *He was a happy bandit,*
> *Nothing did he fear . . .*

Some of the masons were playing cards now on the table cleared of the white china bowls and plates. The stove was going great guns. Gil wanted to go and take a leak, but in turning his head he saw Theo walking across the room and opening the door, most probably on his way to the same place. Gil stayed where he was. Theo closed the door behind him. He went out into the night and fog, dressed in a khaki shirt and blue pants patched with various faded bits of blue, very pleasing to look at; Gil had a similar pair, and valued them highly. He began to undress. He peeled off his shirt, revealing an undershirt from which his muscles bulged through the wide armholes. With his pants round his ankles, bending down, he saw his thighs: they were thick and solid, well developed by bicycling and playing soccer, smooth as marble and just as hard. In his thoughts Gil let his eyes travel up from his thighs to his belly, to his muscular back, to his arms. He felt ashamed of his strength. Had he taken up the challenge to fight, "on the level" perhaps (no punching, just wrestling) or "no holds barred" (boot and fist), he could certainly have beaten Theo; but that one had a reputation for extreme vindictiveness. Out of sheer rage Theo would have been capable of getting up at night to pad over to Gil's bed and cut his throat. It was thanks to this reputation that he was able to go on insulting others as blithely as he did. Gil refused to run the risk of having his throat cut. He stepped out of his pants. Standing for a moment in front of his bed in his red shorts and white undershirt, he gently scratched his thighs. He hoped that his buddies would observe his muscles and understand that he had only refused to fight out of generosity, so as not to make an older man look like a fool. He got into bed. His cheek on the bolster, Gil thought of Theo with disgust, that feeling growing more intense as he realized that in days past, as a young man, Theo surely had been a very handsome man. He was still pretty vigorous. Sometimes, at work, he would make awkward, punning references to what he thought was the proverbial virility of the men of the building trade. His face, with its hard, manly, still unspoilt features, was covered as with a net of minuscule wrinkles. His dark eyes, small but brilliant, mostly expressed sarcasm, but on certain days Gil had caught them looking at him, overflowing with an extraordinary tenderness; and that more often than not toward evening, when the gang was getting ready to leave. Theo would be scouring his hands with a little soft sand, and then he would straighten his back to take a good look at the work in progress: at the rising wall, at the discarded trowels, the planks, the wheelbarrows, the buckets. Over all these, and over the workmen, a gray, impalpable dust was settling, turning the yard into a single object, seemingly finished, the result of the day's commotion. The peace of the evening appeared due to this achievement, a deserted yard, powdered a uniform gray. Stiff after their day's work, worn out and silent, the masons would drift off with slow, almost funereal steps. None of them were more than forty years old. Tired, kit bag over left shoulder, right hand in pants pocket, they were leaving the day for the night. Their belts uneasily held up pants made for suspenders; every ten meters they would give them a hitch, tucking the front under the belt while letting the back gape wide, always showing that little triangular flap and its two buttons intended for fastening to a pair of suspenders. In this sluggish calm they would return to their quarters. None of them would be going to the girls or the bistro before Saturday, but, once abed and at peace, they would let their manhood take its rest and under the sheets store up its black forces and white juices; would go to sleep on their side and pass a dreamless night, one bare arm with its powder-dusted hand stretched out over the edge of the bed, showing the delicate pulsation of the blood in bluish veins. Theo would trail along beside Gil. Every evening he offered him a cigarette before setting out to catch up with the others, and sometimes—and then his expression would change—he would give him a great slap on the shoulder.

"Well, buddy? How's it going?"

Gil would reply with his usual, noncommittal shrug. He would barely manage a smile. On the bolster, Gil felt his cheeks grow hot. He had lain there with his eyes wide open, and by reason of his ever increasing need to empty his bladder, his anger was aggravated by impatience. The rims of his eyelids were burning. A blow received straightens a man up and makes the body move forward, to return that blow, or a punch—to jump, to get a hard-on, to dance: to be alive. But a blow received may also cause you to bend over, to shake, to fall down, to die. When we see life, we call it beautiful. When we see death, we call it ugly. But it is more beautiful still to see oneself living at great speed, right up to the moment of death. Detectives, poets, domestic servants and priests rely on abjection. From it, they draw their power. It circulates in their veins. It nourishes them.

"Being a cop's just a job like any other."

Giving this answer to the slightly scornful friend of long standing who was asking him why he had joined the police force, Mario knew that he was lying. He did not much care for women, although it was easy for him to get a piece of the action from prostitutes. The fact of Dédé's presence made the hatred he felt all around him in his life as a policeman seem like a heavy burden. Being a cop embarrassed him. He wanted to ignore the fact, but it enveloped him. Worse, it flowed in his veins. He was afraid of being poisoned by it. Slowly at first, then with increasing force, he became involved with Dédé. Dédé could be the antidote. The Police in his veins circulated a little less strongly, grew weaker. He felt a little less guilty. The blood in his veins was then less black, and this made him a target for the scorn of the hoodlums and the vengeance of Tony.

Was it true that the prison of Bougen was filled with beautiful female spies? Mario kept hoping that he would be called in for a case involving a theft of documents concerning national defense matters.

In Dédé's room, Rue Saint-Pierre, Mario was sitting, feet on the floor, on the divan bed covered with a plain, fringed, blue-cotton bedspread pulled over unmade sheets. Dédé jumped onto the bed to kneel beside the immobile profile of Mario's face and torso. The detective didn't say anything. Not a muscle in his face moved. Never before had Dédé seen him look so hard, drawn, and sad; his lips were dry and set in a mean expression.

"And now what? What's going to happen? I'll go down to the port, take a good look around . . . I'll see if he's there. What d'you say?"

Mario's face remained grim. A strange heat seemed to animate it, without heightening its color; it was pale, but the lines were set so hard and so rigidly drawn and patterened that they lit the face up with an infinity of stars. It looked as if Mario's whole life were surging upward, mounting from his calves, parts, torso, heart, anus, guts, arms, elbows, and neck, right up into the face, where it grew desperate at not being able to escape, to go on, to disappear into the night and come to an end in a shower of sparks. His cheeks were a little hollowed, making the chin look firmer. He wasn't frowning; his eyeballs were slightly protuberant, and his eyelid looked like a small, amber rosebud attached to the stem of his nose. In the front of his mouth Mario was rolling around an ever increasing amount of spittle, not daring, not knowing how to swallow it. His fear and his hatred mingled and massed there, at the farthest reaches of himself. His blue eyes looked almost black, under brows which had never appeared so light, so blond. Their very brightness troubled Dédé's peace of mind. (The boy was far more peaceful than his friend was agitated—profoundly agitated, as if he alone had dredged up to the surface all the mud deposited in both of them; and this new force of purpose in the detective made him look both desperate and grave, with a touch of that restrained irritation so typical a trait in accredited heroes. Dédé seemed to have recognized this and could find no better means of displaying his gratitude than by accepting, with elegant simplicity, his purification, his becoming endowed with the vernal grace of April woodlands.) We were saying—that extreme brightness of Mario's eyebrows troubled the young fellow, as he saw so light a color casting such shadows, over so dark and stormy an expression. Desolation appears greater when pinpointed by light. And the whiteness of the brows troubled his peace of mind, the purity of it: not because he knew that Mario went in fear of his life because of the return of a certain stevedore he had once arrested, but because he was watching the detective manifest unmistakable signs of acute mental struggle—by making him understand, in some indefinite way, that there was hope of seeing joy return to his friend's face as long as it still showed signs of such brightness. That "ray of light" on Mario's face was, in point of fact, a shadow. Dédé put a bare forearm—his shirtsleeves were rolled up above the elbow—on Mario's shoulder and gazed attentively at his ear. For a moment he contemplated the attractions of Mario's hair, razor-cut from the nape of the neck to the temples: recently cut, it gave off a delicate, silky light. He blew gently on the ear, to free it of some blond hairs, longer ones, that fell from the forehead. None of this caused Mario's expression to change.

"What a drag, you looking so grouchy! What do you think they're going to do, those guys?"

For a couple of seconds he was silent, as if reflecting; then he added:

"And it's really too damn bad you didn't think of having them arrested. Why didn't you?"

He leaned back a little way to get a better view of Mario's profile, whose face and eyes did not move. Mario was not even thinking. He was simply allowing his stare to lose itself, to dissolve, and to let his whole body be carried away in this dissolution. Only a short while ago Robert had informed him that five of the most determined characters among the dockers had sworn they'd "get" him. Tony, whom he had arrested in a manner these sons of Brest regarded as unfair, had been released from the prison of Bougen the previous evening.

"What would you like me to do?"

Without shifting his knees, Dédé had managed to lean back even farther. He now had the posture of a young female saint at the very moment of a visitation, fallen on her knees at the foot of an oak tree, crushed by the revelation, by the splendor of Grace, then bending over backward in order to save her face from a vision that is searing her eyelashes, her very eyeballs, blinding her. He smiled. Gently he put his arm round the detective's neck. With little kisses he pecked at, without ever touching them, his forehead, temples, and eyes, the rounded tip of the nose, his lips, yet always without actually touching them; Mario felt like being subjected to a thousand prickly points of flame, darting and flickering to and fro. He thought:

"He's covering me with mimosa blossoms."

Only his eyelids fluttered, no other part of his body moved, nor did his hands, still resting on his knees, nor did his pecker grow lively. He was, nevertheless, touched by the kid's unaccustomed tenderness. It reached him in a thousand small shocks, sad only in their tentativeness, and warm, and he permitted it slowly to swell and lighten his body. But Dédé was pecking at a rock. The intervals between kisses grew longer, the youngster withdrew his face, still smiling, and started to whistle. Imitating the twitter of sparrows on all sides of Mario's rigid and massive head, from eye to mouth, from neck to nostrils, he moved his small mouth, now shaped like a chicken's ass, whistling now like a blackbird, now like an oriole. His eyes were smiling. He was having a good time, sounding like all the birds in a grove. It made him feel quite soft inside to think that he was all these birds, and that at the same time he was offering them up on this burning but immobile head, locked in stone. Dédé tried to delight and fascinate him with these birds. But Mario felt a kind of anguish, being confronted with that terrifying thing: the smile of a bird. Then, again, he thought with some relief:

"He's powdering me with mimosa blossoms."

Thus, to the birdsong was added a light pollen. Mario felt vaguely like being held captive in one of those fine-meshed widows' veils that are dotted with pea-sized black knots. Then he retired into himself to regain that region of flux and innocence that can be called limbo. In his very anguish he escaped from his enemies. He had the right to be a policeman, a copper. He had a right, to let himself slip back into the old complicity that united him with this little sixteen-year-old stoolie. Dédé was hoping that a smile might open that head, to let the birds in: but the rock refused to smile, to flower, to be covered with nests. Mario was closing up. He was aware of the kid's airy whistlings, but he was—that part of him that was ever-watchful Mario—so far gone into himself, trying to face up to fear and to destroy it by examining it, that it would take him a while to return as far as his muscles and to make them move again. He felt that there, behind the severity of his face, his pallor, his immobility, his doors, his walls, he was safe. Around him rose the ramparts of The Police Force, and he was protected by all that only apparent strictness. Dédé kissed him on the corner of his mouth, very quickly, then bounded back to the foot of the bed. Perching in front of Mario, he smiled.

"What's happening, for crissakes? You sick, or in love, or what?"

In spite of his desire, he had never even thought of going to bed with Dédé, nor had he ever made the slightest equivocal gesture in that direction. His chiefs and colleagues knew of his association with the kid, who to them was merely an auxiliary nonentity.

Dédé had no answer for Mario's sarcasm, but his smile faded a little, without disappearing altogether. His face was pink.

"You must be out of your gourd."

"Well I haven't hurt you, have I? I just planted a few friendly kisses on you. You've been sitting there scowling long enough. Just trying to cheer you up."

"So I haven't got a right to sit and think things over, eh?"

"But it's such a drag when you're like that. And anyway, how do you know for
sure that that Tony's really out to get you . . ."

Mario made an irritated gesture. His mouth hardened.

"You don't think I'm getting cold feet, do you?"

"I didn't say that."

Dédé sounded angry.

"I didn't say that."

He was standing in front of Mario. His voice was hoarse, a little vulgar, deep,
with a slight country accent. It was the kind of voice that knows how to talk to
horses. Mario turned his head. He looked at Dédé for a couple of seconds. All he
would proceed to say during the ensuing scene would be tight-lipped and stern,
as if trying to put the full force of his will into his expression, so that the youngster
would realize, once and for all, that he, Mario Lambert, inspector of the mobile
squad, assigned to the Commissariat of Brest, went in no fear for his future. For
a year now he had been working with Dédé who provided him with information
on the secret life of the docks and told him about the thefts, the pilfering of coffee,
minerals, other goods. The men on the waterfront paid little attention to the kid.

"Get going."

Planted in front of him, feet apart and looking stockier than before, Dédé gazed
at the policeman, somewhat sulkily. Then he swiveled round on one foot, keeping
his legs extended like a compass, and, in reaching over to the window where his
coat was hanging on the hasp, moved his shoulders and chest with surprising speed
and strength, displacing the weight of an invisible vault of heaven. For the first
time Mario realized that Dédé was strong, that he had grown up into a young man.
He felt ashamed about having given in to fear in his presence, but then very
quickly retreated into the shell of The Police, which justifies every kind of
behavior. The window opened on to a narrow lane. Facing it, on the other side,
was the gray wall of a garage. Dédé put on his coat. When he turned around again,
briskly as before, Mario got up and stood in front of him, hands in pockets.

"Now, did you get it straight? No need to go in too close. I've told you, no one
suspects that you're in with me, but it's better if you don't let them spot you."

"Don't worry, Mario."

Dédé was getting ready to leave. He wound a red, woolen muffler round his
neck and put on a small, gray cap, the kind still worn by lads in the villages. He
pulled out a cigarette from a number of loose ones in his coat pocket and nimbly
popped it into Mario's mouth, then one into his own, without cracking a smile in
spite of what it brought to mind. And then, in a suddenly grave, almost solemn
fashion, he donned his gloves, the only symbol of his minimal enough affluence.
Dédé loved, almost venerated these poor objects and would never just carry them
in his hand, but always put them on with great care. He knew that they were the
only detail by which he himself, from the depths of his self-imposed—therefore
ethical—dereliction, touched upon the world of society and wealth. By these
clearly purposeful motions he put himself into his proper place again. It amazed
him now that he had dared that kiss, and all the games that had preceded it. Like

any other mistake, it made him feel ashamed. Never before had he shown Mario, nor Mario him, any sign of affection. Dédé was serious by nature. In his dealings with the detective, he seriously went about collecting his clues, and reported them as seriously every week in some secluded spot that had been agreed on over the phone. For the first time in his life he had given in to his own imagination.

"Stone cold sober, too," he thought.

In saying that Dédé was a serious person, we do not mean that this was a quality he thought desirable. It was rather that his inherent gravity made it hard for him to ever force himself into a semblance of gaiety. He struck a match and held out the little flame to Mario, with a gravity greater than his ignorance of the rites. Since Mario was the taller, the little fellow offered up his face at the same time, in all innocence, partly shadowed by the screen of his hands.

"And what are you going to do?"

"Me . . . ? Nothing. What d'you suppose. I'll just be waiting for you to get back."

Once again Dédé looked at Mario. He gazed at him for a couple of seconds, his mouth half open and dry. "I'm scared," he thought. He took a pull at his cigarette and said: "All right." He turned to the mirror to adjust the peak of his cap, to bend it over a little more to the left. In the mirror he could see the whole room in which he had now lived for over a year. It was small, cold, and on the walls there were some photographs of prizefighters and female movie stars, clipped out of the papers. The only luxury item was the light fixture above the divan: an electric bulb in a pale pink glass tulip. He did not despise Mario for being scared. Quite some time ago he had understood the nobility of self-acknowledged fear, what he called the jitters, or cold feet . . .

Often enough he had been forced to take to his heels in order to escape from some dangerous and armed foe. He hoped that Mario would accept the challenge to fight, having decided himself, should a good occasion arise, to knock off the docker who had just come out of the joint. To save Mario would be to save himself. And it was natural enough for anyone to be scared of Tony the Docker. He was a fierce and unscrupulous brute. On the other hand, it seemed strange to Dédé that a mere criminal should cause The Police to tremble, and for the first time he had his doubts that this invisible and ideal force which he served and behind which he sheltered might just consist of weak humans. And, as this truth dawned on him, through a little crack in himself, he felt both weaker and—strangely enough—stronger. For the first time he was taking thought, and this frightened him a little.

"What about your chief? Haven't you told him?"

"Don't you worry about that. I've told you your job: now get on with it." Mario dimly feared the boy might betray him. The voice in which he answered showed signs of softening, but he caught himself quickly, even before opening his mouth, and the words came out tough and dry. Dédé looked at his wristwatch.

"It's getting on for four," he said. "It's dark already. And there's *some* fog rolling in . . . Visibility five meters."

"Well, what are you waiting for?"

Mario's voice was suddenly more commanding. He was the boss. Two quick steps had been quite sufficient to take him across the room and bring him, with the same ease of movement, in front of the mirror, where he combed his hair, and once more became that powerful shadow, raw-boned and muscular, cheerful and young, which corresponded to his proper form, and sometimes to that of Dédé as well. (As he watched Mario approach their meeting place, Dédé sometimes told him, with a grin: "I like what I see, and I'd like to be it," but at other times his pride rebelled against such identification. That, then, was when he would attempt some timid gesture of revolt, but a smile or a concise order would put him right back where he belonged, in Mario's shadow.)

"All right."

He tried to sound tough, but for his own ears only. Stock-still for a second, to prove his absolute independence to himself, he let a puff of smoke drift in the direction of the window at which he was staring; one hand in his pocket he then turned abruptly toward Mario and, looking him straight in the eye, extended his other hand, stiffly, at arm's length.

"So long."

He sounded positively funereal. With a more natural calm, Mario replied:

"So long, buddy. Get back as soon as you can."

"And don't you feel too blue. T'ain't worth it."

He stood by the door. He opened it. The few items of clothing hanging from the door hook billowed out, sumptuously, while the stench from the open latrines on the outside landing penetrated the room. Mario noticed this sudden magnificent swirling of materials. With slight embarrassment he heard himself saying:

"Stop playacting."

He was moved, but he could not permit himself to be moved. His sensitivity, carefully hidden and not really aware of formal and definitive beauty, but very much so of flashes of what we know only by the name "poetry," sometimes overtook and stunned him for a few seconds: it might be some docker, smiling such a smile as he was pocketing a pinch of tea in the warehouse, under his very eyes, that Mario felt like going on without a word, caught himself hesitating, almost regretting that he was the policeman instead of the thief: this hesitation never lasted long. He had hardly taken a step before the enormity of his behavior struck him. The law and order whose servant he was might be overthrown irreparably. A huge breach had already occurred. They might say he refrained from arresting the thief for purely esthetic reasons. At first his habitual watchdog temper would be checked by the grace of the docker, but once Mario became aware of the working of that charm, it was then obviously out of sheer hatred for the thief's beauty that he finally arrested him.

Dédé turned his head, signaling a last farewell from the corner of his eye, but his friend took this to be a wink of complicity at Dédé's own mirror image. Dédé had scarcely closed the door when he felt his muscles melt, his extremities soften as in the execution of a graceful bow. It was the same feeling he had experienced while playing around Mario's face: he had been overcome by a weakness, quickly restrained, that had awakened in him a longing—his neck already bending forward, languidly—to rest his head on Mario's thick thigh.

"Dédé!"

He opened the door again.

"What is it?"

Mario came toward him, looked him straight in the eye. He said, in a gentle whisper:

"You know I trust you, don't you, buddy?"

Surprise in his eyes, mouth half open, Dédé looked at the detective without answering, without seeming to understand.

"Come back in for a minute . . ."

Gently Mario drew him into the room and shut the door.

"I know you'll do your best to find out what's going on But, as I said, I trust you. Nobody must get to know that I am here in your room. All right?"

The detective put his large, gold-beringed hand on the little informer's shoulder, then pulled him close to his chest:

"We've been working together for quite some time now, eh, buddy? Now you're on your own. I count on you."

He kissed him on the side of the head and let him go. This was only the second time since they had gotten to know one another that he had called the boy "buddy." Mario considered this fairly low-class language, but it was effective in sealing their friendship. Dédé took off down the stairs. Natural young tough that he was, it did not take him long to shake off his gloom. He stepped out into the street. Mario had listened to his familiar footfall—bouncy, sure, and steady—as he descended the wooden staircase of the miserable little hotel. In two strides, for the room was small and Mario a big man, he was by the window. He pulled aside the thick, tulle curtain, yellowed by smoke and dirt. Before him were the narrow street and the wall. It was dark. Tony's power was growing. He was turning into every shadow, every patch of the thickening fog into which Dédé was now plunging.

Querelle jumped ashore from the patrol boat. Other sailors came after him, Vic among them. They were coming from *Le Vengeur.* The boat would be there to take them back on board shortly before eleven. The fog was very dense, so substantial that it seemed as if the day itself had taken on material form. Having conquered the city, it might well decide to last longer than twenty-four hours. Without saying a word to Querelle, Vic walked off toward the Customs shed through which the sailors passed before ascending the steps that lead up to the level of the road, the quayside, as we have mentioned before, being immediately below. Instead of following Vic, Querelle merged into the fog, heading toward the sea wall. A cunning grin on his face, he waited a moment, then started walking along the wall, running his bare palm over its surface. It did not take long before he felt something brush against his fingers. Taking hold of the string, he tied the end of it round the opium package he had been carrying under his peacoat. He gave the string three sharp little tugs, and up it went, over the wall face, slowly, all the way to Vic.

The Admiral in command of the port was quite shaken the next morning when he was told that a young sailor had been found on the ramparts with his throat cut.

Nowhere had Querelle been seen in Vic's company. In the boat they had not spoken to one another, or certainly not at any length. That same evening, in the shadow of a smokestack, Querelle had given Vic a quick briefing. As soon as Querelle reached the road, he took the ball of string and the package back from Vic. Walking by Vic's side, with the sailor's blue coat sleeve, stiff and heavy from the fog's moisture, brushing against his own, Querelle felt the presence of Murder in every cell of his body. At first this came upon him slowly, a little like the mounting of an amorous affect, and, it seemed, through the same channel—or rather, through the *reverse* of that channel. In order to avoid the city and to enhance the bravado of their venture, Querelle decided to follow the rampart wall. Through the fog, his voice reached Vic:

"Get over here."

They continued along this road as far as the Castle (where Anne of Brittany once resided), then they crossed the Cours Dajot. No one saw them. They were smoking cigarettes. Querelle was smiling.

"You told nobody, right?"

"Hell, no. I'm not crazy."

The tree-lined walk was deserted. Besides, no one would have thought twice about two sailors coming out of the postern gate of the rampart road and continuing into the trees, now almost obliterated by the fog, through the brambles, the dead foliage, past ditches and mud, along paths meandering toward some dank thicket. Anyone would have thought they were just two young guys chasing a bit of skirt.

"Let's go round the other side. You see? That way we get around the fort."

Querelle went on smiling, smoking. Vic was matching Querelle's long, heavy stride, and as long as he kept pace with him, he was filled with surprising confidence. Querelle's taciturn and powerful presence instilled in Vic a feeling of authority similar to the one he had experienced the times they had pulled stickup jobs together. Querelle smiled. He let it rise inside him, that emotion he knew so well, which very soon now, at a good spot, there where the trees stood closer together and where the fog was dense, would take full command of him, driving out all conscience, all inhibition, and would make his body go through the perfect, quick, and certain motions of the criminal. He said:

"It's my brother who'll take care of the rest. He's our partner."

"Didn't know he was in Brest, your bro."

Querelle was silent. His eyes became fixed, as if to observe even more attentively the rising of that emotion within him. The smile left his face. His lungs filled with air. He burst. Now he was nothing.

"Yeah, he's in Brest all right. At La Féria."

"La Féria? No kidding! What's he do there? La Féria's a weird kind of joint."

"How so?"

No longer was any part of Querelle present within his body. It was empty. Facing Vic, there was no one. The murderer was about to attain his perfection, because here, in the dark of the night, there now loomed up a group of trees forming a kind of chamber, or chapel, with the path running through it like an aisle. Inside the package containing the opium there were also some pieces of jewelry, once obtained with Vic's assistance.

"Well, you know what they say. You know it as well as I do."

"So what? He's screwing the Madam."

A fraction of Querelle returned to the tips of his fingers, to his lips: the furtive ghost of Querelle once again saw the face and overwhelming presence of Mario combined with Norbert. A wall that had to be dealt with, still, and Querelle paled and dissolved at the foot of it. It had to be scaled, or climbed, or broken through, with a heave of the shoulder.

"Me, too, I've got my jewels," he thought.

The rings and the gold bracelets belonged to him alone. They invested him with sufficient authority to perform a sacred rite. Querelle was now no more than a tenuous breath suspended from his lips and free to detach itself from the body, to cling to the closest and spikiest branch.

"Jewels. That copper, he's covered in jewels. I've got my jewels, too. And I don't show them off."

He was free to leave his body, that audacious scaffolding for his balls. *Their* weight and beauty he knew. With one hand, calmly, he opened the folding knife he had in the pocket of his peacoat.

"Well then the proprietor must've screwed him first."

"And so? If that's his game."

"Shee-it."

Vic sounded shocked.

"If someone proposed that to you, would you say 'sure, go ahead'?"

"Why not, if I felt like it. I've done worse things than that."

A wan smile appeared on Querelle's face.

"If you saw my brother, you'd fall for him. You'd let him do it."

"They say it hurts."

"You bet'cha."

Querelle stopped.

"Smoke?"

The breath, about to be exhaled, flowed back into him who became Querelle once more. Without moving his hand, with a fixed stare, paradoxically directed inward at himself, he saw himself making the sign of the Cross. After that sign, given to warn the audience that the artiste is about to perform a feat of mortal danger, there was no looking back. He had to remain totally attentive in order to go through the motions of murder: he had to avoid any brutal gesture that might surprise the sailor, because Vic most probably wasn't used to being murdered, yet, and might cry out. The criminal has to contend with life and death, both: once they start shouting, one might stick them anywhere. The last time, in Cádiz, the victim had soiled Querelle's collar. Querelle turned to Vic and offered him a cigarette and lighter, with a seemingly awkward gesture hampered by the parcel he was holding under his arm.

"Go ahead, light one for me too."

Vic turned his back to keep the wind out.

"Yeah, he'd like you, you're such a sweet little kitten. And if you could suck his prick as hard as you're pulling on the old coffin nail, boy he could really swing with that!"

Vic blew out a puff of smoke. Holding out the lighted cigarette to Querelle, he said:

"Well, yeah, I don't think he'd get a chance."

Querelle sniggered.

"Oh, no? And what about me, I wouldn't get a chance either?"

"Oh, come off it . . ."

Vic wanted to move on, but Querelle held him back, stretching out one leg as if to trip him. Baring his teeth, cigarette clamped between them, he went on:

"Hey? Hey . . . Tell me something, ain't I as good as Mario? Ain't I?"

"What Mario?"

"What Mario? Well . . . It's thanks to you that I got over that wall, right?"

"Yeah, so what? What the hell are you driving at?"

"So you don't want to?"

"Come off it, stop horsing around . . ."

Vic would never add anything to that. Querelle grabbed him by the throat, letting his package fall onto the path. As it fell, he whipped out his knife and severed the sailor's carotid artery. As Vic had the collar of his peacoat turned up, the blood, instead of spurting over Querelle, ran down the inside of his coat and over his jersey. His eyes bulging the dying man staggered, his hand moving in a most delicate gesture, letting go, abandoning himself in an almost voluptuous posture that recalled, even in this land of fog, the dulcet clime of the bedchamber in which the Armenian had been murdered—whose image Vic's gesture now recreated in Querelle's memory. Querelle supported him firmly with his left arm and gently lowered him down onto the grass where he expired.

The murderer straightened his back. He was a thing, in a world where danger does not exist, because one is a thing. Beautiful, immobile, dark thing, within whose cavities, the void becoming vocal, Querelle could hear it surge forth to escape with the sound, to surround him and to protect him. Vic was not dead, he was a youth whom that astonishing thing, sonorous and empty, with a mouth half open and half hidden, with sunken, severe eyes, with hair and garments turned to stone, with knees perhaps enveloped in a fleece thick and curled like an Assyrian beard, whom this thing with its unreal fingers, wrapped in fog, had just done to death. The tenuous breath to which Querelle had been reduced was still clinging to the spiky branch of an acacia. Anxiously, it waited. The assassin snorted twice, very quickly, like a prizefighter, and moved his lips so that Querelle might enter, flow into the mouth, rise to the eyes, seep down to the fingers, fill the thing again.

Querelle turned his head, gently, not moving his chest. He heard nothing. He bent down to pull out a handful of grass turf to clean the blade of his knife. He thought he was squashing strawberries into freshly whipped cream, wallowing in them. He raised himself up from his crouched position, threw the bunch of bloodstained grass onto the dead man's body, and, after bending down a second time to retrieve his package of opium, resumed his walk under the trees alone. That the criminal at the instant of committing his crime believes that he'll never be caught is a mistaken assumption. He refuses, no doubt, to see the terrible consequences of his act at all clearly, yet he *knows* that the act does condemn him to death. We find the word "analysis" a little embarrassing. There are other ways of uncovering the workings of this self-condemnation. Let us simply call Querelle a happy moral suicide. Unable to know whether he'll be caught or not, the criminal lives in a state of anxiety, which he can only get rid of by negating, that is to say, by expiating his deed. And *that* is to say, by suffering the full penalty (for it would seem that it is the very impossibility of confessing to murders that provokes the panic, the metaphysical or religious terror in the criminal). At the bottom of a dry moat, at the foot of the ramparts, Querelle was leaning against a tree, cut off from the world by fog and night. He had put the knife back in his pocket. His beret he was holding in front of him, with both hands, at the level of his belt, the pompon against his belly. The smile was gone. He was now, in fact, appearing before the Criminal Court that he made up for himself after every murder. As soon as he had committed the crime, Querelle had felt the hand of an imaginary policeman on his shoulder, and from the site of the slaughter all the way to this desolate place he had walked with a heavy tread, crushed by his appalling fate. After some hundred meters he abandoned the path to plunge in among the trees and brambles and down a slope to the old moat below the battlements girding the city. He had the frightened look and downcast mien of a guilty man under arrest, yet within him the certainty—and this joined him to the policeman, in a shameful yet friendly fashion—that he was a hero. The ground was sloping and covered with thorny shrubs.

"Well, here we go," he thought. And, almost at once: "Yassir, this is it, folks. Back to the worm farm."

When he reached the bottom of the moat, Querelle stopped for a moment. A light wind was stirring the dry, brittle, pointed tips of the grasses, making them rustle quietly. The strange lightness of the sound only made his situation seem more bizarre. He walked on through the fog, still heading away from the scene of the crime. The grass and the wind went on making their gentle noise, soft as the sound of air in an athlete's nostrils, or the step of an acrobat ... Querelle, now clad in bright blue, silk tights, proceeded slowly, his figure molded by the azure garment, waist accentuated by a steel-studded leather belt. He felt the silent presence of every muscle working in unison with all the others to create the effect of a statue carved out of turbulent silence. Two police officers walked on either side of him, invisible, triumphant, and friendly, full of tenderness and cruelty toward their prey. Querelle continued a few more meters, through the fog and the whispering grasses. He was looking for a quiet place, solitary as a cell, sufficiently secluded and dignified to serve as a place of judgment.

"Sure hope they don't pick up my tracks," he thought.

He regretted that he had not simply turned around and walked backward in his own footsteps, thus raising the grass he had trodden down. But he perceived, quickly, the absurdity of his fear, while hoping his steps would be so light that every blade of grass would be intelligent enough to stand up again of its own accord. But the corpse surely wouldn't be discovered until later on, in the early morning hours. Yes, it would have to wait for the working men on their way to their jobs: *they* are the ones who come across what criminals leave by the roadside. The foggy weather did not trouble him. He noticed the marshy stench prevailing in the area. The outstretched arms of pestilence enfolded him. He kept on going. For a moment he was afraid a couple of lovers might have come down here among the trees, but this time of the year that seemed quite unlikely. Leaves and grass were damp, and the gaps between the branches interlaced with cobwebs moistened his face with their droplets as he passed through them. For a few seconds, to the astonished eyes of the assassin, the forest appeared most enchanted and lovely, vaulted and girded by hanging creeper plants gilded by a mysterious sun hanging in a sky both dim and clear and of an immensely distant blue, the womb of every dawn. Finally Querelle found himself by the trunk of a huge tree. He went up to it, cautiously walked around it, then leaned against it, turning his back to the place of murder where the corpse lay waiting. He took off his beret and held it in the way we have described. Above him, he knew, a tangle of black branches and twigs was penetrating and holding the fog. And from within him rose, up to his waking consciousness, all the details of the charges against him. In the hush of an over-heated room brimming with eyes and ears and fiery mouths, Querelle clearly heard the deep and droning and by its very banality most vengeful voice of the Presiding Judge:

"You have brutally slaughtered an accomplice of yours. The motives for this deed are only too evident . . ." (Here the Judge's voice and the Judge himself blurred. Querelle refused to see those motives, to disentangle, to find them in himself. He relaxed his attention to the proceedings and pressed himself more closely against the tree. The entire magnificence of the ceremonial appeared in his mind's eye, and he saw the Public Prosecutor rising to his feet.)

"We demand the head of this man! Blood calls for blood!"

Querelle was standing in the box. Braced against the tree he extracted further details of this trial in which his head was at stake. He felt good. Intertwining its branches above him, the tree protected him. From far off, he could hear frogs croaking away, but on the whole everything was so calm that the anguish in court suddenly became enhanced by the anguish of loneliness and silence. As the crime itself was the point of departure (total silence, the silence unto death desired by Querelle), they had spun around him (or, rather, it had issued from himself, this tenuous and immaterial extension of death) a thread of silence, to bind him captive. He concentrated more intensely on his vision. He made it more precise.

He was there, yet he was not. He was assisting with the projection of that guilty man into the Criminal Court. He was both watching and directing the show. At times the long and pointed reverie was cut across by some clear and practical thought: "There really aren't any stains on me?" or "Supposing there's someone up there on the road . . . ," but then a quick smile appeared on his face and drove his fear away. Yet he was not able to pride himself too much on that smile's power to dissipate the gloom: the smile might also bring on the fear, first to one's teeth bared by receding lips, giving birth to a monster whose snout would take on exactly the shape of one's smile, and then that monster would grow inside one, to envelop and inhabit you, ending up being far more dangerous just because of its very nature of a phantom begotten of a smile in the dark. Querelle wasn't smiling much now. Tree and fog protected him against night and retribution. He returned to the courtroom. Sovereign at the foot of the tree, he made his imaginary double go through the stances of fear, rebellion, confidence and terror, shudders, blenchings. Recollections of what he had read came to his aid. He knew there ought to be an "incident" in the courtroom. His lawyer rose to speak. Querelle wanted to lose consciousness for a moment, to take refuge in the droning in his ears. He felt he ought to delay the closing scene. Finally, the Court reconvened. Querelle felt himself grow pale.

"The Court pronounces the death sentence."

Everything around him disappeared. He himself and the trees shrunk, and he was astonished to find that he was wan and weak with this new turn of events, just as startled as we are when we learn that Weidmann was not a giant who could tower above the tops of cedar trees, but a rather timid young man of waxen and pimply complexion, standing only 1.70 meters tall among the husky police officers. All Querelle was conscious of was his terrible misfortune of being certifiably alive, and of the loud buzzing in his ears.

Querelle shivered. His shoulders were getting a little cold, as were his thighs and feet. He was standing at the base of the tree, beret in hand, packet of opium under his arm, protected by the thick, cloth uniform and the stiff collar of his peacoat. He put on his beret. In some indefinite way he sensed that all was not yet finished. He still had to accomplish the last formality: his own execution.

"Gotta do it, I guess!"

Saying "sensed," we intend to convey the kind of premonition one celebrated murderer, a short while after his apparently totally unexpected arrest, meant when he told the judge: "I *sensed* that I was about to be nabbed . . ." Querelle shook himself, walked a few steps straight ahead, and, using his hands, scrambled back up the slope where the grass was singing. Some branches grazed against his cheeks and hands: it was then that he felt a profound sadness, a longing for maternal caresses, because those thorny branches appeared gentle, velvety with the fog adhering to them, and they reminded him of the soft radiance of a woman's breast. A couple of seconds later he was back again on the path, then on the road, and he re-entered the city by a different gate from the one he had emerged from with the other sailor. Something seemed to be missing from his side.

"It's dull, with no one to talk to."

He smiled, but very faintly. He was leaving, back there in the fog, on the grass, a certain object, a small heap of calm and night emanating from an invisible and gentle dawn, an object, sacred or damned, waiting at the foot of the outer walls for permission to enter the city, after expiation, after the probationary period imposed for purification and humility. The corpse would have that boring face he knew, all its lines smoothed away. With long, supple strides, that same free and easy, slightly rolling gait that made people say "There's a guy steps like an hombre," Querelle, his soul at peace, took the road leading to La Féria.

That episode we wanted to present in slow motion. Our aim was not to horrify the reader, but to give the act of murder something of the quality of an animated cartoon—which in any case is exactly the art form we would most like to be able to use, to show the deformations of our protagonist's musculature and soul. In any case, and in order not to annoy the reader too much—and trusting him to complete, with his very own malaise, the contradictory and twisted windings of our own vision of the murder—there is a great deal we have left out. It would be easy to have the murderer experience a vision of his brother. Or to have him killed by his brother. Or to make him kill or condemn his brother. There are a great number of themes on which one might embroider some revolting tapestry like that. Nor do we want to go on about the secret and obscene desires inhabiting the one going to his death. Vic or Querelle, take your pick. We abandon the reader to this confusion of his innards. But let us consider this: after committing his first murder Querelle experienced a feeling of being dead, that is to say, of existing somewhere in the depths—more exactly, at the bottom of a coffin; of wandering aimlessly about some trite tomb in some trite cemetery, and there imagining the quotidian lives of the living, who appeared to him curiously senseless since *he* was no longer there to be their pretext, their center, their generous heart. However, his human form, or "fleshly envelope," went on busying itself on the earth's surface, among all those senseless people. And Querelle proceeded to arrange another murder. As no act is perfect to the extent that an alibi could rid us from our responsibility for it, Querelle saw in each crime, be it only a theft, *one* detail which (in his eyes only) became a mistake that might lead to his undoing. To live in the midst of his mistakes gave him a feeling of lightness, of a cruel instability, as he seemed to be flitting from one bending reed to another.

From the time he reached the first lights of the town Querelle had already resumed his habitual smile. When he entered the main parlor of the brothel he was just a husky sailorboy, clear-eyed and looking for some action. He hesitated for a few seconds in the midst of the music, but one of the women lost no time in getting to him. She was tall and blonde, very skinny, wearing a black-tulle dress pulled in over the region of her cunt—and hiding it in order to evoke it better—by a triangle of black, longhaired fur, probably rabbit, threadbare and almost worn bald in places. Querelle stroked the fur with a light finger while looking the girl in the eye, but refused to accompany her upstairs.

After delivering the package of opium to Nono and receiving his five thousand francs Querelle knew that the time had come for him to "execute himself."

This would be capital punishment. If a logical chain of events had not brought Querelle to La Féria, the murderer would no doubt have contrived—secretly, within himself—another sacrificial rite. Once more he smiled, looking at the thick nape of the brothelkeeper's neck as that one bent over, on the divan, to examine the opium. He looked at his slightly protruding ears, the bald and shiny top of his head, the powerful arch of his body. When Norbert looked up again, he confronted Querelle with a face both fleshy and bony, heavy-jowled and broken-nosed. Everything about the man, in his forties, gave an impression of brutal vigor. The head belonged to a wrestler's body, hairy, tattooed perhaps, most certainly odorous. "Capital punishment, for sure."

"Now then. What's your game? What do you want with the Madam? Tell me."

Querelle discarded his grin in order to appear to smile expressly at this question and to wrap up his answer in another smile which this question alone could have provoked—and which this smile alone would succeed in rendering inoffensive. And so, he laughed out loud as he replied, with a free and easy shake of the head and in a tone of voice designed to make it impossible for Nono to take umbrage:

"I like her."

From that moment on Norbert found all the details of Querelle's face totally enchanting. This wasn't the first time a well-built lad had asked for the Madam in order to sleep with the brothelkeeper. One thing intrigued him: which one would get to bugger the other?

"All right."

He pulled out a die from his waistcoat pocket.

"You go? I go?"

"Go ahead."

Norbert bent down and threw the die on the floor. He rolled a five. Querelle took the die. He felt certain of his skill. Nono's well-trained eye noticed that Querelle was going to cheat, but before he could intervene the number "two" was sung out by the sailor, almost triumphantly. For a moment Norbert remained undecided. Was he dealing with some kind of joker? At first he had thought that Querelle was really after his own brother's mistress. This fraudulent trick had proved that was not so. Nor did the guy look like a fruit. Perturbed all the same, by the anxiety this beast of prey showed in going to its own perdition, he shrugged lightly as he rose to his feet and chuckled. Querelle, too, stood up. He looked around, amused, smiling the more he relished the inner sensation of marching to the torture chamber. He was doing it with despair in his soul, yet with an unexpressed inner certitude that this execution was necessary for him to go on living. Into what would he be transformed? A fairy. He was terrified at the thought. And what exactly is a fairy? What stuff is it made of? What particular light shows it up? What new monster does one become, and how does one then feel about the monstrosity of oneself? One is said to "like that," when one gives oneself up to the police. That copper's good looks were really at the back of everything. It is sometimes said that the smallest event can transform a life, and this one was of such significance.

"No kissing, that's for sure," he thought. And: "I'll just stick my ass out, that's all." That last expression had for him much the same resonance as "I'll stick my prick out."

What new body would be his? To his despair, however, was added the comforting certainty that the execution would wash him clean of the murder, which he now thought of as an ill-digested morsel of food. At last he would have to pay for that somber feast that death-dealing always is. It is always a dirty business; one has to wash oneself afterward. And wash so thoroughly that nothing of oneself remains. Be reborn. Die, to be reborn. After that he would not be afraid of anybody. Sure, the police could still track him down and have his head cut off: thus it was necessary to take precautions not to give oneself away, but in front of the fantasy court of justice he had created for himself Querelle would no longer have anything to answer for, since he who committed that murder would be dead. The abandoned corpse, would it get past the city gates? Querelle could hear that long, rigid object, always wrapped in its narrow fog shroud, complaining, murmuring some exquisite tune. It was Vic's dead body, bewailing its fate. It desired the honors of funeral rites and interment. Norbert turned the key in the lock of the door. It was a big, shiny key, and it was reflected in the mirror opposite the door.

"Take your pants down."

The brothelkeeper's tone was indifferent. Already he had ceased to have any feelings for a guy who interfered with the laws of chance. Querelle remained standing in the middle of the room, his legs wide apart. The idea of women had never bothered him much. Sometimes, at night, in his hammock, his hand would mechanically seek out his prick, caress it, jack off quietly. He watched Nono unbuttoning. There was a moment's silence, and his gaze became fixed on the boss's finger as he was prying one of the buttons out of its buttonhole.

"Well, have you made up your mind?"

Querelle smiled. He began desultorily, to undo the flap of his sailor's pants. He said:

"You'll take it easy, you hear? They say you can get hurt."

"Well, hell, it won't be the first time . . ."

Norbert sounded dry, almost mean. A flash of anger ran through Querelle's body: he looked extremely beautiful now, with his head held up, shoulders motionless and tense, buttocks tight, hips very straight (drawn in by the strain in the legs that was raising the buttocks), yet of a slimness that enhanced the overall impression of cruelty. Unbuttoned, his flap fell forward over his thighs, like a child's bib. His eyes were glittering. His face, even his hair seemed to be gleaming with hatred.

"Listen, buddy, I'm telling you it's the first time all right. So don't you try any monkey business."

Norbert, struck by this sudden outburst as by a whiplash, felt his wrestler's muscles tense for action, ready to recoil, and answered right back:

"Don't come on so high and mighty. That don't wash with me. You don't think I'm some kind of hick, do you now? I saw you, man. You cheated."

And, with the force of his bodily mass added to the force of his anger at finding himself defied, he came close enough to Querelle to touch him with the whole of his body, from brow to knee. Querelle stood his ground. In a still deeper voice, Norbert went on, impassively:

"And I think that's enough of that. Don't you? It wasn't me who asked you. Get ready."

That was a command such as Querelle had never before received. It came from no recognized, conventional, and detached authority, but from an imperative that had issued from within himself. His own strength and vitality were ordering him to bend over. He felt like punching Norbert in the mouth. The muscles of his body, of his arms, thighs, calves were ready for action, contracted, flexed, taut, almost on tiptoes. Speaking right into Norbert's teeth, into his very breath, Querelle said:

"Man, you're mistaken. It's your old lady I was after."

"And what else is new."

Norbert grabbed him by the shoulders and tried to swing him around. Querelle wanted to push him away, but his pants had started gravitating toward his ankles. To retain them, he opened his legs a bit wider. They glared at each other. The sailor knew he was the stronger one, even in spite of Norbert's athletic build. Nevertheless he yanked up his pants and stepped back a pace. He relaxed his face muscles, raised his eyebrows, frowned a little, then shook his head lightly, to indicate resignation:

"All right," he said.

Both men, still facing each other, relaxed and simultaneously put their hands behind their backs. This perfectly synchronized double gesture surprised both of them. There was an element of understanding there. Querelle grinned, looking pleased.

"So you've been a sailor."

Norbert snorted, then answered, testily, in a voice still somewhat shaken by anger:

"Zephir."

Querelle was struck by the exceptional quality of the man's voice. It was solid. It was, at one and the same time, a marble column issuing out of his mouth, holding him up, and against which he rested. It was, above all, to this voice that Querelle had submitted.

"What's that?"

"Zephir. The Battalion, if you prefer."

Their hands moved to unfasten their belts, and sailors' belts are, for practical reasons, buckled behind their backs—to avoid, for example, an unsightly pot-belly effect when wearing a tight-fitting rig. Thus, certain adventurous characters for no other motive than their own memories of Navy days, or their submission to the glamour of the naval uniform, retain or adopt that particular eccentricity. Querelle felt a whole lot friendlier. Since the brothelkeeper belonged to the same family as himself, with roots stretching far down into the same shadowy and perfumed lands, this very scene was something like one of those trite little escapades in the tents of the African Battalion—which no one mentions later when meeting again on civvy street. Enough had been said. Now Querelle had to execute himself. That's what he would do.

"Get over there, to the bed."

As the wind subsides at sea, all anger had subsided. Norbert's voice was flat. Querelle pulled his leather belt out of the loops and held it in his hand. His pants had slipped down over his calves, leaving his knees bare, and, on the red carpet, they looked like a sluggish pool in which he was standing.

"Come on. Turn round. It won't take long."

Querelle faced about. He bent over, supporting himself on clenched fists—one closed round the belt buckle—on the edge of the divan. Norbert felt disheveled and unobserved. With a light and calm touch he liberated his prick from his underpants and held it for a moment, heavy and extended in his hand. He saw his reflection in the mirror in front of him and knew it was repeated twenty times in this room. He was strong. He was The Master. Total silence reigned. Advancing calmly, Norbert rested his hand on his prick as if it were some strong and flexible tree branch—leaning, as it were, on himself. Querelle was waiting, head bowed, blood mounting to his face; Nono looked at the sailor's buttocks: they were small and hard, round, dry, and covered with a thick brown fleece which continued on to the thighs and—but there, more sparsely—up to the small of the back, where the striped undershirt just peeped out from under the raised jersey. The shading on certain drawings of female rumps is achieved by incurving strokes of the brush, not unlike those bands of different colors on old-fashioned stockings: that is how I would like the reader to visualize the bared parts of Querelle's thighs. What gave them a look of indecency was that they could have been reproduced by those incurving strokes, with their emphasis on rounded curves, and the graininess of the skin, the slightly dirty gray of the curling hairs. The monstrousness of male love affairs appears in the uncovering of that part of the body, framed by undershirt and dropped pants.

"That's the way I like you."

Querelle did not reply. The smell of the opium packet lying on the bed disgusted him. And there the rod was already, entering. He recalled the Armenian he had strangled in Beirut, his softness, his lizard- or birdlike gentleness. Querelle asked himself whether he should try to please the executioner with caresses. Having no fear of ridicule now, he might as well try out that sweetness the murdered pederast had exuded.

"He did call me the fanciest names I ever did hear, that's for sure. One of the softest, he was, too," he thought.

But what gestures of affection were appropriate? What caresses? His muscles did not know which way to bend to obtain a curve. Norbert was crushing him. Slowly he penetrated him up to the point where his belly touched Querelle, whom he was holding close, with sudden, fearsome intensity, his hands clasped round the sailor's belly. He was surprised how warm it was inside of Querelle. He pushed in farther, very carefully, the better to savor his pleasure and his strength. Querelle was astonished at suffering so little pain.

"He's not hurting me. Have to admit he knows how to do it."

What he felt was a new *nature* entering into him and establishing itself there, and he was exquisitely aware of his being changed into a *catamite*.

"What's he going to say to me afterward? Hope he doesn't want to talk."

In a vague way he felt grateful toward Norbert for protecting him, in thus covering him. A sense of some degree of affection for his executioner occurred to him. He turned his head slightly, hoping, after all, and despite his anxiety, that Norbert might kiss him on the mouth; but he couldn't even manage to see his face. The boss had no tender feelings for him whatsoever, nor would it ever have entered his head that a man could kiss another. Silently, his mouth half open, Norbert was taking care of it, like of any serious and important business. He was holding Querelle with seemingly the same passion a female animal shows when holding the dead body of her young offspring—the attitude by which we comprehend what love is: consciousness of the division of what previously was one, of what it is to be thus divided, while you yourself are watching yourself. The two men heard nothing but the sound of each other's breathing. Querelle felt like weeping over the skin he had sloughed and abandoned—where? at the foot of the city wall of Brest?—but his eyes, open in one of the deep folds of the velvet bedcover, remained dry.

"Here it comes."

At the first thrust, so strong it almost killed him, Querelle whimpered quietly, then more loudly, until he was moaning without restraint or shame. Such lively expression of pleasure gave Norbert reason to feel certain that this sailor was not really a man, in that he was not able to exercise, at the moment of pleasure, the traditionary reserve and restraint of the manly male. The murderer suddenly felt ill at ease, hardly able to formulate the reason for it: "Is that what it's like, being a real fairy?" he thought. But at once he felt floored by the full weight of the French Police Force: without really succeeding. Mario's face was attempting to substitute itself for that of the man who was screwing him. Querelle ejaculated onto the velvet. A little higher up on the cover he softly buried his head with its strangely disordered black curls, untidy and lifeless like the grass on an upturned clump of turf. Norbert had stopped moving. His jaws relaxed, letting go of the downy nape of Querelle's neck which he had been biting. Then the brothelkeeper's massive bulk, very gently and slowly, withdrew from Querelle. Querelle was still holding his belt.

The discovery of the murdered sailor caused no panic, not even surprise. Crimes are no more common in Brest than anywhere else, but by its climate of fog, rain, and thick, low cloud, by the grayness of the granite, the memory of the galley slaves, by the presence, right next to the city but beyond its walls—and for that reason all the more stirring—of Bougen Prison, by the old penitentiary, by the invisible but durable thread that linked the old salts, admirals, sailors, fishermen, to the tropical regions, the city's atmosphere is such, heavy yet luminous, that it seems to us not only conducive, but even essential to the flowering of a murder. Flowering is the word. It appears obvious to us that a knife slashing the fog at any conceivable spot, or a revolver bullet boring a hole in it, at the height of a man, might well burst a bubble full of blood and cause it to stream along the inside walls of the vaporous edifice. No matter where the blow falls, small stars of blood appear in the wounded fog. In whatever direction you extend your hand (already so far from your body that it no longer belongs to you), now invisible, solitary, and anonymous, the back of it will brush against—or your fingers grab hold of—the strong, trembling, naked, hot, ready-for-action, rid-of-its-underwear prick of a docker or sailor who waits there, burning hot and ice cold, transparent and erect, to project a jet of jism into the froggy fog. (Ah, those knockout body fluids: blood, sperm, tears!) Your own face is so close to another, invisible face that you can sense the blush of his affect. And all faces are beautiful, softened, purified by their blurriness, velvety with droplets clinging to cheeks and ears, but the bodies grow thicker and heavier and appear enormously powerful. Under their patched and worn blue-denim pants (let us add, for our own pleasure, that the men on the waterfront still wear red-cloth underwear similar in color to the pants worn by those olden-day galley slaves), the dockers and workmen usually have on another pair which gives the outer pair the heavy look of bronze clothes on statues—and you will perhaps be even more aroused when you realize that the rod in your hand has managed to penetrate so many layers of material, that it needed such care on the part of thick and work-soiled fingers to undo this double row of flybuttons, to prepare your joy—and this double garment makes a man's lower half appear more massive.

The corpse was taken to the morgue in the Naval Hospital. The autopsy revealed nothing not already known. He was buried two days later. Admiral de D . . . du M . . . , Commander of the Port, ordered the police judge to conduct a serious and secret investigation and to keep him informed of its progress on a daily basis. He hoped to be able to avert any scandal that might besmirch the entire Navy. Armed with flashlights, police inspectors searched woods and thickets and all overgrown ditches. They searched meticulously, turning over every little heap of manure they came across. They passed close to the tree where Querelle had gone to his true condemnation. They discovered nothing: no knife, no footprint, not a shred of clothing, not a single blond hair. Nothing but the cheap cigarette lighter Querelle had handed to the young sailor; it lay in the grass, not far from the dead body. The police said they were unable to determine whether it had belonged to the murderer or to his victim. Nothing was learned in an enquiry as to its ownership on board the *Vengeur.* Querelle had picked up that lighter on the eve of the crime, pocketed it, almost automatically, from among the bottles and glasses on the table on which Gil Turko, its owner, had been singing. Theo had given it to Gil.

As the crime had been committed in those woods by the ramparts, the police had a notion that the man they were looking for might well be a pederast. Knowing with what horror society recoils from anything even remotely connected with the idea of homosexuality, it seems surprising that the police should find it so easy to consider that idea. Once a murder has been committed, the police habitually put forward the two motives of robbery or jealousy; but as soon as someone who is or has been a sailor is involved, they simply say to themselves: sexual perversion. They cling to that conclusion with almost painful intensity. To society at large, the police are what the dream is to the quotidian round of events; what it excludes from its own preoccupations, at least as far as possible, polite society authorizes its police force to deal with. This may account for the combined repulsion and attraction with which that force is regarded. Charged with the drainage of dreams, the police catch them in their filters. And that explains why policemen bear such resemblance to those they pursue. It would be a mistake to believe that it is merely the better to trick, track down, and vanquish it more effectively, that those inspectors blend so well with their quarry. Looking closely at Mario's personal life, we notice first of all his habitual visits to the brothel and his friendship with its proprietor. No doubt he finds Nono an informer who is in some ways a useful kind of link between law-abiding society and shady doings, but in talking to him he is also able to acquire (if he did not know them already) the manners and idioms of the underworld—tending to overdo them, later, in moments of danger. Finally, his desire to love Dédé in forbidden ways is an indication: this love alienates him from the police force whose conduct must always be quite beyond reproach. (Those propositions appear contradictory. We shall see how that contradiction resolves itself in actuality.) Up to their necks in work we refuse even to admit, the police live under a curse, particularly the plainclothes men, who, when seen in the middle of (and protected by) the dark blue uniforms of the straight coppers, appear like thin-skinned, translucent lice, small fragile things easily crushed with a fingernail, whose very bodies have become blue from feeding off that other, the dark blue. That curse makes them immerse themselves in their efforts with a vengeance. Whenever the occasion arises, they then bring up the notion of pederasty—in itself, and fortunately, a mystery they are unable to unravel. The inspectors had a vague feeling that the murder of that sailor over by the ramparts was not quite run-of-the-mill: what they should have found there was some "sugar daddy," assassinated, abandoned on the grass, picked clean of his money and valuables. Instead of which they had found the body of the most likely type of suspect, with his money in his pockets. No doubt this anomaly worried them a little, and interfered with the progress of their ruminations, but it did not really bother them overmuch. Mario had not been given any specific orders to participate in the investigation of this case. Thus, at first, he paid only cursory attention to it, being more preoccupied with the danger he was in after Tony's discharge. Had he taken time to interest himself in the case, he would have been no more able than anyone else to explain it in terms of homosexual goings-on. Indeed, neither Mario nor any of the heroes of this book (excepting Lieutenant Seblon, but then Seblon is not *in* the book) is a pederast; for Mario, those people were of two kinds—those who wanted to get laid and paid for it and were known as sugar daddies, and, well, the others who catered to them. But then, quite suddenly, Mario became engrossed in the case. He felt a keen desire to unravel the plot, which he imagined carefully and tightly organized and of potential danger to himself. Dédé had returned without any precise information, yet Mario was sure of the risk he was running: he started going out again, came out into the open with the crazy notion that by his speed and agility he would outdistance death, and that even if he were killed, death would simply pass through him. His courage was designed to dazzle and blind whatever it was that was threatening him. All the same, secretly, he reserved the right to negotiate with the enemy along lines that will eventually become apparent: Mario was merely waiting for the occasion. In that, too, he demonstrated courage. The police made enquiries among all known "queens." There aren't many of those in Brest. Although it is a big naval base, Brest has remained a small, provincial town. The avowed pederasts—self-avowed, that is—manage to remain admirably inconspicuous. They are peaceful citizens of irreproachable outward appearance, even though they may, the long day through, perhaps suffer from a timid itch for a bit of their fun. Nor could any detective have supposed that the murder discovered in the neighborhood of the ramparts might have been the violent and—in terms of time and place—inevitable outcome of a love affair that had developed on board a solid and loyal Navy vessel. No doubt the police knew about the worldwide reputation of La Féria, but the reputation of the boss himself seemed unassailable: they did not know of a single client—docker or other—who had buggered him or whom he had buggered. Yet the notoriety of La Féria was legendary. However, Mario did not consider any of these matters until later, when Nono, in a moment's playful braggadocio, told him about his doings with Querelle. When Querelle emerged from the coal bunkers and came up on deck on the day after that big night, he was black from head to toe. A thick but soft layer of coal dust covered his hair, stiffening it, petrifying every curl, powdering his face and naked torso, the material of his pants, and his bare feet. He crossed the deck to reach his quarters.

"Mustn't worry too much," he was thinking as he walked along. "There's only one thing to be afraid of, and that's the guillotine. Now even that ain't so terrible. They're not going to execute me every day."

His blackface act served him well. Querelle had begun to realize—and to think, for the first time, about doing something about it—the turmoil within Lieutenant Seblon, betrayed by the officer's frowning mien and overly severe tone of voice. Being just a simple sailor, he could not understand the ways of his Lieutenant who would punish him for the slightest infraction and look for the least little pretext for doing so. But one day the officer had happened to pass too close to the machinery and had soiled his hands with axle grease. He had turned to Querelle, who happened to be standing close by. In a suddenly quite humble manner he asked:

"D'you happen to have a rag I could use?"

Querelle produced a clean handkerchief, still folded, from his pocket and held it out to him. The Lieutenant wiped his hands on it and kept it.

"I'll have it washed. Come by and pick it up sometime."

Some days later the Lieutenant found an opportunity of addressing Querelle and, he hoped, of wounding him. Harshly:

"Don't you know it's against regulations to fix the beret that way?"

He grabbed the red pompom on top of the beret and yanked it off the seaman's head. The sun then shone its rays on such a splendid mop of hair that the officer came close to giving himself away. His arm, his sudden gesture turned leaden. In a changed voice, he went on, holding out the beret to the dumbfounded sailor:

"That's what you like, to look like some ruffian. You deserve ... (he hesitated, not really knowing whether to say '... all the genuflections, all the caresses of seraphim's wings, all the perfume of lilies ...'). You deserve to be punished."

Querelle looked him in the eye. Simply and so calmly that it was hurtful, he said:

"Have you finished with my handkerchief, sir?"

"That's right. Well, come along and get it."

Querelle followed the officer to his cabin. The latter started looking for the handkerchief, but did not find it. Querelle waited, immobile, strictly at attention. Then Lieutenant Seblon took one of his own, monogrammed, clean handkerchiefs, white cambric, and offered it to the seaman.

"Sorry. Seems I can't find yours. Do you mind if I give you this one?"

Querelle nodded his indifferent-seeming acceptance.

"I'm sure it'll turn up again. I had it laundered. Now, I'm pretty certain you wouldn't have done that yourself. You don't look like that kind of lad to me."

Querelle was taken aback by the officer's "tough" expression as he uttered those words in an aggressive, almost accusing tone. All the same, he smiled.

"That ain't quite so, sir. I know how to take care of things."

"That's news to me. You're the kind of guy, it seems to me, takes his washing to some little sixteen-year-old Syrian chick, so she can do it and ... (here Lieutenant Seblon's voice quavered. He knew he better not say what he perfectly well knew he would say, after three seconds of silence) ... bring it to you all nicely smoothed and ironed."

"No such luck. I don't know any girls in Beirut. What there is to wash, I do myself."

And then, without understanding why, Querelle noticed a slight relaxation of the officer's rigid attitude. Spontaneously, with the amazing sense for putting their attractions to work for them that young men have, even those to whom any degree of methodical coquetry is quite foreign, he gave his voice a somewhat sly inflection, and his body, relaxing too, became animated from neck to calves—by the almost imperceptible shifting of one foot in front of the other—by a series of short-lived ripples that were truly graceful and reminded Querelle himself of the existence of his buttocks and shoulders. Suddenly he appeared as if drawn in quick, broken lines, and, to the officer, drawn by the very hand of the master.

"Well?"

The Lieutenant looked at him. Querelle was again immobile, yet the grace of his movements remained. He smiled. His eyes were like asterisks.

"Well, in that case . . ."

The Lieutenant spoke in a casual drawl. "Well . . . (and in one breath, managing not to betray too much of his unease) . . . if you're really so good at all that, how would you like to be my steward for a while?"

"I'd like that, sir . . . It's just that I wouldn't be getting any hardship money, then."

It was a straightforward reservation, added onto a straightforward acceptance of the offer. Without knowing that it was love that had inspired them, Querelle was now witnessing, in his mind's eye, the sudden and simultaneous transformation of all potential and actual punishments meted out by the Lieutenant: he saw them lose their primary meaning and take on the nature of "encounters," which, and that for quite some time, were pointing toward a union, an understanding between the two men. They held memories in common. Their relationship, as from that day, had its own past history.

"But why not? I'll take care of that. Don't you worry, you won't stand to lose any pay."

The Lieutenant cherished his belief that he had never revealed his love one little bit, while hoping (at the same time) that he had made it abundantly clear. As soon as the picture became comprehensible to Querelle—the following day, in fact, when he found, in a place where logically it should never have been, in an old croc-skin briefcase, his own handkerchief—stained with axle grease and further starched with some other fluid—he found such games of hide-and-seek most amusing, being able to see through them perfectly well. And that day, when he emerged from the coal bunkers, he felt certain that his surprisingly black face, looking more massive than usual under its light coating of coal dust, would appear beautiful enough for the Lieutenant to lose his cool. Perhaps he would even have "a confession to make"?

"Well, we'll see. Maybe he hasn't even heard . . ."

Within his body, his anxiety was giving rise to a most exquisite sensation. Querelle called his star: his smile. And the star appeared. Querelle kept on moving forward, planting his wide feet firmly on the deck. He gave a slight roll to his hips, narrow as they were!—to provide a little action there in the midriff region, where an inch of his white underpants showed above the wide, plaited leather belt, buckled at the back. He had of course registered, and not without spite, that the Lieutenant's gaze often dwelt on that region of his physique, and he had a natural awareness of his own seductive points. He thought of them in a serious manner, sometimes with a smile, that habitual, sad smile of his. He also swung his shoulders a little, but the motion, like that of his hips and his arms, was more discreet than usual, closer to himself, more internalized, one might say. He was hugging himself: or one might say, he was playing at being huggable. As he approached the Lieutenant's cabin he was hoping that the officer would have noticed the abortive theft of his watch. He longed to be taken up on that.

"I'll handle it. I'll sock him in the mouth . . ."

But while he was turning the doorknob he realized he was hoping that the watch (which he had returned, as soon as he got back on board, to its place in the drawer—while the Lieutenant wasn't looking) had stopped, of its own accord—broken or run down or—he dared to think it—stopped by virtue of a particular kindness of destiny, or even out of a particular kindness on the part of that already once-seduced watch itself.

"Well, so what. If he says just one word about that, I'll take care of him, but good."

The Lieutenant was waiting for him. From the first moment, the caress of the Lieutenant's quick glance at his body and his face, Querelle was confirmed in his power: it was his body that was emitting the ray that ran through the officer's eyes down to the very pit of his stomach. The handsome, blond boy, secretly adored, would very soon appear, naked perhaps, but re-invested with great majesty. The coal dust was not thick enough to quite conceal the brightness of the hair, the eyebrows and the skin, nor the rosy coloration of the lips and ears. It was obviously just a veil, and Querelle raised it now and again by occasionally, coquettishly, one might say artfully blowing on his arms or ruffling a curl of his hair.

"You're a good worker, Querelle. You even go for the rough chores, without even telling me. Who told you to coal?"

The Lieutenant sounded tough and sardonic. He was struggling to suppress his feelings. His eyes were making pitiful and useless efforts not to rest too obviously on Querelle's hips and pelvis. One day when he had offered him a glass of port wine, and Querelle had replied that he couldn't take alcohol on account of a dose of the clap (Querelle had lied: on the spur of the moment, and to whet the Lieutenant's desire, he had pretended to be suffering from a "man's disease," to appear a true "bedroom athlete"), Seblon, ignorant of the nature of this affliction, imagined a festering penis under that blue denim, dripping away like one of those Easter candles inlaid with five grains of incense . . . He was already quite furious with himself for being unable to take his eyes off those muscular and powdered arms, where particles of coal dust clung to hairs still curled and golden. He thought:

"What if it really was Querelle who murdered Vic? But that's impossible. Querelle is too much of a natural beauty to need to assume the beauty of crime. He doesn't need that kind of trimming. One would have to make up all kinds of things about them, secret messages, meetings, embraces, stolen kisses."

Querelle gave him the same answer he had given to the Captain at Arms: "Well . . ."

That glance, quick as it was, Querelle caught it. His smile broadened, and in shifting his feet, he performed a quick, seductive "bump."

"So you don't really like working here, eh?"

Having found himself unable to resist such a trite explanation and wording, the officer experienced yet another surge of self-loathing and blushed to observe Querelle's black nostrils quiver delicately and the pretty middle part of his upper lip join in with more rapid and more subtle tremors—clearly a most delightful outward sign of great efforts to restrain a smile.

"But no, I do like it. But I was down there to help out a buddy. Colas, in fact."

"He could have picked someone else to replace him. You're in a pretty incredible state. Do you really like breathing coal dust all that much?"

"No, but . . . But then, well, for me . . ."

"What's that? What do you want to say?"

Querelle let his smile shine bright. He said:

"Oh, nothing."

That nailed the officer's feet to the floor. It only needed a word, a simple order, to send Querelle to the showers. For a few moments they remained very ill at ease, both of them in a state of suspense. It was Querelle who brought matters to a close.

"Is that all, sir?"

"Yes, that's all. Why ask?"

"Oh, no reason."

The Lieutenant thought he detected a hint of impertinence in the sailor's question, and in his answer as well, both delivered in the sunshine of a blinding smile. His dignity prompted him to dismiss Querelle on the spot, but he could not muster the strength to do that. If bad luck would have Querelle decide to go back down to the coal bunkers again, he thought, his lover would certainly follow him there . . . The half-naked seaman's presence in his cabin was driving him out of his mind. Already he was heading on down to hell, descending the black marble staircase, almost to those depths into which the news of Vic's murder had plunged him earlier. He wanted to engage Querelle in that sumptuous adventure. He wanted him to play his part in it. What secret thought, what startling confession, what dazzling display of light was concealed under those bell-bottoms, blacker now than any pair ever known to man? What shadowy penis hung there, its stem rooted in pale moss? And what was the substance covering all these things? Well, certainly nothing but a little coal dust—familiar enough, in name and consistency; that simple ordinary stuff, so capable of making a face, a pair of hands, appear coarse and dirty—yet it invested this young blond sailorboy with all the mysterious powers of a faun, of a heathen idol, of a volcano, of a Melanesian archipelago. He was himself, yet he was so no longer. The Lieutenant, standing in front of Querelle, whom he desired but did not dare approach, made an almost imperceptible gesture, nervous, quickly withdrawn. Querelle noted all the waves of uneasiness passing across the eyes fixed firmly on his, without letting one of them escape him—and (as if such a weight had, by squashing Querelle, caused his smile to broaden more and more) he kept on smiling under the gaze and the physical mass of the Lieutenant, both bearing down on him so heavily that he had to tense his muscles against them. He understood nonetheless the gravity of that stare, which at that moment expressed total human despair. But at the same time, in his mind, he was shrugging his shoulders and thinking:

"Faggot!"

He despised the officer. He kept on smiling, allowing himself to be lulled by the monstrous and ill-defined notion of "faggot" sweeping back and forth inside his head.

"Faggot, what's a faggot? One who lets other guys screw him in the ass?" he thought. And gradually, while his smile faded, lines of disdain appeared at the corners of his mouth. Then again, another phrase drifted through his mind, inducing a vague feeling of torpor: "Me, I'm one too." A thought he had difficulty in focusing on, though he did not find it repulsive, but of whose sadness he was aware when he realized that he was pulling his buttocks in so tight (or so it seemed to him) that they no longer touched the seat of his trousers. And this fleeting, yet quite depressing thought generated, up his spine, an immediate and rapid series of vibrations which quickly spread out over the entire surface of his black shoulders and covered them with a shawl woven out of shivers. Querelle raised his arm, to smooth back his hair. The gesture was so beautiful, unveiling, as it did, the armpit as pale and as taut as a trout's belly, that the Lieutenant could not prevent his eyes from betraying how very weary he was of this state of unrequited passion. His eyes cried for mercy. Their expression made him look more humble, even, than if he had fallen on his knees. Querelle felt very strong. If he despised the Lieutenant, he felt no impulse to laugh at him, as on other days. It seemed unnecessary to him to exert his charms, as he had an inkling that his true power was of another kind. It rose from the depths of hell, yet from a certain region in hell where the bodies and the faces are beautiful. Querelle felt the coal dust on his body, as women feel, on their arms and hips, the folds of a material that transforms them into queens. It was a makeup that did not interfere with his nakedness, that turned him into a god. But for the moment he was content to merely turn on his smile again. He was sure, now, that the Lieutenant would never ever raise the matter of the watch.

"So what are you going to do now?"

"Don't know, sir. I'm at your service. But, well, the buddies are a hand short, down below."

The officer engaged in some quick thinking. To send Querelle to the shower would be to destroy the most beautiful object his eyes had ever been given to caress. As the seaman would be back again the next day, to be close beside him, it would be better to leave him covered with that black stuff. And sometime during the day he might find an occasion for going below to the bunkers, and there he might surprise this giant morsel of darkness at its flagrant, amorous activities.

"All right, then. Get going."

"Very good, Lieutenant. I'll be back tomorrow."

Querelle saluted and turned on his heel. With the anguish of a shipwrecked man watching island shores recede, and yet delighted with the casual tenor of complicity in Querelle's parting words—tender as the first use of a nickname—the officer saw those ravishingly neat buttocks, that chest, those shoulders, and that neck draw away from him, irrevocably, yet not so far that he wouldn't be able to recall them with innumerable and invisible outstretched hands, enfolding those treasures and guarding them with the tenderest solicitude. Querelle went back to his coaling, as was his habit now, after murders. If on the first occasion he had thought that he would thus escape recognition by possible witnesses, at subsequent times he simply remembered the feeling of astounding power and security that that black powder, covering him from head to toe, had given him, and thus he sought it out again. His strength lay in his beauty and in his daring to still add to that beauty the appearance of cruelty inherent in masks; he was strong—and so invisible and calm, crouching in the shadow of his power, in the remotest corner of himself—strong, because he was menacing, yet knew himself to be so gentle; he was strong, a black savage, born into a tribe in which murder ennobled a man.

"And besides, hell, I've got all that jewelry!"

Querelle knew that the possession of certain wealth—gold, especially—gives one the right to kill. At that level, killing is done in "the interests of the State." He was a black among the whites, and the more mysterious, monstrous, beyond the laws of this world, as he owed this singularity to a hardly intentional blackface act, being covered in mere coal dust—but he himself, Querelle, was proof that there is more to coal dust than meets the eye: that it has the power to transform, just by being sprinkled over his skin, the soul of a man. He gained strength by being a blaze of light to himself, an incarnation of night to the others; he gained strength from working in the farthest depths of the ship. Lastly, he was experiencing the gentleness of funereal things, their light solemnity. He came, in the end, to veil his face and wear black mourning garb for his victim, secretly, in his own fashion. Though he had dared to do so on former occasions, today he could not bring himself to recapitulate the details of the murder. On his way back to the bunkers all he said to himself was:

"He didn't say anything about the watch."

Had the Lieutenant not been trying to involve Querelle in that story he was imagining around Vic's murder, perhaps he would have been more surprised at the way his steward contributed to the strange doings of this day by voluntarily joining the work party in the coal bunkers. But the day was proving too distracting as it was for him to attempt an interpretation of this additional mystery. And when the two police inspectors charged with the inquiry on board came to interrogate him about the men, he did not mention his idea that Querelle might be the suspect. However, he found himself in more kinds of trouble: if, to his fellow officers, the Lieutenant's preciosity of speech and gesture, the sometimes overly sensuous tones of his voice, appeared merely as signs of distinction—accustomed as they were to the smooth and unctuous mannerisms of their blessed families—the inspectors made no mistake and instantly saw what they had here, a faggot. Although he still worked on the contrary impression when dealing with crewmen, either by stressing the hardness of his metallic voice or by giving exceedingly laconic commands—sometimes in sheer telegraphese—the police officers shook his self-confidence. Faced with them, their authority, he immediately felt guilty and slipped into acting like a distracted girl, giving further indications of his guilt feelings.

Mario decided to open the proceedings:

"I'm sorry to take up your time, Lieutenant . . ."

"And so you should be."

That remark, apparently accidental, certainly inadvertent, made him appear both cynical and rude. The inspector thought that he was trying to be funny, and this set him on edge. While the Lieutenant's embarrassment grew, Mario, who had been somewhat intimidated at first, started putting his questions more bluntly. To the fairly obvious:

"Did you ever notice any goings-on between Vic and any particular buddy of his?" Seblon gave the reply—cut in half by a frog-in-the-throat that did not go unnoticed by the questioners—:

"How exactly does one recognize such affairs?"

His own, obviously overstated retort made him blush. His embarrassment grew. To Mario, the strangeness of the officer's replies was only too apparent. Since the Lieutenant's strength lay in his speech—his weakness, too—he now tried to regain the upper hand by this sorely undermined verbal ability. He said:

"How can I keep track of what the boys do in their own time? Even if that crewman, Vic, got murdered because of some unsavory involvement, I just wouldn't know about it."

"Of course not, Lieutenant. But, sometimes one happens to hear something."

"You must be joking. I do not eavesdrop on my men. And you better realize that even if some of the young fellows did have dealings with revolting types such as you have in mind, they wouldn't boast about them. I should imagine their meetings are shrouded in such secrecy . . ."

He realized that he wasn't far from singing the praises of homosexual affairs. He would have liked to keep his mouth shut, but being aware that a sudden silence would appear strange to the inspector, he added, in an offhand manner:

"Those disgusting characters are wonderfully organized . . ."

That was too much. He himself noticed the ambivalence of the opening statement, with the "wonderfully" striking a note of joyous defiance. The inspectors felt they had had enough. Without being able to distinguish exactly what it was that betrayed him, it seemed to them that his manner of speaking took pleasure in the manners and morals of precisely those elements whom he pretended to condemn. Their thoughts might have been expressed in clichés like: "He talks about them quite sympathetically, doesn't he?" or "It doesn't sound like he'd really detest them all that much." In short, he appeared suspect. Fortunately for him, he had an alibi, for he had been on board the night of the crime. When the interview was over, but before the two police officers had left the cabin, the Lieutenant wanted to put on his cloak of navy blue, and then did so with such coquetry—which he at once, and clumsily, corrected—that the total effect was not of just "putting it on," that would have been far too manly, but rather that of "wrapping himself in it"—which, indeed, was the way he thought of it himself. Again, he experienced embarrassment, and he made up his mind (once more) never to touch a piece of material again in public. Querelle donated ten francs, when they came round to collect for a wreath for Vic. And now some excerpts, picked at random, from the private diary.

This journal can only be a book of prayers.

God grant that I may envelop myself in my chilly gestures, in a chilly fashion, like some very languid Englishman in his traveling rug, an eccentric lady in her shawl. To confront men with, You have given me a gilded rapier, chevrons, medals, gestures of command: these accessories are my salvation. They allow me to weave about me some invisible lace, of intentionally coarse design. That coarseness exhausts me, even though I find it comforting. When I grow old, I shall take refuge in the last resort, behind the ridiculous façade of rimless, steel pince-nez, celluloid collars, a stammer, and starched cuffs.

Querelle told his comrades that he is a "victim" of the recruitment posters! So am I, a victim of those posters, and a victim's victim.

What sudden joy! I am all joy. My hands, mechanically at first, described, in empty space, at the height of my chest—two female breasts, grafting them on as it were. I was happy. Now I repeat the gesture, such bliss. Such great abundance. I am overflowing. I stop: I am her, overflowing. I start over. I caress these two aerial boobs. They are beautiful. They are heavy, my palms support them. It happened when I stood leaning against the rail, at night, looking across, listening to the noises of Alexandria. I caress my breasts, my hips. I feel my buns getting rounder, more voluptuous. Egypt lies behind me now: the sands, the Sphinx, the Pharaohs, the Nile, the Arabs, the Casbah, and the wonderful adventure of being her. I would like them *a little pear-shaped.*

Once again, I dragged the door curtains in with me, quite unwittingly. I felt how they wanted to envelop me in their folds, and I could not resist making a splendid gesture, to free myself of them. The gesture of a swimmer parting the water.

The Thief's Journal

◄O►

This book had been announced from the very beginning of Genet's literary career, and it seemed the inevitable conclusion of his fictional oeuvre. In it he gives the most straightforward of the accounts of his life of crime and comes up to the present, the period during which he was actually composing the text.

The straightforwardness, however, is only on the surface. Dedicated to Jean-Paul Sartre and Simone de Beauvoir, The Thief's Journal *is a highly philosophical text that echoes (or perhaps inspired) many of the phrases that appear in Sartre's* Saint Genet. *In the second part of the following selection, Genet speculates on the meaning of sainthood.*

Two of Genet's lovers appear under their own names or nicknames as characters in the book. "Java" was Genet's nickname for a sailor whom he had met in 1947 and with whom he would remain intimate for the next six years. The other lover, who entered Genet's life two years earlier, was Lucien Sénémaud, who also inspired the poem The Fisherman of Suquet.

The book was not published until 1949. It was brought out by the prestigious publishing house of Gallimard, in a generally available edition. For the first time Genet's work was available to the public at large. In the coming years, Gallimard would reissue all of Genet's works in a handsome, uniform edition.

CONVICTS' GARB IS striped pink and white. Though it was at my heart's bidding that I chose the universe wherein I delight, I at least have the power of finding therein the many meanings I wish to find: *there is a close relationship between flowers and convicts.* The fragility and delicacy of the former are of the same nature as the brutal insensitivity of the latter.[1] Should I have to portray a convict—or a criminal—I shall so bedeck him with flowers that, as he disappears beneath them, he will himself become a flower, a gigantic and new one. Toward what is known as evil, I lovingly pursued an adventure which led me to prison. Though they may

[1]My excitement is the oscillation from one to the other.

not always be handsome, men doomed to evil possess the manly virtues. Of their own volition, or owing to an accident which has been chosen for them, they plunge lucidly and without complaining into a reproachful, ignominious element, like that into which love, if it is profound, hurls human beings. Erotic play discloses a nameless world which is revealed by the nocturnal language of lovers. Such language is not written down. It is whispered into the ear at night in a hoarse voice. At dawn it is forgotten. Repudiating the virtues of your world, criminals hopelessly agree to organize a forbidden universe. They agree to live in it. The air there is nauseating: they can breathe it. But—criminals are remote from you—as in love, they turn away and turn me away from the world and its laws. Their smells of sweat, sperm, and blood. In short, to my body and my thirsty soul it offers devotion. It was because their world contains these erotic conditions that I was bent on evil. My adventure, never governed by rebellion or a feeling of injustice, will be merely one long mating, burdened and complicated by a heavy, strange, erotic ceremonial (figurative ceremonies leading to jail and anticipating it). Though it be the sanction, in my eyes the justification too, of the foulest crime, it will be the sign of the most utter degradation. That ultimate point of the most utter degradation. That ultimate point to which the censure of men leads was to appear to me the ideal place for the purest, that is, the most turbid amatory harmony, where illustrious ash weddings are celebrated. Desiring to hymn them, I use what is offered me by the form of the most exquisite natural sensibility, which is already aroused by the garb of convicts. The material evokes, both by its colors and roughness, certain flowers whose petals are slightly fuzzy, which detail is sufficient for me to associate the idea of strength and shame with what is most naturally precious and fragile. This association, which tells me things about myself, would not suggest itself to another mind; mine cannot avoid it. Thus I offered my tenderness to the convicts; I wanted to call them by charming names, to designate their crimes with, for modesty's sake, the subtlest metaphor (beneath which veil I would not have been unaware of the murderer's rich muscularity, of the violence of his sexual organ). Is it not by the following image that I prefer to imagine them in Guiana: the strongest, with a horn, the "hardest," veiled by mosquito netting? And each flower within me leaves behind so solemn a sadness that all of them must signify sorrow, death. Thus I sought love as it pertained to the penal colony. Each of my passions led me to hope for it, gave me a glimpse of it, offers me criminals, offers me to them or impels me to crime. As I write this book, the last convicts are returning to France. The newspapers have been reporting the matter. The heir of kings feels a like emptiness if the republic deprives him of his anointment. The end of the penal colony prevents us from attaining with our living minds the mythical underground regions. Our most dramatic movement has been clipped away: our exodus, the embarkation, the procession on the sea, which was performed with bowed head. The return, this same procession in reverse, is without meaning. Within me, the destruction of the colony corresponds to a kind of punishment of punishment: I am castrated, I am shorn of my infamy. Unconcerned about beheading our dreams of their glories, they awaken us prematurely. The home prisons have their power: it is not the same. It is minor. It has none of that elegant, slightly bowed grace. The atmosphere there is so heavy that you have to drag yourself about. You creep along. The home prisons are more stiffly erect, more darkly and severely; the slow, solemn agony of the penal colony was a more perfect blossoming of abjection.[2] So that now the home jails, bloated with evil males, are black with them, as with blood that has been shot through with carbonic gas. (I have written "black." The outfit of the convicts—captives, captivity, even prisoners, words too noble to name us—forces the word upon me: the outfit is made of brown homespun.) It is toward them that my desire will turn. I am aware that there is often a semblance of the burlesque in the colony or in prison. On the bulky, resonant base of their wooden shoes, the frame of the condemned men is always somewhat shaky. In front of a wheelbarrow, it suddenly breaks up stupidly. In the presence of a guard they bow their heads and hold in their hands the big, straw, sun bonnet—which the younger ones decorate (I should prefer it so) with a stolen rose granted by the guard—or a brown-homespun beret. They strike poses of wretched humility. If they are beaten, something within them must nevertheless stiffen: the coward, the sneak, cowardice, sneakiness are—when kept in a state of the hardest, purest cowardice and sneakiness—hardened by a "dousing," as soft iron is hardened by dousing. They persist in servility, despite everything. Though I do not neglect the deformed and misshapen, it is the handsomest criminals whom my tenderness adorns.

Crime, I said to myself, had a long wait before producing such perfect successes as Pilorge and Angel Sun. In order to finish them off (the term is a cruel one!) it was necessary for a host of coincidences to concur: to the beauty of their faces, to the strength and elegance of their bodies there had to be added their taste for crime, the circumstances which make the criminal, the moral vigor capable of accepting such a destiny, and, finally, punishment, its cruelty, the intrinsic quality which enables a criminal to glory in it, and, over all of this, areas of darkness. If the hero join combat with night and conquer it, may shreds of it remain upon him! The same hesitation, the same crystallization of happy circumstances governs the success of a pure sleuth. I cherish them both. But if I love their crime, it is for the punishment it involves, "the penalty" (for I cannot suppose that they have not anticipated it. One of them, the former boxer Ledoux, answered the inspectors smilingly: "My crimes? It's before committing them that I might have regretted them") in which I want to accompany them so that, come what may, my love may be filled to overflowing.

I do not want to conceal in this journal the other reasons which made me a thief, the simplest being the need to eat, though revolt, bitterness, anger, or any similar sentiment never entered into my choice. With fanatical care, "jealous care," I

---

[2] Its abolition is so great a loss to me that I secretly recompose, within me and for myself alone, a colony more vicious than that of Guiana. I add that the home prisons can be said to be "in the shade." The colony is in the sun. Everything transpires there in a cruel light which I cannot refrain from choosing as a sign of lucidity.

prepared for my adventure as one arranges a couch or a room for love; I was *hot* for crime.

•   •   •

I GIVE THE NAME violence to a boldness lying idle and enamored of danger. It can be seen in a look, a walk, a smile, and it is in you that it creates an eddying. It unnerves you. This violence is a calm that disturbs you. One sometimes says: "A guy with class!" Pilorge's delicate features were of an extreme violence. Their delicacy in particular was violent. Violence of the design of Stilitano's only hand, simply lying on the table, still, rendering the repose disturbing and dangerous. I have worked with thieves and pimps whose authority bent me to their will, but few proved to be really bold, whereas the one who was most so—Guy—was without violence. Stilitano, Pilorge, and Michaelis were cowards. Java too. Even when at rest, motionless and smiling, there escaped from them through the eyes, the nostrils, the mouth, the palm of the hand, the bulging basket, through that brutal hillock of the calf under the wool or denim, a radiant and somber anger, visible as a haze.

But, almost always, there is nothing to indicate it, save the absence of the usual signs. René's face is charming at first. The downward curve of his nose gives him a roguish look, though the somewhat leaden paleness of his anxious face makes you uneasy. His eyes are hard, his movements calm and sure. In the cans he calmly beats up the queers; he frisks them, robs them, sometimes, as a finishing touch, he kicks them in the kisser with his heel. I don't like him, but his calmness masters me. He operates, in the dead of night, around the urinals, the lawns, the shrubbery, under the trees on the Champs-Elysées, near the stations, at the Porte Maillot, in the Bois de Boulogne (always at night) with a seriousness from which romanticism is excluded. When he comes in, at two or three in the morning, I feel him stocked with adventures. Every part of his body, which is nocturnal, has been involved: his hands, his arms, his legs, the back of his neck. But he, unaware of these marvels, tells me about them in forthright language. From his pockets he takes rings, wedding bands, watches, the evening's loot. He puts them in a big glass which will soon be full. He is not surprised by queers or their ways, which merely facilitate his jobs. When he sits on my bed, my ear snatches at scraps of adventure: An officer in underwear whose wallet he steals[3] and who, pointing with his forefinger, orders: "Get out!" René-the-wise-guy's answer: "You think you're in the army?" Too hard a punch on an old man's skull. The one who fainted when René, who was all excited, opened a drawer in which there was a supply of phials of morphine. The queer who was broke and whom he made get down on his knees before him. I am attentive to these accounts. My Antwerp life grows stronger, carrying on in a firmer body, in accordance with manly methods. I encourage René, I give him

---

[3] He says: "I did his wallet."

advice, he listens to me. I tell him never to talk first. "Let the guy come up to you, keep him dangling. Act a little surprised when he suggests that you do it. Figure out who to act dumb with."

Every night I get a few scraps of information. My imagination does not get lost in them. My excitement seems to be due to my assuming within me the role of both victim and criminal. Indeed, as a matter of fact, I emit, I project at night the victim and criminal born of me; I bring them together somewhere, and toward morning I am thrilled to learn that the victim came very close to getting the death penalty and the criminal to being sent to the colony or guillotined. Thus my excitement extends as far as that region of myself, which is Guiana.

Without their wishing it, the gestures and destinies of these men are stormy. Their soul endures a violence which it has not desired and which it has domesticated. Those whose usual climate is violence are simple in relation to themselves. Each of the movements which make up this swift and devastating life is simple and straight, as clean as the stroke of a great draftsman—but when these strokes are encountered in movement, then the storm breaks, the lightning that kills them or me. Yet, what is their violence compared to mine, which was to accept theirs, to make it mine, to wish it for myself, to intercept it, to utilize it, to force it upon myself, to know it, to premeditate it, to discern and assume its perils? But what was mine, willed and necessary for my defense, my toughness, my rigor, compared to the violence they underwent like a malediction, risen from an inner fire simultaneously with an outer light which sets them ablaze and illuminates us? We know that their adventures are childish. They themselves are fools. They are ready to kill or be killed over a card game in which an opponent—or they themselves—was cheating. Yet, thanks to such guys, tragedies are possible.

This kind of definition—by so many opposing examples—of violence shows you that I shall not make use of words the better to depict an event or its hero, but so that they may tell you something about myself. In order to understand me, the reader's complicity will be necessary. Nevertheless, I shall warn him whenever my lyricism makes me lose my footing.

Stilitano was big and strong. His gait was both supple and heavy, brisk and slow, sinuous; he was nimble. A large part of his power over me—and over the whores of the Barrio Chino—lay in the spittle he passed from one cheek to the other and which he would sometimes draw out in front of his mouth like a veil. "But where does he get that spit," I would ask myself, "where does he bring it up from? Mine will never have the unctuousness or color of his. It will merely be spun glassware, transparent and fragile." It was therefore natural for me to imagine what his penis would be if he smeared it for my benefit with so fine a substance, with that precious cobweb, a tissue which I secretly called the veil of the palace. He wore an old gray cap with a broken visor. When he tossed it on the floor of our room, it suddenly became the carcass of a poor partridge with a clipped wing, but when he put it on, pulling it down a bit over the ear, the opposite edge of the visor rose up to reveal the most glorious of blond locks. Shall I speak of his lovely bright eyes, modestly lowered—yet it could be said of Stilitano: "His bearing is immodest"—over which there closed eyelids and lashes so blond, so luminous and thick, that they brought in not the shade of evening but the shade of evil. After all, what meaning would there be in the sight that staggers me when, in a harbor, I see a sail, little by little, by fits and starts, spreading out and with difficulty rising on the mast of a ship, hesitantly at first, then resolutely, if these movements were not the very symbol of the movements of my love for Stilitano? I met him in Barcelona. He was living among beggars, thieves, fairies, and whores. He was handsome, but it remains to be seen whether he owed all that beauty to my fallen state. My clothes were dirty and shabby. I was hungry and cold. This was the most miserable period of my life.

1932. Spain at the time was covered with vermin, its beggars. They went from village to village, to Andalusia because it is warm, to Catalonia because it is rich, but the whole country was favorable to us. I was thus a louse, and conscious of being one. In Barcelona we hung around the Calle Mediodia and the Calle Carmen. We sometimes slept six in a bed without sheets, and at dawn we would go begging in the markets. We would leave the Barrio Chino in a group and scatter over the Parallelo, carrying shopping baskets, for the housewives would give us a leek or turnip rather than a coin. At noon we would return, and with the gleanings we would make our soup. It is the life of vermin that I am going to describe. In Barcelona I saw male couples in which the more loving of the two would say to the other:

"I'll take the basket this morning."

He would take it and leave. One day Salvador gently pulled the basket from my hands and said, "I'm going to beg for you."

It was snowing. He went out into the freezing street, wearing a torn and tattered jacket—the pockets were ripped and hung down—and a shirt stiff with dirt. His face was poor and unhappy, shifty, pale, and filthy, for we dared not wash since it was so cold. Around noon, he returned with the vegetables and a bit of fat. Here I draw attention to one of those lacerations—horrible, for I shall provoke them despite the danger—by which beauty was revealed to me. An immense—and brotherly—love swelled my body and bore me toward Salvador. Leaving the hotel shortly after him, I would see him a way off beseeching the women. I knew the formula, as I had already begged for others and myself: it mixes Christian religion with charity; it merges the poor person with God; it is so humble an emanation from the heart that I think it scents with violet the straight, light breath of the beggar who utters it. All over Spain at the time they were saying:

"Por Dios."

Without hearing him, I would imagine Salvador murmuring it at all the stalls, to all the housewives. I would keep an eye on him as the pimp keeps an eye on his whore, but with such tenderness in my heart! Thus, Spain and my life as a beggar familiarized me with the stateliness of abjection, for it took a great deal of pride (that is, of love) to embellish those filthy, despised creatures. It took a great deal of talent, which came to me little by little. Though I may be unable to describe its mechanism to you, at least I can say that I slowly forced myself to consider that wretched life as a deliberate necessity. Never did I try to make of it something other than what it was, I did not try to adorn it, to mask it, but, on the contrary, I wanted to affirm it in its exact sordidness, and the most sordid signs became for me signs of grandeur.

I was dismayed when, one evening, while searching me after a raid—I am speaking of a scene which preceded the one with which this book begins—the astonished detective took from my pocket, among other things, a tube of Vaseline. We dared joke about it since it contained mentholated Vaseline. The whole record office, and I too, though painfully, writhed with laughter at the following:

"You take it in the nose?"

"Watch out you don't catch cold. You'd give your guy whooping cough."

I translate but lamely, in the language of a Paris hustler, the malicious irony of the vivid and venomous Spanish phrases. It concerned a tube of Vaseline, one of whose ends was partially rolled up. Which amounts to saying that it had been put to use. Amidst the elegant objects taken from the pockets of the men who had been picked up in the raid, it was the very sign of abjection, of that which is concealed with the greatest of care, but yet the sign of a secret grace which was soon to save me from contempt. When I was locked up in a cell, and as soon as I had sufficiently regained my spirits to rise above the misfortune of my arrest, the image of the tube of Vaseline never left me. The policemen had shown it to me victoriously, since they could thereby flourish their revenge, their hatred, their contempt. But lo and behold! that dirty, wretched object whose purpose seemed to the world—to that concentrated delegation of the world which is the police and, above all, that particular gathering of Spanish police, smelling of garlic, sweat, and oil, but substantial looking, stout of muscle and strong in their moral assurance—utterly vile, became extremely precious to me. Unlike many objects which my tenderness singles out, this one was not at all haloed; it remained on the table a little, gray, leaden tube of Vaseline, broken and livid, whose astonishing discreteness, and its essential correspondence with all the commonplace things in the record office of a prison (the bench, the inkwell, the regulations, the scales, the odor), would, through the general indifference, have distressed me, had not the very content of the tube made me think, by bringing to mind an oil lamp (perhaps because of its unctuous character), of a night-light beside a coffin.

In describing it, I recreate the little object, but the following image cuts in: beneath a lamppost, in a street of the city where I am writing, the pallid face of a little, old woman, a round, flat, little face, like the moon, very pale; I cannot tell whether it was sad or hypocritical. She approached me, told me she was very poor and asked for a little money. The gentleness of that moon-fish face told me at once: the old woman had just got out of prison.

."She's a thief," I said to myself. As I walked away from her, a kind of intense reverie, living deep within me and not at the edge of my mind, led me to think that it was perhaps my mother whom I had just met. I know nothing of her who abandoned me in the cradle, but I hoped it was that old thief who begged at night.

"What if it were she?" I thought as I walked away from the old woman. Oh! if it were, I would cover her with flowers, with gladioli, and roses, and with kisses! I would weep with tenderness over those moon-fish eyes, over that round, foolish face! "And why," I went on, "why weep over it?" It did not take my mind long to replace these customary marks of tenderness by some other gesture, even the vilest and most contemptible, which I empowered to mean as much as the kisses, or the tears, or the flowers.

"I'd be glad to slobber over her," I thought, overflowing with love. (Does the word *glaïeul* [gladiolus] mentioned above bring into play the word *glaviaux* [gobs of spit]?) To slobber over her hair or vomit into her hands. But I would adore that thief who is my mother.

The tube of Vaseline, which was intended to grease my prick and those of my lovers, summoned up the face of her who, during a reverie that moved through the dark alleys of the city, was the most cherished of mothers. It had served me in the preparation of so many secret joys, in places worthy of its discrete banality, that it had become the condition of my happiness, as my sperm-spotted handkerchief testified. Lying on the table, it was a banner telling the invisible legions of my triumph over the police. I was in a cell. I knew that all night long my tube of Vaseline would be exposed to the scorn—the contrary of a Perpetual Adoration— of a group of strong, handsome, husky policemen. So strong that if the weakest of them barely squeezed his fingers together, there would shoot forth, first with a slight fart, brief and dirty, a ribbon of gum which would continue to emerge in a ridiculous silence. Nevertheless, I was sure that this puny and most humble object would hold its own against them; by its mere presence it would be able to exasperate all the police in the world; it would draw down upon itself contempt, hatred, white and dumb rages. It would perhaps be slightly bantering—like a tragic hero amused at stirring up the wrath of the gods—indestructible, like him, faithful to my happiness, and proud. I would like to hymn it with the newest words in the French language. But I would have also liked to fight for it, to organize massacres in its honor and bedeck a countryside at twilight with red bunting.[4]

The beauty of a moral act depends on the beauty of its expression. To say that it is beautiful is to decide that it will be so. It remains to be proven so. This is the task of images, that is, of the correspondences with the splendors of the physical world. The act is beautiful if it provokes, and in our throat reveals, song. Sometimes the consciousness with which we have pondered a reputedly vile act, the power of expression which must signify it, impel us to song. This means that treachery is beautiful if it makes us sing. To betray thieves would be not only to find myself again in the moral world, I thought, but also to find myself once more in homosexuality. As I grow strong, I am my own god. I dictate. Applied to men, the word beauty indicates to me the harmonious quality of a face and body to which is sometimes added manly grace. Beauty is then accompanied by magnificent, masterly, sovereign gestures. We imagine that they are determined by very special moral attitudes, and by the cultivation of such virtues in ourselves we hope

---

[4] I would indeed rather have shed blood than repudiate that silly object.

to endow our poor faces and sick bodies with the vigor that our lovers possess naturally. Alas, these virtues, which they themselves never possess, are our weakness.

Now as I write, I muse on my lovers. I would like them to be smeared with my Vaseline, with that soft, slightly mentholated substance; I would like their muscles to bathe in that delicate transparence without which the tool of the handsomest is less lovely.

When a limb has been removed, the remaining one is said to grow stronger. I had hoped that the vigor of the arm which Stilitano had lost might be concentrated in his penis. For a long time I imagined a solid member, like a blackjack, capable of the most outrageous impudence, though what first intrigued me was what Stilitano allowed me to know of it: the mere crease, though curiously precise in the left leg, of his blue denim trousers. This detail might have haunted my dreams less had Stilitano not, at odd moments, put his left hand on it, and had he not, like ladies making a curtsey, indicated the crease by delicately pinching the cloth with his nails. I do not think he ever lost his self-possession, but with me he was particularly calm. With a slightly impertinent smile, though quite nonchalantly, he would watch me adore him. I know that he will love me.

Before Salvador, basket in hand, crossed the threshold of our hotel, I was so excited that I kissed him in the street, but he pushed me aside:

"You're crazy! People'll take us for *mariconas!*"

He spoke French fairly well, having learned it in the region around Perpignan where he used to go for the grape harvesting. Deeply wounded, I turned away. His face was purple. His complexion was that of winter cabbage. Salvador did not smile. He was shocked. "That's what I get," he must have thought, "for getting up so early to go begging in the snow. He doesn't know how to behave." His hair was wet and shaggy. Behind the window, faces were staring at us, for the lower part of the hotel was occupied by a café that opened on the street and through which you had to pass in order to go up to the rooms. Salvador wiped his face with his sleeve and went in. I hesitated. Then I followed. I was twenty years old. If the drop that hesitates at the edge of a nostril has the limpidity of a tear, why shouldn't I drink it with the same eagerness? I was already sufficiently involved in the rehabilitation of the ignoble. Were it not for fear of revolting Salvador, I would have done it in the café. He, however, sniffled, and I gathered that he was swallowing his snot. Basket in arm, passing the beggars and the guttersnipes, he moved toward the kitchen. He preceded me.

"What's the matter with you?" I said.

"You're attracting attention."

"What's wrong?"

"People don't kiss that way on the sidewalk. Tonight, if you like . . ."

He said it all with a charmless pout and the same disdain. I had simply wanted to show my gratitude, to warm him with my poor tenderness.

"But what were you thinking?"

Someone bumped into him without apologizing, separating him from me. I did not follow him to the kitchen. I went over to a bench where there was a vacant seat near the stove. Though I adored vigorous beauty, I didn't bother my head much about how I would bring myself to love this homely, squalid beggar who was bullied by the less bold, how I would come to care for his angular buttocks . . . and what if, unfortuantely, he were to have a magnificent tool?

The Barrio Chino was, at the time, a kind of haunt thronged less with Spaniards than with foreigners, all of them down-and-out bums. We were sometimes dressed in almond green or jonquil yellow, silk shirts and shabby sneakers, and our hair was so plastered down that it looked as if it would crack. We did not have leaders but rather directors. I am unable to explain how they became what they were. Probably it was as a result of profitable operations in the sale of our meager booty. They attended to our affairs and let us know about jobs, for which they took a reasonable commission. We did not form loosely organized bands, but amidst that vast, filthy disorder, in a neighborhood stinking of oil, piss, and shit, a few waifs and strays relied on others more clever than themselves. The squalor sparkled with the youth of many of our number and with the more mysterious brilliance of a few who really scintillated, youngsters whose bodies, gazes, and gestures were charged with a magnetism which made of us their object. That is how I was staggered by one of them. In order to do justice to the one-armed Stilitano I shall wait a few pages. Let it be known from the start that he was devoid of any Christian virtue. All his brilliance, all his power, had their source between his legs. His penis, and that which completes it, the whole apparatus, was so beautiful that the only thing I can call it is a generative organ. One might have thought he was dead, for he rarely, and slowly, got excited: he watched. He generated in the darkness of a well-buttoned fly, though buttoned by only one hand, the luminosity with which its bearer will be aglow.

My relations with Salvador lasted for six months. It was not the most intoxicating but rather the most fecund of loves. I had managed to love that sickly body, gray face, and ridiculously sparse beard. Salvador took care of me, but at night, by candlelight, I hunted for lice, our pets, in the seams of his trousers. The lice inhabited us. They imparted to our clothes an animation, a presence, which, when they had gone, left our garments lifeless. We liked to know—and feel—that the translucent bugs were swarming; though not tamed, they were so much a part of us that a third person's louse disgusted us. We chased them away but with the hope that during the day the nits would have hatched. We crushed them with our nails, without disgust and without hatred. We did not throw their corpses—or remains—into the garbage; we let them fall, bleeding with our blood, into our untidy underclothes. The lice were the only sign of our prosperity, of the very underside of prosperity, but it was logical that by making our state perform an operation which justified it, we were, by the same token, justifying the sign of this state. Having become as useful for the knowledge of our decline as jewels for the knowledge of what is called triumph, the lice were precious. They were both our shame and our glory. I lived for a long time in a room without windows, except a transom on the corridor, where, in the evening, five little faces, cruel and tender, smiling or screwed up with the cramp of a difficult position, dripping with sweat, would hunt for those insects of whose virtue we partook. It was good that, in the depths of such wretchedness, I was the lover of the poorest and homeliest. I thereby had a rare privilege. I had difficulty, but every victory I achieved—my filthy hands, proudly exposed, helped me proudly expose my beard and long hair—gave me strength—or weakness, and here it amounts to the same thing—for the following victory, which in your language would naturally be called a comedown. Yet, light and brilliance being necessary to our lives, a sunbeam did cross the pane and its filth and penetrate the dimness; we had the hoarfrost, the silver thaw, for these elements, though they may spell calamity, evoke joys whose sign, detached in our room, was adequate for us: all we knew of Christmas and New Year's festivities was what always accompanies them and what makes them dearer to merrymakers: frost.

The cultivation of sores by beggars is also their means of getting a little money—on which to live—but though they may be led to this out of a certain inertia in their state of poverty, the pride required for holding one's head up, above contempt, is a manly virtue. Like a rock in a river, pride breaks through and divides contempt, bursts it. Entering further into abjection, pride will be stronger (if the beggar is myself) when I have the knowledge—strength or weakness—to take advantage of such a fate. It is essential, as this leprosy gains on me, that I gain on it and that, in the end, I win out. Shall I therefore become increasingly vile, more and more an object of disgust, up to that final point which is something still unknown but which must be governed by an aesthetic as well as moral inquiry? It is said that leprosy, to which I compare our state, causes an irritation of the tissues; the sick person scratches himself; he gets an erection. Masturbation becomes frequent. In his solitary eroticism the leper consoles himself and hymns his disease. Poverty made us erect. All across Spain we carried a secret, veiled magnificence unmixed with arrogance. Our gestures grew humbler and humbler, fainter and fainter, as the embers of humility which kept us alive glowed more intensely. Thus developed my talent for giving a sublime meaning to so beggarly an appearance. (I am not yet speaking of literary talent.) It proved to have been a very useful discipline for me and still enables me to smile tenderly at the humblest among the dregs, whether human or material, including vomit, including the saliva I let drool on my mother's face, including your excrement. I shall preserve within me the idea of myself as beggar.

I wanted to be like that woman who, at home, hidden away from people, sheltered her daughter, a kind of hideous, misshapen monster, stupid and white, who grunted and walked on all fours. When the mother gave birth, her despair was probably such that it became the very essence of her life. She decided to love this monster, to love the ugliness that had come out of her belly in which it had been elaborated, and to erect it devotedly. Within herself she ordained an altar where she preserved the idea of Monster. With devoted care, with hands gentle despite the calluses of her daily toil, with the willful zeal of the hopeless, she set herself up against the world, and against the world she set up the monster, which took on the proportions of the world and its power. It was on the basis of the monster that new principles were ordained, principles constantly combated by the forces of the world which came charging into her but which stopped at the walls of her dwelling where her daughter was confined.[5]

But, for it was sometimes necessary to steal, we also knew the clear, earthly beauties of boldness. Before we went to sleep, the chief, the liege lord, would give us advice. For example, we would go with fake papers to various consulates in order to be repatriated. The consul, moved or annoyed by our woes and wretchedness, and our filth, would give us a train ticket to a border post. Our chief would resell it at the Barcelona station. He also let us know of thefts to commit in churches—which Spaniards would not dare do—or in elegant villas; and it was he himself who brought us the Dutch and English sailors to whom we had to prostitute ourselves for a few pesetas.

Thus we sometimes stole, and each burglary allowed us to breathe for a moment at the surface. A vigil of arms precedes each nocturnal expedition. The nervousness provoked by fear, and sometimes by anxiety, makes for a state akin to religious moods. At such times I tend to see omens in the slightest accidents. Things become signs of chance. I want to charm the unknown powers upon which the success of the adventure seems to me to depend. I try to charm them by moral acts, chiefly by charity. I give more readily and more freely to beggars, I give my seat to old people, I stand aside to let them pass, I help blind men cross the street, and so on. In this way, I seem to recognize that over the act of stealing rules a god to whom moral actions are agreeable. These attempts to throw out a net, on the chance that this god of whom I know nothing will be caught in it, exhaust me, disturb me, and also favor the religious state. To the act of stealing they communicate the gravity of a ritual act. It will really be performed in the heart of darkness, to which is added that it may be rather at night, while people are asleep, in a place that is closed and perhaps itself masked in black. The walking on tiptoe, the silence, the invisibility which we need even in broad daylight, the groping hands organizing in the darkness gestures of an unwonted complexity and wariness. Merely to turn a doorknob requires a host of movements, each as brilliant as the facet of a jewel. When I discover gold, it seems to me that I have unearthed it; I have ransacked continents, South Sea islands; I am surrounded by Negroes; they threaten my defenseless body with their poisoned spears, but then the virtue of the gold acts, and a great vigor crushes or exalts me, the spears are lowered, the Negroes recognize me and I am one of the tribe. The perfect act: inadvertently putting my hand into the pocket of a handsome sleeping Negro, feeling his prick stiffen beneath my fingers and withdrawing my hand closed over a gold coin discovered in and stolen from his pocket—the prudence, the whispering voice, the

---

[5] I learned from the newspapers that, after forty years of devotion, this mother sprayed her sleeping daughter, and then the whole house, with gasoline—or petroleum—and set fire to the house. The monster (the daughter) died. The old woman (age seventy-five) was rescued from the flames and was saved, that is, she was brought to trial.

alert ear, the invisible, nervous presence of the accomplice and the understanding of his slightest sign, all concentrate our being within us, compress us, make of us a very ball of presence, which so well explains Guy's remark:

"You feel yourself living."

But within myself, this total presence, which is transformed into a bomb of what seems to me terrific power imparts to the act of gravity, a terminal oneness—the burglary, while being performed, is always the last, not that you think you are not going to perform another after that one—you don't think—but because such a gathering of self cannot take place (not in life, for to push it further would be to pass out of life); and this oneness of an act which develops (as the rose puts forth its corolla) into conscious gestures, sure of their efficacy, of their fragility and yet of the violence which they give to the act, here too confers upon it the value of a religious rite. Often I even dedicate it to someone. The first time, it was Stilitano who had the benefit of such homage. I think it was by him that I was initiated, that is, my obsession with his body kept me from flinching. To his beauty, to his tranquil immodesty, I dedicated my first thefts. To the singularity too of that splendid cripple whose hand, cut off at the wrist, was rotting away somewhere, under a chestnut tree, so he told me, in a forest of Central Europe. During the theft, my body is exposed. I know that it is sparkling with all my gestures. The world is attentive to all my movements, if it wants me to trip up. I shall pay dearly for a mistake, but if there is a mistake and I catch it in time, it seems to me that there will be joy in our Father's dwelling. Or, I fall, and there is woe upon woe and then prison. But as for the savages, the convict who risked "the Getaway" will then meet them by means of the procedure briefly described above in my inner adventure. If, going through the virgin forest, he comes upon a place guarded by ancient tribes, he will either be killed by them or be saved. It is by a long, long road that I choose to go back to primitive life. What I need first is condemnation by my race.

Salvador was not a source of pride to me. When he did steal, he merely filched trifles from stands in front of shop windows. At night, in the cafés where we huddled together, he would sadly worm himself in among the most handsome. That kind of life exhausted him. When I entered, I would be ashamed to find him hunched over, squatting on a bench, his shoulders huddled up in the green and yellow, cotton blanket with which he would go out begging on wintry days. He would also be wearing an old, black-woolen shawl which I refused to put on. Indeed, though my mind endured, even desired, humility, my violent, young body rejected it. Salvador would speak in a sad, reticent voice:

"Would you like us to go back to France? We'll work in the country."

I said no. He did not understand my loathing—no, my hatred—of France, nor that my adventure, if it stopped in Barcelona, was bound to continue deeply, more and more deeply, in the remotest regions of myself.

"But I'll do all the work. You'll take it easy."

"No."

I would leave him on his bench to his cheerless poverty. I would go over to the stove or the bar and smoke the butts I had gleaned during the day, with a scornful young Andalusian whose dirty, white, woolen sweater exaggerated his torso and muscles. After rubbing his hands together, the way old men do, Salvador would leave his bench and go to the community kitchen to prepare a soup and put a fish on the grill. Once he suggested that we go down to Huelva for the orange picking. It was an evening when he had received so many humiliations, so many rebuffs while begging for me that he dared reproach me for my poor success at the Criolla.

"Really, when you pick up a client, it's *you* who ought to pay *him*."

We quarreled in front of the proprietor of the hotel, who wanted to put us out. Salvador and I therefore decided to steal two blankets the following day and hide in a southbound freight train. But I was so clever that that very evening I brought back the cape of a customs officer. As I passed the docks where they mount guard, one of the officers called me. I did what he required, in the sentry box. After coming (perhaps, without daring to tell me so, he wanted to wash at a little fountain), he left me alone for a moment and I ran off with his big black woolen cape. I wrapped myself up in it in order to return to the hotel, and I knew the happiness of the equivocal, not yet the joy of betrayal, though the insidious confusion which would make me deny fundamental oppositions was already forming. As I opened the door of the café, I saw Salvador. He was the saddest-looking of beggars. His face had the quality, and almost the texture, of the sawdust that covered the floor of the café. Immediately I recognized Stilitano standing in the midst of the ronda players. Our eyes met. His gaze lingered on me, who blushed. I took off the black cape, and at once they started haggling over it. Without yet taking part, Stilitano watched the wretched bargaining.

"Make it snappy, if you want it," I said. "Make up your minds. The customs man is sure to come looking for me."

The players got a little more active. They were used to such reasons. When the general shuffle brought me to his side, Stilitano said to me in French:

"You from Paris?"

"Yes. Why?"

"For no reason."

Although it was he who had made the first advance, I knew, as I answered, the almost desperate nature of the gesture the invert dares when he approaches a young man. To mask my confusion, I had the pretext of being breathless, I had the bustle of the moment. He said, "You did pretty well for yourself."

I knew that this praise was cleverly calculated, but how handsome Stilitano was amidst the beggars (I didn't know his name yet)! One of his arms, at the extremity of which was an enormous bandage, was folded on his chest as if in a sling, but I knew that the hand was missing. Stilitano was an habitué of neither the café nor even the street.

"What'll the cape cost me?"

"Will you pay me for it?"

"Why not?"

"With what?"

"Are you scared?"

"Where are you from?"

"Serbia. I'm back from the Foreign Legion. I'm a deserter."

I was relieved. Destroyed. The emotion created within me a void which was at once filled by the memory of a nuptial scene. In a dance hall where soldiers were dancing among themselves, I watched their waltz. It seemed to me at the time that the invisibility of two legionnaires became total. They were charmed away by emotion. Though their dance was chaste at the beginning of "Ramona," would it remain so when, in our presence, they wedded by exchanging a smile, as lovers exchange rings? To all the injunctions of an invisible clergy the Legion answered, "I do." Each one of them was the couple wearing both a net veil and a dress uniform (white leather, scarlet and green shoulder braid). They haltingly exchanged their manly tenderness and wifely modesty. To maintain the emotion at a high pitch, they slowed up and slackened their dance, while their pricks, numbed by the fatigue of a long march, recklessly threatened and challenged each other behind a barricade of rough denim. The patent-leather vizors of their képis kept striking together. I knew I was being mastered by Stilitano. I wanted to play sly:

"That doesn't prove you can pay."

"Trust me."

Such a hard-looking face, such a strapping body, were asking me to trust them. Salvador was watching us. He was aware of our understanding and realized that we had already decided upon his ruin, his loneliness. Fierce and pure, I was the theater of a fairyland restored to life. When the waltz ended, the two soldiers disengaged themselves. And each of those two halves of a solemn and dizzy block hesitated, and, happy to be escaping from invisibility, went off, downcast, toward some girl for the next waltz.

"I'll give you two days to pay me," I said. "I need dough. I was in the Legion too. And I deserted. Like you."

"You'll get it."

I handed him the cape. He took it with his only hand and gave it back to me. He smiled, though imperiously, and said, "Roll it up." And joshingly added, "While waiting to roll me one."

Everyone knows the expression: "to roll a skate."[6] Without batting an eyelash, I did as he said. The cape immediately disappeared into one of the hotel proprietor's hiding places. Perhaps this simple theft brightened my face, or Stilitano simply wanted to act nice; he added: "You going to treat an ex-Bel-Abbès boy to a drink?"

A glass of wine cost two sous. I had four in my pocket, but I owed them to Salvador, who was watching us.

"I'm broke," Stilitano said proudly.

The card players were forming new groups which for a moment separated us

---

[6] *Rouler un patin* (to roll a skate) is French slang meaning to kiss with the tongue.—Translator's note.

from Salvador. I muttered between my teeth, "I've got four sous and I'm going to slip them to you, but you're the one who'll pay."

Stilitano smiled. I was lost. We sat down at a table. He had already begun to talk about the Legion when, staring hard at me, he suddenly broke off.

"I've got a feeling I've seen you somewhere before."

As for me, I had retained the memory.

I had to grab hold of invisible tackle. I could have cooed. Words, or the tone of my voice, would have not merely expressed my ardor, I would not have merely sung, my throat would have uttered the call of indeed the most amorous of wild game. Perhaps my neck would have bristled with white feathers. A catastrophe is always possible. Metamorphosis lies in wait for us. Panic protected me.

I have lived in the fear of metamorphoses. It is in order to make the reader fully conscious, as he sees love swooping down on me—it is not mere rhetoric which requires the comparison—like a falcon—of the most exquisite of frights that I employ the idea of a turtledove. I do not know what I felt at the moment, but today all I need do is summon up the vision of Stilitano for my distress to appear at once in the relationship of a cruel bird to its victim. (Were it not that I felt my neck swell out with a gentle cooing, I would have spoken rather of a robin redbreast.)

A curious creature would appear if each of my emotions became the animal it evokes: anger rumbles within my cobra neck; the same cobra swells up my prick; my steeds and merry-go-rounds are born of my insolence. . . . Of a turtledove I retained only a hoarseness, which Stilitano noticed. I coughed.

Behind the Parallelo was an empty lot where the hoodlums played cards. (The Parallelo is an avenue in Barcelona parallel to the famous Ramblas. Between these two wide thoroughfares, a multitude of dark, dirty, narrow streets make up the Barrio Chino.) Squatting on the ground, they would organize games; they would lay out the cards on a square piece of cloth or in the dust. A young Gypsy was running one of the games, and I came to risk the few sous I had in my pocket. I am not a gambler. Rich casinos do not attract me. The atmosphere of electric chandeliers bores me. The affected casualness of the elegant gambler nauseates me. And the impossibility of acting upon the balls, roulettes, and little horses discourages me, but I loved the dust, filth, and haste of the hoodlums. When I bugger . . . ,[7] as I bend farther forward I get a profile view of his face crushed against the pillow, of his pain. I see the wincing of his features, but also their radiant anguish. I often watched this on the grimy faces of the squatting urchins. This whole population was keyed up for winning or losing. Every thigh was quivering with fatigue or anxiety. The weather that day was threatening. I was caught up in the youthful impatience of the young Spaniards. I played and I won. I won every hand. I didn't say a word during the game. Besides, the Gypsy was a stranger to me. Custom permitted me to pocket my money and leave. The boy was so

[7]Since the hero, whom at first I called by his real name, is my current lover (1948), prudence advises me to leave a blank in place of his name.

good-looking that by leaving him in that way I felt I was lacking in respect for the beauty, suddenly become sad, of his face, which was drooping with heat and boredom. I kindly gave him back his money. Slightly astonished, he took it and simply thanked me.

"Hello, Pépé," a kinky, swarthy-looking cripple called out as he limped by.

"Pépé," I said to myself, "his name is Pépé." And I left, for I had just noticed his delicate, almost feminine little hand. But hardly had I gone a few steps in that crowd of thieves, whores, beggars, and queers than I felt someone touching me on the shoulder. It was Pépé. He had just left the game. He spoke to me in Spanish:

"My name is Pépé."

"Mine is Juan."

"Come, let's have a drink."

He was no taller than I. His face, which I had seen from above when he was squatting, looked less flattened. The features were finer.

"He's a girl," I thought, summoning up the image of his slender hand, and I felt that his company would bore me. He had just decided that we would drink the money I had won. We made the round of the bars, and all the while we were together he was quite charming. He wore a very low-necked, blue jersey instead of a shirt. From the opening emerged a solid neck, as broad as his head. When he turned it without moving his chest, an enormous tendon stood out. I tried to imagine his body, and, despite the almost frail hands, I imagined it to be solid, for his thighs filled out the light cloth of his trousers. The weather was warm. The storm did not break. The nervousness of the players around us heightened. The whores seemed heavier. The dust and sun were oppressive. We drank hardly any liquor, but rather lemonade. We sat near the peddlers and exchanged an occasional word. He kept smiling, with a slight weariness. He seemed to be indulging me. Did he suspect that I liked his cute face? I don't know, but he didn't let on. Besides, I had the same sly sort of look as he; I seemed a threat to the well-dressed passerby; I had his youth and his filth, and I was French. Toward evening he wanted to gamble, but it was too late to start a game as all the places were taken. We strolled about a bit among the players. When he brushed by the whores, Pépé would kid them. Sometimes he would pinch them. The heat grew more oppressive. The sky was flush with the ground. The nervousness of the crowd became irritating. Impatience prevailed over the Gypsy who had not decided which game to join. He was fingering the money in his pocket. Suddenly he took me by the arm.

"*Venga!*"

He led me a few steps away to the one comfort station on the Parallelo. It was run by an old woman. Surprised by the suddenness of his decision, I questioned him:

"What are you going to do?"

"Wait for me."

"Why?"

He answered with a Spanish word which I did not understand. I told him so and, in front of the old woman who was waiting for her two sous, he burst out laughing and made the gesture of jerking off. When he came out, his face had a bit of color. He was still smiling.

"It's all right now. I'm ready."

That was how I learned that, on big occasions, players went there to jerk off in order to be calmer and more sure of themselves. We went back to the lot. Pépé chose a group. He lost. He lost all he had. I tried to restrain him; it was too late. As authorized by custom, he asked the man running the bank to give him a stake from the kitty for the next game. The man refused. It seemed to me then that the very thing that constituted the Gypsy's gentleness turned sour, as milk turns, and became the most ferocious rage I have ever seen. He whisked away the bank. The man bounded up and tried to kick him. Pépé dodged. He handed me the money, but hardly had I pocketed it than his knife was open. He planted it in the heart of the Spaniard, a tall, bronzed fellow, who fell to the ground and who, despite his tan, turned pale, contracted, writhed, and expired in the dust. For the first time I saw someone give up the ghost. Pépé had disappeared, but when, turning my eyes away from the corpse, I looked up, there, gazing at it with a faint smile, was Stilitano. The sun was about to set. The dead man and the handsomest of humans seemed to me merged in the same golden dust amidst a throng of sailors, soldiers, hoodlums, and thieves from all parts of the world. The Earth did not revolve: carrying Stilitano, it trembled about the sun. At the same moment I came to know death and love. This vision, however, was very brief, for I could not stay there because I was afraid I might have been spotted with Pépé and lest a friend of the dead man snatch away the money which I kept in my pocket, but as I moved off, my memory kept alive and commented upon the following scene, which seemed to me grandiose: "The murder, by a charming child, of a grown man whose tan could turn pale, take on the hue of death, the whole ironically observed by a tall, blond youngster to whom I had just become secretly engaged." Rapid as my glance at him was, I had time to take in Stilitano's superb muscularity and to see, between his lips, rolling in his half-open mouth, a white, heavy blob of spit, thick as a white worm, which he shifted about, stretching it from top to bottom until it veiled his mouth. He stood barefoot in the dust. His legs were contained in a pair of worn and shabby faded, blue-denim trousers. The sleeves of his green shirt were rolled up, one of them above an amputated hand; the wrist, where the resewn skin still revealed a pale, pink scar, was slightly shrunken.

Beneath a tragic sky, I was to cross the loveliest landscapes in the world when Stilitano took my hand at night. What was the nature of that fluid which passed with a shock from him to me? I walked along dangerous shores, emerged into dismal plains, heard the sea. Hardly had I touched him, when the stairway changed: he was master of the world. With the memory of those brief moments, I could describe to you walks, breathless flights, pursuits, in countries of the world where I shall never go.

•   •   •

Stilitano smiled and laughed at me.

"Are you stringing me along?"

"A little," he said.

"Go right ahead."

He smiled again and raised his eyebrows.

"Why?"

"You know that you're a good-looking kid. And you think you don't have to give a damn about anyone."

"I've got a right to. I'm a nice guy."

"You're sure?"

He burst out laughing.

"Sure. No mistake. I'm so likable that sometimes I can't get rid of people. In order to shake them off I sometimes have to do them dirt."

"What kind of dirt?"

"You want to know? Just wait, you'll see me on the job. You'll have time to see what it's like. Where are you staying?"

"Here."

"Don't. The police'll be around. They'll look here first. Come with me."

I told Salvador that I couldn't stay at the hotel that night and that a former member of the Legion was offering me his room. He turned pale. The humility of his pain made me feel ashamed. In order to leave him without remorse I insulted him. I was able to since he loved me to the point of devotion. He gave me a woebegone look, but it was charged with a poor wretch's hatred. I replied with the word: "Fruit." I joined Stilitano, who was waiting for me outside. His hotel was in the darkest alley in the neighborhood. He had been living there for some days. A stairway from the corridor which opened out to the sidewalk led to the rooms. As we were going up, he said to me, "D'you want us to shack up together?"

"If we feel like it."

"You're right. We'll stay out of trouble easier."

In front of the door of the corridor he said to me, "Hand me the box."

We had only one box of matches between us.

"It's empty," I said.

He swore. Stilitano took me by the hand, putting his own behind his back, for I was at his right.

"Follow me," he said. "And stop talking. The staircase has ears."

Gently he led me from step to step. I no longer knew where we were going. A wondrously supple athlete was leading me about in the night. A more ancient and more Greek Antigone was making me scale a dark, steep Calvary. My hand was confident, and I was ashamed to stumble at times against a rock or root, or to lose my footing. My ravisher was carrying me off.

"He's going to think I'm clumsy."

However, he thoughtfully and patiently helped me, and the silence he enjoined upon me, the secrecy with which he surrounded the evening, our first night, made me for a moment believe in his love for me. The house smelled neither better nor worse than the others in the Barrio Chino, but the horrible odor of this one will always remain for me the very odor not only of love but of tenderness and confidence. After making love, the animal odor of my lover lingers in my nostrils a long time. Probably some particles remain clinging to the hairs which line the interior, and it is a bit of his body that I encounter and recreate in me when I sniff. When my sense of smell remembers Stilitano's odor, the odor of his armpits, of his mouth, though it may suddenly come upon them with a disquieting veracity, I believe them capable of inspiring me with the wildest rashness. (Sometimes at night I meet a youngster and go with him to his room. At the foot of the stairs, for my trade lives in shady hotels, he takes me by the hand. He guides me as skillfully as did Stilitano.)

"Watch out."

He mumbled these words, which were too sweet for me. Because of the position of our arms I was pressed against his body. For a moment I felt the movement of his mobile buttocks. Out of respect, I moved a little to the side. We mounted, narrowly limited by a fragile wall which must have contained the sleep of the whores, thieves, pimps, and beggars of the hotel. I was a child being carefully led by his father. (Today I am a father led to love by his child.)

At the fourth landing, I entered his grubby little room. My whole respiratory rhythm was upset. I was in the throes of love. In the Parallelo bars Stilitano introduced me to his cronies. There were so many *mariconas* among the people of the Barrio Chino that no one seemed to notice that I liked men. Together, he and I pulled off a few easy jobs which provided us with what we needed. I lived with him, I slept in his bed, but this big fellow was so exquisitely modest that never did I see him entirely. Had I obtained what I so keenly wanted from him, Stilitano would have remained in my eyes the firm and charming master, though neither his strength nor his charm would have gratified my desire for all the manly types: the soldier, the sailor, the adventurer, the thief, the criminal. By remaining inaccessible, he became the epitome of those whom I have named and who stagger me. I was therefore chaste. At times, he was so cruel as to require that I button the waistband of his trousers, and my hand would tremble. He pretended not to see anything and was amused. (I shall speak later of the character of my hands and of the meaning of this trembling. It is not without reason that in India sacred or disgusting persons and objects are said to be Untouchable.) Unable to see it, I invented the biggest and loveliest prick in the world. I endowed it with qualities: heavy, strong, and nervous, sober, with a tendency toward pride and yet serene. Beneath my fingers, I felt, sculpted in oak, its full veins, its palpitations, its heat, its pinkness, and at times the racing pulsation of the sperm. It occupied less my nights than my days. Behind Stilitano's fly it was the sacred Black Stone to which Heliogabalus offered up his imperial wealth. Stilitano was happy to have me at his beck and call and he introduced me to his friends as his right arm. Now, it was his right hand that had been amputated. I would repeat to myself delightedly that I certainly was his right arm; I was the one who took the place of the strongest limb. If he had a girlfriend among the whores of the Calle Carmen, I was unaware of it. He exaggerated his contempt for fairies. We lived together in this way for a few days. One evening when I was at the Criolla, one of the whores told me to leave. She said that a customs officer had been around looking for me. It must have been the one I had first satisfied and then robbed. I went back to the hotel and told Stilitano about it. He said he would attend to the matter and then left.

I was born in Paris on December 19, 1910. As a ward of the *Assistance Publique*,[8] it was impossible for me to know anything about my background. When I was twenty-one, I obtained a birth certificate. My mother's name was Gabrielle Genet. My father remains unknown. I came into the world at 22 Rue d'Assas.

"I'll find out something about my origin," I said to myself, and went to the Rue d'Assas. Number 22 was occupied by the Maternity Hospital. They refused to give me any information. I was brought up in Le Morvan by peasants. Whenever I come across *genêt* [broom] blossoms on the heaths—especially at twilight on my way back from a visit to the ruins of Tiffauges where Gilles de Rais lived—I feel a deep sense of kinship with them. I regard them solemnly, with tenderness. My emotion seems ordained by all nature. I am alone in the world, and I am not sure that I am not the king—perhaps the sprite—of these flowers. They render homage as I pass, bow without bowing, but recognize me. They know that I am their living, moving, agile representative, conqueror of the wind. They are my natural emblem, but through them I have roots in that French soil which is fed by the powdered bones of the children and youths buggered, massacred, and burned by Gilles de Rais.

Through that thorny plant of the Cevennes,[9] I take part in the criminal adventures of Vacher. Thus, through her whose name I bear, the vegetable kingdom is my familiar. I can regard all flowers without pity; they are members of my family. If, through them, I rejoin the nether realms—though it is to the bracken and their marshes, to the algae, that I should like to descend—I withdraw further from men.[10]

The atmosphere of the planet Uranus appears to be so heavy that the ferns there are creepers; the animals drag along, crushed by the weight of the gases. I want to mingle with these humiliated creatures which are always on their bellies. If metempsychosis should grant me a new dwelling place, I choose that forlorn planet, I inhabit it with the convicts of my race. Amidst hideous reptiles, I pursue an eternal, miserable death in a darkness where the leaves will be black, the waters of the marshes thick and cold. Sleep will be denied me. On the contrary, I recognize, with increasing lucidity, the unclean fraternity of the smiling alligators.

It was not at any precise period of my life that I decided to be a thief. My laziness and daydreaming having led me to the Mettray Reformatory, where I was supposed to remain until "the age of twenty-one," I ran away and enlisted for five

---

[8]The French national agency in charge of the care of foundlings.—Translator's note.
[9]The very day he met me, Jean Cocteau called me "his Spanish *genêt*" (*genêt d'Espagne*—rush-leaved broom). He did not know what that country had made of me.
[10]Botanists know a variety of *genêt* which they call winged broom (*genêt ailé*).

years so as to collect a bonus for voluntary enlistment. After a few days I deserted, taking with me some valises belonging to Negro officers.

For a time I lived by theft, but prostitution was better suited to my indolence. I was twenty years old. I had therefore known the army when I came to Spain. The dignity conferred by the uniform, the isolation from the world which it imposes, and the soldier's trade itself afforded me a certain peace—though the army is on the *fringe* of society—and self-confidence. My situation as a naturally humiliated child was, for some months, tempered. I knew at last the sweetness of being welcomed by men. My life of poverty in Spain was a kind of degradation, a fall involving shame. I was fallen. Not that during my stay in the army I would have been a pure soldier, governed by the rigorous virtues which create castes (my homosexuality would have been enough for me to incur disapproval), but there was still going on within my mind a secret labor which one day came to light. It is perhaps their moral solitude—to which I aspire—that makes me admire traitors and love them—this taste for solitude being the sign of my pride, and pride the manifestation of my strength, the employment and proof of this strength. For I shall have broken the stoutest of bonds, the bonds of love. And I so need love from which to draw vigor enough to destroy it! It was in the army that I witnessed for the first time (at least I think it was) the despair of one of my robbed victims. To rob soldiers was to betray, for I was breaking the bonds of love uniting me with the soldier who had been robbed.

Plaustener was good-looking, strong and confident. He got up on his bed in order to look in his pack. He tried to find in it the hundred-franc note which I had taken a quarter of an hour earlier. His gestures were those of a clown. He was on the wrong track. He imagined the most unlikely hiding places: the mess kit from which he had nevertheless just eaten, the brush bag, the grease can. He was ridiculous. He kept saying, "I'm not crazy. I wouldn't have put it there."

Not knowing whether he was crazy, he checked; he found nothing. Hoping to counter the evidence, he resigned himself and stretched out on his bed only to get up again and search in places where he had already looked. I saw his certainty, the certainty of a man four-square on his thighs and sure of muscle, crumble, pulverize, powder him with a softness he had never had, chip away his sharp angles. I was present at this silent transformation. I feigned indifference. However, this self-confident, young soldier seemed to me so pitiful in his ignorance that his fear, almost his wonderment, with respect to a malignity of which he had been unaware—not thinking it would dare reveal itself to him for the first time by actually taking him for victim—his shame too, almost softened me so far as to make me want to give him back the hundred-franc note which I had hidden, folded up into sixteen parts, in a crack of the barracks wall, near the clothes drier. The head of a robbed man is hideous. The robbed men's heads which frame him give the thief an arrogant solitude. I dared say, in a curt tone, "You're funny to watch. You look as if you've got the runs. Go to the can and pull the chain."

This reflection saved me from myself.

I felt a curious sweetness; a kind of freedom lightened me, gave my body as it lay on the bed an extraordinary agility. Was that what betrayal was? I had just violently detached myself from an unclean comradeship to which my affectionate nature had been leading me, and I was astonished at thereby feeling great strength. I had just broken with the army, had just shattered the bonds of friendship.

The tapestry known as *Lady with the Unicorn* excited me for reasons which I shall not attempt to go into here. But when I crossed the border from Czechoslovakia into Poland, it was a summer afternoon. The border ran through a field of ripe rye, the blondness of which was as blond as the hair of young Poles; it had the somewhat buttery softness of Poland, about which I knew that in the course of history it was more sinned against than sinning. I was with another fellow who, like me, had been expelled by the Czech police, but I very soon lost sight of him; perhaps he had strayed off behind a bush or wanted to get rid of me. He disappeared. The rye field was bounded on the Polish side by a wood at whose edge was nothing but motionless birches; on the Czech side, by another wood, but of fir trees. I remained a long time squatting at the edge, intently wondering what lay hidden in the field. What if I crossed it? Were customs officers hidden in the rye? Invisible hares must have been running through it. I was uneasy. At noon, beneath a pure sky, all nature was offering me a puzzle, and offering it to me blandly.

"If something happens," I said to myself, "it will be the appearance of a unicorn. Such a moment and such a place can only produce a unicorn."

Fear, and the kind of emotion I always feel when I cross a border, conjured up at noon, beneath a leaden sun, the first fairyland. I ventured forth into that golden sea as one enters the water. I went through the rye standing up. I advanced slowly, surely, with the certainty of being the heraldic character for whom a natural blazon has been formed: azure, field of gold, sun, forests. This imagery, of which I was a part, was complicated by the Polish imagery.

"In this noonday sky the white eagle should soar invisible!"

When I got to the birches, I was in Poland. An enchantment of another order was about to be offered me. The *Lady with the Unicorn* is to me the lofty expression of this crossing the line at noontide. I had just experienced, as a result of fear, an uneasiness in the presence of the mystery of diurnal nature, at a time when the French countryside where I wandered about, chiefly at night, was peopled all over with the ghost of Vacher, the killer of shepherds. As I walked through it, I would listen within me to the accordion tunes he must have played there, and I would mentally invite the children to come and offer themselves to the cutthroat's hands. However, I have just referred to this in order to try to tell you at what period of my life nature disturbed me, giving rise within me to the spontaneous creation of a fabulous fauna, or of situations and accidents whose fearful and enchanted prisoner I was.[11]

---

[11]The first line of verse which to my amazement I found myself composing was the following: "Harvester of stolen breath." I am reminded of it by what I have written above.

The crossing of borders and the excitement it arouses in me were to enable me to apprehend directly the essence of the nation I was entering. I would penetrate less into a country than to the interior of an image. Naturally, I wished to possess it, but also by acting upon it. Military attire being that which best denotes it, this was what I hoped to tamper with. For the foreigner, there are no other means than espionage. Mixed in with it, perhaps, was the concern about polluting, through treason, an institution which regards integrity—or loyalty—as its essential quality. Perhaps I also wanted to alienate myself further from my own country. (The explanations I am giving occur to me spontaneously. They seem valid for my case. They are to be accepted for mine alone.) In any event, I mean that as a result of a certain frame of mind which is natural to enchantment (being further exalted by my emotion in the presence of nature, endowed with a power recognized by men) I was ready to act, not in accordance with the rules of morality but in accordance with certain laws of a fictional aesthetic which makes the spy out to be a restless, invisible, though powerful character. In short, a preoccupation of this kind gave, in certain cases, a practical justification to my entering a country to which nothing obliged me to go, except, however, expulsion from a neighboring country.

It is with regard to my feeling in the presence of nature that I speak of espionage, but when I was deserted by Stilitano, the thought of it was to occur to me as a consolation, as if to anchor me to your soil where loneliness and poverty made me not walk but fly. For I am so poor, and I have already been accused of so many thefts, that when I leave a room too quietly on tiptoe, holding my breath, I am not sure, even now, that I am not carrying off with me the holes in the curtains or hangings. I do not know how informed Stilitano was about military secrets or what he might have learned in the Legion, in a colonel's office. But he was thinking of turning spy. Neither the profit to be derived from the operation nor even the danger appealed to me. Only the idea of treason already had that power which was taking greater and greater hold of me.

"Who'll we sell them to?"

"Germany."

But after a few moments' reflection he decided:

"Italy."

"But you're Serbian. They're your enemies."

"So what?"

Had we gone through with this adventure, it would have drawn me out to some extent from the abjection in which I was caught. Espionage is a practice of which states are so ashamed that they ennoble it for its being shameful. We would have profited from this nobleness. Except that in our case it was a matter of treason. Later on, when I was arrested in Italy and the officers questioned me about the protection of our frontiers, I was able to discover a dialectic capable of justifying my disclosures. In the present case I would have been backed up by Stilitano. I could not but wish, through these revelations, to be the abettor of a terrible catastrophe. Stilitano might have betrayed his country and I mine out of love for Stilitano. When I speak to you later about Java, you will find the same characteristics, indeed almost the same face as Stilitano's; and as the two sides of a triangle meet at the apex which is in the sky, Stilitano and Java go off to meet a star forever extinguished: Marc Aubert.[12]

Though the blue-woolen cape I had stolen from the customs officer had already afforded me a kind of presentiment of a conclusion wherein law and outlaw merge, one lurking beneath the other but feeling, with a touch of nostalgia, the virtue of its opposite, to Stilitano it would offer an adventure less spiritual or subtle but more deeply involved in daily life, better utilized. It will not yet be a question of treason. Stilitano was a power. His egotism sharply marked out his natural frontiers. (Stilitano was a power to *me*.)

When he entered late at night, he told me that the whole matter was settled. He had met the customs officer.

"He won't bother you. It's all over. You can go out without worrying."

"But what about the cape?"

"I'm keeping it."

Feeling that a strange mingling of baseness and charm from which I was naturally excluded had just taken place that night, I dared not ask for further details.

"Get started!"

With a gesture of his vivid hand, he motioned to me that he wanted to undress. As on other evenings, I got down on my knees to unhook the bunch of grapes. Inside his trousers was pinned one of those imitation bunches of thin cellulose grapes stuffed with cotton wool. (They are as big as greengage plums; elegant Spanish women of the period wore them on their loose-brimmed, straw sun bonnets.) Whenever some queer at the Criolla, excited by the swelling, put his hand on Stilitano's basket, his horrified fingers would encounter this object, which he feared might be actual balls.

The Criolla was not only a fairy joint. Some boys in dresses danced there, but women did too. Whores brought their pimps and their clients. Stilitano would have made a lot of money were it not that he spat on queers. He despised them. He was amused at their annoyance about his grapes. The game lasted a few days. So I unhooked the bunch, which was fastened to his blue trousers by a safety pin, but, instead of putting it on the mantelpiece as usual and laughing (for we would burst out laughing and joke during the operation), I could not restrain myself from keeping it in my cupped hands and laying my cheek against it. Stilitano's face above me turned hideous.

[12]This face also merges with that of Rasseneur, a crook with whom I worked around 1936. I recently read in the weekly *Detective Magazine* that he has been given a life sentence, whereas that very same week a petition of writers asked, for the very same punishment, that the President of the Republic grant me a reprieve. The photo of Rasseneur in court was on the second page. The journalist stated ironically that he seemed quite pleased about being shipped off. That doesn't surprise me. At the Santé Prison he was a little king. He'll be a big shot at Riom or Clairvaux. Rasseneur is, I think, from Nantes. He also robbed homosexuals. I learned from a friend that a car, driven by one of his victims, looked all over Paris for him for a long time in order to run him over "accidentally." There is a terrible fairy vengeance.

"Drop it, you bitch!"

In order to open the fly, I had squatted on my haunches, but Stilitano's rage, had my usual fervor been insufficient, made me fall to my knees. That was the position I used to take mentally in spite of myself. I stopped moving. Stilitano struck me with his two feet and his one fist. I could have got away. I stayed there.

"The key's in the door," I thought. Through the fork of the feet that were kicking me furiously I saw it sticking out of the keyhole, and I would have liked to turn it with a double turn so as to be locked in alone with my executioner. I made no attempt to understand the reason for his anger, which was so disproportionate to its cause, for my mind was unconcerned with psychological motives. As for Stilitano, from that day on he stopped wearing the bunch of grapes. Toward morning, having entered the room earlier than he, I waited for him. In the silence, I heard the mysterious rustling of the sheet of yellow newspaper that replaced the missing windowpane.

"That's subtle," I said to myself.

I was discovering a lot of new words. In the silence of the room and of my heart, in the waiting for Stilitano, this slight noise disturbed me, for before I came to understand its meaning there elapsed a brief period of anxiety. Who—or what—is calling such fleeting attention to itself in a poor man's room?

"It's a newspaper printed in Spanish," I said to myself again. "It's only natural that I don't understand the sound it's making."

Then I really felt I was in exile, and my nervousness was going to make me permeable to what—for want of other words—I shall call poetry.

The bunch of grapes on the mantelpiece nauseated me. One night Stilitano got up to throw it into the toilet. During the time he had worn it, it had not marred his beauty. On the contrary, in the evening, slightly encumbering his legs, it had given them a slight bend and his step a slightly rounded and gentle constraint, and when he walked near me, in front or behind, I felt a delicious agitation because my hands had prepared it. I still think it was by virtue of the insidious power of these grapes that I grew attached to Stilitano. I did not detach myself until the day when, in a dance hall, while dancing with a sailor, I happened to slip my hand under his collar. This seemingly most innocent of gestures was to reveal a fatal virtue. My hand, lying flat on the young man's back, knew that it was gently and piously hidden by the sign of the candor of sailors. It felt as if something were flapping against it, and my hand could not keep from thinking that Java was flapping his wing. It is still too soon to talk about him.

I shall prudently refrain from comment upon this mysterious wearing of the bunch of grapes; yet it pleases me to see in Stilitano a queer who hates himself.

"He wants to baffle and hurt, to disgust the very people who desire him," I say to myself when I think of him. As I ponder it more carefully, I am more disturbed by the idea—which I find pregnant with meaning—that Stilitano had bought a fake wound for that most noble spot (I know that he was magnificently hung) in order to save his lopped-off hand from scorn. Thus, by means of a very crude subterfuge here I am talking again about beggars and their misfortunes. Behind a real or sham physical ailment which draws attention to itself and is thereby forgotten is hidden a more secret malady of the soul. I list the secret wounds:

decayed teeth,
foul breath,
a hand cut off,
smelly feet, etc. . . .

to conceal them and to kindle our pride we had

a gouged eye,
a peg leg, etc.

We are fallen during the time we bear the marks of the fall, and to be aware of the imposture is of little avail. Using only the pride imposed by poverty, we aroused pity by cultivating the most repulsive wounds. We became a reproach to your happiness.

I aggravated this foul adventure by an attitude that became an actual disposition. One day, just for the fun of it, Stilitano said to me, "I'm going to have to stick my prick up your ass."

"It would hurt," I said with a laugh.

"Not a bit. I'll put trees in it."

"Trees" are put into shoes. I pretended to myself that he would put "trees" into his cock so that it would get even bigger, until it became a monstrous, unnamable organ, cultivated specially for my loathing, and not for my pleasure. I accepted this make-believe explanation without disgust.

Meanwhile, Stilitano and I were having a hard time. When, thanks to a few queers, I brought in a little money, he showed such pride that I sometimes wonder whether he is not great, in my memory, because of the bragging of which I was the pretext and chief confidant. The quality of my love required that he prove his virility. If he was the splendid beast gleaming in the darkness of his ferocity, let him devote himself to sport worthy of it. I incited him to theft.

We decided to rob a store together. In order to cut the telephone wire, which, most imprudently, was near the door, a pair of pliers was needed. We entered one of the many Barcelona bazaars where there were hardware departments.

"Manage not to move if you see me swipe something."

"What'll I do?"

"Nothing. Just look."

Stilitano was wearing white sneakers, his blue trousers, and a khaki shirt. At first I noticed nothing, but when we left, I was amazed to see, at the flap of his shirt pocket, a kind of small lizard, both restless and still, hanging by the teeth. It was the steel pliers that we needed and that Stilitano had just stolen.

"That he charms monkeys, men, and women," I said to myself, "is comprehensible, but what can be the nature of the magnetism, born of his glib muscles and his curls, of that blond amber, that can enthrall objects?"

However, there was no doubt about the fact that objects were obedient to him. Which amounts to saying that he understood them. So well did he know the nature of steel, and the nature of that particular fragment of polished steel called pliers, that it remained, to the point of fatigue, docile, loving, clinging to his shirt to which he had known, with precision, how to hook it, biting desperately into the cloth with its thin jaws so as not to fall. At times, however, these objects, which are irritated by a clumsy movement, would hurt him. Stilitano used to cut himself, his fingertips were finely gashed, his nail was black and crushed, but this heightened his beauty. (The purple of sunsets, according to physicists, is the result of a greater thickness of air which is crossed only by short waves. At midday, when nothing is happening in the sky, an apparition of this kind would disturb us less; the wonder is that it occurs in the evening, at the most poignant time of day, when the sun *sets*, when it disappears to pursue a mysterious destiny, when perhaps it dies. The physical phenomenon that fills the sky with such pomp is possible only at the moment that most exalts the imagination: at the setting of the most brilliant of the heavenly bodies.) Ordinary objects, those used every day, will adorn Stilitano. His very acts of cowardice melt my rigor. I liked his taste for laziness. He was leaky, as one says of a vessel. When we had the pliers, he slipped out.

"There may be a dog around."

We thought of putting it out of the way with a piece of poisoned meat.

"Rich people's dogs don't eat just any old thing."

Suddenly Stilitano thought of the legendary Gypsy trick: the thief was said to wear a pair of trousers smeared with lion's fat. Stilitano knew that this was unobtainable, but the idea excited him. He stopped talking. He was probably imagining himself in a thicket, at night, stalking his prey, wearing a pair of trousers stiff with fat. He was strong with the lion's strength, savage as a consequence of being thus prepared for war, the stake, the spit, and the grave. In his armor of grease and imagination he was resplendent. I do not know whether he was aware of the beauty of adorning himself with the strength and boldness of a Gypsy, nor whether he was thrilled at the idea of thus penetrating the secrets of the tribe.

"Would you like to be a Gypsy?" I once asked him.

"Me?"

"Yes, you."

"I wouldn't mind. Only I wouldn't want to stay in a caravan."

Thus he did dream occasionally. I thought I had discovered the flaw in his petrified shell through which a bit of my tenderness might slip in. Stilitano was too little excited by nocturnal adventures for me to feel any real exhilaration in his company when we slunk along walls, lanes, and gardens, when we scaled fences, when we robbed. I have no significant memory of any such excitement. It was with Guy, in France, that I was to have the profound revelation of what burglary was.

(When we were locked in the little storeroom, waiting for night and the moment to enter the empty offices of the Municipal Pawnshop in B., Guy suddenly seemed to me secret, inscrutable. He was no longer the ordinary guy you happen upon somewhere or other; he was a kind of destroying angel. He tried to smile. He even broke out into a silent laugh, but his

eyebrows were knitted. From within this little fairy where a hoodlum was confined there sprang forth a determined and terrifying fellow, ready for anything—and primarily for murder if anyone dared to hinder his action. He was laughing, and I thought I could read in his eyes a will to murder which might be exercised on me. The longer he stared at me, the more I had the feeling that he read in me the same determined will to be exercised against him. So he grew taut. His eyes were harder, his temples metallic, his facial muscles more knotted. In response, I hardened accordingly. I prepared an arsenal. I watched him. If someone had entered at that moment, we would, I felt, uncertain as we were of one another, have killed each other out of fear lest one of us oppose the terrible decision of the other.)

I continued doing other jobs with Stilitano. We knew a night watchman who tipped us off. Thanks to him, we lived off our burglaries alone for a long time. The boldness of a thief's life—and its light—would have meant nothing if Stilitano at my side had not been proof of it. My life became magnificent by men's standards since I had a friend whose beauty derived from the idea of luxury. I was the valet whose job was to look after, to dust, polish, and wax, an object of great value which, however, through the miracle of friendship, belonged to me.

"When I walk along the street," I wondered, "am I being envied by the loveliest and wealthiest of *señoritas?* What roguish prince, what *infanta* in rags, can walk about and have so handsome a lover?"

I speak of this period with emotion, and I magnify it, but if glamorous words, I mean words charged in my mind with more glamour than meaning, occur to me, they do so perhaps because the poverty they express, which was mine too, is likewise a source of wonder. I want to rehabilitate this period by writing of it with the names of things most noble. My victory is verbal and I owe it to the richness of the terms, but may the poverty that counsels such choices be blessed. In Stilitano's company, during the period when I was to experience moral abjection, I stopped desiring it, and I hated that which must be its sign: my lice, rags, and filth. Perhaps his power alone was enough for Stilitano to inspire respect without having to perform a bold deed; nevertheless, I would have liked our life together to be more brilliant, though it was sweet for me to encounter in his shadow (his shadow, dark as a Negro's must be, was my seraglio) the looks of admiration of the whores and their men when I knew that we were both poor thieves. I kept inciting him to ever more perilous adventures.

"We need a revolver," I said to him.

"Would you know what to do with it?"

"With you around, I wouldn't be afraid to bump a guy off."

Since I was his right arm, I would have been the one to execute. But the more I obeyed serious orders, the greater was my intimacy with him who issued them. He, however, smiled. In a gang (an association of evildoers) the young boys and inverts are the ones who display boldness. They are the instigators of dangerous jobs. They play the role of the fecundating sting. The potency of the males, the age, authority, friendship, and presence of the elders, fortify and reassure them. The males are dependent only upon themselves. They are their own heaven, and, knowing their weakness, they hesitate. Applied to my particular case, it seemed to me that the men, the toughs, were composed of a kind of feminine fog in which I would still like to lose myself so that I might feel more intensely that I was a solid block.

A certain distinction of manner, a more assured gait, proved to me my success, my ascension into the secular domain. In Stilitano's presence, I walked in the wake of a duke. I was his faithful but jealous dog. My bearing grew proud. Along the Ramblas, toward evening, we passed a woman and her son. The boy was good-looking. He was about fifteen. My eyes lingered on his blond hair. We walked by them and I turned around. The youngster showed no reaction. Stilitano likewise turned around to see whom I was looking at. It was at that moment, when both Stilitano's eyes and mine were staring after her son, that the mother drew him to her, or drew herself to him, as if to protect him from the danger of our two gazes, of which, however, she was unaware. I was jealous of Stilitano whose mere movement of the head had, so it seemed to me, just been sensed as a danger by the mother's back.

One day, while I was waiting for him in a bar on the Parallelo (the bar was, at the time, the meeting place of all the hardened French criminals: pimps, crooks, racketeers, escaped convicts. Argot, sung with somewhat of a Marseille accent, and a few years behind Montmartre argot, was its official tongue. Twenty-one and poker were played there rather than ronda), Stilitano blew in. He was welcomed by the Parisian pimps with their customary, slightly ceremonious politeness. Severely, but with smiling eyes, he solemnly placed his solemn behind on the straw-bottomed chair whose wood groaned with the shamelessness of a beast of burden. This wailing of the seat expressed perfectly my respect for the sober posterior of Stilitano, whose charm was neither all nor always contained there, though it would assemble in that spot—or rather on it—and would there accumulate and delegate its most caressing waves—and masses of lead!—to give the rump a reverberating undulation and weight.

I refuse to be prisoner of a verbal automatism, but here again I must have recourse to a religious image: this posterior was a Station. Stilitano sat down. With his usual elegant lassitude—"I palmed them," he would say on all and every occasion—he dealt the cards for the poker game, from which I was excluded. None of the gentlemen would have required that I leave the game, but of my own accord, out of courtesy, I went to sit down behind Stilitano. As I was about to take my seat, I saw a louse on the collar of his jacket. Stilitano was handsome and strong, and welcome at a gathering of similar males whose authority likewise lay in their muscles and their awareness of their revolvers. The louse on Stilitano's collar, still invisible to the other men, was not a small, stray spot; it was moving; it shifted about with disturbing velocity, as if crossing and measuring its domain—its space rather. But it was not only at home; on Stilitano's collar it was the sign that he belonged to an unmistakably verminous world, despite his eau de Cologne and silk shirt. I examined him more closely: his hair near the neck was too long, dirty, and irregularly cut.

"If the louse continues, it'll fall on his sleeve or into his glass. The pimps'll see it. . . ."

As if out of tenderness, I leaned on Stilitano's shoulder and gradually worked my hand up to his collar, but I was unable to complete my movement. With a shrug, Stilitano disengaged himself, and the insect continued its meanderings. A Pigalle pimp (who was said to be tied up with an international band of white slavers) made the following remark:

"There's a nice one climbing on you."

All eyes turned—without, however, losing sight of the game—to the collar of Stilitano, who, twisting his neck, managed to see the insect.

"You're the one who's been picking them up," he said to me as he crushed it.

"Why me?"

"I'm telling you it's you."

The tone of his voice was unanswerably arrogant, but his eyes were smiling. The men continued their card game.

It was the same day that Stilitano informed me that Pépé had just been arrested. He was in the Montjuich jail.

"Who told you?"

"I read it in the paper."

"How long can they give him?"

"Life."

We made no other comment.

This journal is not a mere literary diversion. The further I progress, reducing to order what my past life suggests, and the more I persist in the rigor of composition—of the chapters, of the sentences, of the book itself—the more do I feel myself hardening in my will to utilize, for virtuous ends, my former hardships. I feel their power.

In the urinals, which Stilitano never entered, the behavior of the faggots would make matters clear: they would perform their dance, the remarkable movement of a snake standing on its tail and undulating, swaying from side to side, tilted slightly backward, so as to cast a furtive glance at my prick which was out of my fly. I would go off with the one who looked most prosperous.

In my time, the Ramblas were frequented by two young *mariconas* who carried a tame little monkey on their shoulders. It was an easy pretext for approaching clients: the monkey would jump up on the man they pointed out to it. One of the *mariconas* was called Pedro. He was pale and thin. His waist was very supple, his step quick. His eyes in particular were splendid, his lashes immense.

In fun, I asked him which was the monkey, he or the animal he carried on his shoulder. We started quarreling. I punched him. His eyelashes remained stuck to my knuckles; they were false. I had just discovered the existence of fakes.

Stilitano got money occasionally from the whores. Most often he stole it from them, either by taking the change when they paid for something, or at night from their handbags, when they were on the bidet. He would go through the Barrio Chino and the Parallelo heckling all the women, sometimes irritating them, sometimes fondling them, but always ironic. When he returned to the room, toward morning, he would bring back a bundle of children's magazines full of gaudy pictures. He would sometimes go a long roundabout way in order to buy them at a newsstand that was open late at night. He would read the stories which, in those days, corresponded to the Tarzan adventures in today's comic books. The hero of these stories is lovingly drawn. The artist took the utmost pains with the imposing physique of this knight, who was almost always nude or obscenely dressed. Then Stilitano would fall asleep. He would manage so that his body did not touch mine. The bed was very narrow. As he put out the light, he would say,

"Night, kid!"

And upon awakening:

"Morning, kid!"[13]

Our room was very tiny. It was dirty. The wash basin was filthy. No one in the Barrio Chino would have dreamed of cleaning his room, his belongings or his linen—except his shirt and, most often, only the collar. Once a week, to pay the room rent, Stilitano screwed the landlady who, on other days, called him Señor.

One evening he had a fight. We were going through the Calle Carmen. It was just about dark. Spaniards' bodies sometimes have a kind of undulating flexibility and their stances are occasionally equivocal. In broad daylight Stilitano would not have made a mistake. In this incipient darkness he grazed three men who were talking quietly but whose gesticulations were both brisk and languorous. As he neared them, Stilitano, in his most insolent tone of voice, hurled a few coarse words at them. Three quick and vigorous pimps replied to the insults. Stilitano stood there, taken aback. The three men approached.

"Do you take us for *mariconas*, talking to us like that?"

Although he recognized his blunder, Stilitano wanted to strut in my presence.

"Suppose I do?"

"*Maricona* yourself."

A few women drew up, and some men. A circle gathered around us. A fight seemed inevitable. One of the young men provoked Stilitano outright.

"If you're not fruit, come on and fight."

Before getting to the point of fists or weapons, hoodlums gab it out for a while. It's not that they try to softpedal the conflict; rather, they work themselves up to combat. Some other Spaniards, their friends, were egging the three pimps on. Stilitano felt he was in danger. My presence no longer bothered him. He said:

"After all, boys, you're not going to fight with a cripple."

He held out his stump. But he did it with such simplicity, such sobriety, that this vile hamming, instead of disgusting me with him, ennobled him. He withdrew, not

[13] I used to toss my things any old place when we went to bed, but Stilitano laid his out on a chair, carefully arranging the trousers, jacket, and shirt so that nothing would be creased. He seemed thereby to be endowing his clothes with life, as if wanting them to get a night's rest after a hard day.

to the sound of jeers, but to a murmur expressing the discomfort of decent men discovering the misery about them. Stilitano stepped back slowly, protected by his outstretched stump, which was placed simply in front of him. The absence of the hand was as real and effective as a royal attribute, as the hand of justice.

Those who one of their number called the Carolinas paraded to the site of a demolished street urinal. During the 1933 riots, the insurgents tore out one of the dirtiest, but most beloved pissoirs. It was near the harbor and the barracks, and its sheet iron had been corroded by the hot urine of thousands of soldiers. When its ultimate death was certified, the Carolinas—not all, but a formally chosen delegation—in shawls, mantillas, silk dresses, and fitted jackets, went to the site to place a bunch of red roses tied together with a crepe veil. The procession started from the Parallelo, crossed the Calle São Paolo and went down the Ramblas de Las Flores until it reached the statue of Columbus. The faggots were perhaps thirty in number, at eight A.M., at sunrise. I saw them going by. I accompanied them from a distance. I knew that my place was in their midst, not because I was one of them, but because their shrill voices, their cries, their extravagant gestures seemed to me to have no other aim than to try to pierce the shell of the world's contempt. The Carolinas were great. They were the Daughters of Shame.

When they reached the harbor, they turned right, toward the barracks, and upon the rusty, stinking sheet iron of the pissoir that lay battered on the heap of dead scrap iron they placed the flowers.

I was not in the procession. I belonged to the ironic and indulgent crowd that was entertained by it. Pedro airily admitted to his false lashes, the Carolinas to their wild larks.

Meanwhile, Stilitano, by denying himself to my pleasure, became the symbol of chastity, of frigidity itself. If he did screw the whores often, I was unaware of it. When he lay down to sleep in our bed, he had the modesty to arrange his shirt tail so artfully that I saw nothing of his penis. The purity of his features corrected even the eroticism of his walk. He became the representation of a glacier. I would have liked to offer myself to the most bestial of Negroes, to the most flat-nosed and most powerful face, so that within me, having no room for anything but sexuality, my love for Stilitano might be further stylized. I was therefore able to venture into his presence the most absurd and humiliating postures.

We often went to the Criolla together. Hitherto, it had never occurred to him to exploit me. When I brought back to him the pesetas I had earned around the pissoirs, Stilitano decided that I would work in the Criolla.

"Would you like me to dress up as a woman?" I murmured.

Would I have dared, supported by his powerful shoulder, to walk the streets in a spangled skirt between the Calle Carmen and the Calle Mediodia? Except for foreign sailors, no one would have been surprised, but neither Stilitano nor I would have known how to choose the dress or the hairdo, for taste is required. Perhaps that was what held us back. I still remembered the sighs of Pedro, with whom I had once teamed up, when he went to get dressed.

"When I see those rags hanging there, I get the blues! I feel as if I were going into a vestry to get ready to conduct a funeral. They've got a priestish smell. Like incense. Like urine. Look at them hanging! I wonder how I manage to get into those damned sausage skins."

"Will I have to have things like that? Maybe I'll even have to sew and cut with my man's help. And wear a bow, or maybe several, in my hair."

With horror I saw myself decked out in enormous bows, not of ribbons, but of sausage meat in the form of pricks.

"It'll be a drooping, dangling bow," added a mocking inner voice. An old man's droopy ding-dong. A bow limp, or impish! And in what hair? In an artificial wig or in my own dirty, curly hair?

As for my dress, I knew it would be sober and that I would wear it with modesty, whereas what was needed to carry the thing off was a kind of wild extravagance. Nevertheless, I cherished the dream of sewing on a cloth rose. It would emboss the dress and would be the feminine counterpart of Stilitano's bunch of grapes.

(Long afterward, when I ran into him in Antwerp, I spoke to Stilitano about the fake bunch hidden in his fly. He then told me that a Spanish whore used to wear a muslin rose pinned on at cunt level. "To replace her lost flower," he said.)

In Pedro's room, I looked at the skirts with melancholy. He gave me a few addresses of women's outfitters, where I would find dresses to fit me.

"You'll have a *toilette*, Juan."[14]

I was sickened by this butcher's word (I was thinking that the *toilette* was also the greasy tissue enveloping the guts in animals' bellies). It was then that Stilitano, perhaps hurt by the idea of his friend in fancy dress, refused.

"There's no need for it," he said. "You'll manage well enough to make pickups."

Alas, the boss of the Criolla demanded that I appear as a young lady.

As a young lady!

> *Myself a young lady*
> *I alight on my hip. . . .*

I then realized how hard it is to reach the light by puncturing the abscess of shame. I once managed to appear in woman's dress with Pedro, to exhibit myself with him. I went one evening, and we were invited by a group of French officers. At their table was a lady of about fifty. She smiled at me sweetly, with indulgence, and unable to contain herself any longer, she asked me:

"Do you like men?"

"Yes, madame, I do."

"And . . . when did it start?"

I did not slap anyone, but my voice was so shaken that I realized how angry and ashamed I was. In order to pull myself together, I robbed one of the officers that very same night.

---

[14]The term *la toilette* also refers to certain kinds of wrappings or casings, for example, a tailor's or dressmaker's wrapper for garments, as well as to the caul over mutton.—Translator's note.

"At least," I said to myself, "if my shame is real, it hides a sharper, more dangerous element, a kind of sting that will always threaten anyone who provokes it. It might not have been laid over me like a trap, might not have been intentional, but since it is what it is, I want it to conceal me so that I can lie in wait beneath it."

At Carnival time, it was easy to go about in woman's dress, and I stole an Andalusian petticoat with a bodice from a hotel room. Disguised by the mantilla and fan, one evening I walked across town quickly in order to get to the Criolla. So that my break with your world would be less brutal, I kept my trousers on under the skirt. Hardly had I reached the bar when someone ripped the train of my dress. I turned around in a fury.

"I beg your pardon. Excuse me."

The foot of a blond young man had got caught in the lace. I hardly had strength enough to mumble, "Watch what you're doing." The face of the clumsy young man, who was both smiling and excusing himself, was so pale that I blushed. Someone next to me said to me in a low voice, "Excuse him, señora, he limps."

"I won't have people limping on my dress!" screamed the beautiful actress who smoldered within me. But the people around us were laughing. "I won't have people limping on my toilette!" I screamed to myself. Formulated within me, in my stomach, as it seemed to me, or in the intestines, which are enveloped by the "toilette," this phrase must have been expressed by a terrible glare. Furious and humiliated, I left under the laughter of the men and the Carolinas. I went straight to the sea and drowned the skirt, bodice, mantilla and fan. The whole city was joyous, drunk with the Carnival that was cut off from the earth and alone in the middle of the Ocean. I was poor and sad.

* * *

By the gravity of the means and the splendor of the materials which the poet used to draw near to men, I measure the distance that separated him from them. The depth of my abjection forced him to perform this convict's labor. But my abjection was his despair. And despair was strength itself—and at the same time the matter for putting an end to it. But if the work is of great beauty, requiring the vigor of the deepest despair, the poet had to love men to undertake such an effort. And he had to succeed. It is right for men to shun a profound work if it is the cry of a man monstrously engulfed within himself.

By the gravity of the means I require to thrust you from me, measure the tenderness I feel for you. Judge to what degree I love you from the barricades I erect in my life and work (since the work of art should be only the proof of my saintliness, not only must this saintliness be real so that it may fecundate the work, but also that I may brace myself, on a work already strong with saintliness, for a greater effort toward an unknown destination) so that your breath—I am corruptible to an extreme—may not rot me. My tenderness is of fragile stuff. And the breath of men would disturb the methods for seeking a new paradise. I shall impose a candid vision of evil, even though I lose my life, my honor, and my glory in this quest.

Creating is not a somewhat frivolous game. The creator has committed himself to the fearful adventure of taking upon himself, to the very end, the perils risked by his creatures. We cannot suppose a creation that does not spring from love. How can a man place before himself something as strong as himself which he will have to scorn or hate? But the creator will then charge himself with the weight of his characters' sins. Jesus became man. He expiated. Later, like God, after creating men, He delivered them from their sins: He was whipped, spat upon, mocked, nailed. That is the meaning of the expression: "He suffers in his flesh." Let us ignore the theologians. "Taking upon Himself the sins of the world" means exactly this: experiencing potentially and in their effects all sins; it means having subscribed to evil. Every creator must thus shoulder—the expression seems feeble—must make his own, to the point of knowing it to be his substance, circulating in his arteries, the evil given by him, which his heroes choose freely. We wish to regard this as one of the many uses of the generous myth of Creation and Redemption. Though the creator grants his characters free will, self-determination, he hopes, deep down in his heart, that they will choose Good. Every lover does likewise, hoping to be loved for his own sake.

I wish for a moment to focus attention on the reality of supreme happiness in despair: when one is suddenly alone, confronting one's sudden ruin, when one witnesses the irremediable destruction of one's work and self. I would give all the wealth of this world—indeed it must be given—to experience the desperate—and secret—state which no one knows I know. Hitler, alone, in the cellar of his palace, during the last minutes of the defeat of Germany, surely experienced that moment of pure light—fragile and solid lucidity—the awareness of his fall.

My pride has been colored with the crimson of my shame.

Though saintliness is my goal, I cannot tell what it is. My point of departure is the word itself, which indicates the state closest to moral perfection. Of which I know nothing, save that without it my life would be vain. Unable to give a definition of saintliness—no more than I can of beauty—I want at every moment to create it, that is, to act so that everything I do may lead me to it, though it is unknown to me, so that at every moment I may be guided by a will to saintliness until I am so luminous that people will say, "He is a saint," or, more likely, "He was a saint." I am being led to it by a constant groping. No method exists. It is only obscurely and with no other proofs than the certainty of achieving saintliness that I make the gestures leading me to it. Possibly it may be won by a mathematical discipline, but I fear it would be a facile, well-mannered saintliness, with familiar features, in short, academic. But this is to achieve a mere semblance. Starting from the elementary principles of morality and religion, the saint arrives at his goal if he sheds them. Like beauty—and poetry, with which I merge it—saintliness is individual. Its expression is original. However, it seems to me that its sole basis is renunciation. I therefore also associate it with freedom. But I wish to be a saint chiefly because the word indicates the loftiest human attitude, and I shall do everything to succeed. I shall use my pride and sacrifice it therein.

Tragedy is a joyous moment. Feelings of joy will be conveyed by smiles, by a lightness of the whole body, and of the face. The hero is unaware of the seriousness of a tragic theme. Though he may catch a glimpse of it, he must not see it. Indifference is native to him. In popular dance halls there are sober young men, indifferent to the music which they seem to be leading rather than following. Others joyously strew among prostitutes the syphilis which they have reaped from one of them. With the decaying of their splendid bodies, foretold by wax figures in fair booths, they go off calmly, with a smile on their lips. If it be to death that he goes—a necessary end—unless it be to happiness—he does so as if to the most perfect, therefore most happy, self-fulfillment. He goes off with joyous heart. The hero cannot sulk at a heroic death. He is a hero only because of that death. It is the condition so bitterly sought by creatures without glory; itself is glory; it is (this death and the accumulation of the apparent misfortunes leading to it) the crowning of a predisposed life, but, above all, the gaze of our own image in an ideal mirror which shows us as eternally resplendent (until the dying away of the light which will bear our name).

His temple bled. Two soldiers had just fought for some long forgotten reason, and it was the younger who fell, his temple smashed by the iron fist of the other, who watched the blood flow and become a tuft of primroses. The flowering spread rapidly. It reached the face, which was soon covered with thousands of those compact flowers, sweet and violet as the wine vomited by soldiers. Finally, the entire body of the young man lying in the dust was a bank of flowers whose primroses grew big enough to be daisies through which the wind blew. Only one arm remained visible and moved, but the wind stirred all the grasses. Soon all the victor could see was a single hand making a clumsy sign of farewell and hopeless friendship. Eventually the hand disappeared, caught in the flowering compost. The wind died down slowly, regretfully. The sky grew dark after having first lit up the eye of the brutal, murderous young soldier. He did not weep. He sat down on the flower bed that his friend had become. The wind stirred a bit, but a bit less. The soldier brushed his hair from his eyes and rested. He fell asleep.

The smile of tragedy is also governed by a kind of humor with respect to the Gods. The tragic hero delicately flouts his destiny. He fulfills it so nicely that this time the object is not man but the Gods.

Having already been convicted of theft, I can be convicted again without proof, merely upon a casual accusation, just on suspicion. The law then says that I am capable of the deed. I am in danger not only when I steal, but every moment of my life, because I have stolen. My life is clouded by a vague anxiety which both weighs upon it and lightens it. To preserve the limpidity and keenness of my gaze, my consciousness must be sensitive to every act so that I can quickly correct it and change its meaning. This anxiety keeps me on the alert. It gives me the surprised attitude of a deer caught in the clearing. But the anxiety, which is a kind of dizziness, also sweeps me along, makes my head buzz, and lets me trip and fall in an element of darkness where I lie low if I hear the ground beneath the leaves resounding with a hoof.

I have been told that among the ancients Mercury was the god of thieves, who thus knew which power to invoke. But we have no one. It would seem logical to pray to the devil, but no thief would dare do so seriously. To make a compact with him would be to commit oneself too deeply. He is too opposed to God, who, we know, is the final victor. A murderer himself would not dare pray to the devil.

In order to desert Lucien I shall organize an avalanche of catastrophes around the desertion so that he will seem to be swept away by them. He will be a straw in the midst of the tornado. Even if he learns that I have willed his misfortune and hates me, his hatred will not affect me. Remorse, or the expression of reproach in his lovely eyes, will have no power to move me, since I shall be in the center of a hopeless sadness. I shall lose things which are dearer to me than Lucien, and which are less dear than my scruples. Thus, I would readily kill Lucien to engulf my shame in great pomp. Alas, a religious fear turns me from murder and draws me to it. Murder might very well transform me into a priest, and the victim into God. In order to destroy the efficacy of murder, perhaps I need only reduce it to the extreme by the practical necessity of a criminal act. I can kill a man for a few million francs. The glamour of gold can combat that of murder.

Was the former boxer Ledoux dimly aware of this by any chance? He killed an accomplice in order to take revenge. He created a disorder in the dead man's room to make it seem like theft and, seeing a five-franc note lying on the table, Ledoux took it and explained to his astonished girlfriend:

"I'm keeping it for luck. Nobody'll say I committed murder without getting something out of it."

I shall fortify my mind rather quickly. When you think about murder, the important thing is not to let your eyelids droop or your nostrils dilate tragically, but to examine the idea very leisurely, with your eyes staring wide open, drawn up by the wrinkling of your forehead as if in naïve astonishment, in wonder. No remorse, no prospective sorrow can then appear at the corner of your eyes, nor can precipices hollow out under your feet. A bantering smile, a pleasant tune whistled between my teeth, a bit of irony in the fingers curled around the cigarette would be enough to renew my contact with desolation in satanic solitude (unless I should be very fond of some murderer of whom that gesture, smile, and pleasant tune are characteristic). After stealing B.R.'s ring:

"What if he learns about it?" I asked myself. "I sold it to someone he knows!" I imagine, for he likes me, his grief and my shame. So I envisage the worst: death. His.

On the Boulevard Haussmann I saw the spot where certain burglars had been arrested. To flee from the store, one of them had tried to break through the glass. By accumulating damage around his arrest, he thought he was giving it an importance that would detract from the fact preceding it: the burglary. He was already trying to surround his person with a bloody, astonishing, intimidating pomp, in the midst of which he himself remained pitiful. The criminal magnifies his exploit. He wants to disappear amid great display, in an enormous setting brought on by destiny. At the same time, he decomposes his deed into rigid moments, he dismembers it.

"What care I for men's contempt when my blood . . ."

Could I, unblushingly, still admire handsome criminals if I did not know their nature? If they have had the misfortune to serve the beauty of many poems, I wish to help them. The utilization of crime by an artist is impious. Someone risks his life, his glory, only to be used as ornament for a dilettante. Even though the hero be imaginary, a living creature inspired him. I refuse to take delight in his sufferings if I have not yet shared them. I shall first incur the scorn of men, their judgment. I distrust the saintliness of Vincent de Paul. He should have been willing to commit the galley slave's crime instead of merely taking his place in irons.

The tone of this book is likely to scandalize the best spirits and not the worst. I am not trying to be scandalous. I am assembling these notes for a few young men. I should like them to consider these remarks as the recording of a highly delicate ascesis. The experience is painful and I have not yet completed it. That its point of departure may be a romantic reverie matters little if I work at it rigorously, as at a mathematical problem, if I derive from it materials useful for the elaboration of a work of art, or for the achievement of a moral perfection (for the destruction, perhaps, of these very materials, for their dissolution) approaching that saintliness which to me is still only the most beautiful word in human language.

Limited by the world, which I oppose, jagged by it, I shall be all the more handsome and sparkling as the angles which wound me and give me shape are more acute and the jagging more cruel.

Acts must be carried through to their completion. Whatever their point of departure, the end will be beautiful. It is because an action has not been completed that it is vile.

When I turned my head, my eyes were dazzled by the gray triangle formed by the two legs of the murderer, one of whose feet was resting on the low ledge of the wall while the other stood motionless in the dust of the yard. The two legs were clothed in rough, stiff, dreary homespun. I was dazzled a second time for, having taken from between my teeth the white rose whose stem I had been chewing, I carelessly tossed it away (in the face, perhaps, of a hoodlum) and it caught, with sly cunning, in the fly forming the severe angle of gray cloth. This simple gesture escaped the guard. It even escaped the other prisoners and the murderer, who felt only a very slight shock. When he looked at his trousers, he blushed with shame. Did he think it was a gob of spit or the sign of a pleasure granted him by the mere fact of being for a moment beneath the brightest sky in France? In short, his face turned crimson and, with a casual gesture, trying to conceal the act, he plucked out the absurd rose, which was stealthily clinging by the tip of a thorn, and stuffed it into his pocket.

I call saintliness not a state, but the moral procedure that leads me to it. It is the ideal point of a morality which I cannot talk about since I do not see it. It withdraws when I approach it. I desire it and fear it. This procedure may appear stupid. Yet, though painful, it is joyful. It's a gay girl. It foolishly assumes the figure of a Carolina carried off in her skirts and screaming with happiness.

I make a sacrifice, rather than of solitude, the highest virtue. It is the creative virtue par excellence. There must be damnation in it. Will anyone be surprised when I claim that crime can help me ensure my moral vigor?

When might I finally leap into the heart of the image, be myself the light which carries it to your eyes? When might I be in the heart of poetry?

I run the risk of going astray by confounding saintliness with solitude. But am I not, by this sentence, running the risk of restoring to saintliness the Christian meaning which I want to remove from it?

This quest for transparency may be vain. If attained, it would be repose. Ceasing to be "I," ceasing to be "you," the subsisting smile is a uniform smile cast upon all things.

The very day of my arrival at the Santé Prison—for one of my many stays there—I was brought up before the warden: I had babbled at the reception desk about a friend I had recognized going by. I was given two weeks of solitary confinement and was taken away at once. Three days later an assistant slipped me some butts. They had been sent to me by the prisoenrs in the cell to which I had been assigned, though I hadn't yet set foot in it. When I got out of the hole, I thanked them. Guy said to me:

"We saw there was someone new. It was written on the door. Genet. We didn't know who Genet was. We didn't see you come. We realized you were in solitary, so we slipped you the butts."

Because my name was down in the register for that cell, its occupants already knew that they were involved in an unknown penalty incurred for an offense in which they had no part. Guy was the soul of the cell. This curly-headed and fair-skinned, buttery adolescent was its inflexible conscience, its rigor. Every time he addressed me I felt the meaning of that strange expression:

"A load in the loins from a tommy gun."

He was arrested by the police. The following dialogue took place in my presence:

"You're the one who did the job on the Rue de Flandre."

"No, it wasn't me."

"It was you. The concierge recognizes you."

"It's someone who looks like me."

"She says his name is Guy."

"It's someone who looks like me and has the same name."

"She recognizes your clothes."

"He looks like me, has the same name, and the same clothes."

"He's got the same hair."

"He looks like me, has the same name, the same clothes, and the same hair."

"They found your fingerprints."

"He looks like me, has the same name, the same clothes, the same hair, and the same fingerprints."

"That can keep on."

"To the very end."

"It was you who did the job."

"No, it wasn't me."

A letter from him contained the following passage (I had just been locked up again in the Santé): "Dear Jean, I'm too broke to send you a package. I don't have any dough, but I'd like to tell you something that I hope you'll be glad to hear. For the first time I felt like jerking off while thinking about you and I came. At least you can be sure you've got a pal outside who's thinking about you. . . ."

I sometimes reproach him for his familiarity with Inspector Richardeau. I try to explain to him that a detective is even lower than a stool pigeon. Guy hardly listens to me. He takes short steps when he walks. He is aware, around his neck, of the loose collar of his very soft, silk shirt and, on his shoulders, of his well-cut jacket. He holds his head high and looks straight ahead, in front of him, severely, at the sad, gray, gloomy Rue de Barbès, though a pimp, behind the curtains in a rooming house, can see him pass by.

"You're really right," he says. "They're all bastards."

A moment later, when I thought he was no longer thinking about what I had been saying (a certain time elapsed without his thinking, so that he might thereby better feel a silver chain weighing at his wrist, or his mind empty in order to make room for this idea) he muttered:

"Yes, but a cop's not the same thing."

"Oh? You think so?"

Despite my arguments, which aimed at merging the cop and the stool pigeon, and at proving the former more blameworthy, I felt as Guy did, though I did not admit it to him, that it wasn't the same thing. I secretly love, yes, I love the police. I wouldn't tell him how excited I used to be in Marseille whenever I walked by the policemen's canteen on Belzunce Square. The interior was full of Marseille cops, in uniform and in plainclothes. The canteen fascinated me. They were snakes coiled up and rubbing against each other in a familiarity untroubled—and perhaps furthered—by abjectness.

Guy walked along impassively. Did he know that the pattern of his mouth was too flabby? It gave his face a childlike prettiness. Though naturally blond, his hair was dyed dark. He wanted to pass as a Corsican—after a while he started believing he really was one—and I suspected that he liked makeup.

"They're after me," he said.

A thief's activity is a succession of cramped though blazing gestures. Coming from a scorched interior, each gesture is painful and pitiful. It is only after a theft, and thanks to literature, that the thief chants his gesture. His success chants within his body a hymn which his mouth later repeats. His failure enchants his distress. To my smile and my shrug, Guy replied:

"I look too young. You have to look like a man with the other guys."

I admired his utterly unbending will. He told me that one of his bursts of laughter would betray him. I felt the same pity for him as I would for a lion that was made by its trainer to walk a tightrope.

Concerning Armand, of whom I speak little (modesty prevents me, as does perhaps the difficulty of telling who he was and what he meant to me, from giving an exact notion of the value of his moral authority), his kindness was, I think, a sort of element in which my secret (unavowable) qualities found their justification.

It was after I had left him, after I had put up the frontier between him and me, that I felt this. He seemed to me intelligent. That is, he had dared, not unconsciously, to depart from moral rules, with the deceptive ease of men who are unaware of them. In fact, he had done so at the cost of a mighty effort, with the certainty of losing a priceless treasure, though with the further certainty of creating another, more precious than the one he had lost.

One evening, in a bar, we learned that a gang of international crooks had surrendered to the police—"like cowards, without a fight," as the Belgian papers put it—and everyone was commenting upon their behavior.

"They didn't have guts," said Robert. "Don't you agree?"

Stilitano didn't answer. He was afraid of discussing fear or boldness in my presence.

"You're not answering. Don't you agree? They claim they pulled off big jobs, bank robberies, train robberies, and then they give themselves up to the cops like good little boys. They could have defended themselves to the last bullet. At any rate, they're done for, since they're going to be extradited. France wants them. They'll get theirs. I'd have . . ."

"Stop shooting your mouth off!"

Armand's anger was sudden. He was glaring indignantly.

Robert replied, more humbly:

"Why, don't you agree with me?"

"When I was your age, I'd done more jobs than you and still I never talked about men, especially those who'd been nabbed. All that's left for them now is the trial. You're not big enough to judge."

This explanatory tone made Robert a bit bolder. He dared answer:

"Still and all, they got cold feet. If they did all they're said to have done. . . ."

"You lousy little bastard, it's just because they did all they're said to have done that they got cold feet, as you say. Do you know what they wanted? Eh, do you? Well, I'll tell you. The moment they saw it was all up, they wanted to give themselves a treat that they never in their lives had time for: getting cold feet. You get it? It was a treat for them to be able to surrender to the police. It gave them a rest."

Stilitano didn't bat an eyelash. I thought I could tell by his wry smile that he was familiar with the meaning of Armand's answer. Not in that assertive, heroic, insolent form, but in a more diffuse style. Robert didn't answer. He didn't understand the explanation at all, except that it had just placed him slightly outside the circle of the three of us.

I would have discovered this justification by myself, though later on. Armand's kindness consisted of allowing me to feel at ease in it. He understood everything. (I mean that he had solved my problems.) Not that I am suggesting that the explanation he dared give of the gangsters' surrender was valid in their case, but it was so for me—had it been a question of justifying my surrender in such circumstances. His kindness also consisted of his transforming into a revel, into a solemn and ridiculous display, a contemptible desertion of duty. Armand's concern was rehabilitation. Not of others or of himself, but of moral wretchedness. He conferred upon it the attributes which are the expression of the pleasures of the official world.

I am far from having his stature, his muscles, and their fur, but there are days when I look at myself in a mirror and seem to see in my face something of his severe kindness. Then I feel proud of myself and of my ponderous, pushed-in mug. I don't know in what pauper's grave he lies buried, or whether he's still up and about, strolling around with his strong, supple body. He is the only one whose real name I want to transcribe. To betray him even so little would be too much. When he got up from his chair, he reigned over the world. Had he been slapped, physically insulted, he would not have flinched. He would have remained intact, just as great. He filled out all the space in our bed with his legs open in a wide, obtuse angle, where I would find only a small space to curl up. I slept in the shadow of his meat, which would sometimes fall over my eyes, and, upon awakening, I would sometimes find my forehead adorned with a massive and curious brown horn. When he awoke, his foot would push me out of bed, not brutally but with an imperious pressure. He wouldn't speak. He smoked while I prepared the coffee and toast of this Tabernacle where knowledge rested—and where it was distilled.

One evening, we learned in the course of a distasteful conversation that Armand used to go from Marseille to Brussels, from town to town, from café to café, making lace-paper cutouts in front of the customers in order to earn money enough to eat. The docker who told us that didn't joke about it. He spoke very simply and straightforwardly about the doilies and fancy handkerchiefs, the delicate linen work produced with a pair of scissors and folded paper.

"I've seen Armand at it. I've seen him do his act," he said.

The idea of my calm, hulking master doing woman's work moved me. No ridicule could touch him. I don't know which prison he had been in, whether he had been released or had escaped, but what I did learn about him pointed to that school of all delicacies: the shores of the Maroni River in Guiana or the penitentiaries of France.

As he listened to the docker, Stilitano smiled maliciously. I feared lest he try to wound Armand: I was right. The machine-made lace which he palmed off on pious ladies was a sign of nobility. It indicated Stilitano's superiority over Armand. Yet I dared not beg him not to mention the matter. To show such moral elegance toward a crony would have revealed within me, in my heart, weird landscapes, so softly lighted that a flick of the thumb would have ruffled them. I pretended to be indifferent.

"You learn something new every day," said Stilitano.

"There's nothing wrong with that."

"That's what I say. One gets along however one can."

No doubt, to reassure myself, to bolster my insecurity, I had to assume that my lovers were wrought of tough matter. Here I was learning that the one who impressed me most was composed of human woes. Today the memory which recurs to me most often is that of Armand, whom I never saw in that occupation, approaching tables in restaurants and cutting out—in Venetian point—his paper lace. Perhaps it was then that he discovered, without anyone's help, the elegance, not of what is called manners, but of the *manifold* play of attitudes. Whether out of laziness, or because he wanted to humble me, or because he felt a need for a ceremonial to enhance his person, he required that I light his cigarette in my mouth and then put it into his. I wasn't even supposed to wait for his desire to manifest itself, but to anticipate it. I did this in the beginning, but, being a smoker myself, in order to do things more quickly and not make any waste motions, I put two cigarettes into my mouth, lit them, and then handed one to Armand. He brutally forbade this procedure, which he considered inelegant. As before, I had to take one cigarette from the pack, light it, put it into his mouth, and then take another for myself.

Since going into mourning means first submitting to a sorrow from which I shall escape, for I transform it into the strength necessary for departing from conventional morality, I cannot steal flowers and lay them on the grave of someone who was dear to me. Stealing defines a moral attitude which cannot be achieved without effort; it is a heroic act. Sorrow at the loss of a beloved person reveals to us our bonds with mankind. It requires of the survivor that he observe, above all, a strict dignity. So much so that our concern about this dignity will make us steal flowers if we cannot buy them. This act was the result of desperation at being unable to carry out the customary formality of farewell to the dead. Guy came to see me to tell me how Maurice B. had just been shot down.

"We need some wreaths."

"Why?"

"For the funeral."

His speech was clipped. He was afraid that if he lengthened the syllables his whole soul might droop. And perhaps he thought it was not a time for tears and wailing. What wreaths was he talking about, what funeral, what ceremony?

"The burial. We need flowers."

"Do you have any dough?"

"Not a penny. We'll take up a collection."

"Where?"

"Not in church, of course. Among our pals. In the bars."

"Everyone's broke."

It was not a burial for a dead man that Guy was demanding, but, more important, that the pomp of the world be accorded his hoodlum friend who had been shot down by a cop. He wished to weave for the humblest the richest of floral mantles. To honor the friend, but above all to glorify those who are the most wretched by employing the means used by those who regard them as such and are even responsible for their being so.

"Doesn't it make you sore to know that cops who get killed get first-class funerals?"

"Does that bother you?"

"Doesn't it you? And when they bury judges, the whole court walks behind."

Guy was excited. He was lit up with indignation. He was generous and without restraint.

"Nobody's got any dough."

"Got to find some."

"Go swipe some flowers with his pals."

"You're crazy!"

He spoke in a hollow voice, ashamedly, perhaps regretfully. A madman can pay homage to his dead with astonishing funerals. He can and must invent rites. Guy already had the pathetic attitude of a dog shitting. It squeezes, its gaze is fixed, its four paws are close together beneath its arched body; and it trembles, from head to reeking turd. I remember my shame, in addition to my surprise at witnessing so useless a gesture, when one Sunday, at the cemetery, my foster mother, after looking about her, tore a clump of marigolds from an unknown and quite fresh grave and replanted them on the grave of her daughter. Stealing flowers anywhere to cover the coffin of a loved one is a gesture—Guy was aware of this—which does not gratify the thief. No humor is tolerated in such a situation.

"Well, what are you going to do?"

"I'm going to rob, but fast. A stickup."

"Have anything in mind?"

"No."

"Well?"

At night, with two friends, he pilfered some flowers from the Montparnasse Cemetery. They went over the wall on the Rue Froidevaux, near the urinal. It was, so Guy told me later, a lark. Perhaps, as always when he committed a burglary, he took a crap. At night, if it's dark, he lets down his pants, usually behind the main entrance, or at the bottom of the stairway, in the yard. This familiar act restores his assurance. He knows that in French slang a turd is known as a "watchman."

"I'm going to post a watchman," he says. We then go up more calmly. The place is less strange to us.

They went looking for roses with a flashlight. It seems they were hardly able to distinguish them from the foliage. A joyous intoxication made them steal, run, and joke among the monuments. "You can't imagine what it was like," he said to me. The women were given the job of weaving the wreaths and making the bouquets. It was their men who made the nicest ones.

In the morning everything was wilted. They threw the flowers into the garbage, and the concierge must have wondered what kind of orgy had taken place that night in rooms where no bouquet ever entered, except, occasionally, an orchid. Most of the pimps did not dare attend so poor a funeral. Their dignity, their insolence, required worldly solemnity. They sent their women. Guy went. When he came back, he told me how sad it had been.

"We looked ratty! It's too bad you didn't come. There were only whores and tramps."

"Oh! you know, I see them every day."

"It's not that, Jean. It was so that someone would answer when the mutes asked for the family. I felt ashamed."

(When I was in the Mettray Reformatory, I was ordered to attend the burial of a youngster who had died in the infirmary. We accompanied him to the little cemetery of the reformatory. The grave diggers were children. After they lowered the coffin, I swear that, if anyone had asked, as they do in the city, for "the family," I would have stepped forward, tiny in my mourning.)

Guy stretched a bit; then he smiled.

"Why were you ashamed?"

"It was too crummy. A pauper's funeral."

"We sure got tight. We drank all night long. I'm glad to be back. At least I'll be able to take off my shoes."

When I was young, I wanted to rob churches. Later on, I experienced the joy of removing rugs, vases, and sometimes paintings. In M ..., G ... didn't notice the beauty of the laces. When I told him that the surplices and altar cloths were very valuable, his broad forehead wrinkled. He wanted a figure. In the sacristy I muttered, "I don't know."

"How much, fifty?"

I didn't answer. I was in a hurry to get out of that room where priests get dressed, undressed, button their cassocks, and knot their albs.

"Well, how much? Fifty?"

His impatience got the better of me and I answered, "More, a hundred thousand."

G . . .'s fingers trembled, they got heavy. They were damaging the cloths and the angular laces. As for his face, which was in a bad light and was excited with greed, I don't know whether to call it hideous or splendid. We calmed down along the banks of the Loire. We sat down in the grass while waiting for the first freight train.

"You're lucky to know about those things. I'd have left the lace behind."

It was then that Guy suggested that he and I work more closely together. "All you'll have to do is let me know about the jobs and I'll do them," he said. I refused. In burglary, you cannot carry out what someone else has conceived. The one who does a job must be clever enough to allow for the unforeseen in a given project. All Guy saw in a thief's life was the splendid and brilliant, the scarlet and golden. To me, it is somber and subterranean. I see it as hazardous and perilous, just as he does, but with a peril different from breaking one's bones by falling from a roof or being pursued in a car and smashing up against a wall or being killed by a 6/35 bullet. I'm not cut out for those lordly spectacles in which you disguise yourself as a cardinal in order to steal the relics of a basilica, in which you take an airplane to outwit a rival gang. I don't care for such luxurious games.

When he stole a car, Guy would manage to drive off just when the owner appeared. He got a kick out of seeing the face of the man watching his car docilely going off with the thief. It was a treat for him. He would burst into an enormous, metallic laugh, a bit forced and artificial, and would drive off like the wind. It was rare for me not to suffer at the sight of the victim and his stupefaction, at his rage and shame.

When I got out of prison we met at a pimps' bar. At *La Villa*. The walls were covered with autographed photos, pictures of dance-hall hostesses, but chiefly of boxers and dancers. He had no money. He himself had just escaped.

"Don't you know of something to do?"

"I do."

I told him in a low voice that I intended to rob a friend who owned some *objets d'art* that could be sold abroad. (I had just written a novel entitled *Our Lady of the Flowers*, and its publication had won me some wealthy connections.)

"Do we have to beat the guy up?"

"No need. Listen."

I took a deep breath, I leaned over to him. I changed the position of my hands on the rail of the bar. I shifted my leg. In short, I was getting ready to jump.

"Listen. We could send the guy to jail for a week."

I can't exactly say that Guy's features moved, yet his whole physiognomy was transformed. Perhaps his face hardened and grew motionless. I was suddenly frightened by the harshness of his blue stare. Guy bent his head over a little to the side, without ceasing to look me in the face, or, more exactly, to stare at me, to hold me fast. I suddenly realized the meaning of the expression: "I'm going to pin you down!" His voice, when it answered, was low and even, but leveled at my stomach. It shot from his mouth with the rigidity of a column, of a ram. Its constrained monotone made it seem compressed, compact.

"What? Are *you* saying that, Jean? Are *you* telling me to send a guy to the jug?"

My face remained as motionless as his, just as hard, though more deliberately tense. To the gathering clouds in his stormy face I opposed mine of stone, to his thunder and lightning, my angles and points. Knowing that his rigor would burst and give way to contempt, I faced it, for a moment. I quickly thought of how I could save myself without his suspecting that I had planned a vile act. I had to have time on my side. I said nothing. I was letting his amazement and contempt pour over me.

"I can bump a guy off. I'll beat your guy up and rob him, if you want me to. All you've got to do is say so. Well, tell me, Jean, you want me to bump him off?"

I stared at him and still said nothing. I assumed that my face was impenetrable. Guy must have seen how tense I was, must have thought I was at the point of an extremely dramatic moment, in fact, of checked will, of a decision which astonished him enough to move him. But I feared his severity, the more so since never had he seemed to me more virile than that evening. As he sat on the high stool, his strong, thick, rough hand rested on his muscular thighs which bulged beneath the smooth cloth of his trousers. In some indefinable element of meanness, stupidity, virility, elegance, pomp, and viscosity which he had in common with them, he was the equal of the pimps around us, and their friend. He dwarfed me. "They" dwarfed me.

"You realize what it is to send a guy there? We've both had it. Go on, we can't do that."

Had he himself betrayed and ratted on his friends? His intimacy with a police inspector had made me fear—and hope—that he was a squealer. Made me fear, for I was running the risk of being reported, made me fear further, for he would be preceding me in betrayal. Made me hope, for I would have a companion and support in vileness. I understood the loneliness and despair of the traveler who has lost his shadow. I remained silent and stared at him. My face was motionless. The time was not ripe for me to change tactics. "Let him flounder about in astonishment until he loses footing." However, I still could not help seeing his contempt, for he said, "But Jean, I regard you as my brother. Do you realize? If any guy, a guy from here, wanted to have you thrown in, I'd attend to him. And you, you tell me . . ."

He lowered his voice, for some of the pimps had drawn near. (Some of the whores too might have overheard us. The bar was packed.) My stare tried to get harder. My eyebrows knitted. I was chewing away at the inside of my lips and was still saying nothing.

"You know, if it had been anyone else but you who suggested that . . ."

In spite of the shell of will with which I was protecting myself, I was humiliated by the brotherly gentleness of his contempt. His words and the tone of his voice left me undecided. Was he or was he not a stool pigeon? I'll never know for sure. If he was, he might just as well have been despising me for an act that he himself would have been ready to commit. It was also possible that it repelled him to have me as a companion in vileness because I was less glamorous to him, less sparkling, than some other thief whom he would have accepted, I was aware of his contempt. He could easily have dissolved me, like rock candy. Nevertheless, I had to preserve my rigidity without being too dead set.

"But Jean, if it had been somebody else, I'd have knocked hell out of him. I don't know why I let you say it. No, I don't know why."

"All right, that'll do."

He lifted his head. His jaw dropped. My tone had surprised him.

"Huh?"

"I said that'll do."

I bent over closer and put my hand on his shoulder.

"Guy, my boy, you're all right. I was worried when I saw you so chummy with R. (the detective). I'm letting you know it. I had the jitters. I was scared you might have become a squealer."

"You're crazy. I was in cahoots with him, first because he's as crooked as they come, and then so that he'd get me some papers. He's a guy whose palm you can grease."

"All right, now I feel sure, but yesterday, when I saw you having a drink together, I swear it didn't look so good. Because I've never been able to stomach squealers. Do you realize that suspecting you was like being hit on the head? Thinking that you might've turned stool pigeon?"

I wasn't as careful as he had been when reproaching me, and I raised my voice a bit. The relief of no longer being despised restored my breath, made me bounce too high and too fast. I was carried away by the joy of emerging from contempt, also of being saved from a brawl which would have set all the pimps in the bar against me, and of dominating Guy in turn with an authority conferred upon me by my mastery of language. A kind of self-pity enabled me to speak effortlessly with inflections that moved me, for I had lost, though I landed on my feet. My toughness and intransigence had shown a crack, and the matter of the burglary (which neither of us dared bring up again) was definitely out of the question. We were surrounded by very precious pimps. They were speaking loudly, though very politely. Guy talked to me about his woman. I answered as best I could. I was veiled in a great sadness which was pierced at times by the lightning of my rage. Loneliness (whose image might be a kind of fog or vapor emanating from me), torn apart for a moment by hope, closed over me again. I might have had a comrade in freedom (for I'm quite sure that Guy is an informer); he was denied me. I would have loved to betray with him. For I want to be able to love my accomplices. This extraordinarily lonely situation (of being a thief) must not leave me walled in with a graceless boy. During the act, fear, which is the matter (or rather the light) of which I am almost completely composed, may cause me to collapse in the arms of my accomplice. I do not think that I choose him to be big and strong so as to be protected in case of failure, but rather that an overpowering fear may throw me into the hollow of his arms, or thighs, those havens of delight. This choice, which often enables fear to give way so completely and turn to tenderness, is a dangerous one. I abandon myself too readily to those beautiful shoulders, to that back, those hips. Guy was tempting when we worked.

Guy came to see me in a state of terror. It was impossible to tell whether his panic was real. His face was pitiful that morning. He was more at ease in the corridors and on the stairways of the Santé with pimps whose prestige lay in the dressing gowns they put on to visit their lawyers. Did the security of prison give him a lighter bearing?

"I'm in the shit and I've got to get out of it. Show me a job to do so I can beat it to the sticks."

He persisted in living among pimps, and I recognized in his nervousness and in the fatal movement of his head the tragic tone of faggots and actresses. "Is it possible," I wondered, "that the 'men' in Montmartre are fooled by him?"

"You come blowing in without notice. I don't have jobs on tap."

"Anything, Jean. I'll bump someone off if I have to. I'm ready to drill a guy for just a little loose cash. Yesterday I nearly landed myself in the jug."

"That doesn't get me anywhere," I said smilingly.

"You don't realize. You live in a swell hotel."

He irritated me. What have I to fear of smart hotels, chandeliers, reception rooms, the friendship of men? Comfort may give me a certain boldness of spirit. And with my spirit already far off, I am sure that my body will follow.

Suddenly he looked at me and smiled.

"The gentleman receives me downstairs. Can't we go to your room? Is your kid there?"

"He is."

"Is he nice? Who is he?"

"You'll see."

When he had left us, I asked Lucien what he thought of Guy. Secretly I would have been happy had they loved each other.

"He's a queer-looking bird, with his hat. Gets himself up like a scarecrow."

And he immediately spoke of something else. Neither Guy's tattoos, nor his adventures, nor his boldness would have interested Lucien. All he saw was how ridiculously he was dressed. The elegance of hoodlums may be questioned by a man of taste. But they deck themselves out during the day, and especially at night, with as much care as a tart, and there is something touching about their seriousness. They want to shine. Egoism reduces their personalities to their bodies alone (the poverty of the home of a pimp who is better dressed than a prince). But what did this quest for elegance, almost always achieved, reveal about Guy? What does it mean when the details are that ridiculous little hat, that tight jacket, the pocket handkerchief? Nevertheless, though he lacked Lucien's childlike grace and discreet manner, his passionate temperament, warmer heart, and more ardent, burning life still made him dear to me. He was capable, as he said, of committing murder, of ruining himself in an evening for a friend or for himself alone. He had guts. And perhaps all of Lucien's qualities do not have, in my eyes, the value of a single virtue of this ridiculous hoodlum.

My love for Lucien and my happiness in this love are beginning to induce me to recognize a morality more in conformity with your world. Not that I am more generous (I have always been that), but the rigid goal toward which I am moving, fierce as the iron shaft at the top of a glacier, so desirable, so dear to my pride and my despair, seems to me too great a threat to my love. Lucien is not aware that I am headed for infernal regions. I still like to go where he takes me. How much more intoxicating, to the point of dizziness, falling, and vomiting, would be the love I bear him if Lucien were a thief and a traitor. But would he love me then? Do I not owe his tenderness and his delicate merging within me to his submission to the moral order? Yet I would like to bind myself to some iron monster, smiling though icy, who kills, steals, and delivers father and mother to the judges. I also desire this so as to be myself the monstrous exception which a monster, delegate of God, allows himself to be, and which satisfies my pride as well as my taste for moral solitude. Lucien's love fills me with joy, but if I go to Montmartre, where I lived for a long time, what I see there, and the squalor I sense, quicken my heartbeat, strain my body and soul. I know, better than anyone else, that there is nothing in disreputable neighborhoods; they are without mystery; yet they remain mysterious to me. To live again in such places so as to be in harmony with the underworld would require an impossible return to the past, for the pale-faced corner hoodlums have pale souls, and the most dreadful pimps are distressingly stupid. But at night, when Lucien has gone back to his room, I curl up fearfully under the sheets and want to feel against me the tougher, more dangerous, and more tender body of a thief. I am planning for the near future a perilous outlaw's life in the most dissolute quarters of the most dissolute of ports. I shall abandon Lucien. Let him become whatever he can. I shall go away. I shall go to Barcelona, to Rio or elsewhere, but first to prison. I shall find Sek Gorgui there. The big Negro will stretch out gently on my back. Gently, but with sure precision, his tool will enter me. It will not tremble. It will not jerk hastily like mine. That presence within me will so fill me that I shall forget to come. The Negro, vaster than night, will cover me over. All his muscles will be conscious, however, of being the tributaries of a virility converging at that hard and violently charged point, his whole body quivering with goodness and self-interest, which exist only for my happiness. We shall be motionless. He will drive deeper. A kind of sleep will lay the Negro out on my shoulders; I shall be crushed by his darkness, which will gradually dilute me. With my mouth open, I shall know he is in a torpor, held in that dark axis by his steel pivot. I shall be giddy. I shall have no further responsibility. I shall gaze over the world with the clear gaze that the eagle imparted to Ganymede.

* * *

The more I love Lucien, the more I lose my taste for theft and thieves. I am glad that I love him, but a great sadness, fragile as a shadow and heavy as the Negro, spreads over my entire life, just barely rests upon it, grazes it and crushes it, enters my open mouth: it is regret for my legend. My love for Lucien acquaints me with the loathsome sweetness of nostalgia. I can abandon him by leaving France. I would then have to merge him in my hatred of my country. But the charming child has the eyes, hair, chest, and legs of the ideal hoodlums whom I adore and whom I would feel I was abandoning in abandoning him. His charm saves him.

This evening, as I was running my fingers through his curls, he said to me dreamily:

"I'd really like to see my kid."

Instead of making him seem hard, these words softened him. (Once when his ship put ashore, he made a girl pregnant.) My eyes rest upon him more gravely, more tenderly too. I gaze at this proud-faced, smiling youngster with his keen, gentle, roguish eyes as if he were a young wife. The wound I inflict upon this male compels me to a sudden respect, to new delicacies, and the dull, remote, and almost narrow wound makes him languid, like the memory of the pains of child-birth. He smiles at me. More happiness fills me. I feel that my responsibility has become greater, as if—literally—heaven had just blessed our union. But will he, later on, with his girlfriends, be able to forget what he was for me? What will it do to his soul? What ache never to be cured? Will he have, in this respect, the indifference of Guy, the same smile accompanying the shrug with which he shakes off, letting it drift in the wake of his swift walk, that dull and heavy pain, the melancholy of the wounded male? Will a certain casualness toward all things be born of it?

II

POETRY

The Fisherman of Suquet

◄o►

The Fisherman of Suquet *was written in 1945 and celebrates Genet's love for Lucien Sénémaud. The young man was not a professional fisherman, but like other boys in Cannes he fished in the nearby bay of Suquet.*

If the poem is Genet's most accomplished, perhaps its success is due to its dramatic form. Genet was not at his best in straightforward lyric outbursts. In this poem, as in his novels, his feelings are deployed and separated out; they are assigned to different figures, the Thief, the Night, the Tree, the Artillery Man, and so on.

The special tone of Genet's poetry comes from its combination of shocking, very modern subject matter and old-fashioned strict verse forms. In the case of this poem, homosexual love and violence are unveiled through rhymed alexandrines of great purity. Cocteau was an obvious influence on Genet's poetry, and indeed, when they first met, Genet recited to Cocteau, from memory, a long poem by the Master.

A SECRET ACCORD, a gentleman's agreement was worked out between my mouth and the cock of this eighteen-year-old fisherman. Although it was still tucked away in his blue shorts:

Time, air, and the landscape around him were
dimming. Stretched out on the sand, what I could detect between
his limbs (the spread branches of his legs) was hardening.

The sand retained his footprints but also registered
the heft and weight of a penis excited by the troubling
evening heat. Every grain glittered.

"What's your name?"
"What about yours?"

. . .

After that night the thief tenderly loved the kid—
sly, spirited, imaginative, rugged—whose body, just by drawing
near, made everything tremble—water, sky, rocks, houses, boys, girls.
Even the page I'm writing on now.

My patience is a medal pinned to your lapel.

Gold dust floats around you. Isolates you from me.

With your sunstruck face you're as shadowy as a Gypsy.

His eyes: autumn's smoky dress drawn over thistles and blackthorn.

His cock: my lips compressed to cover my sharp teeth.

His hands clarify things. Then obscure them. Kindle and douse
them.

His big left toe with the ingrown nail reams my nostril or mouth.
It's too big at first but soon he gets the foot in, then the
whole leg.

You long to fish where water flows from ice,
In my hidden pools held back by rings,
O plunge your arms into my handsome eyes,
Metallic traps armed with double springs.
Under lofty pines and storm-torn skies,
Angler glinting with wet blond scales,
In your eyes my wickerwork hand pales
As I watch the world's saddest fish flee, fled,
From the shallows where I crumble bread.

Aspen: your heel, hung from the top bough,
Pink, poised, grabs the rising sun and nails
It to a branch. Aspen, your sough-
ing, a mouth organ, makes my teeth hum. Your nails
Claw the sky, tear the tender cortex,
Then you bedeck yourself blandly
In the snow's softest fringe. The tree raises high
A torso deeply wounded, revived
With feathers. My lips force the sap to rise.

. . .

When the sun slowly burns away the haze
That covers the slopes of your shapely calves,
I make my pilgrimage to the rocks where I saw the blaze,
Blond soldier kneeling in the light.
A snake wakes up when the dead start to talk.
Aroused by my broken foot the partridges take wing.
At sunset I'll see the gold
Seekers panning under the mad moon,
As the grave robbers draw straws.

How dark your feet are, your polished slippers!
Your feet frozen in my pools of tears.
Your Carmelite feet powdered and discalced,
Your blessèd feet reflecting bits of heavenly blue,
Tonight your feet will brand my white shoulders
(Which are forests the moon fills with wolves),
O my fisherman in the budding willow grove,
Headsman in a mail of stars and studs,
Upright, sustained by the breakwater's white arm.

Attached to the erect green tree—your face upside down
(Gold tree plus love cub make up a double-headed emblem)—
You hang by just one foot, cuddly koala,
From the greenery and play
On your harmonica a slow waltz,
Which hums out of the blue, but do your eyes see
From the mizzenmast the astounding dawn?
O naked angler with the subtle heart,
Come down from the tree but beware my rumorous leaves.

Farewell, Queen of Heaven, farewell the skin-
Deep flower carved into my hand.
O my silence haunted by a ghost your hands,
Your eyes, silence. The paleness of your skin.
Silence once more these waves on the flight
Of stairs where you pace out the night.
A pure angelus rings out from under his arch.
Farewell, sun. From my heart it takes flight,
Falls into a grisly nocturnal march.

At night my fisherman came down out of the blue
Houses and my hands held him tight.
He smiled. The sea snared our feet, drew

Us out. Hung from his belt by bright
Drenched hair dangled a bunch of heads
(His belt was studded and gleamed in the moonlight)
The heads of eight sullen girls shocked that they were dead.
The fisherman admired himself in the mirroring night.

The treasures of the night are buried under your feet,
Go easily along the glowing path of coals.
Peace be with you.
Through nettles, gorse, blackthorn, forests, your step
Measures out the shadows.
And each of your feet, each step
Buries me under jasmine in a porcelain tomb.
You darken the world.
Tonight's treasures: Ireland and its Troubles,
muskrats scurrying across the moors, an arch
of light, the wine you keep repeating, the
wedding in the valley, a hanged man
swinging from an apple tree in flower, then that
part, approached heart in mouth, guarded
in your shorts by hawthorn in flower.

The pilgrims arrive from every side.
They wind around your hips where the sun sets,
With difficulty scale the wooded slopes of your thighs
Where it's night even by day.

Through the grasslands under your unbuckled
Belt we arrive at last, throat dry,
body sore, feet tired, close to Him.
Next to His brilliance even Time is veiled
    In mourning and, above the crepe, sun, moon,
        stars, your eyes, your tears may even be shining.
Time makes shadows before Him.
Nothing but strange violet flowers will
Sprout from these gnarled bulbs.
We press clasped hands to our heart
Fists in our mouth.

What's it to love you? I'm afraid to see this water flow
Between my poor fingers. I don't dare swallow you.
My mouth is sketching in an imaginary column.
It goes down lightly on a fog in autumn.
I enter love as I might go into the water,

Hands stretched out, blind; my swallowed
Sobs harden your presence within me
Where your presence is heavy, eternal. I love you.

But He's melting in my mouth. Nothing but verse—.
Words for what miss, worm for which garden? What dream lulls him,
makes him cocoon, lightly torments him, gives him this slow,
soft stomachache?

—Are you rejecting me?
But think of the affection he must summon up in order to come back
to me when his dreams offer him so much elsewhere!
How many tossed bouquets of cut flowers in order to forget
his luxuriant groves!

I caress the little mound of crestfallen flesh which curls
up in my hand, and I look you in the eyes; there, far away, I see
in your eyes the gentle animal that lends this gentleness to your cock.

You try to swim upstream to me. A few waves reach me. This foam
in your eyes proves it. But the heaviest part of you remains down
in your depths. And that's where you sink.
If I lend an ear I hear your voice calling me, but it is so
tangled up with the sirens' song that I wouldn't know how to
extricate it in order to pull one pure note toward my ear.

But I won't abandon you.

Pulling out?

He pulls out of me.

All the kisses instead of making it up just add to the night
which engulfs me and falls around me.

Die by my hand. Die before my very eyes.

I have to make the situation as obscure as possible (and
tense to the breaking point) so that the drama will be inevitable,
so that we can chalk it up to necessity.

Black blood flows already from his mouth and from his open
mouth his white ghost flees again.

THE THIEF

There where night crochets her flowers and, wistful,
Disrobes, the butcher clutches my roses by the fistful.
O night, take this child my tears disclosed
And make a poem in which his penis is enclosed.

NIGHT

My treasures undone by his frail hands
Pour in your godlike sleep down to your heels
His sigh masks the titwillow's plaint,
Thief whose nose bleeds on my lacquered nails.

THE THIEF

The mistral moans and moves but misses me. They're killing me.
Killing me slowly. I'm afraid. Don't be afraid, come
Through the morning meadows, headstrong, come-
Ly cock, bring me the morning star and the sea.

THE TREE

If you stroll past, thief, humming your song
Armed legions will spring forth from my bark.
Don't resist my hard heart nor my welcoming boughs
I'll watch you die, trampled under their boots.

THE THIEF

Sometimes he wakes up and goes through my pockets
He robs me and, though he's threatened with poison,
My eagle surveys him, carries him off like a lamb to
High rocks and fleeces him deep in my hollow past. .

THE TREE

Casting lightning your fair ray breaks me in two.
You'd like it if your tricks worked on me.
Thief, your slippery hand will be caught one day.
A tree has arrayed itself in its hardy destiny.

THE THIEF

From each of my fingertips a leaf flutters!
All this green commotion, seething foliage.
The rapist's pale face flushes red.
The star of the Levant signals from his curly head.

THE NIGHT

But what are you talking about? The fishermen go home
Like the sea to the bottom of the abyss (their eyes).
The tide is on time, and the foam at the edge
Of laughing lips is for you a precious prize.

THE ARTILLERY MAN

With my feet wrapped in wool socks
I cross the woods in my leather leggings.
Neither the sea nor your shit, not even your breath,
Thief, can keep everything from trembling under me.

THE THIEF

You're a hypocrite, immortal equestrienne
In an organdy dress on a wounded horse!
Your beautiful fingers are shedding lost petals
Farewell my great garden tended by the heavens!
And so I remain alone, forgotten by the man who sleeps in my
arms. The sea is calm. I don't dare budge. His scrutiny would
be worse than his dreamed desertion of me. Perhaps he'd even vomit
on my chest.

And what would I do then? Pick through his vomit? Root through
the wine, meat, bile, these violets and these roses that dilute
and untie the threads of blood?

Broken rapier, foils of fire!
The sea torments me while the moon stands guard.
Blood in the sea pours out of my ear.
Fisherman with the melancholy regard
Your leaden eyes in a sky scudding free
Once again drain my abscesses without pity
For I'm sinking and turning into a swamp
Where the night goes to discolor the will-
o'-the-wisp that flickers over my voyage out.

III

THEATER

The Maids

◄o►

Genet talked about The Maids *as early as 1945. During the summer of 1946 he mounted a campaign to convince the famous stage director (and actor) Louis Jouvet to direct his play. When Jouvet read the first draft, the play was in three acts, requiring several sets and a large cast. At Jouvet's suggestion, the script was tightened into a one-act, one-set play with just three actors. This concentration is the main reason the play is so forceful.*

The play was premiered in Paris on April 19, 1947, at the Théâtre de l'Athénée. It was presented on the same program with a play by Jean Giradoux, The Apollo of Belloc. *Genet's play provoked a scandal in the press, which was sharply divided about its merits. Audiences too reacted at the extremes, either cheering or booing the performances. At the time the play premiered, French theatergoers were used to poetic realism of the sort propounded by Giradoux or Anouilh, or they laughed at ribald and highly conventional, naughty comedies. Genet's stark tale of vengeance and cold hate certainly puzzled and confused them.*

Genet was not happy with the initial production, which to his mind was far too glossy. The actresses who played the maids were far too young and pretty for his taste (they were both mistresses of Jouvet), and the sets by Christian Bérard and costumes by Lanvin seemed far too commercial for the script. When Genet later published the play, he haughtily falsified the facts by suggesting in his preface that Jouvet had begged him for the script. (Genet dismissed Jouvet without even naming him.)

The play was revived on January 13, 1954, in Paris by Tania Balachova in an earlier draft from the one that Jouvet had used. The two versions were also published together in 1954 with an important preface by Genet in which he dismissed European theater in favor of Oriental ritual and stylization.

People often say that Genet wanted the two maids to be played by men. Although Sartre refers to this idea, and claims Genet mentioned it to him, Genet

would later strenuously deny that he had ever thought of having the roles as-
sumed by male actors.

The plot is based on a real-life incident. In the 1930s, two sisters, Christine
and Léa Papin, twenty-eight and twenty-one years old, killed the bourgeois family
for whom they worked in the provincial town of Mans. The family had been ex-
tremely harsh with the sisters, despite their irreproachable conduct as servants.
One night the electricity in the house failed. The family was away and the maids
were left in charge of the household. When the mother and daughter returned,
they scolded the maids, who, seized by a paroxysm of rage, tore out the eyes of the
mother and daughter and killed them. They then mutilated the corpses further,
bathing one in the blood of the other. Having finished their work, they washed
their tools, bathed, and went to sleep in the same bed, declaring "Now we've made
a fine mess of it!"

Genet borrowed from the real-life story the madness and mutual dependence of
the servant-sisters as well as their vision of murder as a sort of ritual, but all
other details in Genet's play differ from the historical facts.

M ADAME'S BEDROOM. Louis Quinze furniture. Lace. Rear, a window
opening on the front of the house opposite. Right, a bed. Left, a door and
a dressing table. Flowers in profusion. The time is evening.

(Claire, wearing a slip, is standing with her back to the dressing table. Her
gestures—arm extended—and tone are exaggeratedly tragic.)

CLAIRE: Those gloves! Those eternal gloves! I've told you time and again to
leave them in the kitchen. You probably hope to seduce the milkman with
them. No, no, don't lie; that won't get you anywhere! Hang them over the
sink. When *will* you understand that this room is not to be sullied. Every-
thing, yes, everything that comes out of the kitchen is spit! So stop it!
(During this speech, Solange has been playing with a pair of rubber gloves and ob-
serving her gloved hands, which are alternately spread fanwise and folded in the
form of a bouquet.) Make yourself quite at home. Preen like a peacock. And
above all, don't hurry, we've plenty of time. Go! *(Solange's posture changes*
and she leaves humbly, holding the rubber gloves with her fingertips. Claire sits
down at the dressing table. She sniffs at the flowers, runs her hand over the toilet
articles, brushes her hair, pats her face.) Get my dress ready. Quick! Time
presses. Are you there? *(She turns round.)* Claire! Claire! *(Solange enters.)*
SOLANGE: I beg Madame's pardon, I was preparing her tea. *(She pronounces*
it "tay.")
CLAIRE: Lay out my things. The white spangled dress. The fan. The emeralds.
SOLANGE: Very well, Madame. All Madame's jewels?

CLAIRE: Put them out and I shall choose. And, of course, my patent-leather slippers. The ones you've had your eye on for years. *(Solange takes a few jewel boxes from the closet, opens them, and lays them out on the bed.)* For your wedding, no doubt. Admit he seduced you! Just look at you! How big you are! Admit it! *(Solange squats on the rug, spits on the patent-leather slippers, and polishes them.)* I've told you, Claire, without spit. Let it sleep in you, my child, let it stagnate. Ah! Ah! *(She giggles nervously.)* May the lost wayfarer drown in it. Ah! Ah! You *are* hideous. Lean forward and look at yourself in my shoes. Do you think I find it pleasant to know that my foot is shrouded by the veils of your saliva? By the mists of your swamps?

SOLANGE: *(On her knees, and very humble)* I wish Madame to be lovely.

CLAIRE: I shall be. *(She primps in front of the mirror.)* You hate me, don't you? You crush me with your attentions and your humbleness; you smother me with gladioli and mimosa. *(She stands up and, lowering her tone)* There are too many flowers. The room is needlessly cluttered. It's *impossible. (She looks at herself again in the glass.)* I shall be lovely. Lovelier than you'll ever be. With a face and body like that, you'll never seduce Mario. *(Dropping the tragic tone)* A ridiculous young milkman despises us, and if we're going to have a kid by him—

SOLANGE: Oh! I've never—

CLAIRE: *(Resuming)* Be quiet, you fool. My dress!

SOLANGE: *(She looks in the closet, pushing aside a few dresses.)* The red dress. Madame will wear the red dress.

CLAIRE: I said the white dress, the one with spangles.

SOLANGE: *(Firmly)* I'm sorry. Madame will wear the scarlet velvet dress this evening.

CLAIRE: *(Naively)* Ah? Why?

SOLANGE: *(Coldly)* It's impossible to forget Madame's bosom under the velvet folds. And the jet brooch, when Madame was sighing and telling Monsieur of my devotion! Your widowhood really requires that you be entirely in black.

CLAIRE: Eh?

SOLANGE: Need I say more? A word to the wise—

CLAIRE: Ah! So you want to talk. . . . Very well. Threaten me. Insult your mistress, Solange. you want to talk about Monsieur's misfortunes, don't you? Fool. It was hardly the moment to allude to him, but I can turn this matter to fine account! You're smiling? Do you doubt it?

SOLANGE: The time is not yet ripe to unearth—

CLAIRE: What a word! My infamy? My infamy! To unearth!

SOLANGE: Madame!

CLAIRE: Am I to be at your mercy for having denounced Monsieur to the police, for having sold him? And yet I'd have done even worse, or better. You think I haven't suffered? Claire, I forced my hand to pen the letter—without mistakes in spelling or syntax, without crossing anything out—the letter that sent my lover to prison. And you, instead of standing by me, you mock me. You force your colors on me! You speak of widowhood! He isn't dead. Claire, Monsieur will be led from prison to prison, perhaps even to Devil's Island, where I, his mistress, mad with grief, shall follow him. I shall be in the convoy. I shall share his glory. You speak of widowhood and deny me the white gown—the mourning of queens. You're unaware of that, Claire—

SOLANGE: *(Coldly)* Madame will wear the red dress.

CLAIRE: *(Simply)* Quite. *(Severely)* Hand me the dress. Oh! I'm so alone and friendless. I can see in your eyes that you loathe me. You don't care what happens to me.

SOLANGE: I'll follow you everywhere. I love you.

CLAIRE: No doubt. As one loves a mistress. You love and respect me. And you're hoping for a legacy, a codicil in your favor—

SOLANGE: I'd do all in my power—

CLAIRE: *(Ironically)* I know. You'd go through fire for me. *(Solange helps Claire put on her dress.)* Fasten it. Don't pull so hard. Don't try to bind me. *(Solange kneels at Claire's feet and arranges the folds of the dress.)* Avoid pawing me. You smell like an animal. You've brought those odors from some foul attic, where the lackeys visit us at night. The maid's room! The garret! *(Graciously)* Claire, if I speak of the smell of garrets, it is for memory's sake. And of the twin beds where two sisters fall asleep, dreaming of one another. There, *(She points to a spot in the room.)* there, the two iron beds with the night table between them. There, *(She points to a spot opposite.)* the pinewood dresser with the little altar to the Holy Virgin! That's right, isn't it?

SOLANGE: We're so unhappy. I could cry! If you go on—

CLAIRE: It *is* right, isn't it! Let's skip the business of your prayers and kneeling. I shan't even mention the paper flowers. . . . *(She laughs.)* Paper flowers! And the branch of holy boxwood! *(She points to the flowers in the room.)* Just look at these flowers open in my honor! Claire, am I not a lovelier Virgin?

SOLANGE: *(As if in adoration)* Be quiet—

CLAIRE: And there, *(She points to a very high spot at the window.)* that notorious skylight from which a half-naked milkman jumps to your bed!

SOLANGE: Madame is forgetting herself, Madame—

CLAIRE: And what about your hands? Don't *you* forget your hands. How often have I *(She hesitates)* murmured: they befoul the sink.

SOLANGE: The fall!

CLAIRE: Eh?

SOLANGE: *(Arranging the dress on Claire's hips)* The fall of your dress. I'm arranging your fall from grace.

CLAIRE: Get away, you bungler! *(She kicks Solange in the temple with her Louis Quinze heel. Solange, who is kneeling, staggers and draws back.)*

SOLANGE: Oh! Me a burglar?

CLAIRE: I said bungler; and if you must whimper, do it in our garret. Here, in my bedroom, I will have only noble tears. A time will come when the hem of my gown will be studded with them, but those will be precious tears. Arrange my train, you clod.

SOLANGE: *(In ecstasy)* Madame's being carried away!

CLAIRE: By the devil! He's carrying me away in his fragrant arms. He's lifting me up, I leave the ground, I'm off. . . . *(She stamps with her heel.)* And I stay behind. Get my necklace! But hurry, we won't have time. If the gown's too long, make a hem with some safety pins. *(Solange gets up and goes to take the necklace from a jewel case, but Claire rushes ahead of her and seizes the jewels. Her fingers graze those of Solange, and she recoils in horror.)* Keep your hands off mine! I can't stand your touching me. Hurry up!

SOLANGE: There's no need to overdo it. Your eyes are ablaze.

CLAIRE: *(Shocked astonishment)* What's that you said?

SOLANGE: Limits, boundaries, Madame. Frontiers are not conventions but laws. Here, my lands; there, your shore—

CLAIRE: What language, my dear. Claire, do you mean that I've already crossed the seas? Are you offering me the dreary exile of your imagination? You're taking revenge, aren't you? You feel the time coming when, no longer a maid—

SOLANGE: You see straight through me. You divine my thoughts.

CLAIRE: *(Increasingly carried away)*—the time coming when, no longer a maid, you become vengeance itself, but, Claire, don't forget—Claire, are you listening?—don't forget, it was the maid who hatched schemes of vengeance, and I—Claire, you're not listening.

SOLANGE: *(Absentmindedly)* I'm listening.

CLAIRE: And I contain within me both vengeance and the maid and give them a chance for life, a chance for salvation. Claire, it's a burden, it's terribly painful to be a mistress, to contain all the springs of hatred, to be the dunghill on which you grow. You want to see me naked every day. I *am* beautiful, am I not? And the desperation of my love makes me even more so, but you have no idea what strength I need!

SOLANGE: *(Contemptuously)* Your lover!

CLAIRE: My unhappy lover heightens my nobility. Yes. Yes, my child. All that you'll ever know is your own baseness.

SOLANGE: That'll do! Now hurry! Are you ready?

CLAIRE: Are you?

SOLANGE: *(She steps back to the wardrobe.)* I'm ready—I'm tired of being an object of disgust. I hate you, too. I despise you. I hate your scented bosom. Your . . . *ivory* bosom! Your . . . *golden* thighs! Your . . . *amber* feet! I hate you! *(She spits on the red dress.)*

CLAIRE: *(Aghast)* Oh! . . . Oh! . . . But. . . .

SOLANGE: *(Walking up to her)* Yes, my proud beauty. You think you can always do just as you like. You think you can deprive me forever of the beauty of the sky, that you can choose your perfumes and powders, your nail polish and silk and velvet and lace, and deprive *me* of them? That you can steal the milkman from me? Admit it! Admit about the milkman. His youth and vigor excite you, don't they? Admit about the milkman. For Solange says: to hell with you!

CLAIRE: *(Panic-stricken)* Claire! Claire!

SOLANGE: Eh?

CLAIRE: *(In a murmur)* Claire, Solange, Claire.

SOLANGE: Ah! Yes, Claire, Claire says: to hell with you! Claire is here, more dazzling than ever. Radiant! *(She slaps Claire.)*

CLAIRE: Oh! . . . Oh! Claire. . . . You. . . . Oh!

SOLANGE: Madame thought she was protected by her barricade of flowers, saved by some special destiny, by a sacrifice. But she reckoned without a maid's rebellion. Behold her wrath, Madame. She turns your pretty speeches to nought. She'll cut the ground from under your fine adventure. Your Monsieur was just a cheap thief, and you—

CLAIRE: I forbid you! Confound your impudence!

SOLANGE: Twaddle! She forbids me! It's Madame who's confounded. Her face is all convulsed. Would you like a mirror? Here. *(She hands Claire a mirror.)*

CLAIRE: *(Regarding herself with satisfaction)* I see the marks of a slap, but now I'm more beautiful than ever!

SOLANGE: Yes, a slap!

CLAIRE: Danger is my halo, Claire; and you, you dwell in darkness. . . .

SOLANGE: But the darkness is dangerous—I know. I've heard all that before. I can tell by your face what I'm supposed to answer. So I'll finish it up. Now, here are the two maids, the faithful servants! They're standing in front of you. Despise them. Look more beautiful. We no longer fear you. We're merged, enveloped in our fumes, in our revels, in our hatred of you. The mold is setting. We're talking shape, Madame. Don't laugh—ah! above all, don't laugh at my grandiloquence. . . .

CLAIRE: Get out!

SOLANGE: But only to be of further service to Madame! I'm going back to my kitchen, back to my gloves, and the smell of my teeth. To my belching sink. You have your flowers, I my sink. I'm the maid. You, at least, you can't defile me. But! But! . . . *(She advances on Claire, threateningly.)* But before I go back, I'm going to finish the job. *(Suddenly an alarm clock goes off. Solange stops. The two actresses, in a state of agitation, run together. They huddle and listen.)* Already?

CLAIRE: Let's hurry! Madame'll be back. *(She starts to unfasten her dress.)* Help me. It's over already. And you didn't get to the end.

SOLANGE: *(Helping her; in a sad tone of voice)* The same thing happens every time. And it's all your fault, you're never ready. I can't finish you off.

CLAIRE: We waste too much time with the preliminaries. But we've still. . . .

SOLANGE: *(As she helps Claire out of her dress)* Watch at the window.

CLAIRE: We've still got a little time left. I set the clock so we'd be able to put the things in order. *(She drops wearily into the armchair.)*

SOLANGE: *(Gently)* It's so close this evening. It's been close all day.

CLAIRE: *(Gently)* Yes.

SOLANGE: Is that what's killing us, Claire?

CLAIRE: Yes.

SOLANGE: It's time now.

CLAIRE: Yes. *(She gets up wearily.)* I'm going to make the tea.

SOLANGE: Watch at the window.

CLAIRE: There's time. *(She wipes her face.)*

SOLANGE: Still looking at yourself . . . Claire, dear. . . .

CLAIRE: Let me alone, I'm exhausted.

SOLANGE: *(Sternly)* Watch at the window. Thanks to you, the whole place is in a mess again. And I've got to clean Madame's gown. *(She stares at her sister.)* Well, what's the matter with you? You can be like me now. Be yourself again. Come on, Claire, be my sister again.

CLAIRE: I'm finished. That light's killing me. Do you think the people opposite. . . .

SOLANGE: Who cares! You don't expect us to . . . *(She hesitates.)* organize things in the dark? Have a rest. Shut your eyes. Shut your eyes, Claire.

CLAIRE: *(She puts on her short black dress.)* Oh! When I say I'm exhausted, it's just a way of talking. Don't use it to pity me. Stop trying to dominate me.

SOLANGE: I've never tried to dominate you. I only want you to rest. You'll help me more by resting.

CLAIRE: I understand, don't explain.

SOLANGE: Yes, I will explain. It was you who started it. When you mentioned the milkman. You think I couldn't see what you were driving at? If Mario—

CLAIRE: Oh!

SOLANGE: If the milkman says indecent things to me, he does to you, too. But you loved mingling. . . .

CLAIRE: *(Shrugging her shoulders)* You'd better see whether everything's in order. Look, the key of the secretary was like this *(She arranges the key)* and, as Monsieur says—

SOLANGE: *(Violently)* You loved mingling your insults—

CLAIRE: He's always finding the maids' hairs all over the pinks and roses!

SOLANGE: And things about our private life with—

CLAIRE: With? With? With what? Say it! Go on, name it! The ceremony? Besides, we've no time to start a discussion now. She'll be back, back, back! But, Solange, this time we've got her. I envy you; I wish I could have seen the expression on her face when she heard about her lover's arrest. For once in my life, I did a good job. You've got to admit it. If it weren't for me, if it hadn't been for my anonymous letter, you'd have missed a pretty sight: the lover handcuffed and Madame in tears. It's enough to kill her. This morning she could hardly stand up.

SOLANGE: Fine. She can drop dead! And I'll inherit! Not to have to set foot again in that filthy garret, with those two idiots, that cook and that butler.

CLAIRE: I really liked our garret.

SOLANGE: Just to contradict me. Don't start getting sentimental about it. I loathe it and I see it as it really is, bare and mean. And shabby. But what of it! We're just scum!

CLAIRE: Ah! No, don't start that again. Better watch at the window. I can't see a thing. It's too dark outside.

SOLANGE: Let me talk. Let me get it out of my system. I liked the garret because it was plain and I didn't have to put on a show. No hangings to push aside, no rugs to shake, no furniture to caress—with my eyes or with a rag, no mirrors, no balcony. Nothing forced us to make pretty gestures. Don't worry, you'll be able to go on playing queen, playing at Marie Antoinette, strolling about the apartment at night.

CLAIRE: You're mad! I've never strolled about the apartment.

SOLANGE: *(Ironically)* Oh, no. Mademoiselle has never gone strolling! Wrapped in the curtains or the lace bedcover. Oh no! Looking at herself in the mirrors, strutting on the balcony at two in the morning, and greeting the populace which has turned out to parade beneath her windows. Never, oh no, never.

CLAIRE: But, Solange—

SOLANGE: It's too dark at night for spying on Madame, and you thought you were invisible on your balcony. What do you take me for? Don't try to tell me you walk in your sleep. At the stage we've reached you can admit it.

CLAIRE: But, Solange, you're shouting. Please, please lower your voice. Madame may come in without making a sound. . . . *(She runs to the window and lifts the curtain.)*

SOLANGE: All right, I've had my say. Let go of the curtains. Oh, I can't stand the way you lift them. Let go of them. It upsets me; that's how Monsieur did it when he was spying on the police, the morning he was arrested.

CLAIRE: So you're scared now? The slightest gesture makes you feel like a murderer trying to slip away by the service stairway.

SOLANGE: Go on, be sarcastic, work me up! Go on, be sarcastic! Nobody loves me! Nobody loves us!

CLAIRE: *She* does, *she* loves us. She's kind. Madame is kind! Madame adores us.

SOLANGE: She loves us the way she loves her armchair. Not even *that* much! Like her bidet, rather. Like her pink enamel lavatory seat. And we, we can't love one another. Filth. . . .

CLAIRE: Ah! . . .

SOLANGE: . . . doesn't love filth. D'you think I'm going to put up with it, that I'm going to keep playing this game and then at night go back to my folding cot? The game! Will we even be able to go on with it? And if I have to stop spitting on someone who calls me Claire, I'll simply choke! My spurt of saliva is my spray of diamonds!

CLAIRE: *(She stands up and cries.)* Speak more softly, please, please. Speak—speak of Madame's kindness.

SOLANGE: Her kindness, is it? It's easy to be kind, and smiling, and sweet—ah! that sweetness of hers!—when you're beautiful and rich. But what if you're only a maid? The best you can do is to give yourself airs while you're doing the cleaning or washing up. You twirl a feather duster like a fan. You make fancy gestures with the dishcloth. Or like *you*, you treat yourself to historical parades in Madame's apartment.

CLAIRE: Solange! You're starting again! What are you trying to do? We'll never calm down if you talk like that! I could say a thing or two about you.

SOLANGE: You? You?

CLAIRE: Yes, me. If I wanted to. Because, after all. . . .

SOLANGE: All? After all? What are you insinuating? It was you who started talking about that man. Claire, I hate you.

CLAIRE: Same to you and more! But if I wanted to provoke you I wouldn't have to use the milkman as an excuse. I've got something better on you and you know it.

SOLANGE: Who's going to get the better of who? Eh? Well, say something!

CLAIRE: Go on, start it! You hit first. It's you who's backing out, Solange. You don't dare accuse me of the worst: my letters. Pages and pages of them. The garret was littered with them. I invented the most fantastic stories and you used them for your own purposes. You frittered away my frenzy. Yesterday, when you were Madame, I could see how delighted you were at the chance they gave you to stow away on the *Lamartinière*, to flee France in the company of your lover—

SOLANGE: Claire—

CLAIRE: Your lover, to Devil's Island, to Guiana. You were delighted that my letters allowed you to be the prostitute kneeling at the feet of the thief. You were happy to sacrifice yourself, to bear the cross of the impenitent thief, to wipe his face, to stand by him, to take his place in the galleys so that he could rest. And you felt yourself growing. Your brow rose higher than mine, it rose above the palm trees.

SOLANGE: But what about you, just before, when you were talking about following him. . . .

CLAIRE: Right. I don't deny it. I took up where you left off. But with less violence than you. Even in the garret, amidst all the letters, you started swaying back and forth with the pitching of the boat.

SOLANGE: You didn't see yourself—

CLAIRE: I did. I'm more sensible than you. You're the one who concocted the story. Turn your head. Ha! If only you could see yourself, Solange. Your face is still lit up by the sun setting through the virgin forest! You're planning his escape! *(She laughs nervously.)* You certainly do work yourself up! But don't let it worry you; it would be cruel to disturb your blissful voyage. I hate you for other reasons, and you know what they are.

SOLANGE: *(Lowering her voice)* I'm not afraid of you. I know you hate me and that you're a sneak, but be careful now. I'm older than you.

CLAIRE: So what?—Older! And stronger too? You're trying to put me off by making me talk about that man. Hmph! You think I haven't found you out? You tried to kill her.

SOLANGE: Are you accusing me?

CLAIRE: Don't deny it. I saw you.

(A long silence)

And I was frightened. Frightened, Solange. Through her, it was me you were aiming at. I'm the one who's in danger. When we finish the ceremony, I'll protect my neck.

(A long silence. Solange shrugs her shoulders.)

SOLANGE: *(With decision)* Is that all? Yes, I did try. I wanted to free you. I couldn't bear it any longer. It made me suffocate to see you suffocating, to see you turning red and green, rotting away in that woman's bittersweetness. Blame me for it, you're right. I loved you too much. Had I killed her, you'd have been the first to denounce me. You'd have turned me over to the police, yes, you.

CLAIRE: *(She seizes her by the wrists.)* Solange. . . .

SOLANGE: *(Freeing herself)* What are *you* afraid of? It's *my* concern.

CLAIRE: Solange, my little sister, she'll be back soon.

SOLANGE: I didn't kill anyone. I was a coward, you realize. I did the best I could, but she turned over in her sleep. *(Rising exaltation)* She was breathing softly. She swelled out the sheets: it was Madame.

CLAIRE: Stop it.

SOLANGE: Now you want to stop me. You wanted to know, didn't you? Well, wait, I've got some more to tell you. You'll see what your sister's made of. What stuff she's made of. What a servant girl really is. I wanted to strangle her—

CLAIRE: Let me alone. Think of what comes after.

SOLANGE: Nothing comes after. I'm sick and tired of kneeling in pews. In church I'd have had the red velvet of abbesses or the stone of the penitents, but my bearing at least would have been noble. Look, just look at how she suffers. How she suffers in beauty. Grief transfigures her, doesn't it? Beautifies her? When she learned that her lover was a thief, she stood up to the police. She exulted. Now she is forlorn and splendid, supported under each arm by two devoted servants whose hearts bleed to see her grief. Did you see it? Her grief sparkling with the glint of her jewels, with the satin of her gowns, in the glow of the chandelier! Claire, I wanted to make up for the poverty of my grief by the splendor of my crime. Afterward, I'd have set fire to the lot.

CLAIRE: Solange, calm down. The fire might not have caught. You'd have been found out. You know what happens to incendiaries.

SOLANGE: I know everything. I kept my eye and ear to the keyhole. No servant ever listened at doors as I did. I know everything. Incendiary! It's a splendid title.

CLAIRE: Be quiet. I'm stifling. You're stifling me. *(She wants to open the window.)* Oh! Let's have some air!

SOLANGE: Get away from the window. Open the anteroom and the kitchen doors. *(Claire opens both doors.)* Go and see whether the water's boiling.

CLAIRE: All alone?

SOLANGE: Wait, all right, wait till she comes. She's bringing her stars, her tears, her smiles, her sighs. She'll corrupt us with her sweetness. *(The telephone rings. The two sisters listen.)*

CLAIRE: *(At the telephone)* Monsieur? It's Monsieur! . . . This is Claire, Monsieur. . . . *(Solange wants to hear too, but Claire pushes her away.)* Very well. I'll inform Madame. Madame will be overjoyed to hear that Monsieur is free. . . . Yes, Monsieur. . . . Very well. . . . Good-bye, Monsieur. *(She wants to hang up, but her hand trembles, and she lays the receiver on the table.)*

The Balcony

◄O►

Genet wrote the first version of The Balcony *and the first version of* The
Blacks *in the spring and summer of 1955.* The Balcony *takes place mainly in
Le Grand Balcon, a brothel in which clients act out their fantasies with whores.
The characters on stage make repeated references to the revolution that is taking
place offstage. The madam who heads this house of illusions is called Irma. One
of Irma's prostitutes, Chantal, escapes the whorehouse and joins the revolutionar-
ies, for whom she becomes the symbol of Liberty. When they take the palace and
presumably kill the Queen and her court, the Police Chief replaces these dignitar-
ies with their equivalents from* The Balcony: *Irma becomes the Queen; the
gas-company employee, the minor functionary, and the gendarme who pay to act
out their fantasies as judge, bishop, and general, are now appointed to those very
positions.*

For years Genet had wanted to write a play about Spain, and The Balcony
*grew out of this desire: "My point of departure was situated in Spain, Franco's
Spain, and the revolutionary who castrates himself was all those Republicans
when they had admitted their defeat. And then my play continued to grow in its
own direction and Spain in another." Certainly the Police Chief can be seen as a
reference to Franco, Roger to the republican revolutionaries, Chantal as the short-
lived Republic, and Irma as Spain itself. Genet was fascinated with two different
newspaper accounts he had read, one about Franco's plans to build a huge tomb
for himself in the Valley of the Fallen; the other story was about the Aga Khan's
projected tomb in Aswan, Egypt.* The Balcony *incorporates this theme in the
construction of a tomb by and for the still-living Police Chief.*

*The opening scenes of the play, given here, are the most brilliant and so inher-
ently theatrical that nothing that follows can top them. Although they take place
in a brothel, Genet did not want them to be tacky, and he was furious when the
lurid side of the text was emphasized in the world premiere. In April 1957,* The
Balcony *was staged in London at the Arts Theatre, a small, club production di-
rected by Peter Zadek. The Arts Theatre was chosen because, as a club, it did*

not fall under the aegis of the Lord Chamberlain, the censor in control of profes-
sional London theater.

When Genet saw Zadek's production during the dress rehearsal he went into a
fury. He announced, "I have been betrayed." He tried to restage the play, but
Zadek had him barred from the theater. When Genet returned to Paris the next
day, he gave a press conference and announced, "My play The Balcony *takes*
place in a 'house of prostitution,' but the characters belong as little to the reality
of a brothel as the characters in Hamlet *belong to the world of the court. . . .*
The real theme of the play is illusion. Everything is false, the General, the Arch-
bishop, the Police Chief, and everything must be treated with extreme delicacy.
But instead of ennobling the play, they've vulgarized it."

Genet was never content with The Balcony *himself, however. Between 1955*
and 1961 he published five different versions of the play. Although he wrote the
first draft with little editing, he rewrote the play almost obsessively. In the opin-
ion of the play's editor, Marc Barbezat, Genet, over a ten-year period, destroyed
the scripts with his incessant revisions. The scenes presented here are the ones he
touched the least because, from the very beginning, they were the most successful.

The play was rapturously received in the United States, where it opened at
New York's off-Broadway Circle in the Square early in March 1960. José Quin-
tero directed a cast that included a sexy Salome Jens as the General's horse and
Sylvia Miles as the whore posing as a thief. Quintero shortened the play radi-
cally, which may account for its success. By October 16, 1961, The Balcony, *with*
583 performances, had become the longest-running play in Off-Broadway history
up till then. It continued to play until the beginning of 1962, by which time it had
racked up 672 performances.

SCENE ONE

O N THE CEILING, *a chandelier, which will remain the same in each scene. The*
set seems to represent a sacristy, formed by three blood red, cloth folding screens. The one
at the rear has a built-in door. Above, a huge Spanish crucifix, drawn in trompe l'oeil.
On the right wall, a mirror, with a carved gilt frame, reflects an unmade bed which, if
the room were arranged logically, would be in the first rows of the orchestra. A table with
a large jug. A yellow armchair. On the chair, a pair of black trousers, a shirt and a
jacket. THE BISHOP, *in miter and gilded cope, is sitting in the chair. He is obviously*
larger than life. The role is played by an actor wearing tragedian's cothurni about twenty
inches high. His shoulders, on which the cope lies, are inordinately broadened so that
when the curtain rises he looks huge and stiff, like a scarecrow. He wears garish makeup.
At the side, a woman, rather young, highly madeup and wearing a lace dressing gown, is
drying her hands with a towel. Standing by is another woman, IRMA. *She is about forty,*

dark, severe-looking, and is wearing a black tailored suit and a hat with a tight string (like a chin strap).

THE BISHOP: *(Sitting in the chair, middle of the stage; in a low but fervent voice)* In truth, the mark of a prelate is not mildness or unction, but the most rigorous intelligence. Our heart is our undoing. We think we are master of our kindness; we are the slaves of a serene laxity. It is something quite other than intelligence that is involved. . . . *(He hesitates.)* It may be cruelty. And beyond that cruelty—and through it—a skillful, vigorous course toward Absence. Toward Death. God? *(Smiling)* I can read your mind! *(To his miter)* Miter, bishop's bonnet, when my eyes close for the last time, it is you that I shall see behind my eyelids, you, my beautiful gilded hat . . . you, my handsome ornaments, copes, laces. . . .

IRMA: *(Bluntly)* An agreement's an agreement. When a deal's been made. . . .
(Throughout the scene she hardly moves. She is standing very near the door.)

THE BISHOP: *(Very gently, waving her aside with a gesture)* And when the die is cast. . . .

IRMA: No. Twenty. Twenty and no nonsense. Or I'll lose my temper. And that's not like me. . . . Now, if you have any difficulties. . . .

THE BISHOP: *(Curtly, and tossing away the miter)* Thank you.

IRMA: And don't break anything. We need that. *(To the woman)* Put it away.
(She lays the miter on the table, near the jug.)

THE BISHOP: *(After a deep sigh)* I've been told that this house is going to be besieged. The rebels have already crossed the river.

IRMA: There's blood everywhere. . . . You can slip round behind the Archbishop's Palace. Then, down Fishmarket Street. . . .
(Suddenly a scream of pain, uttered by a woman offstage.)

IRMA: *(Annoyed)* But I told them to be quiet. Good thing I remembered to cover the windows with padded curtains.
(Suddenly amiable, insidious)
Well, and what was it this evening? A blessing? A prayer? A mass? A perpetual adoration?

THE BISHOP: *(Gravely)* Let's not talk about that now. It's over. I'm concerned only about getting home. . . . You say the city's splashed with blood. . . .

THE WOMAN: There was a blessing, Madame. Then, my confession. . . .

IRMA: And after that?

THE BISHOP: That'll do!

THE WOMAN: That was all. At the end, my absolution.

IRMA: Won't anyone be able to witness it? Just once?

THE BISHOP: *(Frightened)* No, no. Those things must remain secret, and they shall. It's indecent enough to talk about them while I'm being undressed. Nobody. And all the doors must be closed. Firmly closed, shut, buttoned, laced, hooked, sewn. . . .

IRMA: I merely asked. . . .

THE BISHOP: Sewn, Madame.

IRMA: *(Annoyed)* You'll allow me at least, won't you, to feel a little uneasy . . . professionally? I said twenty.

THE BISHOP: *(His voice suddenly grows clear and sharp, as if he were awakening. He displays a little annoyance.)* We didn't tire ourselves. Barely six sins, and far from my favorite ones.

THE WOMAN: Six, but deadly ones! And it was a job finding *those.*

THE BISHOP: *(Uneasy)* What? You mean they were false?

THE WOMAN: They were real, all right! I mean it was a job committing them. If only you realized what it takes, what a person has to go through, in order to reach the point of disobedience.

THE BISHOP: I can imagine, my child. The order of the world is so lax that you can do as you please there—or almost. But if your sins were false, you may say so now.

IRMA: Oh no! I can hear you complaining already the next time you come. No. They were real. *(To the woman)* Untie his laces. Take off his shoes. And when you dress him, be careful he doesn't catch cold. *(To the Bishop)* Would you like a toddy, a hot drink?

THE BISHOP: Thank you. I haven't time. I must be going.
    (Dreamily)
Yes, six, but deadly ones!

IRMA: Come here, we'll undress you!

THE BISHOP: *(Pleading, almost on his knees)* No, no, not yet.

IRMA: It's time. Come on! Quick! Make it snappy!
    (While they talk, the women undress him. Or rather they merely remove pins and untie cords that seem to secure the cope, stole, and surplice.)

THE BISHOP: *(To the woman)* About the sins, you really did commit them?

THE WOMAN: I did.

THE BISHOP: You really made the gestures? All the gestures?

THE WOMAN: I did.

THE BISHOP: When you moved toward me with your face forward, was it really aglow with the light of the flames?

THE WOMAN: It was.

THE BISHOP: And when my ringed hand came down on your forehead, forgiving it. . . .

THE WOMAN: It was.

THE BISHOP: And when my gaze pierced your lovely eyes?

THE WOMAN: It was.

IRMA: Was there at least a glimmer of repentance in her lovely eyes, my Lord?

THE BISHOP: *(Standing up)* A fleeting glimmer. But was I seeking repentance in them? I saw there the greedy longing for transgression. In flooding it, evil all at once baptized it. Her big eyes opened on the abyss . . . a deathly pallor lit up—yes, Madame—lit up her face. But our holiness lies only in our being able to forgive you your sins. Even if they're only make-believe.

THE WOMAN: *(Suddenly coy)* And what if my sins were real?

THE BISHOP: *(In a different, less theatrical tone)* You're mad! I hope you really didn't do all that!

IRMA: *(To the Bishop)* Don't listen to her. As for her sins, don't worry. Here there's no. . . .

THE BISHOP: *(Interrupting her)* I'm quite aware of that. Here there's no possibility of doing evil. You live in evil. In the absence of remorse. How could you do evil? The Devil makes believe. That's how one recognizes him. He's the great Actor. And that's why the Church has anathematized actors.

THE WOMAN: Reality frightens you, doesn't it?

THE BISHOP: If your sins were real, they would be crimes, and I'd be in a fine mess.

THE WOMAN: Would you go to the police?

> *(IRMA continues to undress him. However, he still has the cope on his shoulders.)*

IRMA: Stop plaguing her with all those questions.

> *(The same terrible scream is heard again.)*

They're at it again! I'll go and shut them up.

THE BISHOP: That wasn't a make-believe scream.

IRMA: *(Anxiously)* I don't know. . . . Who knows and what does it matter?

THE BISHOP: *(Going slowly to the mirror. He stands in front of it)* Now answer, mirror, answer me. Do I come here to discover evil and innocence? *(To Irma, very gently)* Leave the room! I want to be by myself.

IRMA: It's late. And the later it gets, the more dangerous it'll be . . .

THE BISHOP: *(Pleading)* Just one more minute.

IRMA: You've been here two hours and twenty minutes. In other words, twenty minutes too long. . . .

THE BISHOP: *(Suddenly incensed)* I want to be by myself. Eavesdrop, if you want to—I know you do, anyway—and don't come back till I've finished. *(The two women leave with a sigh, looking as if they were out of patience.* THE BISHOP *remains alone.)*

THE BISHOP: *(After making a visible effort to calm himself, in front of the mirror and holding his surplice)* Now answer, mirror, answer me. Do I come here to discover evil and innocence? And in your gilt-edged glass, what was I? Never—I affirm it before God Who sees me—I never desired the episcopal throne. To become bishop, to work my way up—by means of virtues or vices—would have been to turn away from the ultimate dignity of bishop. I shall explain: *(THE BISHOP speaks in a tone of great precision, as if pursuing a line of logical reasoning.)* In order to become a bishop, I should have had to make a zealous effort not to be one, but to do what would have resulted in my being one. Having become a bishop, in order to be one I should have had—in order to be one for myself, of course!—I should have had to be constantly aware of being one so as to perform my function. *(He seizes the flap of his surplice and kisses it.)* Oh laces, laces, fashioned by a thousand little hands to veil ever so many panting bosoms, buxom bosoms, and faces, and hair, you illustrate me with branches and flowers! Let us continue. But—there's the crux!

(He laughs.)

So I speak Latin!—a function is a function. It's not a mode of being. But a bishop—that's a mode of being. It's a trust. A burden. Miters, lace, gold cloth and glass trinkets, genuflexions. . . . To hell with the function!

(Crackling of machine-gun fire.)

IRMA: *(Putting her head through the door)* Have you finished?

THE BISHOP: For Christ's sake, leave me alone. Get the hell out! I'm probing myself.

(IRMA shuts the door.)

THE BISHOP: *(To the mirror)* The majesty, the dignity, that light up my person, do not emanate from the attributions of my function—no more, good heavens! than from my personal merits—the majesty, the dignity that light me up come from a more mysterious brilliance: the fact that the bishop precedes me. Do I make myself clear, mirror, gilded image, ornate as a box of Mexican cigars? And I wish to be bishop in solitude, for appearance alone. . . . And in order to destroy all function, I want to cause a scandal and feel you up, you slut, you bitch, you trollop, you tramp. . . .

IRMA: *(Entering)* That'll do now. You've got to leave.

THE BISHOP: You're crazy! I haven't finished.

(Both women have entered.)

IRMA: I'm not trying to pick an argument, and you know it, but you've no time to waste. . . .

THE BISHOP: *(Ironically)* What you mean is that you need the room for someone else and you've got to arrange the mirrors and jugs.

IRMA: *(Very irritated)* That's no business of yours. I've given you every attention while you've been here. And I repeat that it's dangerous for anyone to loiter in the streets.

(Sound of gunfire in the distance.)

THE BISHOP: *(Bitterly)* That's not true. You don't give a damn about my safety. When the job's finished, you don't give a damn about anyone!

IRMA: *(To the girl)* Stop listening to him and undress him.

IRMA: *(To the Bishop, who has stepped down from his cothurni and has now assumed the normal size of an actor, of the most ordinary of actors)* Lend a hand. You're stiff.

THE BISHOP: *(With a foolish look)* Stiff? I'm stiff? A solemn stiffness! Final immobility. . . .

IRMA: *(To the girl)* Hand him his jacket. . . .

THE BISHOP: *(Looking at his clothes, which are heaped on the floor)* Ornaments, laces, through you I re-enter myself. I reconquer a domain. I beleaguer a very ancient place from which I was driven. I install myself in a clearing where suicide at last becomes possible. The judgment depends on me, and here I stand, face to face with my death.

IRMA: That's all very fine, but you've got to go. You left your car at the front door, near the power station.

THE BISHOP: *(To Irma)* Because our Chief of Police, that wretched incompetent, is letting us be slaughtered by the rabble!

(Turning to the mirror and declaiming) Ornaments! Miters! Laces! You, above all, oh gilded cope, you protect me from the world. Where are my legs, where are my arms? Under your scalloped, lustrous flaps, what have my hands been doing? Fit only for fluttering gestures, they've become mere stumps of wings—not of angels, but of partridges!—rigid cope, you make it possible for the most tender and luminous sweetness to ripen in warmth and darkness. My charity, a charity that will flood the world—it was under this carapace that I distilled it. . . . Would my hand emerge at times, knifelike, to bless? Or cut, mow down? My hand, the head of a turtle, would push aside the flaps. A turtle or a cautious snake? And go back into the rock. Underneath, my hand would dream. . . . Ornaments, gilded copes. . . .

(The stage moves from left to right, as if it were plunging into the wings. The following set then appears.)

SCENE TWO

Same chandelier. Three brown folding screens. Bare walls. At right, same mirror, in which is reflected the same unmade bed as in the first scene. A woman, young and beautiful, seems to be chained, with her wrists bound. Her muslin dress is torn. Her breasts are visible. Standing in front of her is the executioner. He is a giant, stripped to the waist. Very muscular. His whip has been slipped through the loop of his belt, in back, so that he seems to have a tail. A JUDGE, who, when he stands up, will seem larger than life (he, too, is mounted on cothurni, which are invisible beneath his robe, and his face is made up) is crawling, on his stomach, toward the woman, who shrinks as he approaches.

THE THIEF: *(Holding out her foot)* Not yet! Lick it! Lick it first. . . .

(THE JUDGE makes an effort to continue crawling. Then he stands up and, slowly and painfully, though apparently happy, goes and sits down on a stool. THE THIEF (the woman described above) drops her domineering attitude and becomes humble.)

THE JUDGE: *(Severely)* For you're a thief! You were caught. . . . Who? The police. . . . Have you forgotten that your movements are hedged about by a strong and subtle network, my strong-arm cops? They're watchful, swivel-eyed insects that lie in wait for you. All of you! And they bring you captive, all of you, to the Bench. . . . What have you to say for yourself?

You were caught. . . . Under your skirt. . . . *(To the Executioner)* Put your hand under her skirt. You'll find the pocket, the notorious Kangaroo Pocket. . . . *(To the Thief)* that you fill with any old junk you pick up. Because you're an idiot to boot. . . . *(To the Executioner)* What was there in that notorious Kangaroo Pocket? In that enormous paunch?

THE EXECUTIONER: Bottles of scent, my Lord, a flashlight, a bottle of Fly-tox, some oranges, several pairs of socks, bearskins, a Turkish towel, a scarf. *(To the Judge)* Do you hear me? I said: a scarf.

THE JUDGE: *(With a start)* A scarf? Aha, so that's it? Why the scarf? Eh? What were you going to do with it? Whom were you planning to strangle? Answer. Who? . . . Are you a thief or a strangler? *(Very gently, imploringly)* Tell me, my child, I beg of you, tell me you're a thief.

THE THIEF: Yes, my Lord.

THE EXECUTIONER: No!

THE THIEF: *(Looking at him in surprise)* No?

THE EXECUTIONER: That's for later.

THE THIEF: Eh?

THE EXECUTIONER: I mean the confession is supposed to come later. Plead not guilty.

THE THIEF: What, and get beaten again!

THE JUDGE: *(Mealymouthed)* Exactly, my child: and get beaten. You must first deny, then admit and repent. I want to see hot tears gush from your lovely eyes. Oh! I want you to be drenched in them. The power of tears! . . . Where's my statute book? *(He fishes under his robe and pulls out a book.)*

THE THIEF: I've already cried. . . .

THE JUDGE: *(He seems to be reading.)* Under the blows. I want tears of repentance. When I see you wet as a meadow I'll be utterly satisfied!

THE THIEF: It's not easy. I tried to cry before. . . .

THE JUDGE: *(No longer reading. In a half-theatrical, almost familiar tone)* You're quite young. Are you new here? *(Anxiously)* At least you're not a minor?

THE THIEF: Oh no, sir.

THE JUDGE: Call me my Lord. How long have you been here?

THE EXECUTIONER: Since the day before yesterday, my Lord.

THE JUDGE: *(Reassuming the theatrical tone and resuming the reading)* Let her speak. I like that pulling voice of hers, that voice without resonance. . . . Look here: you've got to be a model thief if I'm to be a model judge. If you're a fake thief, I become a fake judge. Is that clear?

THE THIEF: Oh yes, my Lord.

THE JUDGE: *(He continues reading.)* Good. Thus far everything has gone off well. My executioner has hit hard . . . for he too has his function. We are bound together, you, he, and I. For example, if he didn't hit, how could I stop him from hitting? Therefore, he must strike so that I can intervene and demonstrate my authority. And you must deny your guilt so that he can beat you.

(A noise is heard, as of something having fallen in the next room. In a natural tone)

What's that? Are all the doors firmly shut? Can anyone see us, or hear us?

THE EXECUTIONER: No, no, you needn't worry. I bolted the door.

(He goes to examine a huge bolt on the rear door.)

And the corridor's out of bounds.

THE JUDGE: *(In a natural tone)* Are you sure?

THE EXECUTIONER: You can take my word for it.

(He puts his hand into his pocket.)

Can I have a smoke?

THE JUDGE: *(In a natural tone)* The smell of tobacco inspires me. Smoke away.

(Same noise as before.)

Oh, what *is* that? What *is* it? Can't they leave me in peace?

(He gets up.)

What's going on?

THE EXECUTIONER: *(Curtly)* Nothing at all. Someone must have dropped something. You're getting nervous.

THE JUDGE: *(In a natural tone)* That may be, but my nervousness makes me aware of things. It keeps me on the alert.

(He gets up and moves towards the wall.)

May I have a look?

THE EXECUTIONER: Just a quick one, because it's getting late.

(THE EXECUTIONER shrugs his shoulders and exchanges a wink with the Thief.)

THE JUDGE: *(After looking)* It's lit up. Brightly lit, but empty.

THE EXECUTIONER: *(Shrugging his shoulders)* Empty!

THE JUDGE: *(In an even more familiar tone)* You seem anxious. Has anything new happened?

THE EXECUTIONER: This afternoon, just before you arrived, the rebels took three key positions. They set fire to several places. Not a single fireman came out. Everything went up in flames. The Palace. . . .

THE JUDGE: What about the Chief of Police? Twiddling his thumbs as usual?

THE THIEF: There's been no news of him for four hours. If he can get away, he's sure to come here. He's expected at any moment.

THE JUDGE: *(To the Thief, and sitting down)* In any case, he'd better not plan to come by way of Queen's Bridge. It was blown up last night.

THE THIEF: We know that. We heard the explosion from here.

THE JUDGE: *(Resuming his theatrical tone. He reads the statute book.)* All right. Let's get on with it. Thus, taking advantage of the sleep of the just, taking advantage of a moment's inattention, you rob them, you ransack, you pilfer and purloin. . . .

THE THIEF: No, my Lord, never. . . .

THE EXECUTIONER: Shall I tan her hide?

THE THIEF: *(Crying out)* Arthur!

THE EXECUTIONER: What's eating you? Don't address me. Answer his Lordship. And call me Mr. Executioner.

THE THIEF: Yes, Mr. Executioner.

THE JUDGE: *(Reading)* I condinue: did you steal?

THE THIEF: I did, I did, my Lord.

THE JUDGE: *(Reading)* Good. Now answer quickly, and to the point: what else did you steal?

THE THIEF: Bread, because I was hungry.

THE JUDGE: *(He draws himself up and lays down the book.)* Sublime! Sublime function! I'll have all that to judge. Oh, child, you reconcile me with the world. A judge! I'm going to be judge of your acts! On me depends the weighing, the balance. The world is an apple. I cut it in two: the good, the bad. And you agree, thank you, you agree to be the bad! *(Facing the audience)* Right before your eyes: nothing in my hands, nothing up my sleeve, remove the rot and cast it off. But it's a painful occupation. If every judgment were delivered seriously, each one would cost me my life. That's why I'm dead. I inhabit that region of exact freedom. I, King of Hell, weigh those who are dead, like me. She's a dead person, like myself.

THE THIEF: You frighten me, sir.

THE JUDGE: *(Very bombastically)* Be still. In the depths of Hell I sort out the humans who venture there. Some to the flames, the others to the boredom of the fields of asphodel. You, thief, spy, she-dog, Minos is speaking to you, Minos weighs you. *(To the Executioner)* Cerberus?

THE EXECUTIONER: *(Imitating the dog)* Bow-wow, bow-wow!

THE JUDGE: You're handsome! And the sight of a fresh victim makes you even handsomer. *(He curls up the Executioner's lips.)* Show your fangs. Dreadful. White. *(Suddenly he seems anxious. To the Thief)* But at least you're not lying about those thefts—you did commit them, didn't you?

THE EXECUTIONER: Don't worry. She committed them, all right. She wouldn't have dared not to. I'd have made her.

THE JUDGE: I'm almost happy. Continue. What did you steal? *(Suddenly, machine-gun fire.)*

THE JUDGE: There's simply no end to it. Not a moment's rest.

THE THIEF: I told you: the rebellion has spread all over the north of the city. . . .

THE EXECUTIONER: Shut up!

THE JUDGE: *(Irritated)* Are you going to answer, yes or no? What else have you stolen? Where? When? How? How much? Why? For whom?

THE THIEF: I very often entered houses when the maids were off. I used the tradesmen's entrance. . . . I stole from drawers, I broke into children's piggy banks. *(She is visibly trying to find words.)* Once I dressed up as a lady. I put on a dark brown suit, a black straw hat with cherries, a veil, and a pair of black shoes—with Cuban heels—then I went in. . . .

THE JUDGE: *(In a rush)* Where? Where? Where? Where—where—where? Where did you go in?

THE THIEF: I can't remember. Forgive me.

THE EXECUTIONER: Shall I let her have it?

THE JUDGE: Not yet. *(To the girl)* Where did you go in? Tell me where?

THE THIEF: *(In a panic):* But I swear to you, I don't remember.

THE EXECUTIONER: Shall I let her have it? Shall I, my Lord?

THE JUDGE: *(To the Executioner, and going up to him)* Ah! ah! Your pleasure depends on me. You like to thrash, eh? I', pleased with you, Executioner! Masterly mountain of meat, hunk of beef that's set in motion at a word from me! *(He pretends to look at himself in the Executioner.)* Mirror that glorifies me! Image that I can touch, I love you. Never would I have the strength or skill to leave streaks of fire on her back. Besides, what could I do with such strength and skill? *(He touches him.)* Are you there? You're all there, my huge arm, too heavy for me, too big, too fat for my shoulder, walking at my side all by itself! Arm, hundredweight of meat, without you I'd be nothing. . . . *(To the Thief)* And without you too, my child. You're my two perfect complements. . . . Ah, what a fine trio we make! *(To the Thief)* But you, you have a privilege that he hasn't, nor I either, that of priority. My being a judge is an emanation of your being a thief. You need only refuse—but you'd better not!—need only refuse to be who you are—what you are, therefore who you are—for me to cease to be . . . to vanish, evaporated. Burst. Volatilized. Denied. Hence: good born of. . . . What then? What then? But you won't refuse, will you? You won't refuse to be a thief? That would be wicked. It would be criminal. You'd deprive me of being! *(Imploringly)* Say it, my child, my love, you won't refuse?

THE THIEF: *(Coyly)* I might.

THE JUDGE: What's that? What's that you say? You'd refuse? Tell me where. And tell me again what you've stolen.

THE THIEF: *(Curtly, and getting up)* I won't.

THE JUDGE: Tell me where. Don't be cruel. . . .

THE THIEF: Your tone is getting too familiar. I won't have it!

THE JUDGE: Miss. . . . Madame. I beg of you. *(He falls to his knees.)* Look, I beseech you. Don't leave me in this position, waiting to be a judge. If there were no judge, what would become of us, but what if there were no thieves?

THE THIEF: *(Ironically)* And what if there weren't?

THE JUDGE: It would be awful. But you won't do that to me, will you? Please understand me: I don't mind your hiding, for as long as you can and as long as my nerves can bear it, behind the refusal to confess—it's all right to be mean and make me yearn, even prance, make me dance, drool, sweat, whinny with impatience, crawl . . . do you want me to crawl?

THE EXECUTIONER: *(To the Judge)* Crawl.

THE JUDGE: I'm proud!

THE EXECUTIONER: *(Threateningly)* Crawl!

    (THE JUDGE, who was on his knees, lies flat on his stomach and crawls slowly toward the Thief. As he crawls forward, THE THIEF moves back.)

THE EXECUTIONER: Good. Continue.

THE JUDGE: *(To the Thief)* You're quite right, you rascal, to make me crawl after my judgeship, but if you were to refuse for good, you hussy, it would be criminal. . . .

THE THIEF: *(Haughtily)* Call me Madame, and ask politely.

THE JUDGE: Will I get what I want?

THE THIEF: *(Coyly)* It costs a lot—stealing does.

THE JUDGE: I'll pay! I'll pay whatever I have to, Madame. But if I no longer had to divide the Good from the Evil, of what use would I be? I ask you?

THE THIEF: I ask myself.

THE JUDGE: *(Is infinitely sad)* A while ago I was going to be Minos. My Cerberus was barking. *(To the Executioner)* Do you remember? *(THE EXECUTIONER interrupts the Judge by cracking his whip.)* You were so cruel, so mean! So good! And me, I was pitiless. I was going to fill Hell with the souls of the damned, to fill prisons. Prisons! Prisons! Prisons, dungeons, blessed places where evil is impossible since they are the crossroads of all the malediction in the world. One cannot commit evil in evil. Now, what I desire above all is not to condemn, but to judge. . . . *(He tries to get up.)*

THE EXECUTIONER: Crawl! And hurry up, I've got to go and get dressed.

THE JUDGE: *(To the girl)* Madame! Madame, please, I beg of you. I'll willing to lick your shoes, but tell me you're a thief. . . .

THE THIEF: *(In a cry)* Not yet! Lick! Lick! Lick first!

    (The stage moves from left to right, as at the end of the preceding scene, and plunges into the right wing. In the distance, machine-gun fire.)

SCENE THREE

Three dark green folding screens, arranged as in the preceding scenes. The same chandelier. The same mirror reflecting the unmade bed. On an armchair, a horse of the kind used by folk dancers, with a little kilted skirt. In the room, a timid-looking gentleman: the GENERAL. *He removes his jacket, then his bowler hat and his gloves.* IRMA *is near him.*

THE GENERAL: *(He points to the hat, jacket, and gloves.)* Have that cleared out.

IRMA: It'll be folded and wrapped.

THE GENERAL: Have it removed from sight.

IRMA: It'll be put away. Even burned.

THE GENERAL: Yes, yes, of course, I'd like it to burn! Like cities at twilight.

IRMA: Did you notice anything on the way?

THE GENERAL: I ran very serious risks. The populace has blown up dams. Whole areas are flooded. The arsenal in particular. So that all the powder supplies are wet. And the weapons rusty. I had to make some rather wide detours—though I didn't trip over a single drowned body.

IRMA: I wouldn't take the liberty of asking you your opinions. Everyone is free, and I'm not concerned with politics.

THE GENERAL: Then let's talk of something else. The important thing is how I'm going to get out of this place. It'll be late by the time I leave. . . .

IRMA: About it's being late. . . .

THE GENERAL: That does it.

(He reaches into his pocket, takes out some bank notes, counts them and gives some to IRMA. She keeps them in her hand.)

THE GENERAL: I'm not keen about being shot down in the dark when I leave. For, of course, there won't be anyone to escort me?

IRMA: I'm afraid not. Unfortunately Arthur's not free. *(A long pause)*

THE GENERAL: *(Suddenly impatient)* But . . . isn't she coming?

IRMA: I can't imagine what she's doing. I gave instructions that everything was to be ready by the time you arrived. The horse is already here. . . . I'll ring.

THE GENERAL: Don't, I'll attend to that. *(He rings.)* I like to ring! Ringing's authoritative. Ah, to ring out commands.

IRMA: In a little while, General. Oh, I'm so sorry, here am I giving you your rank. . . . In a little while you'll. . . .

THE GENERAL: Sh! Don't say it.

IRMA: You have such force, such youth! such dash!

THE GENERAL: And spurs. Will I have spurs? I said they were to be fixed to my boots. Oxblood boots, right?

IRMA: Yes, General. And patent leather.

THE GENERAL: Oxblood. Patent leather, very well, but with mud?

IRMA: With mud and perhaps a little blood. I've had the decorations prepared.

THE GENERAL: Authentic ones?

IRMA: Authentic ones. *(Suddenly a woman's long scream)*

THE GENERAL: What's that?

(He starts going to the right wall and is already bending down to look, as if there were a small crack, but IRMA steps in front of him.)

IRMA: Nothing. There's always some carelessness, on both sides.

THE GENERAL: But that cry? A woman's cry. A call for help perhaps? My heart skips a beat. . . . I spring forward. . . .

IRMA: *(Icily)* I want no trouble here. Calm down. For the time being, you're in mufti.

THE GENERAL: That's right.

(A woman's scream again)

THE GENERAL: All the same, it's disturbing. Besides, it'll be awkward.

IRMA: What on earth can she be doing?

(She goes to ring, but by the rear door enters a very beautiful young woman, red-headed, hair undone, disheveled. Her bosom is almost bare. She is wearing a black

corset, black stockings, and very high heeled shoes. She is holding a general's uniform, complete with sword, cocked hat, and boots.)

THE GENERAL: *(Severely)* So you finally got here? Half an hour late. That's more than's needed to lose a battle.

IRMA: She'll redeem herself, General, I know her.

THE GENERAL: *(Looking at the boots)* What about the blood? I don't see any blood.

IRMA: It dried. Don't forget that it's the blood of your past battles. Well, then, I'll leave you. Do you have everything you need?

THE GENERAL: *(Looking to the right and left)* You're forgetting. . . .

IRMA: Good God! Yes. I was forgetting.

(She lays on the chair the towels she has been carrying on her arm. Then she leaves by the rear. THE GENERAL goes to the door, then locks it. But no sooner is the door closed than someone knocks. THE GIRL goes to open it. Behind, and standing slightly back, THE EXECUTIONER, sweating, wiping himself with a towel.)

THE EXECUTIONER: Is Mme Irma here?

THE GIRL: *(Curtly)* In the Rose Garden. *(Correcting herself)* I'm sorry, in the Funeral Chapel.

(She closes the door.)

THE GENERAL: *(Irritated)* I'll be left in peace, I hope. And you're late. Where the hell were you? Didn't they give you your feed bag? You're smiling, are you? Smiling at your rider? You recognize his hand, gentle but firm? *(He strokes her.)* My proud steed! My handsome mare, we've had many a spirited gallop together!

THE GIRL: And that's not all! I want to trip through the world with my nervous legs and well-shod hooves. Take off your trousers and shoes so I can dress you.

THE GENERAL: *(He has taken the cane.)* All right, but first, down on your knees! Come on, come on, bend you knees, bend them. . . .

(THE GIRL rears, utters a whinny of pleasure and kneels like a circus horse before the General.)

THE GENERAL: Bravo! Bravo, Dove! You haven't forgotten a thing. And now, you're going to help me and answer my questions. It's fitting and proper for a nice filly to help her master unbutton himself and take off his gloves, and to be at his beck and call. Now start by untying my laces.

(During the entire scene that follows, THE GIRL helps THE GENERAL remove his clothes and then dress up as a general. When he is completely dressed, he will be seen to have taken on gigantic proportions, by means of trick effects: invisible footgear, broadened shoulders, excessive makeup.)

THE GIRL: Left foot still swollen?

THE GENERAL: Yes. It's my leading foot. The one that prances. Like your hoof when you toss your head.

THE GIRL: What am I doing? Unbutton yourself.

THE GENERAL: Are you a horse or an illiterate? If you're a horse, you toss your head. Help me. Pull. Don't pull so hard. See here, you're not a plough horse.

THE GIRL: I do what I have to do.

THE GENERAL: Are you rebelling? Already? Wait till I'm ready. When I put the bit into your mouth. . . .

THE GIRL: Oh no, not that.

THE GENERAL: A general reprimanded by his horse! You'll have the bit, the bridle, the harness, the saddlegirth, and I, in boots and helmet, will whip and plunge!

THE GIRL: The bit is awful. It makes the gums and the corners of the lips bleed. I'll drool blood.

THE GENERAL: Foam pink and spit fire! But what a gallop! Along the rye fields, through the alfalfa, over the meadows and dusty roads, over hill and dale, awake or asleep, from dawn to twilight and from twilight. . . .

THE GIRL: Tuck in your shirt. Pull up your braces. It's quite a job dressing a victorious general who's to be buried. Do you want the saber?

THE GENERAL: Let it lie on the table, like Lafayette's. Conspicuously, but hide the clothes. Where? How should *I* know? Surely there's a hiding place somewhere.

(THE GIRL bundles up his clothes and hides them behind the armchair.)

THE GENERAL: The tunic? Good. Got all the medals? Count 'em.

THE GIRL: *(After counting them, very quickly)* They're all here, sir.

THE GENERAL: What about the war? Where's the war?

THE GIRL: *(Very softly)* It's approaching, sir. It's evening in an apple orchard. The sky is calm and pink. The earth is bathed in a sudden peace—the moan of doves—the peace that precedes battles. The air is very still. An apple has fallen to the grass. A yellow apple. Things are holding their breath. War is declared. The evening is very mild. . . .

THE GENERAL: But suddenly?

THE GIRL: We're at the edge of the meadow. I keep myself from flinging out, from whinnying. Your thighs are warm and you're pressing my flanks. Death. . . .

THE GENERAL: But suddenly?

THE GIRL: Death has pricked up her ears. She puts a finger to her lips, asking for silence. Things are lit up with an ultimate goodness. You yourself no longer heed my presence. . . .

THE GENERAL: But suddenly?

THE GIRL: Button up by yourself, sir. The water lay motionless in the pools. The wind itself was awaiting an order to unfurl the flags. . . .

THE GENERAL: But suddenly?

THE GIRL: Suddenly? Eh? Suddenly? *(She seems to be trying to find the right words.)* Ah yes, suddenly all was fire and sword! Widows! Miles of crepe had to be woven to put on the standards. The mothers and wives remained dry-eyed behind their veils. The bells came clattering down the bombed towers. As I rounded a corner I was frightened by a blue cloth. I reared, but, steadied by your gentle and masterful hand, I ceased to quiver. I started forward again. How I loved you, my hero!

THE GENERAL: But . . . the dead? Weren't there any dead?

THE GIRL: The soldiers died kissing the standard. You were all victory and kindness. One evening, remember. . . .

THE GENERAL: I was so mild that I began to snow. To snow on my men, to shroud them in the softest of winding-sheets. To snow. Moskova!

THE GIRL: Splinters of shell had gashed the lemons. Now death was in action. She moved nimbly from one to the other, deepening a wound, dimming an eye, tearing off an arm, opening an artery, discoloring a face, cutting short a cry, a song. Death was ready to drop. Finally, exhausted, herself dead with fatigue, she grew drowsy and rested lightly on your shoulder, where she fell asleep.

THE GENERAL: *(Drunk with joy)* Stop, stop, it's not time for that yet, but I feel it'll be magnificent. The crossbelt? Good. *(He looks at himself in the mirror.)* Austerlitz! General! Man of war and in full regalia, behold me in my pure appearance. Nothing, no contingent trails behind me. I appear, purely and simply. If I went through wars without dying, went through sufferings without dying, if I was prompted, without dying, it was for this minute close to death.

(Suddenly he stops; he seems troubled by an idea.)

Tell me, Dove?

THE GIRL: What is it, sir?

THE GENERAL: What's the Chief of Police been doing?

(THE GIRL shakes her head.)

Nothing? Still nothing? In short, everything slips through his fingers. And what about us, are we wasting our time?

THE GIRL: *(Imperiously)* Not at all. And, in any case, it's no business of ours. Continue. You were saying: for this minute close to death . . . and then?

THE GENERAL: *(Hesitating)* . . . close to death . . . where I shall be nothing, though reflected *ad infinitum* in these mirrors, nothing but my image. . . . Quite right, comb your mane. Curry yourself. I require a well-groomed filly. So, in a little while, to the blare of trumpets, we shall descend—I on your back—to death and glory, for I am about to die. It is indeed a descent to the grave. . . .

THE GIRL: But, sir, you've been dead since yesterday.

THE GENERAL: I know . . . but a formal and picturesque descent, by unexpected stairways. . . .

THE GIRL: You are a dead general, but an eloquent one.

THE GENERAL: Because I'm dead, prating horse. What is now speaking, and so beautifully, is Example. I am now only the image of my former self. Your turn, now. Lower your head and hide your eyes, for I want to be a general in solitude. Not even for myself, but for my image, and my image for its image, and so on. In short, we'll be among equals. Dove, are you ready?

(THE GIRL nods.)

Come now. Put on your bay dress, horse, my fine Arab steed.

(THE GENERAL slips the mock-horse over her head. Then he cracks his whip.)

We're off!

(He bows to his image in the mirror.)

Farewell, general!

(Then he stretches out in the armchair with his feet on another chair and bows to the audience, holding himself rigid as a corpse. THE GIRL places herself in front of the chair and, on the spot, makes the movements of a horse in motion.)

THE GIRL: The procession has begun. . . . We're passing through the City. . . . We're going along the river. I'm sad. . . . The sky is overcast. The nation weeps for that splendid hero who died in battle. . . .

THE GENERAL: *(Starting)* Dove!

THE GIRL: *(Turning around, in tears)* Sir?

THE GENERAL: Add that I died with my boots on!

(He then resumes his pose.)

THE GIRL: My hero died with his boots on! The procession continues. Your aides-de-camp precede me. . . . Then come I, Dove, your war-horse. . . . The military band plays a funeral march. . . .

(Marching in place, THE GIRL sings Chopin's Funeral March, *which is continued by an invisible orchestra [with brasses]. Far off, machine-gun fire.)*

IV

ESSAY

The Studio of Alberto Giacometti

◄○►

Genet published this essay for the first time in a catalogue, Behind the Looking Glass, *published by the Maeght Gallery in 1957 to coincide with an exhibition of Giacometti's work in Paris. The essay begins on a hushed, dejected—even a terrified—note as Genet remarks on our powerlessness over the visual world. He observes that Giacometti makes the visual world all the more intolerable because he shows us what would be left of humanity if everything false were stripped away.*

Genet was fascinated throughout his writing career with death as a theme, and he sees Giacometti as a sculptor whose works should be buried below ground as offerings to the dead rather than erected above ground to be viewed by the living. At about the same time Genet wrote this essay, he proposed in another essay that theatrical works should be performed just once, in a cemetery, and for the dead.

The friendship between Giacometti and Genet flourished between 1954 and 1957. Meeting Giacometti was certainly one factor that led to Genet's return to creativity, which occurred in 1955. Genet's three full-length plays and his two best essays, The Studio of Alberto Giacometti *and* The High-Wire Artist, *were composed between 1955 and 1957, although he continued to revise the plays after this two-year period.*

Genet met Giacometti through Sartre, who had devoted a major essay to the sculptor in 1954. Giacometti liked Genet's sparkling, mordant conversation, and this essay records some of their blunt, amusing exchanges. Giacometti was initially attracted to Genet's bald head (Giacometti thought hair was a lie), turned-up nose, and intense eyes. When he first saw Genet from a distance in a café, he wanted the writer to pose for him.

Genet had been exposed to the amazing fertility and occasional glibness of Cocteau and Sartre; now he met an artist who worked day and night and was never satisfied with his statues or paintings. Giacometti's high standards became Genet's own, and indeed Giacometti can be seen as a model for the perfectionism of Genet the playwright.

Before World War II, the Swiss-born Giacometti had been known as the major Surrealist sculptor, but after 1945 he returned to the human figure and produced statues with huge feet, thin bodies, and small heads. After 1950, Giacometti concentrated on rendering likenesses of his wife and his brother, primarily in paintings and drawings.

Giacometti did four drawings and three paintings of Genet between 1954 and 1957. The most successful of these works is the great portrait of 1955, which belongs to the Centre Georges Pompidou in Paris. Genet sat for Giacometti more than forty days. A second portrait hangs in the Tate Gallery in London. While Giacometti was observing Genet, Genet was observing Giacometti. His notes resulted in this essay, which became Giacometti's favorite commentary on his work.

E VERY MAN MAY have felt a certain dismay, if not alarm, at seeing the world and its history apparently caught in an inescapable and ever-widening movement that seems likely to alter, for ever more vulgar ends, only the world's visible manifestations. This visible world is what it is, and our action upon it cannot make it radically different. Hence our nostalgic dreams of a universe in which man, instead of acting so furiously upon visible appearance, would attempt to rid himself of it—not only to refuse any action upon it, but to strip himself bare enough to discover that secret site within ourselves that would capacitate an entirely different human enterprise. More specifically, an altogether different moral enterprise. But after all, it is perhaps to this inhuman condition, to this inescapable arrangement, that we owe our nostalgia for a civilization that attempts to venture elsewhere than into the realm of the measurable. It is Giacometti's work that makes our universe even more unendurable to me, so much has this artist seemingly managed to discard what stood in his way in order to discover what is left of man when false pretenses are removed. But Giacometti too may have required this inhuman condition that has been imposed upon us, may have needed his nostalgia to become so great it would grant him the strength to succeed in his pursuit. Whatever the case, his entire oeuvre seems to me to be such a pursuit, bearing not only on man but on any object, even the most ordinary. And when he has succeeded in stripping the object or the chosen being of its utilitarian appearances, the image of it that he gives us is magnificent. A deserved but foreseeable recompense.

Beauty has no other origin than the singular wound, different in every case, hidden or visible, which each man bears within himself, which he preserves, and into which he withdraws when he would quit the world for a temporary but authentic solitude. Such art, then, is a far cry from what is called miserabilism. Giacometti's art seems to me determined to discover this secret wound in each being and even in each thing, in order for it to illuminate them.

• • •

When Osiris suddenly appeared—for the niche was cut right into the wall—under the green light, I was scared. Were my eyes, naturally, informed first? No. First my shoulders and the back of my neck, crushed by a hand or a mass that compelled me to sink into the Egyptian ages and, mentally, to bow down and even to crouch before this tiny statue with its hard gaze, its hard smile. Here indeed was a god. Of the inexorable. (I am speaking, as may have been realized, of the figure of Osiris standing in the crypt of the Louvre.) I was scared because no mistake was possible: this was a god. Some of Giacometti's statues produce an emotion analogous to that terror, and a fascination almost as great.

They still give me this odd feeling: they are familiar, they walk in the street, yet they are in the depths of time, at the source of all being; they keep approaching and retreating in a sovereign immobility. If my gaze attempts to tame them, to approach them, then—but not furiously, not ranting or raging, simply by means of a distance between them and myself that I had not noticed, a distance so compressed and reduced it made them seem quite close—they take their distance and keep it: it is because this distance between them and myself has suddenly unfolded. Where are they going? Though their image remains visible, where are they? (I am speaking in particular of the eight large statues exhibited this summer in Venice.)

It is hard for me to understand what in art is called an innovator. Should a work be understood by future generations? But why? And what would that mean? That they might use it? For what? I don't see it. But I do see—though dimly still—that any work of art that seeks to attain awesome proportions, must, with infinite patience and application from its very inception, come down through the ages and join, if it can, the immemorial darkness populated by the dead, who will recognize themselves in this work.

No, no, the work of art is not intended for future generations. It is offered to the innumerable people of the dead. Who welcome it. Or reject it. But these dead I was speaking of have never been alive. Or I'm forgetting. They were alive enough to be forgotten, and the purpose of their life was to make them pass over to that calm shore where they wait for a sign—from here—that they recognize.

Though present here, where are these figures of Giacometti's I was talking about, if not in death? From which they escape to approach us each time our eyes summon them.

I say to Giacometti:

JG It takes guts to keep one of your statues at home.
AG Why?
    I hesitate to answer. What I am about to say will make me seem ridiculous.
JG One of your statues in a room, and the room is a temple.
    He seems a bit disconcerted.

A G Do you think that's a good thing?

J G I don't know. What do you think?

The chest and especially the shoulders of two of them have the delicacy of a skeleton that crumbles if you touch it. The curve of the shoulder—where it joins the arm—is exquisite . . . (excuse me, but) is powerfully exquisite in its strength. I touch the shoulder and close my eyes: the happiness of my fingers is indescribable. First of all, they have never touched bronze before. Then, someone strong is guiding them, reassuring them.

He talks in a rough and ready fashion, seems to prefer words and intonations closest to everyday conversation. Like a man making barrels.

A G You saw them when they were plaster . . . You remember them, in plaster?

J G Yes.

A G Do you think they lose something, cast in bronze?

J G No. Not at all.

A G Do you think they gain something?

Again I hesitate to say what best expresses my feelings.

J G You'll think I'm being ridiculous all over again, but they make a strange impression. I wouldn't say they gain, but the bronze has gained something. For the first time in its life the bronze has won out. Your women are bronze's victory. Over itself, maybe.

A G That must be it.

He smiles. And all the wrinkled skin of his face starts to laugh. In a peculiar way. The eyes laugh, of course, but the forehead too (his entire person has the gray color of his studio). Out of sympathy, perhaps, he has assumed the color of dust. His teeth laugh—wide apart and gray too—the wind passes through them.

He looks at one of his statues:

A G Sort of misshapen, isn't it?

He uses this word often. He's sort of misshapen himself. He scratches his gray, bristling head. It's Annette who has trimmed his hair. He pulls up his gray trousers which were drooping over his shoes. Six seconds ago he was laughing, but he has just touched one of the statues he has been working on: for half a minute he will exist entirely in the transition from his fingers to the lump of clay. I don't interest him at all.

Apropos of bronze. During a dinner party one of his friends, teasing him probably—who was it?—says: "Tell the truth: could a normally constituted brain exist inside a head that flat?"

Giacometti knew that a brain could not live in a bronze skull, even if it had the exact measurements of Monsieur René Coty's. And since the head will be cast in bronze, and in order for the head to live, and the bronze too, then it must . . . It's obvious, isn't it?

Giacometti still insists: his ideal is the little rubber fetish figurine sold to South Americans in the lobby of the Folies-Bergères.

AG When I walk down the street and see a girl walking ahead of me, all dressed up, I see a girl. When she is in the room and naked before me, I see a goddess.

JG For me a naked woman is a naked woman. She doesn't make much of an impression. I certainly can't see her as a goddess. But I see your statues the way you see naked girls.

AG You think I manage to show them the way I see them?

This afternoon we are in the studio. I notice two canvases—two heads—of an extraordinary acuity, they seem to be moving, coming toward me, ceaseless in this movement toward me from some unknown depth of the canvas that keeps emitting this trenchant countenance.

AG It's a start, don't you think?

He looks questioningly into my face. Then, reassured:

AG I did them the other night. From memory . . . I did some drawings too (he hesitates) . . . but they're not good. You want to see them?

The question so astonished me I must have answered oddly. This is the first time in the four years I've been seeing him on a regular basis that he's offered to show me anything he's done. The rest of the time he notices—with some surprise—that I see and that I admire what I see.

So he opens a box and takes out six drawings, four of which are splendid. One of those that moved me least represents a tiny figure at the very bottom of a huge white sheet.

AG I'm not very pleased with this, but it's the first time I've dared do anything like it.

Maybe he means: "To emphasize so large a white surface by means of so tiny a figure"? Or else: "To show that the proportions of a figure resist the destructive powers of a huge surface"? Or else . . .

Whatever he was trying to do, his words move me, coming from a man who never stops daring. This tiny figure is one of his triumphs. What is it that Giacometti has had to overcome, what is it that threatens him so?

When I said, just now: "for the dead" I also meant that such a countless host could finally see what they could not see when they were alive, standing skeletons. It takes art, then—not fluid, quite rigid on the contrary—but endowed with the strange power of penetrating this realm of death, of seeping through the porous walls of the realm of shades. The injustice—and our grief—would be excessive if a single one of them were deprived of the knowledge of a single one of us, and ours would be a hollow victory if all it granted us was a future glory. To the people of the dead, Giacometti's oeuvre communicates the knowledge of each being's and each thing's solitude, and the knowledge that this solitude is our surest glory.

A work of art is not approached—who ever thought it was?—like a person, like a living being, nor like any other natural phenomenon. A poem, a painting, a statue have to be examined with a certain number of qualities. But let's talk about painting.

Even a living face does not yield itself so readily, yet it doesn't take too great an effort to discover its meaning. I believe—I'm guessing—I believe that you have to isolate it. If my gaze manages to release it from all that surrounds it, if my gaze (my attention) keeps this face from blending with the rest of the world, so that it can escape for a while into ever vaguer meanings, and if, on the contrary, that solitude is obtained by which my gaze severs it from the world, then it is its meaning alone that will appear and accumulate within this face—or this person, or this being, or this phenomenon. What I'm saying is that the knowledge of a face, if it is to be esthetic, must refuse to be historical.

To examine a painting requires a larger effort, a more complex operation. It is actually the painter—or the sculptor—who has performed for us the operation described above. So it is the solitude of the represented person or object that is restored to us, and for us really to perceive it and be touched by it, we viewers must experience the space not of its continuity but of its discontinuity.

Each object creates its infinite space.

If I look at a painting, as I have said, it appears to me in its absolute object-solitude as a painting. But this is not what concerned me. It is what its canvas is to represent. So it is both the image that is on the canvas and the real object it represents that I want to apprehend in their solitude. So at first I must try to isolate the painting in its meaning as object (canvas, frame, etc.), so that it will cease belonging to the huge family of painting (to which I will restore it later on) but so that the image on the canvas will attach itself to my experience of space, to my knowledge of the solitude of objects, of beings or of events as I described them earlier.

If you have never been amazed by this solitude you will not know the beauty of painting. If you claim you do, you're lying.

Each statue, clearly, is different. I know only the statues of women for which

Annette has posed, and the busts of Diego—and each goddess and this god—here I hesitate: if, in the presence of these women, I feel I am in the presence of goddesses—of goddesses and not of statues of a goddess—the bust of Diego never attains this height, until now it has never retreated—to return again at a terrible speed—to that distance I mentioned. Instead it might be the bust of a priest belonging to a very high rank in the church. Not a god. But each very different statue still belongs to the same proud and somber family. Familiar and very close. Inaccessible.

Giacometti, to whom I am reading this text, asks me why I find this difference in intensity between the statues of women and the busts of Diego.

JG Maybe—(I hesitate for a while in answering) . . . maybe because, in spite of everything, woman naturally seems more distant to you . . . or else you want to make her retreat . . .

Unintentionally, without actually saying anything to him about it, I evoke the image of the Mother, so highly regarded—or what do I know?

AG Yes, maybe that's it.

He goes on reading, while my thoughts unravel, but then he looks up, takes his filthy twisted glasses off his nose.

AG Maybe it's because the statues of Annette show the whole person, while Diego is only his bust. He is cut off. Hence more conventional. And it is this convention that makes him less remote.

This seems like a good explanation.
JG You're right. It "socializes" him.

Tonight, writing this note, I am less convinced by what he said, for I don't know how he would do the legs. Or rather the rest of the body, for in such a sculpture, each organ or limb is so much the extension of all the rest, forming the indissoluble individual, that it even loses his name. "This" arm cannot be imagined without the body that continues and signifies it in the extreme (the body being the extension of the arm) and yet I know no arm more intensely, more specifically an arm than this one.

This resemblance, it seems to me, is not due to the artist's "manner." It is because each figure has the same—doubtless nocturnal—origin, though certainly located in the world.
Where?

*   *   *

About four years ago, I was in a train. Opposite me in the compartment was sitting a dreadful little old man. Filthy and obviously nasty, as certain of his observations were to prove. Refusing to pursue a conversation that gave me no pleasure, I wanted to read, but in spite of myself I stared at this little old man: he was extremely ugly. Our eyes met, as they say, and whether this was a momentary or prolonged sensation I no longer know, but I suddenly had the painful—yes, painful—conviction that any man was "worth" exactly—excuse me, but it's "exactly" that I want to emphasize—as much as any other. "Anyone," I said to myself, "can be loved beyond his ugliness, his foolishness, his nastiness."

It was a glance, brief or prolonged, that had met my own and that had made me aware of it. And whatever makes it possible that a man can be loved beyond his ugliness or his nastiness is precisely what makes it possible to love his ugliness or his nastiness. Let there be no mistake: there was no question of any goodness proceeding from me, but of a recognition. Giacometti's gaze has long since seen this, and he restores it to us. I say what I feel: that kinship manifested by his figures seems to me to be that precious point at which the human being is restored to what is most irreducible in him: his solitude in being exactly equivalent to any other.

If—Giacometti's figures being incorruptible—accident is eliminated, what then remains?

Giacometti's bronze dog is admirable. And finer still when its strange substance: plaster, wires or wadding, came apart. The curve of the front paw, without marked articulation and yet apparent, is so beautiful that it alone determines the dog's lithe gait. For he prowls and sniffs, muzzle level with the ground. He is gaunt.

I had forgotten the splendid cat: in plaster, from muzzle to tip of the tail, almost horizontal and capable of passing through a mousehole. Its rigid horizontality perfectly reproduces the form a cat retains, even when curled into a ball.

When I express astonishment that there should be an animal—it is the only one among his figures:

AG It's me. One day I saw myself in the street like that. I was the dog.

> If it was initially chosen as a sign of poverty and solitude, it seems to me that this dog is drawn as a harmonious paraph, the curve of the spine corresponding to the curve of the paw, but this paraph is still the supreme magnification of solitude.

This secret region, this solitude in which beings—and things, too—take refuge, is what gives so much beauty to the street; for example: I am sitting in the bus, and all I have to do is look outside. The bus follows the downward slope of the street, moving fast enough so that I have no chance to linger over a face or a gesture, my speed requires a corresponding speed in my gaze, so that no face, no body, no attitude is prepared *for me:* they are naked. I register: one very tall, thin man, stoop shouldered, hollow-chested, glasses and a long nose; a stout housewife walking slowly, heavily, sadly; an old man who is not a good specimen, a single tree next to a single tree next to a single tree . . . ; an office worker, another, a crowd of office workers, a whole city populated by stoop-shouldered office workers, all character- ized by this one detail that my gaze registers: a downward turn of the mouth, a weariness of the shoulders . . . each attitude, perhaps because of the vehicle's speed and that of my eye, is so quickly sketched, its arabesque so quickly grasped that each human being is revealed to me in whatever is newest, most irreplaceable about him—and it is always a wound—thanks to the solitude in which this wound locates him, this wound of which he is barely conscious and yet which is the source of his entire being. Thus I cross a city sketched by Rembrandt, in which each person and each thing is grasped in its truth, which leaves all plastic beauty far behind.

The city—constituted of solitude—would be wonderfully *taken from life,* except that my bus passes lovers crossing a square: they have their arms around each other's waists, and the girl has devised this charming gesture of putting her tiny hand in the hip pocket of the boy's blue jeans, and look how this one graceful and studied gesture vulgarizes a page of masterpieces.

Solitude, as I understand it, does not signify an unhappy state, but rather secret royalty, profound incommunicability yet a more or less obscure knowledge of an invulnerable singularity.

I can't stop touching the statues: I look away and my hand continues its discoveries of its own accord: neck, head, nape of the neck, shoulders . . . The sensations flow to my fingertips. Each one is different, so that my hand traverses an extremely varied and vivid landscape.

The Emperor (listening, I think, to *The Magic Flute*) to Mozart: All those notes! All those notes!

Mozart: Sire, there is not one too many.

So my fingers repeat what Giacometti's have done, but whereas his were seeking support in the wet plaster or the clay, mine confidently follow in their tracks. And—at last!—my hand lives, my hand sees.

The beauty of Giacometti's sculptures seems to me to reside in this incessant, uninterrupted oscillation from the remotest distance to the closest familiarity: this oscillation never ends, and that is how it can be said that the sculptures are in motion.

We go out for a drink. Coffee for him. He stops to take a better look at the intense beauty of the Rue d'Alésia, where the transparent foliage of the acacias—slender, pointed leaves more yellow than green in the sunlight—seem to powder the street with gold.

AG Lovely that . . . Lovely.

He walks on, limping. He says he was quite happy when he learned that his operation—after an accident—would leave him lame. Which is why I shall venture this: his statues always seem to take refuge, ultimately, in some secret infirmity their solitude grants them.

Giacometti and I—and a few Parisians as well—know that there exists in Paris, where she resides, a being of great elegance, slender, proud, upright, singular, and gray—a very tender gray—it is the Rue Oberkampf, who casually changes her name and farther along is known as the Rue de Ménilmontant. Lovely as a spire, she rises to the sky. If you decide to follow her by car from the Boulevard Voltaire, as she rises she opens up, but oddly: instead of separating, the houses crowd closer together, offering very plain facades and gables, all quite ordinary but somehow transfigured by the personality of this street, tinged by a sort of remote yet familiar kindness. Recently some ridiculous dark blue disks with red bars across them were installed to indicate that cars cannot be parked here. Spoiled? Not at all: nothing—but nothing! could degrade this beauty.

So what has happened? What is the source of the street's noble sweetness? How can it be so tender yet so remote, and why is it that one approaches it so respectfully? May Giacometti forgive me, but it seems to me that this almost vertical street is nothing more nor less than one of his tall statues, at once anxious, tremulous, and serene.

Down to the statues' feet . . .

Here a word: except for his walking men, all Giacometti's statues have their feet somehow caught in a single, sloping, rather thick block that looks something like a pedestal. From there, the body supports, at a great distance, high above, a tiny head. This enormous (in proportion to the head) mass of plaster or of bronze might suggest that these feet are loaded with all the materiality of which the head frees itself . . . not at all; an uninterrupted exchange occurs between these massive feet and this tiny head. These ladies are not pulling themselves out of an oppressive mud: at twilight they will come sliding down a slope drowned in shadows.

His statues seem to belong to a bygone age, to have been discovered after time and darkness—which work them over knowingly—have corroded them in order to give them that look, at once mild and severe, of a *passing eternity*. Or again, they emerge from an oven, residue of a terrible firing: flames extinguished, this is what remained.

But what flames!

Giacometti tells me that once it occurred to him to model a statue and bury it.

(One immediately thinks: "May the earth lie lightly upon it.") Not so that it would be discovered, or if so, then much later, when he himself and even the memory of his name have disappeared.

Was burying it a way of offering it to the dead?

On the solitude of objects.

AG. One day, in my bedroom, I was looking at a napkin left on a chair and I suddenly realized that not only was each object alone, but that it had a weight—or actually a weightlessness—that kept it from weighing on any other. The napkin was alone, so alone that I felt I could take away the chair without changing the napkin's position. It had its own place, its own weight, even its own silence. The world was light, light . . .

If he had to give a present to someone he admires or loves, perhaps he would send—certain thereby of honoring that person—a curled wood shaving from the carpenter's shop or a piece of bark from a birch tree.

His canvases. Seen in the studio (which is rather dark: Giacometti so respects every kind of matter that he would be annoyed if Annette were to clean the dust from his windowpanes), where I can't step very far back from them, the portrait first seems a tangle of curved lines, commas, circles cut by a secant, more or less pink, gray, or black—a strange green is mixed in there too—a delicate labyrinth that he happened to be making, in which he was probably getting lost. But it occurs to me to take the picture out into the courtyard: the result is terrifying. As I step back (I will go so far as to open the courtyard door, walk out into the street, retreating some twenty or twenty-five yards) the face, with all its modeling, emerges, predominates—according to that phenomenon already described and so characteristic of Giacometti's faces—comes toward me, bears down upon me, and rushes back into the canvas from which it had set out, acquiring a presence, a reality, a relief which are truly terrible.

I mentioned "its modeling," but it is something else. For he never seems to be concerned with tones or shading or conventional values. He actually produces a linear network that would be nothing more than drawings within the drawing. But—and here I no longer understand—even though he has never tried to render relief by shadows or tones, or by any pictorial convention, this is where he obtains the most extraordinary relief. "Relief"? If I look more closely at the canvas, this word no longer applies. Rather it is a matter of an unbreakable hardness that the face has acquired. As if it had an extremely high molecular weight. It has not begun living like certain faces that we call "lifelike" because they are grasped at a particular moment of their movements, because they are identified by an accident that belongs only to their history. Quite the contrary: faces painted by Giacometti seem to have accumulated life so intensely that they haven't a moment left to live, not a gesture left to make, and (not that they have just died) that they finally know death because too much life has amassed within them. Seen from twenty yards away, each portrait is a little mass of life, hard as a pebble, full as an egg, which might effortlessly feed a hundred other portraits.

How he paints: he refuses to establish a difference in "level"—or in plane—between the different parts of the face. The same line, or the same group of lines can serve for the cheek, the eye, and the eyebrow. For him the eyes are not blue, the cheeks pink, the eyebrows black and curving: there is a single continuous line that is constituted by the cheek, the eye, and the eyebrow. There is not the shadow of the nose over the cheek, or rather if it exists, that shadow must be treated as a part of the face, with the same lines, the same curves, valid here or there.

Set down amid old bottles of turpentine, his palette, the last few days: a mud puddle of various grays.

This ability to isolate an object and to bring to its surface its own, its only meanings is possible only by the historical elimination of the viewer. An exceptional effort is required in order to erase any history whatever, so that the viewer becomes not a sort of eternal present but rather a dizzying and uninterrupted rush from a past toward a future, an oscillation from one extreme to the other, obviating rest.

If I look at the wardrobe in order to know, *ultimately,* what it is, I eliminate everything that is not the wardrobe. And the effort I make turns me into a strange being: this being, this observer ceases to be present, and even to be a present observer: he cannot stop receding into a boundless past, a boundless future. He ceases to be there so that the wardrobe might remain, and so that between the wardrobe and himself all affective or utilitarian relations are abolished.

(September '57) I discovered Giacometti's most beautiful statue—I am talking about three years ago—under a table, leaning down to retrieve my cigarette butt. It was there in the dust, he was hiding it, a visitor's clumsy foot might have chipped it.

AG If it's really strong, it will show itself, even if I hide it.
AG It's lovely . . . lovely!

He still has a slight Grisons accent . . . "Lovely!" and his eyes open wide, he smiles warmly; he is talking about the dust covering all the old turpentine bottles cluttering a table in the studio.

The bedroom, Annette's and his, which used to have a dirt floor, is tiled now, lovely red tiles. Rain used to flood the room. Grimly, he resigned himself to the tiles. The prettiest, but the simplest kind. He says he will never live anywhere but in this studio and this bedroom. If it were possible, he would like them to be even more modest.

One day, at lunch with Sartre, I repeated my phrase about the statues: "the bronze has won."

"That's what would please him most," Sartre said. "His dream would be to vanish completely behind his work. He would be even happier if the bronze had appeared of its own accord."

If I want to tame a work of art, I frequently use a trick: I adopt, however artificially, a state of naïveté, I talk about it—and I also talk to it—in the most ordinary tone of voice; I even play dumb a little. At first I come closer. I'm referring here to the noblest works—and try to make myself more naïve, clumsier than I am. This is how I try to overcome my shyness.

"Funny thing, that red . . . it's red all right, and that blue there . . . and the paint that looks like mud . . ."

The work loses something of its formality, its solemnity. By means of a familiar *reconnaissance*, I gradually approach its secret . . . With Giacometti's oeuvre, this is no help at all. The work is already too far away. Impossible to fake a good-natured stupidity. Severe, it commands me to go back to that solitary point from which it must be regarded.

His drawings. He draws only with pen or hard pencil—the paper is often pierced, torn. The curves are hard, they have no softness, nothing gentle about them. It seems that for him a line is a man: he treats it as an equal. The broken lines are sharp and give his drawings—a result, too, of the pencil's granitic and paradoxically muted substance—a sparkling aspect. Diamonds. And diamonds even more because of the way he uses white space. In his landscapes, for example, the entire page is a diamond, one side of which is visible thanks to the subtle, broken lines, while the side on which the light falls—from which the light is reflected, more precisely—lets you see nothing but white. This produces extraordinary jewels—one is reminded of Cézanne's watercolors—thanks to these white spaces, in which an invisible drawing is suggested, the sensation of space obtained with a strength rendering it almost measurable. (I was thinking in particular of the interiors, with the ceiling lamp and the palm trees, but since then he has done a series of four drawings of a table in a vaulted room that far surpass the ones I was describing.) Extraordinarily faceted jewels. And it is the blank space—the white page—that Giacometti has cut.

Apropos of the four big drawings of a table.

In certain canvases (Monet, Bonnard . . .), the air circulates. In the drawings I am talking about, how to put it . . . the space circulates. The light too. Without any of the usual oppositions of value—dark/light—the light radiates and a few lines sculpt it.

* * *

Giacometti's struggles with a Japanese face. Professor Yanihara, whose portrait he was doing, had to postpone his departure by two months because Giacometti was never satisfied by the drawing he started over every day. The professor returned to Japan without his portrait. This face without any unevenness, but serious and gentle, must have tempted his genius. The remaining drawings are wonderfully intense: a few faint gray lines on a dark gray, almost black ground. And that same accumulation of life I mentioned earlier. No way of squeezing in one more grain of life. They are at that final point at which life resembles inanimate matter. Faces pumped full.

I am posing. He draws very carefully—though without having "arranged" it—the stove and its pipe, which are behind me. He knows he must be precise, faithful to the reality of objects.

A G You must do just what is in front of you.
      I say yes. Then, after a moment of silence:
A G And besides that, you must do a picture.

He misses the brothels, which have vanished. I think they had—and their memory still has—too large a place in his life for him not to speak of them. It seems to me that he went to them almost as a worshiper. He went there to find himself kneeling before a remote and implacable divinity. Between each naked whore and himself there may have been that distance that each of his statues constantly establishes between themselves and us. Each statue seems to withdraw—or to advance—into a darkness so remote and dense that it merges with death: so each whore must have merged with a mysterious darkness in which she was sovereign. And he, abandoned on the shore from which he sees her both diminishing and growing larger at the same moment.
    I venture this as well: is it not in the brothel that woman can revel in a wound that will never deliver her from solitude? Is it not the brothel that will rid her of any utilitarian function, thereby affording her a sort of purity?

Several of his large statues are gilded.

The whole time he was struggling with Yanihara's face (one can imagine that face offering itself and refusing to let its image pass onto the canvas, as if it had to protect its unique identity), I had the moving spectacle of a man who never made mistakes but who invariably got lost. He kept sinking deeper into impossible, ineluctable regions. He has climbed back out of them recently. His work is still shadowed and still blinded by them. (The four big drawings of the table come immediately after this period.)

SARTRE I saw something of him during the Japanese period—that was a bad time, things weren't working out.

JG He always says that. He's never satisfied.
SARTRE That time, he was really desperate.

I wrote "infinitely precious objects . . ." about his drawings. I also wanted to say that the white spaces give the page an Oriental look, the lines being used not for any signifying value of their own, but only to assign meaning to the empty spaces. The lines are there only to give shape and solidity to the empty spaces. Look closely: it is not the line that is elegant, but the empty space, contained by it. It is not the line that is complete, but the empty space.

And why is that?
    Maybe because, besides the palm tree or the ceiling lamp—and besides the very special space in which they are drawn—that he wants to restore, Giacometti is trying to give an apparent reality to what was only absence—or if you prefer, indeterminate uniformity, *i.e.*, blank space, and even, still more profoundly, the sheet of paper. It seems, once again, that he has taken as his task to ennoble a sheet of white paper that, without his lines, would never have existed.
    Am I wrong? It's possible.
    Yet when he pins the blank sheet in front of him, I get the impression that he has as much respect and reserve confronting its mystery as confronting the object he's going to draw.
    (I had already noted that his drawings suggested a certain typographical arrangement: Mallarmé's *Coup de dés*.)
    The entire oeuvre of the sculptor and the graphic artist could be entitled: "The Invisible Object."

Not only do the statues come toward you as if they were very far away, from the depths of an extremely remote horizon, but, wherever you happen to be in relation to them, they manage to make you, looking at them, do so from below. They are, far away on a remote horizon, upon an eminence, and you are at the foot of this rising ground. They come, eager to meet you, and to pass you.

For I keep coming back to these women, cast in bronze now (usually gilded and patinated): around them space vibrates. Nothing is any longer at rest. Perhaps because each angle (made with Giacometti's thumb when he was modeling the clay) or curve, or lump, or crest, or torn tip of metal are themselves not at rest. Each of them still emits the sensibility that created them. No point, no ridge that outlines or lacerates space is dead.

Yet the backs of these women may be more human than their fronts. The nape of the neck, the shoulders, the small of the back, the buttocks seem to have been modeled more "lovingly" than any of the fronts. Seen from three-quarters, this oscillation from woman to goddess may be what is most disturbing: sometimes the emotion is unbearable.

For I cannot help returning to this race of gilded—and sometimes painted—sentries who, standing erect, motionless, keep watch.

Beside them, Maillol's statues, or Rodin's, seem so ready to belch and doze off.

Giacometti's statues (these women) keep their vigil for a dead man.

The threadlike walking man. His lifted foot. He will never stop. And he walks firmly on the ground, that is, on a sphere.

When it was learned that Giacometti was doing my portrait (I have a full, more or less round face) people said: "He'll give you a face like a knife blade." The clay bust isn't done yet, but I think I know why he has used, in the various drawings, lines that seem to take flight from the median line of the face—nose, mouth, chin—toward the ears and, if possible, all the way to the nape of the neck. This is apparently because a face offers the full strength of its meaning when it faces front, and because everything must start from this center in order to feed and fortify what is behind, what is hidden. I am sorry to put it so badly, but I have the impression—as when someone pulls his hair back from his forehead and temples—that the painter is pulling the meaning of the face back (behind the canvas).

The busts of Diego *can* be seen from all sides: three-quarters, profile, back . . . , they *should* be seen from the front. The meaning of the face—its profound resemblance—instead of accumulating on the front, escapes, plunges into infinity, into a place that is never reached, behind the bust.

(It goes without saying that I am mainly trying to describe or define an emotion, not to explain the artist's techniques.)

One of Giacometti's often-repeated observations: "You must value . . ."

I don't think he ever, not even once in his life, cast a contemptuous glance on anyone or anything. Each was to be regarded in its most precious solitude.

AG I'll never manage to put into a portrait all the strength there is in a head. Just being alive already requires so much will, so much energy . . .

In front of his statues, one more feeling: these are all beautiful persons, yet their sadness and their solitude seem to me comparable to the sadness and the solitude of a deformed man who, suddenly naked, sees his deformity displayed at the very moment he would offer it to the world in order to indicate his solitude and his glory. Unfailing, both.

Some of Jouhandeau's characters have this naked majesty: Prudence Hautechaume.

* * *

The joy, familiar yet constantly new, of closing my eyes and running my fingers over the surface of a statue. It's very likely, I tell myself, that any bronze statue affords the fingers the same delight. Visiting friends who own two small Donatellos, exact replicas, I try to repeat the experience: the bronze no longer responds: mute, dead.

Giacometti, or the sculptor for the blind.

But even ten years ago, I had experienced the same pleasure when my hand, fingers and palm, moved over his candelabra. Indeed it is Giacometti's hands, not his eyes, that create his objects, his figures. He does not dream them, he feels them.

He is enamored of his models. He loved the Japanese professor.

His concern for composition on the sheet of paper seems to correspond closely to the feeling I indicated earlier: to ennoble the page, the canvas.

In the café. While Giacometti is reading, a wretched, nearly blind Arab causes something of a scandal by calling another customer an asshole . . . The insulted party stares hard and nastily at the blind man, grinding his teeth as if he were chewing his rage. The Arab is gaunt, maybe feebleminded. He bumps into an invisible but solid wall. He understands nothing of the world in which he is blind, weak, and stupid, and he insults it in one or another of its manifestations.

"If you didn't have that white cane! . . ." shouts the Frenchman whom the Arab has called an asshole. I secretly marvel that a white cane can make this blind man holier than a king, stronger than the burliest butcher.

I offer the Arab a cigarette. His fingers grope for it, find it almost by accident. He is short, gaunt, filthy, and a little drunk too, stammering, drooling. His beard is sparse and unshaved. There seem to be no legs in his pants. He can scarcely stand up. He is wearing a wedding ring. I say a few words in his language:

"Are you married?"

Giacometti keeps reading, and I dare not disturb him. He may be annoyed by my dealings with the Arab.

"No . . . No wife."

While he says this, the Arab makes an up-and-down gesture with his hand to let me know that he masturbates.

"No . . . no wife . . . I've got my hand . . . and besides my hand . . . no, there's nothing, nothing but my towel . . . or the sheets . . :

His blank, faded, sightless eyes keep moving.

". . . and I'll be punished . . . God will punish me . . . you don't know all I've done . . .

Giacometti has finished reading, he takes off his twisted, mended glasses and puts them in his pocket. We leave. I want to say something about the incident but what would he answer, what would I say? I know he knows as well as I do that this wretch preserves, sustains—with rage, with fury—that focus which makes him·

identical to everyone and more precious than the rest of the world: what remains when he has withdrawn into himself, as far as possible, just as when the sea recedes and abandons the shore.

I mention this incident because it seems to me that Giacometti's statues have withdrawn—abandoning the shore—to that secret focus that I can neither describe nor specify, but which makes every man, when he withdraws there, more precious than the rest of the world.

Long before this, Giacometti had told me about his love affair with an old beggar woman, as charming as she was filthy and ragged, whose tumors covering her half-bald skull he could probably see at the very moment she was "entertaining" him.

AG I really liked her, you know? When she stayed away for two or three days, I would go out into the street to see if she was coming . . . She was worth all the beautiful women in the world, you know?
JG You should have married her—introduced to everyone as Mme Giacometti.
    He looked at me, smiled faintly.
AG Think so? If I did that, I'd be pretty strange, no?
JG Yes.

There must be a link between these severe and solitary figures and Giacometti's taste for whores. Thank God not everything can be explained, and I can't quite see what this link is, but I can feel it. One day he told me:

AG What I like about the girls is that they're useless. They're there, that's all.
    I may be mistaken but I don't think he's ever painted one of them. If he were to do so, he would find himself confronting a being with her solitude to which would be added yet another solitude, deriving from despair, or from emptiness.

Strange feet or pedestals! I've come back to them. Just as much (at least, at first glance) as the laws of sculpture (knowledge and restoration of space), it appears here that Giacometti, may he forgive me! obeys an intimate ritual by which he gives his statue an assertive, grounded, feudal base. The action of this base on us is magical . . . (you will tell me that the whole figure is magical, yes, but the anxiety, the spell this fabulous clubfoot produces is not of the same order as the rest of the figure. Frankly, I believe that there is a break here in Giacometti's *métier:* admirable in both styles, but opposite. Through the head, the shoulders, the arms, the pelvis he enlightens us. Through the feet he casts a spell.)

If he could, Giacometti would reduce himself to powder, to dust, and how happy that would make him!

"But the girls?"

It is unlikely that dust can win the hearts of whores. He might creep into the folds of their skin, so they might have a touch of squalor.

Since Giacometti gives me a choice—after a hesitation that would end only after my death or his—I decide on a small head of myself (a parenthesis here): and indeed this head is quite small. Isolated on the canvas, it is no more than seven centimeters high and three and a half or four centimeters wide, yet it has *the strength, the weight, and the dimensions* of my actual head. When I take the picture out of the studio to look at it, I am embarrassed for I know I am as much there on the canvas as facing it, looking at it—so I decide on this tiny head (stuffed with life and so heavy it seems like a little lead bullet on its trajectory.

AG All right, I'm giving it to you. (He looks at me.) No kidding. It's yours. (He looks at the canvas and says with more energy now, as if he were tearing out a fingernail:) It's yours. You can take it . . . But later . . . I have to add a piece of canvas at the top.

Now that he points it out, this amelioration is essential, but as much for the canvas itself, which my tiny head diminishes, as for that head that will thereby assume its full weight.

I am sitting very straight, motionless, rigid (if I move, he quickly calls me to order, to silence, and to immobility) on a very uncomfortable kitchen chair.

AG (looking at me in amazement): "How handsome you are!" He touches the canvas with his brush two or three times without, apparently, taking his eyes off me. Then he murmurs again, as though to himself: "How handsome you are." Then he adds this observation which amazes him still more: "Like everyone, you know? Neither more, nor less."

AG When I am out walking, I never think about my work.

This may be true but as soon as he comes into his studio, he is at work. In an odd way, moreover: He is at at once straining toward the statue's realization—hence not here, inaccessible—and present. He is constantly modeling.

Since these days the statues are very tall, standing in front of them—they are made of brown clay—his fingers move up and down like those of a gardener grafting or trimming a rambler rosebush. His fingers run down the statue. And the whole studio vibrates and lives. I have the strange impression that just because he is here, even without his touching them, the old, already finished statues are changed, transformed, because he is working on one of their sisters. This ground-floor studio, moreover, is about to collapse from one moment to the next. All the wood is worm-eaten, there is nothing but gray dust, the statues are made of plaster with the string, oakum, pieces of wire showing through, the canvases, painted gray, have long since lost that peacefulness they had at the art-supply store, here everything is spotted and broken-down, everything is precarious and about to collapse, everything is tending to dissolve, everything drifts: now, all this is somehow apprehended in an absolute reality. When I have left the studio, when I am out in the street, it is then that nothing of what is around me is real anymore. Shall I say it? In this studio, a man is slowly dying, consuming himself, and before our eyes turning himself into goddesses.

Giacometti does not work for his contemporaries, nor for the generations to come: he makes statues that ultimately delight the dead.

Have I said this already? Every object Giacometti draws or paints offers us, bestows upon us his friendliest, most affectionate thought. It never appears in a disconcerting form, never seeks to be monstrous! Quite the contrary, from a great distance it brings a sort of reassuring friendship and tranquillity. Or, if his statues disturb, it is because they are so pure, so rare. To be in harmony with such objects (apple, bottle, ceiling light, table, palm tree) demands the refusal of any and all compromise.

I write that a sort of friendship radiates from the objects, that these afford us a friendly thought . . . This is speaking rather generally. It might be true of Vermeer. Giacometti is something else: it is not because he has made himself "more human"—because usable and constantly used by man—that the object Giacometti paints moves and reassures us, it is not because it is clothed in the best, the gentlest, the most sensitive of human presences, but on the contrary, because it is "this object" in all its naïve freshness as object. Itself and nothing else. Itself in its total solitude.

　　This is not very well put, is it? Try something else: it seems to me that in order to approach objects, Giacometti's eye then his pencil strip themselves of all servile premeditation. On the pretext of ennobling—or debasing, in the current fashion—the object, he (Giacometti) refuses to endue the object with the slightest tinge—however delicate, cruel, or high keyed—of the human.

　　Looking at a ceiling fixture, a hanging lamp, he says: "It's a ceiling fixture, that's what it is." And nothing more.

　　And this sudden observation illuminates the painter. The ceiling fixture. It will exist on the sheet of paper, in all its naïve nakedness.

　　What respect for objects! Each has its beauty because each is "alone" in being—the irreplaceable is in it.

　　Giacometti's art, then, is not a social art that would establish a social link between objects—man and his secretions—but rather an art of superior beggars and bums, so pure that they could be united by a recognition of the solitude of every being and of every object. "I am alone," the object seems to say, "hence caught within a necessity against which you are powerless. If I am only what I am, I am indestructible. Being what I am, and unconditionally, my solitude knows yours."

V

FILM

The Penal Colony

◄○►

Although Genet wrote several long film scripts, few of them saw the light of the projector. In 1950, his twenty-minute black-and-white homosexual erotic film, A Song of Love, *was produced, but Genet subsequently renounced it. Genet had been writing scenarios from the very beginning of his career and would continue to write them into the last decade of his life.*

One of Genet's favorite projects was The Penal Colony. *It was never realized, either as a play or as a film. At one point he even considered turning it into a novel. An altogether different work with the same title was conceived as part of a cycle of plays that began with* The Screens.

In the notes to the director in The Penal Colony, *Genet wrote in passing some of his most trenchant remarks about cinema. Genet's comments have been culled from his parenthetical reflections in the script.*

COMMENTS ON THE CINEMA

OF THE ACTORS
The adventure into which I plunge them does not astonish them, but they live it out through acts, through gestures, not through thinking about it. In that way I can escape the danger of putting together a realistic narrative according to the usual methods by which each character *knows* what he's expressing at the very moment he expresses it, and knows the overtones that his expression *should* have on his protagonist and on us. . . .

If my characters have the right size, the right shoulder width, look, and smile, I'll take responsibility for everything else, asking them only to perform a series of gestures which anyone at all could do, but a series of gestures minutely calculated by me. Of course it's possible that this way of working might remove all spontaneity from the narrative. I prefer rigidity to a natural stupidity without art and without originality. . . .

OF THE CAMERA

Cinema is essentially shameless. Since it has the ability to enlarge gestures, let's make use of it. The camera can open a fly and dig into it for its secrets. If I think that's necessary to do, I will not deprive myself of such an invasion. I will use it to record, doubtlessly, the trembling of a lip, but also the very particular textures of mucous membranes, their humidity. The blown-up appearance of a bubble of saliva in the corner of a mouth can bring to the spectator, during the unfolding of a scene, an emotion that will give to this drama a weight, a new density. . . .

THE ACTORS' FACES

No one will have a prominent face—that is, sharp features that point toward the outside world—but rather a face with features that are concentrated, shoved together, that push down toward the inner self—in short, mongoloid: the eyes hollowed out, the nose pushed in. That's what I want, first of all because such faces are more childlike. Even if they were adult men (but were they ever?) my heroes, lulled gently in the womb of the penal colony, would not turn out toward the world: on the contrary, they're folded back on themselves. Finally, sharp-featured faces, irregular, would snag passing events with their sharp points. If events don't slide like oil across my actors' faces then they're going to launch a revolt. Why do I need to describe a revolt in order to express myself?. . . .

It would be tiresome to repeat my insults against actors and to give once again my reasons for disliking them, so I'll say quickly and brutally that I'm disgusted by their gestures and their faces worn down by an abuse of expressions that are always faked, always put on, never convincing. Their faces, their washed-away features reek of the boredom exuded by old café waiters or headwaiters. If I'd used professional actors here I would have ended up with a penal colony of actors. But who would ever be able to believe that these miserable rags could one day have enough passion, deviance, or just the bad luck of a difficult life to commit a crime? What I expect actors to do in order to incarnate my characters is not to act but to perform simply, within the limits of their physical appearance and their personal tics, a series of very simple gestures such as walking, running, whistling, etc. They will not have to pretend. Choose as you [the director] like one actor rather than another, and if one recognizes in the performance traces of a background (professor, judge, sailor, a social dancer, tenor, etc.), that's all the same to me—the penal colony was made up of professors, officers, judges (rather few), sailors, dancers, and tenors. But no one will have to pretend to be something or to have been something. The universe in which error is possible doesn't interest me much, but how can we live in a universe in which evil binds together beings and acts?

OF HIS FILM SCRIPT

I have chosen, doubtlessly too arbitrarily, to place my penitentiary in the center of a desert and to deprive it completely of women; even the guards, even the black soldiers, don't have the right to bring along their wives. Am I cheating? Yes, if the public wonders about it, asks the question, and I don't know how to answer it.

Fiction must obey realistic demands. It respects not the traditional world but a more secret verisimilitude. The narrative entitled *The Penal Colony* is therefore a homosexual drama and nothing else. Nevertheless I wonder if the truth, and the lyric violence of images, will give a poetic power that is large enough to captivate even the spectator who is rather distant from such a strange notion. . . . The only homosexual in this story is me. I am only trying to propose a particular theme and to light it in such a way that it will enter—without hesitation, without a fuss, and without being refused—any old conscious mind.

VI

MEMOIR

Prisoner of Love

◄○►

In the summer of 1983, probably in July, Genet began to write Prisoner of Love *in Morocco. He linked his composition of this book about America and the Middle East with his feeling of total alienation from France. Genet was conscious that he was writing in a new style. When he was interviewed in Vienna at this time, Genet refused to speak about his earlier novels. He was reluctant to discuss them because he feared being drawn back into the past and into his old "literary" style.*

THE PAGE THAT was blank to begin with is now crossed from top to bottom with tiny black characters—letters, words, commas, exclamation marks—and it's because of them the page is said to be legible. But a kind of uneasiness, a feeling close to nausea, an irresolution that stays my hand—these make me wonder: do these black marks add up to reality? The white of the paper is an artifice that's replaced the translucency of parchment and the ocher surface of clay tablets; but the ocher and the translucency and the whiteness may all possess more reality than the signs that mar them.

Was the Palestinian revolution really written on the void, an artifice superimposed on nothingness, and is the white page, and every little blank space between the words, more real than the black characters themselves? Reading between the lines is a level art; reading between the words a precipitous one. If the reality of time spent among—not with—the Palestinians resided anywhere, it would survive between all the words that claim to give an account of it. They claim to give an account of it, but in fact it buries itself, slots itself exactly into the spaces, recorded there rather than in the words that serve only to blot it out. Another way of putting it: the space between the words contains more reality than does the time it takes to read them. Perhaps it's the same as the time, dense and real, enclosed between the characters in Hebrew.

When I said the blacks were the characters on the white page of America, that was too easy an image: the truth really lies where I can never quite know it, in a love between two Americans of different color.

So did I fail to understand the Palestinian revolution? Yes, completely. I think I realized that when Leila advised me to go to the West Bank. I refused, because the occupied territories were only a play acted out second by second by occupied and occupier. The reality lay in involvement, fertile in hate and love; in people's daily lives; in silence, like translucency, punctuated by words and phrases.

In Palestine, even more than anywhere else, the women struck me as having a quality the men lacked. Every man, though just as decent, brave, and considerate, was limited by his own virtues. The women—they weren't allowed on the bases, but they did all the work in the camps—added to all their virtues a dimension that seemed to subtend a great peal of laughter. If the act they put on one day to protect a priest had been performed by men it would never have carried conviction. Perhaps it was women, not men, who invented the segregation of women.

By the time we'd had our very light lunch it was about half-past twelve. The sun shone down vertically on Jerash and the men were taking a siesta. Nabila and I were the only two people awake and, not wanting to be in the shade, we decided to go to the camp at Baqa nearby. At that time Nabila was still an American. She got divorced later so as to stay with the Palestinians. She was thirty years old, with the beauty of a heroine in a Western. In blue-denim jeans and jacket, her black hair falling loose to the waist but cut in a fringe in front, she was a shocking figure to be walking around the camp at that hour. Some Palestinian women in national dress spoke to her, and must have been astonished to hear the boyish figure answer like an Arab of their own sex and with a Palestinian accent.

Whenever three women get talking, after a few polite exchanges they are joined by five more, and then seven or eight. Although I was with Nabila I was forgotten, or rather treated as nonexistent. Five minutes later we went into a Palestinian woman's house for a glass of tea—an excuse for continuing the conversation in a room that was cool and out of the sun. The women spread out a blanket for the two of us to sit on, added a few cushions, but remained standing themselves as they made the tea or coffee. No one took any notice of me except Nabila, who, remembering I was beside her, passed me a little glass. All the talk was in Arabic. My only interlocutors were the four walls and the whitewashed ceiling.

Something told me my situation was not what I'd have expected from my previous knowledge of the East: here was I, a man, alone with a group of Arab women. And everything seemed to reinforce this topsy-turvy vision of the Orient. All but three of the women were married, probably each to a different man. Perched there like a pasha on my cushions, I was in a rather dubious position. I interrupted the torrent of words they were exchanging with Nabila and asked her to translate.

"You're all married. Where are you husbands?"

"In the mountains!"

"Mine works in the camp!"

"So does mine."

"What would they say if they knew a man was here alone with you, sprawled on their blankets and cushions?"

They all burst out laughing.

"They *will* know!" said one. "We'll tell them, to embarrass them and have a good laugh at their expense. We'll tease our wonderful warriors! And perhaps they'll get cross and pretend to find boys more amusing."

The women all seemed to have nothing to do, and to talk a lot as they did it. But in fact each of them looked after one or two male offspring, changing their diapers and nursing or bottle-feeding them so that they would grow up into heroes and die at twenty, not in the Holy Land but for it. That's what they told me.

This was at Baqa Camp in 1970.

The fame of heroes owes little to the extent of their conquests and all to the success of the tributes paid to them. The *Iliad* counts for more than Agamemnon's war; the steles of the Chaldes for more than the armies of Nineveh. Trajan's Column, *La Chanson de Roland*, the murals depicting the Armada, the Vendôme column—all the images of wars have been created after the battles themselves thanks to looting or the energy of artists, and left standing thanks to oversight on the part of rain or rebellion. But what survives is the evidence, rarely accurate but always stirring, vouchsafed to the future by the victors.

Without warning we were on the alert. Europe received a jolt, and I'm still amazed. Three years before—I quote—"some film directors in Tel Aviv had scattered boots, helmets, guns, bayonets, and human footprints on the sands to simulate a debacle later edited in a studio in Los Angeles."

There was nothing new about the representation of battles, whether victories or defeats. Each side had its tricks and its experts, and artists attached to its army to cover the Egyptian campaigns. Draftsmen and painters depicted after the event whatever the victor permitted. In 1967, I was told, Israel prepared, shot, and cut in advance a film showing Egypt's defeat, and on the seventh day showed it to all the world's television, proclaiming their victory over the Arabs. When Nasser died, the brilliance of his funeral eclipsed his death. The cradle, the football, you could call it the coffin, pitched and tossed in the air and practically flew over the heads of the crowd, which though visibly angry was perhaps at the same time amused.

Hussein, Boumédienne, Kosygin, Chaban-Delmas, Haile Selassie the Lion of Judah, and other heads of state or government were lifted up by fists packing—flesh and bone together—fifteen kilos; by shoulders inured to the crates of Cairo shipping agents or the assembly lines of truck factories. The celebrities were picked up and then set down on the rostrum as delicately as a silk stocking held between finger and thumb. But the toughs of Egypt kept the coffin for themselves.

It was a good game. The ball disappeared into the scrum, then reappeared in another corner of the screen. Several players grappled for possession. Whose furious kick would send it flying into eternity? The pallbearers walked faster and faster, as if dead drunk, their mad rush forcing the Koran to follow. Legs, feet, throats, and the bier all got carried away. The bearers hurried the coffin along more nimbly than the All Blacks, and then it was swallowed up in the crowd. The whole world was following the match on the screen, and could imagine the bier passing from foot to foot, fist to shoulder, crotch to hair, until from the soil of Egypt the crowds, the pallbearers, the reciters of the Koran, the coffin, and the rugby players all vanished, leaving nothing but haste ever accelerating until it reached the grave. The sound of the gun salute was drowned by falling spadefuls of earth. Despite the guard, two or three thousand feet, relieved of their load, danced on the grave till morning, moving at the absolute speed that must belong to the One God. I couldn't help thinking of a World Cup in Oriental Funerals: this one would certainly have scored.

Not long after, in September 1970, when Hussein of Jordan was in danger of being beaten by the fedayeen, America came to his aid. Neither Nasser's morale nor his heart having held out, the rugby match at once muscular and sentimental that we saw on television was a ceremony designed to wipe out the debacle of 1967 and conceal those ushered in by 1970. Was the deceased only in hiding? The earnestness of the spectacle on the screen was as naïve as the kisses showered on the lips, hair, gold chain, earring, and eyes of a player who's just scored a goal. Is the spectator's applause for the goal or for the kisses? Has one out of ten sweating lads disappeared beneath the rest? Is he hiding? The Raïs's body had vanished. He who was the sun of a people would merge into the cedar of his coffin, and all would be ratified by time. The Arab people was skewered on an age of nations. The countries of the world were getting restive. New wars would be needed. Nasser would come in handy again, transfigured by comic strips.

Even before I got there I knew my visit to the banks of the Jordan, to the Palestinian bases, could never be clearly expressed. I had greeted the revolt as a musical ear recognizes a right note. I often left my tent and slept under the trees, looking up at a Milky Way that seemed quite close through the branches. At night the armed sentries moving around over grass and leaves made no sound. They tried to merge into the tree trunks. They listened.

The Milky Way rose out of the lights of Galilee and arched over me and the Jordan Valley before breaking up over the desert of Saudi Arabia. Lying there in my blanket I may have entered into the sight more than the Palestinians themselves, for whom the sky was a commonplace. Imagining their dreams, for they had dreams, as best I could, I realized I was separated from them by the life I'd lived, a life that was blasé compared with theirs. Cradle and innocence were words so chastely linked, for them, that to avoid corrupting either they avoided looking up. They mustn't see that the beauty of the sky was born and had its cradle in the moving lights of Israel.

In one of Shakespeare's tragedies, the archers loose their arrows against the sky, and I wouldn't have been surprised if some of the fedayeen, feet firmly on the ground, but angered at so much beauty arching out of the land of Israel, had taken aim and fired their bullets at the Milky Way—China and the socialist countries supplied them with enough ammunition to bring down half the firmament. But could they fire at stars rising out of their own cradle, Palestine?

"There was only one procession. Mine. I led it on Good Friday in a white surplice and black cope. I really haven't got time to talk to you," said the priest, already red with anger.

"I saw two. One with a banner of the Virgin Mary . . ."

"No. What you refer to as the second procession and the Virgin Mary—they were no such thing. Those louts marching along blowing bugles? Fishermen of some sort who'd have done better to stick to their own concerns. They enjoy causing a scandal."

But two processions had passed one another before my very eyes, the first led by the Lebanese priest, the second preceded by the blue and white banner of the saint and, according to the irate cleric, made up of hooligans and sailors quick-marching to the harbor.

I heard later, from a Benedictine, that there really were two processions. The first, despite the accompanying band, moved slowly, with an assumed melancholy. A group of musicians and male and female singers were performing what should have been a joyful requiem when this lachrymose parade was intercepted by another, composed of jaunty young men charging along blowing bugles. At their head was a stout young fellow holding up a picture of the Virgin Mary.

I recognized her from the folded hands, the white-edged clouds against the blue sky, the golden stars as in a Murillo, and the toes resting on a sharp-looking crescent. But I ought to have realized the truth from the stars, the blue of the sky, the quick marching, the bugles, the gaiety, the sweaters and rubber boots of the sailors, the absence of women—in fact the whole procession, and in particular, as my informant pointed out, the stars and the moon, ought to have enlightened me.

Although they described a perfect orbit around the lady, the stars were exactly the same in number as those in Ursa Minor. The blue was that of the sea. The fringed clouds were gentle waves. The crescent was Islam. The buglers played a merry tune because they were on the right road, and they didn't think twice about cutting the other mournful procession in two. The strapping lads in their gum-boots were fishermen, and the picture of the woman, who didn't have a halo like the Virgin Mary, symbolized the Pole Star.

This was what the Benedictine told me to start with. He went on to say that the lady in the picture was neither virginal nor Christian but belonged to the pre-Islamic "Peoples of the Sea." Her origins were pagan, and she'd been worshipped by sailors for thousands of years. In the dimmest of nights she infallibly showed them the North, and because of her the worst-rigged ship was sure to reach harbor safe and sound.

But the Benedictine couldn't tell me why the second procession was so cheerful that particular day, the day the Son died, leaving behind one who'd been a mother at sixteen and was very like the lady on the banner. Since he didn't want to go into it, I told myself, silently, that perhaps the buglers' high spirits that Good Friday represented the triumph of paganism over the religion of the Son.

That night at Ajloun I saw the Pole Star to my right in its place in Ursa Minor and the Milky Way dissolving into the Arabian desert, and I couldn't but wonder that, in a Muslim country where, as I still believed, woman was something remote, I was able to conjure up in my mind's eye before falling asleep a procession of men, apparently unmarried, who'd captured the image of a beautiful lady. But she represented the Pole Star, eternally fixed immeasurable distances away in the ether, and belonged, like every woman,[1] to a different constellation. The fishermen were masturbators rather than mates, and the word polar applied as much to the woman as to the star.

Though I was lying still in my blankets as I looked up into the sky, following the light, I felt myself swept into a maelstrom, swirled around and yet soothed by strong but gentle arms. A little way off, through the darkness, I could hear the Jordan flowing. I was freezing cold.

It was for fun as much as anything that I'd accepted the invitation to spend a few days with the Palestinians. But I was to stay nearly two years. Every night as I waited half dead for the capsule of Nembutal to send me to sleep, I lay with my eyes open and my mind clear, neither afraid nor surprised, but amused to be there. On either side of the river men and women had been on the alert for ages. Why should I be any different?

Meager though it seemed at the time, I'd had the privilege of being born in the capital of an empire that circled the globe, while at the same time the Palestinians were being stripped of their lands, their houses, and even their beds. But they'd come a long way since then!

"Stars, that's what we were. Japan, Norway, Düsseldorf, the United States, Holland—don't be surprised if I count them up on my fingers—England, Belgium, Korea, Sweden, places we'd never even heard of and couldn't find on the map—they all sent people to film us and photograph us and interview us. 'Camera,' 'in shot,' 'tracking shot,' 'voice off'—but gradually the fedayeen found themselves 'out of shot' and learned that the visitors spoke 'voice off.'

"A journalist who'd been driven around for a few yards by Khaled Abu Khaled would claim to be a friend of Palestine. We learned the names of towns we'd never dreamed of, and how to use apparatus we'd never seen before. But no one on the bases or in the camps ever actually saw a foreign film or photograph, television program or newspaper article about us. We knew *we* existed; we must be doing surprising things since people came from such far-off places to see us—but did the far-off places exist?

[1]The Palestinians, who were often invited to China, will quote the Thoughts of Mao at me; one of those most frequently quoted refers to women as "half of the stars."

"And the journalists used to stay about two hours: they had to catch a plane in Amman to cover the Lord Mayor's Show in London in six hours' time. Most of them thought Abu Amar and Yasser Arafat were two different people, possibly enemies. Those who got that right would multiply the numbers of Fatah and the ALP[2] by three or four because they counted all the members' pseudonyms as well as their ordinary names.

"We were admired so long as our struggle stayed within the limits set by the West. But nowadays there's no question of going to Munich, Amsterdam, Bangkok, and Oslo. We did get as far as Oslo once, and it snowed so hard we could make snowballs as it fell and chuck them at one another. In our own sands, on our own hills, we were a fable. When we went down the steps of the Jordan at night to lay mines, and came up again next morning, were we ascending from Hell or descending from Heaven? Whenever a European, man or woman, looked at us . . ."

This story had to be transmitted through another fedayee acting as interpreter, but the fedayee who told it gave me the impression he'd recited it often. It all came out so pat I was able to grasp what he said without waiting for the translation. Did he see that from my expression? At any rate he started to address me directly.

"Whenever Europeans looked at us their eyes shone. Now I understand why. It was with desire, because their looking at us produced a reaction in our bodies before we realized it. Even with our backs turned we could feel your eyes drilling through the backs of our necks. We automatically adopted a heroic and therefore attractive pose. Legs, thighs, chest, neck—everything helped to work the charm. We weren't aiming to attract anyone in particular, but since your eyes provoked us and you'd turned us into stars, we responded to your hopes and expectations.

"But you'd turned us into monsters, too. You called us terrorists! We were terrorist stars. What journalist wouldn't have signed a fat check to get Carlos to sit and drink one or two or ten whiskies with him! To get drunk together and have Carlos call him by his name! Or if not Carlos, Abu el-Az."

"Who's he?"

In 1971 Hussein's prime minister, Wasfi Tall, was killed in Cairo—had his throat cut, I believe—by a Palestinian who scooped up his blood and drank it. His name was Abu el-Az. He's in prison now in Lebanon, held by the Phalangists. The fedayee who was talking to me was one of his colleagues—I shan't give his name. I'd thought before then that "drinking someone's blood" was just a figure of speech for "killing," but according to his friend, Wasfi Tall's murderer had lapped up his gore.

"Israel calls everyone in the PLO terrorists, leaders and fedayeen alike. They show no sign of the admiration they must feel for you.

"As far as terrorism is concerned, we're nothing compared to them. Or compared to the Americans and the Europeans. If the whole world's a kingdom of terror, we know whom to thank. But you terrorize by proxy. At least the terrorists I'm talking about risk their own skins. That's the difference."

[2]Palestine Liberation Army.

. . .

After the 1970 agreement, the streets of Amman were policed by patrols of fe-
dayeen and Bedouin, often mixed. The airy, quizzical fedayeen could read and
understand all the international signs and symbols, while the Bedouin turned them
over gingerly in their slender, desert aristo fingers and handed back residence
permits, passes, safe-conducts, driving licenses, and car papers upside down. Their
dismay was obvious. And after being humiliated by the Palestinians in 1970, they
were only too delighted to kill them in June 1971. There was no reason for the
slaughter, but there was joy in it.

Today almost the whole of Amman is like the district which is still called Jebel
Amman and remains the most fashionable part of the city. The walls of the houses
were built of stone embossed on the outer surface, sometimes in the style called
diamond point. In 1970 the solidity of this luxury district was in sharp contrast to
the canvas and corrugated iron of the camps. The fact that the tents were of many
colors, because of the patches, made them pleasing to look at, especially to a
Western observer. If they looked at them from far enough away and on a misty
day, people thought the camps must be happy places because of the way the colors
of the patches seemed to match: those who lived beneath such harmony must be
happy, or they wouldn't have taken the trouble to make their camps such a joy to
the eye.

Who, reading this in the middle of 1984, when it was written, can help saying
the Palestinian camps have increased and multiplied? Just as they did before,
perhaps four thousand years ago or more, they seem to have sprung up all over
the world, in Afghanistan, Morocco, Algeria, Ethiopia, Eritrea. Whole nations
don't become nomads by choice or because they can't keep still. We see them
through the windows of airplanes or as we leaf through glossy magazines. The
shiny pictures lend the camps an air of peace that diffuses itself through the whole
cabin, whereas really they are just the discarded refuse of "settled" nations. These,
not knowing how to get rid of their "liquid waste," discharge it into a valley or on
to a hillside, preferably somewhere between the tropics and the equator.

From the sky, from the pressurized air of the cabin, we can see quite plainly that
while the fortified countries and cities, tied to the ground like Gulliver, made use
of their nomads—the privateers, the navigators, the Magellans, Vasco da Gamas,
and Ibn Battutas; the explorers, the centurions, the surveyors—they despised them
too. And it got better and more comfortable still for the banks when, thanks to the
gold in their cellars, money could "circulate" by means of bits of paper.

We oughtn't to have let their ornamental appearance persuade us the tents were
happy places. We shouldn't be taken in by sunny photographs. A gust of wind blew
the canvas, the zinc, and the corrugated iron all away, and I saw the misery plain.

The words sailors use were probably arrived at quite naturally; but what a strange
language they spoke when they were lost. They weren't yet poets—landsmen
moving over and resting on peaceful earth, with plenty of time to imagine the wide
expanses of ocean and its abysses and whirlpools. They were just simple mariners

traveling around the world without a hope, unless heaven or their mothers' prayers intervened, of an unexpected return to known shores and familiar hearths. Yet what curious words they found for a beach or a piece of wood or canvas—words like fo'c'sle and poop and topgallant.

The surprising thing is not the wildness of their invention, but that the words still live on in our language instead of having sunk like a wreck. Invented in wandering and solitude, and therefore in fear, they still make us reel and our vocabulary pitch and toss.

When you go from Klagenfurt to Munich you take a little train that snakes loop after loop through the hills, and the Austrian ticket collector walks down the corridor with the gait of a sailor in a rough sea. It's the only relic of the sea in the mountains of the Tyrol, all that remains of a terrestrial and maritime empire on which the sun never set. But Maximilian and Charlotte had the same rolling gait when they sailed to Mexico.

"The deep" is as expressive a term as most of the old but unforgotten phrases used in navigation. When sailors lost their way in loneliness and fog, water and endless pitching, perhaps hoping never to emerge, they also ventured verbally, making such discoveries as shoals, Finisterres, breakers, tribes, baobabs, Niagaras, dogfish. It was in a vocabulary that would have sounded strange in the ears of their widows, remarried by now to some shoemaker, that they told travelers' tales no one can explore without both dread and delight.

Perhaps the waters of the deep are as impenetrable as the darkest night: no eye can pierce its thousand walls, and color there is first impossible and then superfluous.

Amman can be described in these terms. It's made up of seven hills and nine valleys, the latter consisting of deep crevasses that banks and mosques can never fill. When you come down from the best districts of the city—the highest and most wealthy—you descend into the deep, surprised at being able to do so without a diving suit. You notice your legs are more sprightly, your knees more supple, your heartbeat quieter, but the shouts of the passersby and the noise of the traffic—and sometimes of bullets—seem to struggle against one another like rival teams in some new game. Now the shouting predominates for a moment, now the traffic din, producing a confusion in which nothing is clear except what's called a muffled roar, though it's really your own hearing that's impaired.

So much for your ears. As for the eye, in the shops of the "deep" it encounters windows all gray with dust. Of course the dust was still Arab even though the goods I saw on display were Japanese, but the even layer of particles, soft to the eye as the down in an ass's ear, was a kind of darkness. Not total darkness, though. A sort of submarine gloom. You might say the gray dust made Amman a city of the deep.

What did it mean, the soft film falling on the latest models of Japanese electronics from that most chic of archipelagos? Did it signify the rejection of an absurd but creeping sophistication? An attempt to bury it forever? Was it the symbol of the inevitable future awaiting everything? A way of taming the fiercest technology?

But would astronomy ever have become almost as pointless a branch of knowledge as theology if sailors, despite their dread of the deep and its reefs, hadn't told of the heavens and its galaxies?

From Amman, city of the kingdom of David, a Nabatean, Roman, Arab city going back into the mists of time, there arose an age-old accumulation of stench.

When we gave up believing in a Providence that steered us by the shoulder, we had to fall back on chance.

It was by chance I found out about the two networks by which some young men from North Africa who wanted to die for Fatah—the only organization every Arab had heard of in 1968—made their way to Egypt. Bourguiba, preferring diplomacy to war, had banned the volunteers from Tunisia, though they did pass through. Did he shut his eyes to it? Did approaching senility make him take too long an afternoon nap?

Some strange words ask to be understood more than others equally unfamiliar. Even if you hear them only once, their music stays with you. The word "fedayeen" was one of these. In the train from Sousse to Sfax I met a group of six young men, laughing and eating cheese and sardines. They were in high spirits because the recruiting board had found them unfit for military service. From what they said I gathered they had pretended to be mentally defective or mad, or deaf from self-abuse. They must have been about twenty. I left them behind when I got off the train at Sfax, but a few hours later met them once more by a fountain, again eating food out of tins. Instead of returning my smile or my greeting they seemed embarrassed. Some started to study the holes in their Gruyère. Others, who had recognized me, began a whispered but urgent conversation from which I learned— unless someone told me directly—that they'd got off the train at Sfax too, but onto the rails rather than the platform, so as not to be seen by the station master.

The next day a truck took them to Médenine, where they stayed in a small hotel. They crossed the Libyan frontier during the night.

This was in the early summer of 1968. I often used to go to Sfax. A waiter in my hotel asked me if I liked Tunisia. That's how, after a preliminary exchange of glances, amorous encounters always begin. I said I didn't.

"Come with me this evening," he said.

We met outside a bookshop.

"I'll read, and translate to you as I go along."

The shopkeeper handed us some slim volumes of Arabic poetry hitherto safely concealed, as he thought, under piles of other books. Then he opened a door and showed us into a small room, where the young man read me the first poems dedicated to Fatah and the fedayeen. What impressed me most was the elaborate decoration at the beginning, to the right, of each line of verse.

"Why are they hidden?" I asked.

"The police don't allow them to circulate openly. The southern part of the country is being developed by engineers from America and Vietnam. Bourguiba doesn't want any trouble with the U.S. or Israel. And our government has recognized Saigon. Come with us tomorrow. Three of us are driving forty kilometers out of town."

"What for?"

"You'll see. And hear."

The poems, at least in translation, left me unmoved, except for the beauty of the calligraphy. They were about struggle and disaster, but I couldn't make anything of the imagery, which was all about doves and damsels and honey.

The next day at about five in the evening the youths drove me out into the desert. They stopped the car where two tracks crossed. At six o'clock we listened to Bourguiba delivering a speech in Arabic on the radio. Every so often the boys would interrupt with sarcastic comments. Afterward we started to drive back to Sfax.

"What did you come all the way out here for?" I asked.

"For two years we've amused ourselves listening to Bourguiba speechify in the desert," they said.

Then, more seriously, they showed me a place where two tracks met in the sand. One went south with the caravans of female camels, the other went north through Tunisia. Both came from Mauretania, Morocco, and Algeria and led to Tripoli, Cairo, and the Palestinian camps. Those who took the northern route hitchhiked or jumped rides on the train. The ticket collectors looked the other way, as I was told by a ticket collector himself. The young men who went south mingled with the Bedouin caravans. King Idriss's border was open to them, and after a few weeks' military training in Tripoli they went on to Cairo by train, and then on again, I forget how, to Damascus or Amman.

I don't mean to say a whole flood of fighters from four or five North African countries used this illegal detour to come to the aid of the Palestinian camps. But that was how I learned of the appeal the Palestine resistance exercised on the Arab nation as a whole, and of the reverberations and almost immediate response it awakened. Of course the fedayeen had to be helped to reject the Zionist occupation, America or no America; but I sensed additional motives. Each of the Arab peoples wanted to throw off old yokes: when Algeria, Tunisia, and Morocco shook their leaves, they'd brought down the French who'd been hiding in the foliage. Cuba had got rid of its Americans in the same way. In South Vietnam they were only hanging by a cobweb. And Mecca, not so much sought after as it has become since, still didn't have many pilgrims.

It was about then that the minister Ben Salah introduced the figures 49 and 51 into Tunisian conversation. Fifty-one percent of the country's profit went to the government, forty-nine percent to private individuals. Fifty-one percent of the population was male, forty-nine percent female. Perhaps as a joke Ben Salah cut the merchants down to size: souks and French trees were pruned back and carpet sellers grew thin and seemed to be searching the ground for their lost branches. Bourguiba's sky blue eye was fixed exclusively on Washington. Meanwhile, in

every village along the coast and from north to south, potters indefatigably turned
out millions of jars—replicas of the age-old amphorae that sponge fishers are
always finding at the bottom of the sea, full of oil preserved by the mud since the
days of ancient Carthage. Every morning there were more jars, still warm from the
just-quenched oven. I could see Tunisia dwindling away: all its clay being sold to
girls from Norway in the form of terra-cotta amphorae. In the end, I thought, it'll
disappear altogether.

A few weeks later, about the middle of May 1968, I came across the same slim
volumes of Arabic poems to the glory of Fatah, but without the decorations, in the
courtyard of the Sorbonne in Paris. I think the stand they were on was close to
Mao's. That August the Soviet Union nipped the Prague Spring in the bud.

The young Tunisians I saw in the south of the country then were about eighteen
or twenty: the rutting season, the age of conquest for its own sake and for the sake
of sex; the age for making fun of the moral values your parents talk about and
never practice. The younger generation were all the more wild and even brazen
because Nasser encouraged their rebelliousness, and because they were preparing
to die. As you'll have realized, while some of the young men in Tunisia were as
I've described, the rest were preparing to be a nation of waiters—a hierarchy of
waiters and headwaiters in cafés and restaurants. Floor waiters in hotels were the
highest on the ladder to Heaven. They went about almost naked, and those who
were good-looking, even though some of them were married, would often leave
the country, traveling first class with some Swiss banker, or more rarely some Swiss
banker's wife.

So 1968 ended, and in Amman the Palestinians' struggle against King Hussein,
muted at first, grew more intense.

I'm still itching to say a few more words about amphorae. I saw them being
made. The clay was on the wheel and the potter was turning it with his foot. He
reminded me of a countrywoman working a sewing machine. But when the
amphora was almost finished the potter took it off the wheel, threw it into a box
and broke it. An assistant kneaded the still malleable pieces together and added
them to the mass of clay still waiting to be worked.

What had happened was that at the last moment the potter had made an
irreparable mistake. Because he was tired, or for some other reason, one of his
fingers, or more likely his thumb, had pressed down too hard and produced a hole
or some similar flaw in the side of the jar. So he had to start all over again, or the
amphora wouldn't live up to its supposed three thousand years.

Even now—they'll never grow up—Japanese potters still play with accidents.
Whether it arises from the clay, the wheel, the kiln, or the glaze, they watch out
for any irregularity and sometimes even emphasize it. In any case they use it as
a starting point for a new adventure. The shape and color may be perfectly
classical, but spoiled by a scratch or being under- or overfired. So they pursue and
develop the flaw, struggling fiercely, lovingly with and against it until it becomes

deliberate, an expression of themselves. If they succeed they're overjoyed: the result is modern. Never Tunisian. But not many Swiss bankers take up with Japanese potters.

To the other reasons I've given for the more lively part of Tunisian youth going to fight with the Palestinians, we might add that it was fed up with age-old amphorae.

In their own country the young Tunisians I mentioned before could easily look around and find others to lord it over: the fellahs from some god-forsaken part of the south as yet unrecorded on the rainfall map couldn't express themselves very well; French tourists were equally impressed by dusky eyes and by their gift of the gab. Their rapid prattle sounded as if it might owe something to amphetamines, but in fact this forked generation had merely learned to string phrases together from French television newsreaders: "Problems concerning the social fabric and rising delinquency aside, it will depend entirely upon ourselves to succeed at all levels in obtaining the highest possible output, creating a market in quality products even though the imminence of new scientific developments might call for ultrasophisticated state-of-the-art equipment." But outside Tunisia none of these squirts ever breathed a word, either in Arabic or in French. It was deeds that were needed, and gutsy ones—but siesta starts at two in the afternoon.

Bourguiba was asleep on his back.

It had been so pleasant dreaming about the Palestinians, and nobody knew yet, except in Israel, that all the Arab countries of Asia would expel them. No one knew, but everyone wanted them to be driven out and was secretly working for it.

One Palestinian alone was enough to cause a commotion. Their arrival in Tunis in 1982 was a facer for the languid Tunisians, part Turk, part wop, part Breton: more than a thousand Palestinians and, in their midst, Arafat himself.

It's at this point, neither sooner nor later, that I must say what Fatah was. But already those who dreamed up the various names of the Palestine movements were using Arabic as if they were both philologists and children. So while I'm going to try to explain the word, I know I can never bring out all its meaning.

The consonants *F*, *T*, and *H*, in that order, form a triliteral root meaning fissure, chink, opening; also a breakthrough before a victory, a victory willed by God. Fatah also means lock, and is connected with the word for key, which in Arabic is *meftab*—the three basic letters preceded by *me*. The same triliteral root gives Fatiha, that which opens, the name of the first surat of the Koran. The first surat itself begins with Bismillah.

Fatah, then, or rather F.T.H., corresponds to the initials of the Falestine (Palestine) Tharir (liberation) Haka (movement). In their French or logical order the three letters would give Haftha, which if it exists at all is meaningless. To get F.T.H. the order had to be reversed. Some overgrown children must have had a good laugh over that.

I see three hidden meanings in the three words Fatah, *meftab*, and Fatiha.

Fatah—chink, fissure, opening—suggests the expectation, the almost passive expectation, of a God-willed victory. *Mefta*—key—suggests almost visibly a key in an opening or lock. Fatiha also means an opening, but a religious one, the first chapter of the Koran. So behind the three words derived from the same root as Fatah lurk the ideas of struggle (for victory), sexual violence (the key in the lock), and battle won through the grace of God.

The reader probably sees this digression as a mere diversion, but I was so intrigued by the choice and composition of the word Fatah that I extracted the three above meanings from it, having put them there myself. The word itself occurs three times in the Koran.

The image of the fedayee grows more and more indelible: he turns into the path, and I'll no longer be able to see his face, only his back and his shadow. It's when I can neither talk to him anymore, nor he to me, that I'll need to talk about him.

The disappearance seems to be not only a vanishing but also a need to fill the gap with something different, perhaps the opposite of what is gone. As if there were a hole where the fedayee disappeared, a drawing, a photograph, any sort of portrait, seems to call him back in every sense of the term. It calls him back from afar—again, in every sense of the word. Did he vanish deliberately in order that the portrait might appear?

Giacometti used to paint best around midnight. He spent the day gazing intently, steadily. I don't mean he was absorbing the features of the model—that's something different. Every day Alberto looked for the last time, recording the last image of the world.

I first met the Palestinians in 1970. Some of the leaders got excited and almost insisted I finish this book. But I was afraid the end of the book might coincide with the end of the resistance. Not that my book would show it as it actually was. But what if my decision to make my years with the resistance public were a sign that it was soon to disappear? Some inexpressible feeling warned me that the rebellion was fading, flagging, was about to turn into the path and disappear. It would be made into epics. I looked at the resistance as if it were going to vanish at any moment.

To anyone looking at their pictures on television or in the papers, the Palestinians seemed to girdle the earth so fast they were everywhere at once. But they saw themselves as swallowed up by all the worlds they traveled through. Perhaps both we and they are wrong, or rather caught between an old illusion and a new variety, as when Ptolemy's ancient theory collided with Copernicus's novel and probably equally temporary truth.

The Palestinians imagined they were being hounded on all sides—by Zionism, imperialism, and Americanism. One day toward evening when things were at their quietest, we were safe inside the stone walls of our apartment in the middle of the Palestine Red Crescent building in Amman and I was writing down some addresses from Alfredo's dictation. Suddenly the air was rent by a cry, or rather a shriek. It was the lady of fifty.

She was a Palestinian who'd gone to live in Nebraska when she was very young and got rich there. What I remember about her is her face, her American accent, and her black clothes. She always dressed entirely in black, whether it was a blouse and a full skirt or a blouse and a narrow skirt; whether she chose a long seroual or a coat lined or edged with fur; whether the material was thick or thin. Her shoes and stockings, her jet necklaces, her hair and the scarf she tied over it—all were black. Her face was stern, her speech brief, curt, and guttural. The director of the Red Crescent had arranged for her to have a bedroom and the use of the lounge in our flat. All he told us about her was that one day in Nebraska, at home watching television, she saw some pictures of fedayeen who'd been killed by King Hussein's Bedouin. She switched off the television and the electricity, collected her handbag, passport, and checkbook, bolted and barred the front door, called in at the bank, went to the travel agent's and booked a ticket to Amman, and finally took a taxi straight from Amman airport and came and offered her services to the Red Crescent.[3]

The Red Crescent were in a quandary, because apart from signing checks—and she ruined herself doing that—this immensely wealthy Palestinian could do only one thing: even in the most uncomfortable conditions, sit in front of the television and watch American films.

We didn't talk to her much. She spoke only American and just a bit of Arabic. But we found out from her shriek, the meaning of which we learned soon afterward, how stupefied the Palestinians were when they suddenly found out that the whole world was against them.

Twiddling the knobs of the television to find something to pass the time, she could only find dialogue in Arabic. Then she thought she'd been rescued from the boredom of the evening, from Alfredo's and my silence and from the distant murmur of Amman, when someone on the screen spoke a whole sentence in Brooklyn slang. But—and this was why she'd shrieked—the other person answered in Hebrew: the television had picked up Tel Aviv. Her Palestinian hand, trembling with rage, cut off the sound in midsentence.

Silence fell again. The Palestinians might whiz nonstop from Oslo to Lisbon, but they knew they were being kept track of in the hatred language.

The villas in Jebel Amman had very large rooms. Each house had four salons: a Louis Quinze, a Directory, an Oriental, and a Modern—and sometimes even a "modern style" or *art nouveau* one as well. The nursery was done out in chintz, the nanny's room in cretonne. The domestics—cooks, gardeners, valets, and so on— slept out in the suburbs, in the camp at Wahadat, or twenty kilometers away in the camp at Baqa. Special servants' buses took them out every evening, standing

---

[3]The Muslim counterpart to the Red Cross.

up and already asleep, and brought them back again the next morning, standing up and not yet awake. A night porter stayed on duty to have tea and rolls ready for the masters when they woke up.

In this world of refugees, masters and servants were equal. The word refugee, later to become a title of distinction, was now a title deed to one of the strong, stone-built, wind-proof villas. But it was a title that threatened, though not yet too ominously, the camps of shreds and patches.

"I'm your equal because I'm a refugee. I'm your superior because my house is built of stone. Don't do anything to hurt or disturb me—I'm a refugee and a Muslim just like you."

Caught up in the to-ing and fro-ing between camp and villa, the servants seemed to bear their indignity proudly. But the year 1970 upset everybody. Wealthy Palestinians let their servants sleep in for a while. Others, by way of precaution, started to eat the same food as their staff. In September, democracy became fashionable almost overnight. Surreptitiously at first, then openly, the daughters of the house made their own beds or even emptied the ashtrays in the lounge. The reason was that all the menservants had taken up their guns ready for the fighting in Amman. They became heroes or, better still, died and became martyrs. For various reasons, that time was always to be known as Black September.

Many German families offered to take in wounded fedayeen from mobile hospitals like the one run by Dr. Dieter. All I'll say of him here is that in 1971 he set up a training school for nurses in the camp at Gaza. He took me to the camp one day after finishing his rounds among the sick and wounded. We went into one of the houses, all of which consisted of a single room. We were greeted by the political officer of the camp and the mothers and fathers of all the girls who wanted to learn the rudiments of nursing.

Naturally we drank tea, and then Dr. Dieter, standing at a blackboard fixed to the wall, began his lecture by drawing a rough sketch of a male body, complete with sexual organs. Not only did nobody laugh or smile; there was a sort of holy hush. The interpreter was a Lebanese. Dieter demonstrated the circulation of the blood with colored chalks, showing the veins in blue and the arteries in red. He put in the heart and lungs and other vital parts, and indicated where tourniquets should be applied. After the brain, skull, lungs, aorta, arteries, and thighs he came to the male sexual organs.

"A bullet or shell splinter can lodge here," he said.

So he drew a bullet near the penis. He didn't attempt to conceal anything, with his hand or his voice or his words. Both the official and the families approved of his frankness. His main concern was the shortage of doctors and nurses, male and female, in the camps.

"After twenty lessons the girls will know the basic necessities, but I shan't award certificates—the political and military chiefs are against it. The girls are being trained to go with the fedayeen and look after the wounded, not to Jebel Amman to administer aspirin and footbaths to the wives of millionaires."

There are lots of Palestinians in the Rhineland. They work in factories and speak good German, with the verbs at the ends of the sentences. The young ones born of German mothers learn Arabic and the history of Palestine, and call all the butchers in Düsseldorf, with their bloody aprons, Hussein.

As soon as I arrived on the bases at Ajloun I noticed a sergeant who was both a Palestinian and black, and whom the fedayeen spoke to or answered, if not scornfully, at least with a tinge of irony. Was it the color of his skin? A fedayee who spoke French told me it wasn't, but he smiled as he said it.

It was the month of Ramadan, and the soldiers could be divided up into very devout, not very devout, and indifferent. The latter ate during the fast.

One evening the sergeant, knowing I was a Christian, laid a cloth on the grass and set out a bowl of soup and a pot of vegetables. He himself remained standing, obeying the Koran. I had to choose quickly. To refuse would be to snub a black; to accept would make the favor too obvious. Eating just a little struck me as an elegant compromise. A few bits of bread dipped in the soup were all I wanted anyway. There were a couple of soldiers standing behind me, and when I'd eaten what I thought was a polite amount I got up, and the sergeant told the soldiers to finish what I'd left.

I could feel my cheeks flushing. I ought to have told the sergeant the fedayeen must eat with me, not after, and above all not finish my leavings—but how could I say that to a black? The main thing was not to make too much fuss. I said nothing. Should I sit down with the fedayeen and ask them for a bit of bread? The fedayeen had noticed what was happening. But not the black sergeant, as far as I could see.

When they look back, do the Palestinians see themselves with the same features and gestures, the same attitudes of body and limbs, in the same getup, as fifteen years ago? Do they see themselves from behind, for instance, or in profile? That image of themselves they conjure up amid the events of the past—is it younger?

Which of them remembers the scene I witnessed under the trees at Ajloun a few days after the fighting in Amman? The fedayeen had built a little arbor with a roof of leaves, and inside was a table—three planks laid shakily on four roughly stripped branches—with four benches fixed in the ground around it. The month of Ramadan had brought the expected surprise of a crescent moon open toward the west. We'd eaten our evening meal out on the moss near the arbor and were sitting replete around a bowl still warm but empty, listening to someone reciting verses from the Koran. So it must have been about eight o'clock.

"The man's a monster," Mahjoub told me. That evening he'd seemed the hungriest of us all. "He's the first head of state since Nero to set fire to his own capital."

What national pride I still possessed allowed me to reply:

"Excuse me, Dr. Mahjoub—we did just as well as Nero long before Hussein. A hundred years ago Adolphe Thiers asked the Prussian army to shell Versailles,

Paris, and the Commune. He did the job even more thoroughly than Hussein. And he was just as small."

The evening star was out. Mahjoub, slightly taken aback, went to bed in his tent. A dozen or so soldiers aged between about fifteen and twenty-three almost filled the arbor, but they made room for me. One fedayee stayed on sentry duty by the door. Then two men came in. They were fighters, still quite young but with downy moustaches on their upper lips to show how tough they were. They weighed one another up, as the phrase goes, each trying to intimidate the other. Then they sat down facing one another, lowering themselves casually but stiffly onto the benches and hitching up their trousers to preserve a nonexistent crease.

I was sitting silent and alert, as I'd been told, on the third bench. The newcomer sitting next to me took his hand out of the left-hand pocket of his leopard trousers and, with a movement at once very human and yet seeming to belong to some rare ceremonial, produced a small pack of fifty cards which he got his partner to cut. Then he fanned the cards out in front of them. One of the two swept them up and arranged them in a pack again, examined it, then shuffled the cards in the usual way and dealt them out between the two of them. Both looked serious and almost pale with suspicion. Their lips were tight, their jaws set. I can still hear the silence. Card playing was officially forbidden on the bases: Mahjoub had referred to it as "a middle-class pastime for middle-class people."

The game began. Gambling, and for a stake, filled both their faces with greed. They were equally matched, and first one and then the other grabbed the kitty. Around the two heroes, everyone tried to catch a brief glimpse of their swiftly concealed hands. Against all the rules, the onlookers behind each contestant made signals to the player opposite, who pretended to take no notice. I think they must have been playing a game something like poker. I was impressed by the way they both stared blankly at their hands, concealing their agitation and anxiety; by their brief hesitation over whether to take one, two, or three cards; and by the speed of those thin fingers, the bones so fine it seemed they might break when the winner turned the cards over and gathered them in. One of the players dropped a card on the floor and picked it up so nonchalantly it reminded me of a film in slow motion. The indifference, even disdain, on his face when he saw what it was made me think it must be an ace.

I thought people would think he'd been cheating, imitating an "accident" familiar to cardsharpers. What little Arabic I knew consisted mainly of threats and insults. But the words *charmouta* and *battai*, muttered between the players' clenched teeth and lips gleaming with saliva, were quickly bitten back.

The two players stood up and shook hands across the table, without a word, without a smile. Such dreary ceremony can be seen only in the casinos of Europe or Lebanon. Tennis matches can end like this too, but only in Australia. Sometimes a laugh is provided by a well-dressed lout who bends the cards lengthwise, either backward or forward. According to its position on the table a card may be either the boat in which the cheat himself sails, or the first half of the beast with two backs, or a woman pressed down on the beach and opening herself up. If the croupier notices the resulting smiles where no smiles should be, he brings out a fresh pack of cards, his face and eyes as expressionless as someone doing up his fly in public.

Obon is the name the Japanese give to another kind of game. Obon is the feast of the dead, who come back among the living for three times twenty-four hours. But the person who's returned from the grave is present only through the deliberately clumsy actions of the living. I interpret these as meaning: "We are alive and we laugh at the dead. They can't take offense because they're only skeletons condemned to remain in a hole in the ground."

It's merely their absence that the children, those underminers of ceremony, will bring up and install in their apartments. "We'll stay in the graveyard—we shan't be in anyone's way. We'll only be present if your awkwardness gives us away." The invisible dead are seated on the finest cushions and offered good things to eat and gold-tipped cigarettes to smoke such as Liane de Pougy was offered when she was twenty-three.

The kids pretend to limp. It seems that in the month leading up to Obon they practice limping, the better to leave the absent corpse behind in the races. These come to a sudden end—shinbones, skulls, thighbones, and fingerbones fall to the ground, and all the living laugh. An act of irony and affection had been enough to give the dead person a taste of life.

The game of cards, which only existed because of the shockingly realistic gestures of the fedayeen—they'd played at playing, without any cards, without aces or knaves, clubs or spades, kings or queens—reminded me that all the Palestinians' activities were like the Obon feast, where the only thing that was absent, that could not appear, was what the ceremony, however lacking in solemnity, was in aid of.

The science of shrieking seems almost as well known in the Arab world as the art of giving birth standing up, with the woman, her legs apart, holding on to a rope attached to the ceiling.

"Jean, did you hear that woman? She must be an Arab. That shriek's exactly like the one my grandmother let out when she did my father out of his inheritance."

"What was the inheritance?"

"The eighth part of an olive grove."

"What does that amount to?"

"Three and a half kilos of olives."

It doesn't take Muhammad many words to tell of his poverty, his father's dependency, the shriek of the old Arab woman. The shriek itself may have been natural, but its shrillness was learned when she was a girl. No one teaches R'Guiba, the watchman, how to shout a warning—he learns it in his youth when his voice is still high, and it comes back to him when he's on watch and some danger threatens, even after his voice has broken.

The Syrians often let out the same cry as the shamming Palestinians when a one of swords or any of the same suit comes up. All except the seven are of ill omen:

the one means excess, the two softness, the three distance, the four absence or loneliness, the five defeat, the six effort, and the seven—the famous Seven of Swords⁴—means hope, and it's the one card in the pack that's greeted with kisses. The eight means complaint, the nine masturbation, and the ten desolation and tears—and the cry that met this card, dejected rather than aggressive, was not at all like the cry of delight that greeted the appearance of clubs, the symbols of happiness.

At the camp at Baqa, the humiliated got their own back. The Japanese, Italians, French, Germans, and Norwegians were the first film cameramen, photographers, and sound engineers on the scene. The air, which had been light, became heavy.

Those who'd never been asked to pose themselves but who would be stars if they got a picture of a star—which here meant every Palestinian wearing combat dress and carrying a Kalashnikov—thought they had their victims just where they wanted them. With the irritability more or less natural to the inhabitants of a vexed archipelago, the Japanese threatened in English to go back to Tokyo without any pictures and leave Japan ignorant of the Palestinian Revolution. Little did they know that the famous terrorists of Lodz were in training ten kilometers away, with maps of Israel and plans of the airport in their overalls pockets.

The French made one fedayee pose twelve times for a single picture. Dr. Alfredo put a stop to this farce with three sharp words.

To show they knew how to take low-angle shots, the Italians told the fighters to unload their guns and take aim, then threw themselves down and took pictures lying on the ground. But the spirit of revenge produced a delightful chaos.

A photographer is seldom photographed, a fedayee often, but if he has to pose he'll die of boredom before he dies of fatigue.

Some artists think they see a halo of solitary grandeur around a man in a photograph, but it's only the weariness and depression caused by the antics of the photographer. One Swiss made the handsomest of the fedayeen stand on an upturned tub so that he could take him silhouetted against the sunset!

What is still called order, but is really physical and spiritual exhaustion, comes into existence of its own accord when what is rightly called mediocrity is in the ascendant.

Betrayal is made up of both curiosity and fascination.

But what if it were true that writing is a lie? What if it merely enabled us to conceal what was, and any account is, only eyewash? Without actually saying the opposite of what was, writing presents only its visible, acceptable and, so to speak, silent face, because it is incapable of really showing the other one.

The various scenes in which Hamza's mother appears are in a way flat. They ooze love and friendship and pity, but how can one simultaneously express all the

⁴Mary of the Seven Swords, stepdaughter of Lady Music. (*The Satin Shoe*, Paul Claudel).

contradictory emanations issuing from the witnesses? The same is true for every page in this book where there is only one voice. And like all the other voices, my own is faked, and while the reader may guess as much, he can never know what tricks it employs.

The only fairly true causes of my writing this book were the nuts I picked from the hedges at Ajloun. But this sentence tries to hide the book, as each sentence tries to hide the one before, leaving on the page nothing but error: something of what often happened but what I could never subtly enough describe—though it's subtly enough I cease to understand it.

Hicham had never been shown any consideration by anyone, old or young. No one took any notice of him, not because he was nothing, but because he did nothing. But one day his knee hurt him and he put himself down for medical inspection the following day. He went, and was given the number fourteen. Fifteen was a fedayee officer, a captain. After seeing thirteen patients, Dr. Dieter read out Hicham's name and number, but he was so flustered by hearing his own name pronounced by a doctor he didn't realize it referred to him. He nudged number fifteen, the officer who was supposed to come after him.

"No—you first," said Dieter. "You with the bad knee."

An official told Hicham to go first, and so he did. And I was told that after that day, when a German doctor made him go before a captain, Hicham started to throw his weight about. He knew he hadn't gone up in rank, but the fact that the official had briefly given him precedence made him throw out his chest. Not long afterward he relapsed into obscurity again: the officers forgot to return his salute. There was no such thing as pride to be seen in Baqa Camp.

Outside the arbor, under the trees, indifferent to the phantom game of cards, ten or so fedayeen waited their turn for a shave. They looked tired, but fairly relaxed. The lengthy ceremonial had begun. First every man had to bring a little bundle of dead branches. A fire was lit with a handful of leaves and the water put to boil in an old tin can. They were on such friendly terms with each other they might easily have taken it in turns with the one mirror and shaved themselves. But the mirror was only as big as the palm of a man's hand, and it was a sort of rest, added to that of the evening itself, to leave your beard and your face in the hands of the fedayee known as the barber. The touch of a hand, whether friendly or indifferent, but anyway different from one's own, was the start of a wave that soothed every organ in the seated body and reached right down to the weary toes. They took turns to be shaved. The whole thing usually lasted from eight o'clock to ten, and took place three times a week.

But why the game of cards?

"I leave the fighters completely free."

Mahjoub and I were walking under the trees at night.

"I should hope so."

"The only thing I've forbidden is cards."

"But why cards?"

"The Palestinian people wanted a revolution. When they find out the bases on the Jordan are gambling dens, they'll know brothels will be next."

I defended as best I could amusements I personally wasn't interested in, but was sorry Mahjoub took it on himself to ban something that helped the men pass the time."

"Gambling often leads to fighting."

It was easy to quote chess as an example of the pitiless struggle between the U.S.S.R. and the Western powers. Mahjoub said a curt good night and went to bed. The fedayeen knew. The show they'd put on for me demonstrated their disillusion, for to play only with gestures when your hands ought to be holding kings and queens and knaves, all the symbols of power, makes you feel a fraud, and brings you dangerously close to schizophrenia. Playing cards without cards every night is a kind of dry masturbation.

At this point I must warn the reader that my memory is accurate as far as facts and dates and events are concerned, but that the conversations here are reconstructed. Less than a century ago it was still quite normal to "describe" conversations, and I admit I've followed that method. The dialogue you'll read in this book is in fact reconstituted, I hope faithfully. But it can never be as complex as real exchanges, since it's only the work of a more or less talented restorer, like Viollet-le-Duc. But you mustn't think I don't respect the fedayeen. I'll have done my best to reproduce the timbre and expression of their voices, and their words. Mahjoub and I really did have that conversation; it's just as authentic as the game of cards without cards, where the game existed only through the accurate mimicry of hand and finger and joint.

Is it because of my age or through lack of skill that when I describe something that happened in the past I see myself not as I am but as I was? And that I see myself—examine myself, rather—from outside, like a stranger; in the same way as one sees those who die at a certain age as always being that age, or the age they were when the event you remember them for happened? And is it a privilege of my present age or the misfortune of my whole life that I always see myself from behind, when in fact I've always had my back to the wall?

I seem to understand now certain acts and events that surprised me when they happened there on the banks of the Jordan, opposite Israel—acts and events unrelated to anything, inaccessible islets I couldn't fit together then but which now form a clear and coherent archipelago.

I first went to Damascus when I was eighteen years old.

Arab card games are very different from those played by the French and the English. They're closer to the Spanish—an inheritance from Islam preserved by the fingers of urchins playing La Ronda.

Mahjoub in Jordan and one-armed General Gouraud in Damascus both banned card playing for different reasons, as they thought. Gouraud must have been afraid of clandestine gatherings that must *ipso facto* be anti-French. So the Syrians played cards at night in the little mosques of Damascus, by the light of a candle end or a wick dipped in a drop of oil. My presence must have reassured them. If some sappers on patrol in the narrow streets were surprised by the light and came to see what it was, I could explain we were there for religious reasons, to pray for France.

After the game, to make sure I wouldn't forget them, the Syrians would show me the ruins. I'm sure they'd been deliberately left as they were by Gouraud, the big boss, who refused to have them cleared away so that the citizens of Damascus should shake in their shoes forever. In the morning, at the dawn prayer, the players used to go home linking little or forefingers. I can still see the Swords and the Seven of Swords.

In the very small fraction of Fatah that I knew, I counted up eight Khaled Abu Khaleds. The number of *noms de guerre* was astonishing. False names were originally intended to conceal a fighter; now they adorned him. His choice was a pointer to his fantasies, which were paralleled by such designations as Chevara (a contraction of Che Guevara), Lumumba, and Hadj Muhammad. Every name was a thin, sometimes transparent, mask beneath which there was another name, another mask, of the same or different stuff but of another color, through which could be glimpsed a further name. Khaled just concealed a Maloudi, itself imperfectly covering an Abu Bakr, which again was superimposed on a Kader. The layers of names corresponded to layers of personas, and what they hid might be someone quite simple but was usually someone complex and weary. In such cases the name might belong to a deed admissible in one place and forbidden in another.

I, in my ignorance, accepted appearance and reality with equal politeness, and felt slightly irritated whenever I discovered someone's original name. A lot could be said about those two words, appearance and reality! Some of the names were invented, some came from garbled memories of American films; all tried to cover up whatever might remain of the misdeed.

I thought I could hear echoes of it in the phraseologies and absurdly sweeping slogans attributed to the sort of figures that haunt the imagination of nations in revolt.

Who said what?

"I'd make a treaty with the devil to fight against you."

"Who sups with the devil must use a long spoon."

"You don't ask for freedom. You take it."

"We'll fight two or three or four or five or ten Vietnams if necessary."

"We have lost a battle but not the war."

"I do not confuse the American people, whom I love and admire, with their reactionary government."

The paternity of such sayings is not very clear. The fourth is supposed to belong to Guevara. The fathers of the third were Abd el-Kadr and Abd el-Krim, and of the second Churchill, Stalin, and Roosevelt. It's said the first had Lumumba for a sire but was legitimized by Arafat, and this made it possible for Khaled to say to me:

"Israel is the devil we have to work with to conquer Israel."

It seemed to me he said it in one go, without any punctuation or pause for breath until the burst of laughter at the end. Take it as it is, and as you like.

One very conventional image reigned, trivial as the posters in the Paris Métro.

"From campfire to campfire there echoed calls to arms, *noms de guerre,* and songs. Anyone who was twenty then saw the world as being consumed or at least licked by flakes of fire, like the *R* of Revolution ever being devoured but never burned away by eternal flames."

What I saw at once was that every "nation," the better to justify its rebellion in the present, sought proof of its own singularity in the distant past. Every uprising revealed some deep genealogy whose strength was not in its almost nonexistent branches but in its roots, so that the rebels springing forth everywhere seemed to be celebrating some sort of cult of the dead. Words, phrases, whole languages were disinterred.

One day in Beirut, when I'd managed to make some sort of a joke, a Lebanese smiled at me and said almost fondly:

"You're getting to be a real Phoenician!"

"Why a Phoenician? Can't I be an Arab?"

"No, not any more. We haven't been Arabs since Syria invaded Lebanon." That was in 1976. "The Syrians are Arabs. The Lebanese Christians are Phoenicians."

The youngest generation were a lot of moles. What an example, after two thousand years of traveling the earth's surface on horseback, on foot, or by sea, to go back and burrow among molehills for the remains of some temple! Not only the search itself but also the wholesale identifying of one people with another, root and branch, struck me as undignified, a pretentious vulgarity worthy of Paris. It's a form of laziness to think nobility is proved by ancestry, and when I knew them, the Palestinians didn't go in for it. The danger then was that they might see Israel as a sort of superego.

1972 was before the Syrians' battle for the Palestinian camp at Tal-el-Zaatar. That didn't take place till 1976. But the Palestinians did show me the Phalangist barracks overlooking the camp.

This book could be called *Souvenirs,* and I'll lead the reader back and forth in time as well as, inevitably, in space. The space will be the whole world, the time chiefly the period between 1970 and 1984.

Pierre Gemayel's militia, modeled on Hitler's SA and founded at about the same time, was called the Phalange—Kataeb in Arabic. Black shirts, brown shirts, blue shirts—the famous "Azul legion" that froze to death among the fairy-tale snows of white Russia—green shirts, gray shirts, shirts of steel . . . In the place of the Nazis' anthem I heard the Phalangists'.

In 1970 the tall lads marched along singing the praises of the Immaculate Conception. I was enchanted. I could calculate their cruelty from their stupidity. Something halfway between monks and hoodlums, they swung along, chins jutting out, to a military march, some obliging musician having converted the tempo of the hymn into the solemn beat of an irresistible advance into immortality. From their full, slightly Negroid lips the songs issued forth with a fine foolishness. The Virgin Mary must have trembled at the thought of all those adolescent dead about to land in Heaven at any moment. But it was tragic too, the obvious virility of the young men lauding the gentleness of an invisible goddess, a smart young woman smothered in wreaths of white roses. Marching along in quick time, the strapping youths struck me as unreal, of another world—which as a matter of fact was where they soon went.

They marched in martial fashion. But wars aren't fought by marching in martial fashion. Real warriors probably never march in time. I was trying to impart some dignity to the ponderous, rather theatrical gait of the Kataeb—like something from the Beirut Opera. It was dictated by a leader for whom this sort of outmoded spectacle was appropriate; he never marched himself, but he did think in double time.

The newspaper seller's two sons answered me shyly. They were both Phalangists, and as they spoke they each touched, or rather clutched, a gold medal of the Virgin of Lourdes in the same way as a native of Mali on the banks of the Niger might clutch his gri-gri—a few magic words in Arabic on very thin paper, perhaps Rizla, rolled up in a red-woolen holder.

"Why are you touching that?"

"To remind me to say my morning prayer from the Koran."

The Cross and the image of the Virgin Mary, especially if they are engraved, or better still embossed, in gold—the Phalangists touch such talismans to preserve their strength. But what is it they are really touching—the Cross, the Virgin Mary, gold, or the sex of the world? If a Phalangist kills anyone, he doesn't do so of his own accord but on orders from God and in defence of His Mother, His Son, and the gold presented by one of the Magi. The Phalangists' God is the Lord of Hosts who makes haste to help them against the threat of the Other—Allah.

In 1972 I saw a member of the Kataeb kiss a young Lebanese woman. Between her tanned breasts, evidence of topless sunbathing, shone the little, gold gibbet, studded with diamonds and rubies. But instead of Christ it had a black, egg-shaped pearl. The young man's lips seemed to swallow the pearl, his tongue to caress the skin of the girl's breast. She laughed. Three Phalangists in turn bowed their heads in that communion, and without a trace of self-consciousness the girl said:

"May Jesus protect you and His Mother give you victory."

Having pronounced this blessing she went chastely on her way.

Francisco Franco was in power. On my way to the abbey of Montserrat I went through rocks, boulders, and ripe wheat. Churches are always decorated in red for Pentecost, and the columns in the chapel were hung with cerise-silk banners embroidered with gold, or what glitters like gold these days. The abbot assisted in the celebration of the mass.

After having looked on with some emotion—the significance of which, before my meeting with Hamza and his mother, will appear later—as the black Virgin proffered her child (as it might have been some hoodlum showing a black phallus),

I sat down on a bench. The church was full of men and women in mourning. Most of the congregation were very young. The abbot and his two acolytes, heirs of Cisneros the grand inquisitor, wore copes of cerise silk. Children's voices, crystal frail and slightly raw, sang a mass by Palestrina. I kept thinking how the name started with the same six letters as Palestine. Then came the famous kiss of peace: after the elevation the abbot kissed each of the acolytes on both cheeks, and they conveyed the salutation to each of the monks sitting in the choir. Then two choristers opened the screen doors and his reverence came down among the congregation, kissing some of us. I was one of those who received a kiss, but I broke the chain of fraternity by not passing it on. The clergy emerged from the choir and went down the nave toward the main doors, followed by the congregation, men and women mingled together and I among them.

Then, for me alone, a wonderful thing happened. The doors seemed to open by themselves, as if pushed from without—the opposite of what happened on Palm Sunday, when the clergy, having gone out through the sacristy, knocked at the church door three times in memory of the Messiah's entry into Jerusalem, asking to be let into the nave. Now, at Whitsuntide, the doors opened inward, while inside the lighted chapel the abbot with his crozier and all the clergy wanted to be let out.

The countryside started at the church porch, and to a triumphal tune the procession moved through the wheat and through the rye, as far as the rocks that the first Saracens in Spain shrank from scaling in about the year 730. For some time everyone had been singing the *Veni Creator Spiritus*. And I remembered—I thought it had significance only for me—that it was sung at weddings as well as at Whitsun.

The monks and the acolytes sprinkled the fields with holy water, and the abbot, thinking to bring the country peace, blessed it with one hand, the index and middle finger raised and singing at the top of his voice. He sounded crazy to me—the whole crowd was crazy, almost delirious. A little rain, just a few drops, would have been a relief to all of us. But the Catalan countryside cowered there in the sun like every other living thing in Spain. God who created heaven and earth must have had some fun carving out those red, phalloid rocks which perhaps, despite the legend, were crowned with Arabs the moment they appeared, but which the abbot now blessed as freely as he blessed the wheat.

The sun blazed down. It was noon. Suddenly we turned our backs on nature, over which and for which the nuptial chant, Latin and Gregorian, had risen up, and were led by our shepherd back to the church. But our going back into the shade was not so much a return into the Temple as the closing in around us of a night forest, where groves and thickets and clearings lay waiting for us in the moonlight.

A ring of young men and girls in the woods on a moonlit night—are they there to pray, or, when all Islam is governed by lunar cycles, to fuse their strength together into a single malediction? Is it Christian to place the feet of married couples on the inside of the Crescent? I could think of nothing to compare with what I was feeling. Something other than the Eternal was present. What terror was ever like this? Mont Blanc advancing upon me? Grock entering the circus ring and producing a child's violin from his trousers? Or a policeman's hand falling on my shoulder? And the hand saying quietly: "Got you!"

The word paganism sounds a challenge to any society. The word atheist is less dangerous—it's too close to Christian moralism, or at least the kind that reduces Christ to the thorn in His kingly and godly crown, to be a threat. But paganism puts the unbeliever back amid the so-called "mists of time," when God didn't yet exist. A sort of intoxication and magnanimity allows a pagan to approach every-thing, himself included, with equal respect and without undue humility. To approach, and perhaps to contemplate. No doubt I overrate paganism, which I seem to have been confusing with animism. But in describing that ceremony at Montserrat, I tell of the cave I emerge from, the cave I sometimes find myself in again through some fleeting emotion.

I tried in the *Review of Palestinian Studies* to show what was left of Chatila and Sabra after the Phalangists had been there for three nights. They crucified one woman alive. I saw the body, with the arms outstretched and covered with flies, especially round the tips of her hands: there were ten blackening clots of blood where they had cut off the top joints of her fingers.

Was that how the Phalangists got their name, I wondered. In that place, at that time, in Chatila on September 19, 1982, it seemed to me it must have been a game. To cut off someone's fingers with secateurs like a gardener trimming a yew—these Phalangist jokers were just gardeners lurking about, converting a landscape garden into a formal one. But this impression disappeared as soon as I had time to think it over, and then I saw quite a different scene in my mind's eye. You don't lop off either branches or fingers for nothing.

Their windows were shut but the panes were broken, and when they heard the gunfire and saw the camps lit up by flares, the women knew they were trapped. Jewel cases were emptied out onto the tables. Like people pulling on gloves so as not to be late for a party, the women stuck rings on all the fingers and even the thumbs of both hands, perhaps five or six rings to a finger. And then, covered with gold, did they try to escape? One, hoping to buy the pity of a drunken soldier, took a cheap ring set with an imitation sapphire off her forefinger. The Phalangist, drunk already, grew drunker still at the sight of all her jewelry, and to save time took out his knife (or a pair of secateurs found near the house), cut off the top two joints of her fingers, and pocketed them and their adornments.

Pierre Gemayel went to see Adolf Hitler in Berlin, and what he saw there—brawny, blond young men in brown shirts—made up his mind: he would have his own militia, based on a football team. As a Lebanese Christian he wasn't taken seriously by the other Christians, for whom force could come only from finance. The Maronites' mockery drove Pierre and his son Bechir straight into the arms of the Israelis and led the Phalangists to make use of cruelty, a shadow of force more effective in those parts than force itself. Neither Pierre nor his son could have exercised power if some other power—Israel—hadn't sponsored and backed them up. And Israel and its cruelty were sponsored in turn by the United States.

So I was getting to know them better, these Phalangists who kissed gold crosses between girls' breasts, whose thick lips clung to medals of the Virgin on gold chains, and lingered over the hand of a Patriarch devoutly masturbating the shaft of his golden crozier.

I opened my eyes wide to gaze at the "Real Presence" in the monstrance, where sumptuously, humbly but boldly the "bread" was displayed. How many individual shipwrecks the Church is made up of . . .

The Muhammadan steeds rode hell for leather. Were they running away? We stood behind the abbot in the chapel. The black Virgin and her Negro Jesus had resumed their former pose. But would I be experiencing the thrill I felt that Whitsun if I hadn't given a twenty-year-old Muslim a lift in my taxi from Barcelona, and he hadn't stayed on with me throughout the ceremonies?

The original kiss bestowed by the abbot in the chapel and multiplied like the Nazarene's loaves by the lakeside or like the petals of a flower, each subsequent kiss having the same virtue as the first, reminds me of the chief of the pseudotribe giving each of the sixteen worthies fewer kisses than the one before.

"To each according to his deserts." But perhaps the noblest of the sixteen worries was he who was given a single kiss. I knew nothing about it. Perhaps just a single kiss was the sign of the highest veneration, in a progression descending by intervals of sixteen to the One?

One night just before dawn in January 1971, four months after Black September, three separate groups of fedayeen who'd been on the march for some time, transferring from one base to another, were singing to each other from their various hills. Between each song I could hear the silence of the morning, dense with all the daytime sounds that hadn't yet burst forth. I was with the group nearest the Jordan. As I squatted down, resting, I was drinking tea—noisily, for it was hot and in those parts it's the custom to proclaim the pleasures of tongue and palate. I was also eating olives and unleavened bread. The fedayeen were chatting in Arabic and laughing, unaware of the fact that not far away was the spot where John the Baptist baptized Christ.

The three hilltops, each invisible to the other two, hailed one another in turn—it was about then, or a little later, that Boulez was working on *Répons*—and in the east the yet unrisen sun was tingeing the black sky with blue. Even the uncertain voices of the young lions of fourteen were pitched low to improve the polyphonic effect (usually they all sang in unison), and also to prove their general maturity, their fighting spirit, their courage, their heroism—and perhaps also, by this discreet emulation, to prove their love for the heroes.

One group would be silent, waiting for the other two to answer, which they always did together, though each of the three groups sang in a different mode. In certain passages, though, a boy fighter would decide to add some trills a couple or two and a half tones higher than the rest; then the others would fall silent, as if making way for an elder. The contrast between the voices underlined the contrast between the terrestrial kingdom Israel and the landless land with no other prop than the warbling of its soldiers.

"Were these kids fighters, then—fedayeen, terrorists, who steal out in the dead of the night or in broad daylight and plant bombs all over the world?"

In between the verses winging from hill to hill I thought all was utterly silent. But then between the second and third verses I heard the voice of a stream. I never made out whether it was near or far away, but from its murmur I took it to be clear and secret, and it rose up modestly between two hills and two groups of singers. It was only between the fifth and sixth verses that the stream's voice rose and filled the whole valley. Then, as if meaning spread from the stream of water to the stream of voices, the singing grew hoarser and louder, driving out the childish tones and becoming rough, imperious and, finally, quite wrathful.

It seemed absurd that a dictator should silence lovers. But probably they hadn't heard either the stream or the torrent.

The night wasn't dark enough: I could make out the shapes of trees, kitbags, guns. When my eyes got used to a very dim patch and I peered hard, I could see, instead of the patch, a long, shadowy path ending in a sort of intersection from which other even darker paths branched out. The call to love came not from voices or things, perhaps not even from myself, but from the configuration of nature in the darkness. A daylight landscape, too, sometimes issues the order to love.

The improvised trills—all the singing was improvised—were devoid of consonants and mostly very high pitched. It was as if three scattered Queens of the Night, wearing faint moustaches and battle dress, came together in the morning to carol with the confidence, recklessness, and detachment of prima donnas, oblivious of their weapons and their clothes. Oblivious too of the fact that they were really soldiers, who at any moment might be silenced for ever by a hail of bullets from Jordan as accurate and melodious as their own singing. Perhaps the Queens believed their camouflage uniform made their singing infrasonic?

The legendary pre-Islamic hero Antar, buried deep in memory, might have come to life again at any moment. I remembered how at eighty years old he rose in his stirrups to sing the praises of his dead beloved and of their happy home. And a blind man, guided only by the voice, drew his bow and slew Antar with an arrow in the groin. The voice had replaced the sightless eyes to guide the dart.

The voices, that morning at least, were as sure as the sound of oboes, flutes, and flageolets—sounds so true you could smell the wood the instruments were made of, feel its grain. Just as in Stravinsky's own voice, cracked yet delightful, I recognized the sound of the instruments in *The Soldier's Tale*. I remember the rough, so-called guttural Arabic consonants being contracted, elided, or prolonged till they were soft as velvet.

A great light in the east: day came to the hills before the sun rose. I was under some old olive trees that I knew well.

We made our way round another hill, the same one as before, though I'd thought we were several hills further on. This was a pathetic trick to make the enemy think the Palestinians were everywhere at once. For ten years, against the hypersensitive equipment of Israel, the Palestinians used ruses that were both dangerous and useless, but often amusing and even poetic.

To my question, "What song were you singing?" Khaled replied:

"Everyone invents his own. One group introduces a subject, the group that answers first gives the next subject, the third group gives the first an answer that's also a question, and so on."

"What's it usually about?"

"Love, of course! And occasionally the revolution."

I made another discovery: some voices, inflexions, and quarter-tones sounded familiar. For the first time in my life I was hearing Arab singing coming freely out of people's mouths and chests, borne on a living breath that machines—discs, cassettes, radios—killed at the very first note.

That morning I'd heard a great improvisation performed among the mountains, in the midst of danger; yet heedless of the death that lurked everywhere for warrior musicians whose bodies might soon lie decomposing in the midday sun.

Let us not dwell on the well-known fact that memory is unreliable. It unintentionally modifies events, forgets dates, imposes its own chronology, and omits or alters the present of the writer or speaker. It magnifies what was insignificant: everyone likes to witness things that are unusual and have never been described before. Anyone who knows a strange fact shares in its singularity.

And every writer of memoirs would prefer to stick to his original plan. Fancy having gone so far only to find that what lies beyond the horizon is just as ordinary as here! Then the writer of memoirs wants to show what no one else has ever seen in that ordinariness. For we're conceited, and like to make people think the journey we made yesterday was worth writing up today. Few races are naturally musical: every people and every family needs its own bard. But the writer of memoirs, though he doesn't advertise the fact, wants to be *his* own bard: it's within himself that his tiny, never-finished drama takes place. Would Homer have written or recited the *Iliad* without Achilles's wrath? But what would we know about Achilles's wrath without Homer? If some undistinguished poet had sung of Achilles, what would have become of the glorious, peaceful but shortish life Zeus allowed him?

English aristocrats and English mechanics alike can all whistle Vivaldi and the songs of sparrows and other English birds. The Palestinians were inventing songs that had been as it were forgotten, that they found lying hidden in themselves before they sang them. And perhaps all music, even the newest, is not so much something discovered as something that re-emerges from where it lay buried in the memory, inaudible as a melody cut in a disc of flesh. A composer lets me hear a song that has always been shut up silent within me.

A few days later I saw Khaled again. I thought I'd recognized his voice in one of the choirs on the three hills. What subjects had he chosen?

"I'm getting married in a month's time," he answered, smiling, "so the two hills opposite mine were making fun of my fiancée. They said she was ugly and stupid and had a hump and couldn't read or write. And I had to defend her. I told them when the revolution's over I'll throw them all in jail."

He unslung his carbine from his shoulder and added it to the pile of guns stacked on their butts on the grass. His teeth flashed under his moustache.

I wrote that in February 1984, fourteen years after the singing on the hills. I never made any notes at the time, along the roads or tracks or on the bases. Nor anywhere else. I record an event because I was present when it happened and I was lastingly affected by it. I think my life is made up of impressions as strong as that, or even stronger.

"Why not now?"

"You know very well we haven't got any prisons."

"What about a mobile one?"

"Design one for us!"

"So then what happened?"

"They answered, and the sun came up, and we sang the dawn prayer. Then they pulled my leg about what they said I used to get up to on the sly with King Hussein and Golda."

"And then?"

"I doubled their sentences."

"What happened next?"

"They said they'd really been singing about their hill, which was called The Fiancée (*Laroussi*)."

He was silent, smiling slightly. Then he asked shyly:

"It was a good song, wasn't it?"

Looking at his hand, with its thick palm and powerful thumb, I realized the strength of his song and of his spirit.

"Maybe you didn't catch all the words? At one point I described all the cities in Europe where we've carried out attacks. Did you hear how I sang 'München,' in German, in all sorts of different keys?"

"And you described it?"

"Yes, street by street."

"Do you know it?"

"After singing about it for so long, yes—like the back of my hand."

Still smiling, he told me more about his views on the art of singing, and added seriously:

"The stream was an awful nuisance."

"In what way?"

"It got in our way. Once it took over it wouldn't let anyone else get a word in."

So he had noticed the voice I'd thought so secret and unobtrusive that mine was *the only ear to hear it.*

But if such elusive sensations are perceptible to organs other than mine, perhaps what I took to be my own exclusive knowledge is available to everyone, and I have no secret life . . .

In the evening the fedayeen usually rested from the day's work: fetching and carrying supplies and guarding the base, the gun emplacements, the radio and telephone network, and everything else to do with security; not to mention the permanent alert against the ever-dangerous Jordanian villages. One evening Khaled Abu Khaled asked me about the fighting methods of the *Black Panthers.*

My answer was slowed down by the meagreness of my Arabic vocabulary. He was surprised to hear about the activities of the urban guerrillas.

"Why do they do that? Haven't they got any mountains in America?"

Perhaps because it seemed to lack depth, the Panther movement spread fast among the blacks, and among young whites impressed by the guts of its leaders and grass-roots activists and by its novel and strongly antiestablishment symbolism. Afro hairdos, steel combs, and special handshakes were also the insignia of other black movements more oriented toward Africa—an imaginary Africa that combined Islam and spirit worship. The Panthers didn't reject those emblems, but added to them the slogan "All Power to the People"; the image of a Black Panther on a blue background; leather jackets and blue berets; and above all the open carrying of weapons.

To say the Party had no ideology because its "Ten Points" were either vague or inconsistent and its Marxism-Leninism was unorthodox is neither here nor there. The main object of a revolution is the liberation of man—in this case the American black—not the interpretation and application of some transcendental ideology. While Marxism-Leninism is officially atheist, revolutionary movements like those of the Panthers and the Palestinians seem not to be, though their more or less secret goal may be to wear God down, slowly flatten Him out until He's so drained of blood and transparent as not to be at all. A long but possibly efficient strategy.

Everything the Panthers did was aimed at liberating the blacks. They used rousing images to promote the slogan "Black is Beautiful," which impressed even black cops and Uncle Toms. But swept along, it may be, by the momentum of its own power, the movement overshot the goal it had set itself.

It grew weak, with the harsh weakness then in fashion, shooting cops and being shot by them.

It grew weak through its rainbow fringe, its fund-raising methods, the quantity and inevitable evanescence of its TV images, its use of a rough yet moving rhetoric not backed up by rigorous thought, its empty theatricality—or theatricality *tout court!*—and its rapidly exhausted symbolism.

To take the elements one at a time: the rainbow fringe probably acted as a kind of barrier between the Panthers and the whites, but in addition to being frivolous it also infiltrated the Panthers themselves.

As for the movement's fund-raising methods, enthusiasm was quickly aroused among rich bohemians, black and white: checks flowed in, jazz and theater groups contributed the takings from several performances. The Panthers were tempted to spend money on lawyers and lawsuits, and there were various unavoidable expenses. But they were also tempted to squander money, and they yielded to the temptation.

Television images had the advantage of being mobile, but they were still only two-dimensional, and had more to do with dreams than with hard fact.

The Panthers' rhetoric enchanted the young—both black and white took it up. But the words "Folken," "Man," and "Power to the People" soon came to be a thoughtless habit.

Theatricality, like TV, belongs to the realm of imagination, though it uses ritual means.

The Panthers' symbolism was too easily deciphered to last. It was accepted quickly, but rejected because too easily understood. Despite this, and precisely because its hold was precarious, it was adopted by the young in the first instance— by young blacks who replaced marijuana with outrageous hairstyles and by young whites still used to a language of Victorian prudishness. They laughed when first Johnson and then Nixon were publicly called motherfuckers, and supported the Panthers because they were the "in" thing. The blacks were no longer seen as submissive people whose rights had to be defended for them, but determined fighters, impulsive and unpredictable but ready to fight to the death for a movement that was part of the struggle of their race all over the world.

Maybe the explosion was made possible by the Vietnam War and the resistance the Viets put up against the Yanks. The fact that Panther leaders were allowed to speak—or were not prevented from speaking—at antiwar meetings seemed to give them a right to take part in the country's affairs. Later—and this shouldn't be underrated—some black veterans joined the Party when they came home, bringing with them their anger, their violence, and their knowledge of firearms.

Probably the Panthers' most definite achievement was to spotlight the fact that the blacks really existed. I had the opportunity of seeing this for myself. At the Democratic convention in Chicago in 1968, the blacks were still if not timid at least cautious. They avoided broad daylight and definite statement. Politically they made themselves invisible. But in 1970 they all held their heads high and their hair stood on end, though the real, fundamental activity of the Panthers was almost over.

If the white administration hoped to destroy them by inflation followed by deflation, it was soon proved wrong. The Panthers made use of the inflation period to carry out many acts, perform many gestures that became symbols all the stronger for being weak. They were quickly adopted by all the blacks and by white youth. A great wind swept over the ghetto, carrying away shame, invisibility, and four centuries of humiliation. But when the wind dropped people saw it had been only a little breeze, friendly, almost gentle.

• • •

The image I want to record here came to me in a crowd of others which gradually yielded to it in vividness, force, and persuasiveness as my decision to write became clear and concentrated on that image alone—the image of night at the Pole.

The Lufthansa plane took off from Hamburg on the evening of December 21, 1967 and took us first to Copenhagen, where because of a fault in the navigation equipment we had to go back to Hamburg. We left again on the morning of the twenty-second. Apart from three Americans, five Germans, and myself, all the passengers were taciturn Japanese. Nothing of note happened till we got to Anchorage, but there, just before we landed, the air hostess spoke a few greetings in English and German, and then said *"sayonara."*

The clear voice, the long-expected strangeness of the language, the limpid vowels gliding over the consonants, the word itself floating through the darkness while the plane was just about to leave Western longitudes, gave me the feeling of utter newness that we call presentiment.

The plane took off again. Or did it? The engines were running, but I hadn't felt the jolt, great or small, that usually accompanies takeoff. And it was so dark I couldn't see if we were moving or not. Everyone was silent, sleeping perhaps or taking their own pulse. Through the window I could see a red sidelight on the wingtip. One of the hostesses told me we'd passed the Pole and were "coming down" on the eastern part of the globe.

The fatigue of the journey, the change of route, the movement of the plane, the darkness that seemed to stretch as far as Japan, the thought of being on the east of the world, the idea that at any moment there might be an accident whereas every other moment proved there hadn't been one yet, the echo in my mind of the word *"sayonara"*—all these things kept me awake.

The word made me feel my body being stripped bit by bit of a thick, black layer of Judaeo-Christian morality, until it was left naked and white. I was amazed at my own passiveness. I was a mere witness of the operation, conscious of the well-being it produced without taking part in the process. I knew I had to be careful: the thing would only be a complete success if I didn't interfere. The relief I felt was rather a cheat. Perhaps someone else was watching me.

I'd fought so long against that morality my struggle had become grotesque. But it was vain. Yet a word of Japanese spoken in the fluent voice of a girl had been enough to trigger off the operation. What also struck me as surprising was that in my past struggles I'd never invented, or by learning Japanese discovered, that simple, rather amusing word, the meaning of which I still didn't know. I was intrigued by the medicinal power of a mere word irrespective of its content. A little while later it seemed to me that *"sayonara"* (as the "r" sound doesn't exist in Japanese it sounded like "sayonala") was the first touch of cotton wool that was going to cleanse my wretched body—wretched because of the long, degrading siege it had had to withstand from Judaeo-Christian ethics.

This deliverance, which I'd expected to be lengthy, irksome, and deep, as if carried out with a scalpel, began with a sort of game—an unfamiliar word placed cunningly after some English and German ones. And that welcome, addressed to all the passengers, was the start for me of a cleanup that, while only superficial, would free me from a moral system that clung to the skin rather than burned into the flesh. I ought to have realized before that it would be got rid of not by a solemn surgical operation but by the application of good, strong soap. My inside wasn't affected.

Nevertheless I got up to go and have a crap in the rear of the plane, hoping to get rid of a tapeworm three thousand years long. I obtained almost immediate relief: all would be well—my liberation had begun by tweaking the nose of propriety. An agile aesthetic had loosened the grasp of an onerous ethic. But I didn't know anything about Zen, and I don't know why I wrote that. The plane flew on through the night, but I had no doubt that when I got to Tokyo I'd be naked and smiling, ready and willing to slice off the heads of first one and then another customs officer or else laugh in their faces.

The customs people didn't even look at the little Japanese girl whose death I'd both hoped for and feared. I'd thought her fragile bones and already flattened features cried out to be crushed. The German crew's heavy boots matched the muscles in their hips and thighs, the sturdiness of their torsos, the tendons in their necks, their grim expressions.

"Such frailty is a kind of aggression and just asks to be suppressed."

But I probably had that thought in some other form, presumably haunted by images of emaciated Jews naked or almost naked in the concentration camps, where their weakness was regarded as a provocation.

"To look so frail and crushed is a sort of plea to be crushed. If we were to crush her, who would know? There are already more than a hundred million Japanese alive today."

But she was still alive and speaking Japanese.

All decisions are made blindly. If even one judgment left the judges exhausted after sentence was pronounced, their officers aghast, the public flabbergasted, and the criminal free, unreason would have been at the root of both judgment and freedom. Fancy taking as much trouble over a judgment as some idiot does over a poem! Where will you find a man determined to earn his living by not judging? How many forsake the narrow byways of the law to wear themselves out arriving at an elaborate judgment which may only prove that to plan carefully is a recipe for failure? A judge hidden in anonymity is a judge only in name. When the judge calls the criminal's name out he stands up, and they are immediately linked by a strange biology that makes them both opposite and complementary. The one cannot exist without the other. Which is the sun and which the shadow? It's well known some criminals have been great men.

Everything happens in the dark. At the point of death, however insubstantial those words and however unimportant the event itself, the condemned man still wants to determine for himself the meaning of his life, lived in a darkness he tried not to lighten but to make more black.

• • •

Stony Brook is a university about sixty kilometers from New York. The university buildings and the houses where the professors and students live stand in the middle of a forest. The Panthers and I were to give a couple of lectures there, one for the students and the other for the professors. The idea was to talk about Bobby Seale and his imprisonment, and the real risk that he might be sentenced to death. We were also going to discuss Nixon's determination to wipe out the Black Panther Party, and the black problem in general; to try to sell some copies of the party weekly; and to collect one lecture fee of five hundred dollars from the professors and another of one thousand dollars from the students. And we meant to see if we could recruit some sympathizers from among the small number of black students.

Just as I was getting into the car to leave party headquarters in the Bronx, I asked David Hilliard if he was coming with us.

He smiled faintly and said he wasn't, adding what seemed to me an enigmatic comment:

"There are still too many trees."

I left, together with Zaïd and Nappier, but all through the journey I kept thinking of what he had said. "There are still too many trees." So, for a black only thirty years old, a tree still didn't mean what it did to a white—a riot of green, with birds and nests and carvings of hearts and names intertwined. Instead it meant a gibbet. The sight of a tree revived a terror that was not quite a thing of the past, which left the mouth dry and the vocal cords impotent. A white sitting astride the beam holding the noose at the ready—that was the first thing that struck a Negro about to be lynched? And what separates us from the blacks today is not so much the color of our skin or the type of our hair as the phantom-ridden psyche we never see except when a black lets fall some joking and to us cryptic phrase. It not only seems cryptic; it is so. The blacks are obsessionally complicated about themselves. They've turned their suffering into a resource.

The professors at Stony Brook were very relaxed and gave us a warm welcome. They couldn't understand why I didn't try to distance myself from the Panthers by using a less violent rhetoric. I ought to have calmed down the Panther leaders, made them understand . . . Both checks were made out to me, though they were given to the Panthers. I was touched by this fine distinction. A blond lady professor said:

"We have to protest against the shooting down of the Panthers—at the rate things are going it'll be our own sons next."

On reflection I have to say this: from its foundation in October 1966 right up to the end of 1970 the Black Panther Party kept on surpassing itself with an almost uninterrupted stream of images. In April 1970 the Panthers' strength was still as great as ever. University professors could find no arguments against them, and so inevitable was their revolt that the whites, whether academics or laymen, were reduced to mere attempts at exorcism. Some called in the police. But the Panther movement, though both cheerful and touching, was never popular. It called for total commitment, for the use of arms, and for verbal invention and insult that slashed the face of the whites. Its violence could only be nurtured by the misery of the ghetto. Its great, internal liberty arose from the war waged on it by the police, the government, the white population, and some of the black middle classes. The movement was so sharp it was bound to wear out quickly—but in a shower and clatter of sparks that made the black problem not only visible but crystal clear.

Very few American intellectuals understood that the Panthers' arguments, not being drawn from the common fund of American democracy, were bound to seem very sketchy, and the Panthers themselves ignorant and simpleminded. They didn't realize that, at the stage the Panthers were at, the force of what was called Panther rhetoric or word mongering resided not in elegant discourse but in strength of affirmation (or denial), in anger of tone and timbre. When the anger led to action there was no turgidity or overemphasis. Anyone who has witnessed political rows among the whites—the Democratic Convention in Chicago in August 1968, for example—and who cares to make a comparison, will have to admit that the whites aren't overburdened with poetic imagination.

It's clear now that the Panthers' party alone couldn't have been responsible for the riot of color in the fabrics and furs affected by the young blacks. The whites knew that beneath this bold provocation there lay a will to live, even at the cost of life itself. The outrageous young blacks of San Francisco, Harlem, and Berkeley were simultaneously concealing and hinting that a weapon was being aimed at the whites. Because of the Panthers, those blacks who were still called "Toms"—the ones with jobs in government or the law, the mayors of mainly black cities, who'd been elected or appointed just for show—were now "seen" and "looked at" and "listened to" by the whites. Not because they took orders from the Panthers or because the Panthers took orders from them, but because the Panthers were feared.

Sometimes the results were unfortunate for the ghetto. Some black leaders who were listened to by the whites were tempted to try to extend their influence and crush offending blacks, for love not of justice but of power. They were able to prop up American law and order. But between 1966 and 1971 the Panthers emerged as young savages threatening the laws and the arts in the name of a Marxist-Leninist religion about as close to Marx or Lenin as Dubuffet is to Cranach.

You had to get some sleep, though, in the end. In the small hours, after discussions and disputes, whisky and marijuana, you had to go to bed. There were plenty of stomach ulcers among the Panthers.

The young black in jail for having taken drugs, then stolen and raped and beaten up a white—you might think he's the son of some polite black man who obeys the laws of Church and State. But in fact, as he himself well knows, he's one who three hundred years ago killed a white; took part in a mass runaway, robbing and pillaging and pursued by hounds; charmed and then raped a white woman, and was hanged without trial. He's one of the leaders of a revolt that took place in 1804, his feet are chained to the walls of his prison, he's one who bows his head and one who refuses to bow his head. White officialdom has provided him with a father he doesn't know, black like himself, but perhaps fated to finalize the break between the original Negro, who has gone on existing, and himself.

This method is at once convenient and inconvenient for the whites. It's convenient because it allows the government to strike down or kill people without being held responsible. But it's inconvenient because responsibility for the "crimes" of the blacks rests with individuals and not with the whole black community, and when an individual is sentenced he is drawn into the American democratic system. So that makes the whites miserable: are they to condemn the Negroes as a whole or just a black? Because of the Panthers, some very good blacks were taken over, but by their action these same Panthers showed that "once a Negro always a Negro."

But a touch of garlic helps . . .

In the Palestinian camps the boys between seven and fifteen who were trained to be soldiers were known as young lions. The arrangement seems very open to criticism. It was useful psychologically, but only up to a point. The boys' minds and bodies might have been hardened through difficult sports of ever-increasing complexity, calling for immediate reactions to overcome cold, heat, hunger, fear, and surprise. But training conditions, however harsh, will always be different from the situation soldiers find themselves in when confronted with other soldiers determined to kill—even if the enemy consists of children. The leaders of the young lions, knowing they are training kids, give even their sternest orders a tinge of almost maternal gentleness.

"Every Palestinian knows how to shoot from the age of ten," Leila told me proudly. She still thought shooting consisted of raising your gun to your shoulder and pulling the trigger. Real shooting means aiming at the enemy and killing him, and the boys—like the fedayeen—were using obsolescent weapons. But where were they supposed to be shooting? At whom? And above all under what conditions?

In the microscopic patch of land allotted to the young lions, more a playground than a battleground, there was a reassuring, nursery atmosphere, never the terror or intolerable cruelty caused by a certain something you'll never know about the enemy. The lessons in guerrilla warfare were rudimentary. I saw the young lions going through the same barbed-wire entanglements so often without being presented by any new problems—i.e., without having to circumvent any surprise that might have been worked out in the recesses of Israeli brains—that the boys seemed to me to serve the same Potemkin-like purpose as the bases themselves. The young lions' camps tried to prove to the journalists from all over the world who came on organized visits that generations of Palestinians were being born with guns in their hands, their eyes on the target, and recapture of the occupied territories in their hearts. Only journalists from the Communist countries were prepared to be taken in.

In its declarations on the subject, Israel always referred to this undying hatred.

(On the maps, a blank surrounded on one side by the blue of the Mediterranean, in the east by Lebanon and in the south by the kingdom of Jordan represented what was known as Palestine until 1948, and was supposed to obliterate what the world now called Israel). Mere photographs of the young lions in their camps were enough to show, if not the vulnerability of Israel, at least the constant danger that threatened it. And yet there was no comparison between Israel's own preparations and actions and these camps of boy soldiers solemnly hoisting their triangular flag every morning. I was present several times at this ceremony. The size of the flag matched that of the kids: it was very small. But no one's surprised when schoolchildren wave tiny, paper flags as a queen goes by, her little smile answered by an even smaller one from the children. In the young lions' camps the symbol of the homeland was feeble, but I daresay that as they grew older the symbols grew larger.

If the training camp was suddenly shrouded in smoke, the children were neither frightened nor surprised; it was part of an organized plan. But what would happen when Israel destroyed the sun and turned broad day into night?

What does it mean—"a touch of garlic helps"? Insipid food can be brightened up by a dash of spice, and some of the young lions, when put in temporary charge of the other boys, would, being older and more depraved, introduce an element of sadistic pleasure. A nasty addition, perhaps, but stimulating.

Cleanliness is congenital to the Palestinians, and anyone facing death can only do so after a thorough washing and scouring.

Again it was Khaled who put me in the picture. Two twenty-year-old fighters—from among those who'd been singing with him in the mountains—were washing one another carefully out in the open not far away from us. The other fedayeen seemed not to notice and certainly not to look at them. By washing and scouring I mean the almost maniacal attention they paid to personal hygiene and to the work it involved, which seemed to be sacred in the sense of paramount. First with a towel and then with their hands they rubbed their skin till it shone, passing the cloth between their toes several times to make sure all the dirt was removed. Then came the private parts, the trunk and the armpits. The two soldiers helped each other, one pouring on clean water after the other had soaped himself.

They were only a few yards away from the other soldiers, but what they were doing separated them forever from the rest, making them at once huge as mountains and distant as ants. Each scoured his own body like a housewife cleaning a saucepan, washing it in detergent and rinsing it till it sparkles. And theirs struck me as different from the usual Muslim ablutions.

Obediently copying the attitude of the fedayeen, I left the two to their solitude and their work, neither of which could be shared. One of them started to sing, and the other joined in. The first picked a small pouch up from the ground nearby, zipped it open, took out a pair of dressmaking shears, and proceeded very carefully, still singing—improvising as usual—to cut his toenails, paying particular attention to the corners, which were liable to make holes in his socks. Then he did his fingernails, and after that, still singing, washed his hands, his face, and his shaven pubis, trying to find, and soon finding, words that applied to Palestine itself.

I don't know why they didn't go down that night into Israel. The prefunerary toilette wasn't called for, and so they became a couple of unconsecrated fedayeen just like the others again. They'd have to start all over again the next time they were chosen.

It was with a roar of laughter designed to show she had the same "collar of Venus" as Lannia Solha that Nabila told me about the death of a Palestinian woman eighty years old. She was very thin round the stomach, and put on a sort of bodice with four rows of splinter grenades inside. She was probably helped by other women of her own age or younger, used to her sex, her thinness, and her white hair. Then, weeping real tears, she approached a group of Amal fighters who were laughing as they rested from shooting Palestinians. The old woman wept and moaned for some time, until the group of Amals kindly went up to her to see if they could help her. She kept mumbling phrases in Arabic that the Shiites couldn't hear, so they had to gather round close.

When I read in the papers about a virgin of sixteen blowing herself up in the middle of a group of Israeli soldiers, it doesn't surprise me very much. It's the lugubrious yet joyful preparations that intrigue me. What string did the old woman or the girl have to pull to detonate the grenades? How was the bodice arranged to make the girl's body look womanly and enticing enough to rouse suspicion in soldiers with a reputation for intelligence?

I was listening on a Walkman in a hotel room, but imagine a real funeral in a church with a coffin surrounded by wreaths and eight candles and a real dead body inside, even if the box is closed—and then the *Requiem* descended on me with full choir and orchestra. The music conjured up not death but a life, the life of the corpse, present or absent, the one for whom the mass is sung. But I was listening through headphones.

Mozart, using the Roman liturgy and Latin phrases that I followed with difficulty, asked for eternal rest, or rather another life. But as there had been no ceremony, and I could see no church door, graveyard, priest, genuflexions, or censer, at the sound of the "Kyrie" I started to hear a pagan madness.

The troglodytes came dancing out of their caves to welcome the dead woman, not in the light of sun or moon but in a pearly mist that generated its own light. The caves looked like the holes in a huge Swiss cheese, and the cavemen, phantoms without your human dimensions, cheerful and even laughing, swarmed around greeting the newcomer, the "maiden" whatever her age, so that she might adapt easily to the afterlife, accept like a welcome gift either death or the new eternal life, happy and proud to have been plucked up out of the world below.

The days of wrath, the tubas, the trembling of the kings—it wasn't a mass but an opera lasting less than an hour, the time it might take someone to die, performed and heard in dread of losing this world and finding oneself in what other? And in what form? The journey through the underworld, the terror of the grave, all that was there, but above all the gaiety, the laughter overlaying the fear, the haste of the dying woman to quit this world and leave us to the bleak courtesies of everyday while she went laughing up—not down but up—to the light. Laughing, and perhaps, who knows, sneezing as well.

That was what I heard, from the "Dies Irae" to the famous eighth bar of the "Lacrimosa" which I could never distinguish from those that followed—music that permitted hilarity and even liberty, that dared all.

When after long days of doubt and anxiety a youth—transsexual is rather a horrible word—decides on a sex change, once the decision is made he is filled with joy at the thought of his new sex, of the breasts he'll really stroke with hands too small and damp, of the disappearance of body hair. But above all, as the old sex fades and, he hopes, finally drops off useless, he'll be possessed with a joy close to madness when he refers to himself as "she" instead of "he," and realizes that grammar also has divided into two, and the feminine half has turned a somersault so that it applies to him, whereas the other half used to be forced on him. The transition to the nonhairy half must be both delightful and terrible. "I am filled with thy joy . . ." "Farewell to half of me—I die to myself . . ."

To leave behind the hated but familiar masculine ways is like forsaking the world and going into a monastery or a leper house. To quit the world of trousers for the world of the brassière is a kind of death, expected but feared. And isn't it also comparable to suicide, with choirs singing the "Tuba mirum"?

A transsexual is thus a sort of monster and hero combined. An angel too, for I don't know if anyone would ever actually use his new sex even once, unless the male member withered quite away, or, worse, fell off, and the whole body and its purpose became one great female organ. He'll start to be frightened when his feet refuse to get smaller: you won't find many high-heeled shoes in size 9 or 10. But happiness will prevail over all else—happiness and joy.

The *Requiem* says as much: joy and fear. And so the Palestinians, the Shiites, and the Fools of God, who all fell laughing upon ancient cavemen and gold court shoes size 9 or 10, came together in a thousand roars of onward-rushing laughter, mingled with the fierce retreat of trombones. Thanks to joy in death or in the new, despite bereavement, and in contrast to ordinary life, all moralities had broken down. What prevailed was the joy of the transsexual, of the *Requiem*, of the kamikaze. Of the hero.

In contrast to the disagreeable practice of drying your Western hands in a blast of hot air to avoid wetting a clean towel, you must have experienced, especially as children, the pleasure of staying out in the rain, preferably in the summer when the water that drenches you is warm. I've never been able to find out which way the wind's blowing by wetting my finger and holding it up, nor the direction of the rain, unless it's as slanting as the last rays of the sun. And when I realized, at the first hail of bullets, that I was going toward them, I laughed like a boy taken by surprise. As I crouched in the shelter of a wall I felt a sudden, idiotic delight at being safe, while certain death awaited two yards beyond the wall. I was enjoying myself. Fear didn't exist. Death was just as much a part of life as the shower of steel and lead nearby. All I could see on the faces of the fedayeen were happy smiles or a calm that might have been blasé. Abu Ghassam, the fedayee who'd grabbed my sleeve and pulled me to safety, looked both irritated and relieved.

"A nice thing," he must have been thinking, "getting shot at without warning, and on top of that having to look after a European." He'd been made responsible for me because he knew some French.

I noticed that none of the soldiers attempted to go into the buildings to find shelter from which to shoot back and perhaps protect the inhabitants, though they were armed and laden with ammunition, with cartridge belts crossed over their chests. All—except me—were very young and unseasoned.

I felt weighed down by a kind of despondency, which in other places and by other people has been called defeatism. The famous last words, "It is finished," probably express my mood better. They weren't even fighting anymore near Jerash. All that was still standing out were the columns of the temples left by the Romans. The front of the house was being riddled with bullets, but as our wall was at right angles to it no one was in any danger. Death was close, but being held at bay. If I moved forward two yards I'd be killed.

And it was there more strongly than anywhere else that I heard the call across a horizontal abyss, more urgent and more apt to enfold me forever than any vertical gulf shrieking my name. As on other days, the shooting went for some time. The young fedayeen laughed. Apart from Abu Ghassam none of them knew any French, but their eyes told me everything.

Would Hamlet have felt the delicious fascination of suicide if he hadn't had an audience, and lines to speak?

But why had the voice of the stream grown so loud that night, so loud that it got on my nerves? Had the choirs and the hills come close to the water without anyone realizing? More likely the singers' voices were tired, or they just started to listen to the voice of the stream, either because they liked the sound of it or because they disliked it.

Two images help me tell you what I remember. First the image of white clouds. Everything I saw in Jordan and Lebanon remains shrouded in dense clouds that still swirl down on me. I seem able to pierce them only when I grope blindly after some vision, though I don't know which. I want it to appear to me as fresh as when I first experienced it as participant or witness: the vision, for example, of four hands drumming on wood, inventing more and more cheerful rhythms on the planks of a coffin. And then the mist parts. Swiftly, or as deliberately as the rise of a theater curtain, the context of the four rhythm-creating hands emerges as clear as when first I saw it. I make out, whisker by whisker, the two black moustaches; the white teeth; the smile that ceases only to come back broader still.

The second image is that of a huge packing case. I open it and find nothing but shavings and sawdust inside. My hands sift through them, I'm almost desperate at the thought of finding nothing else when I know they're used to protect valuables. Then my hand touches something hard and my fingers recognize the faun's head, the handle of the silver teapot that the shavings and sawdust at once guard and conceal. I had to search through the almost impenetrable packing in order that the teapot might reach me undented. The teapot stands for the Palestinian events which I thought were lost in sawdust and clouds, but which were preserved for me in their morning freshness as if someone—my publisher, perhaps?—had wrapped them up safe so that I might describe them to you as they were.

Clouds are very nutritious.

Anyhow, I remember my astonishment and saying to myself: "If the fedayeen really perceive what I think I'm the only one to see, I must hide what I feel, because they often shock me. Then pretence is prudence as much as politeness."

Despite the frankness of their faces, gestures, and actions, despite their openness, I soon realized I caused as much astonishment as I felt, if not more: When so many things are there to be seen, just seen, there are no words to describe them. A fragment of hand on a fragment of branch; an eye that didn't see them but saw me and understood. Everyone knew I knew I was being watched.

"Are they just feigning friendship, pretending we're comrades? Am I visible or transparent? Am I visible because I'm transparent?

"The fact is I'm transparent because I'm too visible—a stone, a clump of moss, but not one of them. I thought I had a lot to hide. They looked like hunters: at once suspicious and sympathetic."

"No man who's not a Palestinian himself ever does much for Palestine. He can leave her behind and go to some nice quiet spot like the Côte d'Or, or Dijon. But a fedayee has to win, die, or betray."

This is a basic truth never to be forgotten. There's only one Jew, a former Israeli, among the leaders of the PLO: Illan Halery. The PLO and the Palestinians trust him because he's completely rejected Zionism.

Either a Palestinian falls and dies or, if he survives, he's sent to prison for a few sessions of torture. After that the desert takes him and keeps him in the camps near Zarka. We'll find out more later what a fedayee's "slack periods" were like.

A team of German doctors is always to be found where there's torturing going on. They may be serving commercial interests back home: supplying the camps with instruments of torture, selling medicines and the latest wonders of physiotherapy, and getting those who don't succumb to torture out of the country to safety. Then they're sent to hospital in Düsseldorf, Cologne, or Hamburg, and if they come out they learn German and snow and the winter wind; they look for a job, and sometimes marry a single wife.

I was told that was what had happened to Hamza. It was a theory held by several Palestinian leaders. But after December 1971 I didn't meet anyone who could tell me for sure that Hamza was still alive.

But what were the "slack periods" like? The expression conceals what is perhaps a Palestinian soldier's guiltiest secret. What are the daydreams of a revolutionary who rebels in the desert with no experience of the West and practically none of his own shadow, the East? Where do they get their assumed names from? What effect does novelty have on them? And so on . . .

The emblem was easy to decipher—a gilt aluminium crown in the kingdom of Jordan. How is one to describe the king? Something Glubb Pasha left behind on the throne. In 1984 people talked about him like this:

"How's the 'Monarch'?"

"What's the 'Monarch' doing?"

"What does the 'Monarch' think?"

"Where's the 'Monarch' gone?"

"The 'Monarch' was in a good temper."

"The 'Monarch' pees standing up—he's the same as everyone else. Does he think he's Bismarck?"

But in the Palestinian camps, in private conversation where people feel safe from the Moukabarats,[5] in European countries where former fedayeen have taken refuge, it wouldn't occur to anyone except the children not to call him just the Butcher of Amman.

"It's not an insult. The poor fellow likes blondes and has an erection when he sees his own massacres through the open window. 'I screw blondes—and screw you too! I murder and slay—and that goes for you as well!' He's got his Circassians and Moukabarats and Bedouin to do it with."

"His Majesty is so natural—it's really touching! I'm often with His Majesty. He sometimes perches his ass right on the edge of his chair, he's so shy! The reason His Majesty's so amiable is that His Majesty was educated in England. His Majesty listens to a few words, then gets up and goes. He says a few words in English, as naturally as the royal princess. And yet His Majesty's a Bedouin."

"His Majesty takes great pride in being no more and no less than a Bedouin from the Hejaz. He enters. All the lights in the room go out. Then he approaches, a little oil lamp with a mauve-silk shade holding out his hand for people to kiss."

"King Hussein relies on this defense: that if he hadn't subdued the Palestinians, Tsahal would now be in Riyadh."

"He's been unlucky. Move your chair closer—walls have ears—and listen.

"His grandfather, King Abdullah, was assassinated as he left the mosque in Jerusalem. Blood."

"His father went mad. Blood."

"Glubb Pasha, his mentor, was kicked out. Blood."

"King Talal, his father, died out of his mind in Switzerland. Blood."

"The Palestinians. Blood."

"Muhammad Daoud, his prime minister, was given a slap in the face by his sixteen-year-old daughter. Blood."

"Wasfi Tall, his other prime minister, was assassinated in Cairo. Blood."

[5]The secret police of the kingdom of Jordan.

"Poor King Hussein, what a lot of corpses in his little arms."

That was the tune being sung in Amman in July 1984.

Prismatic vision might teach us a lot. A few years ago, in various parts of the Arab world, you might come across a lady, a sort of benevolent schoolmistress devoted to those of low degree. She was the same to everyone, man, woman, or child, no matter what their rank: the fact was, she was born a princess of Orleans. Her condescension was invisible to Arab emirs and Arab beggars alike. But she knew she was a princess, related to the royal houses of Europe, and a village famine and a sheikh's family relationship to the Prophet were of equal importance to her.

Who or what made me come back to this house? The wish to see Hamza again after fourteen years? The wish to see his mother, whom I could easily have imagined older and thinner without coming all this way? Or was it the need to prove to myself that I belonged, in spite of myself, to the class, proscribed but secretly desired, of those who when it comes to other people make no distinction between the highest and the humblest? Or was it that without our realizing it an invisible scarf had been woven between us, binding us all to one another?

The princess wouldn't have bothered to join in the mockery of Hussein: he wasn't an Orleans.

A shanty town within a kingdom. In a piece of broken mirror they see their faces and bodies piecemeal, and the majesty they see there takes shape before them in a half sleep; and always this sleep leads up to death.

Everyone prepares for the Palace, and by the age of thirteen they all wear silk scarves made in France and specially designed for the shanty towns of the kingdom: the colors and patterns have to be as obvious as kiss curls. So some trade does take place between the shanty town and the outside world, though it's limited to the sale of scarves, brilliantine, scent, plastic cuff links, and counterfeit watches from a counterfeit Switzerland in exchange for the currency brothels have to offer. The scarves and machine-embroidered shirts must be becoming and set off the little ponces' pretty faces.

Scarves, shirts, and watches all have one function—they are signs informing Palace and police representatives of the character of whoever contacts them. One applicant is determined to risk his life, another offers his mother or sister or both, another the kind of sex marketable in Europe, another some inside knowledge, some ass or eye or amorous whisper—and each ties round his neck the scarf that corresponds to his particular stock-in-trade.

Though born of a chance coupling and raised under the rusty sky of the shanty town, every one of them is good-looking. Their fathers are from the South. The boys soon acquire the arrogance of males destined for tasks and fates outside both the shanty town and the kingdom. Some are fair, with a flashy beauty, a provocation that will last another couple of years.

"It's not only our eyes, Jean. It's our curls (those on their heads), our necks, our thighs as well. You're probably not familiar with the fairness of our thighs?"

• • •

Whether the king's Palace was an abyss into which the shanty town might be drawn, or the shanty town an abyss drawing down the Palace and its paraphernalia, in any case one wonders which was real and which only a reflection. Anyhow, if the Palace was the reflection and the shanty town the reality, the reflection of the reality was only to be found in the Palace, and vice versa. You could see that if you visited first the Palace and then the shanty town. The two powers were so evenly balanced you wondered if it wasn't a case of mutual mesmerism, that familiar, flirtatious but bitter confrontation linking the two palaces. The king's palace seemed to look with envy at the poverty of men and women wearing themselves out in the attempt to survive, longing to betray—but whom?—and knowing that possessions and luxury would go up in smoke if ever they decided they had nothing to lose.

What inspired leap launched the naked child, warmed by the breath of an ox, nailed with nails of brass, hoisted up finally, because he had been betrayed, into universal glory? Isn't a traitor one who goes over to the enemy? That among other things. The Venerable Peter, abbot of Cluny, in order to study the Koran better, decided to have it "translated." Not only did he forget that in passing from one language to another the holy text could only convey what can be expressed just as easily in any tongue—that is everything except that which is holy; but he was probably actually motivated by a secret desire to betray. (This may manifest itself in a sort of stationary dance, rather like the desire to pee.)

The temptation to "go over" goes with unease at having just one simple certainty—a certainty that's bound *ipso facto* to be uncertain. Getting to know the other, who's supposed to be wicked because he's the enemy, makes possible not only battle itself but also close bodily contact between the combatants and between their beliefs. So each doctrine is sometimes the shadow and sometimes the equivalent of the other, sometimes the subject and sometimes the object of new daydreams and thoughts so complex they can't be disentangled. Once we see in the need to "translate" the obvious need to "betray," we shall see the temptation to betray as something desirable, comparable perhaps to erotic exaltation. Anyone who hasn't experienced the ecstasy of betrayal knows nothing about ecstasy at all.

The traitor is not external but inside everyone. The Palace got its soldiers, informers, and whores from that part which was still desirable of a population that had been knocked over backward, and the shanty town responded with all kinds of mockery.

The shanty town, a medley of monsters and woes seen from the Palace, and in turn seeing the palace and *its* woes, knew pleasures unheard of elsewhere. One went about on two legs and a torso, around dusk—a torso from which a wrist stuck out with a hand on the end like a stoup, a begging bowl made of flesh that demanded its mite with three fingers you could see through. The wrist emerged from a ragged mass of crumpled, worn-out, dirty American surplus, merging ever more completely with the mud and shit until it was sold as rags, mud, and muck combined.

Further on, also on two legs, is a female sex organ, bare, shaven, but twitching and damp and always trying to cling onto me. Somewhere else there's a single eye without a socket, fixed and sightless, but sometimes sharp, and hanging from a bit of sky blue wool. Somewhere else again, an arse with its balls hanging bare and weary between a pair of flaccid thighs.

Treason was everywhere. Every kid that looked at me wanted to sell his father or mother; fathers wanted to sell their five-year-old daughters. The weather was fine. The world was disintegrating. The sky existed elsewhere, but here there was only an inexplicable lull in which nothing survived but bodily functions. Beneath the tin roofs the light was gray by day and by night.

A pimp went by dressed like someone in an American film of the thirties. He looked tense, and to keep up his courage he was whistling as though he were walking through a forest at night. This was the middle of the brothel for Arabs who were stony broke. Whether hell or the depths of hell, place of absolute despair or of rest in the midst of perdition, this red-light quarter for some incomprehensible reason prevented the shanty town from sinking further into and merging with the mud on which it had been almost delicately poised. It calmly linked the shanty town to the rest of the world, and hence to the Palace. It was a place for making love, and pimps and madams, whores and customers restricted themselves to what is called normal love and is therefore incomplete. No sodomy or cocksucking here, only quick reciprocal fucking lying down or standing up, without any devouring of arses or dicks or cunts—only married, patriotic, Swiss mountain love.

Erotic fantasies were more intricate and more sought after in the bedrooms and corridors of the Royal Palace, with its mirrors, whole walls of mirrors, in which the smallest caress was repeated to infinity—that infinity where you can make out every detail of a tiny ultimate image. The mirrors were set at strange angles designed to include a view of the shanty town. Need it be said that the residents of the Palace were more sophisticated than those of the shanty town? And did the people in the shanty town know they were there in the mind of the Palace, ministering to its pleasure?

Everyone felt relieved at his own rottenness, soothed at escaping from moral and aesthetic effort. What crawled toward the brothels was a mass of desires craving quick fulfilment, dragging itself along on a thousand legs, seeking and finding some damp and quivering hole where the frustration of a week would vanish in five jolts and in as many seconds.

If a stranger, Arab or otherwise, came here, he'd see the survival of a closely guarded civilization, one with a familiar, almost pious contact with rejection, with what Europe calls dirt. The alarm clock was always set. In five minutes the customer disposed of his dreams. A youth of eighteen who wanted to go into the king's army or join the society of police informers might come across his own father having a crap: then the budding spy would kick his squatting parent's teeth in—or walk by, pretending to believe he was a Norwegian.

The absence of morality scares everyone, but it doesn't put them off. Excrement is consoling, it corresponds to something in our comfortable souls, it stops us from finishing ourselves off. A prick moves, seeks a way to fulfil itself. What's needed for that: to do away with the pride of self, of having a surname, a first name, a family tree, a country, an ideology, a party, a grave, a coffin with two dates—birth and death. Birth and death, those accidental dates; but it's difficult to put down to chance the Transcendent Absolute that governs Heaven and Earth in Islam.

The system of exchange between the Palace, the King, the Court, the Stables, the Horses, the Officials, the Footmen, and the Tanks on the one hand, and the Shanty Town on the other, is a complex one, but though it's not obvious it's sure. It allows the surface of both places to remain unruffled. There's never any friction, and this is why: the splendor of the Palace is a kind of poverty. The rank of the Sun King and his courtiers is purely mythical. The brutality of the police derives simply from their readiness to obey too promptly and too well. The shanty town slows down, tempers, and filters this naïve zeal. The handsome youths, the issue of strange couplings, go through the brothels where faces and bodies are lit up by what used to be. With their good looks goes the utmost scorn, and as they are sturdy too, their masculinity is proud, even regal. To preserve its power the Palace covets the force that comes forth at night from the shanty town.

"I am the force. The tank."

At this point in my fantasy I begin to wonder who was its author. A god perhaps, but not just any old god—the one not to be reborn but born for the first time on a heap of ox and ass dung, to go through this shambles of a world somehow, to rub along somehow, to die on the cross and become the force.

"Could *you* sell your mother?"

"I have! It's easy to sell a cunt when you've emerged from one on all fours."

"What about the Sun?"

"For the moment we're brothers."

The poverty of the villages leads to the capital, to the sky of rusty tin and the rubbish that serves to produce a few handsome boys. The Palace consumes a great deal of youth.

"It's to maintain some sort of order, whether muddy or lacerated by the Sun."

What sort of beauty is it these lads from the shanty town possess? When they're still children, a mother or a whore gives them a piece of broken mirror in which they trap a ray of the sun and reflect it into one of the Palace windows. And by that open window, in the mirror, they discover bit by bit their faces and bodies.

The king was in Paris when the Bedouin troops dug up the bodies of the fedayeen killed between Ajloun and the Syrian frontier, to kill them again, or as the ritual expression put it, "to get rid of a hundred spare bullets." Had he abandoned his massacres for three days in order to try out a new Lamborghini? His brother, the regent, stayed behind in Amman. The camp at Baqa, twenty kilometers from the capital, was suddenly completely surrounded by three rows of tanks. The parleying between the women from the camp and the Jordanian officers lasted two days and two nights. The old women awakened pity, the younger ones desire. They all displayed whatever might still touch the soldiers: children, breasts, eyes, wrinkles.

Of this gesture of sacred prostitution the men of the camp appeared to know nothing. They turned their backs on it; little groups of them went about the muddy alleys in silence, fingering their amber beads and smoking. Imagine the thousands of gold-tipped Virginia cigarettes thrown away as soon as lit. The emirates supplied the Palestinians with cigarettes to teach them the geography of the Gulf.

The men refused to talk to Hussein's officers. I think to this day that the fedayeen (all the men in the camp were fedayeen) had made an agreement with the women, young and old, by which the women were to talk and the men to be silent so as to impress the Jordanian army with their determination, real or assumed. I think now it was assumed. But the Bedouin officers didn't know they were witnessing a performance designed to conceal an escape.

To prevent the Jordanians from entering the camp, the Palestinians had to hold out another day and night. The women yelled, the children they carried on their backs or led by the hand were frightened and yelled even louder. Pushing carriages full of children, bags of rice, and sacks of potatoes, the women went through the barbed-wire fences while the men, still silent, went on fingering their beads.

"We want to go back home."

They were on the road that leads to the Jordan. The officers were very perplexed.

"We can't fire on women and carriages!"

"We're going home."

"What do you mean—'home'?"

"Palestine. We'll walk. We'll cross the Jordan. The Jews are more humane than the Jordanians."

Some of the Circassian officers were tempted to shoot at them and their kids, proposing to walk forty kilometers to cross the Jordan!

"Sire—a word of advice. Don't shoot."

That's what Pompidou is supposed to have said to Hussein.

Though the French ambassador in Amman was rather simple, Pompidou knew through his spies about the women's revolt. A French priest whose name I've forgotten because he's still alive acted as "postbox" between some Palestinian leaders and what may then have been called the French left, which had links with the left in the Vatican. When the Jordanian authorities heard he was in the camp, they ordered the army and political chiefs to hand him over to the Jordanian police.

The Law Courts in Brussels, the Albert Memorial in London, the altar to the Motherland in Rome, and the Opéra in Paris are supposed to be the ugliest buildings in Europe. A sort of grace once mitigated one of them. When a car emerges from the arches of the Louvre facing the avenue de l'Opéra, the Opéra itself, or Palais Garnier, is visible at the end of the street. It has a kind of gray green dome on top, and I think that's what you see first.

When the women of Baqa left the camp claiming they were going home to Palestine, King Hussein was going up part of the avenue de l'Opéra on his way to lunch at the Elysée Palace. I've been told the gray-green dome was the first and perhaps the only thing he saw: it had PALESTINE WILL OVERCOME painted on it in huge, white letters. Male dancers, ballerinas, and stagehands from the Opéra had gone up on the roof and written the message the night before the procession, and the king saw it. Nowhere in the world seemed safe from the terrorists: the Paris Opéra, haunted both by Fantômas and, in its cellars, by the Phantom, was now haunted in its attics by the fedayeen. The brief warning lasted a long while despite rain and sun, and despite orders from Pompidou. He must have laughed.

But twenty times or more on the gray walls of Paris, near the Opéra and elsewhere, I saw Israel's answer to that message. Sprayed on hastily, unobtrusively, almost shyly, it read: "Israel will live." It happened two or three days after what in my memory I still refer to as "Palestine: the last dance at Baqa." How immensely more forceful was this response!—response rather than answer. Or rather, what a contrast between the limited declaration of "will overcome" and the almost eternal claim of "will live." In the field of mere rhetoric, in the twilight of Paris, Israel and its furtive sprayings went immensely far.

If people can understand a nation dying for its country, as the Algerians did, or for its language, as the Flemish of Belgium and the Irish of Ulster are still doing, they ought to be able to accept that the Palestinians are fighting against the Emirs for their lands and their accent. The twenty-one countries in the League, including the Palestinians, all speak Arabic, but the accent, though subtle and not easily perceived by an untrained ear, does exist. The division of the Palestinian camps into districts transferring, reflecting, and preserving the geography of the villages back in Palestine was no more important to them than the preservation of their accent.

This is roughly what Mubarak told me in 1971. When I offered to give an Arab a lift and drive him a hundred and sixty kilometers on his way, he asked me to wait there, and then ran off. He ran more than two kilometers in less than a quarter of an hour, and came back with his only treasure: a not quite new shirt wrapped up in a newspaper. *Filiumque* and another religion bursts into flame. A stress on the first or the penultimate syllable of a word, and two nations refuse to get along. Something that seemed to us of no value had become that man's one treasure, for which he was ready to risk his life.

Accents apart, an extra letter added to a forgotten or garbled word could be enough to cause a tragedy. During the 1982 war, the truck drivers were either Lebanese or Palestinians. An armed Phalangist would hold out his hand with something in it and ask, "What's this?"

According to your answer you would either be waved on or get a bullet in the head. The word for a tomato in Lebanese Arabic is *bandouran*; in Palestinian Arabic it's *bandoura*. One letter more or less was a matter of life or death.

Every district in a camp tried to reproduce a village left behind in Palestine and probably destroyed to make way for a power station. But the old people of the village, who still talked together, had brought their own accent with them when they fled, and sometimes local disputes or even lawsuits too. Nazareth was in one district, and a few narrow streets away Nablus and Haifa. Then the brass tap, and to the right Hebron, to the left a quarter of old El Kods (Jerusalem). Especially around the tap, waiting for their buckets to fill, the women exchanged greetings in their own dialects and accents, like so many banners proclaiming where each patois came from.

There were a few mosques with their cylindrical minarets and two or three domes.

When I was in Amman the dead were buried on their sides, facing Mecca. I attended several funerals, and I know that at Thiais, as at Père-Lachaise, there was a compass showing the direction of Mecca. But the grave, or rather compartment, was more like a narrow pipe, so that people sometimes had to trample on the deceased to make him lie down and sleep.

All over the world and in every age, plays upon words, accents, or even letters have often caused quite bitter conflict. Every thief has had dealings in his time with the sort of judge who's out to get us. They had a special way of reading out our record in court.

"Theft!"—triumphantly.

"Theft!" again.

A pause, and then suddenly in a quiet voice, enunciating every letter and leaving the bench in no doubt of our eternal guilt.

"Theft*s-s-s* . . ."

A pause. Theftss. And that was that.

Once again in the history of the revolt, the women acted as a diversion. First paramount object: not to hand over the Christian priest. Second paramount object: to save the camp. It appealed to their love of adventure, of drama, of dressing up, and using different voices and gestures. The women jumped for joy; the men's role was to lie low and act the coward. On the theme, "Let's pretend to be outraged because the Bedouin want to get at our wives," the women wrote a script and proceeded to perform it.

The regent phoned Hussein. Pompidou made his famous remark. Night fell, as it always does, and five banners depicting from right to left God the Father, the Lamb, the Cross, the Virgin, and the Child appeared according to plan, facing the Jordanian tanks. Then came children in red robes and long, white, lace tops, carrying a kind of golden sun. The whole procession advanced singing, probably in Greek, toward the three lines of tanks.

Every Jordanian soldier was supposed to keep his eyes and ears open in the dark and capture the French priest dead or alive. They'd all goggled before at such ceremonies taking place around the little Greek church in Amman. So they didn't notice an elderly peasant in corduroy trousers and a red scarf round his neck making his way alone through the barbed wire.

The women, with their sleeping children, stayed out by the tanks all night. In the morning, smiling and cheerful, they took the Jordanian officers by the hand and led them into every house in the camp, opening boxes of matches and packets of salt to show there wasn't any priest hidden inside.

A week after Hussein returned home, a reconciliation was celebrated between the fedayeen and the Bedouin army, just roundly tricked by the women as well as by the men, who could now talk and smile freely again. It was like the Field of the Cloth of Gold or some other scene during the Western Middle Ages in which ostensibly friendly kings embraced so warmly you could tell which one was going to stifle the other. Or like the reconciliation between China and Japan, or between the two Germanies, or between France and Algeria, Morocco and Libya, de Gaulle and Adenauer, Arafat and Hussein. I don't see any end to these hypocritical kisses.

We expected a party, and we got one.

Hussein sent boxes and baskets of fruit. Arafat brought hampers of bottles from the Gulf: coconut milk, mango and apricot juice, and so forth. All in the open space outside the camp where the women and howling infants had spent that night.

Did it really all happen as I say it did?

A few months before, a few soldiers and even fewer officers had deserted from the Bedouin Army. I met some of them, including a very fair, young, second lieutenant with blue eyes. If I ask him where he got his fairness and sky blue eyes, I thought, he'll say from the cornfields of Beauce and the Franks who fought in the first Crusade. How could an Arab be fair?

"Where did you get your fair hair?" I asked aloud.

"From my mother. A Yugoslav," he answered in French without an accent.

Some of the officers who'd remained "loyal" to Hussein had probably looked the other way so as not to see the priest leave the camp. He made his way out unmolested in his greenish jacket, his red, knitted muffler, and a cap from the Manufacture d'Armes et de Cycles at Saint-Etienne in the Loire. The Palestinians escorted him to Syria, where he caught a plane to Vietnam.

I went early, with an Egyptian friend, to get a closer view. The wooden tables were covered with white cloths and laden with mountains of oranges and bottles of fruit juice. But the crowd had got up even earlier than I had. There was a battalion of desert Bedouin, each with two bandoliers crossed over his chest; two lots of fedayeen, unarmed; and photographers from all over the world, journalists, and film directors from various Arab and Muslim countries.

The Bedouin dancing is chaste because it takes place between men, mostly holding one another by the elbow or forefinger. But it's also erotic because it takes place between men, and because it's performed before the ladies. So which sex is it that burns with desire for an encounter that can never be?

Can there be a party where no one gets drunk? If a party isn't designed to make people drunk, it's best to turn up intoxicated. Can there be a party where no prohibition is flouted? What about the *Fête de l'Humanité* at La Courneuve?

As alcoholic drinks are sinful according to the Koran, the intoxication that morning came from the singing, the insults, and the dancing. Or, if you prefer, from the insults in the form of singing and dancing.

I was below the open space, looking up at it obliquely.

As the fedayeen stood there almost stiffly in their civilian clothes, the Bedouin soldiers began to dance, accompanied only by their own shouts and cries and the thud of their naked feet on the concrete. So as not to be restricted they'd taken off their shoes, but they still wore their puttees. I knew then that the Bedouin were making use of the dance in the same way as the Palestinians had made use of their wives a week before: the dancing was a display, almost a confession, of the femininity that contrasted so strongly with their burly chests. But these were crisscrossed with bandoliers so full that if one bullet had exploded the whole battalion would have gone up in smoke. And in their acceptance of, even desire for, that annihilation lay the source of their virility and their valor.

This is how they danced. First in a single row, which then split into two. Then a line of ten, twelve, or fourteen soldiers holding arms like Breton bridegrooms would be joined by a similar line, also holding arms, all dressed in long tunics buttoned up down to their calves, or rather their puttees. Each man wore a turban and a moustache, but beneath these there wasn't a row of teeth to be seen. Knowing they were the victors, the Bedouin soldiers didn't smile, though their colonels did. The troops themselves were too shy, and had probably already learned that smiles unleash anger.

To a heavy double beat, reminiscent of Auvergne, the Bedouin threw up their knees and shouted:

"Yaya el malik!" (Long live the king!)

Facing them, but some distance away, Palestinians in civilian clothes performed a clumsy imitation of the Bedouin dance and answered with a laugh:

"Abu Amar!" (Yasser Arafat!)

The rhythm was the same, because "Yaya el malik" is pronounced "Yayal malik." Four syllables uttered by the Jordanians and four uttered by the Palestinians. The same rhythm and almost the same dance, for it was just a vestige, a stump of a dance, the weary echo of a few steps from a forgotten dance, to satisfy bureaucratic requirements and officials with badly knotted ties. There was nothing left of the original gloomy ritual, with the Bedouin advancing menacingly, backed up and protected by their accomplice the desert. Their "yaya" was not so much a tribute to their king as an insult spat out at the Palestinians. The latter were more and more entrammeled in the clumsiness, the inferiority, of their own contribution to the show.

As they danced, the Bedouin were surrounded by the desert and the mists of time. And I wonder even now whether one day, as they dance, weighed down with bullets and gunpowder, ever more vigorous, ever more rigorous, they won't rip apart the Hashemite kingdom they seem to be defending. And after that, destroy America, conquer heaven, meet the fedayeen there, and speak the same language.

Languages may be an easily learned method of communicating ideas, but by "language" shouldn't we really mean something else? Childhood memories: of words, and above all of syntax, conveyed to the young almost before vocabulary, together with stones and straw and the names of grasses, streams, tadpoles, minnows, the seasons, and their changes. And the names of illnesses: a woman was said to be "dying with her chest," a phrase beside which such words as tuberculosis or galloping consumption were banal. The cries and groans we invent while making love, going back to our childhood with its moments of wonder and its flashes of comprehension.

"You're as red as a crayfish!"

But a crayfish isn't red—it's gray, almost black! We've seen it shrinking back in the stream, and it's gray. Yes, but wait—by the time you ate it, it had been in boiling water, which had turned it red and dead. Bedouin and fedayeen didn't speak the same language. But a "red crayfish" would have been just as incomprehensible to either.

The Palestinians, dancing worse and worse, were on the point of collapse. Then came a sharp blast on a whistle: the camp commander had seen what was happening, and he waved them toward the tables and the fruit. Saved! In this context the word means that face was saved: the dancers pretended they were dying of thirst, and fell upon the bottles and the oranges. At no time did Bedouin and Palestinians address a word to each other.

Hatred between factions can be something terrible, even if it's kept up artificially. Some figures: the Bedouin army consisted of 75,000 men in all, from about 75,000 families, which makes a total population of about 750,000. That was the official figure for the "pure Jordanian" population. The Bedouin, who in a way had answered the questions I'd been asking myself a few days earlier, had conquered through dancing.

The Palestinians, isolated by this archaeo-virility, had distanced themselves from the Bedouin and their obscure privileges, but this didn't impress Israel. Meanwhile every life, the only treasure of anyone on either side, was lived in its unique and solitary splendor.

The figures I've quoted date from 1970.

The sun had just risen over Ajloun and was still among the trees.

"You must see her," they said. "Come with us and we'll translate."

At six in the morning I was pretty angry with the thirteen or fourteen lads who'd woken me up.

"Here, we've made you some tea," they said.

They threw off my bedclothes and hauled me out of the tent. If I went a couple of kilometers with them up the path among the hazel trees I'd see the farm and the farmer's wife.

The hills near Ajloun, south of the Jordan, are like the hills in the Morvan, with the odd foxglove or honeysuckle though fewer tractors in the fields and not a single cow.

The land around the buildings was well looked after: that's what I noticed first. In the little kitchen garden in front of the house there was parsley growing, and courgettes, shallots, rhubarb, and black beans, and a creeping vine with bunches of white grapes already basking in the sun.

The farmer's wife was standing in the romanesque arch of the doorway, watching us approach, the band of youngsters and the old man. Judging by her wrinkles and the wisps of gray hair escaping from her black head scarf, I'd have said she was in her sixties.

Later on I'll say that Hamza's mother was actually about fifty in 1970. When I met her again in 1984 she had the face of a woman of eighty—I don't say she "looked" eighty, because creams and salves and massage and various other artificial treatments against wrinkles and excess fat make one forget the ever-swifter flight toward decrepitude and death. I *had* forgotten. In Europe people do forget how a peasant woman's face disintegrates in the sun and the cold, with weariness and poverty and despair. And also how, at the last gasp, there may be a sudden flash of childlike mischief, as at a last little treat.

She held out her hand and greeted me without a smile, but put a finger that had touched my hand to her lips. I did the same, and she greeted each of the fedayeen in the same way, courteous but reserved, almost wary. She ws a Jordanian: neither proud nor ashamed of it, but simply making it plain. As she was alone in the house we couldn't go into the main room, and besides: "There isn't room for five, let alone fifteen."

She spoke easily. Later I was told her Arabic was as fine as that spoken by professors. She went barefoot on the straw. She seldom read a newspaper. The only available space on the farm big enough to hold us all was a perfectly round sheepfold adjoining the house.

"Where are the sheep?"

"One of my sons is out with them. My husband's taken the mule up the mountain."

So the Jordanian farmer I said good morning to without thinking every day was her husband. He used to lend the mule to the fedayeen, who took several barrels every day up to some soldiers posted on a rock, keeping watch over the silent village.

But everything was silent. The Jordanian peasants stayed out of sight. Now and then, through binoculars, I could see a woman in a black head scarf throwing grain to her hens or milking a goat, but she soon went back into her house and shut the door. The men must have been waiting inside with their guns kept trained on successive targets—on the Palestinian bases and patrols.

On the morning before our visit to the farm, two fedayeen had gone smiling into the courtyard of a house where they were celebrating a wedding. Custom prescribed that all visitors, even casual passersby, should be offered food and drink, and the people there were all smiles. Except to the Palestinians, at the sight of whom the smiles faded. They left, feeling hurt.

The farmer's wife offered us all coffee, and went inside to make it—into her main and perhaps her only room. The sheepfold consisted of a circle marked out on the ground and covered with straw. A stone ledge built into the inside of the wall served as a bench. We sat down, the boys joked with each other, and the farmer's wife brought in a tray with a coffeepot and fifteen empty glasses piled up on it.

"But there are sixteen of us."

I thought I hadn't heard right: a woman on her own would never sit down with us here. But we all wanted her to be the sixteenth. Neither offended nor coy, she declined. But she didn't mind sitting on the raised sill of the entrance for a moment. Not a hair strayed out of her head scarf: she must have set herself to rights in the mirror while the coffee was brewing. I was opposite her as she sat outlined in the doorway. I noticed her large feet, bare but as if of bronze, protruding from under a full, black, closely pleated skirt. The oracle of Delphi had just sat down in the sheepfold. When spoken to she answered in a clear, resonant voice. A fighter who knew French translated for me; he told me in a whisper he thought her Arabic was probably the most beautiful he'd ever heard.

"My husband and I both agree that the two halves of our people have only one country—this one. We were only one people when the Turks founded the Empire. We were only one before the French and the English drew lines we don't under-stand over us with their rulers. Palestine was put under the English mandate, and now it's called Israel; they gave us an Emir from the Hejaz—Hussein is his great-grandson. You've brought a Christian to see me: tell him I greet him in friendship. Tell him you are our brothers, and it hurts us to be living in houses while you are living in tents. As for the man who calls himself the king, we can do without him and his family. Instead of looking after his father in his palace, he let him die in a prison for madmen."

Patriotism is generally an inflated assertion of imaginary superiority or suprem-acy. But rereading what I've written here I feel I was convinced by what the farmer's wife said. Or rather I was touched, as by a prayer in a vast church. What I heard was like a chant expressing the aspirations of a whole people. We should always remember that the Palestinians have nothing, neither passport nor territory nor nation, and if they laud and long for all those things it's because they see only the ghosts of them. The Jordanian woman sang without either bombast or plati-tude. Her strong and musical utterance was neither dull nor declaratory but almost drily factual; her voice remained even, as if stating the obvious.

"But Hussein's a Muslim just like you," joked one of the boys, trying to pro-voke her.

"Perhaps, like me, he's fond of the smell of mignonette," she answered. "The resemblance goes no further than that."

She sat in the doorway and spoke in that calm fearless voice for nearly an hour. Then she rose and straightened up, signifying she had work to do on the farm.

I went over and congratulated her on her garden.

"We're from the South," she said. "My father was a Bedouin soldier. He was given the farm a few weeks before he died."

Her voice never showed either pride, humility, or anger. She answered all our questions and remarks with patience and politeness.

"Do you know who taught us to farm?" she said. "The Palestinians, in 1949. They showed us how to turn the soil, how to choose the seeds, and when to water them."

"I noticed your vine," I said. "It's very handsome, but why does it crawl along the ground?"

For the first time, she smiled. Broadly.

"I know that in Algeria and France the vines are propped up and grow like runner beans. You make wine out of them. For us that would be a sin. We eat the grapes. And they taste best when they ripen on the ground."

She touched fingertips with each of us, and watched us go.

It wasn't impossible that, deep down, every Palestinian blamed Palestine for lying down and submitting too easily to a strong and cunning enemy.

"Why didn't she rise up in revolt? Volcanoes might have erupted, thunderbolts might have fallen and set fire to everything . . ."

"Thunderbolts? Haven't you realized yet that Heaven's on the side of the Jews?"

"But just taking it lying down! Where are the famous earthquakes?"

Even their anger, not merely verbal but born out of suffering, increased their determination to fight.

"The West goes out of its way to defend Israel . . ."

"The arrogance of the strong will be met with the violence of the weak."

"Even blind violence?"

"Yes. For a purpose that's both blind and lucid."

"What do you mean?"

"Nothing. I'm just getting worked up."

None of the fedayeen ever lets go of his gun. If it wasn't slung over his shoulder he held it horizontal on his knees or vertical between them, not suspecting this attitude was in itself either an erotic or a mortal threat, or both. Never on any of the bases did I see a fedayee without his gun, except when he was asleep. Whether he was cooking, shaking out his blankets, or reading his letters, the weapon was almost more alive than the soldier himself. So much so that I wonder whether, if the farmer's wife had seen boys without guns coming toward her house, she wouldn't have gone indoors, shocked at the sight of young men walking about naked. But she wasn't surprised: she lived surrounded by soldiers.

When, after leaving her place, we reached the turning by the little hazel copse, the fedayeen ran off and left me by myself on the road. Each tried not to be seen by the others, but I could just make them out from flashes of white shirt when, calm as babies on the pot, they squatted down to defecate. I suppose they wiped themselves clean with leaves plucked from the lower branches. Then back they came on to the road in good order, buttoned up neatly, still carrying their guns and still singing an impromptu marching song. When we got back we made ourselves some tea.

When I thought about her afterward, the farmer's wife sometimes struck me as a woman of great courage and intelligence; but at other times I couldn't help seeing her as a perfect example of dissimulation. Were she and her husband, with the hidden consent of the whole population of Ajloun, acting a part—he pretending, to the point of obsequiousness, to be a friend of the Palestinians, while she more subtly used argument and political acumen? Were they really a couple of collaborators, as the word was used by Frenchmen of other Frenchmen who consorted with the Germans? Had they been instructed to feign sympathy with the fedayeen in order to pass on information to the Jordanian army? If so, perhaps it was they who supplied the details that made the massacres of the fedayeen possible in June '71.

I still wonder why that farmer's wife was so much against Hussein. Was part of her family Palestinian? Did she have a score to settle? Did she remember being rescued from danger by some Palestinians? I still wonder about it.

All the pretense, misunderstanding, and eyewash were quite evident to the journalists, who either went along with it deliberately or were dazzled by the glare given off by all rebellions. But although the very naïveté of the deceits ought to have warned them, I can't remember one newspaper article expressing surprise at the collusion and childishness involved. Perhaps the papers, who'd spent real money sending all those reporters and photographers and cameramen such a long way, insisted on sensational events to justify the expense. No question of applying the Paris cops' motto, "Move on, please, there's nothing to see."

Journalists weren't allowed anywhere near the bases—Halt! Secret! No Entry! The bases were forbidden territory, perhaps because, as everyone guessed, though they didn't dare say so, there wasn't anything to see.

And perhaps this book I'm writing, an upsurge in my memory of some delightful times, is also—but would I say so?—just a collection of past moments designed to conceal the fact that there was nothing to see or hear. Are these pages only a barricade to hide the void, a mass of minor details designed, because they themselves are true, to lend plausibility to the rest?

I felt rather uncomfortable about the way the PLO were using the same devious and cynical methods of keeping military secrets as ordinary states successfully established, though I had to admit I couldn't see any alternative.

As a matter of fat I never saw or heard anything that couldn't perfectly well have been repeated. But mightn't that have been due to my extreme naïveté and fits of absentmindedness? While visiting a base, I was quite capable of poring at length over the maneuvers of a colony of processionary caterpillars, themselves so clueless that they'd chosen to live among fedayeen growing colder and hungrier by the hour. Did Abu Omar see me as a real colleague who happened to be rather featherbrained, or as a dim old man who if anything important happened wouldn't understand, let alone disclose it, but just put it on a par with the comings and goings of the caterpillars?

The fedayee who'd translated the farmer's wife's Arabic so efficiently brought the almost involuntary distance between us to a rather abrupt end. I was invited to a birthday dinner by a former Turkish officer who turned out to be his father.

Until about 1970 Amman, which like other Arab capitals retained the dusty dullness of a small Bedouin township, was still a wreck. Now, after all the storms that have raged around Beirut, Amman is dangerously overblown.

The stream, in a voice that was low at first, has told how all the Arab countries mistrusted the Palestinians. Not one of them bothered to give any real help to that tortured people, tormented by its enemy, Israel, by its own political and revolutionary factions, and by the inner conflicts of each of its citizens. Every country felt threatened by a people without a country.

Lebanon, the so-called Switzerland of the Middle East, would disappear when Beirut disappeared under the bombs. The phrase "carpet of bombs," repeated over and over again by the papers and the radio, was perfectly apt.

And the more Beirut collapsed, its houses bent double as if they had stomachaches, the stronger, the more portly, the fatter, grew Amman. As you went down into the old city you saw little *bureaux de change* check by jowl, straight out of the City of London. As soon as the sun got too hot, their smiling, moustachioed owners put up their steel shutters, went out in their damp, short-sleeved shirts to their air-conditioned Mercedes, and drove home to take an afternoon nap in their villas in Jebel Amman. Nearly all of them, and their wives (in the plural), were fat. The wives looked through *Vogue* and *House and Garden*, ate chocolates and listened to *The Four Seasons* on cassettes. Vivaldi was all the rage when I got there in 1984; Mahler was just arriving as I left.

Ruins achieve glory and everlastingness through those who laid them low. And mending a broken column or a chipped capital is a kind of reparation. Because of its Roman remains, Amman, for all its dust and dirt, had something.

I went through quite a large orchard near Ashrafieh and the fedayee-cum-interpreter was waiting for me at the house. It was not unlike the Nashashibis' place, all on one floor. The main reception room was on the same level as an orchard of apricot trees. Omar's father was sitting in an armchair smoking a hubble-bubble. The carpet was so vast and thick and had such a beautiful pattern I was tempted to take off my shoes.

"But they'll smell my dirty feet, my postman's feet that have trudged for miles . . ."

A small table laden with honey cakes was already set out on the carpet.

"I hope you like oriental pastries."

Omar's father was tall and lean and stern looking. His hair and moustache were white and trimmed quite short.

"Don't listen to my son. He's made up his mind not to like them because there's nothing Marxist-Leninist or scientific about their ingredients or the way they're cooked. Make yourself comfortable."

When I reached the cushions on the far side of the carpet I stretched out and propped myself up on my elbow. Omar, Omar's father, and Mahmud, another fedayee, were all three squatting down in their socks, their three pairs of shoes left on the marble surround. I laughed at the bubbles inside the hookah.

"You find it amusing? Strange?" asked the ex-Turkish officer.

"I feel as if I were looking at my stomach after I've drunk a bottle of Perrier."
Faint smiles from Omar and Mahmud. Very faint. Almost invisible.

"Maybe what you're really thinking is: there's your stomach, but it's my mouth producing the storm in it."

It wasn't what I was thinking, but it did echo my feelings, impossible to put into words, as I reclined there on the carpet under the Murano chandelier, talking to a former Turkish officer whom I later discovered to be eighty years old.

The limits of convention in conversation are very fluid, perhaps as fluid as geographical frontiers, but as with the latter it takes a war, with deaths, casualties, and heroic survivors, to move them. When they do move, it's to make way for new frontiers, which are also traps. So I still know next to nothing about the Moslem Brotherhood.

"Last year, in Cairo, a writer asked me to correct an article he'd written in French," a Moroccan lawyer told me. "It was about forty pages long, but by page two I was completely stunned. The whole thing was full of hate. Things like: 'We must fight everything that isn't Islam. For the time being we'll act through strikes . . . Nothing is more offensive to man but pleasing to God than the fetid breath of a starving atheist or of a brother who's been on hunger strike for ten days.' "

The Moroccan's grimace of disgust struck me as more farfetched than the Egyptian's tirade. He'd refused to correct the article.

But when they spoke to me, a Frenchman, every member of the Moslem Brotherhood kept within the usual bounds. So I never gained access to their infernal secrets, as a reader in the old days might be admitted to the forbidden books in the *enfer* of the Bibliothèque Nationale.

The Turkish officer didn't seem to mind what he said. (And here, in reconstructing Monsieur Mustapha's conversation, I have to go in for a bit of forgery, filling in the gaps with the help I got later from Abu Omar and Mubarak. Otherwise all I'd have would be an unintelligible sketch of ruins drawn in the dark. I reproduce the content correctly, but in references to people who are still alive I've changed first names, surnames, and initials.)

"It was in Constantinople that I began to speak your language. I hope I've improved in it since then. But I was born in Nablus and our family name is Naboulsi. It's a famous family, and since eight minutes past eight this morning I've been eighty years old. In 1912 I was a student in Berlin and an officer in the Ottoman army. In 1915, at the beginning of the war, when I suppose you were a French child and already my enemy, we—"

Here he smiled as sweetly as a saint or a baby: "We—forgive me: that word doesn't link you to me, it excludes you, because in this context we means the Germans and the Turks—we were serving under Kaiser Wilhelm II. We weren't yet fighting your Maréchal Franchet d'Esperey. He came later. So Turkish is my first language, but as well as Arabic I also speak German. And English. You must be the judge of my French. Don't think too badly of me for talking about myself this evening—it's my birthday until midnight. In 1916 I was posted to intelligence."

Each sentence gulped down the one that went before without leaving time for digestion. My job was to listen.

"The war you Europeans say is over will last a long time yet. A Muslim I was and a Muslim I remained in the Empire, though we knew a transcendental God was unfashionable. But now—does being a Muslim mean any more than just saying so? Anyway, I'm still an Arab and a Muslim in the eyes of both Arabs and Muslims. But as regards Palestine . . . As a Turk I was a Palestinian. Now I'm practically nothing. Except perhaps through my youngest son—through Omar. I'm still a Palestinian through someone who's betrayed Islam for Marx.

"I believe, like you, in the virtues of treason, but I believe even more—though, alas, obscurely—in fidelity. As you see, I'm left in peace in my house in Amman, but here I'm a Jordanian, fallen stage by stage from the Khedive to Hussein, from the empire to the provinces."

"Are you still a Turkish officer?"

"You could say so. I have the courtesy title of colonel. That means about as much to me as if Monsieur Pompidou made me a duke in the French Section of the Workers' International or the Prince of Air Inter. In theory I obey the last scion—why don't I say sprig or twig?—of a Hashemite dynasty from the Hejaz, because since 1917 I've had to . . . No, it was 1922, the time when Ataturk did a deal with Europe . . ."

"You don't like Kemal Ataturk?"

"It's not true, the famous scene where he's supposed to have thrown down a copy of the Koran in the Assembly. He'd never have dared—the chamber was full of Muslim deputies. But he proved later on that he hated us."

"At the end of his life he got Antioch and Alexandretta back for Turkey."

"The French gave them to Turkey. They shouldn't have done it. They're Arab territories. The people there still speak Arabic. But as I was saying, after 1922 I had to stop taking orders from the Ottomans and take them from the English, from Abdullah, and from Glubb, who stripped me of my officer's rank because I'd served under Ataturk. He really did it because I'd done my military training in Germany."

"France has had its 'lost soldiers,' too."

"What a fine name! But all soldiers are lost.

"It's only just turned ten. I've still got till midnight. When I came back to Amman, the very town where I'd fought the English under Allenby, my eldest son, Ibrahim, whose mother, my first wife, is German, arranged for me to buy our house back. For that's what I had to do. Then one day I was playing backgammon in a café near your hotel—the Salah-ed-Din, I believe?—when I was recognized. I spent five months in prison. You've been luckier . . . you only spent a few hours with Nabila Nashashibi—one of her brothers told me. After that I was free. Free! Free not to cross the Jordan or see Nablus again. Not that I care, of course."

He put the mouthpiece of the hubble-bubble back in his mouth. I took sneaky advantage of the brief silence.

"But you're still a Turkish officer?"

"Discharged, as they say, a long time ago. My enemy was Ismet Inonu, less brutal but more bitter than Kemal. It was at his funeral in Ankara thirty years ago that I last wore Turkish uniform in public. My first wife keeps it in Bremen. She lives there with my son Ibrahim."

He sang it softly:

"It was at his funeral in Ankara thirty years ago that I last wore Turkish uniform in public."

Then, to another rhythm:

> *It was at his funeral*
> *in Ankara*
> *Thirty years ago*
> *That I last wore, that I last wore, Kara,*
> *Turkish uniform*
> *In public.*

He went on:

"That tune haunts me. It's a sort of cavatina. The first musical table mat we had in Constantinople—Istanbul to you—used to play it."

"When you fought for the Turks against the English, didn't you feel you were fighting the Arabs in Lawrence and Allenby's army?"

"Did I hear you mention feelings? My dear Monsieur Genet, you don't suppose that in the army, where they like to give orders and be obeyed, and to obey, ah yes, to obey, and win medals—you don't suppose people in the army have feelings, do you?"

He and I both laughed politely. Omar and Mahmud didn't join in.

"And nothing was as clear-cut as that small but immodest archaeologist makes out. Lawrence embroidered everything—even when he's sodomized he presents it as heroism. And look at what's happening in Amman and Zarka now: all the officers and men of Palestinian origin have somehow received orders, or at least been advised in pressing terms, to desert from the Jordanian army—which is still made up of groups from Glubb's Arab Legion, young Bedouin and Palestinians—and join the PLA[6] And how many have done so?"[7]

"Not many."

"Very few. But why? Out of disloyalty to the Palestinian homeland? Out of cowardice? To avoid having to fight against former brothers-in-arms? Out of loyalty to King Hussein? I'm a very old soldier, and I know all those things can come into it. I was an Arab officer in the Ottoman army. When your historians talk of Lawrence bringing about a general Arab revolt, let's cheerfully admit it was

[6]Palestine Liberation Army. Not to be confused with the Palestine Liberation Organization, led by Yasser Arafat.

[7]Leila told me that in fact many soldiers and officers deserted. But how many is many?

thanks to gold, to the coffers of gold sent by His Majesty George V. Of course there were solemn discussions in which ambition skulked in the disguise of rhetoric about freedom and independence, patriotism and magnanimity. But despite the fine words, ambition itself was disfigured by demands for posts, governorships, commissions, missions—and other things I can't remember. But I can remember the gold. My blue eyes saw it, my fingers touched it. The discussions! What a joke! About gold! About gold coins in pockets.

"My son told me you went to see a farmer's wife last week. I understand she's the daughter of a Bedouin NCO who was dazzled by British gold. He was dazzled by gold, but so were our emirs, who were also impressed by sashes and garters and ribbons—medals for the puffed-out chests of Bedouin who can be bowled over by a Lebel rifle. Just look at what's going on around you. Or keep your eyes closed, you who see nothing but poetry: Omar belongs to Fatah—do you think the fedayeen rush to join it out of altruism?"

He raised his voice, but it was mournful as he called out to the two young men: "Omar! Omar and Mahmud! Tonight you may smoke."

For my benefit he added, leaning back on his cushions of embroidered silk, "They wouldn't have smoked in the presence of my white hairs when I was a diwan."

We took no notice of this slip of the tongue, and fell silent. Perhaps he thought an apology would only make it worse; perhaps I liked the idea of talking to an old Turk who thanks to his dreams and my passivity saw himself as a former vizir.

Hands were already fishing in pockets for lighters and American cigarettes.

"One day you'll understand what the English were like.

"But look at the Circassians. Let's talk about them for a bit. Abdul-hamid needed a reliable army (Muslim but not Arab) to fight against the rebel Bedouin. So he thought of the Circassians in the Russian Empire. The Khedive offered them the best land in this region—here in Jordan and in what later became Syria—land where springs were few but bountiful. They may have abandoned their land in Golan"—he pronounced it "Jolan"—"to the Jews, but they still have their villages near Amman. And who were the Circassians? A kind of Muslim Cossack good at slaughtering Bedouin. And now they're their generals, ministers, ambassadors, and postmasters who work for Monsieur Hussein and protect him against the Palestinians."

The two young men went behind a pillar to smoke. I saw this same deference to the Arab aristocracy, or what set itself up as that, not only in the faces, words, and behavior of the fedayeen but also when Samia Solh entered the lounge of the Strand Hotel in Beirut. But the description of that evening can wait. The Turk was forging ahead.

"If justice had been done we ought to have lost the war in our officers' messes, with their countless trays of mezze and glasses of arak. We didn't think of anything but food. Amid all he plates and liqueurs and jokes our discussions would have flagged if we hadn't had a star to guide us. What we were debating was this: Should we, as Arab officers in the Turkish army, be hoping for and doing our best to promote the downfall of the Empire and the victory of England and France? I admit what was admissible in our debates, and say nothing about our revolting ambitions should Ludendorff defeat you on the Somme.

"The English had despised us under Muhammad Ali. The French had done so in Algeria and Tunisia. Right through the 1914–18 war, the mosques in Tunisia prayed for our victory. Perhaps because the bey was of Turkish origin. Anyhow, Tunis prayed for Germany and Turkey to conquer your countries. The Italians had despised us since 1896 in Eritrea. Ought we have wished all those Christians success?"

"The Germans were Christians, too."

Monsieur Mustapha paused for a few seconds to whistle the cavatina the musical plate-warmer used to play.

"No Arab country was a German colony. And Boche engineers built our roads and railways. Have you see the Hejaz railway?"

"Not this time. I did when I was eighteen. I did my military service in Damascus."

"In Damascus! You must tell me about it. What year?"

"1928 or '29."

"Did it leave you with happy memories? . . . No, don't talk about that country, or about yourself and your love affairs. I know all about it. Let's get back to the debate that fired our Arab consciences every hour of every day. I remember Ataturk with a certain amount of respect. He didn't like the Arabs and scarcely knew their language,[*] but he saved what he could of the Ottoman world.

"The way you humiliated the Empire, with the last Caliph escaping on an English ship, a prisoner and a deserter like Abd el-Kader! England with its Glubb here, and its Samuel in Palestine. And Frangié in Lebanon, and Aflak and his ridiculous Baas in Syria. And Ibn Saud in Arabia . . ."

"What ought we to have done in '14—and '18?"

Under the Murano chandelier, on the Smyrna carpet, Omar's father stood up and looked at me.

"We knew before 1917, long before the Balfour decision, that during the war some rich landowners . . ."

For the first time I heard the Sursok family mentioned.

". . . some rich landowners had already made contacts with the object of selling whole villages to the Jews, good and bad land all mixed up together. We know the names of the Arab families who gained by it . . ."

"They had friends in the Porte . . ."

"Undoubtedly. And the English, who were anti-Semitic but realistic, wanted a European colony near Suez to help them stand guard over what lay east of Aden."

The ebony and mother-of-pearl clock struck midnight. The Turkish officer had reached the sixteenth hour of his eightieth birthday. Omar asked him respectfully

---

[*]Is this a legend? Ataturk was almost taken prisoner because he spoke Arabic so badly. And I've heard he couldn't understand it very well, either.

whether he hadn't been afraid of offending me, a stranger. The old man looked at me kindly, I thought.

"Not for a moment," he said. "You're from a country that will still be in my heart even after I'm dead: the country of Claude Farrère and Pierre Loti."

They brushed against death every day, every night, hence the airy elegance beside which dancing is heaviness itself. And with them animals and somehow things also were tamed.

Among groups ranging in size from ten to ten thousand, death didn't mean anything any more: you couldn't feel a quadruple grief when four friends died instead of one, a sorrow a hundred times deeper when a hundred died. Paradoxically, the death of a favorite fedayee made him all the more alive, made us see details about him we'd never noticed before, made him speak to us, answer us with new conviction in his voice. For a short time the life, the one life of the now dead fedayee took on a density it had never had before. If while he was still alive the twenty-year-old fedayee had made a few undemanding plans for the next day—washing his clothes, posting a letter—it seemed to me those unfulfilled intentions were accomplished now by the smell of decomposition. A dead man's plans stink as they rot.

But what did they mean to do with this gray head, with its gray skin, gray hair, gray unshaven beard—this gray, pink, round head for ever in their midst? Use it as a witness? My body didn't count. It served only to carry my round, gray head.

It was much simpler with the Black Panthers. They'd found a waif, but instead of being a child the waif was an old man, and a white. Childish as I was about everything, I was so ignorant of American politics it took me a long time to realize Senator Wallace was a racist. It was like the fulfilment of an old childhood dream, in which strangers, foreigners—but probably more like me than my own compatriots—opened up a new life to me.

This childishness, almost innocence, was forced on me by the Panthers' kindness, which it seemed to me they bestowed on me not as a special favor but because it was natural to them. To be adopted like a child when one was an old man was very pleasant: it brought me both real protection and education in affection. The Panthers were well known for their talent as teachers.

The Panthers protected me so well I was never afraid in America—except for them. And as if by magic neither the white administration nor the white police ever made trouble for me. Right at the start, before I was adopted by David Hilliard, someone almost always went with me if I wanted to see Harlem. Until one day I went on my own into a bar that served blacks only. It was probably attached to a brothel, for pretty girls kept coming in with black pimps. I ordered a Coca-Cola. My accent and the order in which I spoke the words made everyone burst out laughing.

I was deep in discussion with the barman and a pimp when two Panthers who were looking for me found me in "the jungle of the cities."

The whites' recoil from the Panthers' weapons, their leather jackets, their revolutionary hairdos, their words, and even their gentle but menacing tone—that was just what the Panthers wanted. They deliberately set out to create a dramatic image. The image was a theater both for enacting a tragedy and for stamping it out—a bitter tragedy about themselves, a bitter tragedy for the whites. They aimed to project their image in the press and on the screen until the whites were haunted by it.

And they succeeded. The theatrical image was backed up by real deaths. The Panthers did some shooting themselves, and the mere sight of the Panthers' guns made the cops fire.

"Was the Panthers' failure due to the fact that they adopted a 'brand image' before they'd earned it in action?"—that's a rough summary of a question I was asked by a paper called *Remparts* (Ramparts). But the world can be changed by other means than the sort of wars in which people die. "Power may be at the end of a gun," but sometimes it's also at the end of the shadow or the image of a gun. The Panthers' demands, as expressed in their "ten points," are both simple and contradictory. They are like a screen behind which what's done is different from what's seen to be done.

Instead of seeking real independence—territorial, political, administrative, and legal—which would have meant a confrontation with white power, the black underwent a metamorphosis in himself. He had been invisible; he became visible. And this visibility was accomplished in various ways. Black is not a color itself, but with a pigmentation showing every shade of density, the black can wear clothes that are veritable feasts of color. Against a black skin, light or dark, matching tones or contrasts of gold and azure, pink and mauve are all equally striking. But the set cannot disguise the tragic scene being played before it. The eyes are alive, and give forth a terrifying eloquence.

Did this metamorphosis bring about any change?

"Yes, when the whites were affected by it. The whites changed because their fears were no longer the same."

Deaths and other acts of aggression showed the blacks as more and more threatening, less and less in awe of the whites. The whites sensed that a real society was coming into being not far away. It had existed before, but then it had been a timid attempt at counterfeiting white society. Now it was breaking away, refusing to be a copy. And not only outwardly, in everyday life, but also inwardly, in the creation of a myth for which Malcolm X, Martin Luther King himself, and N'Krumah all acted as models.

It was almost certain that the Panthers had just won a victory, and by means that seem derisive: silks, velvets, wild horses, and images that brought about a metamorphosis in the black. The method—for the moment—was traditional: international conflict, national liberation and perhaps class struggle.

Was it only a kind of theater?

"Theater as it's usually understood involves an acting area, an audience, re-hearsals. If the Panthers acted, they didn't do so on a stage. Their audience was never passive: if it was black it either became what it really was or booed them; if it was white it was wounded and suffered. No imaginary curtain could be brought down on their performances. Excess in display, in words, and in attitude swept the Panthers to ever new and greater excess.

Perhaps it's time to mention their lack of a country, though what follows is only a suggestion.

For every well-defined people—and even for nomads, for they don't visit their grazing areas merely at random—land is the necessary basis of nationhood. It is more. It's territory, it's matter itself, it's the space in which a strategy may be worked out. Whether still in its natural state, cultivated or industrialized, it is land that makes the notions both of war and of strategic withdrawal possible. Land may or may not be called sacred—the barbaric ceremonies that are supposed to make it so are of little importance. What matters is that it provides a place from which you can make war and to which you can retreat. But both the blacks and the Palestinians are without land. Their two situations are not completely identical, but they are alike in that neither group has any territory of its own.

So where can these virtual martyrs prepare their revolt *from?* The ghetto? But they can't take refuge there—they'd need ramparts, barricades, bunkers, arms, ammunition, the support of the whole black population. Nor can they sally forth from the ghetto to wage war on white territory—all American territory is in the hands of the American whites.

The Panthers' subversion would take place elsewhere and by other means: in people's consciences. Wherever they went, the Americans were the masters, so the Panthers would do their best to terrorize the masters by the only means available to them. Spectacle. And the spectacle would work because it was the product of despair. The tragedy of their situation—the danger of death and death itself; physical terror and nervous dread—taught them how to exaggerate that despair.

But spectacle is only spectacle, and it may lead to mere figment, to no more than a colorful carnival; and that is a risk the Panthers ran. Did they have any choice? But even if they themselves had been the masters, or had had sovereignty over some territory, they probably wouldn't have formed a government complete with president, minister for war, minister of education, field marshals, and Newton as "supreme commander" as soon as he got out of jail.

The few whites who sympathized with the Panthers soon ran out of steam. They could follow them only on the plane of ideas, not into the depths, where a strategy had to be worked out whose only source was the blacks' imagination.

So the Panthers were heading for either madness, metamorphosis of the black community, death, or prison. All those options happened, but the metamorphosis was by far the most important, and that is why the Panthers can be said to have overcome through poetry.

I went back to the tents of Ajloun by the Salt road, and the first thing I saw was Abu Kassem with his arms in the air. He was hanging out his washing on a string tied to a couple of trees. The spring was nearby. Before the Amman massacre, the

Jordanian ministers' servants used to water their horses there. The fedayeen now lived in the ministers' houses. Where had Abu Kassem got the clothespins? And why had he been doing his washing? He answered me, unsmiling, with a quote from the catechism.

"A fedayee can look after himself and can always find whatever he needs. There are the pins—if you've got any washing to do you can use them. You won't find any others—you're not a fedayee."

"Thank you—I never wash. You're joking, Kassem, but you look very grim."

"M'hammad's going to the Ghor tonight."

The Ghor is the Jordan valley:

"Is he your friend?"

"Yes."

"How long have you known he was going?"

"Twenty minutes."

"Is that his washing?"

"His and mine. The men must be clean tonight."

"Are you worried, Kassem?"

"Anxious. I'll be anxious until he comes back or until I have to give up hope."

"You love M'hammad that much, and you a revolutionary?"

"When you're a revolutionary yourself you'll understand. I'm nineteen, I love the revolution, I'm devoted to it and hope to work for it for a long time to come. But here we're in a way off duty. We may be revolutionaries but we're only human. I love all the fedayeen, and you too. But here under the trees all night and day, I can be more friendly with one of the commandos than with the rest if I want to. I can break a bar of chocolate into two, but not into sixteen. So I make my choice."

"You're all revolutionaries, but you like just one of them the best?"

"We're all Palestinians. But I choose to belong to Fatah. Hasn't it ever struck you that revolution and friendship go together?"

"Yes. But what about your leaders?"

"Even if they're revolutionaries, they're like me and have their preferences."

"And would you go so far as to call the friendship you speak of, love?"

"Yes. It is love. Do you think at a time like this I'm afraid of words? Friendship, love? One thing is true—if he dies tonight there'll always be a gulf at my side, a gulf into which I must never fall. My leaders? When I was seventeen they thought I was grown-up enough to be allowed to join Fatah. And I've stayed in Fatah even though my mother needed me. I'm nineteen now, and no less grown-up than I was before. I may be a revolutionary, but in moments of relaxation I turn to friendship—friendship's restful, too. I'll be worried tonight, but I'll get on with my work. I learned two years ago what I have to do when it's my turn to go down to the Jordan, so I know all about it. Now I'd better hang this last vest up to dry."

There were ten or twelve camps in Jordan. Jebel Hussein, Wahadat, Baqa, Gaza Camp, and Irbid were the ones I knew best. Life in the camps was less elegant, that's to say less stripped down to essentials, than on the bases. Less volatile, too.

The women were all very serene, but even the thinnest carried a characteristic feminine weight. I don't mean the physical weight of breasts, hips, and thighs, but that of the womanly gestures conveying certainty and repose.

A lot of foreigners, that is non-Palestinians, not only visited the camps but also went "up," paradoxically, to the "bases" overlooking the Jordan—fortified positions commanding the river from the mountains. The fedayeen came back to the camps to rest—or to get laid, as Westerners say, or to get medicine to cure the effects of that activity.

Nearly every camp had a tiny infirmary-cum-pharmacy full—it was so small—of old cartons of unidentified and useless drugs from Germany, France, Italy, Spain, and Scandinavia. Nobody could read the lists of ingredients or the instructions for use.

When a few tents were burned down at Baqa Camp, Saudi Arabia flew some houses made of corrugated iron straight out from Riyadh as a gift, and the old women greeted their arrival as if they were young princesses, with a sort of impromptu dance. It was like the dance Azeddine invented in honor of his first bicycle. The corrugated iron or aluminium houses reflected the glare of the sun. Imagine a cube with one side missing for the floor and another with a doorway cut in it. In such a room an eighty-year-old couple would have cooked in the midday sun in summer and frozen at night in the winter.

Some Palestinians had the bright idea of filling the corrugations on the roof and sides of one house with loose black earth, held in place with wire netting. Then they sowed seeds in the soil and watered it every evening, producing a carpet of green dotted with poppy flowers. The place became a little grotto pleasant to be in, winter or summer. But there weren't many imitations of those horse-covered hills.

What was to become of you after the storms of fire and steel? What were you to do?

Burn, shriek, turn into a brand, blacken, turn to ashes, let yourself be slowly covered first with dust and then with earth, seeds, moss, leaving behind nothing but your jawbone and teeth, and finally becoming a little funeral mound with flowers growing on it and nothing inside.

When I looked at the Palestinian revolution from a viewpoint higher than my own, it was never desire for territory, for land more or less derelict, and unfenced kitchen gardens and orchards, but a great movement of revolt, a challenge over rights which reached to the limits of Islam, not only involving territorial boundaries but also calling for a revision, probably even a rejection, of a theology as soporific as a Breton cradle.

The dream, but not yet the declared aim, of the fedayeen was clear: to do away with the twenty-two Arab nations and leave everyone wreathed in smiles, childlike at first but soon foolish. But they were running out of ammunition and their main target, America, was endlessly resourceful. Thinking to walk tall, the Palestine revolution was sinking fast. Training people to sacrifice themselves results not in altruism but in a kind of fascination that makes them jump off a cliff not to help but merely to follow those who have already leapt to their deaths. Especially when they foresee, not through thought but through fear, the annihilation to come.

A little further back, when I was talking about the deference, almost sycophancy, in the fedayeen's behavior towards members of the Palestinian traditional or banking aristocracies, I said I'd return to the subject of Samia Solh.

I'd already seen wounded commandos lying between white sheets in a hospital in Southern Lebanon, overawed by elderly women with madeup eyes, lips, and cheeks, who tinkled like tambourines whenever they moved, so many were their gold bracelets, chains, necklaces, and earrings.

"Your janglings will either wake them up or kill them," I said to one.

"Not a bit of it! We wave our arms about because we're Latins. Or at least Mediterranean—Maronites, Phoenicians. We do our best to restrain ourselves, but we can't help showing pity at the sight of all this suffering. And then naturally our jewelry makes a noise! But our martyrs love it. Some of them tell me they've never been as close to anything so rich and beautiful in their lives. Let their poor eyes at least be filled with happiness."

"Don't argue with strangers, Mathilde. Let's go on to the surgical ward."

Later on I had the chance all too often to observe at close quarters such elderly ladies, from what remains of the leading Palestinian families.

Perhaps a goose cassoulet provides the best metaphor for what a handsome old Palestinian lady looked like. The faces and the manners of these rich dames made you think of something cooked very fast at times but mostly simmered very slowly to produce those round cheekbones and retain that pink skin. The misfortunes of their people at once sharpened and softened their features; they were preserved in suffering as the goose's flavor is preserved in its own fat. So they were—one of them especially—adorably and selfishly sweet. The object of their sweetness was to keep sufferings that were too raw at a distance. They kept themselves up-to-date about the sufferings in Chatila as they did about the price of gold and the exchange rate of the dollar—through the stitches of a piece of embroidery or tapestry. They knew about suffering, but through a cushion, or a gown a hundred or a hundred and twenty years old, worked by dead fingers, watched by now sightless eyes. They cultivated politeness as a kind of ornament.

If Venice happened to crop up in conversation they never mentioned Diaghilev. Instead they made elegant reference to the Lagoon, the Grand Canal, the glass factories at Murano, and funerals at which the coffin was borne along in a gondola.

"Like Diaghilev's," you might say.

"I watched it go by from a balcony at the Danieli."

These princesses with wrists strong enough to wear solid gold chains contemplate their people from their chaises lounges, through pearl-handled lorgnettes. They watch the fighting through their windows, and the sadness in their eyes grows ever more affected.

I myself watched the sea and Cyprus in the distance through the window of a prefab, and waited for the fighting, but I didn't turn into a juicy old princess. The resemblance never-troubled me: I didn't fancy either the smooth looks or the easy life of the line of Ali.

Yet like them I'll have looked on at the Palestinians' revolt as if from a window or a box in a theater, and as if through a pearl-handled lorgnette.

How far away I was from the Palestinians. For example, when I was writing this book, out there among the fedayeen, I was always on the other side of a boundary. I knew I was safe, not because of a Celtic physique or a layer of goose fat, but because of even shinier and stronger armor: I didn't belong to, never really identified with, their nation or their movement. My heart was in it; my body was in it; my spirit was in it. Everything was in it at one time or another; but never my total belief, never the whole of myself.

There are so many ways of being married. But what struck me as really strange, every day, day and night, every hour, every second, there under the trees, were the doings of that curious couple, Islam and Marxism. In theory everything about it was incompatible. The Koran and *Das Kapital* were foes. Yet harmony seemed to result from their contradictions. Anyone giving out of generosity seemed to have done so out of a love of justice resulting from an intelligent reading of the German tome. We sailed along madly, sometimes slowly, sometimes fast, with God always bumping into the domed forehead of Marx, who denied him. Allah was everywhere and nowhere, despite all the prayers toward Mecca.

Louis Jouvet was a famous actor in France in the late forties, and when he coolly asked me to write him a play with only two or three characters in it I answered with equal detachment. I realized his provocative question was asked only out of politeness. And I detected the same politeness in Arafat's voice when he said:

"Why don't you write a book?"

"Why not?"

We were only exchanging courtesies; neither of us was bound by promises forgotten before they were uttered. My certainty that there was nothing at all serious either in Arafat's question or in my answer was probably the real reason why I forgot to bring pen and paper with me. I didn't believe in the idea of that or any other book; I meant to concentrate on what I saw and heard; and I was as interested in my own curiosity as in its objects. But without my quite realizing it, everything that happened and every word that was spoken set itself down in my memory.

There was nothing for me to do but look and listen. Not a very laudable occupation. Curious and undecided, I stayed where I was, at Ajloun. And gradually, as with some elderly couples who started off indifferent to one another, my love and the Palestinians' affection made me stay on.

The policy of the superpowers, and the PLO's relations with them, spread over the Palestinian revolt, and us with it, a kind of transcendental influence. A tremor starting in Moscow, Geneva, or Tel Aviv would rumble on via Amman to reach out under the trees and over the mountains to Jerash and Ajloun.

The complex old Arab and Palestinian aristocracies worked alongside the modern authorities, parallel to and, as I once thought, superimposed on them.

From Ajloun, Palestinian patriotism looked like Delacroix's *Liberty on the Barricades*. Distance, as often happens, lent a touch of divinity. But the birth of that patriotism had been obscure, even dubious.

The Arab Peninsula had long been entirely under Turkish rule, mild for some people, harsh according to most. Then between 1916 and 1918 the English, with their coffers full of gold, promised the Arabs independence and the setting up of an Arab kingdom if the Arab-speaking people rose against the Turks and the Germans. But even before this, rivalries among the leading Palestinian, Lebanese, Syrian, and Hejazi families had led to their seeking now Turkish and now English support, not to obtain greater freedom for the new Arab nation, as yet unborn though perhaps about to be conceived, but so that they could cling to power. Among these illustrious clans were the Husseini, Jouzi, N'seybi, and Nashashibi families. Others either awaited the victory of the Emir Faisal or worked against it.

Nothing was said clearly. No leading Palestinian family actually declared itself, but all of them probably had a representative in either the Turkish or the Anglo-French camp.

That had been roughly the setup in 1914.

But the families who'd rashly chosen the English camp, which was also that of the Emir Faisal, were obliged to turn against the English when they found out that the Jewish National Home was to be recognized as an independent state.

With the exception of some wealthy Syrian and Lebanese families such as the Sursoks and the incredible descendants of Abd el-Kadr, all the hereditary "leading" Palestinian families claimed to be at the forefront of the struggle, leading the country simultaneously against Israel and the British.

The Husseini family[9]—sons, grandsons, nephews, and great-nephews of the Grand Mufti of Jerusalem—has produced many martyrs to the Palestinian cause. (When I use words like "martyr" I don't adopt the aura of nobility that the Palestinians attribute to them. From a slightly mocking distance, I merely make use of the vocabulary. I shall give my reasons later.)

Madame Shahid (the name means "martyr"), née Husseini, a niece of the Grand Mufti, told me with what I took to be pride how the Khedives had sorted things out in Jerusalem.

"There was such chaos and muddle around the Holy Sepulcher, such mean and petty rows about who was to celebrate the most masses, who was to occupy the church the longest—Roman Catholics, Russian Orthodox, Greeks, Maronites, those with hair or those with tonsures—and what liturgies they were to follow—the French, Italian, German, Spanish, and Coptic bishops and the Greek and

---

[9]The still numerous Hussein family are connected only distantly, if at all, with the present King of Jordan, though both the Palestinian and the Hejazi families claim to be "Sherifs"—that is, descended from the Prophet.

Russian priests all wanted to use their own languages—that the Khedives decided two or three Muslim families should be put in charge of the keys of the Holy Sepulcher and of the Church of the Ascension. I can remember the sound of the carriage on the cobblestones as my father drove home with the key of Christ's tomb, and how glad my mother was to have him back safe and sound."

The "leading families" still took part in the struggle, but not all their members were equally devoted to the cause. Some merely made use of it, rallying round or distancing themselves as it suited their interests. The Husseini and Nashashibi families both include many heroes, though they were rivals under the Turks.

Members of the Leading Families didn't spare one another. One of their privileges was to tell of anything that might harm their rivals, whether it was true or false. But I never heard any such allegations among the fedayeen. Perhaps I missed them through not understanding the language better. I heard plenty of insults against the army chiefs, though: the fighters made no secret of their contempt. They often talked to me about it, but they never said a word against one another. Judgment was shrewdly conveyed without a word being spoken.

Nor did the fedayeen know anything of the ornaments that generation after generation of the leading families had added to the Muslim epic. None of them could have told me the story Madame Shahid related.

"When Sultan So-and-So [some name I've forgotten] entered Jerusalem he decided, before any other ceremony, to say a prayer. As there was no mosque there yet, the people suggested he should pray in a Christian church, but he refused, saying, 'If I did, some future governor might use it as an excuse to seize the church on the grounds that it had been used to worship Allah.' So he prayed in the open, and it was there that the Muslims later built the Mosque of the Rock."

That story's about as true as the French legend of St. Louis dispensing justice under an oak tree and blessing the acorns.

With such embroideries Madame Shahid, a Palestinian, tried to bolster up the legend of a tolerant Islam. At the same time (the way the English tend the graves in their churchyards) she polished up the reputation of a sultan who might have had some connection with her own family fifteen hundred years ago. Such fairy tales were unknown to the fedayeen.

Lawrence promised Faisal sovereignty for the Arab people, but England didn't keep the promise. The League of Nations gave France mandatory powers over Lebanon and Syria, while England got Palestine, and Jordan went to Iraq. The rivalry between the leading families was transformed into patriotism; their senior members became warlords, regarded as bandit chiefs by England and France, and, after 1933, as Hitler's lackeys in the Middle East. The Palestine resistance was beginning.

One day a hotel porter told me he was waiting to hear from Canada about a job he was hoping to get in a big hotel there, "instead of staying here with no future." As we were talking, a bent old waiter went by and disappeared into the staff quarters.

"That's my future if I stay," said the porter scornfully. "Sixty years a servant."
"And never a day's rebellion!"
He slapped his hand angrily on the desk.
"Yes, sixty years and never a day's rebellion! I'd go anywhere rather than that."

Guests at the Strand Hotel in Beirut included political and military officials of the PLA and PLO, politicians of all nationalities who wanted to meet Arafat, journalists more or less friendly with or accepted by the Resistance, and a few German writers sympathetic to its cause. You might have a whisky or two with Kadoumi's bodyguards in one of the lounges there.

Samia Solh, sister-in-law to Prince Abdullah of Morocco, had just been ushered in by the manager. Just before she sat down she let her ankle-length mink coat, lined with white silk, slip to the floor, forming a sort of plinth. She stepped over it, and a bellboy picked it up and bore it off on outstretched arms to the cloakroom.

I was eighteen when I was taken to see four men who'd been hanged in Cannon Square, here in Beirut. (I was told they were thieves, but I think now they were rebel Druses.) My eyes had been as quick to seek out the dead men's flies as the eyes of the guests were now to fasten first on the famous hips, then on the reputedly very quick tongue and lips of the lovely but dim Samia.

"A week ago I was with Muhammad in Tripoli," she said. "We hit it off straight away."

Not dreaming that ten years later the PLO would be banned from Libya, its offices in Tripoli closed, the Palestinian officers listened to the lady entranced, with a reverence so hushed that her would-be intimate murmur rang out like a lecture at the Collège de France. Her peals of laughter were designed to draw attention to her triple collar of Venus, but they sounded coarse rather than crystalline when punctuated by Khadafi's given name.

No one was allowed to talk to her. Only the radio dared to comment, as it calmly did on the latest massacres on the banks of the Jordan and the ease with which fedayeen were picked off by Israeli soldiers.

No one touched those hips, that throat, those lips. I can understand now—I wondered at the time—how a fedayee might have been excited by all that beauty, the result of massages, applications of dandelion juice, anointings with royal jelly, and other products of shameless chemists. But the attentions the fedayeen paid her that evening were an eye-opener to me. Their tribute wasn't to the vixen wiggling her hips, though. It was to the fact that she brought History into the reinforced concrete hotel. It was in the Strand that the leaders of the PLO used to meet, among them Kamal Aduan, Kamal Nasser, and Abu Yussef Nedjar—I'll tell later on how they were killed by Israelis pretending to be queers, perhaps in retaliation for the murders at Munich during the 1972 Olympics.

"Verdun is very well laid out—a mixture of crosses and crescents forming one huge graveyard. There was slaughter there, carried out by God Himself. Senegalese, Madagascans, Tunisians, Moroccans, Mauritians, New Caledonians, Corsicans, men from Picardy, Tonkin, and Réunion all clashed fatally with Uhlans, Pomeranians, Prussians, Westphalians, Bulgarians, Turks, Serbs, Croats, and men from Togoland. Thousands of peasants from all corners of the globe came here to die, to kill and be killed, to be swallowed up in the mud. So many that certain poets—only poets think such thoughts—have seen the place as a kind of magnet attracting soldiers from everywhere, a magnet pointing to some other Pole Star, symbolized by another virgin.

"Our Palestinian graves have fallen from planes all over the world, with no cemeteries to mark them. Our dead have fallen from one point in the Arab nation to form an imaginary continent. And if Palestine never came down from the Empire of Heaven to dwell upon earth, would we be any less real?"

So sang one of the fedayeen, in Arabic.

"The lash of outrage was urgent. Yet here are we, a divine people, on the brink of exhaustion, sometimes close to catastrophe, and with about as much political power as Monaco," answered another.

"We are the sons of peasants. Placing our cemeteries in heaven; boasting of our mobility; building an abstract empire with one pole in Bangkok and the other in Lisbon and its capital here, with somewhere a garden of artificial flowers lent by Bahrain or Kuwait; terrorizing the whole world; making airports put up triumphal arches for us, tinkling like shop doorbells—all this is to do in reality what smokers of joints only dream of. But has there ever been a dynasty that didn't build its thousand-year reign on a sham?"

So said a third fedayee.

Everywhere Obon, the nonexistent dead Japanese, and the cardgame without cards.

One afternoon under the trees.

"We'll wrap ourselves up a bit more tightly in our blankets and go to sleep. The next day we'll wake up an exact replica of the Jews. We'll have created a Palestinian, not an Arab God, and a Palestinian Adam and Eve, a Palestinian Cain and Abel."

"How far have you got?"

"To the word replica."

"With God, the book, the destruction of the Temple and all that?"

"A New Israel, but in Romania. We'll occupy Romania or Nebraska, and speak Palestinian."

"When you've been a slave it's lovely to be just a down and out. When you've been a Palo[10] it's lovely to turn into a tiger."

---

[10]Palestinian.

"Having been slaves, shall we be terrible masters when the time comes?"

"Soon. In a couple of thousand years. If I forget thee, El Kods . . ."[11]

The two fedayeen were exchanging quips across the camp. All the time they went on smiling, smoothing their moustaches with thumb, forefinger, or tongue, flashing their teeth, lighting cigarettes.

Holding out a lighter, cupping the flame with your hand, moving it near the tip of the other's cigarette, accidentally letting the light go out and then striking it again—all this means more than the mere offer of a smoke when the emirs shower down packets of cigarettes by the million.

Small gestures, whether difficult or easy, can show esteem or real friendship: a smile, the loan of a comb, helping someone brush his hair, a look in a tiny mirror.

But the greenstuff was so ubiquitous and intrusive I longed for a whiff of Bovril.

I see I often mention the trees. That's because it was a long time ago—fifteen years—and they've probably been cut down by now.

They didn't shed their leaves even in the winter, though they did go yellow. Does this strange phenomenon occur anywhere else? Was it really strange?

I talk about the trees because they were the setting of happiness—happiness in arms. In arms because there were bullets in the guns; but I don't remember ever experiencing so deep a peace.

War was all around us. Israel was on the watch, also in arms. The Jordanian army threatened. But every fedayee was just doing what he was fated to do.

All desire was abolished by such liberty. Rifles, machine guns, Katyushkas— every weapon had its target. Yet under the golden trees—peace.

There are the trees again—I haven't really conveyed how fragile they were. The yellow leaves were attached to the branches by a fine, yet real stalk, but the forest itself looked as frail to me as a scaffolding that vanishes when a building's finished. It was insubstantial, more like a sketch of a forest, a makeshift forest with any old leaves, but sheltering soldiers so beautiful to look at they filled it with peace.

Nearly all of them were killed, or taken prisoner and tortured.

Ferraj's group of about twenty fedayeen were camped in the forest some distance from the asphalt road from Jerash to Ajloun.

Abu Omar and I found them sitting on the grass.

Abu Hani was the colonel in command of the whole sector, an area about sixty kilometers long and forty wide, with the Jordan on two sides and the Syrian frontier on the other. The first thing the colonel did if ever there were any visitors was impress them with his rank. I remember him as short and covered with braid, a cane under his arm and stars on his shoulders. His face was too red; he was bad tempered rather than bossy, but inclined to be stupid. Rather like the portraits of Charles I, only not so tall.

[11]El Kods = Jerusalem in Arabic.

Ferraj was twenty-three. He soon steered the conversation in the direction he wanted.

"Are you a Marxist?"

I was rather surprised, but didn't attach much importance either to the question or to the answer.

"Yes," I said.

"Why?"

I was still not really interested. Ferraj's young face looked open and guileless. He was smiling, but anxious to hear what I'd say. After a while I told him nonchalantly:

"Perhaps because I don't believe in God."

Abu Omar translated immediately and correctly.

The colonel jumped. I mean he'd been sitting on the reddish grass or moss like the rest of us, but now he actually leapt to his feet and yelled:

"That's enough!"

He was talking both to the fedayeen and to me.

"Here you can talk about everything. Absolutely everything. But don't call in doubt the existence of God. I won't have any blasphemy. We don't take lessons from the West anymore."

Abu Omar, a practicing Christian, went on translating as calmly as before, though he was rather vexed. Ferraj, looking across at me and not up at the colonel, didn't raise his voice either. He answered gently but with a touch of irony, rather as one might address a harmless madman:

"You don't have to listen. It's quite easy. Your HQ's only a couple of kilometers away—you can be there in a quarter of an hour without even hurrying. And then you won't hear anything. But we're going to keep the Frenchman here till five in the morning, to hear what he's got to say and tell him what we think. We'll be free to say what we like."

So that night I was either going to be given my pass, or rejected.

Abu Hani went off, having said he must have a report on what I said during the night.

"I'm responsible for the discipline in this camp."

The next morning he came back to Ferraj's base and shook hands with me. He claimed to know what had been said.

Our vigil in the tent under the trees had lasted till quite late. Each of the fedayeen asked me questions as he prepared tea or coffee or his own argument.

"But it's you who ought to be talking to me—telling me what you mean by revolution, and how you intend to bring it about."

Perhaps they were carried away by the lateness of the hour, or by a time that was getting more and more confused—the gray, intoxicating time outside space, which upsets the clocks of the memory and seems to set words free.

It was like closing time in a bar, when you can suddenly hear the sound of the pinball machines. Something makes everyone very lucid and interested, and because the waiters are sleepy you go and continue the discussion outside.

Through the walls of the tent we could hear the cries of the jackals. Perhaps because we were so tired, time and space ceased to exist, but the fedayeen, relishing and borne along by their youthful eloquence, went on talking.

Abu Omar translated.

"Because Fatah's not only a war of liberation but also the beginning of a revolution, we'll use the violence to get rid of privilege, starting with Hussein and the Bedouin and the Circassians."

"But how?"

"The oil belongs to the people, not to the princes."

I remember that phrase very clearly. The odd thought struck me, though I partly believed it too, that a very poor people may need to indulge in the luxury of having fat princes over them, waddling through their cool invisible gardens, just as other poor folk save up and even ruin themselves for Christmas. The inhabitants of some countries let themselves be eaten up by fleas at night and flies in the daytime in order to fatten the flocks of their pious rulers.

But my thought was too disagreeable for that night, and I kept it to myself.

Arabian tobacco smoke was pouring out of our mouths and nostrils.

"We must get rid of Hussein, America, Israel, and Islam."

"Why Islam?"

As soon as we arrived I'd noticed his big, black beard and burning eyes, his gleaming black hair and swarthy skin. And his silence, that seemed all the more intense for having now been broken. It was he who'd asked the question, in a voice that was strong but almost crystal clear.

"Why do you have to get rid of Islam? How can you get rid of God?"

He was talking chiefly to me. He went on:

"You're here, not just in an Arab country, or in Jordan, or on the banks of the Jordan, but with the fedayeen. So you must be a friend. When you came"—he smiled—"you from France and I from Syria—you told us you didn't believe in God. But if you ask me, if you didn't believe in Him you wouldn't have come."

He went on smiling.

"I claim to be a good Muslim. If you agree, we'll have a debate, you and I, in front of everyone. Are you game?"

"Yes."

"Stand up then, and we'll meet each other halfway and embrace. Let's start out as friends and stay friends during and after the discussion. A year ago I was sent to China for three months, and this is what I remember from the thoughts of Mao Tse-tung: Before you argue, show that you're friends with a kiss on both cheeks."

He spoke easily. While he was slightly taken aback by the strangeness of my position, you could tell he spoke from absolute certainty himself, demanding answers from God as of right. The fedayeen were utterly silent as he and I went and embraced in the middle of the tent and then returned to our places. We addressed ourselves to the theme that oil was something that must be made use of.

Of course. A few experts would take care of the oil industry. But it seemed the fedayeen thought all Arabia's oil was in one bottomless pit, a sort of Danaïds' well, like the Englishman's chest of gold coins that was never empty despite the Turko-Arab officers' full pockets, holsters, and saddlebags.

"If God didn't exist, you wouldn't be here," said Abu Gamal, the Syrian. "And the world would have had to create itself, and the world would be God, and the world would be good. But it isn't. The world's imperfect, so it can't be God."

Abu Omar translated into French. I answered flippantly: I was tired and rather light-headed.

"If God made the world he made a pretty poor job of it, so it comes to the same thing," I said.

"But we're here to remedy that," said the Syrian. "We're free both to suffer and to cure."

I could see by now that the earth was flat and Lorraine was still called Lotharingia. I felt like invoking Thomas Aquinas. Abu Gamal and I jousted on without either of us suspecting we were heading inevitably for heresy. What mattered to me was not any particular argument, nor even the discussion itself—it struck me as scholastic and colorless—but a sort of kindness and strength, a combination of conviction and openness in which everyone present shared. We *were* free—free to say anything we liked. We mightn't have been actually drunk, but we'd taken off, knowing Abu Hani was sleeping his head off, probably alone, a couple of kilometers away.

Almost roughly I interrupted Ferraj to say something to Abu Gamal.

"When you started by putting the discussion under the aegis of God you cut the ground from under my feet—I don't claim the patronage of anyone so grand. And your God is all the grander because you can increase His dimensions as much as you like. But the reason you also insisted on beginning with the seal of friendship is that even though you're a Muslim you've got more faith in friendship than you have in God. For here we all are, armed, an unbeliever among believers, and yet I'm your friend."

"And where does friendship came from but God? . . . To you, to me, to all of us here this morning. Would you be our friend if God hadn't inspired you with friendship for us, and us with friendship for you?"

"So why doesn't He do the same to Israel?"

"He can whenever He wants to. And I believe he will."

Then we took it in turns to talk about irrigating the desert.

"We'll have to get rid of the princes," said Ferraj. "They own the desert. And we'll have to learn hydraulics. The trouble is the princes are descendants of the Prophet."

"We'll show them they're sons of Adam like the rest of us."

That was Abu Gamal.

Then to me:

"If a Jordanian soldier—a Muslim, that is—threatened you, I'd kill him."

"I'd try to do the same if he threatened you."

"And if he killed you I'd avenge you by killing him," he laughed.
"It must be difficult to stay a Muslim. I respect you for your faith."
"Thank you."
"Respect me for being able to do without it."
A dangerous leap. He hesitated, but in the end no, he wouldn't.
"I'll pray to God to *give* you faith."
Everyone in the tent burst out laughing, even Abu Omar and Abu Gamal. It was nearly four in the morning.

The whole gathering was highly diverted at the notion of all these young drinkers of tea and orange juice spending the night lecturing and being lectured to by an elderly Frenchman, an outsider suddenly set down under the trees in a winter that had begun with Black September. There I was in the midst of a bunch of terrorists whose mere names made newspapers tremble like leaves in their readers' hands. And there were they, laughing without cynicism, verbally inventive, a bit wild, but as proper as a bunch of seventeen-year-old seminarists. Their exploits on land and in the air were reported with fear and disgust, or at least a good imitation of it. But vague moral condemnation didn't bother them. That night, from dark to dawn ...

Time had undergone a curious transformation since I arrived in Ajloun. Every moment had become "precious," so bright you felt you ought to be able to pick it up in pieces. The time of harvest had been followed by the harvest of time.

But I managed to surprise them by swallowing eight capsules of Nembutal.

I slept peacefully in a deep, underground shelter inside the tent. Farcical as it had been to enter the United States after the American consul in Paris had refused me a visa, it was even stranger to be here, sleeping quietly in the midst of this free and easy egalitarianism. But there was nothing dramatic about it. These gentle terrorists might have been camping on the Champs Elysées, with the rest of us watching them through binoculars for fear of getting wet—for they peed both far and high.

Just before I lay down on the blankets spread for me in the shelter, the fifteen or twenty terrorists peered in amazement at my medicine bottle, at the eight Nembutal capsules I took, and at the tranquil expression on my face. As I gulped the poison down they gazed at my Adam's apple with amazement and perhaps admiration. They must have been thinking:

"To put away a dose like that without showing any fear—that must be French courage. We have a hero among us tonight."

The hours we spent in friendly argument, the long nights of stupefied weariness in which we got to know one another, come back to me as a vague babble which I recreate as I write.

Every mosque, however small, had a fountain—a little trickle of water, a bowl, or stagnant pool for the ritual ablutions. In the forest, whether to shave his pubic hair or to prepare himself for prayer, a pious fedayee in his late teens would make himself a miniature Ganges out of leafy branches and a green, plastic pail, a minute

Benares of his own under a cork oak, beech, or fig tree. It was such a good imitation of India that as I went by I could almost hear the Muslim murmur, as he offered up his cupped palms, "Om mani Pad me Om." The Muhammadan forest was full of standing Buddhas.

Unless:

Wherever there was a drop of flowing or standing water there was a spring: here (though less than in Morocco) Islam stumbled over paganism at every step. Here, where Christian beliefs are held to blaspheme a God as solitary as the vice to which the same adjective is applied, paganism provides a touch of darkness at noon, of sunlight in shadow, of dampness drawn up from the Jordan. It's a dampness from which the kind fairy with the magic wand catches hay fever; a dampness that leaves behind it the print of a human foot.

Because they never owned anything, the fedayeen imagined the luxury they wanted to rid the world of. That's what I meant—what I wanted both to say and to conceal—by the "quiet periods" I mentioned above: the daydreams people have to work off somehow when they've neither the strength nor the opportunity to make them come true. It's then they invent the game of revolution, which is what revolt is called when it lasts and begins to be structured, when it stops being poetic negation and becomes political assertion.

If such imaginary activity is to be of any use, it has to exist. But gradually people learn to do without it, like a detachable lining in the West. Then our preoccupation with merely imaginary wealth and power is supposed to help us create weapons with which to destroy real wealth and power when we meet them.

But except for a worn-out cushion on a sofa in some old Turkish house, there wasn't any red velvet in Jordan. So the fedayeen were forced to invent the powers it possesses.

Why that material, that color? Is there really any connection between them and power? It seems there might be. The all but absolute reign of the Sun King called for red velvet, and both the first and the second Emperor of France were crowned amid velvet and red. Other materials are less stifling and their colors more amiable. But red velvet!

The soft stone of which the villas of Amman are built, crushed the commandos, but it didn't weigh as heavily on them as it did on the women and old men left behind in the camps.

Whenever I go back to Amman I feel as if I'm buried alive.

"It's depressing and pathetic. But if it weren't depressing there wouldn't be any poetry—the poetry comes from the poor." (This from Monsieur El Katrani, talking about the Tuileries Gardens in Paris at night.)

Some of the fedayeen asked me to bring them the works of Karl Marx back from Damascus. In particular *Das Kapital.* They didn't know he wrote it sitting on his backside on pink silk cushions—wrote it in fact to fight against soft, pink silk, and soft, mauve silk, and against little tables and vases and chandeliers and chintz, and silent footmen and portly Regency commodes.

In Jordan we had Roman columns, most of them lying flat, having fallen and been set up again and fallen again. But they're not luxury. They're History.

These were the Palestinians' enemies, in order of importance: the Bedouin, the Circassians, King Hussein, the feudal Arabs, the Muslim religion, Israel, Europe, America, the big banks. Jordan won, and so victory went to all the rest, too, from the Bedouin to the big banks.

One night in December 1970 Mahjoub called a meeting in a cave and spoke to the fedayeen.

"You're now observing a cease-fire. I'm supposed to inform you officially. And so I have. But you're fighters, so use your heads. You've got sisters and cousins married to Jordanians—do what's necessary to get hold of their guns. That's just a suggestion—think of better ones for yourselves. Hussein's government has banned any further operations against Israel on the Occupied Territories carried out from bases in Jordan."[12]

The men weren't happy with this. They all made the same objection.

"What's a soldier without his gun?" "A disarmed fighter is like a man naked and impotent."

For three hours Mahjoub tried, in vain, to convince them there in the cave, illuminated by torches and by lighters lighting American cigarettes. As we emerged I must have been the only one affected by the loveliness of the sky, unless the beauty of the night and of the promised land aggravated the fedayeen's pain.

The day after the next they all had to hand in their arms. The dumps had been prepared. If it was a long time till the fighting started again, the greased and dismantled guns would be out of date.

All the fedayeen in Jordan were to be allowed to stay on the alert in the quadrilateral formed by the Jordan river, the Salt–Irbid road, the Syrian frontier and the Salt–Jordan road. Ajloun was roughly in the middle.

Something was going on inside us. Some organ was troubled, and troubled us. Or else we suddenly saw the world more clearly, or thought we did. Then a place, often an empty space without people or animals or so much as a caterpillar, but with moss and pebbles and grasses broken by something in flight, would suddenly all sweetly come together and shift without moving. It has just, or for a long time, been eroticized.

So it was with the fields around Ajloun. They were waiting for a sign. But from whom?

The fedayeen moved silently from one commando camp under the trees to another, some dreaming but armed, others unarmed but on the alert, stealthy. They delivered boxes of grenades, cleaned their revolvers.

---

[12]The PLO had agreed with Hussein that a Palestinian militia should remain, but with their weapons discreetly hidden. We were meeting in the cave, so that Mahjoub could make this clear to the stubborn fedayeen, for whom a weapon not brandished aloft lost its power: what Mahjoub was suggesting was almost as painful to them as being asked to shave off their moustaches.

They were humiliated by defeat. For they'd won glory by making life difficult for Hussein and his Bedouin. They'd hijacked El Al and Swissair planes over the desert. They'd learned of the death of many of their comrades at the hands of the Israeli enemy lurking beyond the Jordan. They'd sensed the menacing silence of the Jordanian villages; perhaps, too, the thoughts of the women and children left behind in the camps. And they weren't yet dry from the shame of not having dared shoot out the tires when a chrome and white Cadillac, with red-leather upholstery, roof open and headlights blazing in broad daylight, was driven by a Bedouin chauffeur in a red-and-white keffieh full tilt past the soldiers, who had to jump out of the way.

"I'm the Emir Jaber's driver and I've come to find out how His Royal Highness's secretary's nephew is—"

The rest was swallowed up in the sound of grinding gears and screaming tires.

Although it was done very discreetly, we could tell from the security precautions set up in the middle of the night that the Soviet ambassador to Cairo was about to arrive for a meeting with Arafat at some still secret destination in the Ajloun hills.

He came by helicopter.

We weren't really surprised by the unannounced visit: the Palestinian problem had ceased to be merely regional, and the great powers were beginning to take an interest in the recently created and still insignificant PLO.

But we wanted to use the occasion to try to see things from a higher vantage point, though it wouldn't be easy to attain vertical takeoff right away. Every fedayee felt free ranging over this area on foot or by car, never letting go of the surface. It was the surface that concerned us, and we learned its contours as we moved over them. Each fedayee's horizon was taught him by his eyes and feet. He had only to look in front of him to see where he was going, and behind him to see where he'd come from. Neither a radio nor a newspaper linked him to the rest of the revolution; just occasionally an order for a mission.

They were all taken aback, even the leaders, when I said I was going to attend the meeting in Kuwait.

"What are you going to do in Kuwait? Stay with us. Who else will be there anyway? Mostly Europeans. They'll all be talking in English, and you don't speak English."

"I've got a visa for Kuwait in my passport and my room is booked. And here's the letter inviting me."

"All right, if you're obstinate—a couple of fedayeen will drive you to Deraa."

"Why two?"

"We always go in pairs, as a precaution. Cross the frontier at Deraa as best you can, and from there two others will drive you to Damascus. You can catch a plane from there to Kuwait. On your way back after the conference there'll be a car at Damascus Airport to drive you to Deraa, and you'll find a couple of fedayeen waiting there to bring you back here."

It was decided I should stay in Ajloun.

But, above our heads, PLO diplomacy was active, even though it came up against Hussein and his advisers in the American embassy. The comings and goings of diplomats between Amman, Tel Aviv, and Washington were common knowledge, not in factual detail but through gossip. We came and went in the area I've described, regarding ourselves as free, though for security reasons we always moved at ground level. We were obeying the orders of colonels who never rose any higher than their maps, which had ascended from the horizontal to so high on the wall that you needed a pointer to show the north—the Jordan river and the towns just within the occupied territories.

Did the Palestinians realize that by omitting the name and geography of Israel from their maps they were at the same time abolishing Palestine? They either colored Israel blue and threw it into the sea, or made it black and turned it into the Greeks' kingdom of the Shades.

Arafat and the rest of the PLO, with their agreements and their disagreements, functioned at quite a different altitude altogether: they flew from one capital to another. Perhaps Palestine was no longer a country to them, but something to be expressed in fractions, a tiny element in a grand operation being waged between East and West.

But we all knew deep down that the peace we felt, the peace we enjoyed, was due to the PLO.

We hadn't heard about Kissinger's trip to Peking, or his return to Pakistan the next day. How could we have known, on this cliff edge, that China's aid to the PLO was being reduced? What was China, viewed from here? First and foremost a name: Mao.

Many Palestinians—ordinary fedayeen as well as important leaders—were invited to Peking. And to Moscow. I still believe they confused China itself with the organized crowds and ardent demonstrations that sent them home with accounts and images of some sort of paradise. I was told dozens of times how marvelous the old men looked as, grave or smiling, they silently performed their Swedish drill every morning in T'ien an Men Square. The fedayeen also told me about the athletic ancients' long, thin beards. Here a beard is more like an article of clothing.

I may never know whether I ought to call it the Palestinian Resistance or the Palestinian Revolution. And should I really use capitals? There aren't any capital letters in written Arabic.

At the beginning of this book I tried to describe a game of cards in an arbor. As I said, all the gestures were genuine but the cards were not. Not only were they not on the table, but they weren't anywhere; it wasn't a game of cards at all. The cards were neither present nor absent. For me they were like God: they didn't exist.

All that pretense for its own sake—the invitation to me, the preparations, the performance itself, the excitement designed to show me what was missing—can you imagine what it would do to anyone who went through those motions every evening? Withdrawal symptoms for cards, as if they were cocaine. The end of the game was its beginning: nothing at the start and nothing at the finish. What I was seeing was an absence of images: no bastos, no knights, no swords. I wonder if Claudel knew the game the Moors used to play in Spain?

Didn't the new occupiers know what would happen to the Palestinian people when they drove them out of Palestine? That unless they destroyed themselves they'd occupy another territory belonging to another people?

"Why haven't they just melted away?"

To which one could only reply:

"Has a people on the march ever melted away? Tell me where. And how."

I still don't know what the fedayeen's own inmost feelings were, but as far as I could see their land—Palestine—was not merely out of reach. Although they sought it as gamblers do cards and atheists God, it had never existed. Vestiges of it remained, very distorted, in old people's memories. But in our memory things are usually seen as smaller than they really were, and increasingly so with age. Unless, on the other hand, recollection lights them up and makes them larger than life. In either case the dimensions of memory are seldom accurate.

And here everything had changed—the names of things, all their dents and protuberances. Every blade of grass had been grazed; more of the forest was eaten up every day in the form of paper, books, and newspapers. The fedayeen's goal had been transformed into something impossible for them to imagine. Everything they did was in danger of becoming useless because they'd substituted the rehearsal for the performance. The card players, their hands full of ghosts, knew that however handsome and sure of themselves they were, their actions perpetuated a game with neither beginning nor end. Absence was in their hands just as it was under their feet.

"Some officers clearly hankered after the solid equipment, the steel carapaces, and complex instruments of the military academies in Europe, America, and the USSR. They mistrusted the word guerrilla—that 'little war' in which you had to find allies in fog, damp, and the height of rivers, in the rainy season, the long grass, the owl's cry, and the phases of the sun and moon. They knew you could command only if you stood to attention and gave orders to someone doing the same. But military academies are not places for getting discipline, obedience, and victory out of half-educated men, mischievous Arabs at home among mosses and lichens. How to glide from tree to tree and rock to rock, freezing at the slightest sound—no ordinary officer could have taught that."

That's still the opinion of some Palestinians, who miss the combined guile and integrity of battle, and perhaps sometimes its comradeship.

"The Bedouin on the one hand and the Israelis on the other all slaughter civilians with tanks and planes. A hundred guerrilla fighters have only to slip into Israel and shells rain down on the civilians in the Palestinian camps.

"In the Moroccan Navy, sailors with syphilis are called 'Admirals.' Their medical cards are marked with crosses and stars. The first cross indicating the pox is greeted with ecstasy, like a goal at a football match, as proof of virility. The first score is a sacred stigma.

"Everyone—doctors, nurses, and cooks—took excellent care of us. I was a four-star admiral. Five stars meant the Empire. And death. The famous leper king, who's known even in Islam, had two stigmata: one from his anointing and the other from leprosy. I wonder whether the fiercest officers, the ones who wanted heavy artillery, tanks, cannon, and even the atomic bomb, hadn't really got their eye on a state funeral rather than on dying for their country."

It wasn't only the graduates of Saint-Cyr who thought guerrilla warfare lacked nobility. The Soviet Union also refused to take it seriously and referred to it as terrorism. If the Palestinian army is ever to win it'll have to become a ponderous machine, with every colonel's chest covered with gongs from all the right countries.

One evening when the Ramadan fast ended, two of the leaders gave a party near a spring close to the river Jordan. There was only a bit more honey cake than usual and some freer laughter. They welcomed one guest, a long-haired young man called Ishmael, by throwing their arms round him.

I was too used to nicknames and aliases to be surprised at this one.

(It was here, not far away from the place between the Damia and Allenby bridges where John had once baptized Jesus, that the fedayeen decided to change my first name to Ali.)

Ishmael had straight brown locks like Napoleon's down to his shoulders.

"He's a Palestinian who's doing his military service in the Israeli army. He speaks perfect Hebrew," one of the leaders told me.

I said I thought the young man's profile was more Jewish than Arab.

"He's a Druse, but for goodness' sake don't mention it. As soon as he saw you were a Frenchman his expression changed." (I still don't know what he meant by this.) "He takes great risks to pass us information."

As I ate I smiled, and asked Ishmael, in French, to sing us the Israeli national anthem.

He looked surprised, as if he understood, but he had the presence of mind to ask for my question to be translated into Arabic. In answer to something Mahjoub said, he had spoken in English:

"Classical war, I don't know. Classical or romantic."

This struck me as rather affected.

When he left at nightfall to get back into Israel without being spotted by the Jewish sentries, he kissed everyone good-bye except me.

His profile was Hebraic but his speech rhythms were Western.

Not long before, at Jerash, a Sudanese lieutenant of thirty had been astonished to hear me speak, and Abu Omar reply, in French.

"Everything that happens here is because of you," said the Sudanese. "You're responsible for the Pompidou government."

He said other things too, which I've forgotten. But I'll never forget that black face, with its gleaming hair and cheeks slashed with tribal scars, speaking to me not only in French but in slang, with a suburban accent and a Maurice Chevalier vocabulary. And to talk to me he airily stuck his hands in his trouser pockets.

When Abu Omar explained to him in Arabic that I wasn't at all close to the French government, he calmed down and we became great friends. Whenever I met him it was a smile that approached, and I knew he was cooking up some new story specially for me.

"It's very lucky we can understand one another. If it weren't for us Sudanese, you wouldn't speak French, only some provincial patois."

"Explain."

"Every province in France used to speak its own jargon—you were barbarians. When you were strong enough to land in our country you were still only the linguistic equivalent of a game of patience. The Basque soldiers spoke Basque, the Corsicans Corsican. And soldiers from Alsace, Brittany, Nice, Picardy, the Morvan, and the Artois all poured into Madagascar, Indochina, and the Sudan. But to conquer us you needed a common language. So they all had to learn Parisian French—the language of their officers, trained at Saint-Cyr. Wandering about two by two in the native quarter they had to have at least a few key expressions:

" 'The Legion! Help!'

" 'Here, boys!'

" 'Two of us are in trouble!'

" 'Get a move on!'

" 'The Zouaves! Help.' "

It was an amusing theory, correct or no. Jules Ferry was Minister of Education before he became Minister for the Colonies.

The light, sensitive French that gradually spread all over France may have been born of the terrified trembling bequeathed to mainland France by little soldiers from Brittany, Corsica, and the Basque country, conquering and dying in the colonies. Dialect had to go away so that an almost perfect language might be fashioned beyond the seas and come home.

The counterpart to this epic is perhaps the following passage, from Morocco in 1917:

"My fine fellows! Raring to go! When I told them I was going to give them arms and ammunitions they'd have worshipped me if I'd let them. But I'm always as cool as a cucumber. The man who'll get round me hasn't been conceived yet, let alone born. They like a scrap, my lads, and I lead them to it. They expected sabers and I give them guns. They'll wipe out all the Boches. They've got as far as the Somme, guns blazing."

This summarizes the main points of a speech printed in *L'Illustration*. "They" got as far as the Somme. "They" got off the train, marched a couple of hundred yards in silence, breathing loudly. There were about a thousand of them. The first wave lay down without a word, then the second wave, then the third. "They" died in slow motion. A gust of wind laden with gas shut them up for good. Just north of Abbeville lay a huge, gray, Moroccan carpet.

It was Mubarak who told me all this. As a Sudanese officer he tended to sympathize with Khadafi. I had no news of him for some time. As with Hamza, I knew only his first name. After some hesitation he chose Habash instead of Arafat. I wish I could tell you how handsome he was, how gentle, with those cheeks slashed with sacrificial scars.

It was George Habash's FPLP[13] that kept three plane-loads of passengers sweltering in the sun for three days at Zarka airport.

Coming back to the fedayeen bases after a fortnight in Damascus, I found them very thinly spread out, and was struck by the weakness of the new arrangement. Was it the work of someone foolish, inexperienced, obstinate—some Palestinian no good at either strategy or tactics?

It made me think of a papier-mâché wall. What could you expect when there were only six or seven of you all alone, with six or seven small guns? Physically, even the enemy was a kilometer away from the area allotted to the fedayeen. But they were well trained, equipped with heavy artillery, and helped by ballistics experts. It was rumored that Hussein's army had American and Israeli aides. (In 1984 some Palestinians confirmed this. Jordanian officers scornfully denied it.)

I thought of that fedayeen position fourteen years later amid the ruins of Beirut, when Jacqueline was telling me about a trip she'd made to southern Lebanon.

"After the massacres at Sabra and Chatila, Palestinian soldiers and civilians were shut up for hours in cells or hotel rooms in Tyre and Sidon. Then, in Tyre and Sidon and the coast villages in between, came the ceremony of the hoods. Israeli officers and men made the inhabitants of villages and districts file past a man wearing a hood over his head. The spy didn't say anything for fear of being recognized—he just pointed a gloved finger at the guilty parties. What were they guilty of? Of being Palestinians, or Lebanese friends of Palestinians, or likely to become so, or knowing how to handle explosives."

"Weren't any of the hooded men recognized?"

"No. At first it was rumored that they were renegade Palestinians, but a few days later the truth, or what might have been the truth, came out. It was an Israeli soldier under the hood, and he just pointed people out at random. The other members of a victim's family were also suspect, so they kept quiet. By the time it leaked out that the renegade Palestinian was really an Israeli, the damage was done. No one dared denounce the trick in case after all the man had been a Palestinian, some friend or relation."

"And did the play acting last long?"

"Two or three weeks. Long enough. Everyone suspected everyone else. Then came the business of the rooms."

It was a Lebanese woman who told me about that. The Palestinians—soldiers, civilians, and women—would be crammed into one cell or room. Then cries of

---

[13]Popular Front for the Liberation of Palestine.

terror and moans in Arabic, weeping, shrieks, and finally death rattles would be heard from outside. Amid all this came the sound of Arab voices alleging atrocious crimes and vendettas against their Arab relatives; and of fedayeen accusing thir officers of betraying their comrades and giving away military secrets.

All this was rehearsed and tape-recorded by Arabic-speaking Israeli soldiers, then played into the rooms. At every so-called act of treachery a kind of incidental music of amused, sarcastic, or affectedly contemptuous laughter could be heard, with Israeli officers making comments in Hebrew on the confessions. During the next two days the same recording would be broadcast through loudspeakers in village squares.

The object was to intimidate the Lebanese people, Shiite or otherwise, and in particular the Palestinians. This was in September 1982. Perhaps that enormous bluff, the Arabic cry of "Remember Deir Yassin!" was recorded in a studio in Tel Aviv.

It was the memory of this that caused a Frenchman to say:

"The big Israeli demonstration in 1982 against the Lebanese war was planned before the invasion began. Everything was worked out in advance: the invasion, the raids on Beirut, the murder of Bechir Gemayel, the massacres at Chatila, the ostentatious horror of world press and television—even the world's revulsion, the demonstration itself, and the final whitewash. All to make Israel's face look less dirty—"

This made his wife say, "Ssh . . ."

"They made us run away from Deir Yassin with a truck and a loudspeaker."

I've often thought about that radio producer, perhaps an NCO in Tsahal, re-rehearsing a shriek or death rattle that didn't ring true. Perhaps he got the cast to wear Arab dress, to make their moans more convincing. Maybe he was a well-known director from the Habima Theater in Tel Aviv.

But let's get back to 1971. The location of all those thin-spread fedayeen bases in and around Ajloun was known to within a yard by the Jordanian army. And the Circassian officers, with the help of their Bedouin troops, had set up loudspeakers transmitting voices that, under cover of distance, indistinctness, and dark, might be taken for the voices of Palestinian resistance leaders.

"We're all encircled. Surrender is inevitable. We must hand our weapons over to the king's army. The king has promised that every fedayee who presents himself unarmed will have his gun returned to him the next day. The fight is over. No one will be ill treated. I speak in the name of the king and of Abu Amar [Yasser Arafat]."

Imagine the effect, on often very young soldiers, of those voices at once distant and close; giant voices thundering through the dark forest and mountains between ten o'clock and midnight; the voice of the mountains themselves. The voices came from the other side of the Jordan. The quality of the sound was so poor they were unidentifiable.

It was in July 1971 that Hussein's troops encircled the fedayeen. Officially three or four hundred of them were killed, while thousands were sent as prisoners to various jails in the kingdom or the camp at Zarka. The rest managed to escape through Irbid to Syria. Some crossed the Jordan and were disarmed; these got a very friendly welcome from Israeli officers and men. But having fled after listening to their leaders' alleged betrayal, they must have felt very lonely living with their own real treason.

Two Frenchmen who'd been fighting as and with the fedayeen got as far as Irbid. They lie buried in the cemetery there, among the Palestinian martyrs.

To me there is something other than fear and cowardice in the fedayeen's flight; something great. What they were running away from was the sudden appearance of the unexpected. Death, the expected, hadn't come. They were prepared for bullets, wounds, and suffering. They weren't prepared for midnight clamor that later turned out to be the sound of a helicopter still on the ground, but magnified tenfold and with some artillery and machine-gun fire thrown in. No real bullets or shells, though, and after a while a sudden silence in which to hear their treacherous leaders telling them too to betray.

Panic is really the word, and I should write it quickly, for it was that which made legs run of their own accord, fleeing not death but the unexpected. Perhaps that was what embarrassed me so much when I saw the *achebals,* the young lions, in training: they couldn't be trained for the inadmissible—for fleeing into Israel, as one might commit suicide.

"Against Israel I'd make a pact with the devil."

There it was twice: the voice of the leaders telling the fedayee to be a traitor, and sending him into a real alliance with the devil, Israel.

Trying to escape and find some refuge from the voice, perhaps they didn't realize they'd crossed into Israel. Perhaps they thought they were still in Palestine—which in fact they were.

I mentioned panic, but I don't know if people still fear Pan—if the god still summons them on the unequal reeds of his flute, with notes so persuasive that whoever hears and tries to follow them may end up none knows where.

Mist rose up and veiled the moon. If the huge voice reverberating from hill to hill was the voice of God, the fedayeen, ignorant of the miracles of electricity and acoustics, ran to shelter in His bosom. Perhaps the French slang expression, *jouer des flûtes* (literally "make with the pins," that is, run away) has some such divine origin.

Even if the body, the arms and legs, didn't realize it, the fear had come from across the Atlantic. I often went to Amman, where the Boeings used to fly over my hotel, bringing gifts of arms from America to Hussein.

The two young Frenchmen buried in Irbid—the first name of both was Guy— were about twenty years old. Their woman friend, also French, was with them. They used to help the Palestinians rebuild their collapsed walls, thus learning bricklaying and Arabic simultaneously. I met the two Guys at Wahadat: they were like two children of May 1968—liberated but full of antiquated platitudes.

"Hussein must be brought down because he's a fascist. And he must be replaced with a regime that's revolutionary but not Soviet."

"What sort of regime?"

"One based on the Situationists, for instance."

But describing dramatic moments of the resistance, as I've been doing, doesn't give any idea of its everyday atmosphere. That was youthful and lighthearted. If I had to use one image for it I'd suggest this:

Not a series of shocks, but one long, drawn-out, almost imperceptible earthquake traversing the whole country. Or: A great yet almost silent roar of laughter from a whole nation holding its sides, yet full of reverence when Leila Khaled, grenade at the ready, ordered the Jewish crew of the El Al plane to land in Damascus. Then there were the three planes—they belonged to Swissair, I think—full of Americans of both sexes, that landed at Zarka on Habash's orders and stood there side by side in the sun for three days.

A few days later came what might be called the children's revolt. Some Palestinian boys and girls of about sixteen, together with a few young Jordanians of both sexes, all laughing and smiling and shouting, *"Yaya el Malek!"* (Long live the king!) went up to a line of Jordanian tanks in the streets of Amman and offered the occupants of one of them a bunch of flowers. The men in the tank, surprised but pleased, opened the turret and stretched out their arms to take the bouquet. But one of the girls dropped it inside at the feet of the crew, together with a grenade, and the tank exploded. The girl's friends whisked her away into a side street, where she waited to get her breath back and to be supplied with a further series of flowers and grenades.

It was in Amman, of course, that I heard about it. Was the resistance starting to go in for such ingenious cruelties? Was an official uprising in preparation? Had the things I was told about really happened? At any rate, the slap in the face the king's prime minister had received from his daughter was echoing still.

Those children make me think of a fox devouring a chicken. The fox's muzzle is covered with blood. It looks up and bares its perfect teeth—white, shiny, and sharp. You expect it to beam like a baby at any moment.

An ancient people restored to youth by rebellion and to rebellion by youth can seem very sinister.

I remember like an owl. Memories come back in "bursts of images." Writing this book, I see my own image far, far away, dwarf size, and more and more difficult to recognize with age. This isn't a complaint. I'm just trying to convey the idea of age and of the form poetry takes when one is old: I grow smaller and smaller in my own eyes and see the horizon speeding toward me, the line into which I shall merge, behind which I shall vanish, from which I shall never return.

Going through Jerash on my way back from Damascus, I thought I'd look up Dieter, the German doctor who'd started a little hospital in the camp at Gaza. I was met by another doctor, a Lebanese with a kind face.

"Dr. Dieter isn't here anymore," he said. "He's in Germany. You were a friend of his, weren't you? Well, he was sent to prison and tortured, and the West German ambassador finally managed to get him repatriated.

"This is what happened. One day the Jordanian army entered the camp at Gaza, looking for fedayeen probably, and beat up the women and children—anyone they found alive. When they heard there were casualties, Dieter, together with the male nurse and the nun who worked in the hospital here, all set out for Gaza with their instrument cases and urgent medical supplies—surgical spirit, bandages, and so on. But as soon as they started to tend the wounded they were surrounded by troops. The Jordanians laid about them in their usual way, and Dieter and the two nurses were put in the prison you went to with Nabila Nashashibi and Dr. Alfredo. I advise you not to make yourself too conspicuous in Amman."

If only he'd put up some resistance . . . But for all his devotion to the sick and his enormous energy and endurance, Dieter was a very ethereal kind of German. He'd sit up late at night with patients who came to see him just because they were lonely, helping them with a few words or an aspirin. He was fair haired, uncompromising, and delicate.

I'd already heard in Damascus that the Bedouin had won. The Lebanese doctor's story told me something else: the Palestinians were lost.

The head man at Baqa camp, an Arab said to be a hundred years old, used to set out very early for his constitutional. Barefoot, wearing a white *abaya* and with a white scarf wound round his wrinkled head, he'd leave his house at or even before dawn. Obedient to the call from a nearby minaret, he'd stop to say the first prayer of the day, then continue slowly and peacefully on his way toward the Jordanian lines. All the Jordanian officers and men would say good morning to the still hale centenarian, but he didn't return their greeting until he was on his way back, when he went through the Bedouin lines for the second time.

"I let them give me a little cup of coffee. One of the officers has been in Tunisia and he puts some orange-flower water in it. Very nice."

"The officer?"

"The coffee. It bucks me up for the journey home."

At sunset the old boy made his way calmly back to the camp. The Jordanians could see his white figure, almost upright without the aid of a stick, growing ever smaller in the distance, until at last it vanished into the dusk, together with its long black shadow.

He counted the steps on the outward journey, and checked them on the way back. They were the first steps of a smiling, sly, and still cautious resistance. From his paces the distance between the camp and the first lines of the Jordanian army, and thus the right bearings for the guns, could be calculated. The fedayeen used to bring the old man a tin bowl of soup, and he'd sometimes listen for the first shots before going off to bed in his tiny room.

One day I tried to find out if he'd counted up right or if his age was only a legend. Karim often talked to him, so I asked Karim. He said the old chief was sixty, not a hundred, but because of his deep wrinkles and white moustache and eyebrows he was able to conceal his real age. He used his furrowed brow for cover as the fedayeen used the ravines.

Nothing escaped him. When he came back he'd seen and remembered everything: the state of the Jordanians' weaponry, the color of their shoes, changes in the vegetation, the names and numbers of the enemy's tanks. And times, down to hours and minutes—he could repeat them all. He had two wives in a large tent on the other side of the camp. Seven of the fedayeen on the bases were his sons.

The Legion of Honor is worn on the left, isn't it? No one noticed that he wore it, among other medals, on his right breast. Was it dangerous for him to wear it in the desert? How did he die? Of old age? Weariness? A bullet? Perhaps he isn't dead at all! His boldness was breathtaking.

His eyes used to smile whenever they lighted on me: I was an impostor, too. I had neither pencil nor paper and didn't write anything down, but perhaps he observed me and guessed.

September 28, 1970, was just a point on the straight line measured by the Gregorian calendar, but for millions it became a password charged with emotion.

In her youth Golda Meir was elected "Miss Palestine." Palestine was "Flastine" to the "Flestini" themselves.

These lines, this whole book, are only a diversion, producing quick emotions quickly over. Others were produced in me by the words "Islam" and "Muslim."

You get to Ajloun by the road that goes from Baqa past the American satellite-tracking radar to the Jordan.

A month after the battle, every reminder of the Palestinians had been burned or buried or taken away, apart from empty or half-empty cigarette packets and charred shrubs. The fedayeen had been either killed, taken prisoner, or left at the Saudi Arabian frontier after a spell in Jordanian jails that were worse torture to them than the desert. The experts from the FBI were more comfortable there in those unair-conditioned days.

In the countryside, all the wheat and the rye, the barley and the beans, had been slashed to pieces in the battle. It wasn't until Beirut in 1976 and 1982 that I saw nature so molested again, burned to the bone; and found out that the bone of pines and firs were black.

I've read that there are nearly always vestiges at the scene of a crime that can act as clues. In 1972, in a little Circassian village on the Golan Heights, after six years of Israeli occupation, I picked up three scraps of letters. They were written in Arabic, and had all been sent from Damascus by a Syrian soldier who'd fled and taken refuge there. They didn't have much in them apart from a lot of quotations from the Koran suggesting God had saved his life so that there might be one soldier praising His mercy. In any case, either the family they were addressed to were dead, or the letters hadn't been delivered. Israeli soldiers had been the first to read them, and they'd just left them there.

The hamlet consisted of four little houses with green shutters and red-tiled roofs. They were all deserted, their doors and windows hanging open. There were villages like that in Normandy after the landing at Avranches. Looted by the Yanks.

What was strange at Ajloun was that they hadn't been able to take away the holes in the ground. I could still see the three little shelters where I'd slept with the fedayeen. The walls and ceilings were black with smoke. A few bits of brown blanket lay strewn about with the dead. I could tell where the latter were from a stone propping up a piece of paper, or a plastic-coated identity card. I recognized the oblong blue green cards at once, each with a photograph of the fedayee who owned it in the top, right-hand corner, and his assumed name written in Arabic.

As I went through the village I noticed the silence had gone even before I saw the peasants and their wives. The air was full of rustling and cackling, whinnying and chatter. No one returned my greeting, but no one did or said anything unfriendly either. I'd returned from among the Palestinian enemy like one rising from the dead.

When I got to Amman the whole Palestinian resistance was in complete disarray. The semblance of unity that the PLO lent it shortly afterward was still lacking, and the eleven different groups were riven with dissension and resentment amounting almost to hatred. Only Fatah, though it too suffered from internal carpings and rivalries, showed a united front, if only in condemning all the other groups.

I'm still surprised at what happened after July 1971; that is, after the fighting at Ajloun, Jerash, and Irbid. A kind of bitterness entered into relations between the fedayeen. There were two I knew who were about twenty years old. They'd been friends at the same base on the Jordan, but one had remained a fedayee while the other had been promoted to a slightly higher rank. One day at Baqa I heard the fedayee asking for leave to go and see his wife, who was ill in Amman twenty kilometers away. This was the dialogue as I remember it:

"*Salam Allah alikoum.*"

"*. . . koum salam.*"

"Ali, can I have twenty-four hours' leave? My wife's pregnant."

"So is mine, but I'm staying here. You're on duty tonight."

"I'll get someone to take my place."

"Who's supposed to be on duty, you or him?"

"I've got two or three mates ready to replace me."

"No."

The more the one pleaded, the more the other, as if by a normal and necessary mutation, spoke like a petty tyrant. It wasn't a mere matter of discipline and security—it was the routine antagonism between officers and ordinary ranks. Two males confronting one another while fighting for a common homeland still a long way out of sight.

I've found out since that the hatred born between them that day is still very much alive. Now, it seems, they both speak excellent English, and you can hear echoes of their untiring hostility in their exchanges in English and American newspapers.

Is hatred there from the start, needing two friends to make its way?

Anything from or to do with Palestine disappeared, at first via Syria. I think it was about then, at the end of 1971, that the second wave of Palestinian fedayeen began to infiltrate Lebanon. Others, perhaps more wisely, managed through a

Jordanian father- or brother-in-law to buy some land in the neighborhood of Amman. They're said to be the richest men in Jordan.

When you're alone with them you find they still retain some words from the real revolutionary period—1968 to 1971—just as a peasant who rises to be a managing director in Paris may still use an occasional phrase from the dialect of his childhood. But they sense you used to be on the same side as they were then, and a thin veil comes down over their blushes lest this should no longer be the case. Without waiting to be asked, they tell you how much it cost them to buy their house in Jebel Amman.

It took me several years to realize how some of the leaders—well-known ones whose names are mentioned in Western newspapers—became dollar millionaires. It was tacitly known or half known that the seas of the Resistance had thrown up not a few bits of flotsam and jetsam but a whole strongbox in which each of them had one or more drawers containing proofs of his fortune in Switzerland or elsewhere. Each knew what the others had, too, because their fortunes were often the result of a division of the spoils.

The fighters knew all about it. Title deeds are easily hidden, but not a forest or a villa or a map. The high command knew, too. Perhaps they made use of it. Everyone in Fatah was familiar with Abu Hassan and his sports cars and pretty girls. I met him two or three times. The first occasion was rather embarrassing for him as I had to ask for his identity card in front of some amused fedayeen. Half amused himself but also half annoyed, he went through his pockets, and flushed when he drew from his windbreaker the same green card as is carried by every fedayee. He was energetic and athletic, the all-powerful leader and organizer of Black September. I've been told Arafat exploited his vanity for the sake of the PLO. When I heard of his and Boudia's death when his car was blown up, it was like learning of a defeat.

But slowly and surely I came to see the real meaning of it all.

My conclusion was more or less this. It's natural that soldiers' eyes should light up with desire for possession when they break into some luxurious place, and even more natural that some of their leaders should be corrupted through handling kilos of unused greenbacks. When a revolutionary movement meets with success, such things become proof that one was in on it from the start. It's difficult to distinguish total devotion to a cause from a quest for position, ambition for money or power.

It's bound to be one or the other, especially when the aspirant has let it be known that he "offers himself up body and soul in the service of the revolution and of the common good."

This last is a literal translation of what I heard a leader say in July 1984 to justify his wealth.

The latecomers—revolutionaries of the thirteenth hour, who come running when the revolution is already a state—they have to fight barehanded against those who learned to savor the sweet taste of power during the Long March.

When Zuher Monshen, supreme chief of the Saïka, was assassinated in a luxury hotel in Cannes, I was struck by such a flash of enlightenment I was afraid I might actually glow—a visual sign of how he'd embezzled funds intended to provide arms and food for the fedayeen. It happened so suddenly that I thought, briefly, I was the only person who'd found out. But some PLO leaders in Rome and Paris added to my confusion by laughing and saying, as they smoked their exclusive cigars:

"But we all knew about that. We used to call him the Bottomless Pits."

If they all knew, what did Monshen himself know that kept everyone quiet while he was still alive?

Rereading what I've written, I see I've already started to make judgments. I'm a long way past the stage of pretending to drown when I'm only up to the chin in water.

Hitler's first, inexorable duty every morning when he woke up was to look the same: the almost horizontal toothbrush moustache, every whisper sprouting from his nostrils, everything had to remain the same. The black forelock was no more allowed to switch to the wrong side of the shiny forehead than the arms of the swastika were allowed to turn toward the left. And so with the gleam in the eye, angry or ingratiating as required, with the famous voice, and with other things that can't be said. What would the dignitaries of the Reich and the Axis ambassadors have done if they'd seen a clean-shaven, blond, young Finn leap out of bed?

It must have been like that whenever someone has become a symbol: take the Negus, from his built-up soles to his solar topi, from his socks to his sunshade; take Marlene, from her gold ankle chain to her cigarette holder. Imagine Churchill without a cigar! Or a cigar without Churchill! Can a keffiyeh be wound round anybody else's head than Arafat's? He made me, like everyone else, a present of a brand new one, with the usual "Do this in remembrance of me." He couldn't give away signed photographs like an actor, so he gave away a piece of himself. For Westerners he remains a keffiyeh with a stubble.

I was very surprised when I met him. From in front he looked as I'd expected, but when he turned his head to answer me and showed his left profile I saw a different man. The right profile was grim and harsh, the left very mild, with an almost feminine smile underlined by his nervous habit of tossing back his black-and-white keffiyeh. Its fringes and bobbles would fall over his shoulders, sometimes over his eyes, like the hair of an angry youth.

He was affable, and stared into space when he wasn't drinking coffee, but when I saw him from only a few feet away I realized what an effort you had to make—blindly, so to speak, in the darkness of the body—in order to look always the same to others and to yourself. What if a frog went to sleep and woke up a bullfinch? Would Arafat thinking be Arafat changing? It wasn't only to him the fedayeen owed the days of quiet, almost of rejoicing, that I've tried to describe. Not only to him. But it was he alone who was responsible for the defeat.

Was his lack of action thought, and so a continuation of action? That great spider, silently and imperceptibly spinning out his shimmering web as he drank coffee after coffee, gazing into the distance and letting me talk without listening to what I said—had he really got his eye on the other big spider, Golda Meir, weaving her real toils? He proffered a few words, wary as a fly picking its way over the web. Was that what he really was?

VII

LETTERS

To Sartre

◄○►

This letter, regarding the nature of homosexuality, was probably written in 1952. It is a counterargument to Sartre's more voluntarist theory, presented in Saint Genet.

*M*Y DEAR SARTRE,

We didn't have time to talk. As for pederasty, here's a theory I propose to you. It's still just thrown together. Tell me what you think.

We must speak not at first about the sexual instinct but about a law that is linked to the continuation of life.

Starting with this law an *instinct* directs us, obscurely, from childhood on toward woman. Eroticism is diffuse, directed toward oneself, then toward no matter which living creature (or almost) and then slowly becomes differentiated and directs us toward women.

Toward puberty, sexual desire, contained by instinct, is definitely fixed on woman. It becomes attached to feminine characteristics. It abandons, rejects manly characteristics. It perceives them as signs of sterility. Once this moment has arrived or is about to arrive, the psyche proposes a series of symbolic themes. These theories will be themes of life, that is, of actions. And only social actions. The definitive choice of woman implies not only a social agreement, but also it is starting with this law that a social order is established. The psyche proposes to man those acts he must perform and . . . man is active.

But from childhood on, a trauma throws the soul into confusion. I think it happens like this: after a certain shock, I refuse to live. But, incapable of thinking about my death in clear, rational terms, I look at it symbolically by refusing to continue the world. Instinct then leads me toward my own sex. My pleasure will be *endless*. I will not embody the principle of continuity. It is a sulky attitude. Slowly instinct leads me toward masculine attributes. Slowly my psyche will propose to me funereal themes. Actually, first I know I'm capable of not continuing this world in which I live, then I continue, indefinitely, the gestures of the dead. These funereal themes, they too demand to be active, accomplished; if not, there will be an explosion of madness! The proposed themes symbolic of death will thus be very narrow (the extraordinary limitation of the pederastic universe) (suicide, murder, theft, all antisocial acts, capable of giving me a death that if it isn't real is at least symbolic or social—prison).

If one of these themes is *active*, in fact achieved, it will cause my real death. Therefore it's necessary that I achieve it only in the imaginative realm, but if it's in the imagination, that means on the level of the erotic life (endlessly started over, and pointless) or in daydreams that resolve nothing.

The only thing that remains then is to activate these funereal themes in the imagination and to accomplish them in an act: the poem. The functions of a poem, then, will be:

1. To deliver me from a funereal theme that haunts me.
2. To transform it into an act (imaginary).
3. To remove what was singular and limited in the act and to give it a universal significance.
4. To reintegrate my funereal psyche into a social reality.
5. To put childhood behind and to arrive at maturity that is manly, hence social.

That, I believe, is the only possible solution for pederasty. But each of these themes must be superseded, that is lived to the limit of the act (but we'll talk some more about that).

In any event, the significance of homosexuality is this: A refusal to continue the world. Then, to alter sexuality. The child or the adolescent who refuses the world and turns toward his own sex, knowing that he himself is a man, in struggling against this useless manliness is going to try to dissolve it, alter it; there's only one way, which is to pervert it through pseudofeminine behavior. That's the meaning of drag queens' feminine gestures and intonations. It's not, as people think, nostalgia about the idea of the woman one might have been that feminizes; rather it's the bitter need to mock virility. It should be added—something which is only true of our situation—that to refuse life implies taking on a lonely and passive attitude: to be a woman who in society is submissive and waits for man to put her in her place.

Significance of pederastic love: it's the possession of an object (the beloved) who will have no other fate than the fate of the lover. The beloved becomes the object ordained to "represent" *death* (the lover) in life. That's why I want him to be handsome. He has the *visible* attributes when I will be dead. I commission him to live in my stead, my heir apparent. The beloved doesn't love me, he "reproduces" me. But in this way I sterilize him, I cut him off from his own destiny.

• • •

You see it's not so much in terms of sexuality that I explain the faggot, but in direct terms of death. When I'll see you I'll try to tell you what I can about eunuchs and castrati. It's similar. Except that their death dates from their operation.

But it seems obvious to me that the asocial acts of the fag are necessary since their life is lead in death, or rather in what causes death, thus in principle in a climate of treason.

And all these funereal themes will come back in fags' behavior. I'll give you examples galore.

As for the appearance, at certain moments, of pederasty in the life of a normal man, it's provoked by the sudden (or slow) collapse of the life force. A fatigue, a fear to live: a *sudden refusal of the responsibility* to live. Not important, the eroticism of different desires. And . . .

All of this, is presented too rapidly, but I'm going to the country, I won't be seeing you, so give me your opinion.

If a fag speaks intelligently sometimes of a social problem, it's because he imitates his fragmentary mind (you know what I mean) or the faculties of a mind at the height of a continuity of content. But in politics nothing new can be contributed by a homosexual. . . . He cannot *think* about the social problem in an original fashion (Gide and Communism!). Yes, there is Walt Whitman (but you know very well that's just a lyrical outpouring without any positive content).

My friendship to Michelle.

Your,
Genet

As for the hatred of fags: you'll tell me that the Other is a caricature. You're right. But tell me the meaning of this caricature: when I see one isn't it that I'm living—hatefully, wickedly—through a fault that is in me and that I—?

A poem is only the *activity* of a funereal theme. It is (definitely) its socialization, a struggle against death. The themes of life propose action and forbid the poem.

To Java

◄○►

*"Java" was Genet's companion and lover for five years, roughly from 1947 to
1952. They lived together in small hotels in Montmartre. Often Java would go
out on the town while Genet remained at home, writing all night. When Java re-
turned at dawn, Genet would read to him what he had written.*

*They had first met when Genet was introduced to Java by a mutual friend.
At that time the young man was working on a yacht called* Java, *and Genet in-
evitably assigned this raffish nickname to his new lover.*

*After they drifted apart, Genet wrote this letter, remarkable for its tenderness
and the glimpse it gives of the aging Genet.*

OFTEN I THINK about you. When we see each other next we will probably
not say anything important but all those little everyday things that people say to
those for whom they feel a lot of affection. I would like to speak with you as though
we saw each other last eight days ago.

I live a life that is apparently very complicated, because of my trips, snags,
detours, returns, but in fact it's really very simple. I have very fond memories of
a few guys and you know very well that you are one of them for me.

Don't think that I haven't changed: I am a little old man, stunted and wrinkled,
who drags himself from one country to another, not being able to find one where
he can stop. I'm not complaining. I was born a vagabond. At heart I am probably
more Slavic than you are. My true homeland is any old train station. I have a
suitcase, linen, and four photos: Lucien, Jean Decarnin, Abdullah, and you. I come
to Paris as seldom as possible, because I do not like people to speak French around
me. Tomorrow I will be in Munich. The train station is full of Greeks, of Wops,
Arabs, Spaniards, and Japanese.

And your parents, you never talk about them to me?

How old are you? Thirty-six or thirty-seven? As for me, I'm not ashamed of
being fifty and of appearing sixty; it's even rather restful. Perhaps we even went
past each other without either of us recognizing the other one.

If I must come back to Paris, it will be just for a few days, but I will send you a note and try to see you.

Java, I like you. Try to be happy. Kiss your daughter for me. I kiss you very hard, my little one.

Jean

Is your wife still vexed with me?

This letter is a little longer than I should be sending you. But while I was writing to you my ideas about you became more familiar. I've reopened my letter in order to tell you that. It's as though we saw each other just last night. Is your daughter named Sonia? There are some words in your letter that I can't make out. Kiss her for me, Dédé.

VIII

INTERVIEW

Interview with Madeleine Gobeil

◄○►

Madeleine Gobeil, a beginning Canadian journalist, met Genet through a mutual friend, Simone de Beauvoir. She asked Genet to submit to an interview for the American men's magazine Playboy. *Genet asked her how much the magazine would be paying her and demanded that she split the fee with him. The interview took place in January 1964, in Paris. A very abridged version was published soon afterward by the magazine. The much longer version included here is based on the typed transcript approved by Gobeil. This is its first unabridged publication in English. In it, Genet refers to the then-recent assassination of Kennedy by Oswald (whom Genet sympathized with as a loner) and to the case of Caryl Chessman, an American prison writer popular at the time.*

*In January 1964, Genet was in a serene state of mind that would soon be abruptly broken. He had recently written his three major plays (*The Blacks, The Balcony, *and* The Screens*) and he had had a long, intense love affair with Abdallah the high-wire artist, who had been replaced in Genet's affections by Jacky Maglia, a race driver whom Genet had known since the boy was eight or nine years old. In fact Jacky was the stepson of Lucien Sénémaud, the "Fisherman of Suquet," one of Genet's loves from the 1940s.*

Two months after this interview took place, a neglected Abdallah committed suicide. The shattered Genet renounced literature for years to come—a dark, suicidal period from which he did not emerge until 1970 and with his political commitment to the Black Panthers and the Palestinians.

MADELEINE GOBEIL: Jean Genet, today you are a famous writer, translated and produced in many languages. Your play, *The Blacks* has been running for three years in New York. A film based on *The Balcony* has evoked numerous controversies. English and American critical response to *Our Lady of the Flowers* is excellent. Just before your last book came out, a six-hundred-page essay was published by the celebrated French philosopher, Jean-Paul Sartre. And yet, what we mainly know about your work, your trademark, so to speak, is the phrase "thief, traitor, coward, homosexual." It seems almost like an advertising jingle. What do you have to say about this?

JEAN GENET: There is nothing wrong with discovering deep motivations and exploiting them; that's what advertisement knows how to do. If I had wanted to make this slogan into an advertising campaign, I probably would have succeeded.

At the time my books came out (almost twenty years ago now), there is no doubt, I accentuated everything you just said and that for reasons that weren't always very pure hearted, that is to say, not always for reasons of a poetical order. Publicity thus came into the picture. Without being perfectly conscious, I was doing self-promotion. Nonetheless, for this enterprise, I did choose to use means that were not so simple, which even put me in danger. To call myself publically a homosexual, thief, traitor, coward unmasked me, put me in a situation such that I could not sleep easily nor create work that was easily assimilated by society. In short, by saying something so apparently media-mongering, I went right out and put myself in a position in which society could not reach me immediately.

GOBEIL: Why did you decide to be a thief, traitor, and homosexual?

GENET: I did not decide, I didn't make any decision. But there are certain facts. If I started out stealing, it was because I was hungry. Later I had to justify my act, to come to terms with it, so to speak. As for homosexuality, I have no idea. What can one know? Do we know why a man chooses such or such a position in which to make love? Homosexuality was imposed on me just as was the color of my eyes, the number of my feet. As a kid, I was already conscious of the attraction other boys held for me; I never felt any attraction for women. It was only after I became conscious of this attraction that I "decided," freely "chose" in the Sartrian sense of the word. In other words, or more simply stated, I had to get used to it all, while knowing that society didn't approve.

GOBEIL: When did you leave prison for the last time?

GENET: In 1945, I think.

GOBEIL: How many years did you spend there during your life?

GENET: All in all, if you count the time I was in reform school, it was about seven years.

GOBEIL: Was it in prison that your work evolved? Nehru said that his time in prison was the best time for thinking in his life.

GENET: Then let him go back!

GOBEIL: Do you still steal today?

GENET: And you, Miss?

GOBEIL: . . .

GENET: You don't steal, you've never stolen?

GOBEIL: . . .

GENET: Of course, I don't steal in the same manner as I used to. Now I receive

large royalties for my books, at least royalties that to me seem large. And these sums are certainly the result of my first thefts. So I do continue to steal. What I mean is that I continue to be dishonest with regard to a society that itself pretends to believe that I am not.

GOBEIL: Until you were thirty years old, you bummed across Europe, from jail to jail. You describe this period in a *Thief's Journal.* Do you consider yourself to be a good thief?

GENET: A "good thief" . . . It's amusing to hear those two words together. Good thief . . . You probably mean to ask me if I was an able thief. I was not awkward. But there is something in the operation that consists of lifting a portion of hypocrisy (but I am unable to think clearly, the microphone is bothering me. I see the tape recorder and the tape running and I feel I must be polite, not with regard to you, because with you I'm sure I could always get out of trouble, but with regard to the tape running silently without my intervention). So, there is, in the act of stealing, an obligation to hide oneself. If you hide, you dissimulate a part of your action, you cannot own up to it. To confess it in front of judges is dangerous. You must deny things before judges, you must deny by hiding. When you do something while hiding, you always do it awkwardly; what I mean is that you don't make use of all your qualities. Some of them are necessarily directed toward negating the act being undertaken. For me, the act of stealing entails a lot of concern about making my acts public, to "publish" them out of vanity, conceit, or sincerity. In each thief there is a part of Hamlet questioning himself, his actions, but he must question himself in public. Thus he commits his thefts awkwardly.

GOBEIL: Doesn't this awkwardness come from your particularly cerebral way of looking at the issue? Newspapers acclaim great thiefs, they tell of prestigious crimes . . . Take, for example, the great train robbery that put Scotland Yard in a panic, a theft that brought millions of dollars to the perpetrators.

GENET: Millions of dollars? It was policemen who set everything up! There's no doubt in my mind, it was either officers or retired captains or ones on duty, or people in the civil service. But a real thief who accepts being a thief, who works alone, he must fail.

GOBEIL: Do you mean people like the pathetic characters of your novels who commit miserable crimes against other homosexuals, for example, or who rob the poor box in the church? Films and the press rarely evoke this kind of criminal.

GENET: I've never been to America, but from what I've seen in films, I think that, in order to preserve themselves, to stay intact, Americans have had to invent the kind of gangsters that personify evil. Naturally such gangsters can only be imaginary. America has erected such an imaginary gangster so that you cannot identify her, America, with evil. On the one hand there is America the good, the America of the Constitution, the America known to us in France, in the West, in the East, everywhere, and there is, on the other hand, evil, an absolute gangster, and usually Italian by the way. America has invented a type of gangster who doesn't exist, except perhaps among its union bosses. From what I know, American civilization is quite dull. You can judge a country by its outlaws. The ones we know from books and films are so brutal you would never want to meet them. They are boring. And yet there must be some very fine and sensitive bandits.

GOBEIL: Sartre explains that you have decided to live evil out to the extreme limit. What does this mean?

GENET: To live out evil in such a way that you would never be contaminated by the social forces that symbolize what is good. I did not mean I wanted to live out evil to the point of my own death, but in such a way that I would be obliged to find refuge, if I needed to take refuge anywhere, only in evil and nowhere else, never in what is called good.

GOBEIL: And yet, as a famous writer you can take your place in society on the side of what is considered good. Do you go out in the world, to social occasions?

GENET: Never. Society never makes a mistake. Let us say first of all that I don't like to go out. There is no great merit in this. People don't invite me either, because they quickly feel that I do not belong.

GOBEIL: Do you feel solidarity with criminals, those who are humiliated?

GENET: Not at all. Of course no solidarity, because, by God, if there was such a thing, that would be the beginning of morality, and thus the return to goodness. If, for example, loyalty existed between two or three criminals, it would be the beginning of a moral convention, and hence the beginning of something good.

GOBEIL: When you read an account of a crime, such as that of Oswald, what do you feel?

GENET: Ah! If that's what you mean, then I do feel solidarity. Not that I have a particular hatred for President Kennedy—he doesn't interest me at all. But this lone man, who decided to oppose himself to a highly organized society in a world that condemns evil, oh yes, I am rather on his side. I sympathize with him in the same way I would sympathize with a great artist who is alone in the face of society, no more and no less. I am for every man alone. But no matter how much I feel morally in favor of every lone man, lone men remain alone. No matter how much I am with him, Oswald was alone when he committed his crime. No matter how much I feel for Rembrandt, when he was painting, he was alone.

GOBEIL: Are you still in contact with old cellmates?

GENET: Not at all. Look at the situation. I earn royalties from all over the world, you come to interview me from *Playboy*, and they are all still in prison. What kind of contact could we have? For them I am a man who has betrayed them, that's all.

GOBEIL: Is this a betrayal?

GENET: I certainly betrayed something. But I had to do it for something that I felt was more precious. I had to betray stealing because theft is a singular action, which I turned on, for the benefit of a more universal operation, which is poetry. I had to do it. I had to betray the thief that I was in order to be the poet I hope to have become. But "going straight" hasn't made me any happier.

GOBEIL: You betrayed criminals and yet you are spurned by honest people. Do you like living in general disgrace?

GENET: It doesn't displease me, but it's a question of temperament. It's out of conceit, and this is not the best aspect of my personality. I like being in disgrace, just as, all things being equal, Lucifer likes being in God's bad graces. But this is pride, a bit foolish. I ought not to stop at this. It is a naïve and romantic attitude.

GOBEIL: So what effect have criminals had on you?

GENET: Ask rather what judges have brought me. . . . To become a judge you must follow law courses. You start such studies at around eighteen or nineteen years old in the most generous period of adolescence. There are people in the world who know that they will earn their living by judging other human beings, and all this without putting themselves in danger. This is what criminals have brought to me: they made me reflect on the morality of judges. But don't rely on this, in any criminal there is a judge, unfortunately— although the opposite is not true.

GOBEIL: Isn't your goal to liquidate all morality?

GENET: I would very much like to throw off conventional morals, those that are crystallized and that impede growth, that impede life. But an artist is never completely destructive. The very concern to create a harmonious sentence supposes some kind of morality, that is to say a relationship between the author and a possible reader. I write in order to be read. One doesn't write for nothing. In an esthetic philosophy, there is always a morality. I feel that your idea of me is derived from a body of work written twenty years ago. I am not trying to give an image of myself that is repulsive or fascinating or even admissible. I am hard at work.

GOBEIL: We'll get back to your moral conception as an artist, especially as the author of *The Maids* and *The Blacks*. Let us return to your opposition to conventional morality. In your personal life, do you, for example, make use of narcotics?

GENET: I have a practically visceral horror of drug addicts. To take drugs is to refuse consciousness. Drugs provoke a larval state: I become a leaf among other leaves, a caterpillar among others, and not an individual being.

GOBEIL: Did you ever take any?

GENET: Yes, and it did not produce any effects except the unhappiness inherent in the feeling of capitulation.

GOBEIL: People say you never drink. Why?

GENET: Because I am not an American writer. The other evening I was dining with Sartre and Simone de Beauvoir and they were drinking double whiskies. Beauvoir said to me: "The way we have of losing ourselves each night in alcohol doesn't interest you because you are already completely lost." Little alcoholic lapses don't do much for me. I have lived in a long unconsciousness for a long time

GOBEIL: You do eat at least?

GENET: I like to eat when I come back from England. The only two things that link me to the French nation are the language and the food.

GOBEIL: Your book *Our Lady of the Flowers*, which some people call your masterpiece, is a poetic narration of a long masturbation in a jail cell. This is the period when you were affirming that poetry is "the art of creating shit and making people swallow it." You spared your reader no description. You used all the words of the erotic vocabulary. You even evoked religious ceremonies that ended in fornication. Didn't you ever have problems with censorship?

GENET: The censorship of so-called "obscene" words doesn't exist in France. If my most recent play, *The Screens*, isn't produced in France (it was in Germany and will be in America), it is because the French find something in it that isn't there but which they think is: namely the problem of the Algerian war. It is still too painful for them. I would have to be protected by the police and they would certainly not protect Jean Genet. As for the so-called "obscene" words, all I can say is this: these words exist. If they exist then they must be used, otherwise, they shouldn't have been invented. Without me, these words would have just a half-life. The role of a great artist is to valorize any word. You've reminded me of a definition I used to give of poetry, though I would no longer define it in this way today. If you want to understand something, not a great deal, but a little something of the world, you have to rid yourself of resentment. Resentment is something I still have a bit of toward society, but less and less, and I hope eventually not to have any at all. In the end, I don't care. But when I wrote that, I was still caught up in resentment, and poetry consisted of transforming seemingly vile materials into noble-seeming materials and this with the help of language. Today the problem is different. *You* don't interest me any more as an enemy. Ten or fifteen years ago I was against you. Now I am neither for you nor against you, I exist in the same time frame as you and my problem is no longer to oppose you but to do something in which we are both caught up, you as well as me. Today I feel that if readers are sexually provoked by my books, it is because they were badly written, because the poetic emotion ought to be so powerful that no reader could be moved in a sexual manner. Insofar as my books are pornographic, I don't repudiate them, I just think I lacked class.

GOBEIL: Do you know the works of Nabokov and D. H. Lawrence?

GENET: I've read nothing of these authors.

GOBEIL: Did you have an interest in Henry Miller, whose books were called "obscene" and long banned in America?

GENET: I don't know Miller very well. What I do know of him doesn't interest me much. It is full of talk. He's a man who won't stop talking.

GOBEIL: In your opinion, why was Henry Miller banned for so long in America?

GENET: I am incapable of entering into the head of an American censor.

GOBEIL: Let us speak, if you wish, of a book that is translated in America, *Our Lady of the Flowers.* You wrote it in prison?

GENET: Yes, and it even gave me pleasure to write it in prison. My dream would have been to have been in cahoots with a publisher who would have brought it out under plain wrappers in a very limited edition of three or four hundred. The book would have made its way into unsuspecting minds. Unfortunately, it wasn't possible. It had to go unsuspecting to a real publisher who sold it to homosexuals and writers, but they're about the same when you come down to it: they were people who knew what they were getting. But I would have liked for my book to fall into the hands of Catholic bankers or policemen or concierges, people like that.

GOBEIL: What did you use to write on in prison?

GENET: We were given paper with which we were to make a hundred or two hundred bags. It was on this paper that I wrote the beginning of *Our Lady of the Flowers.* It was during the war, I didn't expect to leave prison ever. I don't mean to say that I wrote the truth, but I did write sincerely, with passion and rage, a rage that was even less contained, as I was sure the book would never be read. One day we were conducted from the prison, La Santé, to the courthouse. When I returned to my cell, the manuscript had dissapeared. I was called to the prison director's office and he condemmed me to three days in my cell and bread and water for having used paper which "wasn't made to receive masterpieces." I felt humiliated by the theft committed by the director. I ordered some notebooks from the store, and I crawled under my covers and I tried to remember word for word what I had written. I do believe I succeeded.

GOBEIL: Was it long?

GENET: About fifty pages.

GOBEIL: Did your undertaking resemble that of Caryl Chessman?

GENET: Not at all. Chessman always defended himself, he always refused to recognize the acts that could put him on the sidelines of society. Out of prudence he denied the essential. He doesn't interest me at all. That Americans should know how to use Chessman's case both to clear their consciences and to put distance between a thief and a supposed assassin doesn't surprise me at all; it's just their level. He denied a gesture he ought to have claimed proudly. He found a way to delay the death penalty because he knew American law well and he found a way to live ten or twelve years. That is a success, but not a literary success.

GOBEIL: Did you start writing as a way out of solitude?

GENET: No, since I wrote things that made me even more solitary. No, I don't know why I started writing. The fundamental reasons I don't know. Perhaps it is this: the first time I was conscious of the power of writing was when I sent a postcard to a German friend who was then in America. I didn't really know what to tell her. The side on which I was to write was rather sandy and white, a little like snow, and it was this surface that evoked for me the snow naturally absent from prison, and Christmas; and so instead of writing about any old thing, I wrote about the quality of the card. That was the trigger that allowed me to write. Certainly this is not the motive, but it is what gave me the first taste of freedom.

GOBEIL: How did you begin being published?

GENET: A lawyer Guillaume Hanoteau, now a journalist for *Paris Match*, passed one of my poems, *The Man Condemned to Death*, to Jean Cocteau, who published it at his own expense.

GOBEIL: And that is how you made your way in French literature?

GENET: I never tried to become part of French literature.

GOBEIL: It is true that one would like to consider you as a "case history." You speak in your work about saintliness as "the most beautiful word in the French language" and of "the eternal pair, the criminal and the saint." Saintliness . . . your rivals refuse you the right to use this word.

GENET: My detractors cannot see me using a single word, or even a comma without shuddering: Mauriac, in an article even asked that I stop writing. The Christians, and particularly those who are my detractors, are the owners, of the word saintliness and they do not authorize me to use it.

GOBEIL: What does it mean to you?

GENET: And for you, what does it mean?

GOBEIL: The search for perfection in the spiritual domain.

GENET: My detractors do not object to Saint Camus. Why to Saint Genet? Listen, as a child it was difficult for me to imagine—unless I really exaggerated my daydreams—to imagine that I could become president, general, or anything else. I was a bastard, I had no right to the social order. What was left to me if I desired an outstanding destiny? If I wanted to make the most of my freedom, my possibilities, or as you say, my gifts, not knowing my gift as a writer, if indeed I have such a gift? The only thing left that was desirable was to be a saint, nothing else, that is to say the negation of a human being.

GOBEIL: What relationship do you see between saint and criminal?

GENET: Solitude. Don't you have the feeling that the greatest saints resemble criminals, if one looks closely? Saintliness frightens people. There is no visible agreement between society and the saint.

GOBEIL: Listening to you, reading your works, is a bit surprising. It is strange enough that a man such as you (a bastard coming from a foundling home) did not become a purely intuitive writer. And yet, you argue, you construct. It would be difficult to find a relationship between you and American writers such as Faulkner or Hemingway.

GENET: I ask myself—and I do not think of myself as a nationalist—I ask myself if I am not this way because of French culture, which has surrounded me since my youth. When I was fifteen years old, this was a culture spread across all of France, perhaps across Europe. We French people knew that we were the masters of the world, not only the material world, but of culture as well.

GOBEIL: Even a bastard child could be taken up by a whole culture?

GENET: It was difficult to escape it. My books are perhaps the fruit of a culture that has existed for a very long time and of which I was perhaps more a victim than a beneficiary.

GOBEIL: A victim?

GENET: Strong feeling and fresh intuitions were silenced because they were continually butting up against a mode of cultural expression that cut them down, castrated them as it were. Perhaps with my temperament, if I had been born in the United States, I would have been a very fine, very sensitive poet; whereas I am above all a polemicist. I have to add that no culture is ever complete, whole. European writers, just like American ones, choose, more or less clearly, a means of expression that responds to a demand. Europe demands an appearance of culture, America presents itself as hearty and instinctive. In both cases, we lie. We lie about a truth we sense but cannot express otherwise. America, generally speaking, has given itself a brutal and intuive form while Europe has tried to be cultured and reasonable.

GOBEIL: In your opinion, why did the philosopher Jean-Paul Sartre dedicate a six-hundred-page essay to you?

GENET: Sartre presupposes human freedom and he believes that each individual has all the means at his disposal to take charge of his own destiny. I am the illustration of one of his theories about freedom. He saw a man who, instead of submitting, claimed what was due him, and who was determined to push the consequences to the extreme.

GOBEIL: What do you think of Sartre as a writer and as a friend?

GENET: Sartre repeats himself. He had a few important ideas and exploited them in various forms. When I read him, my mind usually goes faster than his. What surprises me is *The Words*, his most recent book. It demonstrates such a will to get out of the bourgeoisie. In a world in which everyone wants to be the respectable whore, it is very pleasant to meet someone who knows he's a bit of a whore, but who has no need for respectability. I like Sartre because he is funny, amusing, and he understands everything. And it is rather pleasant to be face to face with someone who understands everything with a smile instead of judgmentally. He doesn't accept everything I do, but he enjoys it even when he disagrees. He is a very sensitive person. Ten or fifteen years ago, I saw him blush a few times. And a blushing Sartre is adorable.

GOBEIL: What did you feel while reading the book he devoted to you?

GENET: A kind of disgust—because I saw myself naked and stripped by someone other than myself. In all my books I strip myself but at the same time I disguise myself with words, choices, attitudes, magic. I take pains not to damage myself too much. Sartre stripped me without mercy. He wrote about me in the present tense. My first impulse was to burn the book. Sartre had handed me the manuscript. I finally allowed him to publish it because I've always felt compelled to be responsible for what I evoke. But it took me a long time to recuperate. I was almost unable to continue writing. I could have continued to develop novels mechanically. I could have tried to write porno-graphic novels using automatic writing. Sartre's book created a void that caused a sort of psychological deterioration to set in. This deterioration permitted the meditation that led me to my plays.

GOBEIL: How long did you stay trapped in this void?

GENET: I lived in this miserable state for six years, in the imbecility that underlies most of a life: opening a door, lighting a cigarette. . . . There are just a few moments of light in the life of such a man. The rest is dull shadow.

GOBEIL: But your play *The Maids* dates from 1947 and Sartre's book wasn't published until 1952.

GENET: This is true. Sartre's book did not release something new, it just pushed it further.

GOBEIL: Your plays are very successful, particularly in the United States, where *The Blacks* has run for almost four years. How do you feel about this achievement?

GENET: I still haven't quite taken it in. I am very surprised. Perhaps the United States is not as I imagine it. Everything can happen in America, even an appearance of humanity.

GOBEIL: You wrote four plays, of which three are known to us, *The Maids, The Blacks,* and *The Balcony.* These plays are perplexing. One asks oneself, for example, if in *The Maids,* you are for the hired help against the employers, and in *The Blacks,* if you are for the blacks against the whites, or the contrary. There is a sense of uneasiness.

GENET: I don't care. I wanted to write theater, to crystallize a dramatic and theatrical emotion. If my plays serve the blacks, it doesn't concern me. I don't believe it, as a matter of fact. I think that action, direct combat against colonialism, does more for blacks than a play. In the same way, I think that a maids' union does more for hired help than a play. I tried to give voice to something profound that neither blacks nor any other alienated beings could express. One critic said that maids "don't speak that way." They do speak that way, but only to me, alone at midnight. If you told me blacks don't speak that way, I would have said that if you put your ear to their hearts you would hear that. One has to know how to hear what is not formulated.

GOBEIL: But your plays concern people without privilege.

GENET: It is possible that I wrote these plays against myself. It is possible that I am the whites, the boss, France in *The Screens,* when I try to find what is imbecilic in these qualities. You asked me if I steal. I don't think it has any importance. I never stole from an individual but from a social rank. And I don't give a damn about rank.

GOBEIL: Sartre says that to read you is to spend a night in a brothel. You have had lots of clients, you are famous. What do you do with the money you earn.

GENET: None of your business.

GOBEIL: Do you often grant interviews?

GENET: Never. It took all the persuasion of Simone de Beauvoir for me to grant an interview to a magazine whose very existence was unknown to me. This is the first time in my life I've given an interview that goes beyond a brief encounter at a bistro. I never did anything to publicize my plays in America, for instance. You see, I made a wager: that my work could fend for itself without the help of any publicity. It will succeed if it is powerful, if it is weak, too bad for me.

GOBEIL: But you have succeeded, you've become a personality.

GENET: If I am a personality, I'm an odd one. "Personalities" (the word makes me smile) can go anywhere. I have a visa to go to America, I have had a visa for four years, but I think the consul must have given it to me by accident. I wasn't allowed to use it when they found out who I was.

GOBEIL: Is this because of your criminal record or your homosexuality? Can we discuss this subject?

GENET: I am perfectly willing to talk about homosexuality. It's a subject that pleases me immensely. I know that homosexuality is well looked upon these days in pseudoartistic circles. It is still condemned in bourgeois society. As for me, I owe a lot to it. If you wish to see it as a curse, that is your problem; for my part, I see it as a blessing.

GOBEIL: What has it brought you?

GENET: It is what put me on the path of writing and of understanding people. I'm not saying that it's the only thing, but perhaps if I had not made love with Algerians, I might not have been in favor of the NLF.[1] No, I'm sure I would have been no matter what. But it was perhaps homosexuality that made me understand that Algerians were men like any others.

GOBEIL: Were you ever interested in women?

GENET: Yes, four women have interested me: the Holy Virgin, Joan of Arc, Marie Antoinette, and Madame Curie.

GOBEIL: What role does homosexuality play in your life right now?

GENET: I would like to tell you about its pedagogical role. Obviously, I have made love with all the young men in my care. But I didn't simply focus on making love. I tried to recreate with them the adventure I'd lived through and whose sign is bastardhood, treason, the refusal of society and finally, writing, that is to say a return to society but through other means. Is this an attitude unique to me? Homosexuality, since it places the homosexual outside of the law, obliges him to question social values, and if he decides to care for a young man, he won't do it in a trivial way. He will teach him about the contradictions both of reason and of the heart, which are inherent in a normal society. Right now I am taking a young driver under my wing., Jacky Maglia. I can say this about him: he started out stealing cars, then descended into stealing anything at all. I understood quite quickly that he should devote his life to racing. I bought him cars. He is twenty-one years old now. He is a race driver,

---

[1] The National Liberation Front, the Algerian nationalist party, led the struggle against the French for Algerian independence.

he doesn't steal anymore. He was a deserter, he isn't any more. It was stealing, desertion, and myself who are responsible for his becoming a race driver and returning to society. He has been reintegrated by accomplishment, by exploring the best in himself.

GOBEIL: Do you accompany him when he races?

GENET: I have followed him everywhere, to England, Italy, Belgium, and Germany. I am his timekeeper.

GOBEIL: Are you interested in automobile racing?

GENET: Originally it struck me as stupid, but now it seems very serious and quite beautiful. There is something dramatic and esthetic in a well-run race. The driver is alone, like Oswald. He risks death. It's beautiful when he finishes first. A driver needs qualities such as extreme delicacy and Maglia is a very good driver. Brutes end up dead. Maglia is becoming well known. He will become famous.

GOBEIL: Does he mean a lot to you? Do you love him?

GENET: Do I love him? I love the endeavor. I love what he does and what I have done for him.

GOBEIL: Do you spend a lot of time taking care of him?

GENET: If you care for someone, you have to do it seriously. Last weekend while we were driving from Chartres back to Paris, I didn't smoke in the car because he was driving very tensely at an average of a hundred and seventy kilometers an hour.

GOBEIL: Isn't this way of surrendering to someone else very feminine?

GENET: The femininity that is found in homosexuality envelops the young man and perhaps even allows for more goodness to come out. I was watching a television program about the Vatican. Several cardinals were presented. Two or three of them were asexual and insignificant. Those who were like women were dull and grasping. There was only one, Cardinal Lienart, who gave off a homosexual air, and he seemed good and intelligent.

GOBEIL: Modern man has been criticized for losing his virility. Doesn't homosexuality encourage this tendancy?

GENET: Even if there was a crisis of virility, I wouldn't be very sad about it. Virility is always a game. American actors play at virility. Camus was always striking a virile attitude. To me, virility ought to be a faculty for protecting rather than deflowing girls and women. Obviously, I am not well placed to judge. By denying the usual comedy, the armor is broken open and a man can display a delicacy that otherwise wouldn't see the light of day. It is possible that the liberation of the modern woman obliges men to dismiss old-fashioned attitudes to find ones more in keeping with a less submissive woman. You saw Jacky [Maglia]: he doesn't seem at all effeminate, and yet he interests me because of his sensitivity. When I gave him his first race car, I asked him what he felt. "A bit ashamed," he said to me, "because it is more beautiful than I."

GOBEIL: How long have you known Maglia?

GENET: Since he was quite young. In each case, with young people, I've had to invent, take into account their temperaments, their character, their tastes, each time do something that resembles the creative act—something like what I ask of judges each time they try someone: that the judge be creative and that he not be able to sit in judgment more than four or five times in his whole career, since each time he should be fully creative.

GOBEIL: But when Maglia races in France, it is the very society you don't like that applauds him.

GENET: I know that. Nationalism gets exalted. What saves Maglia is that he risks his life. An image of him can be justified because he knows that each time he races, he risks death. If Maglia let himself get caught in the game of complacency, he would endanger his life, his ability. An attitude that was too conceited would endanger him just as I would be in danger if I took too much of a conceited attitude as a criminal or a writer.

GOBEIL: When you are not at the tracks with Maglia, what do you do?

GENET: The rest of the time I live in a state of semistupidity just like everyone else. From time to time I work on my plays, not every day, I do it in waves, by bursts. Perhaps I'll write an opera with Pierre Boulez, who this year presented an admirable *Wozzeck* by Alban Berg at the Paris Opera.

GOBEIL: Is writing a necessity for you?

GENET: Yes, because I feel responsible for the time allotted me. I want to make something of it, and this something is writing. It is not that I feel responsible in the eyes of other men, or even my own, but perhaps in the eyes of God—who, naturally, I cannot talk much about since I know very little about him.

GOBEIL: You believe in God?

GENET: I think I believe in him. I don't have great faith in the mythologies of catechism. But why should I account for my life by affirming the things that seem to me most precious? Nothing is forcing me. Nothing apparent obliges me. Why then do I feel so strongly that I must do it? Before, the question was resolved by the act of writing. The revolt of my childhood, the revolt that occurred when I was fourteen years old was not a revolt against faith; it was a revolt against my social situation as a humiliated person. This didn't touch my deepest faith.

GOBEIL: And eternal life, do you believe in it?

GENET: This is a question for theologians. Are you a member of Vatican II? This question makes no sense.

GOBEIL: So, what sense do you find in the life of a writer who wanders not from prison to prison, but hotel room to hotel room? You are rich and yet you own nothing. I counted: you have seven books, an alarm clock, a leather jacket, three shirts, a suit, and a suitcase. Is that all?

GENET: Yes, why should I have more?

GOBEIL: Why this satisfaction in poverty?

GENET: (Laughing) It's the virtue of angels. Listen, I don't give a damn. When I

go to London, sometimes my agent books me a room at the Ritz. What do
you want me to do with things and with luxury? I write, that's all.

GOBEIL: In what direction are you aiming your life?

GENET: Toward oblivion. Most of our activities are as vague and dazed as what
a bum experiences. It is very rare for us to make a conscious effort to push
beyond this state of stupor. I push beyond by writing.

Copyright Acknowledgements

◄O►

Note on the Translations

◄o►

The excerpts from the five novels and two plays were translated by Bernard Frechtman; "The Fisherman of Suquet," "The Penal Colony: Comments on the Cinema," and the two letters were translated by Edmund White; "The Studio of Alberto Giacometti" was translated by Richard Howard; *Prisoner of Love* was translated by Barbara Bray; and "An Interview with Madeleine Gobeil" was translated by Rachel Stella.

CPSIA information can be obtained at www.ICGtesting.com
Printed in the USA
LVOW051949070313

323223LV00001B/137/P